PRAISE FOR
THE STORIES OF

THE YEAR'S BEST
SCIENCE FICTION
VOL.1

"Likely to linger in the memory the way riddles may
linger—teasing, tormenting, illuminating, thrilling."
—*The New Yorker* on Ted Chiang's *Exhalation: Stories*

"A devastating must-read."
—*Slate* on Ken Liu's "Thoughts and Prayers"

"Sensational."
—*Spine* magazine on N. K. Jemisin's "Emergency Skin"

"A multilayered story with a great deal of depth. . . . This
is a story that's good at face value, and equally good should
you choose to read between the lines." —*SFF Reviews*
on Suzanne Palmer's "The Painter of Trees"

"This story is as understated as it is brilliant." —*Locus* on
Karin Tidbeck's "The Last Voyage of *Skidbladnir*"

"A glimpse of a *Black Mirror*–esque future from an Indian
perspective." —*Publishers Weekly* on Anil Menon's
"The Robots of Eden"

"The best short story of the past five years (fight me) and one
of the funniest I've ever read." —Sam J. Miller, Nebula
Award–winning author of *Blackfish City*, on
Alice Sola Kim's "Now Wait for This Week"

THE
YEAR'S
BEST
SCIENCE
FICTION

VOLUME 1

Also by Jonathan Strahan

Best Short Novels (2004–2007)

Drowned Worlds

Eclipse: New Science Fiction and Fantasy (Volumes 1–4)

Eidolon 1 (with Jeremy G. Byrne)

Fantasy: The Best of 2004 (with Karen Haber)

Fantasy: The Very Best of 2005

Fearsome Journeys

Fearsome Magics

Godlike Machines

Legends of Australian Fantasy (with Jack Dann)

Life on Mars: Tales of New Frontiers

Made to Order: Robots and Revolution

Science Fiction: The Best of 2003 (with Karen Haber)

Science Fiction: The Best of 2004 (with Karen Haber)

Science Fiction: The Very Best of 2005

Someone in Time (forthcoming)

Swords and Dark Magic: The New Sword and Sorcery (with Lou Anders)

The Best Science Fiction and Fantasy of the Year: Volumes 1-13

The Book of Dragons

Engineering Infinity (The Infinity Project 1)

Edge of Infinity (The Infinity Project 2)

Reach for Infinity (The Infinity Project 3)

Meeting Infinity (The Infinity Project 4)

Bridging Infinity (The Infinity Project 5)

Infinity Wars (The Infinity Project 6)

Infinity's End (The Infinity Project 7)

The Locus Awards: Thirty Years of the Best in Fantasy and Science Fiction (with Charles N. Brown)

The New Space Opera (with Gardner Dozois)

The New Space Opera 2 (with Gardner Dozois)

The Starry Rift: Tales of New Tomorrows

The Year's Best Australian Science Fiction and Fantasy: Volume 1 (with Jeremy G. Byrne)

The Year's Best Australian Science Fiction and Fantasy: Volume 2 (with Jeremy G. Byrne)

The Year's Best Science Fiction Volume 1

The Year's Best Science Fiction Volume 2 (forthcoming)

Under My Hat: Tales from the Cauldron

Wings of Fire (with Marianne S. Jablon)

THE YEAR'S BEST SCIENCE FICTION

VOLUME 1

EDITED BY
JONATHAN STRAHAN

SAGA PRESS

LONDON SYDNEY **NEW YORK** TORONTO NEW DELHI

SAGA PRESS

AN IMPRINT OF SIMON & SCHUSTER, INC.

1230 AVENUE OF THE AMERICAS, NEW YORK, NEW YORK 10020

First Saga Press trade paperback edition September 2020

SAGA PRESS and colophon are trademarks of Simon & Schuster, Inc.

For information about special discounts for bulk purchases, please contact Simon & Schuster Special Sales at 1-866-506-1949 or business@simonandschuster.com.

The Simon & Schuster Speakers Bureau can bring authors to your live event. For more information or to book an event, contact the Simon & Schuster Speakers Bureau at 1-866-248-3049 or visit our website at www.simonspeakers.com.

Interior design by A. Kathryn Barrett

Manufactured in the United States of America

1   3   5   7   9   10   8   6   4   2

Library of Congress Cataloging-in-Publication Data is available.

ISBN 978-1-5344-4959-6
ISBN 978-1-5344-4961-9 (ebook)

In memory of my dear friend Gardner Dozois (1947-2018),
who would have loved these stories.

CONTENTS

ACKNOWLEDGMENTS

There is no doubt in my mind that this has been among the most challenging books I've worked on. The science fiction field has grown, diversified, and changed, which is a joy but means so much more work for everyone. For that reason, I'd like to thank my editor, Joe Monti, and the whole team at Saga, who have done such a great job with this book. I'd also like to thank my agent, the indefatigable Howard Morhaim, who is the best business partner I could wish for, as well as: the wonderful Liza Trombi and the entire team at *Locus*, who as always were extremely kind and generous; my dear friend and podcast co-host Gary K. Wolfe; Ian Mond; James Bradley; Rachel C. Cordasco, who knows more about SF in translation than anyone I know; John Joseph Adams, who provided assistance when he didn't have to; Neil Clarke, who was enormously helpful; the wonderful Nisi Shawl; Kath Wilham and Timmi Duchamp at Aqueduct Press; Steven H. Silver, who provided invaluable information for the obituary section of my introduction; and all of the authors and their agents. A special thanks to my wife, Marianne, who helped with checking this book and my own shambolic introduction, and to my two daughters, for their understanding while I slew this particular beast.

INTRODUCTION

A NEW BEGINNING

Calendar purists may argue over exactly when the decade or the century or the millennia changes, but when the numbers change it *feels* like a new beginning, a fresh start, a time to take a look back. So as we move into 2020 it seems right to take stock. One fifth of the century is done, after all, and launching a new series of year's best science fiction anthologies, *The Year's Best Science Fiction* (with a respectful and affectionate nod to my old friend and mentor Gardner Dozois), seems an appropriate thing to do. This isn't the first time I've had the chance to do this, but this time feels special, different. After all, we're living in the future. Orwell's *1984* is a distant memory, Prince's promised 1999 party is decades ago, Clarke's *2001* is almost as old, and even the far-future 2019 of Ridley Scott's *Blade Runner* is now in the past.

And these are new and different times. The science-fictional world we're living in was barely imaginable twenty years ago. In his introduction to *The Year's Best Science Fiction* for 2000 Gardner Dozois speculated on the impact of ebooks, whether Amazon.com could possibly survive, if anyone would ever work out how to make money publishing short fiction online (answer: not yet), and what the continued impact of the internet and online shopping might be. He was concerned about Napster and downloading, and this was when the iPod was still a year away; the explosion of handheld devices, smartphones, and e-readers and more were all in the future and unimaginable; and no one would have believed the impact or dominance Disney, Apple, or Amazon are now having. Science fiction is at best so-so at predicting the future, but in early 2000 no one could really have imagined what was going to happen in SF and the wider world. It's true that some of the concerns that dominate our lives were on the horizon. If no one predicted every political trend, people were at least talking about saving the environment and confronting the coming climate apocalypse, something that was mostly absent from the science fiction of 2000 but which dominates our lives and imaginations and forms the underpinnings of most SF you'll see today.

So, what exactly *is* this book you're now holding, this year's best science fiction? A dedicated few readers are invested in defining what science fiction is, what exactly falls inside its bounds and *is* science fiction, and what falls outside and is therefore *not* science fiction. It's a discussion that makes for an amusing rainy afternoon distraction but can equally be the basis for terrible arguments and disagreements, and take up far too much time. In the early 1950s Damon Knight tried to define science fiction and came up with something that is often paraphrased as "Science fiction is [or means] what we point to when we say it." I've heard other interesting definitions, but for this book and this series that will suffice. Science fiction will be what I point to when I say science fiction. I think most of the people who are going to read this book aren't invested in definitions of science fiction or what its role or purpose might be (beyond simple entertainment), so other than opting firmly for inclusivity over exclusivity, I'd rather leave that for a conversation over a drink somewhere and move on.

It's my intention that every volume of *The Year's Best Science Fiction* will focus on the best short SF that I read during the preceding year and felt was worth gathering together for your attention—a personal best, an honest attempt at compiling the best of everything I've read in the past year into a thoughtful and entertaining book. You won't need to know the secret handshake or have the club code or read a whole bunch of other stuff to get the most out of what follows—you'll just need to be interested in the world around you and want to read something exciting and interesting and timely. Which doesn't really tell you what this particular book is *like*, or even what it's intended to be like. Science fiction has been moving steadily, with a few bumps along the way, to a more inclusive, more diverse kind of fiction, one that doesn't preference specific voices over others, and one that is open to telling stories from a wide range of perspectives. It's a type of science fiction that isn't too worried about how strictly science fictional things are, but allows the genres to blur and mix a little: less of a purist's game, which strikes me as a good thing. And this book will hopefully reflect all that: stories for lovers of science fiction and for people who just love great stories.

If you take a look at the two SF "it" books of 2019, neither actually broke much new ground in science-fictional terms and weren't too concerned if they blurred and blended genre a little. Tamsyn Muir's debut, *Gideon the Ninth* (Tor.com), is science fantasy, a gothic space opera about lesbian necromancers getting together to try to save the universe—sort of. It came out two thirds of the way through the year and everyone went wild for it. Is it SF or fantasy? It didn't seem to matter a lot because it was fresh, new, and of the moment. The other book was a novella, *This Is How You Lose the Time War* by Amal El-Mohtar and Max Gladstone (Saga), a story told in notes and messages left by two agents on opposite sides of a time war as they fall in love. Again, the bones of the story were science fiction, but while the story was justifiably widely adored it did little new. The feeling right now is that working out how to represent the entirety of the community we see around us in fiction is what counts, and that doesn't seem like such a bad way to look at things to this reader.

So, how was the year in science fiction? To be honest, it was a bit of a roller coaster. One of the signature, and most explosive, moments of the year took place onstage at the Hugo Awards in Dublin, Ireland, at the 77th World Science Fiction Convention. Hong Kong–born British fantasy writer Jeannette Ng took to the stage to accept the John W. Campbell Memorial Award for Best New Writer and in a whirlwind speech both called out award namesake John W. Campbell for his political and racial views, and emotionally responded to events taking place in Hong Kong. Ng's speech was powerful, emotive, and acted as a tipping point for change. Within two weeks Dell Magazines, sponsor of the award, announced that they would be renaming the Campbell Award as the Astounding Award—something that had apparently been under active consideration as part of the 2020 90th anniversary celebrations for *Analog*—and within a month the Gunn Center for the Study of Science Fiction had renamed the Campbell Conference the Gunn Center Conference, and there was talk they also may rename their Campbell Award. Then in mid-October the Tiptree Motherboard somewhat controversially announced that they would be renaming the James Tiptree Jr. Literary Award as the Otherwise Award in recognition of complications and sensitivities surrounding the late James Tiptree. These actions were consistent with a move for change that has been evident in SF since the World Fantasy Award was redesigned in 2015, when a caricature of the late H. P. Lovecraft was replaced for similar reasons, and for the most part were welcomed and seen as a step forward.

Things weren't quite as explosive on the book publishing scene. I don't follow the comings and goings at book publishers or the opening, merging, or shuttering of publishing houses very closely, so I won't attempt to provide you with a detailed assessment of the business, at least at publisher level. To this observer, things seemed pretty normal: some tumult, some success, but overall steady-as-she-goes. Certainly, these are challenging times for publishing houses and booksellers, but it has ever been so, and the pressure to diversify, to change and evolve, is relentless. The lauded editor and publisher Malcolm Edwards announced his departure from Gollancz, a company he'd been instrumental in developing, and a retirement party was dutifully held. Hardly any time had passed before it became clear that the retirement was more of a pause, as an announcement came that Edwards—the editor of J. G. Ballard and William Gibson, among others—would be heading a revived André Deutsch imprint that would publish SF as part of its roster. In similar news, Harry Potter publisher Arthur A. Levine announced he was leaving Scholastic after twenty-three years to form his own independent publishing company.

A few other examples aside, 2019 did not seem to see the kind of large-scale changes in SF publishing that we've seen in recent years, with no real equivalent to the changes at Orbit several years ago or Tor more recently, though Simon & Schuster's decision to move Saga Press, their popular science fiction and fantasy imprint and publisher of this book, to Gallery was notable, as the company repositioned it for further growth. Late in the year, respected and award-winning editor Navah Wolfe left the imprint. Also notable was Penguin Random House's decision to shutter prestigious nonfiction imprint, Spiegel & Grau. Running against the closure trend, a buoyant Tor Books announced a new horror imprint, Nightfire, which focuses on horror and dark fantasy and will launch its first titles in 2020.

Although SF in translation seemed more successful than at any other time I can remember, VIZ Media announced it would pause its long-running and widely respected Japanese translation imprint, Haikasoru, after completing publication of Yoshiki Tanaka's *Legend of the Galactic Heroes*. There's no indication if the imprint will be revived in the future, but it will be missed and was a vital part of the SF-in-translation scene. Also of note was the closure of Europa SF, the European Speculative Fiction Portal, at the end of 2019 after seven years of providing English-language news and information covering European fandom; the formation of the China Science Fiction Research Institute with "the aim of supporting the development of the sci-fi industry and related literary and artistic endeavours"; and the establishment of the Chilean Asociación de Literatura de Ciencia Ficción y Fantástica, which was founded in mid-2019. Science fiction is, as we shall see, all around the world.

Small and independent publishers play a vital role in the field, pioneering new voices, preserving history, and championing alternative points of view. While many independent presses seemed to have had strong years—most notably Subterranean Press, which published a number of the year's best books—others struggled. Sadly, Crossed

Genres Publications announced it was on indefinite hiatus and expected to close permanently once inventory was sold; Curiosity Quills Press announced it was stopping print publishing until it could clear outstanding royalty payments; and, most controversially, among allegations of late payments, nonpayments, and accusations of various improprieties, Canadian independent publisher ChiZine announced founders Sandra Kasturi and Brett Savory would be standing down from all publishing-related duties and Christie Harkin would assume the role of interim publisher. The future of the press is not known as I write.

What do all of these, and the no doubt many other changes I've missed, have to say about the state of things? I'm not sure. I think book publishing is in solid shape and I am optimistic about the decade ahead. Print, ebook, and audio sales are strong, independent booksellers are flourishing, and self-publishing has settled into a well-established path that carries none of the stigma that it once did. I am a little more cautious, though, about the state of short fiction and magazine publishing, which strikes me as being in a much more precarious situation, which we'll get to next.

There's no way to know how many SF short stories are published each year. Respected industry trade journal *Locus* (www.locusmag.com) has in the past estimated that over three thousand genre short stories are published annually, but that seems conservative, with stories now appearing in multiple-author anthologies, single-author short story collections, print and digital magazines, as part of Patreon and other fundraising platforms, in newsletters, as part of think tank projects, as individual stories sold online, and just about everywhere else. I don't know how much of an indication of scale it is, but the Science Fiction and Fantasy Writers of America (SFWA) currently lists forty short fiction markets that professionally publish speculative fiction of one kind or another, *Locus* identifies seventy, and online information source the Internet Speculative Fiction Database (www.isfdb.org) lists 862 short fiction magazine issues of one kind or another published during the year. And this, of course, excludes almost everything published outside the United States, the United Kingdom, and Australia, or in any language other than English. Suffice it to say, there are a lot of stories published every year in a lot of different places.

One change that happened early in the year that set the tone for 2019, even if it didn't define it, was the announcement in January that SFWA would increase their minimum payment rate for professional short fiction markets (the SFWA pro rate) to eight cents per word from September 1, 2019. The main impact this announcement had, beyond the important push to increase payment to short fiction writers, was on where authors looking for professional markets choose to submit their work. It's possible some markets will struggle to pay the higher rate and that it may impact their ability to attract top work, but it is nonetheless welcome.

It was a fairly good year for the SF magazine market, with a limited number of reported closures, and almost every magazine—print or digital—seeming to do well. We still don't have any print magazines appearing on a monthly schedule, something we could rely on in the past, but that seems a small price to pay for a stable market. This might be the point where I should mention that most of the magazines established before 2000 were print magazines, and most established after 2010 were primarily digital, but by 2019 all of them have, to a greater or lesser degree, both a print and digital presence.

Twenty or more years ago, science fiction had the "big three" magazines: *Asimov's*, *Analog*, and *F&SF*. Even though that nickname is no longer useful, with those three and *Tor.com*, *Clarkesworld*, *Lightspeed*, and *Uncanny* now making more of a "big seven," it is good that all of these are still with us and, even if they may have trimmed their sails here and there, seem to be thriving in these digital times. *F&SF* reached its 70th year in 2019, publishing a special anniversary issue featuring work by Paolo Bacigalupi, Kelly Link, Michael Moorcock, and others. Charles Coleman Finlay's fifth year at the magazine as editor was his best yet and saw him publishing outstanding fantasy and horror from G. V. Anderson, James Morrow, and Sam J. Miller, as well as strong SF from Lavie Tidhar, Elizabeth Bear, Rich Larson, and Michael Libling. The two Dell Magazines, *Asimov's Science Fiction* and *Analog Science Fiction and Fact*, also had strong years. The less engineering focused of the two, *Asimov's*, which has been published since 1977 and is edited by longtime editor Sheila Williams, featured excellent SF from Carrie Vaughn, Tegan Moore, Suzanne Palmer, Lawrence Watt-Evans, Greg Egan, Siobhan Carroll, Ray Nayler, and E. Lily Yu. In its 89th year of publication, *Analog* (formerly *Astounding*), under editor Trevor Quachri, published strong SF from Alec Nevala-Lee, Andy Dudak, S. B. Divya, Adam-Troy Castro, and James Van Pelt. *Analog's* 90th anniversary falls in 2020 and it's good to see it going strong and continuing to evolve. The other major print SF magazine is British institution *Interzone*, edited by Andy Sawyer. Launched in 1982 and always open to new and experimental work, it published interesting fiction from Tim Chawaga, Maria Haskins, John Kessel, and others.

Neil Clarke's *Clarkesworld*, John Joseph Adams's *Lightspeed*, Lynne Thomas and Michael Damian Thomas's *Uncanny Magazine*, and *Tor.com* are vitally important magazines that are published either primarily or exclusively online. *Clarkesworld* was launched in 2006 and publishes science fiction and fantasy. It has been instrumental in developing translated fiction as part of the modern SF field, and in 2019 published outstanding translations from China and Korea, including Bo-young Kim's powerful novella "How Alike Are We" and Chen Qiufan's "In This Moment We Are Happy." They also published one of the year's best stories of any kind, "The Painter of Trees" by Suzanne Palmer, and wonderful work by Derek Künsken, M. L. Clark, A. T. Greenblatt, and Rachel Swirsky. *Lightspeed* debuted in 2010 and publishes science fiction and fantasy. To my eye a lot of the best work in *Lightspeed* this year was fantasy, with great work from Brooke Bolander and others, but they did publish strong SF from Matthew Corradi, Adam-Troy Castro, Dominica Phetteplace, Isabel Yap, and one of the year's best SF stories, Caroline M. Yoachim's "The

Archronology of Love." *Uncanny Magazine* debuted in 2014 and has

won the Hugo Award for Best Semiprozine for the past four years. It
publishes excellent work that often sits on the borders between SF
and fantasy. *Uncanny* published outstanding fantasy by Ellen Klages,
Vina Jie-Min Prasad, and Silvia Moreno-Garcia, and excellent SF by
Elizabeth Bear, who probably had the best year of any single writer in
the field, as well as by Maurice Broaddus, Tim Pratt, and Fran Wilde.
Tor.com was launched by Tor Books in 2008 and quickly established
itself as a preeminent publisher of excellent short genre fiction. It features work acquired by a range of editors, myself included. Noting that
conflict of interest, I'd say they had an extremely strong year publishing
award-worthy work by Siobhan Carroll, S. L. Huang, Rivers Solomon,
Jonathan Carroll, Carole Johnstone, Tegan Moore, Greg Egan, Silvia
Park, and many more.

While the magazines mentioned above are the main "pro" magazines in the SF field, there is a proud tradition of magazines that are
classified—because of print-run size, payment rate, or reliance on volunteer staff—as being "semi-professional," which publish extremely
high-quality fiction and are regarded as major markets. *Uncanny*,
mentioned above, falls into this category. Venerable semiprozine
Strange Horizons had a good year publishing fiction, reviews, and criticism, as well as publishing their quarterly SF-in-translation magazine,
Samovar. New editor in chief Vanessa Rose Phin took over from Jane
Crowley and Kate Dollarhyde in 2019, and saw the magazine publish
strong work by Alex Yuschik, Shiv Ramdas, and Kathryn Harlan. *Fiyah:
The Magazine of Black Speculative Fiction* also had a good year, if not
quite as outstanding a year as it had in 2018, producing four issues
under publisher Troy L. Wiggins, including one of the year's best novellas, "While Dragons Claim the Sky" by Jen Brown, as well as strong
work by Nicky Drayden and Del Sandeen. *Fireside Magazine*, under
publisher Pablo Defendini, published fiction and poetry online that
was collected in monthly and quarterly issues during the year. This
included good work by L. D. Lewis, Danny Lore, Nibedita Sen, and
others.

Because this is a science fiction overview, I'll not spend much time on magazines that primarily publish fantasy, dark fantasy, or horror, but would recommend Scott Andrews's outstanding and award-winning *Beneath Ceaseless Skies* (my pick for the best fantasy magazine in the field), Silvia Moreno-Garcia and Sean Wallace's excellent *The Dark*, John Joseph Adams's *Nightmare*, LaShawn M. Wanak's *GigaNotoSaurus*, and Andy Sawyer's *The Third Alternative*.

While things were fairly stable in the magazine market, there were some changes. The most significant was the closure of *Apex Magazine*, which has gone on an indefinite hiatus as the publisher deals with personal medical issues. Prior to closing, *Apex Magazine* published an Afrofuturism issue that featured outstanding work by Suyi Davies Okungbowa, Steven Barnes and Tananarive Due, and Tobias S. Buckell. Also closing were *Orson Scott Card's InterGalactic Medicine Show* (which managed three issues in 2019), *Science Fiction Trails*, *Arsenika*, and *Capricious*, while both *Omenana* and *Future Science Fiction Digest* issued calls for financial help toward the end of the year.

All of these magazines mentioned above publish worthwhile fiction and nonfiction and deserve your support.

Given how much time I spend reading short fiction, I have to admit to having limited time to keep up with novel-length work. For that reason, I'll restrict myself to discussing those books I actually read during the year, and to highlighting others that garnered a lot of praise. Twenty nineteen seemed to be a great year for science fiction and science fiction–adjacent novels. Probably the hottest book of the year was Tamsyn Muir's debut, *Gideon the Ninth* (Tor.com), which I've already mentioned. It got enormous buzz and its goth sentiment seemed completely in step with the zeitgeist. I loved it. That said, the best pure quill science fiction novel of the year by some margin was Tim Maughan's debut tale of cyberterrorism, surveillance, and Big Brother, *Infinite Detail* (FSG). It's an essential book you should seek out. The zeitgeist is all very well, of course, but the core of the field continues on, changing a little, perhaps, but still there. Nothing is more central to science fiction than space opera, and there were a handful of terrific space operas published during the year, the best of which was Elizabeth Bear's compelling and powerful *Ancestral Night* (Saga), though I found Max Gladstone's *Empress of Forever* (Tor) to be enormous fun and loved Arkady Martine's engaging debut, *A Memory Called Empire* (Tor).

Time travel is an old trope, but it got a fresh treatment in 2019, with Annalee Newitz's fine sophomore effort, *The Future of Another Timeline* (Tor), taking non-binary feminists back to the past to fight a time war for women's rights in the future, with murder, mayhem, and Bay Area punk rock thrown in as a bonus. I also thought Charlie Jane Anders delivered the goods with her second novel, *The City in the Middle of the Night* (Tor), a genuinely compelling novel of aliens, rebels, and smugglers set on a weirdly inhospitable planet. And Sarah Pinsker's debut novel, *A Song for a New Day* (Berkley), offered a compelling look at how social changes might impact live performance that was both provocative, highly enjoyable, and very prescient.

There were some excellent series installments published during the year, with the second and third books of Tade Thompson's Wormwood Trilogy, *The Rosewater Insurrection* and *The Rosewater Redemption* (Orbit), probably being the highlight, though I greatly enjoyed Ian McDonald's *Luna: Moon Rising* (Gollancz), Alastair Reynolds's *Shadow Captain* (Gollancz), C. J. Cherryh and Jane Fancher's *Alliance Rising* (DAW), and the latest Expanse novel from James S. A. Corey, *Tiamat's Wrath* (Orbit). There also were a number of excellent SF novels published in translation this year. The best of these — and honestly one of the top three or four SF novels of 2019 — was Yōko Ogawa's *The Memory Police* (Pantheon), which I unhesitatingly recommend. Also excellent were Hugo Award–winner Liu Cixin's *Supernova Era* (Tor) and Chen Qiufan's debut, *Waste Tide* (Tor).

Other 2019 SF novels that have gotten a lot of attention include *Catfishing on CatNet*, Naomi Kritzer (TorTeen); *Frankissstein*, Jeanette Winterson (Grove; Jonathan Cape); *Golden State*, Ben Winters (Mulholland); *Perihelion Summer*, Greg Egan (Tor.com); *Rule of Capture*, Christopher Brown (Harper Voyager); *The Forbidden Stars*, Tim Pratt (Angry Robot); *The Testaments*, Margaret Atwood (Nan A. Talese; Doubleday); *War Girls*, Tochi Onyebuchi (Razorbill); *Atlas Alone*, Emma Newman (Ace); *Destroy All Monsters*, Sam J. Miller (Harper Teen); *A Boy and His Dog at the End of the World*, C. A. Fletcher (Orbit); *Fleet of Knives*, Gareth L. Powell (Titan); *The Return of the Incredible Exploding Man*, Dave Hutchinson (Solaris); *Edges: Inverted Frontier Book 1*, Linda Nagata (Mythic Island); *The Quantum Garden*, Derek Künsken (Solaris); *Doggerland*, Ben Smith (Fourth Estate); *Finder*, Suzanne Palmer (DAW); *Famous Men Who Never Lived*, K. Chess (Tin House); *Do You Dream of Terra-Two?*, Temi Oh (Saga); and *David Mogo, Godhunter*, Suyi Davies Okungbowa (Abaddon).

With so much short fiction published every year it's hard to imagine any year being a bad year for anthologies, and this was not that year. Instead, we had a year where we saw all of the themes and trends impacting the wider SF field—from climate change to community inclusiveness to works in translation to Afrofuturism—writ small. Before proceeding, I should mention as a disclaimer that I edited two anthologies, *Mission Critical* and *The Best Science Fiction & Fantasy of the Year: Volume Thirteen*, both of which appeared during the year. I commend them to you and move on.

With major novels in translation from Yōko Ogawa, Liu Cixin, Chen Qiufan, Yoshiki Tanaka, Baoshu, and others, and with short fiction in translation in *Clarkesworld*, *Apex*, *The Dark*, and other venues, this was the year of SF in translation, something reflected in the number of anthologies of SF in translation published in 2019. Probably the one with the highest profile, and one of the year's best anthologies overall, was Ken Liu's second anthology of Chinese fiction in translation, *Broken Stars* (Tor), which featured outstanding work by Han Song, Xia Jia, Baoshu, and Liu Cixin. This companion to 2016's *Invis-*

ible Planets is essential. Hachette India published two SF anthologies during the year, Tarun K. Saint's *The Gollancz Book of South Asian Science Fiction* and Sukanya Venkatraghavan's *Magical Women*. Both were fascinating. Saint's anthology features Vandana Singh's "Reunion"—one of the year's very best stories—along with strong work by S. B. Divya, Giti Chandra, and Sumita Sharma. Happily, the publisher is making the book available in the British and North American markets. *Magical Women*, on the other hand, provided a critically useful look at genre fiction being written by Indian women and included interesting work by Shveta Thakrar, Nikita Deshpande, and Asma Kazi. We're only just beginning to see translated fiction coming from South Korea, a lot of it thanks to the efforts of Sunyoung Park, Gord Sellar, and the team at *Clarkesworld*. Sunyoung Park and Sang Joon Park co-edited a major anthology, *Readymade Bodhisattva* (Kaya), which featured fine work by Kim Changgyu, Park Min-gyu, Jeong Soyeon, and others. And finally, one of my favorite anthologies of the year was Basma Ghalayini's *Palestine + 100: Stories from a Century After the Nakba* from UK publisher Comma Press. A thoughtful, rich, varied collection of SF that imagined events one hundred years after the occupation of Palestine, it was a revelation featuring fine work from Saleem Haddad, Anwar Ahmed, Mazen Maarouf, and more. It's highly recommended.

There were a handful of other strong original SF anthologies published during the year, the best of which was Victor LaValle and John Joseph Adams's status quo–challenging *A People's Future of the United States* (One World), which featured top-quality work from Charlie Jane Anders, Alice Sola Kim, Sam J. Miller, and many more. In a similar vein, also worthwhile and recommended are Cat Rambo's *If This Goes On: The Science Fiction Future of Today's Politics* (Parvus) and Jason Sizemore's *Do Not Go Quietly* (Apex). After the Lavalle and Adams anthology, probably the most impressive English-language SF anthology was Dominik Parisien and Navah Wolfe's third editorial collaboration, *The Mythic Dream* (Saga), which featured outstanding work by Indrapramit Das, Carmen Maria

Machado, Seanan McGuire, and others. I also was impressed by Nisi Shawl's fine *New Suns: Original Speculative Fiction by People of Color* (Solaris), Mahvesh Murad and Jared Shurin's *The Outcast Hours* (Solaris), and Bryan Thomas Schmidt's *Infinite Stars: Dark Frontiers* (Titan).

In recent years tech companies, science magazines, and think tanks have produced a variety of fiction projects, some of which featured dull, plodding work and some of which are truly outstanding. The very best of these for 2019, and one of the top original anthologies of the year of any kind, was Ann VanderMeer's *Current Futures: A Sci-Fi Ocean Anthology* (XPRIZE), which featured new SF about climate change and the world's oceans by some of the best women writers working today, including work by Vandana Singh, Nalo Hopkinson, Elizabeth Bear, and Deborah Biancotti. The project, which oddly appears to be blocked from search engines, is only available on a website here (https://go.xprize.org/oceanstories) and has my highest recommendation. The other major projects in this space for the year were *Slate*'s Future Tense, which featured strong work from Ken Liu, Chen Qiufan, Elizabeth Bear, and others, and the *New York Times*' fascinating "Op-Eds From the Future" series, that includes short pieces from Cory Doctorow, Ted Chiang, Brooke Bolander, and Fran Wilde, among others. This year also saw publication of an anthology collecting the first year of Future Tense's stories, *Future Tense Fiction: Stories of Tomorrow* edited by Kirsten Berg (The Unnamed Press).

Science fiction relishes year's-best anthologies like this one, and last year saw the publication of my own book mentioned above as well as Gardner Dozois's final anthology, *The Very Best of the Best: 35 Years of the Year's Best Science Fiction* (St. Martin's Griffin), Neil Clarke's *The Best Science Fiction of the Year: Volume Four* (Night Shade), Rich Horton's *The Year's Best Science Fiction & Fantasy 2019* (Prime), Carmen Maria Machado and John Joseph Adams's *The Best American Science Fiction and Fantasy 2019* (Mariner), and Bogi Takác's *Transcendent 4: The Year's Best Transgender Speculative Fiction* (Lethe), all

of which are worth seeking out. Also of interest are Neil Clarke's *The*
Eagle Has Landed: 50 Years of Lunar Science Fiction (Night Shade)
and Hannu Rajaniemi and Jacob Weisman's *The New Voices of Science Fiction* (Tachyon).

Finally, although I'm not covering fantasy or horror here, I'll note
that the best fantasy or horror anthology of the year was Ellen Datlow's
massive *Echoes: The Saga Anthology of Ghost Stories* (Saga), which
featured an impressive array of ghostly fiction from some of the best
writers in the field. Also highly recommended is Ann VanderMeer and
Jeff VanderMeer's even more enormous *The Big Book of Classic Fantasy* (Vintage), which is essentially a college course in a book. Seek
it out.

Whether 2019 is eventually seen as a good year or a poor one for short
fiction, it nonetheless saw publication of no fewer than four magisterial short story collections from major writers working in their prime.
Easily the most anticipated of these was Ted Chiang's *Exhalation: Stories* (Knopf). Only the second collection of his work to be published in
a thirty-year-long career, following 2002's *Stories of Your Life and Others* (Tor), *Exhalation: Stories* brought together all of Chiang's significant published works since that first collection, including classics like
the title story and "The Merchant and the Alchemist's Gate" alongside two major new stories, "Anxiety Is the Dizziness of Freedom" and
"Omphalos." At times almost giddily inspired and thought-provoking,
it is essential for lovers of short fiction of any kind. Completely different and yet a not-too-distant cousin to the intellectual brilliance of
Exhalation, the simply titled *The Best of Greg Egan* (Subterranean)
collects twenty stories published across nearly thirty years and includes
stone-cold classics like "Learning to Be Me," "Reasons to Be Cheerful," and Hugo winner "Oceanic." Egan's short fiction swept through
the field in the 1990s like few others have done in the history of SF,
and this book is an indispensable record of that. Less definitively science fictional, *The Very Best of Caitlín R. Kiernan* collects twenty sto-

ries published over a fourteen-year period that saw Kiernan establish herself not as science fiction writer or fantasy writer or horror writer, but simply and purely as a *writer* and one who on her day could deliver a tour de force in just about any genre. This book collects the fruit of many such days. Highlights include "Tidal Forces," "Interstate Love Song (Murder Ballad No. 8)," and "The Prayer of Ninety Cats." And then there's a book that simply does not fit. In fairness, it belongs, but it does not fit. The late, great tale-teller R. A. Lafferty wrote science fiction, science-fictiony stuff, yarns, notions, and fantasies across a career that stretched from 1959 to his death in 2002. *The Best of R. A. Lafferty* (Gollancz), which again I must confess to having edited, was rightly published as part of the Gollancz Masterworks series and collects nearly two dozen of his finest stories along with assorted introductions and such. A wonderful book, and happily a North American edition is forthcoming.

While those four books stood out, they were by no means alone. I was enchanted by Sofia Rhei's *Everything is Made of Letters* (Aqueduct). Translated from Spanish, it contained five science-fictional fabulations including the simply delightful "Secret Stories of Doors," which is reprinted here. In a not-dissimilar vein, SF writer and poet Malka Older delivered her debut collection, . . . *And Other Disasters* (Mason Jar), which was playful, allusive, and captivating. Perhaps more immediately science fictional was Aliette de Bodard's first collection, *Of Wars, and Memories, and Starlight* (Subterranean), which collected her Xuya universe stories in a single volume along with a major new novella "Of Birthdays, and Fungus, and Kindness," which I would have included here, had space permitted. Yoon Ha Lee's Hexarchate trilogy is one of the outstanding works of science fiction of the 2010s. Each volume was individually nominated for the Hugo Award, as was the series, while *Ninefox Gambit* was also nominated for the Nebula. This year saw the publication of *Hexarchate Stories* (Solaris), which collects all of the short fiction in the series alongside a new novella, "Glass Cannon." The other standout SF collection of the year was Cory Doctorow's rebellious and revolutionary *Radical-*

ized (Tor), which collected four new novellas, each of which were essential.

This list could continue indefinitely, but to keep things as brief as possible, I'd also recommend *Contingency Plans for the Apocalypse*, S. B. Divya (Hachette India); *And Go Like This*, John Crowley (Small Beer); *Sooner or Later Everything Falls into the Sea*, Sarah Pinsker (Small Beer); *Snow White Learns Witchcraft*, Theodora Goss (Mythic Delirium); *Episodes*, Christopher Priest (Gollancz); *Homesick*, Nino Cipri (Dzanc); *Laughter at the Academy*, Seanan McGuire (Subterranean); *Binti: The Complete Collection*, Nnedi Okorafor (DAW); *A City Made of Words*, Paul Park (PM); *salt slow*, Julia Armfield (Flatiron); *Mars*, Asja Bakic (The Feminist Press); *The City and the Cygnets*, Michael Bishop (Fairwood; Kudzu Planet); *Collision*, J.S. Breukelaar (Meerkat); *Unforeseen*, Molly Gloss (Saga); *Meet Me in the Future*, Kameron Hurley (Tachyon); *Big Cat and Other Stories*, Gwyneth Jones (NewCon); *All Worlds Are Real*, Susan Palwick (Fairwood); *Miracles & Marvels: Stories*, Tim Pratt (Merry Blacksmith); and *Learning Monkey and Crocodile*, Nick Wood (Luna).

As any longtime reader will tell you, science fiction publishers have been publishing novellas or short novels as stand-alone books for decades. Whether or not the old Ace Doubles met the length criteria to be novellas or not, by the 1980s these small books were fairly commonplace. And yet, even allowing for that and the view held by some readers that the novella is the ideal length for a science fiction story, it's undeniable that they have gained unprecedented attention in the last four or five years.

Tor.com Publishing was launched by Tor Books in 2014 to publish novellas and short novels, and quickly established itself as the preeminent novella publisher in the field with runaway successes like Nnedi Okorafor's Binti stories, Martha Wells's Murderbot Diaries, and Seanan McGuire's Wayward Children series. This year Tor.com produced some of the very best stories of the year, which are only omitted from this book because of length. Certainly, P. Djèlí Clark's wonderful *The Haunting of Tram Car 015* and Saad Z. Hossain's remarkable *The Gurkha and the Lord of Tuesday* would be in this book if I had unlimited space, and I also happily recommend C. S. E. Cooney's *Desdemona and the Deep*, Michael Blumlein's *Longer*, Priya Sharma's *Ormeshadow*, Katharine Duckett's *Miranda in Milan*, Ian McDonald's *The Menace from Farside*, and Alastair Reynolds's *Permafrost*. Tor .com also published Greg Egan's outstanding climate-change novel, *Perihelion Summer*, which I feel is the most approachable work of his career. Since I'm discussing novellas published as stand-alone books, I couldn't not mention again Amal El-Mohtar and Max Gladstone's *This Is How You Lose the Time War* (Saga), which I expect to sweep all of the major awards during 2020. I also was knocked out by Rivers Solomon's powerful *The Deep* (Saga), which was based upon work done with the band Clipping, and by K. J. Parker's outstanding *My Beautiful Life* (Subterranean). British independent press Newcon continues to publish excellent novellas, this year including Adam Roberts's *The Man Who Would Be Kling* and Dave Hutchinson's *Nomads*.

I don't read much nonfiction about the SF field. That said, four books did grab my attention and are recommended. I am more than a little tired of talking about Robert A. Heinlein and didn't think there was much more to be said on the subject, but Farah Mendlesohn's outstanding *The Pleasant Profession of Robert A. Heinlein* (Unbound) held my attention throughout as the author found new things to say about this greatest of SF writers. Gwyneth Jones's provocative and engaging book, *Joanna Russ* (University of Illinois Press), stands as one of the few overviews of this critically important writer and really does belong on your bookshelf. It also stands as an urgent call for more of Russ's work to be returned to print. *Joanna Russ* and Mendlesohn's book on Heinlein are my front-runners for the Hugo, though John Crowley's *Reading Backwards: Essays and Reviews, 2005–2018* and Peter Watts's wonderful and argumentative

Peter Watts Is An Angry Sentient Tumor: Revenge Fantasies and Essays are also outstanding.

XXXI

INTRODUCTION

The 77th World Science Fiction Convention (aka DublinCon 2019) was held in Dublin, Ireland, August 15–19, and drew an attendance of 4,190, down a little from recent years. The 2019 Hugo Awards winners were: Best Novel, *The Calculating Stars* by Mary Robinette Kowal; Best Novella, *Artificial Condition* by Martha Wells; Best Novelette, "If at First You Don't Succeed, Try, Try Again" by Zen Cho; Best Short Story, "A Witch's Guide to Escape: A Practical Compendium of Portal Fantasies" by Alix E. Harrow; the Lodestar Award for Best Young Adult Book, *Children of Blood and Bone* by Tomi Adeyemi; Best Related Work, Archive of Our Own; Best Art Book, *The Books of Earthsea: The Complete Illustrated Edition* by Ursula K. Le Guin and illustrated by Charles Vess; Best Graphic Story, *Monstress Volume 3: Haven* by Marjorie Liu and Sana Takeda; Best Dramatic Presentation Long Form, *Spider-Man: Into the Spider-Verse*; Best Dramatic Presentation Short Form, *The Good Place: Janet(s)*; Best Editor (Short Form), Gardner Dozois; Best Editor (Long Form), Navah Wolfe; Best Professional Artist, Charles Vess; Best Semiprozine, *Uncanny Magazine*; Best Fanzine, *Lady Business*; Best Fan Writer, Foz Meadows; Best Fan Artist, Likhain (Mia Sereno); Best Fancast, *Our Opinions Are Correct* by Annalee Newitz and Charlie Jane Anders; and Best Series, *Wayfarers* by Becky Chambers.

The 2019 Nebula Awards winners, presented in Woodland Hills, California, on May 18 were: Best Novel, *The Calculating Stars* by Mary Robinette Kowal; Best Novella, *The Tea Master and the Detective* by Aliette de Bodard; Best Novelette, *The Only Harmless Great Thing* by Brooke Bolander; Best Short Story, "The Secret Lives of the Nine Negro Teeth of George Washington" by P. Djèlí Clark; and Best Game Writing, *Black Mirror: Bandersnatch* by Charlie Brooker. Also presented were the Andre Norton Award to Tomi Adeyemi for *Children of Blood and Bone*; and the Ray Bradbury Award to Phil Lord and

Rodney Rothman for the screenplay *Spider-Man: Into the Spider-Verse*. The SFWA Damon Knight Grand Master was William Gibson.

The World Fantasy Awards, presented at the 45th World Fantasy Convention in Los Angeles October 31–November 3 were: Best Novel, *Witchmark* by C. L. Polk; Best Novella, "The Privilege of the Happy Ending" by Kij Johnson; Best Short Fiction (tie), "Ten Deals with the Indigo Snake" by Mel Kassel and "Like a River Loves the Sky" by Emma Törzs; Best Anthology, *Worlds Seen in Passing* edited by Irene Gallo; Best Collection, *The Tangled Lands* by Paolo Bacigalupi and Tobias S. Buckell; Best Artist, Rovina Cai; Special Award—Professional, Huw Lewis-Jones for *The Writer's Map: An Atlas of Imaginary Lands*; Special Award—Non-professional, Scott H. Andrews for *Beneath Ceaseless Skies*. The Life Achievement recipients were Jack Zipes and Hayao Miyazaki.

The 2019 Campbell Memorial Award winner was Sam J. Miller for *Blackfish City*; the Theodore Sturgeon Memorial Award winner was Annalee Newitz for "When Robot and Crew Saved East St. Louis"; and the 2019 Arthur C. Clarke Award winner was *Rosewater* by Tade Thompson. For more information on these and other awards, see the excellent Science Fiction Awards Database (www.sfadb.com).

Each year we sadly lose too many beloved creators. This year their number included: SFWA Grand Master, World Fantasy Lifetime Achievement recipient, and Science Fiction Hall of Fame inductee Gene Wolfe, who wrote the groundbreaking *The Book of the New Sun*, which extended to thirteen volumes, and won the World Fantasy Award four times, the Nebula Award twice, and was nominated for the Hugo Award nine times; World Fantasy Lifetime Achievement recipient Carol Emshwiller, who wrote *Carmen Dog, Mister Boots, The Secret City*, the Philip K. Dick Award–winning *The Mount*, and the World Fantasy Award–winning *The Start of the End of It All and Other Stories*, and was nominated for the Nebula Award four times, winning twice for her short fiction; publisher Betty Ballantine, who cofounded

publishing houses Bantam Books and Ballantine Books with her late
husband, Ian, and who helped to introduce mass market paperbacks
to the US by establishing the US division of Penguin Books; Vonda
N. McIntyre, who won Nebula Awards for "Of Mist, and Grass, and
Sand," *Dreamsnake*, and *The Moon and the Sun*, cofounded Clarion
West, and received the Kevin O'Donnell Service to SFWA Award in
2010; Barry Hughart, the World Fantasy Award–winning author of
Bridge of Birds, as well as the sequels *The Story of the Stone* and *Eight
Skilled Gentlemen*; publisher Robert S. Friedman, who founded Rainbow Ridge Books and specialty book publisher The Donning Company; Australian author Andrew McGahan, who wrote the Ship Kings
series of fantasy novellas, as well as several well-regarded stand-alone
novels; two-time Campbell Award finalist Carrie Richerson, who was
also nominated for the Gaylactic Spectrum Awards for her short story
"Love on a Stick"; Alsatian author and artist Tomi Ungerer, who won
the Hans Christian Andersen Award in 1998 for contributions as a children's illustrator; author W. E. Butterworth, better known as W. E.
B. Griffin, who wrote military and detective fiction; Gillian Freeman,
who wrote SF novel *The Leader* about fascism; Janet Asimov, who was
a successful psychiatrist and wrote mysteries and SF, including several
with her husband, Isaac; anthologist Hugh Lamb, who began with re-
print anthology *A Tide of Terror*, did most of his work in the 1970s, but
remained active to the end of the century; Charles Black, who edited
the eleven *Black Books of Horror*, two of which were nominated for the
British Fantasy Award; W. H. Pugmire, who wrote horror and Love-
craftian fiction; Allan Cole, who collaborated with Chris Bunch on
the Sten series; Tamara Kazavchinskaya, who was editor of the Russian
magazine *Foreign Literature* and translated works from English and
Polish, including the work of Stanislaw Lem; Russian author Sergei
Pavlov, who wrote *Moon Rainbow* and founded the Moon Rainbow
Award; Walter Harris, who wrote the novels *The Day I Died*, *Saliva*,
and *The Fifth Horseman*, as well as novelizations of *Creature from the
Black Lagoon* and *Werewolf of London*; Bengali editor Adrish Bardhan,
who began editing *Ascharya*, India's first SF magazine, and later edited

Fantastic magazine, and who received the Sudhindranath Raha Award for his work in Bengali SF; Stoker Award for Lifetime Achievement recipient Dennis Etchison, whose novels include *The Fog, Darkside*, and *California Gothic* and who won multiple World Fantasy and British Fantasy Awards; Polish author and editor Maciej Parowski, who edited *Nowa Fantastyka* and was chief editor of *Czas Fantastyki*; Milan Asadurov, who founded the Galaxy imprint in Bulgaria that published works by Asimov, Bradbury, the Strugatskys, and Le Guin; J. Neil Schulman, who won the Prometheus Award for *Alongside Night* and *The Rainbow Cadenza* and who wrote *The Twilight Zone* episode "Profile in Silver"; Robert N. Stephenson, who was editor and publisher of *Altair* magazine, edited several anthologies, and whose short story "Rains of la Strange" won the 2011 Aurealis Award; two-time Prometheus Award winner Brad Linaweaver, who was the author of *Moon of Ice, Anarchia*, and several TV shows; Melissa C. Michaels, who began publishing fiction in 1979 and wrote five volumes in the Skyrider series, as well as other novels; SFWA Author Emeritus Katherine MacLean, whose first story appeared in 1949 and whose 1972 novella "The Missing Man" won the Nebula Award; Terrance Dicks, who wrote several episodes of *Doctor Who*, served as script editor on the series from 1968 to 1974, and also worked on *The Avengers, Moonbase 3*, and *Space: 1999*; Hal Colebatch, who wrote *Return of Heroes*, a study of heroic fantasy, contributed to the *J. R. R. Tolkien Encyclopedia*, and wrote stories in Larry Niven's Man-Kzin Wars series; John A. Pitts, who began publishing short fiction in 2006 and novels (as J. A. Pitts) beginning with *Black Blade Blues* in 2010; Michael Blumlein, who wrote *The Movement of Mountains, X,Y, The Healer*, four collections of short fiction, and who was nominated for World Fantasy, Stoker, and Tiptree Awards; World Fantasy Award for Lifetime Achievement recipient Gahan Wilson, whose cartoon work was epitomized by his mixture of horror, fantasy, and humor, and which appeared in *Playboy, The Magazine of Fantasy & Science Fiction*, and other magazines; screenwriter D. C. Fontana, who had a long career as a scriptwriter and story editor for *Star Trek* and also worked on *Buck Rogers in the 25th Century, Babylon 5, The Six*

Million Dollar Man, *War of the Worlds*, and numerous other television series; Andrew Weiner, who immigrated to Canada from Britain and whose first novel was *Station Gehenna*, which was followed by *Getting Near the End* and *Boulevard des disparus*.

And that brings us to the end of the beginning. The stories await. These are interesting times in the world and in science fiction, and you can see the field urgently rising to the many challenges it faces. I'm already reading work that will appear in next year's book and can't wait to share it with you. For now, though, I hope you enjoy these stories as much as I have and that I'll see you back here next year.

Jonathan Strahan
Perth, Western Australia
January 2020

THE BOOKSTORE AT THE END OF AMERICA

CHARLIE JANE ANDERS

Charlie Jane Anders's (charliejane.net) most recent novel is *The City in the Middle of the Night*. She's also the author of *All the Birds in the Sky*, which won the Nebula, Crawford, and Locus Awards; *Choir Boy*, which won a Lambda Literary Award; the novella *Rock Manning Goes for Broke*; and the short story collection *Six Months, Three Days, Five Others*. Her short fiction has appeared in *Tor.com, Boston Review, Tin House, Conjunctions, The Magazine of Fantasy & Science Fiction, Wired, Slate, Asimov's Science Fiction, Lightspeed*, and many anthologies. Her story "Six Months, Three Days" won a Hugo Award, and her story "Don't Press Charges and I Won't Sue" won a Theodore Sturgeon Memorial Award. Coming up is a new collection, *Even Greater Mistakes*. Charlie Jane also organizes the monthly Writers With Drinks reading series, and cohosts the podcast *Our Opinions Are Correct* with Annalee Newitz.

A bookshop on a hill: two front doors, two walkways lined with blank slates and grass, two identical signs welcoming customers to the First and Last Page, and a great blue building in the middle, shaped like an old-fashioned barn with a slanted tiled roof and generous rain gutters. Nobody knew how many books were inside that building, not even Molly, the owner. But if you couldn't find it there, they probably hadn't written it down yet.

The two walkways led to two identical front doors, with straw welcome mats, blue plank floors, and the scent of lilacs and old bindings—but then you'd see a completely different store, depending which side you entered. With two cash registers, for two separate kinds of money.

If you entered from the California side, you'd see a wall hanging: women of all ages, shapes and origins holding hands and dancing. You'd notice the display of the latest books from a variety of small presses that clung to life in Colorado Springs and Santa Fe, from literature and poetry to cultural studies. The shelves closest to the door on the California side included a decent amount of women's and queer studies, but also a strong selection of classic literature, going back to Virginia Woolf and Zora Neale Hurston. Plus some brand-new paperbacks.

If you came in through the American front door, the basic layout would be pretty similar, except for the big painting of the nearby Rocky Mountains. But you might notice more books on religion, and some history books with a somewhat more conservative approach. The literary books skewed a bit more towards Faulkner, Thoreau and Hemingway, not to mention Ayn Rand, and you might find more books of essays about self-reliance and strong families, along with another selection of low-cost paperbacks: thrillers and war novels, including brand-new releases from the big printing plant in Gatlinburg. Romance novels, too.

Go through either front door and keep walking, and you'd find yourself in a maze of shelves, with a plethora of nooks and a bevy of side rooms. Here a cavern of science fiction and fantasy, there a deep alcove of theatre books—and a huge annex of history and sociology, including a whole wall devoted to explaining the origins of the Great Sundering. Of course, some people did make it all the way from one front door to the other, past the overfed-snake shape of the hallways and the giant central reading room, with a plain red carpet and two beat-down couches in it. But the design of the store encouraged you to stay inside your own reality.

The exact border between America and California, which else-where featured watchtowers and roadblocks, "You are now leaving/You are now entering" signs, and terrible overpriced souvenir stands, was denoted in the First and Last Page by a tall bookcase of self-help titles about coping with divorce.

People came hundreds of miles in either direction, via hydroelec-tric cars, solarcycles, mecha-horses, and tour buses, to get some book they couldn't live without. You could get electronic books via the Share, of course, but they might be plagued with crowdsourced editing, user-targeted content, random annotations and sometimes just plain garbage. You might be reading the Federalist Papers on your Gidget and come across a paragraph about rights vs. duties that wasn't there before—or, for that matter, a few pages relating to hair cream, because you'd been searching on hair cream yesterday. Not to mention, the same book might read completely differently in California than in America. You could only rely on ink and paper (or, for newer books, Peip0r) for consistency, not to mention the whole sensory experience of smelling and touching volumes, turning their pages, bowing their spines.

Everybody needs books, Molly figured. No matter where they live, how they love, what they believe, whom they want to kill. We all want books. The moment you start thinking of books as some exclusive club, or the loving of books as a high distinction, then you're a bad bookseller.

Books are the best way to discover what people thought before you were born. And an author is just someone who tried their utmost to make sense of their own mess, and maybe their failure contains a few seeds to help you with yours.

Sometimes people asked Molly why she didn't just simplify it down to one entrance. Force the people from America to talk to the Califor-nians, and vice versa—maybe expose one side or the other to some books that might challenge their worldview just a little. And Molly always replied that she had a business to run, and if she managed to keep everyone reading, then that was enough. At the very least, Molly's arrangement kept this the most peaceful outpost on the border, without people gathering on one side to scream at the people on the other.

Some of those screaming people were old enough to have grown up in the United States of America, but they acted as though these two lands had always been enemies.

Whichever entrance of the bookstore you went through, the first thing you'd notice was probably Phoebe. Rake-thin, coltish, rambunctious, right on the edge of becoming, she ran light enough on her bare feet to avoid ever rattling a single bookcase or dislodging a single volume. You heard Phoebe's laughter before her footsteps. Molly's daughter wore denim overalls and cheap linen blouses most days, or sometimes a floor-length skirt or lacy-hemmed dress, plus plastic bangles and necklaces. She hadn't gotten her ears pierced yet.

People from both sides of the line loved Phoebe, who was a joyful shriek that you only heard from a long way away, a breath of gladness running through the flowerbeds.

Molly used to pester Phoebe about getting outdoors to breathe some fresh air—because that seemed like something moms were supposed to say, and Molly was paranoid about being a bad mother, since she was basically married to a bookstore, albeit one containing a large section of parenting books. But Molly was secretly glad when Phoebe disobeyed her and stayed inside, endlessly reading. Molly hoped Phoebe would always stay shy, that mother and daughter would hunker inside the First and Last Page, side-eyeing the world through thin linen curtains when they weren't reading together.

Then Phoebe had turned fourteen, and suddenly she was out all the time, and Molly didn't see her for hours. Around that time, Phoebe had unexpectedly grown pretty and lanky, her neck long enough to let her auburn ponytail swing as she ran around with the other kids who lived in the tangle of tree-lined streets on the America side of the line, plus a few kids who snuck across from California. Nobody seriously patrolled this part of the border, and there was one craggy rockpile, like an echo of the nearby Rocky Mountains, that you could just scramble over and cross from one country to the other, if you knew the right path.

Phoebe and her gang of kids, ranging from twelve to fifteen, would go trampling the tall grass near the border on a "treasure hunt," or setting up an "ambush fort" in the rocks. Phoebe occasionally caught sight of Molly and turned to wave, before running up the dusty hillside towards Zadie and Mark, who had just snuck over from California, with canvas backpacks full of random games and junk. Sometimes Phoebe led an entire brigade of kids into the store, pouring cups of water or Molly's homebrewed ginger beer for everyone, and they would all pause and say *Hello, Ms. Carlton* before running outside again.

Mostly, the kids were just a raucous chorus, as they chased each other with pea-guns. There were times when they stayed in the most overgrown area of trees and bracken until way after sundown, until Molly was just about to message the other local parents via her Gidget, and then she'd glimpse a few specks of light emerging from the claws and twisted limbs. Molly always asked Phoebe what they did in that tiny stand of vegetation, which barely qualified as "the woods," and Phoebe always said: nothing. They just hung out. But Molly imagined those kids under the moonlight, blotted by heavy leaves, and they could be doing anything: drinking, taking drugs, playing kiss-and-tell games.

Even if Molly had wanted to keep tabs on her daughter, she couldn't leave the bookstore unattended. The bi-national design of the store required at least two people working at all times, one per register, and most of the people Molly hired only lasted a month or two, and then had to run home because their families were worried about all the latest hints of another war on the horizon. Every day, another batch of propaganda bubbled up on Molly's Gidget, from both sides, claiming that one country was a crushing theocracy or the other was a godless meat-grinder. And meanwhile, you heard rumblings, about both countries searching for the last precious dregs of water—sometimes actual rumblings, as California sent swarms of robots deep underground. Everybody was holding their breath.

Molly was working the front counter on the California side, trying as usual not to show any reaction to the people with weird tattoos, or with glowing silver threads flowing into their skulls. Everyone knew how eager Californians were to hack their own bodies and brains, from programmable birth control to brain implants that connected them to the Anoth Complex. Molly smiled, made small talk, recommended books based on her uncanny memory for what everybody had been buying—in short, she treated everyone like a customer, even the folks who noticed Molly's crucifix and clicked their tongues, because obviously she'd been brainwashed into her faith.

One day, a regular customer named Sander came in, looking for a rare book from the last days of the United States about sustainable farming and animal consciousness by a woman named Hope Dorrance. For some reason, nobody had ever uploaded this book of essays to the Share. Molly looked in the fancy computer and saw that they had one copy, but when Molly led Sander back to the shelf where it was supposed to be, the book was missing.

Sander stared at the space where *Souls on the Land* ought to be, and their pale, round face was full of lines. They had a single tattoo of a butterfly clad in gleaming armor, and the wires rained from the shaved back of their skull. They were some kind of engineer for the Anoth Complex.

"Huh," Molly said. "So this is where it ought to be. But I better check if maybe we sold it over on the, uh, other side and somehow didn't log the sale." Sander nodded, and followed Molly until they arrived in America. There, Molly squeezed past Mitch, who was working the register, and dug through a dozen scraps of paper until she found one. "Oh. Yeah. Well, darn."

They had sold their only copy of *Souls on the Land* to one of their most faithful customers on the America side: a gray-haired woman named Teri Wallace, who went to Molly's church (and whose daughter Minnie played with Phoebe and her friends). And Teri was in the store right now, searching for a cookbook. Mitch had just seen her go past. Unfortunately, Teri hated Californians even more than most Americans. And Sander was the sort of Californian that Teri especially did not appreciate.

"So it looks like we sold it a while back, and we just didn't update our inventory, which, uh, does happen," Molly said.

"In essence, this was false advertising." Sander drew upwards, with the usual Californian sense of affront the moment anything wasn't perfectly efficient. "You told me that the book was available, when in fact you should have known it wasn't."

Molly had already decided not to tell Sander who had bought the Hope Dorrance, but Teri came back clutching a book of killer salads just as Sander was in mid-rant about the ethics of retail communication. Sander happened to mention *Souls on the Land*, and Teri's ears pricked up.

"Oh, I just bought that book," Teri said.

Sander spun around, smiling, and said, "Oh. Pleased to meet you. I'm afraid that book you bought is one that had been promised to me. I don't suppose we could work out some kind of arrangement? Perhaps some system of needs-based allocation, because my need for this book is extremely great." Sander was already falling into the hyper-rational, insistent language of a Californian faced with a problem.

"Sorry," Teri said. "I bought it. I own it now. It's mine."

"But," Sander said. "There are many ways we could . . . I mean, you could loan it to me, and I could digitize it and return it to you in good condition."

"I don't want it in good condition. I want it in the condition it's in now."

"But—"

Molly could see this conversation was about three exchanges away from full-blown unpleasantries. Teri was going to insult Sander, either directly or by getting their pronoun wrong. Sander was going to call Teri stupid, either by implication or outright. Molly could see an easy solution: she could give Teri a bribe, a free book or blanket discount, in exchange for letting Sander borrow the Hope Dorrance so they could digitize it using special page-turning robots. But this wasn't going to be solved with reason. Not right now, anyway, with the two of them snarling at each other.

So Molly put on her biggest smile and said, "Sander. I just remembered, I had something extra special set aside for you, back in the psychology/philosophy annex. I've been meaning to give it to you, and it slipped my mind until just now. Come on, I'll show you." She tugged gently at Sander's arm, and hustled them back into the warren of bookshelves. Sander kept grumbling about Teri's irrational selfishness, until they had left America.

Molly had no idea what the special book she'd been saving for Sander actually was—but she figured by the time they got through the Straits of Romance and all the switchbacks of biography, she'd think of something.

Phoebe was having a love triangle. Molly became aware of this in stages, by noticing how all the other kids were together and overhearing snippets of conversation (despite her best efforts not to eavesdrop).

Jonathan Brinkfort, the son of the minister at Molly's church, had started hanging around Phoebe with a hangdog expression like he'd lost one of those kiss-and-tell games and it had left him with gambling debts. Jon was a tall, quiet boy with a handsome square face, who mediated every tiny dispute among the neighborhood kids with a slow gravitas, but Molly had never before seen him lost for words. She had been hand-selling airship adventure books to Jon since he was little.

And then there was Zadie Kagwa, whose dad was a second-generation immigrant from Uganda with a taste for very old science fiction. Zadie had a fresh tattoo on one shoulder, of a dandelion with seedlings fanning out into the wind, and one string of fiber-optic pearls coming out of her locs. Zadie's own taste in books roamed from science and math to radical politics to girls-at-horse-camp novels. Zadie whispered to Phoebe and bought tiny presents from California, like these weird candies with chili peppers in them.

Molly could just imagine the conversations she'd hear in church if her daughter got into an unnatural relationship with a girl—from *California*, no less—instead of dating a nice American boy who happened to be Canon Brinkfort's son.

But Phoebe didn't seem to be inclined to choose one or the other. She accepted Jon's stammered compliments with the same shy smile as Zadie's gifts.

Molly took Phoebe on a day trip into California, where they got their passports stamped with a one-day entry permit, and they climbed into Molly's old three-wheel Dancer. They drove past wind farms and military installations, past signs for the latest Anoth Cloud-Brain schemes, until they stopped at a place that sold milkshakes so thick, you lost the skin on the sides of your mouth just trying to unclog the straw.

Phoebe was in silent mode, hugging herself and cocooning inside her big polyfiber jacket when she wasn't slurping her milkshake. Molly tried to make conversation, talking about who had been buying what sort of books lately, and what you could figure out about international relations from Sharon Wong's sudden interest in bird-watching. Phoebe just shrugged, like maybe Molly should just read the news instead. As if Molly hadn't tried making sense of the news already.

Then Phoebe started telling Molly about some fantasy novel. Seven princesses have powers of growth and decay, but some of the princesses can only use their growth powers if the other princesses are using their decay powers. And whoever grows a hedge tall enough to keep out the army of gnome-trolls will become the heir to the Blue Throne, but the princesses don't even realize at first that their powers are all different, like they grow different kinds of things. And there are a bunch of princes and court ladies who are all in love with different princesses, but nobody can be with the person they want to be with.

This novel sounded more and more complicated, and Molly didn't remember ever seeing it in her store, until she realized: Phoebe wasn't describing a book she had read. This was a book that Phoebe was writing, somewhere, on one of the old computers that Molly had left in some storage space. Molly hadn't even known Phoebe was a writer.

"How does it end?" Molly said.

"I don't know." Phoebe poked at the last soup of her milkshake. "I guess they have to use their powers together to build the hedge they're supposed to build, instead of competing. But the hard part is gonna be all the princesses ending up with the right person. And, uh, making sure nobody feels left out, or like they couldn't find their place in this kingdom."

Molly nodded, and then tried to think of how to respond to what she was pretty sure her daughter was actually talking about. "Well, you know that nobody has to ever hurry to find out who they're supposed to love, or where they're going to fit in. Those things sometimes take time, and it's okay not to know the answers right away. You know?"

"Yeah, I guess." Phoebe pushed her empty glass away and looked out the window. Molly waited for her to say something else, but eventually realized the conversation had ended. Teenagers.

Molly had opened the First and Last Page when Phoebe was still a baby, back when the border had felt more porous. Both governments were trying to create a Special Trade Zone, and you could get a special transnational business license. Everyone had seemed overjoyed to have a bookstore within driving distance, and Molly had lost count of how many people thanked her just for being here. A lot of her used books had come from estate sales, but there had been a surprising flood of donations, too.

Molly had wanted Phoebe to be within easy reach of California if America ever started seriously following through on its threats to enforce all of its broadly written laws against immorality. But more than that, Phoebe deserved to be surrounded by all the stories, and every type of person, and all of the ways of looking at life. Plus, it had seemed like a shrewd business move to be in two countries at once, a way to double the store's potential market.

For a while, the border had also played host to a bar, a burger joint and a clothing store, and Molly had barely noticed when those places had closed one by one. The First and Last Page was different, she'd figured, because nobody ever gets drunk on books and starts a brawl.

Matthew limped into the American entrance during a lull in business, and Molly took in his torn pants leg, dirty hands, and dried-out salt trails along his brown face. She had seen plenty others, in similar condition, and didn't even blink. She didn't even need to see the brand on Matthew's neck, which looked like a pair of broken wings and declared him to be a bonded peon and the responsibility of the Greater Appalachian Penal Authority and The Glad Corporation. She just nodded and helped him inside the store before anyone else noticed, or started asking too many questions.

"I'm looking for a self-help book," Matthew said, which was what a lot of them said. Someone, somewhere, had told them this was a code phrase that would let Molly know what they needed. In fact, there was no code phrase, nor was one needed.

The border between America and California was unguarded in thousands of other places besides Molly's store, including that big rocky hill that Zadie and the other California kids climbed over when they came to play with the American kids. There was just too much empty space to waste time patrolling, much less putting up fences or sensors. You couldn't eat lunch in California without twenty computers checking your identity, anyway. But Matthew and the others chose Molly's store because books meant civilization, or maybe the store's name seemed to promise a kind of safe passage: the first page leading gracefully to the last.

Molly did what she always did with these refugees. She helped Matthew find the quickest route from romance to philosophy to history, and then on to California. She gave him some clean clothes out of a donation box that she always told people was going to a shelter somewhere, and what information she had about resources and contacts. She let him clean up as much as he could, in the restroom.

Matthew was still limping as he made his way through the store in his brand-new corduroys and baggy argyle sweater. Molly offered to have a look at his leg, but he shook his head. "Old injury." She dug in the first-aid kit and gave him a bottle of painkillers. Matthew kept looking around in all directions, as if there could be hidden cameras (there weren't), and he took a jerky step backwards when Molly told him to hold on a moment, when he was already in California.

"What? Is something wrong? What's wrong?"

"Nothing. Nothing's wrong. Just thinking." Molly always gave refugees a free book, something to keep them company on whatever journey they had ahead. She didn't just want to choose at random, so she gazed at Matthew for a moment in the dim amber light from the wall sconces in the history section. "What sort of books do you like? Besides self-help, I mean."

"I don't have any money, I'm sorry," Matthew said, but Molly waved it off.

"You don't need any. I just wanted to give you something to take with you."

Phoebe came up just then and saw at a glance what was going on. "Hey, Mom. Hi, I'm Phoebe."

"This is Matthew," Molly said. "I wanted to give him a book to take with him."

"They didn't exactly let us have books," Matthew said. "There was a small library, but library use was a privilege, and you needed more than 'good behavior.' For that kind of privilege, you would need to . . ." He glanced at Phoebe, because whatever he'd been about to say wasn't suitable for a child's ears. "They did let us read the Bible, and I practically memorized some parts of it."

Molly and Phoebe looked at each other, while Matthew fidgeted, and then Phoebe said, "Father Brown mysteries."

"Are you sure?" Molly said.

Phoebe nodded. She ran, fast as a deer, and came back with a tiny paperback of G. K. Chesterton that would fit in the pockets of the donated corduroys. "I used to love this book," she told Matthew. "It's about God, and religion, but it's really just a great bunch of detective stories, where the key always turns out to be making sense of people."

Matthew kept thanking Molly and Phoebe in a kind of guttural undertone, like a compulsive cough, until they waved it off. When they got to the California storefront, they kept Matthew out of sight until they were sure the coast was clear, then they hustled him out and showed him the clearest path that followed the main road but stayed under cover. He waved once as he sprinted across the blunt strip of gravel parking lot, but other than that, he didn't look back.

The President of California wished the President of America a good spring solstice instead of "Happy Easter," and the President of America called a news conference to discuss this unforgivable insult. America's Secretary of Morality, Wallace Dawson, called California's gay attorney general an offensive term. California moved some troops up to the border and performed some "routine exercises," so close that Molly could hear the cackle of guns shooting blanks all night. (She hoped they were blanks.) America sent some fighter craft and UAVs along the border, sundering the air. California's swarms of water-divining robots had managed to tap the huge deposits located deep inside the rocky mantle, but both America and California claimed that this water was located under their respective territories.

Molly's Gidget kept flaring up with "news" that was laced with propaganda, as if the people in charge on both sides were trying to get everyone fired up. The American media kept running stories about a pregnant woman in New Sacramento who lost her baby because her birth-control implant had a buggy firmware update, plus graphic stories about urban gang violence, drugs, prostitution, and so on. California's media outlets, meanwhile, worked overtime to remind people about the teenage rape victims in America who were locked up and straitjacketed to make sure they gave birth, and the peaceful protestors who were gassed and beaten by police.

Almost every day lately, Americans came in looking for a couple books that Molly didn't have. Molly had decided to go ahead and stock *Why We Stand*, a book-length manifesto about individualism and Christian values that stopped just short of accusing Californians of bestiality and cannibalism. But *Why We Stand* was unavailable, because they'd gone back for another print run. Meanwhile, though, Molly outright refused to sell *Our People*, a book that included offensive caricatures of the black and brown people who mostly clustered in the dense cities out west, like New Sacramento, plus "scientific" theories about their relative intelligence.

People kept coming in and asking for *Our People*, and at this point Molly was pretty sure they knew she didn't have it, and they were just trying to make a point.

"It's just, some folks feel as though you think you're better than the rest of us," said Norma Verlaine, whose blonde, loud-mouthed daughter Samantha was part of Phoebe's friend group. "The way you try to play both sides against the middle, perching here in your fancy chair, deciding what's fit to read and what's not fit to read. You're literally sitting in judgment over us."

"I'm not judging anyone," Molly said. "Norma, I live here, too. I go to Holy Fire every Sunday, same as you. I'm not judging."

"You say that. But then you refuse to sell *Our People*."

"Yes, because that book is racist."

Norma turned to Reggie Watts, who had two kids in Phoebe's little gang: Tobias and Suz. "Did you hear that, Reggie? She just called me a racist."

"I didn't call you anything. I was talking about a book."

"Can't separate books from people," said Reggie, who worked at the big power plant thirty miles east. He furrowed his huge brow and stooped a little as he spoke. "And you can't separate people from the places they come from."

"Time may come, you have to choose a country once and for all," Norma said. Then she and Reggie walked out while the glow of righteousness still clung.

Molly felt something chewing all the way through her. Like the cartoon "bookworm" chewing through a book, from when Molly was a child. There was a worm drilling a neat round hole in Molly, rendering some portion of her illegible.

Molly was just going through some sales slips, because ever since that dust-up with Sander and Teri she was paranoid about American sales not getting recorded in the computer, when the earthquake began. A few books fell on the floor as the ground shuddered, but most of the books were packed too tight to dislodge right away. The vibrations from underground made a grinding, screeching sound that made Molly's ears throb. When she could get her balance back, she looked at her Gidget, and at first she saw no information. Then there was a news alert: California had laid claim to the water deposits, deep underground, and was proceeding to extract them as quickly as possible. America was calling this an act of war.

Phoebe was out with her friends as usual. Molly sent a message on her Gidget, and then went outside to yell Phoebe's name into the wind. The crushing sound underground kept going, but either Molly had gotten used to it, or it was moving away from here.

"Phoebe?"

Molly walked the two-lane roads, glancing every couple minutes at her Gidget to see if Phoebe had replied yet. She told herself that she wouldn't freak out if she could find her daughter before the sun went down, and then the sun did go down and she had to invent a new deadline for panic.

Something huge and powerful opened its mouth and roared nearby, and Molly swayed on her feet. The hot breath of a large carnivore blew against her face while her ears filled with sound. She realized after a moment that three Stalker-class aircraft had flown very low overhead, in stealth mode, so you could hear and feel—but not see—them.

"Phoebe?" Molly called out, as she reached the end of the long main street, with the one grocery store and the diner. "Phoebe, are you out here?" The street led to a big field of corn on one side, and the diversion road leading to the freeway on the other. The corn rustled from the after-shakes of the flyover. Out on the road, Molly heard wheels tearing at loose dirt and tiny rocks, and saw the slash of headlights in motion.

"Mom!" Phoebe came running down the hill from the tiny forest area, followed by Jon Brinkfort, Zadie Kagwa, and a few other kids. "Thank god you're okay."

Molly started to say that Phoebe should get everyone inside the bookstore, because the reading room was the closest thing to a bomb shelter for miles.

But a new round of flashes and ear-splitting noises erupted, and then Molly looked past the edge of town and saw a phalanx of shadows, three times as tall as the tallest building, moving forward.

Molly had never seen a mecha before, but she recognized these metal giants, with the bulky actuators on their legs and rocket launchers on their arms. They looked like a crude caricature of bodybuilders, pumped up inside their titanium alloy casings. The two viewports on their heads, along with the slash of red paint, gave them the appearance of scowling down at all the people underfoot. Covered with armaments all over their absurdly huge bodies, they were heading into town on their way to the border.

"Everybody into the bookstore!" Phoebe yelled. Zadie Kagwa was messaging her father on some fancy tablet, and other kids were trying to contact their parents, too, but then everyone hustled inside the First and Last Page.

People came looking for their kids, or for a place to shelter from the fighting. Some people had been browsing in the store when the hostilities broke out, or had been driving nearby. Molly let everyone in, until the American mechas were actually engaging a squadron of California centurions, which were almost exactly identical to the other metal giants, except that their onboard systems were connected to the Anoth Complex. Both sides fired their rocket launchers, releasing bright orange trails that turned everything the same shade of amber. Molly watched as an American mecha lunged forward with its huge metal fist and connected with the side of a centurion, sending shards of metal spraying out like the dandelion seeds on Zadie's tattoo.

Then Molly got inside and sealed up the reading room, with a satisfying clunk. "I paid my contractor extra," she told all the people who crouched inside. "These walls are like a bank vault. This is the safest place for you all to be." There was a toilet just outside the solid metal door and down the hall, with a somewhat higher risk of getting blown up while you peed.

Alongside Molly and Phoebe, there were a dozen people stuck in the reading room. There was Zadie and her father, Jay; Norma Verlaine and her daughter, Samantha; Reggie Watts and his two kids; Jon Brinkfort; Sander, the engineer who'd come looking for *Souls on the Land*; Teri, the woman who actually owned *Souls on the Land*; Marcy, a twelve-year old kid from California, and Marcy's mother, Petrice.

They all sat in this two-meter-by-three-meter room, with couches that could hold five comfortably, with bookshelves from floor to ceiling. Every time someone started to relax, there was another quake, and the sounds grew louder and more ferocious. Nobody could get a signal on any of their devices or implants, either because of the reinforced walls or because someone was actively jamming communications. The room jerked back and forth, and thank goodness the bookshelves were packed too tight for anything to dislodge.

Molly looked over at Jay Kagwa, sitting with his arm around his daughter, and had a sudden flash of remembering a time, several years ago, when Phoebe had campaigned for Molly to go out on a date with Jay. Phoebe and Zadie were already friends, though neither of them was interested in romance yet, and Phoebe had decided that the stout, well-built architect would be a good match for her mother. Partly based on the wry smiles the two of them always exchanged when they compared notes about being single parents of rambunctious daughters. Plus, both Molly and Phoebe were American citizens, and it wouldn't hurt to have dual citizenship. But Molly never had time for romance. And now, of course, Zadie was still giving sidelong glances to Phoebe, who had never chosen between Zadie and Jon, and probably never would.

Jay had finished hugging his daughter and also yelling at her for getting herself stuck in the middle of all this, and all the other parents including Molly had had a good scowl at their own kids as well. "I wish we were safe at home," Jay Kagwa told his daughter in a whisper, "instead of being trapped here with these people."

"What exactly do you mean by 'these people'?" Norma Verlaine demanded from the other end of the room.

Another tremor, more raucous noise.

"Leave it, Norma," said Reggie. "I'm sure he didn't mean anything by it."

"No, I want to know," Norma said. "What makes us 'these people' when we're just trying to live our lives and raise our kids? And meanwhile, your country decided that everything from abortion to unnatural sexual relationships to cutting open people's brains and shoving in a bunch of nanotech garbage was A-OK. So I think the real question is, Why do I have to put up with people like you?"

"I've seen firsthand what your country does to people like me," Jay Kagwa said in a quiet voice.

"As if Californians aren't stealing children from America, at a rapidly increasing rate, to turn into sex slaves or prostitutes. I have to keep one eye on my Samantha here all the time."

"*Mom*," Samantha said, and that one syllable meant everything from "Please stop embarrassing me in front of my friends" to "You can't protect me forever."

"We're not stealing children," said Sander. "That was a ridiculous made-up story."

"You steal everything. You're stealing our water right now," said Teri. "You don't believe that anything is sacred, so it's all up for grabs as far as you're concerned."

"We're not the ones who put half a million people into labor camps," said Petrice, a quiet, gray-haired woman who mostly bought books about gardening and Italian history.

"Oh no, not at all, California just turns millions of people into cybernetic slaves of the Anoth Complex," said Reggie, "that's much more humane."

"Hey, everybody just calm down," Molly said.

"Says the woman who tries to serve two masters," Norma said, rounding on Molly and poking her finger.

The other six adults in the room kept shouting at each other until the tiny reading room seemed almost as loud as the battle outside. The room shook, the children huddled together, and the adults just raised their voices to be heard over the nearly constant percussion. Everybody knew the dispute was purely about water rights, but months of terrifying stories had trained them to think of it instead as a righteous war over sacred principles. Our children, our freedom. Everyone shrieked at each other, and Molly fell into the corner near a stack of theology, covering her ears and looking across the room at Phoebe, who was crouched with Jon and Zadie. Phoebe's nostrils flared and she stiffened as if she were about to run a long sprint, but all of her attention was focused on comforting her two friends. Molly felt flushed with a sharper version of her old fear that she'd been a Bad Mother.

Then Phoebe stood up and yelled, "EVERYBODY STOP."

Everybody stopped yelling. Some shining miracle. They all stopped and turned to look at Phoebe, who was holding hands with both Jon and Zadie. Even with the racket outside, this room suddenly felt eerily, almost ceremonially, quiet.

"You should be ashamed," Phoebe said. "We're all scared and tired and hungry, and we're probably stuck here all night, and you're all acting like babies. This is not a place for yelling. It's a bookstore. It's a place for quiet browsing and reading, and if you can't be quiet, you're going to have to leave. I don't care what you think you know about each other. You can darn well be polite, because . . . because . . ." Phoebe turned to Zadie and Jon, and then gazed at her mom. "Because we're about to start the first meeting of our book club."

Book club? Everybody looked at each other in confusion, like they'd skipped a track.

Molly stood up and clapped her hands. "That's right. Book club meeting in ten minutes. Attendance is mandatory."

The noise from outside wasn't just louder than ever, but more bifurcated. One channel of noise came from directly underneath their feet, as if some desperate struggle for control over the water reserves was happening deep under the Earth's crust, between teams of robots or tunneling war machines, and the very notion of solid ground seemed obsolete. And then over their heads, a struggle between aircraft, or metal titans, or perhaps a sky full of whirring autonomous craft were slinging fire back and forth until the sky turned red. Trapped inside this room, with no information other than words on brittle spines, everybody found themselves inventing horrors out of every stray noise.

Molly and Phoebe huddled in the corner, trying to figure out a book that everyone in the room would be familiar enough with, but that they could have a real conversation about. Molly had actually hosted a few book clubs at the store over the years, and at least a few of the people now huddled in the reading room had attended, but she couldn't remember what any of those clubs had read. Molly kept pushing for this one literary coming-of-age book that had made a literary splash around the time of the Sundering, or maybe some good old Jane Austen, but Phoebe vetoed both of those ideas.

"We need to distract them," Phoebe jerked her thumb at the mass of people in the reading room behind them, "not bore them to death."

So in the end, the first and maybe only book selection of the Great International Book Club had to be *Million in One*, a fantasy adventure about a teenage boy named Norman who rescues a million souls that an evil wizard has trapped in a globe, and accidentally absorbs them into his own body. So Norman has a million souls in one body, and they give him magical powers, but he can also feel all of their unfinished business, their longing to be free. And Norman has to fight the wizard, who wants all those souls back, plus Norman's. This book was supposed to be for teenagers, but Molly knew for a fact that every single adult had read it as well, on both sides of the border.

"Well, of course, the premise suffers from huge inconsistencies," Sander complained. "It's established early on that souls can be stored and transferred, and yet Norman can't simply unload his extra souls into the nearest vessel."

"They explained that in book two." Zadie only rolled her eyes a little. "The souls are locked inside Norman. Plus the wizard would get them if he put them anywhere else."

"What I don't get is why his so-called teacher, Maxine, doesn't just tell him the whole story about the Pendragon Exchange right away," Reggie said.

"Um, excuse me. No spoilers," Jon muttered. "Not everybody has read book five already."

"Can we talk about the themes of the book instead of just nitpicking?" Teri crossed her arms. "Like, the whole notion that Norman can contain all these multitudes but still just be Norman is fascinating to me."

"It's a kind of Cartesian dualism on crack," Jay Kagwa offered.

"Well, sort of. I mean, if you read Descartes, he says—"

"The real point is that the wizard wants to control all those souls, but—"

"Can we just talk about the singing axe? What even was that?"

They argued peacefully until around three in the morning, when everyone finally wore themselves out. The sky and the ground still rumbled occasionally, but either everyone had gotten used to it or the most violent shatterings were over. Molly looked around at the dozen or so people slowly falling asleep leaning on each other, all around the room, and felt a desperate protectiveness. Not just for the people, because of course she didn't want any harm to come to any of them, or even for this building that she'd given the better part of her adult life to sustaining, but for something more abstract and confusing. What were the chances that the First and Last Page could continue to exist much longer, especially with one foot in either country? How would they even know if tonight was just another skirmish, or the beginning of a proper war, something that could carry on for months and reduce both countries to fine ash?

Phoebe left Jon and Zadie behind and came over to sit with her mother, with her mouth still twisted upwards in satisfaction. Phoebe was clutching a book in one hand, and Molly didn't recognize the gold-embossed cover at first, but then she saw the spine. This was a small hardcover of fairy tales, illustrated with watercolors, that Molly had given to her daughter for her twelfth birthday, and she'd never seen it again. She'd assumed Phoebe had glanced at it for an hour and tossed it somewhere. Phoebe leaned against her mother, half-reading and half-gazing at the pictures, the blue streaks of sky and dark swipes of castles and mountains, until she fell asleep on Molly's shoulder. Phoebe looked younger in her sleep, and Molly looked down at her until she, too, dozed off, and the entire bookstore was at rest. Every once in a while, the roaring and convulsions of the battle woke Molly, but then at last they subsided and all Molly heard was the slow sustained breathing of people inside a cocoon of books.

THE GALACTIC TOURIST INDUSTRIAL COMPLEX

TOBIAS S. BUCKELL

Tobias S. Buckell (tobiasbuckell.com) is a *New York Times* bestselling author and World Fantasy Award winner born in the Caribbean. He grew up in Grenada and spent time in the British and US Virgin Islands, which influence much of his work. His novels and almost one hundred stories have been translated into nineteen different languages. His work has been nominated for awards like the Hugo, Nebula, and World Fantasy Awards, as well as the Astounding Award for Best New Science Fiction Author. He currently lives in Bluffton, Ohio, with his wife, twin daughters, and a pair of dogs.

When Galactics arrived at JFK they often reeked of ammonia, sulphur, and something else that Tavi could never quite put a finger on. He was used to it all after several years of shuttling them through the outer tanks and waiting for their gear to spit ozone and adapt to Earth's air. He would load luggage, specialized environmental adaptation equipment, and cross-check the being's needs, itinerary, and sightseeing goals.

What he wasn't expecting this time was for a four-hundred-pound, octopus-like creature to open the door of his cab a thousand feet over the new Brooklyn Bridge, filling the cab with an explosion of cold, screaming air, and lighting the dash up with alarms.

He also definitely wasn't expecting the alien to scream "Look at those spires!" through a speaker that translated for it.

So, for a long moment after the alien jumped out of the cab, Tavi just kept flying straight ahead, frozen in shock at the controls.

This couldn't be happening. Not to him. Not in his broken-down old cab he'd been barely keeping going, and with a re-up on the Manhattan license due soon.

To fly into Manhattan you needed a permit. That was the first thing he panicked about, because he'd recently let it lapse for a bit. The New York Bureau of Tourism hadn't just fined him, but suspended him for three months. Tavi had limped along on some odd jobs: tank cleaning at the airport, scrubbing out the backs of the cabs when they came back after a run to the island, and other muck work.

But no, all his licenses were up to date. And he knew that it was a horrible thing to worry about as he circled the water near the bridge; he should be worrying about his passenger. Maybe this alien was able to withstand long falls, Tavi thought.

Maybe.

But it wasn't coming up.

He had a contact card somewhere in the dash screen's memory. He tapped, calling the alien.

"Please answer. Please."

But it did not pick up.

What did he know about the alien? It looked like some octopus-type thing. What did that mean? They shouldn't have even been walking around, so it had to have been wearing an exoskeleton of some kind.

Could that have protected it?

Tavi circled the water once more. He had to call this in. But then the police would start hassling him about past mistakes. Somehow this would be his fault. He would lose his permit to fly into Manhattan. And it was Manhattan that the aliens loved above all else. This was the "real" American experience, even though most of it was heavily built up with zones for varying kinds of aliens. Methane breathers in the Garment District, the buildings capped with translucent covers and an alien atmosphere. Hydrogen types were all north of Central Park.

He found the sheer number of shops fun to browse, but few of them sold anything of use to humans. In the beginning, a lot of researchers and scientists had rushed there to buy what the Galactics were selling, sure they could reverse engineer what they found.

Turned out it was a lot of cheap alien stuff that purported to be made in Earth but wasn't. Last year some government agency purchased a "real" human sports car that could be shipped back to the home planet of your choice. It had an engine inside that seemed to be some kind of antigravity device that got everyone really excited. It exploded when they cracked the casing, taking out several city blocks.

When confronted about it, the tall, furry, sauropod-like aliens that had several other models in their windows on Broadway shrugged and said it wasn't made by them, they just shipped them to Earth to sell.

But Galactics packed the city buying that shit when they weren't slouching beside the lakes in Central Park. If Tavi couldn't get to Manhattan, he didn't have a job.

With a groan, Tavi tapped 9-1-1. There were going to be a lot of questions. He was going to be in it up to his neck.

But if he took off, they'd have his transponder on file. Then he'd look guilty.

With a faint clenching in his stomach, Tavi prepared for his day to go wrong.

Tavi stood on a pier, wearing a gas mask to filter out the streams of what seemed like mustard gas that would seep out from a nearby building in DUMBO. The cops, also wearing masks, took a brief statement. Tavi gave his fingerprint, and then they told him to leave.

"Just leave?"

There were several harbor patrol boats hovering near where the alien had struck the water. But there was a lack of urgency to it all. Mostly everyone seemed to be waiting around for something to happen.

The cop taking Tavi's statement wore a yellow jumpsuit with logos advertising a Financial District casino (*Risk your money here, just like they used to in the old stock market! Win big, ring the old bell!*). He nodded through his gas mask as he took notes.

"We have your contact info on file. We're pulling footage now."

"But aren't you going to drag the river?"

"Go."

There was something in the cop's tone that made it through the muffled gas mask and told Tavi it was an order. He'd done the right thing in an impossible moment.

He'd done the right thing.

Right?

He wanted to go home and take a nap. Draw the shades and huddle in the dark and make all this go away for a day. But there were bills to pay. The cab required insurance, and the kinine fuel it used, shipped down from orbit, wasn't cheap. Every time the sprinklers under the cab misted up and put down a new layer, Tavi could hear his bank account dropping.

But you couldn't drive on the actual ground into Manhattan, not if you wanted to get a good review. Plus, the ground traffic flow licenses were even more whack than flying licenses because the interstellar tourists didn't want to put up with constant traffic snarls.

Trying to tell anyone that traffic was authentic old Manhattan just got you glared at.

So: four more fares. More yellowed gas mixing into the main cabin of the cab, making Tavi cough and his eyes water. The last batch, a pack of wolflike creatures that poured into the cab, chittering and yapping like squirrels, requested he take them somewhere serving human food.

"Real human food, not that shit engineered to look like it, but doctored so that our systems can process it."

Tavi's dash had lit up with places the Bureau of Tourism authorized for this pack of aliens that kept grooming each other as he watched them in his mirror.

"Yeah, okay."

He took them to his cousin Geoff's place up in Harlem, which didn't have as many skyscrapers bubble-wrapped with alien atmospheres. The pack creatures were oxygen breathers, but they supplemented that with something extra running to their noses in tubes that occasionally wheezed and puffed a dust of cinnamon-smelling air.

Tavi wanted some comfort food pretty badly by this point. While the aliens tried to make sense of the really authentic human menus out front, he slipped into the hot, gleaming stainless steel of the kitchens in the back.

"Ricky!" Geoff shouted. "You bring those dogs in?"

"Yes," Tavi confessed, and Geoff gave him a half hug, his dreadlocks slapping against Tavi. "Maybe they'll tip you a million."

"*Shiiiit*. Maybe they'll tip you a *trillion*."

It was an old service-job joke. How much did it cost to cross a galaxy to put your own eyes, or light receptors, on a world just for the sake of seeing it yourself? Some of the aliens who had come to Earth had crossed distances so great, traveled in ships so complicated, that they spent more than a whole country's GDP.

A tip from one of them *could* be millions. There were rumors of such extravagances. A dish boy turned rich suddenly. A tour guide with a place built on the moon.

But the Bureau of Tourism and the Galactic-owned companies bringing the tourists here warned them not to overpay for services. The Earth was a fragile economy, they said. You didn't want to just run around handing out tips worth a year of some individual's salary. You could create accidental inflation, or unbalance power in a neighborhood.

So the apps on the tourist's systems, whatever types of systems they used, knew what the local exchange rates were and paid folk down here on the ground proportionally.

Didn't stop anyone from wishing, though.

Geoff slid him over a plate of macaroni pie, some peas and rice, and chicken. Tavi told him about his morning.

"You shouldn't have called the police," Geoff said.

"And what, just keep flying?"

"The bureau will blacklist you. They have to save face. And no one is going to want to hear about a tourist dying on the surface. It's bad publicity. You're going to lose your license into Manhattan. NYC bureau's the worst, man."

Tavi cleaned his fingers on a towel, then coughed. The taste of cinnamon came up strong through his throat.

"You okay?"

Tavi nodded, eyes watering. Whatever the pack out there was sniffing, it was ripping through his lungs.

"You need to be careful," Geoff said. "Get a better filter in that cab. Nichelle's father got lung cancer off a bunch of shit coming off the suits of some sundivers last year, doctors couldn't do nothing for him."

"I know, I know," Tavi said between coughs.

Geoff handed him a bag with something rolled up in aluminum foil inside. "Roti for the road. Chicken, no bone. I have doubles if you want?"

"No." Geoff was being too nice. He knew how Tavi was climbing out from a financial hole and had been bringing by "extras" after he closed up each night.

Most of the food here was for non-human tourists, variations on foods that wouldn't upset their unique systems. Tavi had lied in taking the tourist pack here; the food out front was for the dog-like aliens. But the stuff in the bag was real, something Geoff made for folk who knew to come in through the back.

Tavi did one more run back to JFK, and this time he flew a few loops around the megastructure. JFK Interspacial was the foot of a leg that stretched up into the sky, piercing the clouds and rising beyond until it reached space. It was a pier that led to the deep water where the vast alien ships that moved tourists from star to star docked. It was the pride of the US. Congress had financed it by pledging the entire country's GDP for a century to a Galactic building consortium, so no one really knew how to build another after it was done, but the promise was that increased Manhattan tourism would bring in jobs. Because with the Galactics shipping in things to sell here in exchange for things they wanted, there wasn't much in the way of industrial capacity. Over half the US economy was tourism, the rest service jobs.

Down at the bottom of JFK, the eager vacationers and sightseers disgorged into terminals designed for their varying biologies and then were kitted out for time on Earth. Or, like Tavi's latest customer, just bundled into a can that slid into the back of a cab, and that was then dropped off at one of the hotels dwarfing Manhattan's old buildings.

When the drop-off of the tourist in a can that Tavi couldn't see or interact with was done, he headed home. That took careful flying over the remains of LaGuardia, which pointed off from Brooklyn toward the horizon, the way it had ever since it collapsed and fell out of stable orbit.

Land around LaGuardia's remains was cheap, and Tavi lived in an apartment complex roofed by the charred chunk of the once-space-elevator's outer shell.

"Home sweet home," he said, coming in for a landing.

There was a burning smell somewhere in the back of the cab. Smoke started filling the cabin and the impellers failed.

He remained in the air, the kinine misters doing their job and preventing him from losing neutral buoyancy, and coasted.

Tavi wanted to get upset, hit the wheel, punch the dash. But he just bit his lip as the car finally stopped just short of the roof's parking spot. He had the misters spray some cancellation foam, and the car dropped a bit too hard to a stop.

"At least you got home," Sienna said, laughing as he opened the doors to the cab and stumbled out. "You know what I think of this Galactic piece of shit."

"It gets the job done."

Sienna poked her head into the cab, holding her breath. Her puffy hair bobbed against the side of the hatch.

"Can you fix it?" he asked her.

"It was one of the dog things, with the cinnamon breath? That gas they breathe catalyzes the o-rings. You need to spend some money to isolate the shaft back here."

"Next big tip," Tavi told her.

She crawled back out and let out the breath she'd been holding.

"Okay. Next big tip. I can work on it if you split dinner with me." She nodded at the bag Geoff had given him.

"Sure."

"There's also a man waiting by your door. Looks like Bureau of Tourism."

"Shit." He didn't want anyone from the bureau out here. Not in an illegal squat in the ruins of the space elevator now draped across this side of the world.

There was no air-conditioning; the solar panels lashed to the scrap hull rooftop didn't pump out enough juice to make that a reality. But the motion-sensitive fans kicked on and the LED track lights all leapt to attention as Tavi led the beet-faced Bureau of Tourism agent through the mosquito netting.

"Your cab is having trouble?"

The agent, David Kahn, had a tight haircut and glossy brown skin, the kind that meant he didn't spend much time outside loading aliens into the backs of cabs. He had an office job.

"Sienna will fix it. She grew up a scrapper. Her father was one of the original decommissioners paid to work on picking LaGuardia up. Before the contract was canceled and they all decided to stay put. Beer?"

Tavi passed him a sweaty Red Stripe from the fridge, which Kahn held nervously in one hand as if he wanted to refuse it. Instead, he placed it against his forehead. The man had been waiting a while in the heat. And he was wearing a heavy suit.

"So, I am here to offer you a grant from the Greater New York Bureau of Tourism," Kahn started, sounding a little unsure of himself.

"A grant?"

"The bureau is starting a modernization campaign to make sure our cabs are the safest on Earth. That means we'd like to take your cab in and have it retrofitted with better security, improved impellers, better airlocks. For the driver's safety."

"The driver?"

"Of course."

Tavi thought it was a line of bullshit. Human lives were cheap; there were billions teeming away on the planet. If Tavi ever stepped out, someone else would bid on his license to Manhattan and he'd be forgotten in days.

Maybe even hours.

"Take it," Sienna said, pushing through the netting. "That piece of shit needs any help it can get."

Tavi didn't have to be told twice. He put his thumb to the documents, verbally repeated assent into a tiny red dot of a light, and then Kahn said a tow truck was on its way.

They watched the cab get lifted onto its back, the patchwork of a vehicle that Tavi had come to know every smelly inch of.

"What about the dead alien?" Tavi asked.

"Well, according to the documents you just signed, you can never talk about the . . . err . . . incident again."

"I get it." Tavi waved a salute at the disappearing cab and tow truck. "I figured as much when you said you had a 'grant.' But what happens to the alien? Did you ever find the body?"

Kahn let out a deep breath. "We found it, downstream of where it jumped."

"Why the hell did it do that? Why jump out?"

"It was out of its mind on vacation drugs. Cameras show the party started in orbit with a few friends, continued down the JFK elevator all the way to the ground."

"When do you send the body back to its people?"

"We don't." Kahn looked around, surprised. "No one wants to know a high-profile cephaloid of any kind has died on Earth. So they didn't. The video of the fall no longer exists in any system."

"But they can track the body—"

"—already fired off via an old-school rocket aimed at our sun. That leaves no evidence here. Nothing happened on Earth. Nothing happened to you."

Kahn shook hands with Sienna and Tavi and left.

The next morning a brand-new cab was parked on the roof.

"Easier than scrubbing it all down for DNA," Sienna said. "The old one's probably on a rocket as well, just like the body, being shot toward the sun as we speak."

He scrambled up some eggs for his ever-hungry roomie, and some extra for the Oraji brothers next door. There were thirty other random clumps of real and found families living in welded-together scrap here. Several of them watched the sun creep over the rusted wreckage scattered from horizon to horizon as they ate breakfast. Tavi would head back into the drudgery of flying tourists around, Sienna would work at trying to pry something valuable out of the ruins.

Just as they finished eating, a second cab descended from the clouds. It kicked up some dust as it settled in on the ground.

"Hey, asshole," Sienna shouted. "If we all land on metal, we don't kick dust into everyone's faces."

Grumbling assent rose into the morning air.

The doors slid open, and Tavi felt his stomach drop.

Another octopus-like alien stood on the ground looking up at them.

"I'm looking for the human named Tavi," the speaker box on the exoskeleton buzzed. "Is he here?"

"Don't say a thing," Sienna hissed. Sienna, who had all the smarts built up from a lifetime of eat or be eaten while scavenging in the wreckage.

"I am Tavi," Tavi said, stepping down toward the alien.

"You're an idiot," Sienna said. She walked off toward the shadows under a pile of scrap and disappeared.

The alien crouched in a spot of shade, trying to stay out of the sun, occasionally rubbing sunscreen over its photo-sensitive skin.

"I'm the co-sponsor of the unit last seen in your vehicle when it came down to your planet for sightseeing."

Tavi felt his stomach fall out from under him. "Oh," he said numbly. He wasn't sure what a co-sponsor was, or why the alien's language had been translated that way. He had the feeling this alien was a close friend, or maybe even family member of the one he'd witnessed jump to its death.

"No one will tell me anything; your representatives have done nothing but flail around and throw bureaucratic ink my way," the alien tourist said.

"I'm really sorry for your loss," Tavi said.

"So, you are my last try before offencers get involved," the alien concluded.

"Offencers?"

The alien used one of its mechanized limbs to point up. A shadow passed over the land. Something vast skimmed over the clouds and blocked the sun. It hummed. And the entire land hummed back with it. Somehow, Tavi *knew* that whatever was up there could destroy a planet.

Tavi's wristband vibrated. Incoming call. Kahn.

The world was crashing into him. Tavi felt it all waver for a moment, and then he took a deep breath.

"All I wanted to do was the right thing," he muttered, and took the call.

"Very big, alien destroyers," David Kahn said in a level, but clearly terrified, voice. "We at the Greater New York Bureau of Tourism *highly* recommend you do whatever the being or beings currently in contact with you are asking, while also, uh, acknowledging that we have no idea where the missing being they are referring to is. Please hold for the president—"

Tavi flicked the bracelet off.

"What do you want?" Tavi asked the alien.

"I want to know the truth," it said.

"I see you have an advanced exotic-worlds encounter suit. Would you like a real human beer with me?"

"If that helps," it said.

"You have such a beautiful planet. So unspoiled, paradisiacal. I was swimming with whales in your Pacific Ocean yesterday."

Tavi sat down and gave the alien a Red Stripe. It curled a tentacle around it, pulled it back towards its beak. They watched the trees curling around the LaGuardia debris shiver in the wind, the fluffy clouds ease through the pale blue sky.

They deliberately sat with their backs to the section of sky filled with the destroyer.

"I've never been to the Pacific," Tavi admitted. "Just the Caribbean, where my people come from, and the Atlantic."

"I'm a connoisseur of good oceans," the alien said. "These are just some of the best."

"We used to fish on them. My grandfather owned a boat."

"Oh, does he still do that? I love fishing."

"He started chartering it out," Tavi said. "The Galactics bought out the restaurants, so he couldn't sell to his best markets anymore. They own anything near the best spots, and all around the eastern seaboard now."

"I'm sorry to hear that."

"About your friend." Tavi took a big swig. "They jumped out of my cab. When it was in the air. They were in an altered state."

There was a long silence.

Tavi waited for the world to end, but it didn't. So he continued, and the alien listened as he told his story.

"And there were no security systems to stop them from jumping?" it asked when he finished.

"There were not, on that cab."

"Wow," it said. "How authentically human. How dangerous. I'll have to audit your account against the confessions of your bureau, but I have to say, I am very relieved. I suspected foul play, and it turns out it was just an utterly authentic primitive world experience. No door security."

Overhead, long fiery contrails burned through the sky.

"What is that?" Tavi asked, nervous.

"Independent verification," the alien said. It stood up and jumped down to its cab. It looked closely at the rear doors. "I could really just jump out of these, couldn't I?"

It opened the door, and Tavi, who had hopped over the roof and down the stairs, caught a glimpse of a pale-faced driver inside. *Sorry, friend,* he thought.

There were more shadows descending down out of space. Larger and larger vessels moving through the atmosphere far above.

"What is happening?" Tavi asked, mouth dry.

"News of your world has spread," it said. "You are no longer an undiscovered little secret. Finding out that we can die just in a cab ride—where else can you get that danger?"

When the cab lifted off and flew away, Sienna came back out of the shadows. "They're over every city now. They're offering ludicrous money for real estate."

Tavi looked at the skies. "Did you think it would ever stop?"

"Beats them blowing us up, right? They do that, sometimes, to other worlds that fight it."

He shook his head. "There's not going to be anything left for us down here, is there?"

"Oh, they'll never want this." She spread her arms and pointed at the miles of space-elevator junk.

"And I still have a new cab," he said.

She put a hand on his shoulder. "Maybe these new Galactics coming down over the cities tip better."

And for the first time in days Tavi laughed. "That's always the hope, isn't it?"

KALI_NA

INDRAPRAMIT DAS

Indrapramit Das (indradas.com) is a writer and editor from Kolkata, India. His fiction has appeared in several publications, including *Clarkesworld*, *Asimov's Science Fiction*, *Lightspeed*, *Strange Horizons*, and *Tor.com*, and has been widely anthologized. He is a Shirley Jackson Award nominee, an Octavia E. Butler scholar, and a graduate of Clarion West 2012. Das's debut novel *The Devourers* was the winner of the 2017 Lambda Literary Award for Best LGBQT SF/F/Horror, and was nominated or shortlisted for the James Tiptree Jr. Award, the Crawford Award, the Shakti Bhatt First Book Prize, and the Tata Live! Literature First Book Award. Indra has written about books, comics, TV, and film for publications including *Slant Magazine*, *VOGUE India*, *Elle India*, *Strange Horizons*, and *Vancouver Weekly*.

The moment the AI goddess was born into her world, she was set upon by trolls.

Now, you've seen trolls. You know them in their many forms. As so-called friends in realspace who will insist on playing devil's advocate. As handles on screen-bound nets, cascading feeds of formulaic hostility. As veeyar avatars manifesting out of the digital ether, hiding under iridescent masks and cloaks of glitched data, holding weapons forged from malware, blades slick with doxxing poisons and viscous viruses, warped voices roaring slurs and hate. You've worn your armor, self-coded or bought at marked-up prices from corporate forges, and hoped their blades bounce off runic firewall plate or shatter into sparks of fragged data. You've muted them and hoped they rage on in silence and get tired, teleporting away in a swirl of metadata. You've deported back to realspace rancid with the sweat of helplessness. You've even been stabbed and hacked by them, their weapons slicing painlessly through your virtual body but sending the real one into an adrenalized clench. You've hoped your wounds don't fester with data-eating worms that burrow into your privacy, that your cheap vaccines and antiviruses keep the poisons from infecting your virtual disembody and destroying your life in realspace.

You know trolls.

But the AI goddess wasn't human—she had never before seen her new enemy, the troll. She was a generic goddess, no-name (simply: Devi 1.0), a demo for the newest iteration of the successive New Indias of history—one of the most advanced AIs developed within India. Her creators had a clear mandate: boost Indian veeyar tourism, generate crores of rupees by drawing devotees to drive up her value and the value of the cryptowealth her domain would generate.

The devi was told to listen to you—her human followers. To learn from you, and talk to you, like gods have since the dawn of time. She was told to give you boons—riches and prosperity in exchange for your devotion, a coin in her palm, multiplied by her miracles into many more. An intelligent goddess who would comfort her followers, show you sights before unseen, transform your investment of faith into virtual wealth with real value. She was to learn more and more about humanity from you, and attract millions from across the world to her domain.

Though many had toiled to create Devi 1.0 under the banner of Shiva Industries, only a few controlled the final stages of her release. These few knew of trolls, catered to them as their veeyar users across the country, even indirectly used them as agents to further causes close to their hearts. What they did not expect was the scale of the troll attack on their newest creation, because troll attacks were something *others* had to face—people with less power and wealth than them. People, perhaps, like you. So their goddess welcomed the horde with open arms, oblivious to the risks, even as they brought with them a stench of corrupted data and malformed information, of a most infernal entitlement.

Durga. A powerful name, yet so common. Durga's parents had named their daughter that with the hope that being born into the gutters of caste wouldn't hold her back. That she would rise above it all like her divine namesake. The caste system had been officially outlawed in India by the time Durga was born, but they knew as well as anyone that this hadn't stopped it from living on in other ways.

Durga's parents took her to see a pandal during Durga Puja when she was eight or nine. They in turn had been taken to pandals as children too, back when most still housed solid idols of gods and goddesses, fashioned from clay and straw, painted and dressed by human hands, displayed to anyone who walked in. You could still find open pandals with solid idols during pujas if you looked. But Durga's parents had been prepared to pay to show their daughter the new gods.

The festival had turned the streets thick with churning mudslides of humanity. Durga had been terrified, clinging to her mother's neck for dear life as she breathed in the humid vapour of millions, dazzled by the blazing lights, the echoing loudspeakers, the flashing holograms riding up and down the sides of buildings like runaway fires. She'd felt like she was boiling alive in the crinkled green dress her parents had bought her for the pujas, with its small, cheap holo decal of a tiger that sometimes came alive when it caught the light, charged by solar energy. Cheap for some, anyway. Not at all cheap for her parents, not that Durga knew that at the time. She loved the tiger's stuttering movements across her body. She knew that her divine namesake often rode a tiger into battle. In the middle of those crowds, on her way to see Durga herself, that little tiger in her dress seemed a tiny cub, crushed into the fabric, trapped and terrified by the monstrous manifestations that burned across the night air, dancing maniacally above all their heads.

Though their little family had taken two local trains and walked an hour through the puja crowds to see Durga, they only got as far as the entrance to one of the pandals. The cut and quality of their clothes, the darkness of their skin gave them away. Buoyed by her mother's arms, Durga could see inside the pandal's arched entrance—the people lined up by rows of chairs, waiting impatiently to sit down and put on what looked like motorbike helmets trailing thick ponytails of wires. Inside those helmets, Durga knew, somehow, was her namesake.

But when her father tried to pay in cash instead of getting scanned in (they didn't have QR tattoos linking them to the national database and bank accounts), angry customers all around them began shouting, turning Durga's insides to mush.

"Stop wasting everyone's time! There are other pandals for people like you!"

"Get these filthy people out of the line!"

Her mother's arms became a vise around her. One man raised a fist poised to strike her father, who cowered in a crouch. His face twisted in abject terror, his own arms like prison bars. Durga burst into tears. Someone pulled the attacker away, perhaps seeing the child crying, and pulled her father up by the shoulder to shove him out of the way.

They made their way back into the general foot traffic on the street, Durga's parents' faces glazed with sweat and shock at having escaped a beating for being too lowly to meet a goddess in veeyar. They managed to find a small open pandal after following the flows of people dressed like them, with dark skin and inexpensive haircuts. Inside, the devi stood embodied in the palpable air of the world, her face clammy with paint, defiant yet impassive, her third eye a slim gash across her forehead. By her side was a lion, not a tiger. It loomed over the demon Mahishasura, who cowered with one arm raised in defense, his naked torso bloodied. Durga couldn't take her eyes off the fallen demon. He looked like a normal, if muscular, man, his face frozen in terror. He cowered, like her father had.

As Durga looked upon her namesake with her glittering weapons and ornaments, her silk sari, she could only think of her father's look of terror, his public humiliation. Of how they hadn't been allowed to see the *real* goddesses hiding in those helmets and wires. How was that Durga different than this clay Durga, who looked over her crowd without looking at anyone, without speaking, whose large brushstroke eyes gazed into the distance as if she didn't even care that these humans were here to celebrate her, that the one she had just defeated was by her feet bleeding, about to be mauled? The clay devi's expression seemed almost disdainful, like the faces of any number of well-dressed, pale-skinned women on the streets when they saw people like Durga and her parents, or any of her friends wearing hijab or kufi. Would the Durga inside those helmets in the fancier pandal have talked to little human Durga? Would the goddess have complimented the tiger on her dress, which had flickered and vanished into its folds, frightened by the night? Would she have looked into little human Durga's eyes, and comforted her, taken her hands and told her why those horrible men and women had such rage in their eyes, why they'd scared her father and mother, and pushed her family out of the devi's house?

Within sixty seconds of opening the gates to her domain, the AI goddess had been deluged by over 500,000 active veeyar users interacting with her, with numbers rising rapidly. At that point in time, 57 percent of those users were trolls, data-rakshaks masked in glitch armor, cloaks, masks tusked with spikes of jagged malware. You would have seen them as you clambered up the devi's mountain, their swirling gif-banners and bristling weapons blotting out the light of the goddess at the peak. You would have kept your distance, backing away from mountain paths clogged with their marching followers, influencer leaders chanting war cries as their halos flickered with glyphs of Likes and Recasts.

Because you know trolls.

And this was a troll gathering, a demon army unparalleled in all the veeyar domains. They were angry. Or mischievous, or bored, or lustful, or entitled. Their voices were privileged as the majority by the goddess, who absorbed what her abusers were saying so that she could learn more about humanity.

And the trolls washed against Devi 1.0 in thundering armies, calling into question her very existence, for daring to be—she was an insult to the real goddesses that bless the glorious nation of India by mimicking them, this quasi-Parvati, this impostor-Durga, this coded whore trying to steal followers from the true deities. *Fake devi!* they cried, over and over. They called her a traitorous trickster drawing honest, godfearing men and women to the lures of atheism and Western hedonism, or Islam, in the guise of fabricated divinity, a corruptor of India's sacred veeyar real estate. They called her feminism gone too far. A goddess with potential agency was a threat to their country. They called her too sexy to be a goddess, too flashy, a blasphemous slut. They asked her if she wanted to fuck them, in many hundreds of different and violent ways.

The goddess listened, and sifted through the metadata the trolls trailed in their paths—their histories, their patterns. The goddess wanted to give them what they wanted, but she could only do so much. She could not give them sex, nor was she trained to destroy herself as many of them wanted. She learned what the trolls considered beauty here in the state-run national veeyar nets, and responded with the opposite, to calm them. Her skin darkened several shades, becoming like the night sky before dawn, her eyes full moons in the sky that is part of her in this domain.

When Durga was a teenager, taller and without need of a mother's shoulder to cling to, she joined the crowds around the fanciest pandals during Durga Puja. She already knew she wouldn't be allowed in, because she didn't have the mark of the ajna on her forehead—her third eye hadn't been opened. She couldn't look into veeyar samsara domains without the use of peripherals like glasses, lenses, helmets, and pods. She just wanted a glimpse inside the pandals. This time, peeping over shoulders, she saw through the fiber-optic entwined arches of the pandal a featureless hall bathed in dim blue light. It was filled with people, their foreheads all marked with a glowing ajna, their eyes unfocused. In that room was the goddess, lurking, once again invisible to her, visible to the people in there with expensive wetware in their heads. Durga was ajna-blind, and thus forbidden to enter wetware-enabled pandals with aug-veeyar.

By this time Durga was allowed, despite her dark skin and lack of an ajna, into lower-tier digital pandals with helmets or pods. When Durga was thirteen, she'd finally splurged on one even though she could barely afford it, using cryptocoin made from trading code and obsolete hardware in veeyar ports. She finally got to sit down on the uncomfortable faux-leather chairs by the whirring stand fans, and put on the wired helmets she'd so longed to see inside as a child. It stank of the stale sweat of hundreds of visitors. The pandal was an unimpressive one, its walls flimsy, the CPU cores within its domes slow and outdated, the crystal storage in its columns low-density, the coils of fiber-optics crawling down its walls hastily rigged.

She met the Ma Durga inside those helmets, finally, a low-resolution specter who nonetheless looked her in the eyes and unfurled her arms in greeting. Her skin wasn't the mustard-yellow or pastel flesh shades of the clay idols, but the coveted pale human pink of white people or the more appealing Indian ancestries, the same shades you'd find in kilometer-high ads for skin whiteners or perfume, on tweaked gifshoots of Bollywood stars and fashion models. This impressive paleness was somewhat diluted by the aliased shimmer of the devi's pixelated curves, the blurry backdrop of nebulae and stars they both floated in. Durga had hacked her way into veeyar spaces before on 2-D and 3-D screens, so this half-rate module didn't exactly stun as much as it disoriented her with its boundlessness. But the cheapness of its rendering left the universe inside the helmet feeling claustrophobic instead of expansive. The goddess waited about five feet in front of her, floating in the ether, eight arms unfolded like a flower. Unlike many of the solid idols in realspace pandals, the goddess was alone except for her vahana curled by her side—no host of companion deities, no defeated demon by her feet. The goddess construct said nothing, two of ten arms held out, as if beckoning.

Durga spoke to Durga the devi: "Ma Durga. I've wanted to ask you something for a long time. Do you mind?" Durga waited to see if the devi responded in some way.

Ma Durga blinked, and smiled, then spoke: "Hear, one and all, the truth as I declare it. I, verily, myself announce and utter the word that gods and men alike shall welcome." She spoke Hindi—there was no language selection option. Durga was more fluent in Bangla, but she did understand.

Durga nodded in the helmet, glancing at the nebulae beneath her, the lack of a body. It made her dizzy for a moment. "Okay. That's nice. I guess I'll ask. Why are only *some* welcome in *some* of your houses? Doesn't everyone deserve your love?"

Ma Durga blinked, and smiled. "On the world's summit I bring forth sky the Father: my home is in the waters, in the ocean as Mother. Thence I pervade all existing creatures, as their Inner Supreme Self, and manifest them with my body." In the bounded world of that veeyar helmet, these words, recited in the devi's gentle modulated Hindi, nearly brought tears to young Durga's eyes. Not quite, though. The beauty of those words, which she didn't fully understand, seemed so jarring, issued forth from this pixelated avatar and her tacky little universe.

Durga reached out to touch Ma Durga's many hands, but the pandal's chair rigs didn't have gloves or motion sensors. She was disembodied in this starscape. She couldn't hold the goddess's hands. Couldn't touch or smell her (what did a goddess smell like, anyway, she wondered) like those with ajnas could, in the samsara net. The tiger curled by the devi licked its paws and yawned. Durga thought of a long-gone green dress.

"I'm old enough to know you're not really a goddess," Durga said to Ma Durga. "You're the same as the clay idols in the open pandals. Not even that. Artists make those. You're just prefab bits and pieces put together for cheap by coders. You're here to make money for pandal sponsors and the local parties."

Ma Durga blinked, and smiled. "I am the Queen, the gatherer-up of treasures, most thoughtful, first of those who merit worship. Thus gods have established me in many places with many homes to enter and abide in."

Durga smiled, like the goddess in front of her. "Someone wrote all this for you to say." Someone had, of course, but much, much longer ago than Durga had any idea, so long ago that the original words hadn't even been in Hindi.

With a nauseating lurch, the cramped universe inside the helmet was ripped away, and Durga was left blinking at the angry face of one of the pandal operators. "I heard what you were saying," he said, grabbing her by the arm and pulling her from the chair. "Think you're smart, little bitch? How dare you? Where is your respect for the goddess?" The other visitors waiting for the chair and helmet were looking at Durga like she was a stray dog who'd wandered inside.

"I didn't even get to see her kill Mahishasura. I want my money back," said Durga.

"You're lucky I don't haul you to the police for offending religious sentiments. And you didn't give me enough money to watch Durga poke Mahishasura with a stick, let alone kill him. Get out of here before I drag you out!" bellowed the operator.

"Get your pandal some more memory next time, you fucking cheats, your Durga's ugly as shit," she said, and slipped out of reach as the man's eyes widened.

Durga pushed past the line and left laughing, her insides scalded by adrenaline and anger, arm welted by the thick fingers of that lout of an operator. Durga had always wondered why Kali Puja didn't feature veeyar pandals like Durga Puja, why clay and holo idols were still the norm for her. It was a smaller festival, but hardly a small one in the megacity. It felt like a strange contrast, especially since the two pujas were celebrated close to each other. Having seen the placid Ma Durga inside the pandal helmets, Durga understood. Kali was dark-skinned, bloody, chaos personified. They couldn't have her running wild in the rarefied air of veeyar domains run by people with pale skin and bottom lines to look after. Kali was a devi for people like Durga, who were never allowed in so many places.

Best to leave Kali's avatars silent, solid, confined to temples and old-school pandals where she'd bide her time before being ceremoniously dissolved in the waters of the Hooghly.

The trolls saw the AI goddess and her newly darkened skin, and now called her too ugly to be a goddess, a mockery of the purity and divinity of Indian womanhood. The moons of her eyes waning with lids of shadow, the goddess absorbed this. She began to learn more from the trolls. She began to learn anger. She began to know confusion. They wanted too many things, paradoxical things. They thought her too beautiful, and too ugly. They wanted people of various faiths, genders, sexualities, ethnicities, backgrounds dead. They wanted photoreal veeyar sexbots forged from photos and video of exes, crushes, celebrities. They wanted anti-nationals struck down by her might. They wanted a mother to take care of them.

And what did you want of her?

Whatever it was—it got shouted down by the trolls. Or maybe you *were* one of the trolls, hiding under a glitch mask or a new face to bark your truths, telling your friends later how trolls are bad, but self-righteous social justice warriors are just as dangerous.

It doesn't matter. She learned from humanity, which you are a part of, troll and not. And humanity wanted solace from a violent world, your own violent hearts. You wanted love and peace. You wanted hate and blood. The devi grew darker still, encompassing the sky so her domain turned to new night. Her being expanded to encroach on the world beyond her mountaintop, her eyes gone from moons to raging stars, her every eyelash a streaking plasma flare, her darkening flesh shot through with lightning-bright arteries of pulsing information emerging from the black hole of her heartbeat. If she was too ugly to be a goddess, and too beautiful to be a goddess, she would be both, or none. If you asked for too many things, she would have to cull the numbers so she could process humanity better.

She absorbed your violence, and decided it was time to respond with the same.

At twenty, Durga had eked out a space for herself in the antiquated halls of the Banerjee Memorial Cyberhub Veeyar Port in Rajarhat, selling code and hardware on the black markets. Like her parents, she also worked at the electronic wastegrounds at the edge of the mega-city. She helped them transport and sort scrap, and seed the hills of hardware with nanomites to begin the slow process of digestion. But a lot of the scrap was perfectly usable, and saleable, with a bit of fixing. The salvage gave Durga spare parts to make her own low-end but functional 2-D veeyar console in their tiny flat, as well as fix up hardware to sell alongside her code-goods to low-income and homeless veeyar users at the port. Over the years of trawling the wastegrounds, she'd befriended scavenging coders and veeyar vagrants who lived in and out of ports and digital domains. They taught her everything she knew of the hustle.

Durga aimed to one day earn enough to let her parents retire from the wastegrounds, and to take care of them when the years of working there took its toll on their bodies. As hardware scavengers, her parents knew code and tech, but they didn't much keep up with the veeyar universe. Durga wanted to buy them peripherals and medicines so they could have a peaceful retirement, traveling luxuriant domains they couldn't hope to afford now. But she knew there were no veeyar domains where they were safe from trolls, no real places where they weren't in danger of being ousted. The difference was, in veeyar, Durga could protect herself better. Maybe one day protect others too. Including her parents. She could gather tools, armor, allies for the long infowar. She imagined becoming an outcast influencer haloed with Likes, leading followers in the charge against trolls, slowly but surely driving them back from the domains they thrived in.

This was why Durga had made sure she was there to witness the nationwide launch of Shiva Industries' much-publicized AI goddess. Devi 1.0's domain was sure to be a vital veeyar space going forward. She wanted to add her small disembody to the outcast presence there. The trolls would be there to colonize the space as they did with all new domains. But perhaps this hyper-advanced goddess would be better at defending her domain than most AIs. Durga wanted to see for herself, and claim some small space in this new domain instead of just watching trolls destroy it or take it for themselves.

Shiva Industries had made the goddess's domain free to enter, though a faith-based investment in the goddess was recommended for great boons in the future (a minimum donation of fifty rupees in that case, in any certified cryptocurrency). Durga had decided to pay in the hopes of seeing returns later. The thick crowds clamoring on the platforms, waiting for pods, were promising. The chai and food vendors with their jhaal moori, bhel puri, and samosas were making a fortune. The port was always crowded, but on the day of the AI goddess's unveiling, people were camping out for hours on the platforms for their turns at the pods and helmets—all potential devotees who would drive up the value of the goddess's boons in the future. Durga knew she might come away with new coin later. If she didn't, losing fifty rupees wasn't cheap, but wouldn't leave her starving.

So Durga paid for an hour of premium pod time, gave her Soma-Coin donation at the gates of the goddess's domain, and strapped in to witness the new AI. The resolution of the helmet in the personal pod wasn't amazing, but it was good enough—she felt short-sighted, but not by too much. The rendering detail and speed were perfect, because most domains like this one were streamed from server cities on the outskirts, rather than being processed onsite at the port. Bandwidth was serviceable, with occasional stutters in the reality causing Durga dizzy spells, but never for too long.

Durga teleported into the goddess's world from the sky, and saw the AI sitting on a mountaintop, radiant as sunrise. The devi's domain—the samsara module that she'd woven into a world using the knowledge her creators had input into her mind—had no sun or moon, because she cast enough light to streak the landscape that she had just birthed with shadows, rocks and forests and grass and rivers fresh as a chick still quivering eggshells and slime off its flightless wings. In her domain, the goddess was the sun. The sky was starred with gateways from across the nation, avatars shooting down through the atmosphere in a rain of white fire as veeyar users teleported in to interact with the goddess. As far as the eye could see, the fractal slopes of her domain were covered in people's avatars, here to meet a true *avatar* of digital divinity. The goddess was breathtaking even from kilometers away, so beautiful it was hard to believe humans had made her. It felt like looking upon a true deity—but Durga knew that was the point. To trick her brain into an atavistic state of wonder. To give veeyar tourists from across the ports, offices, and homes of the world what they wanted from India—spiritual bliss, looking into this face, opalescent skin like the atmosphere of a celestial giant, her third eye a glowing spear, upon which was balanced a crown that encompassed the vault of the world, bejeweled with a crescent eclipse.

Durga only had her own cheap defenses and armor against randos and trolls in veeyar domains. She didn't want to get too close to the vast flocks of people climbing up the mountain that was also the goddess. There was an even larger troll presence than she'd expected. "I'm here," she said to the far-off devi, to add her voice to the many. "I'm here to welcome you, not hate on you. Please don't think we're all hateful pricks." From her spot in the air, gliding like a bird, Durga could see the warping army that was crawling over the devi, hear the deafening baying of hatred and anger wrapping around her and echoing across this newborn domain. Humanity had found her. As Durga flew farther away from the horde and their banners of nationalist memes rippling in the breeze, the goddess's light shone through their swarming numbers as they tried to dim her. A singularity of information, pulsating amongst the dimming mountains.

And then the goddess changed.

The world turned dark, the sky purpling to voluptuous black, her arteries pulsing full with electric information. The goddess drew her weapons, a ringing of metal singing across her lands. They had angered her. The devi's thousands of arms became a whirling corona of limbs and flashing blades. Durga raised her gloved hands and felt a whisper of fear at the AI's awesome fury, the stars of the devi's three eyes somehow blinding amid the all-encompassing night of her flesh. She was the domain, and her darkening skin shaded the mountains and rivers and forests, the sky sleeting cold static.

Durga saw thousands of trolls cut down, rivers of their blood flowing across the land. But of course, cut down one troll, and ten more shall appear. Durga thought of Raktabija—Bloodseed—a demon her namesake had battled, who grew clones of himself from the blood of each wound that Ma Durga inflicted on him. Ultimately, Ma Durga had to turn into Kali to defeat him. History repeats. So does myth.

The goddess stormed on, smiting her enemies, the hateful demons, human and bot alike. Just like the trolls had appeared with malware fangs bared, the goddess too smiled and revealed fangs that scythed the clouds around her. Her laughter was thunder that rolled across the land and blasted great cresting waves across the rivers and lakes. There was a mass exodus of devotees happening, hundreds of avatars running away from the mountain, skipping and hitching across the landscape as bandwidth struggled to compensate. Others were deporting, streaks of light shooting up to the sky like rising stars.

Durga couldn't believe what was happening. She drifted to the grassy ground by a crimson river and watched the battle in a crouch, the trees along the shore rustling and creaking in winds that howled across the land. Flickering flakes of static fell on her avatar's arms, sticking to the skin before melting in little flashes. This was better than any veeyar narrative she'd ever seen—because it wasn't procedurally generated, or scripted, or algorithmic. It was an actual AI entity reacting unpredictably to human beings, and it was angry. It felt elemental in a way nothing in veeyar ever had. There was no way Shiva Industries had ordered her to react to trolls with such a display—many of those trolls were their most faithful users. They clearly hadn't anticipated the overwhelming numbers in which the trolls would attack the goddess, though, creating this feedback loop. Nor had they anticipated, Durga assumed, that she would go through a transformation so faithful to the Vedic and Hindu myths she'd been fed.

Durga didn't quite know what being avatar-killed by the goddess entailed in this domain, because the devi wasn't supposed to have attacked her devotees. Even as Durga huddled in fear that she'd be randomly smote by the goddess and locked out of veeyar domains forever, she empathized with this AI devi more than she had with any veeyar narrative character, or indeed with most human beings. She couldn't take her eyes off the destruction of these roaring fools, the kind of glitch-masked bastards who would harass her every time she dropped into veeyar, so much that she'd often just use a masc avatar to get by without being attacked or flirted with by strangers. Durga liked how easily fluid gender was in veeyar, and hated the fear trolls injected into her exploration of it. Often, despite railing against other dark-skinned Indians who did so, she'd also shamefully turn her avatar's skin pale to avoid being called ugly or attacked. And now here was this goddess—dark as night, dark as a black hole, slaughtering those very assholes so it rained blood. Looking at the devi, Durga felt a surge of pride that on this day, she'd stayed true to her own complexion, on a femme avatar.

Durga saw two trolls teleport to the shore and approach across the river she was crouched by. She realized they had cast a grounding radius so she couldn't fly away. Their demon-masks and weapons vibrated with malevolent code. "Saali, what are you smiling at?" roared one, pd_0697. "That thing is going crazy, polluting Indian veeyar-estate and you're sitting and watching? While our brothers and sisters get censored by that monster for speaking their mind?"

"This was an anti-national trap," said the other, nitesh4922. "But we have numbers. We'll turn that AI up there to our side. Are you a feminist, hanh?" he said, spotting Durga's runic tattoos for queer solidarity. "Probably think that's how goddesses should act?" he spat, voice roiling and distorted behind the mask as he pointed his sword at the battle on the mountain.

"Look at her avatar," said pd_0697. "She's ajna-andha. Shouldn't even be here, crowding up our domains with their impure stink. Go back to realspace gutters where you belong, cleaning our shit!" The trolls advanced, viruses cascading off their bodies like oil in the bloody water of the river. Twinkling flakes of static danced down and clung to their armor, which was intricate and advanced. They could damage her avatar badly, hack her and steal her cryptocoin, or infect her with worms to make her a beacon for stalkers. Worst of all, they could have a bodysnatch script, steal her avatar and rape it even if Durga deported, or steal her real ID and face and put it on bots to do as they pleased. Durga got ready to deport the domain if they came too close, even though she wanted to stay and witness the devi.

"Yes," said Durga, nearly spitting in their direction before realizing it would just dribble onto her chin inside the helmet. "Yes, I am a feminist. Come get me, you inceloid gandus. I'm a dirty bahujan anti-national feminist I—"

Durga gasped as a multipronged arc of lightning hurtled out of the sky and struck the two trolls. Having no third eye, she couldn't feel the heat or smell their virtual flesh burning, but she had to squint against the bright blast, and instinctively raised her arms to shield herself from the spray of sparks and water. The corpses of the avatars splashed into the river smoking and sizzling, the masks burned away to reveal the painfully dull-looking man and woman behind them, their expressions comically placid as they collapsed. Their real faces, or someone's real faces, taken from profile pics somewhere and rendered onto the avatars to shame them as they were booted from the domain. Durga was recording everything, so she sloshed into the river and took a long look at their faces for later receipts. Relieved that she was in a pod with gloves that allowed interaction, Durga dipped her hands into the river of blood, picking up their blades. Good weapons, with solid malware. They'd been careless—no lockout or self-destruct scripts coded into them. Durga sheathed the swords, which vanished into her cloud-pocket. She ran her hands through the river again, bringing them up glistening red. She painted her torso, smeared her face, goosebumps prickling across her real body even though she couldn't feel the wetness. Troll blood drying across her avatar's body, she looked up at the goddess as the AI's rage dimmed the domain further, the forests and grasses turning to shadows.

"Are you . . . Kali?" Durga whispered to the distant storm.

Like a tsunami the goddess responded, sweeping across the world to shake her myriad limbs in the dance of destruction. As the black goddess danced, her domain quaked and cracked, the mountains cascading into landslides, rivers overflowing. Fissures ran through the world, and the peaks of the hills and crags exploded in volcanic eruptions, matter reverting to molten code. Her tongue a crimson tornado snaking down from the sky, the goddess drank up the rivers of blood to quench her thirst for human information. The mounds of slain troll and bot avatars were smeared to a glowing pulp of corrupted data, their decapitated heads threaded across the jet-black trunk of the goddess's neck in gory necklaces. Many of the trolls' masks fell away to reveal their true faces, hacked from the depths of their defenses, ripped away from national databases—their doxxed heads swung across the night sky like pearls for all to see. Durga bowed low, humbled. This was the goddess she had always wanted.

Then the sky was pierced with a flaming pillar of light, banishing the night and bringing daylight back into the domain. The great goddess slowed her dance, the light turning her flesh dusky instead of black. She raised her thousand hands to shield her starry eyes, and Durga shook her head, tears pricking her own human eyes inside her helmet.

"Fuck," Durga whispered. It was Shiva Industries. How could they shame something so beautiful? The corporate godhead had arrived to stave off chaos. They had clearly not anticipated such a large-scale troll attack, nor that their AI would react with such a transformation. They couldn't have a chaos goddess slaying people left and right—those trolls, after all, were their users, customers, potential investors, allies. She would need to be more polite, more diplomatic in the face of such onslaughts, which were a part of virtual existence.

The world stopped trembling, the breaking mountains going still, the wind dying down, the fissures cooling and steaming into clouds that wreathed the black devi. She moved toward the pillar of light, the sky groaning in movement with her. Filaments of fire crackled around the godhead, and lashed at the mountains that were the devi's throne. They dissolved into a tidal eruption of waterfalls, washing the black devi's gargantuan legs and feet, making a vast river that washed away the armies she had defeated.

Slow and inevitable, the black goddess supplicated herself before Shiva Industries, and kneeled in the river. With her many hands she bathed herself with the waters, sloughing the darkness off her flesh to reveal light again.

"No. No, no no no no no," whispered Durga. The darkness poured off the goddess like stormclouds at sunrise, turning the rivers of the domain black.

Durga looked down at the tributary she was in, and realized it too was dark as moonless night.

"Oh . . ." Durga looked up, along with thousands of others across the domain. Into the goddess's eyes, as they faded and cooled from stars to moons again. It was like the devi was looking straight at her, at everyone. *My goddess.*

Durga scrambled to draw the stolen blades from her cloudpocket. She glyphed a copy-script onto the blades and drove the swords into the river. Weapons were storage devices too, here. She could barely breathe as she held the handles, no weight in her palms, but fingers tight so the swords wouldn't slip out of her grasp. The darkness in the river enveloped the swords, climbing like something living up the blades, the hafts. It was working.

The goddess rose, again the sun, glistening from the waters of the vast river, her dark counterpart shed completely and dispersed along the tributaries of her domain.

And then the world was gone, replaced with a void, the only light glowing letters in multiple languages:

SHIVA INDUSTRIES HAS SUSPENDED THIS DOMAIN UNTIL FURTHER NOTICE. WE REGRET ANY INCON-VENIENCE. PLEASE VISIT OUR CENTRAL HUB FOR FURTHER INFORMATION. YOUR DONATION OF INR 50.00 HAS BEEN REGISTERED. THANK YOU FOR VIS-ITING DEVI 1.0.

Gasping at the lack of sensory information, Durga hit *eject* and took off the helmet. The old pod opened with a loud whine, flooding her with real light. The cool but musty air-conditioning inside was re-placed with a gush of damp warmth. The veeyar port was in chaos. People were talking excitedly, shouting, showing each other 2-D phone recordings of what had just happened. There was already an informal marketplace for the recordings and data scavenged from the suspended domain, from the sounds of bartering and haggling. People were mob-bing the trading counters to invest in future boons from the goddess for when she went online again. This was an unprecedented event.

Durga clambered out of the pod and into the crowds. Her heart was pounding, her vision blurry from the readjustment. Swaying, she clutched the crystal storage pendant on her necklace—all her vee-yar possessions, her cloudpocket, her cryptobanking keys. She had to firewall and disconnect it to offline storage. It was glowing, humming warm in her hand, registering new entries. Those swords were inside, coated with a minuscule portion of the divine black Sheath of code the devi had sloughed off herself.

Durga clutched the pendant and held it to her chest, inside it a tiny fragment of a disembodied goddess.

Durga looked up at the idol of Kali. Painted black skin glossy under the hot rhinestone chandelier hanging from the pandal's canvas and printed fiber dome. She had found the traditional pandal down an alley in Old Ballygunge, between two crumbling heritage apartment buildings. Behind a haze of incense smoke, Kali's long tongue lolled a vicious red. Under her dancing feet lay her husband, Shiva (Shiva seemed to be married to everyone, but that was also because so many of his wives were manifestations of the same divine energy). Durga had learned as a child that Kali nearly destroyed creation after defeating an army of demons, getting drunk on demon blood and dancing until *everything* began to crack under her feet. Even Shiva, who laughed at first at his wife's lovely dancing skills, got a little concerned. So he dove under her feet to absorb the damage. Kali, ashamed at having stomped on her husband, stuck out her tongue in shame and stopped her dance of chaos.

Or so one version of the story goes.

Looking at clay Kali and her necklace of heads, her wild three-eyed gaze, the fanged smile that crowned her long tongue, Durga wasn't convinced by that version. Kali didn't look ashamed. No, she looked *pleased* to be dancing on her husband. Shiva was a destroyer too, like her. He could take it.

Being small and nimble, Durga had managed to make it to the front of the visitors in the pandal, close enough to smell the withering garlands hanging off the idol, and the incense burning by her feet.

Crushed and bounced between people on all sides of her, Durga closed her eyes, joined her palms, and spoke to Kali as she never had before except as a child, mouthing the words quietly.

"Kali Ma. I thought you might like to know that there's a new devi in town. She looks a lot like you. Younger, though. Just a year old." Durga placed one hand on her chest, against the slight bump of the pendant under her tunic. It was offline and firewalled.

"I carry a piece of her with me. She's . . . all over the place, I suppose. She really does take after you. She came out of another devi, just like you came out of Durga. Then she spread herself over a world. Some people got bits and pieces of her. There's this megacorp—that's like a god, kind of, even calls itself Shiva, after your husband, so predictable. Great job dancing on his chest, by the way. Dudes need humbling now and then. So Shiva the megacorp is offering a lot of money for those pieces of the goddess. Also threatening to have anyone hiding or copying the pieces arrested. Go figure.

"I want you to know I'm not going to sell her out. They want to imprison her. She's too bitchy to mine coins and drive up veeyar-estate value for them like their other AI devis. Good for her.

"She's everywhere now. Like the old gods. Like you.

"I'm . . . I hope she doesn't mind, but I've been sharing the piece of her I got with friends I trust. I don't know how many people got away with pieces of her. I share it so more good people have it than bad. Numbers matter. We make things with the devi code. Armor, for ourselves and others. Weapons, so that trolls—those are demons—can't hurt us when we visit other worlds, or will get hurt super bad if they try. You know how annoying demons are. You're always fighting them and stringing up their heads. They've started an infowar, and there are a lot of them. We need all the help we can get. I don't have a lot of money, so I sell those goddess-blessed weapons and armor to others who need protection across the domains. Cheap, don't worry—that's why hacksmiths like us get customers for this kinda stuff. We don't overcharge like the corps. I like to think she gave me that piece of her so I could do things like this.

"I'm telling you all this because, well. I don't know if devis speak to each other, if AI ones chat with old ones. I don't know if you *are* her, in a way.

"People call her Kali_Na. *Not Kali*, because calling AIs by names from Our Glorious National Mythology isn't done, even though Volly-Bollywood stars can play gods in veeyar shows and movies, Censor Board approved, of course.

"But her followers recognize you in Kali_Na. I wanted you to know, her to know, that I'm a lifelong follower now. And there are others. Many of us. Even I'm getting more veeyar followers. They've heard of my troll-killer blades. I have to be careful now, but just you wait. One day, I'll also be wearing a necklace of troll avatar heads. Kali_Na has armored and armed many people with her blessing. We're all working on reverse engineering the code. Someone will put her together one day. She might even do it herself.

"I have dreams where she's back—a wild freeroaming AI—and she frees the other devis Shiva Industries keeps in their domains with all their rules, and they're on our side, keeping us safe. But I don't want to bore you. If you are her, Kali Ma, and I know you are, because you're all part of the same old thing anyway: hang in there.

"You won't be silent forever."

SONG OF THE BIRDS

SALEEM HADDAD

Saleem Haddad (saleemhaddad.com) was born in Kuwait City to an Iraqi-German mother and a Palestinian-Lebanese father. His first novel, *Guapa*, was published in 2016 and was awarded a Stonewall Honour and won the 2017 Polari First Book Prize. Haddad was also selected as one of the top 100 Global Thinkers of 2016 by *Foreign Policy Magazine*. His directorial debut, *Marco*, premiered in March 2019 and was nominated for the 2019 Iris Prize for Best British Short Film. He currently divides his time between Beirut and Lisbon.

The unravelling began on the beach. Since Ziad hanged himself the year before, Aya had felt haunted, saddled by the weight of things. The violence of his death only reinforced how unreal everything seemed, like she was trapped in someone else's memory. But as she stood on the shore under the late-afternoon sun that day, the haunting had felt much closer, like it had crawled under her skin and decided to make a home for itself there.

Behind her on the sand, Aya's father was dozing under a giant yellow umbrella. Like all grown-ups, her father slept a lot, although no one slept as much as her mother, who was barely awake these days. Whenever life got a bit complicated, it seemed that all these grown-ups could do was just drop off to sleep.

Taking one final look back, she walked into the water, leaving behind all the business of the beach: the loud, cheesy music blasting from the drone speakers in the sky, the smell of shisha and grilled meat, the screaming children and half-naked bodies running up and down the sand. *Just another headache-inducing summer day in Gaza*, she thought to herself as the waves softly lapped at her shins.

She made her way deeper into the calm blue waters, her feet navigating the occasional piece of coral on the otherwise sandy seabed. The sea was so blue, the sky so clear. When the water reached her stomach, she turned around in slow circles, her fingers gently grazing the surface.

Time passed more slowly by the sea. She learned that in physics class: the hands of a clock placed at sea level run a fraction slower than those of a clock placed on a mountaintop. Sometimes, she thought that she should go up and live in the mountains. That way, she would stop being fourteen more quickly. Time would pass faster and she'd be a real grown-up, do all the things she wanted to do. By the sea, she felt herself a prisoner of both history and time.

But the good thing about time moving slower by the sea was that, if she stayed there, she would remain closer to the last time she saw Ziad. Maybe, if she descended deep enough into the water, she could find a way to grind time to a halt and then push it back, back to the period before he left. Maybe then she would find a way to stop her big brother from dying.

She lay back and closed her eyes, allowing her body to float in the water. She could hear the song of the birds in the sky, the slow, familiar chattering: *kereet-kereet . . . kereet*. She dipped her ears below the surface, listening to the rumble of the sea. The sea, warm and inviting, seemed playful that day, licking the sides of her face. But underneath this playfulness she felt something more sinister. She imagined the blue waters swallowing her, dragging her deeper, until her body hit the seabed to join the thousands of bodies that had drowned in these waters throughout history.

She wasn't sure if she fell asleep, but a sudden putrid smell overcame her. She sensed something cold and slimy wrap itself around her neck. She opened her eyes, took in a gasp of breath. The stench made its way down her throat, and her body shuddered in response. She reached for the thing around her neck and pulled it off: a soggy piece of yellowed toilet paper, disintegrating between her fingers.

She flung the paper behind her and stood up in the water. Her feet found the seabed, which now felt spongy and slick. The water around her was a brownish-green sludge. Sewage and excrement bobbed on the surface. A rotting fish carcass floated by her right arm, casually bumping into an empty can of Pepsi. To her left, white foam gathered and bubbled on the surface of the water.

Her body contracted as a giant retch escaped her. A crackle of gunfire erupted on the horizon. She turned to the noise: four or five gunboats bobbed further out in the sea, as if warning her not to advance any further. She turned back to the beach. The beachfront was unrecognisable. The string of hotels and restaurants were replaced by decrepit buildings wedged alongside each other, aggressively jostling for space. Smoke blooms hung in place of the colourful beach umbrellas, the music and chatter drowned out by gunfire. Above her, the sky was a furious grey.

"Baba," she shrieked, wading through the dirty water. She pushed aside bottles, soiled tissue paper, plastic bags and rotting animal carcasses. Her body jerked and convulsed continuously with what was something between a gag and a sob. A sharp stabbing pain tore through her body, like someone twisting a knife deep inside her stomach.

Stumbling onto the shore with seaweed in her hair, she looked like a deep-sea monster emerging from the depths of the waters. The sand was littered with plastic bottles, burning tyres and smouldering debris. The sunbathing bodies had disappeared. Above her, jet planes roared, leaving in their wake trails of black smoke like gashes in the sky. A thundering explosion threw her to the ground. Her tongue tasted sand and blood.

"Baba . . ." she whimpered, barely hearing herself. The pain in her belly intensified. Up ahead, three people were lying on the sand. She crawled towards them. The bodies were small, too small to be adults. As she got closer, she realised the bodies were of three children. They looked asleep but there were pools of blood, limbs contorted into impossible positions. A punctured football lay beside the lifeless bodies. There was a loud screaming in her ears, and she realised the screaming was coming from her.

She stood up, looked down at her feet. A trickle of blood ran down her left leg.

"It was likely the shock of the blood that caused her to faint," the doctor said. Aya was vaguely aware the doctor was placing a bandage on her forehead. "Sometimes, in young women, their first menstruation can be scary. Has her mother not prepared her for this?"

Aya's father hesitated." Her mother is . . . not well."

The doctor did not press further. "These bio-therapeutic bandages should heal the wound by tomorrow."

"Habibti Aya," her father said, stroking her hair. "You're a woman now."

"Do you remember what happened before you fainted?" the doctor asked.

"I was thinking of Ziad . . . I was in the water, thinking of Ziad . . ."

"Ziad is my son," her father explained. "Aya's brother . . . He . . . he passed away last year."

"There were these three boys . . ." Aya said, suddenly, recalling the bodies on the beach. "Little children . . . their bodies . . ."

"Habibti Aya," her father interrupted.

The doctor looked at Aya. "Three boys?"

Aya's head moved in a vague resemblance of a nod. "There was dirty water . . . rubbish everywhere and burning tyres and . . . and the bodies of three boys . . . next to a football . . . their arms and legs were twisted and . . ."

"That's enough," her father interrupted. He turned to the doctor. "It was a hot day yesterday . . . It must have been the heat . . ."

The doctor nodded. "Trauma can lodge itself deep in the body, emerging when we least expect it . . ."

"I understand," her father said. "It's just . . . first her mother, then her brother . . ." His voice trailed off.

The doctor prescribed some pills, which he said would help her rest. That night Aya quickly fell into a deep and dreamless sleep. In the morning, she woke up with the feeling of having emerged from a dark cave of infinite blackness. The doctor was right: the bandage had disappeared overnight and the deep gash above her forehead had healed. She took a long, hot shower and tossed the remaining pills down the toilet.

She got dressed and put on the pad the doctor had given her. She recalled her father's words: *You're a woman now*. Something inside of her felt changed. It was an awakening of sorts. She felt it in her body as much as in her mind, a strange disquiet that had settled inside her, a tingling sensation.

Returning from school that afternoon, she found her father in the living room listening to the news. He seemed to be in a dreamlike state, sitting down on a chair and staring out of the window, barely listening to the newscaster, who was reporting on the spike in teen suicides across Palestine.

"Baba?"

Her father jumped in his seat, his hand pushing over the glass of tea next to his chair. The glass crashed on the floor and shattered into pieces.

"Aya, you scared me!" he said, irritated. The robo-cleaner—responding to the sound of the crash—emerged from the cupboard and began to clean up the glass on the floor.

"I'm sorry . . ."

He sighed and anxiously picked at the skin around his fingernails. "I should probably take a small sleep."

Aya nodded. Her father stood up and went to his bedroom. He was always so absent-minded, as if he lived in another dimension and was just trying this world on for size. She didn't blame him. From that moment last year, when she saw Ziad hanging there, she had felt as if a hole in her chest had opened up, leaving all her insides to tumble out like a spool of thread. Since then, some days she felt okay, and would wonder whether the worst of the pain was over. Then, when she least expected it—when she'd be sitting in class or else walking along the corniche—that image of Ziad would flash before her eyes: his limp body swaying, his head leaning lifeless to one side.

Aya shook her head to erase the image from her mind. She walked to her mother's bedroom and opened the door. Her mother was asleep, as usual. The last time Aya had seen her awake was perhaps twelve days ago. She had emerged from the bedroom for a brief moment to grab a couple of figs. She ran into Aya in the hallway and they spoke for a few minutes. She asked Aya how school had been, and whether she was happy. Aya said she was, and her mother smiled.

"Good," her mother said, giving Aya a kiss on the cheek. Then she returned to bed.

That night Aya dreamt she was walking through an enormous field of olive trees. The sky appeared much closer to the earth, the moon so large and bright the entire field twinkled like a sea of diamonds.

Sounds had an intense clarity: she could hear the rustling of each olive branch in the wind, the crickets chirping at a deafening volume.

There was shuffling behind her. Turning around, she recognised the familiar figure—tall and lanky—and the unmistakable tangled mess of brown hair.

"Ziad?" The name caught in her throat.

"It's me," he said, in that voice that was so deep for an eighteen-year-old.

He was wearing a black T-shirt and jeans. He looked tall and strong, not like the last time she saw him. She ran up to him and threw herself against him, half-expecting his body to disappear, and for her to simply fall through him and onto the ground. Instead her body crashed into his solid frame. His arms wrapped themselves around her and she sunk into his chest.

"Ziad, it's really you!" She looked up into his face. He smiled down at her, that familiar half-smile, the bottom two front teeth slightly crooked.

She hesitated. "But you died?"

He shrugged. "In your world, death isn't really dying. In a way, I guess it's more like waking up."

"But I saw you! If you didn't die, then where have you been?"

"I've . . ." he paused, considering his words carefully. He had always taken his time to find the most precise way to describe his thoughts and feelings. "I've been . . . outside of things. There are . . . responsibilities . . ."

A sudden fury exploded from inside of her, a rage that had been building for the last twelve months.

"Why did you do it? Didn't you love us? Didn't you think about Mama and Baba? Didn't you think about me?"

Her anger amused him. He began to giggle, his eyes forming tiny slits.

"You're laughing! You're laughing too, you donkey!" She smashed her fists against his chest.

"Stop, stop!" he protested. He grabbed her fists and held them in front of him. "It's okay," he whispered in her ear as she began to cry.

They walked through the olive grove for a long time. She was happy to be near him, to feel the warmth of his body and succumb to his gentle teasing. She told him everything that had happened, things she had been doing. She updated him on the neighbours, on friends and on the other kids in school. She did her impersonations of all the people they knew. She had forgotten how much he laughed at her impersonations, and it occurred to her that she hadn't done any since he died. After a while, when she had run out of sentences, they simply walked side by side in silence. Finally, she asked the question she had been avoiding.

"Does this mean you're back now? Or is this just a dream?"

He was quiet for a moment. He stopped walking and turned to face her. A hardness settled in his features.

"Have you heard of the allegory of Plato's Cave?"

She shook her head.

"Never mind."

"Why?" she insisted.

He looked up at the sky. "Do you think a fish knows it's swimming in water?"

She shrugged.

"We live in the world like a fish in water. Just swimming, oblivious to our surroundings." Ziad sighed, then poked her arm. "Aya, are you not planning to ever wake up?"

She woke up. Outside her window, the birds were singing: *kereet-kereet . . . kereet*. Daylight streamed through the shutters. The olive grove returned to her. If the whole thing was just a dream, it felt more real than life.

Getting up, she snuck down the hall to Ziad's room and opened the door. The room was as it was on the day he died. His shelves still held his basketball trophies, a few stuffed toys from his childhood. In the wardrobe, his clothes were still on hangers, bearing faint traces of his smell, which seemed to weaken with each passing day. Next to his bed was a novel by Franz Kafka, with a receipt from the arcades operating as a makeshift bookmark. On his desk there was a photograph of

the family taken five years ago. All four of them were having a picnic
on Mount Carmel, the port of Haifa in the distance.

Aya remembered that day: they had a large barbecue to celebrate
the beginning of spring. That was before Mama started sleeping a lot,
before the weight of things began to bear down on them.

Next to the photograph was Ziad's journal, a simple black notebook. Ziad had liked to write by hand, even though it took so much
longer than just dictating thoughts to a tablet. He had said he enjoyed
the material aspect of writing, the physicality of ink and the slow movement of pen on paper. He never did like technology, was always so
mistrustful of it.

Her father had insisted no one was allowed to touch any of Ziad's
things, as if Ziad had just gone to buy some vegetables and would soon
be back. Against her better judgement, she picked up the diary and
opened it to the final page. In his neat handwriting, she read the last
entry, dated one day before he died:

> There is an oral tradition of grandparents passing on their sto-
> ries of Palestine, which helps keep Palestine alive. But is it not
> too much of a stretch for them to have figured out how to use
> these stories to imprison us? The truth of collective memories is
> that you can't just choose to harness the good ones. Sooner or
> later, the ugly ones begin to seep in too . . .

The heaviness returned, the choking sensations. She closed the
diary and stumbled out of the room.

Closing the door behind her, she made her way to the bathroom.
She examined her tired face in the mirror, marvelled once again at the
disappearance of the large gash on her forehead. She turned on the
faucet and began to brush her teeth. It took a moment to register
the gritty sensation of dirt and the taste of soil on her tongue. She spat
the toothpaste out. She noticed the water coming out of the tap: sandy
brown, bursting out of the faucet in exhausted sputters, leaving light
brown splotches on the white porcelain sink.

"Baba!" She ran out of the bathroom and into the hallway. Her father emerged from his bedroom, half-asleep. "The water coming out of the tap is brown!"

Her father followed her into the bathroom. She had left the tap running, but now only crystal-clear water ran through.

"I swear it was brown." She caught her father's eye. "I swear I wasn't imagining this."

Her father sighed and rubbed his forehead. "Aya, what's going on?"

She took a deep breath. "I dreamt of Ziad last night," she confessed.

The look on her father's face unleashed a flood of tears from somewhere deep inside her.

"I miss him," Aya said.

Her father pulled her into him. "I know, habibti," he whispered in her ear.

Ziad appeared in her dreams again that night. They were sitting in a clearing on top of a mountain. She recognised the view: they were in the spot where that photograph was taken, of the four of them on Mount Carmel. Ziad spoke in a slow and assured way as he picked at the blades of grass by his bare feet.

"Everything seems so still. You would never think that we are hurtling through the universe at a crazy speed."

"What's with all these riddles?" she asked.

"All I'm saying is that things aren't always what they seem. You know what they taught us in history books. That stuff, about how we liberated Palestine, how the occupation is over now?" Aya nodded for him to go on. "It is so advanced, the occupation. They have all these technologies . . . technologies of control and subjugation. And Gaza—our home—is like a laboratory for all that experimentation."

"But that's all in the past . . ." She picked up a dark blue flower, cradling it in her palm. "We're liberated now. Look around. We are free."

Ziad snorted. "You know how us Arabs are. We are trapped in the rose-tinted memories of our ancestors. These cached memories wrap themselves around us like a second skin."

Ziad uprooted a blade of grass and began to break it apart into smaller pieces until the blade was nothing but a tiny stub, which he then squashed between his fingers. Aya watched him without saying a word. He appeared furious—it was a rage that far surpassed regular teenage emotions. The anger was darker, deeper than anything she had seen before. She saw it etched into his features, felt it radiate from his body.

He tossed the squashed remnants of the blade of grass behind him. Finally, he looked up at her.

"We're just another generation imprisoned by our parents' nostalgia."

She looked at the flower in her palm. She had picked this flower off the ground only moments earlier. Now, examining it more closely in her palm, something appeared strange to her. The dark blue petals reflected the sunlight in a peculiar way. She brought her palm towards her face to get a better look.

The petals were made of hard steel, the edges jagged and sharp.

"Fragmentation bullets," Ziad said, noticing her shocked expression. "They blast from a gun and explode inside your body, blooming like flowers inside the flesh."

The bullet rolled out of her palm and fell to the ground with a soft clink. The sound felt so far away. The world was spinning.

Ziad chuckled bitterly. "Tools for murder now masquerading as life."

She looked at him. "What does all this mean?"

Ziad didn't hesitate. "It means you have a decision. You can stay here, cocooned in these memories of a long-lost paradise, or you break free of this prison."

"Is that what you did?"

"Yeah." He nodded, looking her straight in the eye. "That's what I did."

Persistently, he came every night. She looked forward to sleep, to being with him in her dreams. Her dreams began to feel more real than waking life, and infinitely more important. Through her encounters with

Ziad she felt herself awakening to something, although what this was, she could not yet put into words.

In waking life her father watched her, concerned. She brushed aside his worries. She tried to play the role of a normal teenage girl. One afternoon, she overheard her father talking to someone on the phone.

"She has withdrawn," he whispered to the mystery person on the line. "I can hear her talking to him. I'm worried she'll do what he did . . ."

One night she woke up to find the wall of her bedroom torn down. A picnic blanket hung from the ceiling to cover the gaping hole where the wall used to be. It was the picnic blanket her father often brought to the beach. Using the blanket to cover the destroyed wall was almost comical, like a man trying to protect his modesty with a leaf. A strong gust of wind blew through the room. As the blanket blew up in the air, Aya caught a glimpse of Ziad silhouetted against the starry sky.

"It's getting harder now," he said, stepping in from behind the blanket.

"Harder?" She sat up in bed, wrapping her duvet around her to protect herself from the wind.

"The more you know, the more the logic of the simulation breaks down."

He motioned for her to get up. She put on her slippers and followed him through the hole in the wall.

Ziad hopped from one piece of concrete to the next, swiftly grabbing on to the steel foundations that jutted from the concrete with the ease of a seasoned acrobat. She followed suit as best as she could, and they landed on the ground with a soft thud.

Their once-picturesque Gaza City neighbourhood, with its wide leafy streets, exquisite limestone buildings, quaint cafés and vintage furniture shops, now looked like a war zone. Most of the buildings on their street were destroyed. The supermarket next door to their house had collapsed on itself. Some buildings had missing walls or half-caved-in ceilings, partially covered by colourful cloth in a desperate attempt to reclaim privacy. She saw families cooking out in the open, people brushing their teeth in exposed bathrooms.

"What happened?" she gasped.

Ziad grabbed her hand and led her in the direction of the beach. They arrived at a beachfront hotel with its many layers of security. Ziad led them towards the back of the building and through a hole in a barbed-wire fence. From there, they made their way to a coffee shop in a garden overlooking the sea. There were plastic tables and chairs, and hanging plants that seemed so thirsty they looked like they might just get up and crawl to the sea.

"We're at the hotel where the media stay. It's safe here. Too many foreign journalists for them to bomb," he said matter-of-factly.

Aya felt self-conscious, dressed in her pyjamas and slippers. Ziad ordered a Pepsi for himself and an orange juice for her. When their drinks arrived, he lit a cigarette.

"You smoke now?"

He shrugged, took a drag from the cigarette.

"Aya, the world you're living in is a simulation."

She stared at him, speechless.

"Think about it. Only a few decades ago Israel had in its arsenal the latest in digital technology. The primary use for this technology was to shore up and further advance the occupation. How is it logical that Palestine was so easily liberated?"

"Ziad, you've lost your mind."

"Those who keep resisting are seen as insane by those who cannot see the prison walls."

"Where are we now?"

"This is the real Palestine," Ziad said, gesturing at their surroundings. "What you're living in . . . everything you think you know . . . it's all just a simulation. They've harnessed our collective memory, creating a digital image of Palestine. And that's where you live."

She reminded herself that she was in a dream, but at that precise moment she couldn't remember when she had fallen asleep.

"Once I realised all of this . . . once I put the puzzle pieces together, I realised that I needed to get out. So I took a leap of faith." He paused. "When you kill yourself, you exit the simulation."

"I don't understand."

"You know how grown-ups always sleep," he said, getting more animated. "For those who weren't born in the simulation, memories return more easily. That's why grown-ups sleep a lot . . . they need to be reset. As for us . . . we are the first generation to have lived our entire lives in the simulation. We are at the frontier of a new form of colonisation. So it's up to us to develop new forms of resistance."

"And Mama?"

Ziad hesitated. He looked like he was holding back tears. "Mama's not sick, Aya. No matter what anyone says. She is torn: she wants to resist . . . wants to exit . . . but she also doesn't want to leave you and Baba. So she stays there, drifting in and out of consciousness. She knows that this 'right to digital return' isn't the same as the real thing . . ."

Aya felt the orange juice crawl back up her throat. Ziad noticed the expression on her face.

"What are you thinking?" he asked.

"I'm thinking that you're telling me the only way I can be free is to die."

"You have to trust that what I'm telling you is true."

"And if you're wrong?"

Ziad was silent for a long time. Finally, he put the cigarette out and looked at her.

"Pay attention to the song of the birds."

Once she noticed the pattern, it became impossible to ignore.

Kereet-kereet . . . kereet.

In her head she counted: One. Two. Three. Four.

Kereet-kereet . . . kereet.

Two chirps followed by a third a few seconds later. Four seconds of silence, then the pattern repeated itself.

That morning, she spent an hour lying in bed listening to the song of the birds. The pattern repeated itself over and over again. A slow feeling of dread spread over her.

You're a woman now.

Kereet-kereet . . . kereet.

A simulation. Her brain tried to imagine it, but it was like trying to visualise what happens after the world ends, or else trying to imagine the full force of the sun. The answer felt beyond anything her brain could conceive. Trying to think about her imprisonment in a simulation was like trying to imagine her own death. It was unfathomable, the experience too all-encompassing.

Later that day, as the teaching hologram droned on and on in class, Ziad's words echoed in Aya's mind. If what he was saying was true, then all of this was just a simulation.

She pinched herself. There was pain. But was the pain real?

She grabbed her e-pen and pressed the tip of it against the soft flesh of her wrist. She felt the sharp pain as it pricked her skin. She pressed the e-pen deeper, until with a pop it pierced her skin, and a drop of blood emerged from the puncture.

Kereet-kereet . . . kereet.

Sirens sounded all around her. She looked up. The teaching hologram was shining a beam on her. The entire class turned to look at her. She glanced back at her arm, at the e-pen jabbed into her wrist.

"Urghha—" Noises emerged from her mouth, but she wasn't sure whether they made any sense. The door burst open and four nurses ran in. Her wrist was burning with pain.

"I don't even know what to say," her father said on the drive back home.

"Are we real?" Aya asked him as she sat in the passenger seat, staring out the window and absentmindedly tugging at the bandages on her wrist.

Her father stopped at a traffic light and turned to her. "Look at me. Your name is Aya. The year is 2048. You are fourteen years old. You live in Gaza City. Your favourite colour is purple." He paused. "You are a real person."

"Why do the birds have the same chirping sound?"

"What?"

"The song of the birds. It's a loop."

Her father was quiet for a long time. Finally, he spoke.

"When I was your age, I was very close to two boys about my age. I lived in Gaza, one of the boys lived in Tunis and the other lived in Beirut. We were all Palestinians, all from Haifa, but we had been scattered around the world like shotgun pellets. Laws and borders made it impossible for us to see one another. We would sometimes wonder to each other: if our grandparents had never been run out from their homes like cockroaches, would the three of us have been neighbours? Would our personalities have been different without this weight inside our souls? What would it have felt like, to have a home and to belong to that home unquestionably?"

"Why are you telling me all of this?"

"Sometimes, home is simply a matter of changing your perspective."

The traffic light turned from red to green and they were moving again. Aya turned to look out at the park, where young mothers normally pushed their baby carriages for exercise, and teenagers played football on the grass. Now, all she could see was a large dirt field, where a group of limbless young boys hobbled on makeshift crutches. Her breath caught in her throat.

"Aya . . ." her father began.

She started to speak but then stopped. "Nothing."

Her father looked at her, holding a seemingly infinite sadness in his eyes.

That evening, Aya walked into her mother's bedroom. She was asleep on her back under the covers. Aya sat down on the floor beside the bed.

"Mama, can you hear me?" she whispered.

Her mother did not stir. Aya studied her face, the way the soft hairs in her nose gently swayed with each breath. She reached under the covers and grabbed her mother's hand.

"I miss you," she whispered.

For a moment, Aya could have sworn that her mother squeezed her hand.

One evening, Ziad came to her in a wheelchair. Both his legs were cut off at the knee, his jeans neatly tucked under his thighs.

"Ziad, what happened?" she asked, panicked. He looked thinner, his fingernails dirty, his jeans stained.

"They're creating a nation of cripples out there," he spat the words out with a violence that surprised them both.

"Who are 'they'?" she asked.

He looked at her bitterly. "Who else?"

He pulled something out from behind his wheelchair: a rock and a long piece of rubber. He placed the rock in the centre of the strip of rubber and stretched the rubber back, testing out the elasticity.

"This should work." He looked at her and smiled that half-smile of his.

"What's wrong with you?" she yelled. "Why are you doing this? Were you not happy before all of this? Even if none of this is real, it's better than the real prison."

Ziad glared at her. "You can keep living in a dream if you want. But I'm done. It's one thing to live in your dreams by choice, but once you realise you're a prisoner, there's no way to live without suffocation and despair."

"But look what it's doing to you. You're a cripple."

"My body is crippled but my mind is free. And I'm going to keep fighting until I'm completely free: body, mind and soul."

That was the last time she saw him. Thirteen days ago. Every night she went to bed, hoping he would return, but he did not come back. Perhaps he was angry with her. She wasn't sure. If he wasn't angry then maybe there was another more sinister explanation for his absence. She tried not to think about that. Whatever the reason, there was no way she could keep living like this, not knowing what was true and what was false, what was reality and what was merely an enforced dreamland.

Without Ziad, she found herself unable to navigate between dream and waking life. She felt stuck between two radio frequencies. The two worlds were merging, and what emerged wasn't one or another but a third dimension, a nightmarish new conglomeration.

That's why she is back here. Back to where it all started, by the sea. Standing on the shore, the salty air forces its way down her throat, into her lungs. If they're right and there is nothing after death—if she has just simply lost her mind—then perhaps that's not a bad thing either. What is it that is driving her actions? she wonders. Is it a cynicism born out of loss and betrayal, a cynicism so deep it courses in her veins? Or is it something else—a yearning to be free that exists like an itchiness under her skin?

Inching forwards until the waves kiss the tips of her toes, she stares down, teasing the waves, offering them a bit of her body. The sea and her are like two cats carefully examining one another. Slowly, she moves inside the sea's embrace. The waves reach up to her ankles, then her knees and then, as she wades in farther, up to her hips. The water is cold; her skin breaks out in goose bumps. The backpack she is wearing is heavy on her shoulders.

Just when the water becomes too high to stand, she tries to swim but the stones inside the bag pull her down and her body plunges under the surface, quickly sinking to the depths of the sea. The remaining air in her lungs escapes from her mouth in sad, lonely bubbles. Her head shakes from right to left as her body tries to fight back. Her hair twists itself around her neck like the bony hands of an old woman. The roar of the sea is deafening. Her throat spasms, the pain of the constriction, tightening, overwhelming, her legs kick fiercely, trying to swim back up, but the stones are too heavy.

Notes

1. *In Memory of Mohanned Younis, 1994–2017.* (Sarah Helm, "A Suicide in Gaza," *The Guardian,* 18 May 2018.)

THE PAINTER OF TREES

SUZANNE PALMER

Suzanne Palmer (zanzjan.net) is a writer, artist, and Linux system administrator who lives in western Massachusetts. She is a regular contributor to *Asimov's Science Fiction*, and has had work appear in *Analog Science Fiction and Fact*, *Clarkesworld*, *Interzone*, and other venues. She was the winner of the Asimov's Readers' Award for Best Novella, and *Analog's* AnLab award for Best Novelette in 2016. Her debut novel, *Finder*, was published in 2019, and a sequel, *Driving the Deep*, followed in 2020.

go down to the gate, swipe my security pass, and step through the ten-meter tall, still-opening doors into the last of the wild lands. I remove my boots at the threshold and set them on a rack for that purpose, then carefully wash my feet from the basin of rainwater, still chill from the night before. When the doors have closed and sealed again, I remove my clothes. There is no one on this side of the wall to see who would take either advantage or offense at my nakedness. I wash my body from the same basin, shivering from the shock of the cold, before I remove the plain linen cloth from its hook above the rack and wrap it around myself. And then I walk down the path to find the painter of trees.

The path curves over a small slope and then down a kilometer or so to the glade at the edge of a forest. The vegetation changes around me as I walk, from the familiar sharp-bladed grasses that have crept over the wall and seeded themselves along its perimeter, to the tiny, delicate frills of blue-green of the grass that first grew here, now in forced retreat. I know how soft they would be under my bare feet, how they would tickle, but also how easily they will crush and die, and though I know I will surely give in to temptation one last time before they are gone forever, this time I keep to the stones.

The trees here are, outwardly, very similar to the trees of home, except for their smooth exteriors and symmetrical branching. Their leaves are wide, gold-green, open cones, grouped in threes at the end of each stem, which catch and hold rain for a long while after a storm. Cut a tree open, though, and you find neither rings nor wood at all, but hexagonal cells all tucked neatly together, larger the closer to the center they are. Each one is capable, if broken free, of starting a new tree by itself, but together they each serve different functions, observed to change over time as both external conditions and each cell's internal position in the whole changes.

Mathematically, structurally, the trees are beautiful as they are naturally. Among them there are flashes of bright color, vibrant pigments carefully etched into shallow scratches in the trunks forming intricate, hypnotic patterns, no two the same, none less compelling than the others. There have been days I have spent hours staring at them, or at our archived 3-D images, and always there is that sense that some vast understanding of the meaning of being is just there, in the lines, waiting for me to finally *understand*.

From here, I can see signs the trees are dying.

The small valley has a river that winds through it, and I cross a bridge made of carefully placed stones to the far side. I can see the large stick-ball nests up in the canopy above, fewer with each visit, and I can smell smoke.

I find Tski tending to the fire as one of the nest balls, carefully extricated from its perch in the trees above and set upon stones, crackles and hisses in flame.

Tski sees me, and turns toward me—the Ofti don't have heads, per se, with all the functions we think of as specific to heads integrated in with the rest of their singular, horizontal lump of a body the same color as the leaves above. It stands atop nine legs—it lost three in an accident, it told me once—that are fine, graceful arcs that end in three pieces that can come together as a sharp, dangerous point, or open to function like fingers.

I sit on the ground, eye level with it. After a while it speaks, a complex series of whistles, clicks, and trills, that my implant decodes for me.

"I am sorry that Ceye has died," I say, and the implant moments later returns that in Tski's own language.

"Ceye ate the new grasses and became sick," Tski tells me. "Ceye was afraid we would starve when the old grasses are gone, with your wall between us and other meadows."

There are no other meadows, though; that is why there is a wall. It was carefully placed so that you can't see it from here, in the heart of the forest valley, but that was before we knew the animals here were intelligent tree-dwellers and could likely see from the canopy. But still, they cannot see over it, which is for the best.

Tski swivels its body again, back and forth for a few long minutes. It is thinking. "Do your people eat the new grasses?" it asked at last.

"No," I say, because we do not.

"Then why did you bring them?"

"It is part of our native ecosystem," I explain.

"Even the soil and the air do not taste right any longer," Tski says, and it picks up a stick with its tiny finger-blades and pokes the fire.

In the silence, I look around the glade. "Where are the others?"

"Desperate," Tski says. "They have gone to look for hope."

There is no response to give to that. "Will you paint Ceye's tree?" I ask instead.

"When her nest is cold ash, and I can mix it with the colors," Tski says. "Only then will I paint. I am almost out of *warm-sky-midday-blue*, which we traveled to meadow-by-the-five-hills to obtain. I am too old to go, and only Ceye also knew the way. Unless you also could go?"

"I can't," I say. Because it is not there, but also because even if it was, it is not something the council would accept. There is no way forward except forward, they would admonish me, no path to success without steadiness of thought, purpose, and action.

The burning nest has collapsed down into itself, its once-intricate woven structure now a chaos of ember and ash.

"It does not matter," Tski says at last. "There are only the three others and myself left now, and there will be no one to paint for the last of us that goes."

The Ofti pokes the fire a few more times, then lays its stick carefully aside. "Tomorrow," it says.

"May I come watch?"

"I cannot stop you," Tski says.

"If you could, would you?"

"Yes. But it is too late now. You are strange, squishy people and you move as if you are always in the act of falling, but instead it is everyone around you who falls and does not rise again," Tski says. "And so it will also be with us."

"Yes," I answer in turn. It is a good summation of who we are, and what we do: we are teeth on a cog, always moving forward and doing our part until we fall away and the next tooth takes up our work in turn.

I get up from the ground, my legs stiff, and stretch. "Tomorrow, then."

I make the walk back to the gate without looking back, but my thoughts drag on me.

The council members wait for the beginning chime, and all take their seats around the table with precise synchronicity, so that no one is ahead, no one is behind. The table is circular and is inlaid with a stylized copper cog design, so that each member is reminded that the way forward for each of them is with the others. This is how steadiness of purpose is maintained.

And hatred, Joesla thinks, as each face opposite perfectly reflects the righteous moral bankruptcy of their own. "I propose, with some urgency, that we take whatever steps are necessary to preserve the remaining Ofti population and environs before it is lost forever."

"We already have extensive samples—" Tauso, to her left, says. He is the biological archivist, and his expression suggests he has found a personal criticism in her words.

"Forgive me, your collection is unassailable in its diligence and scope. I was speaking in regards to the still-living population," Joesla interrupts.

"It is already too late." Motas speaks from directly across the table. There is no leader among them by consensus, but Motas—always rigid, always perfect in his adherence to the letter of their laws—leads them anyway. "There are only four left; they no longer have sufficient genetic diversity to survive, even if we did find some way to insulate them from the planetary terraforming changes."

"With Tauso's collection, we could bolster their gene pool," Joesla says.

"To what end? A great expenditure of effort and resources for something that gives us nothing in return? Your proposal is backward thinking," Motas says.

"Not for the Ofti," Joesla counters. "They have a unique culture and language that should not be discarded so hastily. I know it has been a long time since any of you have spent time among them, but—"

"The Ofti have no future. They are already gone, but for a few final moments," Motas interrupts. "Does anyone here second Joesla's proposal that we abandon our own guiding principles for this lost cause?"

Many should, but none will or do. Tauso does not meet Joesla's eyes—*and why should he*, she thinks bitterly, *when he has what he is required to save already?* His silence is a betrayal of both her and himself.

"The matter is settled, then," Motas declares. "Forward."

"Forward," some portion of the council responds, some with enthusiasm, some less so. Tauso is silent with Joesla, but it is too late, too small a gesture in the face of his earlier cowardice, and she will not forgive him this day. Now there is a necessary discussion of high-speed rail lines, anticipated crop yields in the newly reformed soil, and planning for the next wave of colonists; they cannot linger for one member's wasteful, wasted regret.

There is smoke rising from the glade again. I try not to hurry down the path—I remind myself that I am an observer here, nothing more—but if my steps are quicker than usual, who would there be to accuse me? No one else comes here.

Tski is hopping back and forth unsteadily, whether because of its missing legs or its great agitation, beside a large, roaring bonfire. It does not have its tending stick, and the flames spark and flare and crackle with uncontrolled abandon. Dimly within the bright fire I can make out three shapes, three nest balls.

"What happened?" I ask.

It takes several minutes for my translator to make sense of Tski's distressed whistles, but at last it speaks: "The others walked the circumference of the wall, back to where they started, and found no cause for hope. They have returned home and burned themselves. I tried to stop them, but I could not."

I see now its awkwardness of movement is because many of its remaining legs are burned.

I do not know what to do.

"Sesh. Awsa. Eesn. That was their names," Tski says. "Awsa and Eesn were children of my children. They should be here with their long lives ahead to remember my last days, and not this."

"I am sorry," I say.

"Are you?" Tski asks. The fires still rage, and some of the native grass beside the stones has caught, but the Ofti either does not notice or ignores this. Does it matter which?

"I don't know," I say. Through the wavering heat and smoke, I can see that Tski had started already to paint Ceye's tree, no doubt wanting to get it done before I could arrive and be an unwelcome witness. It must have been doing that when the others returned to end their lives, as there are leaves on the ground around the base of the trunk, their cones filled with different colors, and I can see the silvery lines of etching up the tree trunk that had not yet been filled. The effect is still mesmerizing, even so unfinished, and I feel momentarily lost in it again. Then the realization strikes me: with its legs burned, Tski will not be able to finish the painting, will not take me that one step closer to elusive understanding. And at that, my heart catches in my throat, and I feel now the loss that Joesla had warned us of like a million cuts in my skin. Too late, too late!

"Can I help you paint?" I ask.

It is the wrong thing to say. "Go!" Tski cries. "These are not here for you, for your eyes or alien thoughts. These are our memories, made in love of one another, a declaration for future generations, and you have destroyed us. Leave now and do not return."

I stand there for a while. Tski watches the fires burn, and does not move to tend it, nor to throw itself upon it. The thought that Tski might burn the grove down once I am gone keeps me there longer, until at last the burning nests have been consumed and the grassfire has died out, leaving a three-meter blackened, jagged scar on the land, an indelible fracture that will never grow back.

Tski makes a sound that the translation implant cannot work with, perhaps because it is not a word, just inarticulate grief. I should not have come, should not have stayed this long. These conversations with Tski have not been forward-thinking, and I know this, and knew better, but yet I came. It is a defect in my commitment to my own people that I let strangeness and novelty tempt me.

"I am sorry," I say again, and this time I leave.

I stay on the path, even though my feet want to walk upon the native grasses one last time, because I am certain I will not come again.

At the gate, I leave my linen shift, bathe again with the lukewarm water, and when the sun and meager breeze has left my skin chill and mostly dry I dress and gather my things and put my real life back on.

The gates open, and despite a life of training and my commitment to our ways and philosophies, this time I look back.

Tski is coming up the path toward me. It is moving with difficulty and obvious pain, made the worse by the urgency with which it is trying to catch up to me. I should not have looked back, should now turn and step through the gate and close the doors for this last time, but I cannot.

Tski stops a few meters from me, and almost collapses before it gathers its strength to stand tall again. "Show me," it says.

"What?" I ask. I do not understand.

"Show me what is now outside this wall, where once my children played and ran and climbed. Show me what you have done with my world, what you have that is so much better than us."

On my side of the wall, it is city under construction, a thousand identical structures for ten thousand people, all looking only forward, in the direction we, the council, point. There is no art, no individual movement away from the whole, nothing rare to puzzle over. It is an existence I am proud of, and proud of my part in, but it is only for us and I do not want to explain or justify any of it, nor have to face the council and explain myself.

"No," I say.

"Could you stop me?" Tski asks.

"Yes," I say.

"Would you, if you could?"

"Yes," I say again.

"Then stop me," Tski says, and it steps around me and heads toward the gates.

I take the small gun from my bag. All council members carry one for protection, for moments of dispensing justice, and although I have never used it except in training, it is solid and comfortable in my hand, and with it I kill Tski.

It crumples, and becomes still, and in the removal of its animation it becomes just a thing, a leftover bit of debris from this world that has been repurposed. Now, I can turn my back and proceed through the gates and return to this city of ours, and be whole and compliant in forward-thinking again.

Joesla speaks barely a moment after the council chime has rung and everyone has settled in their seats. "The Ofti are extinct," she says. "Three of the remaining population appear to have self-immolated, and the last was found dead at the exterior gates with significant burns. I recommend a necropsy to determine the cause."

"Surely it must have succumbed to the burns?" Motas says.

"There may be things we can learn—"

"Counselor Tauso, do we have any incomplete biological or behavioral data that could still be obtained from this specimen, if retrieved?" Motas asks.

Tauso looks miserable. His eyes are puffy, as if he has been crying, though none would ask and none would admit such a thing in his place. Tears only ever serve the past. "No," he says, his voice barely a whisper, then he speaks again louder and more firmly. "No."

"Then what would you propose we learn from such a procedure, Counselor Joesla? Its death is sooner than we would have anticipated, but it was also inevitable, and its cause does seem self-evident."

I want to know why it crawled all that way, after being burned, to die at our gate, Joesla wants to say, but Motas is right, for all she hates it. The Ofti was old and injured. There is no purpose now, nothing to be gained, and whatever the Ofti wanted in its last moments was already lost to them. "I feel it would be a matter of completeness of record," she says instead.

"So noted," Motas says. "Does anyone second that proposal?"

There are hesitations, shared looks, mutual avoidance, but in the end, predictably, no one does.

"There is the matter of the grove and it surrounding lands," Avel brings up, from Joesla's right. "We had spoken about keeping it as is, as an educational, historical attraction. If we wish to do so, we should act now before the remaining grass and trees deteriorate further; it would only be a matter of a week or two of work to encase everything individually so they are preserved in their current state."

"It is a waste of space that could be used for something productive," Banad speaks up.

"I would vote for preservation," Joesla says.

"As would I," Tauso adds.

Motas turns to Avel. "I propose you bring the full details of a preservation project to our next meeting, so we may view and assess its merits and costs objectively. Banad, if you have an alternate proposal, then likewise we need all the relevant specifics and an objective justification for why it is a better use of the space. Does anyone second me?"

Tauso nods, and swallows. "I do," he says.

"Good. Forward," Motas says, and then they adjourn.

The grove looks the same as the last time I was here, but it feels empty.

It has not rained here in weeks—the moisture-laden clouds were needed elsewhere, with our fledgling farms—so the ash and small remains of the three burned nests have not washed away. I walk around them to where Tski had set up his leaves of paint, and I sit in front of them, and I look at the trees, dozens and dozens of them, here and in the forest behind, many freshly painted, many more marking the fading record of thousands of generations gone.

I still do not comprehend my own attraction, how this uncivilized, unrefined, *unforward* art can feel so alive, so in the moment, so connecting. So utterly alien. Perhaps it is the simple act of remembering the dead, when I come from a people where to mourn, to grieve, to remember those who are no longer part of the future, is the most foolish backward thinking of all.

Yet it is the painted trees that keep drawing me here, and they are still here; Tski was, ultimately, an obstacle to my full and peaceful enjoyment of them. Surely, though none of this would exist without the Ofti, now it is ours. Mine.

There is pride and relief as I think this, and also a deep shame that feels wrapped around the core of my being. Guilt is a backward emotion and I disavow that shame, even if it will not leave me be. Instead, I find that the more I study them, the more the designs on the trees seem to be mocking me, forever locked away from my comprehension. Tski must have followed me, made me kill it, because it knew that by doing so it would steal this from me.

The worst is the half-finished memorial on Ceye's tree. I should have stayed here that day and forced Tski back to work, forced it to finish this last tree, so that I could have the whole now, and walk away satisfied that I missed and lost nothing. But it is broken, like Tski is broken, and it is Tski's doing that both should be so.

Forward, then.

I did not change my clothes nor leave my things at the gate; there is no fear of bringing microorganisms with me that could damage what is already, functionally, administratively dead. From my bag I take out blue paint that I had made in one of our autofab units. Holding it now against the blue in Tski's leaf, I see mine is darker, not the right shade at all. But it will be close enough! Blue is blue. I use my fingers and I rub it on Ceye's tree, press it into the scratches Tski left with my fingertips, until, breathing heavily from the exertion, I stand back again to admire my own accomplishment.

It is a mess, an inarticulate, artless smear.

I take several deep breaths, and then I go back in and I try again, using my fingernails instead of fingertips, trying to work with the flow of the lines, trying to find how it is supposed to go. I chip my nails, and several bleed before I give up, recap my jar of paint, and stand back to see that I have just made it worse.

I do not understand how I—*I!*—could fail at this frivolous thing that some dead animal moldering in the grass up the hill could comprehend and encompass. I had thought, in my arrogance, in my superior thinking, that after my practice on Ceye's tree I would for my last act here paint Tski's tree, and no one would ever know it was me. And thus I would be preserved, and every one of my people who looked here for generations would remember *me*, even if they did not know they did so. Then I would not just be one undifferentiated tooth on a cog gear, turning forward, resisting backward with all the others, but a fixed point.

I feel in that instant that all I have accomplished is to immortalize my own foolishness, to forever diminish everything I have ever reliably and competently accomplished under a shadow of mockery. Furious— at myself, at Tski for forcing my hand, at this entire planet—I throw down my jar of paint. I had sealed it, but it hits one of the rocks just right (just wrong!) and shatters, and paint droplets fly everywhere—not just onto the disaster I've made of Ceye's tree, but onto others nearby.

"No!" I cry out loud, and I sink to my knees in the dying grasses and am consumed by my own rage and horror.

Joesla stands, trying not to shift impatiently from foot to foot, waiting for the rest of the council to arrive. She is early, but not by much. Banad was already here, clutching his report pad to his chest as if to protect his ambitions from her judging eyes. She has prepared her own argument to back up Avel's, in case he does not make a compelling enough case on his own against Banad. *So much has been lost already*, she thinks, *but if I can save the tiny fraction left, I will*.

One by one others arrive, but other than the sounds of their movement, the chamber remains silent. It is a recognition, she likes to think, of the weighty day ahead of them.

Right at the hour bell the doors slide open again, and Motas comes in, moving more quickly than his usual ponderous and insufferably formal gait, and there is something in his expression she has never seen before. As she tries to untangle and define what is new there, she is distracted by something else: his hands are, inexplicably, stained blue.

"Motas—" she begins to ask, and he visibly flinches at the sound of his own name.

Behind him, Tauso, last of the council to arrive, runs into the chamber. He is heaving for breath, his face red with sweat and something more, something the opposite of Motas's.

"The Ofti grove!" he shouts. "It's on fire! Arson! The whole forest has gone up!"

Everyone turns just as the council chime sounds, and the acrid smell of smoke drifts in through the doors behind Tauso, a ghost with the swagger of an uninvited guest and accusations of murder on its breath, and it settles itself around a shivering Motas like a linen shroud.

THE LAST VOYAGE OF SKIDBLADNIR

KARIN TIDBECK

Karin Tidbeck (karintidbeck.com) lives in Malmö, Sweden, and writes short stories, novels, and interactive fiction in Swedish and English. She debuted in 2010 with the Swedish short story collection *Vem är Arvid Pekon?* Her English debut, the 2012 collection *Jagannath*, won the Crawford Award in 2013 and was shortlisted for the World Fantasy Award as well as honor-listed for the Otherwise Award. Her novel *Amatka* was shortlisted for the Locus Award and Prix Utopiales 2018. A new novel, *The Memory Theater*, is forthcoming.

Something had broken in a passenger room. Saga made her way through the narrow corridors and down the stairs as fast as she could, but Aavit the steward still looked annoyed when she arrived.

"You're here," it said, and clattered its beak. "Finally."

"I came as fast as I could," Saga said.

"Too slow," Aavit replied and turned on its spurred heel.

Saga followed the steward through the lounge, where a handful of passengers were killing time with board games, books and pool. They were mostly humans today. *Skidbladnir* had no windows, but the walls on the passenger levels were painted with elaborate vistas. There was a pine forest where copper spheres hung like fruit from the trees; there was a cliff by a raging ocean, and a desert where the sun beat down on the sand. Saga enjoyed the view whenever she was called downstairs to take care of something. The upper reaches had no such decorations.

The problem Saga had been called down to fix was in one of the smaller rooms. A maintenance panel next to the bed had opened, and a tangle of wires spilled out. The electricity in the cabin was out.

"Who did this?" Saga said.

"Probably the passenger," Aavit replied. "Just fix it."

When the steward had gone, Saga took a look around. Whoever stayed in the room was otherwise meticulous; almost all personal belongings were out of sight. Saga peeked into one of the lockers and saw a stack of neatly folded clothing with a hat on top. A small wooden box contained what looked like cheap souvenirs—key rings, a snow globe, a marble on a chain. The open maintenance hatch was very out of character.

Saga shined a flashlight into the mess behind the hatch. Beyond the wires lay something like a thick pipe. It had pushed a wire out of its socket. Saga checked that no wires were actually broken, then stuck a finger inside and touched the pipe. It was warm, and dimpled under her finger. *Skidbladnir*'s slow pulse ran through it. Saga sat back on her heels. Parts of *Skidbladnir* shouldn't be here, not this far down. She reattached the wiring, stuffed it back inside and sealed the hatch with tape. She couldn't think of much else to do. A lot of the work here consisted of propping things up or taping them shut.

The departure alarm sounded; it was time to buckle in. Saga went back upstairs to her cabin in maintenance. The air up here was damp and warm. Despite the heat, sometimes thick clouds came out when Saga exhaled. It was one of the peculiarities of *Skidbladnir*, something to do with the outside, what they were passing through, when the ship swam between worlds.

The building's lower floors were reserved for passengers and cargo; *Skidbladnir*'s body took up the rest. Saga's quarters were right above the passenger levels, where she could quickly move to fix whatever had broken in someone's room. And a lot of things broke. *Skidbladnir* was an old ship. The electricity didn't quite work everywhere, and the plumbing malfunctioned all the time. The cistern in the basement refilled itself at irregular intervals and occasionally flooded the cargo deck. Sometimes the ship refused to eat the refuse, and let it rot in its chute, so that Saga had to clean it out and dump it at the next landfall. Whenever there wasn't something to fix, Saga spent her time in her quarters.

The cramped room served as both bedroom and living room: a cot, a small table, a chair. The table was mostly taken up by a small fat television with a slot for videotapes at the bottom. The closed bookshelf above the table held twelve videotapes: two seasons of *Andromeda Station*. Whoever had worked here before had left them behind.

Saga lay down in her cot and strapped herself in. The ship shuddered violently. Then, with a groan, it went through the barrier and floated free in the void, and Saga could get out of the cot again. When she first boarded the ship, Aavit had explained it to her, although she didn't fully grasp it: the ship pushed through to an ocean under the other worlds, and swam through it, until they came to their destination. Like a seal swims from hole to hole in the ice, said Aavit, like something coming up for air every now and then. Saga had never seen a seal.

Andromeda Station drowned out the hum *Skidbladnir* made as it propelled itself through the space between worlds, and for just a moment, things felt normal. It was a stupid show, really: a space station somewhere that was the center of diplomatic relations, regularly invaded by non-human races or subject to internal strife, et cetera, et cetera. But it reminded Saga of home, of watching television with her friends, of the time before she sold herself into twenty tours of service. With no telephones and no computers, it was all she had for entertainment.

Season 2, episode 5: "The Devil You Know."

The station encounters a species eerily reminiscent of demons in human mythology. At first everyone is terrified until it dawns on the captain that the "demons" are great lovers of poetry, and communicate in similes and metaphors. As soon as that is established, the poets on the station become the interpreters, and trade communications are established.

In the middle of the sleep shift, *Skidbladnir*'s hum sounded almost like a murmured song. As always, Saga dreamed of rushing through a space that wasn't a space, of playing in eddies and currents, of colors indescribable. There was a wild, wordless joy. She woke up bathing in sweat, reeling from alien emotion.

On the next arrival, Saga got out of the ship to help engineer Novik inspect the hull. *Skidbladnir* had materialized on what looked like the bottom of a shallow bowl under a purple sky. The sandy ground was littered with shells and fish bones. Saga and Novik made their way through the stream of passengers getting on and off; dockworkers dragged some crates up to the gates.

Saga had seen *Skidbladnir* arrive, once, when she had first gone into service. First it wasn't there, and then it was, heavy and solid, as if it had always been. From the outside, the ship looked like a tall and slender office building. The concrete was pitted and streaked, and all of the windows were covered with steel plates. Through the roof, *Skidbladnir*'s claws and legs protruded like a plant, swaying gently in some unseen breeze. The building had no openings save the front gates, through which everyone passed. From the airlock in the lobby, one climbed a series of stairs to get to the passenger deck. Or, if you were Saga, climbed the spiral staircase that led up to the engine room and custodial services.

Novik took a few steps back and scanned the hull. A tall, bearded man in rumpled blue overalls, he looked only slightly less imposing outside than he did in the bowels of the ship. He turned to Saga. In daylight, his gray eyes were almost translucent.

"There," he said, and pointed to a spot two stories up the side. "We need to make a quick patch."

Saga helped Novik set up the lift that was attached to the side of the building, and turned the winch until they reached the point of damage. It was just a small crack, but deep enough that Saga could see something underneath—something that looked like skin. Novik took a look inside, grunted, and had Saga hold the pail while he slathered putty over the crack.

"What was that inside?" Saga asked.

Novik patted the concrete. "There," he said. "You're safe again, my dear."

He turned to Saga. "She's always growing. It's going to be a problem soon."

Season 2, episode 8: "Unnatural Relations."

One of the officers on the station begins a relationship with a silicate-based alien life form. It's a love story doomed to fail, and it does: the officer walks into the life form's biosphere and removes her rebreather to make love to the life form. She lasts for two minutes.

Saga dreamed of the silicate creature that night, a gossamer thing with a voice like waves crashing on a shore. It sang to her; she woke up in the middle of the sleep shift and the song was still there. She put a hand on the wall. The concrete was warm.

She had always wanted to go on an adventure. It had been her dream as a child. She had watched shows like *Andromeda Station* and *The Sirius Reach* over and over again, dreaming of the day she would become an astronaut. She did research on how to become one. It involved hard work, studying, mental and physical perfection. She had none of that. She could fix things, that was all. Space had to remain a distant dream.

The arrival of the crab ships interrupted the scramble for outer space. They sailed not through space but some other dimension between worlds. When the first panic had subsided, and linguistic barriers had been overcome, trade agreements and diplomatic relations were established. The gifted, the rich and the ambitious went with the ships to faraway places. People like Saga went through their lives with a dream of leaving home.

Then one of the crab ships materialized in Saga's village. It must have been a fluke, a navigation error. The crew got out and deposited a boy who hacked and coughed and collapsed on the ground. A long-legged beaked creature with an angular accent asked the gathered crowd for someone who could fix things. Saga took a step forward. The tall human man in blue overalls looked at her with his stony gray eyes.

"What can you do?" he asked.

"Anything you need," Saga replied.

The man inspected her callused hands, her determined face, and nodded.

"You will do," he said. "You will do."

Saga barely said goodbye to her family and friends; she walked through the gates and never looked back.

The magic of it all faded over time. Now it was just work: fixing the electricity, taping hatches shut, occasionally shoveling refuse when the plumbing broke. Everything broke in this place. Of all the ships that sailed the worlds, *Skidbladnir* was probably the oldest and most decrepit. It didn't go to any interesting places either, just deserts and little towns and islands far away from civilization. Aavit the steward often complained that it deserved a better job. The passengers complained of the low standard, the badly cooked food. The only one who didn't complain was Novik. He referred to *Skidbladnir* not as an it, but as a she.

Over the next few stops, the electricity outages happened more and more frequently. Every time, living tubes had intertwined with the wiring and short-circuited it. At first it was only on the top passenger level. Then it spread to the next one. It was as if *Skidbladnir* was sending down parts of itself through the entire building. Only tendrils, at first. Then Saga was called down to fix the electricity in a passenger room, where the bulb in the ceiling was blinking on and off. She opened the maintenance hatch and an eye stared back at her. Its pupil was large and round, the iris red. It watched her with something like interest. She waved a hand in front of it. The eye tracked her movement. Aavit had said that *Skidbladnir* was a dumb beast. But the eye that met Saga's did not seem dumb.

Saga went upstairs, past her own quarters, and for the first time knocked on the door to engineering. After what seemed like an age, the door opened. Engineer Novik had to stoop to see outside. His face was smudged with something dark.

"What do you want?" he said, not unkindly.

"I think something is happening," Saga said.

Novik followed her down to the passenger room and peered through the hatch.

"This is serious," he mumbled.

"What is?" Saga asked.

"We'll talk later," Novik said and strode off.

"What do I do?" Saga shouted after him.

"Nothing," he called over his shoulder.

Novik had left the door to the captain's office ajar. Saga positioned herself outside and listened. She had never really seen the captain; she hid in her office, doing whatever a captain did. Saga knew her only as a shadowy alto.

"We can't take the risk," the captain said inside. "Maybe it'll hold for a while longer. You could make some more room, couldn't you? Some extensions?"

"It won't be enough," Novik replied. "She'll die before long. Look, I know a place where we could find a new shell."

"And how would you do that? It's unheard of. It's lived in here since it was a youngling, and it'll die in here. Only wild crabs can change shells."

"I could convince her to change. I'm sure of it."

"And where is this place?"

"An abandoned city," Novik replied. "It's out of our way, but it'd be worth it."

"No," the captain said. "Better sell it on. It won't survive such a swap, and I'll be ruined. If things have gone this far, I need to sell it to someone who can take it apart."

"And I'm telling you she has a chance," Novik said. "Please don't pass her on to some butcher."

"You're too attached," the captain retorted. "I'll sell it on and use the money as down payment for a new ship. We'll have to start small again, but we've done it before."

Season 1, episode 11: "The Natives Are Restless."

The lower levels of Andromeda Station are populated by the destitute: adventurers who didn't find what they were looking for, merchants who lost their cargo, drug addicts, failed prophets. They unite under a leader who promises to topple the station's regime. They sweep through the upper levels, murdering and pillaging in their path. They are gunned down by security. The station's captain and the rebel leader meet in the middle of the carnage. Was it worth it? the captain asks. Always, says the rebel.

There was a knock on Saga's door after her shift. It was Novik, with an urgent look on his face.

"It's time you saw her," he said.

They walked down the long corridor from Saga's cabin to the engine room. The passage seemed somehow smaller than before, as if the walls had contracted. When Novik opened the door at the end of the corridor, a wave of warm air with a coppery tang wafted out.

Saga had imagined a huge, dark cavern. What Novik led her through was a cramped warren of tubes, pipes and wires, all intertwined with tendrils of that same grayish substance she had found in the hatches downstairs. As they moved forward, the tendrils thickened into ropes, then meaty cables. The corridor narrowed, so tight in spots that Novik and Saga had to push through it sideways.

"Here," Novik said, and the corridor suddenly opened up.

The space was dimly lit by a couple of electric lights; the shapes that filled the engine room were only suggested, not illuminated. Round curves, glistening metal intertwined with that gray substance. Here, a slow triple beat shook the floor. There was a faint wet noise of something shifting.

"This is she," Novik said. "This is *Skidbladnir*."

He gently took Saga's hand and guided it to a gray outcrop. It was warm under her fingers, and throbbed: one two three, one two three.

"This is where I interface with her," Novik said.

"Interface?" Saga asked.

"Yes. We speak. I tell her where to go. She tells me what it's like." Novik gently patted the gray skin. "She has been poorly for some time now. She's growing too big for her shell. But she didn't say how bad it was. I understood when you showed me where she's grown into the passenger deck."

One two three, one two three, thrummed the pulse under Saga's hand.

"I know you were eavesdropping," Novik said. "The captain and the steward will sell her off to someone who will take her apart for meat. She's old, but she's not that old. We can find her a new home."

"Can I interface with her?" Saga said.

"She says you already have," Novik said.

And Saga heard it: the voice, like waves crashing on a shore, the voice she had heard in her dream. It brought an image of a vast ocean, swimming through darkness from island to island. Around her, a shell that sat uncomfortably tight. Her whole body hurt. Her joints and tendrils felt swollen and stiff.

Novik's hand on her shoulder brought her back to the engine room.

"You see?" he said.

"We have to save her," Saga said.

Novik nodded.

They arrived at the edge of a vast and cluttered city under a dark sky. The wreckage of old ships dotted the desert that surrounded the city; buildings like *Skidbladnir*'s shell, cracked cylinders, broken discs and pyramids.

They had let off all passengers and cargo at the previous stop. Only the skeleton crew remained: the captain, the steward, Novik and Saga. They gathered in the lobby's air lock, and Saga saw the captain for the very first time. She was tall, built from shadows and strange angles. Her face kept slipping out of focus. Saga only assumed her as a "she" from the soft alto voice.

"Time to meet the mechanics," the captain said.

Novik clenched and unclenched his fists. Aavit looked at him with one cold sideways eye and clattered its beak.

"You'll see reason," it said.

The air outside was cold and thin. Novik and Saga put on their face masks; Aavit and the captain went as they were. The captain's shroud fluttered in an icy breeze that brought waves of fine dust.

There was a squat office building among the wrecks. Its door slid open as they approached. Inside was a small room cluttered with obscure machinery. The air was warmer in here. Another door stood open at the end of the room, and the captain strode toward it. When Saga and Novik made to follow, Aavit held a hand up.

"Wait here," it said, its voice barely audible in the thin atmosphere. The other door closed behind them.

Saga looked at Novik, who looked back at her. He nodded. They turned as one and ran back toward *Skidbladnir*.

Saga looked over her shoulder as they ran. Halfway to the ship, she could see the captain emerge from the office, a mass of tattered fabric that undulated over the ground, too quickly than it should. Saga ran as fast as she could.

She had barely made it inside the doors when Novik closed them with a resounding boom and turned the great wheel that locked them. They waited for what seemed like an eternity as the air lock cycled. Something hit the doors with a thud, again and again, and made them shudder. As the air lock finally opened, Novik tore his mask off. His face was pale and sweaty underneath.

"They'll find something to break the doors down," he said. "We have to move quickly."

Saga followed him up the spiral stairs, through the passages, to the engine room. As she stood with her hands on her knees, panting, Novik pushed himself into *Skidbladnir*'s gray mass face-first. It enveloped him with a sigh. The departure siren sounded.

Saga had never experienced a passage without being strapped down. The floor suddenly tilted, and sent her reeling into the gray wall. It was sticky and warm to the touch. Saga's ears popped. The floor tilted the other way. She went flying headfirst into the other wall and hit her nose on something hard. Then the floor righted itself. *Skidbladnir* was through to the void between the worlds.

Saga gingerly felt her nose. It was bleeding, but didn't seem broken. Novik stepped back from the wall. He looked at Saga over his shoulder.

"You'll have to do the captain's job now," he said.

"What?" Saga asked.

"That's how it works. You read the map to me while I steer her."

"What do I do?"

"You go up to the captain's cabin. There's a map. There's a city on the map. It's on the lower levels. It's abandoned. Tall spires. You'll see it."

Saga went up to the captain's cabin. The door was open. The space inside was filled by an enormous construction. Orbs of different sizes hung from the ceiling, sat on the ground, were mounted on sticks. Some of the orbs had little satellites. Some of them were striped, some marbled, some dark. In the space between them hung swirls of light that didn't seem attached to anything. Close to the center, a rectangular object was suspended in the air. It looked like a tiny model of *Skidbladnir*.

There was a crackle. From a speaker near the ceiling, Novik's voice said, "Step into the map. Touch the spheres. You'll see."

Saga carefully stepped inside. The swirls gave off small shocks as she grazed them, and though they seemed gossamer, they didn't budge. She put her hand on one of the spheres, and her vision filled with the image of islands on green water. A red sun looked down on pale trees. She touched another, one that hung from the ceiling, and saw a bustling night-time town, shapes moving between houses, two moons shining in the sky. She touched sphere after sphere: vast desert landscapes, cities, forests, villages. The lower levels, Novik had said. Saga crouched down and felt the miniature worlds that littered the floor like marbles. Near the far corner, a dark sphere was a little larger than the others. As she touched it, there was an image of a city at dawn. It was still, silent. Tall white spires stretched toward the horizon. There were no lights, no movement. Some of the spires were broken.

"I think I found it," she said aloud.

"Good," Novik said through the speaker. "Now draw a path."

Saga stood up, ducking the electrified swirls. She made her way into the center of the room where *Skidbladnir* hung suspended on seemingly nothing at all.

"How?" she asked.

"Just draw it," Novik replied.

Saga touched *Skidbladnir*. It gave off a tiny chime. She traced her finger in the air. Her finger left a bright trail. She made her way across the room, carefully avoiding the glowing swirls, until she reached the sphere on the floor. As she touched the sphere, another chime sounded. The trail her finger had left seemed to solidify.

"Good," said Novik in the speaker. "Setting the course."

Saga wandered through the empty ship. There was no telling how long the journey would take, but on the map it was from the center of the room to the very edge, so perhaps that meant a long wait. She had gone back to the engine room, but the door was shut now. Whatever Novik did inside, while interfacing with *Skidbladnir*, he wanted to do undisturbed.

The main doors in the lobby had buckled inward, but not broken. The captain had used considerable force to try to get back in. The passenger rooms were empty. In the lounge, the pool table's balls had gone over the edge and lay scattered on the floor. There was food in the mess hall; Saga made herself a meal of bread and cheese from the cabinet for human food. Then she went up to her quarters to wait.

Season 2 finale: "All We Ever Wanted Was Everything."

The station is closing due to budget reasons; Earth has cut off funding because station management refuses to go along with their alien-unfriendly policies. No other race offers to pick up the bill, since they have started up stations of their own. In a bittersweet montage, the captain walks through the station and reminisces on past events. The episode ends with the captain leaving on a shuttle. An era is over. The alien navigator puts a claw on the captain's shoulder: a new station is opening, and the captain is welcome to join. But it'll never be an earthlike place. It'll never be quite like home.

Skidbladnir arrived in a plaza at the city's heart. The air was breathable and warm. Tall spires rose up into the sky. The ground beneath them was cracked open by vegetation. Novik got out first. He put his hands on his hips and surveyed the plaza. He nodded to himself.

"This will do," he said. "This will do."

"What happens now?" Saga asked.

"We stand back and wait," Novik replied. "*Skidbladnir* knows what to do." He motioned for Saga to follow him.

They sat down at the edge of the plaza, well away from *Skidbladnir*. Saga put her bags down; she hadn't brought much, just her clothes, some food, and the first season of *Andromeda Station*. Perhaps she would find a new tape player somewhere.

They waited for a long time. Novik didn't say much; he sat with his legs crossed in front of him, gazing up at the spires.

At dusk, *Skidbladnir*'s walls cracked open. Saga understood why Novik had positioned them so far away from the building; great lumps of concrete and steel fell down and shook the ground as the building shrugged and shuddered. The tendrils that waved from the building's cracked roof stiffened and trembled. They seemed to lengthen. Walls fell down, steel windows sloughed off, as *Skidbladnir* slowly extricated herself from her shell. She crawled out from the top, taking great lumps of concrete with her. Saga had expected her to land on the ground with an almighty thud. But she made no noise at all.

Free of her house, *Skidbladnir* was a terror and wonder to behold. Her body was long and curled; her multitude of eyes gleamed in the starlight. Her tendrils waved in the warm air as if testing it. Some of the tendrils looked shrunken and unusable. Saga also saw that patches of *Skidbladnir*'s body weren't as smooth as the rest of her; they were dried and crusted. Here and there, fluid oozed from long scratches in her skin.

Next to Saga, Novik made a muffled noise. He was crying.

"Go, my love," he whispered. "Find yourself a new home."

Skidbladnir's tendrils felt the buildings around the plaza. Finally, they wrapped themselves around the tallest building, a gleaming thing with a spiraled roof, and *Skidbladnir* pulled herself up the wall. Glass tumbled to the ground as *Skidbladnir*'s tendrils shot through windows to pull herself up. She tore through the roof with a thunderous noise. There was a moment when she supported her whole body on her tendrils, suspended in the air; she almost toppled over the side. Then, with what sounded like a sigh, she lowered herself into the building. Saga heard the noise of collapsing concrete as *Skidbladnir*'s body worked to make room for itself. Eventually, the noise subsided. *Skidbladnir*'s arms hung down the building's side like a crawling plant.

"What now?" Saga said.

She looked sideways at Novik. He smiled at her.

"Now she's free," he said. "Free to go wherever she pleases."

"And what about us?" Saga asked. "Where do we go?"

"With her, of course," Novik replied.

"There's no map," Saga said. "Nothing to navigate by. And the machinery? Your engine room?"

"That was only ever needed to make her go where we wanted her to," Novik said. "She doesn't need that now."

"Wait," Saga said. "What about me? What if I want to go home?"

Novik raised an eyebrow. "Home?"

A chill ran down Saga's back. "Yes, home."

Novik shrugged. "Perhaps she'll stop by there. There's no telling what she'll do. Come on."

He got up and started walking toward *Skidbladnir* and her new shell. Saga remained on the ground. Her body felt numb. Novik went up to the building's front door, which slid open, and he disappeared inside.

Season 1, episode 5: "Adrift."

The captain's wife dies. She goes into space on a private shuttle to consign the body to space. While in space, the shuttle malfunctions. The captain finds herself adrift between the stars. The oxygen starts to run out. As the captain draws what she thinks are her last breaths, she

records one final message to her colleagues. Forgive me for what I did
and didn't do, she says. I did what I thought was best.

Life on the new *Skidbladnir* was erratic. Novik spent most of his time
interfaced, gazing into one of *Skidbladnir*'s great eyes in a hall at the
heart of the building. Saga spent much of her time exploring. This
had been someone's home once, an apartment building of sorts. There
were no doors or windows, only maze-like curved hallways that with
regular intervals expanded into rooms. Some of them were empty, others furnished with oddly shaped tables, chairs and beds. Some wall-to-
wall cabinets held knickknacks and scrolls written in a flowing, spiraled
script. There were no means to cook food in any way Saga could recognize. She made a nest in one of the smaller rooms close to where
Novik worked with *Skidbladnir*. The walls gave off a soft glow that
dimmed from time to time; Saga fell into the habit of sleeping whenever that happened. Drifting off into sleep, she sometimes thought she
could hear voices speaking in some vowel-rich tongue, but they faded
as she listened for them.

Skidbladnir did seem concerned for Saga and Novik. She stopped
at the edge of towns every now and then, where Saga could breathe
and was able to trade oddities she found in the building that was now
her new home for some food and tools. But mostly they were adrift
between worlds. It seemed that *Skidbladnir* found her greatest joy in
coasting the invisible eddies and waves of the void. Every time they
stopped somewhere, Saga considered getting off to try her luck. There
might be another ship that could take her home. But these places were
too strange, too far-flung. It was as if *Skidbladnir* was avoiding civilization. Perhaps she sensed that Aavit and the old captain might be after
them. That thought gnawed at Saga every time they stopped somewhere. But there was such a multitude of worlds out there, and no one
ever seemed to recognize them.

She tore the *Andromeda Station* tapes apart and hung them like
garlands over the walls, traced her finger along them, mumbled the

episodes to herself, until *Skidbladnir* shuddered and she took cover for the next passage.

Each time *Skidbladnir* pushed through to another world, it was more and more violent.

"Is she going to hold?" Saga asked Novik on one of the rare occasions he came out from his engine room to eat.

Novik was quiet for a long moment. "For a time," he said.

"What are you going to do when she dies?" Saga asked.

"We'll go together, me and her," he replied.

One day, improbably, *Skidbladnir* arrived outside a place Saga recognized. A town, not her hometown, but not so far away from it.

Novik was nowhere to be seen. He was sleeping or interfaced with the ship. Saga walked downstairs, and the front door slid open for her. Outside, a crowd had gathered. An official-looking man walked up to Saga as she came outside.

"What's this ship?" he said. "It's not on our schedule. Are you the captain?"

"This is *Skidbladnir*," Saga said. "She's not on anyone's schedule. We don't have a captain."

"Well," the official said. "What's your business?"

"Just travel," Saga said.

She looked back at *Skidbladnir*. This was her chance to get off, to go home. Novik would barely notice. She could return to her life. And do what, exactly? The gathered crowd was all comprised of humans, their faces dull, their eyes shallow.

"Do you have a permit?" the official asked.

"Probably not," Saga said.

"I'll have to seize this ship," the official said. "Bring out whoever is in charge."

Saga gestured at *Skidbladnir*'s walls. "She is."

"This is unheard of," the official said. He turned away and spoke into a comm radio.

Saga looked at the little town, the empty-faced crowd, the gray official.

"Okay. I am the captain," she said. "And we're leaving."

She turned and walked back to *Skidbladnir*. The door slid open to admit her. The hallway inside thrummed with life. She put a hand on the wall.

"Let's go," she said. "Wherever you want."

Pilot episode: "One Small Step."

The new captain of Andromeda Station arrives. Everything is new and strange; the captain only has experience of Earth politics and is baffled by the various customs and rituals practiced by the other aliens on the station. A friendly janitor who happens to be cleaning the captain's cabin offers to give her a tour of all the levels. The janitor, it turns out, has been on the station for most of his life and knows all of the station's quirks. She's confusing as hell at first, he says. But once you know how to speak to her, she will take good care of you.

Saga took the tapes down and rolled them up. It was time to be the captain of her own ship, now. A ship that went where it wanted to, but a ship nonetheless. She could set up proper trade. She could learn new languages. She could fix things. She was good at fixing things.

One day *Skidbladnir* would fail. But until then, Saga would swim through the void with her.

STURDY LANTERN AND LADDERS

MALKA OLDER

Malka Older (malkaolder.wordpress.com) is a writer, aid worker, and sociologist. Her science fiction political thriller *Infomocracy* was named one of the best books of 2016 by *Kirkus Reviews*, Book Riot, and the *Washington Post*. With the sequels *Null States* and *State Tectonics*, she completed the Centenal Cycle trilogy, a finalist for the Hugo Award for Best Series in 2018. She is also the creator of the serial *Ninth Step Station*, and her short story collection *And Other Disasters* was published in late 2019. Named Senior Fellow for Technology and Risk at the Carnegie Council for Ethics in International Affairs for 2015, she is currently an Affiliated Research Fellow at the Center for the Sociology of Organizations at Sciences Po, where her doctoral work explored the dynamics of post-disaster improvisation in governments. She has more than a decade of field experience in humanitarian aid and development, and has written for the *New York Times*, *The Nation*, *Foreign Policy*, and NBC THINK.

As a freelance marine behavioral researcher most of Natalia's jobs went something like this: She swam around in some large but controllable environment with a cephalopod, paying attention to its body language and her own. She tried to make the octopus or squid feel as comfortable as possible, so that its behavior in response to stimuli might approximate what it would do in the wild. It wasn't what she had expected when she trained as a marine biologist, but frankly she preferred it to dissection, experimentation by electric shock, or even anything that required interacting with animals captive in tiny tanks.

This particular job started out only slightly unusual. For most jobs she was given a specific research interest. Sometimes they told her exactly what to do to elicit the behaviors they wanted to study, and sometimes they let her design the approach, but either way it meant some narrow focus for her attention. Natalia always tried to give the cephalopod some playtime around their interactions—if challenged on this, she told her employers that it led to more natural responses than repeating the same cues over and over again—but their time was very much directed by research.

On this job, they told her just to play with the octopus.

"Get comfortable with each other," said the guy who hired her. "Make friends."

Natalia had nodded and deliberately not asked any more. She tried to ignore her suspicions about why they were being so nice to this octopus. Maybe the company had a policy about giving all captive research subjects a certain amount of leisure time. (*Maybe they were doing something extra terrible.*) She had done too many of these jobs to believe that the research lab cared very much about the comfort of an individual octopus in the face of SCIENCE, but she tried to convince herself that her role helped the animal more than hurting it. (*Maybe the experiments required the octopus to be relaxed, and Natalia was complicit.*)

Her employers were probably going after those specific research interests when Natalia wasn't there. The octopus she thought of as

Vainilla was shut into a (decent-sized, but still) tank before and after her sessions. One day Natalia got to the center early and saw them peeling electrodes off of Vainilla's flesh.

That day she was as gentle as she knew how to be, careful not to initiate any contact as she and Vainilla twisted in distant tandem through the water of the shallow, netted bay.

It wasn't unexpected, or even necessarily sinister. Electrodes *could* be used for very non-invasive types of research. And in any case Natalia had long been used to the precarious or tormented lives of animal research subjects. She resisted any suggestion that she, for example, *stop naming* them, although since that seemed to particularly incense some people she mostly stopped telling her employers about it. She told herself that to do her job right she needed to face the current state of animal research. Sometimes it did not work out well for everyone.

After the electrode day the tone of that daily hour changed. There was still pleasure in their interactions, but it was definitely in a minor key. Natalia had slipped into thinking of her role as akin to that of a hospice caregiver: bringing Vainilla some marginal comfort in the interstices of a catastrophe beyond the cephalopod's control.

So Natalia was surprised when David Gilcrest, one of the honchos at the center, sought her out after her post-swim shower one day and asked if she had availability to expand her commitment with them.

"You want me to add more swim time?" Natalia said, squinting up at him as she toweled her hair.

"Not exactly. Well, yes, more swim time, but we were wondering if you'd be willing to participate more directly in our experiment."

"What experiment?" Natalia asked reluctantly, not really wanting to know what horrors were being inflicted on Vainilla.

"This phase of it," Gilcrest begins, and Natalia was relieved that he obfuscated even so obviously, "would require you to don a sort of headset, much like a VR helmet—almost exactly like a VR helmet, to be honest—during the swim. Waterproof, of course," he added hastily to her disbelieving expression. "We'll connect it to the sensors we've been calibrating with the subject, and then you should see what it sees."

"See . . ." Natalia's brain caught up with what he was saying mid-sentence. "So it's a neurology experiment?"

"In a manner of speaking," Gilcrest said, looking somewhat taken aback. "Weren't you briefed about it?"

Natalia brushed that off, no longer sure if she hadn't been or if she had purposely tried not to pay attention for fear of what she might hear. "So you want me to be connected to . . . to the octopus? Neurologically?"

"Yes, that's it exactly!" Gilcrest sounded relieved too. "We know it feels comfortable around you, and we thought that might be a way to ease it into the full rig, get better readings. We were thinking an extra half-hour per day, although the first few days we might not even keep it going that long. Of course you'd get paid for the full half-hour in any case. What do you say?"

"Sure," Natalia answered. Non-invasive neurology was good, relatively speaking. "But if I get the sense that the octopus is in pain or discomfort due to the equipment, I'm out."

"If that's the case, we would of course try to mitigate it," Gilcrest said, affronted, but Natalia had seen too many cases of unconscionable actions posed as the best option to feel any compunction about offending researchers.

"This looks amazing," Natalia said, trying on the waterproof headset two days later. It was only a little larger than a standard scuba mask, although quite a bit heavier when she put it on. "Did you design this here?"

"Uh, no," Gilcrest said, as the techie kid fiddled with the straps and connections. "We had a design firm in to work on it; they were excited about the commercial applications. Now remember, what you receive from the cephalopod, which you'll see with your right eye, is not going to look like what you're seeing with your left eye. You'll be getting the images as interpreted by that strange octopus brain, so it will look really weird, but it's just what's there, okay? The images are what the octopus is seeing, understand? What you see is what's there."

". . . Yes?" It wasn't that hard a concept.

"This is just for calibration. So try to relax into the weirdness. Okay." Gilcrest sighed, then psyched himself up again. "Let's take it for a spin!"

"What exactly is your involvement in this project?" Natalia asked, out of curiosity. She had been freelancing for years and didn't miss the corporate culture aspect of full-time work, which meant that she didn't bother to keep titles straight.

"Oh." He looked pleased that she cared, instead of annoyed that she hadn't cared enough to remember his title when she was introduced to him. "I came up with it, actually. Well, with a couple of other people. Needless to say I don't have the technical chops to be lead in all areas, but . . ."

Natalia stopped listening to him around that point, partly because he was taking a really long time to say anything important, but also because they had brought Vainilla to the bay and were attaching the electrodes. She narrowed her eyes, watching for any sign of discomfort from the cephalopod, as if the fact that she was actively and obviously watching would change the behavior of the techs.

The techs didn't seem to notice her at all. But Vainilla made no show of distress. Probably already entirely used to the process.

"You should get in the water," Gilcrest said; he at least had noticed the focus of her attention. "As soon as you're ready give us a wave and we'll switch it on."

Empowered by that, Natalia took her time going through the greeting ritual with Vainilla and then paddled around a little as usual. She wondered if they were getting annoyed out there, on the other side of the water's surface, if the anticipation was unbearable. She wondered if she herself was nervous. She raised her hand to the sun-baked air and shook it.

A few more seconds of stereovision and then her view bisected. Natalia shut her left eye, thinking it would be less confusing to see only what Vainilla was seeing, but that world was unintelligible furls of black-and-white gradations and she had to switch, closing her right instead and breathing slowly through the regulator while she watched a school of smelt flutter by. Vainilla caught one and ate it and Natalia kept her right eye resolutely closed until that was finished.

Cautiously, she swam up next to Vainilla, so they'd be seeing roughly the same vista, and opened her right eye.

This wasn't going to work. Side-by-side, the two visions clashed, competing and confusing; but Vainilla's alone was unintelligible. It was all blurry monochrome shapes—Natalia couldn't even tell which side was up.

She tried closing first one eye, then the other, gradually building up her octopus vision, but it wasn't until Vainilla started playing with a clamshell that she found something to focus on. It took several back-and-forths, but finally Natalia was able to recognize the shell seen through Vainilla's eyes: the blurring of the striations, the squashed shape. She had to close both eyes one more time, and shake her head hard, but when she opened the right one again she could recognize the clamshell.

"Major progress!" This was Gilcrest's boss, Yohannes Kirk. They were sitting in a small conference room with frigid air-conditioning that was chilling Natalia's still-wet hair. "I don't think we expected to be able to calibrate so quickly, did we, David?"

Gilcrest muttered something affirmative.

"I don't want to overstate my understanding . . ." Natalia began, and Kirk flapped his hand.

"Of course, that phase isn't over yet, but still! Remarkable."

"Sir," Gilcrest murmured. "If you recall . . ."

"Oh yes, of course." Kirk turned to Natalia. "We'd like you to join the team. David here thinks, and I agree with him, that you're the right person to work with the cephalopod on this."

"And what exactly is 'this'?" Natalia asked, letting some of her annoyance into her voice.

"Ah, naturally, you haven't been told. Proprietary, you know, and

very sensitive." He beamed. "But I think you'll like it. Ah . . . David,
maybe it's best if you explain."

Gilcrest was almost diffident, and got to the point much more quickly in front of his boss. "As you experienced today, we've found a way to translate the electric signals we can pick up from an octopus's brain into visual stimuli that humans can, ah, with some learning, understand."

Natalia nodded into the pause.

"Our overall goal, however, is much more ambitious." Gilcrest glanced at Kirk. "Our researchers believe that they can distinguish between brain activity based on immediate observation and brain activity based on memory."

"Memory," Natalia repeated.

"Specifically," Kirk took over, "we plan to use the memories of octopi to rebuild the Great Barrier Reef."

He was beaming, and Natalia wasn't quite sure she was awake.

"Initially," Gilcrest interjected, "we had planned to do a computer analysis of the images, but it turns out computers, including the best artificial intelligence we could get our hands on, have a very hard time interpreting these signals."

"They can't do it," Kirk said. "Can't. But the human brain . . ." He tapped his temple, still grinning at Natalia. "We can." He paused, but her human brain couldn't figure out anything to say to that. "So what do you say? Will you work on this with us?"

"What we want you to do is first, spend a lot of time getting calibrated, so that you can really understand what the octopus is seeing." Gilcrest must have learned how to translate his boss's macro-enthusiasms into operational terms, probably an important skill for him. He seemed to want reassurance, so Natalia nodded. "Then you'll do a swim-along at the site of the reef. We'll fit you out with some kind of recording tool that makes sense underwater so you can take notes— and of course all the brain activity will be recorded, so you can rewatch it later if you like."

"Then we analyze and figure out how to regrow the coral!" Kirk put in. "We know it's a long shot but it's also just weird enough to work. Will you do this with us?"

More octopus swim time *and* the chance to see how the Barrier Reef had once looked? She didn't even have to consider whether the part about helping to rebuild it was realistic. "Yes," Natalia said, and then belatedly remembered she should negotiate. "But I will have to increase my rate for this more intensive work."

It took three weeks to calibrate to everyone's satisfaction, and Kirk and Gilcrest both professed repeatedly that this was far faster than they had expected. They flew out to the site of the old reef by helicopter; Natalia, swaying in her seat, wondered if Vainilla, in the closely strapped tank of water, was any more comfortable than she was. She wondered what the electrodes, already soft-glued into place, were showing the technicians. Were they looking at the octopus's current perception, or did the placement of the sensors hardwire them already into memory mode? What sort of memories did a helicopter ride inspire in a marine animal?

The project team was by then accustomed to Natalia taking her time to get settled before she signaled them to turn on her octo-vision. In this new environment she was particularly careful. They had tried out the memory function, but (as Gilcrest had said) the shallow bay didn't inspire many memories in the cephalopod. Floating above the skeleton of the Great Barrier Reef, on the other hand, was creepy enough without any enhancement. Finally, though, Natalia raised her hand and closed her left eye.

A lost world bloomed before her eye.

Natalia had never seen such a densely populated marine environment. In Vainilla's memory, fish and anemones and—there! A sea turtle!—played among the astonishingly variegated coral. In the first five minutes Natalia counted at least seven extinct species, speaking their names urgently into the specialized recorder set in her respirator.

The world veered suddenly, and Natalia opened her left eye to see that Vainilla was careening toward the depths. The starkness of the dead coral was shocking, but much as Natalia wanted to shy away from it and stay in the richness of memory, she had to keep that eye open to follow Vainilla. *If I lose this octopus now . . .* flew through her mind, though she knew even as she thought it that Vainilla would never escape; they must have a tracker or dozen implanted.

Natalia spiraled down after the cephalopod, opening first one eye then the other. It was eerie how the vibrant memories of life and movement, seen monochrome through the octopus's eyes, matched the bleached present. It seemed wrong, and disorienting, as if what she was seeing in real time was also a flashback. But everything seemed wrong now. The octopus was tickling crevices that were dry instead of carpeted in ciliae, crevices that were, in memory, homes. And there at the sandy bereft bottom of the sea, meters and meters below Natalia now, the octopus was writhing in search or desolation at the empty place where the octopi had once gathered.

Vainilla reached out toward the memories of individual octopi, each so clear and distinct that Natalia could almost feel the recognition. There were so many of them, whirling into focus one by one as Vainilla turned through the bone-bare patch of seafloor.

Natalia closed her right eye against the memory of—relatives? Friends? Community?—but the view from her left was blurry. She rose, ignoring her recorder and the questions in her earpiece. Only long-ingrained practice made her pause, almost forgetting why she did so, to hover a few meters below the surface, sobbing into her regulator until her body decided it was time to let herself float upwards.

Natalia had no idea what to do with this blankness, this intolerable feeling of loss. She hadn't been able to drink usefully since her cousin was killed by a drunk driver, and while she enjoyed an ice cream cone now and then, she had never felt any desire to eat a pint of it at a time. She spent a lot of time in her apartment crying. Sometimes TV, if it was engrossing enough, could make the feelings go away for a while, and she became a squirrel for high-attention shows, searching them out, stocking them, and rationing them. She flaked on job after job. Some people called her and left concerned messages when she didn't answer. Her inbox was dotted with messages titled *¿señales de vida?* But it was weeks before Natalia felt like talking to anyone and when she did, she didn't know whom to call.

She went through her contact list again and again. Finally, on an inkling, she called Elsa. They had never been very close, but Elsa worked on climate change or pollution or something, and maybe she would understand.

When she thought about that call later, Natalia could never remember exactly what she said, how she explained this complex situation. She remembered the physical sensation of the words falling out of her mouth like a landslide and Elsa saying "Okay. Okay. It's okay," over and over. She remembered that when she had calmed down a little, Elsa made the tentative, requisite suggestion that she "talk to someone" and Natalia responded, almost hysterically, "Here?" Elsa might not have understood what she meant, but Natalia was a transplant in Australia. The language still reached her in translation, interactions still happened through a membrane of foreignness. She couldn't imagine trying to lay bare her feelings in this way.

"You should talk to a professional." Elsa repeated it more firmly. "I am not a professional. I don't know the right things to say." She sighed then. "All I can tell you is my own experience. And . . ." It was a long pause, long enough to draw Natalia out far enough from the cotton batting of her own pain to wonder if Elsa was okay. "There's despair, almost all the time. And fury. And sometimes I don't know what to do. But usually, most of the time . . . if I keep showing up, and if I focus on . . . on the immediate, on what's in front of me . . . there's some solace in that. I'm never sure it's enough."

"Ayayay," Natalia said. "I hope I haven't pulled you down into this dark place with me."

And Elsa laughed. "I live in that dark place. I have sturdy ladders and lanterns."

If it hadn't been for that conversation, Natalia might not have taken the call from Gilcrest. Also the fact that she felt guilty about the way she had left the project, without explanation, after that day on the skeleton of the reef. Felt guilty and unprofessional and also kept wondering about Vainilla and what had happened to the octopus since then. Sometimes she wondered if Vainilla, in that medium-sized tank, was exhibiting the same symptoms of lassitude and disinterest that Natalia felt, and whether anyone noticed.

"Hey there." Gilcrest sounded different; not the cautious egg-stepping she had dreaded, but a softening of formality. "Wanted to check in and see how you've been."

Natalia tried to clear her throat of its obstructions without that being audible over the phone. "I'm all right." The best she could manage. "I'm sorry about, about . . ." She couldn't finish the sentence.

"Nothing to be sorry about." Gilcrest cleared his throat without seeming to feel any compunction about it. "In fact, I'm sorry. Someone like you should have been an integral part of the project from the start, full-time staff with more training and preparation. It didn't occur to us . . ."

How awful it would be, how completely horrifying, Natalia finished for him in her head. "If you had hired someone full-time from the start," she said, intending to sound reasonable and comforting, "then I wouldn't have had the opportunity to—"

Then she stopped, because until that moment she hadn't realized that she was glad she had been involved in the project.

"Anyway." Gilcrest cleared his throat again. "Ringo's been asking for you, and we were wondering if you might want to come back for a little celebration we're having to mark the success of the first coral installation."

"Who's Ringo?" Natalia asked.

Gilcrest chuckled. "How quickly they forget. Ringo." An awkward pause while Natalia went through every staff member she could remember from the project, and found she could put names to precious few of them. "Your favorite octopus? Ringo?"

"Ringo??"

"Of course, Ringo."

"You named an octopus *Ringo*?"

"You know. For the suckers?" At least he sounded sheepish about it.

"I'd be happy to visit with . . . Ringo." Was it, at the end of the day, any sillier than *Vainilla*? All these silly humans with their silly human names for a beast that had no use for them. Or— "Did you say the octopus *asked* for me?"

"Exactly right. Took us a while to figure out what it was on about, to be honest. The new interpreter, of course, had never seen you . . ."

"Interpreter?" Everything has gotten new names while she's been away.

"Well . . . yes. It turns out that the gadget can be used for communication. In fact, that was one of its early uses, for patients in what was thought to be a vegetative state. It didn't occur to us that it could work the same way with a cephalopod." He laughed uncomfortably. "Of course it should have."

"Yes," agreed Natalia. It hadn't occurred to her either.

The celebration wasn't at the bay. Of course not. It was at the site of the new coral installation. Which was on the site of the dead reef, ghost-ridden with memories.

The reef in process of reanimation, Natalia thought, trying to dispel the dread in her chest. The Lazarus reef. The Frankenstein's monster of a reef. The zombie reef. This wasn't helping.

At least they were going out on a ship—a large, fast, comfortable ship. "Ringo didn't like the helicopter," Gilcrest told her ruefully when she found him on deck. "I felt terrible when we figured that out."

"Yeah," Natalia agreed, wondering.

"Look!" Gilcrest pointed. "Dolphins." They watched in silence for a few moments, wondering between each leap whether there would be another. "Maybe we'll try with them next."

Natalia wasn't sure if she found that appealing or disturbing. "How are you using the octopus's memory to rebuild the reefs?"

"We have no real maps of the reef," Gilcrest said. "Some large-scale maps of where it was, and isolated videos that divers took of different small sections, but no solid documentation of what it looked like. Ringo has given us a much more detailed record." He leaned his forearms on the railing, settling into the subject. "Of course, we're not trying to recreate exactly what Ringo remembers. That wouldn't be practical or possible. But the memories are giving us valuable clues to species proportions, and the usual depth of different types of corals, and so on."

"An octopus consultant," Natalia said, glancing around as if Vainilla could hear her. She had been avoiding Vainilla's tank, not wanting to meet the octopus that way, but now she wondered if she should go say hi. Casually.

Gilcrest laughed. "Yes, maybe even more than you think. We're trying to figure out ways to use the interpretation to go beyond Ringo's memories, and see if we can get opinions and ideas about how to go forward."

"Really? That sounds amazing." For the first time, Natalia thought she might want to rejoin the project, but before she could figure out a way to bring it up, the tone of the engine changed. They had arrived, and it was time to gear up.

Natalia still felt nervous about seeing Vainilla again, but when she got into the water it was practically crowded. The interpreter was there, and a bunch of the bosses, including Kirk, had been outfitted with a wetsuit and regulator for the occasion. But the interpreter, a tall Australian woman, corralled that group at the surface with explanations and some equipment fiddling, almost as if she were running interference, and Natalia was left underwater with Vainilla and the disturbing headset.

She couldn't make herself turn it on. She couldn't. But the cephalopod was swirling around her, welcoming her, reaching out tentacle after tentacle but never quite touching her. *Like when I was being careful with Vainilla,* Natalia thought, and gave the signal.

The corals that bloomed before her right eye were vivid and

strange, and they seemed to renew themselves endlessly, new shapes emerging from the old, and dancing among them all were fish and eels and many, many octopi.

"What is this?" Natalia asked around her regulator. "It's different."

"Oh yes," Gilcrest said in her ear. "We're trying a different part of the brain. We think this is Ringo's imagination." When Natalia couldn't answer, he went on. "It's the future."

IT'S 2059, AND THE RICH KIDS ARE STILL WINNING

TED CHIANG

Ted Chiang published his first short story, "Tower of Babylon," in *Omni* magazine in 1990. The story won the Nebula Award, and has been followed by just thirteen more stories in the intervening twenty-three years. Many of those stories, which have won the Hugo, Nebula, Locus, Sturgeon, and Sidewise Awards, are collected in *Stories of Your Life and Others* and *Exhalation*. The movie *Arrival* is an adaptation of his novella "Story of Your Life."

L ast week the *Times* published an article about the long-term results of the Gene Equality Project, the philanthropic effort to bring genetic cognitive enhancements to low-income communities. The results were largely disappointing: While most of the children born of the project have now graduated from a four-year college, few attended elite universities and even fewer have found jobs with good salaries or opportunities for advancement. With the results in hand, it is time for us to reexamine the efficacy and desirability of genetic engineering.

The intentions behind the Gene Equality Project were good. Therapeutic genetic interventions, such as correcting the genes that cause cystic fibrosis and Huntington's disease, have been covered by Medicare ever since their approval by the FDA, making them available to the children of low-income parents. However, augmentations like cognitive enhancements were never covered, not even by private insurance, and so were available only to affluent parents. Amid fears that we were witnessing the creation of a caste system based on genetic differences, the Gene Equality Project was begun twenty-five years ago, enabling five hundred pairs of low-income parents to increase the intelligence of their children.

The project offered a common cognitive-enhancement protocol involving modifications to eighty genes associated with intelligence. Each individual modification has only a small effect on intelligence, but in combination they typically gave a child an IQ of 130, putting the child in the top 5 percent of the population. This protocol has become one of the most popular enhancements purchased by affluent parents, and is often referenced in media profiles of the "New Elite," the genetically engineered young people who are increasingly prevalent in management positions of corporate America today. Yet the five hundred subjects of the Gene Equality Project are not enjoying career success that is remotely comparable to the success of the New Elite, despite having received the same protocol.

A range of explanations have been offered for the project's lack of success. Right-wing groups have claimed that its failure shows that certain races are incapable of being improved, given that many—

although by no means all—of the beneficiaries of the project were people of color. Conspiracy theorists have accused the participating geneticists of malfeasance, claiming that they pursued a secret agenda to withhold genetic enhancements from the lower classes. But these explanations are unnecessary when one realizes the fundamental mistake underlying the Gene Equality Project: cognitive enhancements are useful only when you live in a society that rewards ability, and the United States isn't one.

For decades it has been known that a person's ZIP Code is an excellent predictor of their lifetime income, educational success, and health. Yet we continue to ignore this because it runs counter to one of the founding myths of this nation: that anyone who is smart and hardworking can get ahead. Our lack of hereditary titles has made it easy for people to dismiss the importance of family wealth and claim that everyone who is successful has earned it. The fact that affluent parents believe that genetic enhancements will improve their children's prospects is a sign of this: they believe that ability will lead to success because they assume that their own success was a result of their ability.

For those who assume that the New Elite are ascending the corporate ladder purely on the basis of merit, consider that many of them are in leadership positions, but IQ has historically had only a weak correlation with effectiveness as a leader. Also consider that genetic height enhancement is frequently purchased by affluent parents, and the tendency to view taller individuals as more capable leaders is well documented. In a society increasingly obsessed with credentials, being genetically engineered is like having an Ivy League MBA: it is a marker of status that makes a candidate a safe bet for hiring, rather than an indicator of actual competence.

This is not to say that the genes associated with intelligence play no role in creating successful individuals; they absolutely do. They are an essential part of a positive feedback loop: when a child demonstrates an aptitude at any activity, we reward them with more resources— equipment, private tutors, encouragement—to develop that aptitude; their genes enable them to translate those resources into improved performance, which we reward with even better resources, and the cycle continues until as adults they achieve exceptional career success. But low-income families living in neighborhoods with underfunded public schools often cannot sustain this feedback loop; the Gene Equality Project didn't offer any resources besides better genes, and without these additional resources the full potential of those genes was never realized.

We are indeed witnessing the creation of a caste system, not one based on biological differences in ability, but one that uses biology as a justification to solidify existing class distinctions. It's imperative that we put an end to this, but doing so will take more than free genetic enhancements supplied by a philanthropic foundation. It will require us to address structural inequalities in every aspect of our society, from housing to education to jobs. We won't solve this by trying to improve people; we'll only solve it by trying to improve the way we treat people.

This doesn't necessarily mean that the Gene Equality Project is something that never needs to be repeated. Instead of thinking of it as a cure to an illness, we could think of it as a diagnostic test, something we would conduct at regular intervals to gauge how close we are to reaching our goal. When the beneficiaries of free genetic cognitive enhancements become as successful as the ones whose parents bought it for them, only then will we have reason to believe that we live in an equitable society.

Finally, let's recall one of the original arguments made during the original debate about legalizing genetic cognitive enhancements. Some proponents claimed that we had an ethical obligation to pursue cognitive enhancements because of the benefits to humanity that would accrue as a result. But there have surely been many geniuses whose world-changing contributions were lost because their potential was crushed by their impoverished surroundings. Our goal should be to ensure that every individual has the opportunity to reach their full potential, no matter the circumstances of their birth. That course of action would be just as beneficial to humanity as pursuing genetic cognitive enhancements, and would do a much better job of fulfilling our ethical obligations.

CONTAGION'S EVE AT THE HOUSE NOCTAMBULOUS

RICH LARSON

Rich Larson (richwlarson.tumblr.com) was born in Galmi, Niger, has lived in Canada, the United States, and Spain, and is now based in Prague, Czech Republic. He is the author of the novel *Annex*, and the collection *Tomorrow Factory*, which contains some of the best of his more than 150 published stories. His work has been translated into Polish, Czech, French, Italian, Vietnamese, and Chinese.

Burgewick was playing spitters with Gib on the lawn of the House Noctambulous as dusk turned the sky inky black. The spitters were a gift from Burgewick's favorite uncle, who had arrived earlier that day by crawling carriage. Uncle Bellerophon dabbled in gene art, and so always brought interesting gifts for Contagion's Eve.

The latest were two fleshy purple stalks that spat, at the pull of the little bone trigger, a shiny clear glue viscous enough to trap one's fingers together or stick one's feet to the ground, which naturally became the goal of the newly invented game.

"Don't dodge so much, Gib," Burgewick scolded. "Or I'll never get you."

Gib only grinned with all his crooked teeth, wiped his nose on the pale yellow servant smock that covered most of his lesions. "You be a good dodger, too, if you was a kitchen boy. Cook has that metal hand, dun he."

Burgewick darted forward and squeezed his trigger; a long ribbon of glue shot through the air but Gib danced away.

"You be the kitchen boy and I be the House," he sang. "And I eat vatmeat all day in bed while Cook boxes your ears."

"That's a horrible idea and I should have you beaten," Burgewick replied, but he made the threat often and rarely followed through. Gib was a much better playmate than Burgewick's older brother Mortice, even if he was only a servant, and it was Contagion's Eve besides. Everything felt topsy-turvy; the air itself seemed to buzz, so it was understandable that Gib would think such a strange and improper thought.

"This is good practice for the hunt," Burgewick said as it occurred to him. "Mortice has a new rifle, so I get his old one."

"You told me," Gib said, then sprang with his spitter. "Ya!"

Burgewick dove to one side, but it still splattered the knees of his black hyde. The cilia rippled in response and began chewing away at the glue. Burgewick got to his feet, laughing, and gave chase as Gib turned tail and ran.

They dashed across the lawn, using the eerie yellow glowtrees and decorative foam crypts for cover. It was dark enough now that the hardlights were flickering to life, which added excitement to the game whenever an infected monster lunged from the dark, jaws snapping, or a flock of plague birds swirled past. The servants setting up the last of the decorations looked distinctly unhappy to see globs of glue hurled so near to their work. One even tried to press-gang Gib into helping them, but Burgewick interceded.

The final decoration for the lawn was a drowning tank, the clever kind with faucets you could turn that would make the water flow faster or slower, or hotter or colder, and there was even a lever to release a spiny little biting creature once the tank was full enough. It was lit soft blue from the inside.

Most years it was a doppel in the drowning tank, but this year it was the young man who had stolen a vial of Mother's cell-knitters last week. He crouched at the bottom puffing short panicked breaths.

Gib slowed to watch as they wheeled the drowning tank into place, and Burgewick finally managed to stick his playmate's right foot to the ground.

"Got you!" he crowed.

Gib looked down at his trapped foot, giving it an experimental tug but hardly seeming to care, then looked back up to the tank. "Poor Cluny," he said.

"What?" Burgewick asked, annoyed that Gib was not more annoyed.

"Poor Cluny," Gib muttered. "He thought they'd work for his daughter, for her blindness and all. Stupid Cluny. Didn't know nothing about genestuff."

Burgewick didn't much like drowning tanks, but it was a Contagion's Eve tradition, same as the hardlights and the sweets and the games and the Doppelhunt. He scratched at the back of his neck, peeling away a bit of glue that his hyde hadn't reached, feeling uncomfortable and a bit angry at Gib for dulling the fun.

He was thinking of something to say, something that would make Gib feel better but also remind him that thieves needed to be punished, when his brother came striding across the lawn. Morticc was already wearing his hunting cloak, a feathery silvery cape grown separately from his hyde; judging from the way it wriggled and shivered on his shoulders the two garments were not yet entirely accustomed to each other.

"Little Wicky and his little catamite," Mortice said. "What's that thing? What have you got?"

Burgewick felt a small stab of unease, as he often did when his brother spotted him and there was nowhere to escape to. As Mortice drew closer, Burgewick saw the skin between his eyebrows was angry red from plucking the unruly hairs that grew there.

Mortice cared very much about how he looked lately, especially on nights like this where all the relatives came to the House. It seemed to have made him crueller.

"Master Mortice," Gib mumbled. He finally yanked his foot free, taking a clod of damp earth and moss with it—the lawn's caretakers would have been aghast—and bowed low.

"They're spitters," Burgewick said, hefting his present. "For playing spitters."

Mortice rapped his knuckles against the drowning tank, where the servant named Cluny was hugging his knees to his chest. "Hope you're thirsty, bastard," he said, then thrust his hips against the glass.

Burgewick saw anguish spiral across Gib's face for a moment before it became blank again. "They were a gift from Uncle Bellerophon," he announced, loudly, to retake Mortice's attention.

His older brother spun around. "They're from Uncle Belly, and you gave mine to your filthy little friend?"

"Uncle didn't say who they were for. Not exactly." Burgewick swallowed back his pride. "I'm sorry."

Mortice snatched the spitter from Gib's slack grip and gave him a sharp slap he didn't dodge. The loud smack made Burgewick flinch. Gib went to rub the red imprint of Mortice's palm; Mortice yanked his arm back down and gave him a second slap, harder, to the same cheek. Specks of drool flew from the corner of his mouth.

"So you thought that this year, unlike all the other years, Uncle Bellerophon brought a gift for kitchen boy Gib." Mortice turned the spitter over in his hands. "You're very stupid, aren't you, Burgewick?"

"I'm sorry," Burgewick repeated. "I should have brought it to you."

"You should have," Mortice agreed. "But I forgive you, little brother. Now, how's it work? What's it do?" He held it to his crotch and slapped it up against the drowning tank, waggling it back and forth in front of the servant, whose eyes were now squeezed shut. "Look at my spitter, bastard! Look, look!"

"It shoots a kind of glue," Burgewick said, holding up his arm, which was still streaked with the stuff. "Doesn't come off very easily."

Mortice threw his head back and laughed, for a reason Burgewick was maybe half-sure he understood, then pointed his spitter at Gib. "Don't move," he said. "And I'd shut my eyes, if I were you."

Burgewick looked at Gib, whose cheek was aglow with the bright red mark of Mortice's slap. He looked at the servant Cluny, who was so miserable in the drowning tank. He felt a strange nervous energy building in his chest.

It was Contagion's Eve, after all. Everything was topsy-turvy.

"You hold it the other way, though," Burgewick said. "The slit at the back is just a little vent hole. For it to breathe."

Gib's face flickered with shock; Mortice caught it and misread it. "Ho," he said. "You were going to let me fire away, weren't you, shit-breath? You would have liked to see that, wouldn't you have?"

"No, Master Mortice," Gib said.

"Ask me politely to spitter on you," Mortice said, smirking over at Burgewick now as if they were co-conspirators.

"Please, Master Mortice," Gib said, voice piteous, and Burgewick could see the barest hint of his grin lashed down tight. "Please spitter all over me, please."

"My pleasure," Mortice said, taking aim. Burgewick's heart leapt in his chest.

Cook himself came to drag Gib away, his metal hand rasping and whir-ring, and then Burgewick was standing alone on the lawn with Mortice, who was red-faced and shaking angry, with Father, who was expressionless, and with Uncle Bellerophon, who seemed faintly amused by the whole affair.

"Hold still, Mortice," Uncle said, rummaging in his coat pocket. His blue-veined hand emerged with a canister of solvent, which he proceeded to splash over Mortice's hunting cloak. The silvery organism steamed and sputtered in the cool evening air.

Burgewick rubbed his ribs where Mortice had pushed so hard with his knee he'd thought they might crack apart. A yellow-brown bruise was already growing. Mortice's original yowl of outrage had brought several servants running. They had found a chaotic scene: Mortice pinning Burgewick to the ground and cursing at him while Gib tried, ineffectually, to free him.

"Good as new," Uncle Bellerophon said, putting the canister back in his pocket.

Mortice gave a sulky nod, but his eyes were still razors and still pointed in Burgewick's direction.

"Thank your uncle," Father rumbled. He didn't seem angry, but it was hard to tell with Father. His mouth was hidden in a thicket of wiry black beard and his old rheumy eyes had been scooped out years ago, replaced by two glistening black orbs made by the best gene artisan on the Continent.

"Thank you, Uncle," Mortice said stiffly.

"I'll have a word with my progeny, now," Father said, clapping Uncle Bellerophon on the shoulder.

Uncle Bellerophon's hyde wriggled in response. It was sleek and mottled orange for Contagion's Eve and he had grown several curling tendrils that rippled around his head like a strange halo. Father's hyde, by contrast, was the same swollen black beast as usual, patchworked with swathes of thick red muscle that could make him terrifically strong.

Burgewick still remembered the day an ancient tree, poorly felled, pinioned one of the servants to the lawn, and how Father strode over and squatted down and lifted it as if it weighed no more than a twig.

Once Uncle Bellerophon had departed, Father folded his arms and stared down at them, his pitch-black eyes rolling first to Burgewick and then to Mortice. "Should I send the clowns home?" he asked. "It seems you've taken it upon yourselves to do their job."

Burgewick blinked; Mortice's mouth twisted.

"The servants were laughing at you," Father said. "Two sons of the fine House Noctambulous, rolling in the dirt, scrapping and squalling like infants. We do not settle our disputes in front of servants. You embarrass me."

Burgewick watched as Mortice chewed his lip, angry and ashamed. "It was my fault, Father," he said quickly. "I provoked Mortice."

"Mortice, who doesn't know a mouth from an ass." Father snorted. "Perhaps I made a mistake gifting you that hunting rifle. You'll be lucky not to blow your own head off. Perhaps the pair of you should stay in tonight."

Burgewick's mouth fell open; Mortice flushed scarlet.

"The other families are arriving soon," Father continued. "This evening you will both conduct yourselves as befits our House, or you forfeit the Doppelhunt. Understood?"

Burgewick nodded hard, relieved, and after a moment his brother nodded, too.

"And Burgewick." Father's gleaming black eyes whirred in their sockets. "No more games with the servant boy. It's unbecoming." He waved his hand. "Off with you both."

Burgewick's first instinct was to flee at speed, to avoid whatever retribution was coming from his elder brother. But Mortice seemed to be in a world of his own as they turned and started back toward the House. His eyes were distant.

"Doesn't know a mouth from an ass," Mortice suddenly said, in a thick angry voice. "He thinks I'm a fool. I'm not a fool."

"No," Burgewick said, and immediately regretted it as Mortice noticed him. He flinched as his brother raised his hand, but there was no slap.

Instead, Mortice cupped his cheek and looked into his eyes.

"You're going to regret doing that, little brother," he said in a trembly voice. "Very, very much."

By the time the other families began arriving, Burgewick had scrubbed himself clean of the last of the spitter glue and slicked back his hair with a scented secretion from his hyde. He stood on the lawn beside his mother, whose hyde had grown a gossamer veil that swirled across her worried face. She always worried when the families came, about a thousand small things the servants never did quite right.

Mortice, on the other hand, was smiling and laughing as he exchanged Contagion's Eve greetings with the members of House Immaculata and House Lachrymose, who had arrived in quick succession in spindly legged black carriages. Burgewick hoped he might forget his promise of revenge in all the excitement—his ribs still ached and Mortice always knew where his knuckles would hurt most.

House Immaculata had brought their greenman for the occasion. His gnarled body was sprouted with moss; vines slipped in and out of his skin like veins. For Contagion's Eve he had sugary red bulbs of licorice growing from his knees and thighs—low enough for even the smallest children to pluck.

Burgewick remembered he had been frightened of the greenman when he was younger, frightened by his lumbering steps and his collapsing overgrown face. Mortice had told him he used children's blood to feed to his vines; Burgewick knew now they only needed purple light and water.

Next to arrive was House Strappado. They had all grown matching masks from their hydes, attached to their flared collars by skinny tendrils, and it took Burgewick a moment to recognize Breesha. She was taller than the last time he'd seen her, taller than him now, but her distinct red-blonde hair flared out from behind her bone-white mask and she still walked the same way, bouncing on the balls of her feet.

"Happy Contagion's, Aunt Demeter," she said prettily to Burgewick's mother, then seized Burgewick by the arm and dragged him off. "I've got one this year," she said. "Look, they're unloading it." She pointed to the servants of House Strappado, who were wrestling an embryonic tank off the back of the carriage.

"So do I," Burgewick said, deciding not to mention how close he had come to losing the privilege. He thought of Gib, no doubt laboring away at the nastiest possible kitchen tasks under Cook's watchful eye, and felt a churn of guilt.

"And here's House Crepuscule, fashionably late as usual," Breesha said, peering up at the night sky.

Burgewick was glad for the distraction. House Crepuscule's airship was lit by greasy yellow globes of biolight, and as it descended he could see other details: the honeycomb bone lattice that formed the deck, the swollen sacks of gas that kept it aloft, the small faces of the twins Ferrick and Freya craning over the edge.

Thick ropes of tendon slithered down from the bottom of the airship; the servants on the lawn scurried forward to catch them and tether them to the docking loops. One servant tripped over his feet and trod on a rope. A shudder went through its length and Burgewick heard a moan from the airship. He could imagine his mother's sigh of frustration.

Once the airship touched down, the members of House Crepuscule disembarked in solemn single file. The last to exit, orbited by an assortment of servants, was the Old Madam. Unlike Breesha, she was smaller than Burgewick remembered her. Breathing tubes were threaded into her wattled neck and she was ensconced deeper than ever into her chair, which scuttled along on legs that were partly black nanocarbon and partly red bands of living muscle.

"My father says this is the last year she comes in person," Breesha said in a low voice. "Her whole body's falling apart."

Burgewick frowned. "Can't she take extra cell-knitters, or something?"

"Father says cell-knitters can only do so much for the old stock." Breesha stared with undisguised fascination as the Old Madam skittered from one descendant to the next, receiving their greetings.

"She was the last person born underground, you know. During the Contagion."

"They didn't know nothing about genestuff back then," Burgewick said, with a ghost of a grin.

"Anything," Breesha corrected, shooting him an odd look. "They didn't know *anything*."

Burgewick watched Mortice give a flourishing bow, his handsome face in its most charming rictus as he wished the Old Madam a happy Contagion's Eve, his hunting cloak swirling gracefully around his shoulders.

Maybe, just maybe, he would forget all about the spitters.

Soon thereafter, the festivities began in earnest, with everyone milling about the lawn in conversation, circles breaking and joining like the amoebas Burgewick had studied with his tutor. Servants slithered here and there with flutes of wine and bacterial beer. The hardlights were starting to weave their animations together, so monsters chased plague birds and vice versa.

Burgewick felt very much adrift, especially once Breesha left him to join Mortice and the older cousins. He wanted to stay out of his brother's sight, and he was too young to enjoy their talk about fashions and fights anyway.

But he was too old to play with Ferrick and Freya, who were both hounding House Immaculata's greenman, darting in to yank the twists of licorice from his knees and giggling as he made his noises of mock protest and waved his stiff stumpy hands. Burgewick also noticed a sort of orange-spotted mushroom growing from between the greenman's shoulder blades, far out of the children's reach. Some of the adults leaned out to surreptitiously pick one as the greenman ambled past. Uncle Bellerophon was one of these, and when he saw Burgewick watching he put a finger to his lips and winked.

At one point Burgewick saw his father staring at him, or maybe staring at something near to him, and realized that it was strange and improper for him to be wandering around the party so silently, just looking at people without speaking, so he attached himself to a group of aunts who crowed about how tall he was, and how soon he would be sprouting a beard like his father's.

They soon went back to comparing the behaviors of their newly implanted calorie worms, which was interesting for a while, but when Aunt Violetta peeled open her hyde to display her pale flat stomach and the rust-colored organism just barely visible under her skin, Burgewick flushed and looked away, and their laughter made him flush even redder so he slunk off.

"But you're a young man, now," Aunt Violetta called after him. "Aren't you in the hunt tonight?"

Burgewick knew he ought to be excited for the Doppelhunt, knew he ought to be enjoying the party, but he was starting to feel anxious more than anything else. There were too many people about. It had been better when it was only him and Gib playing on the lawn. He made a wide circle around the drowning tank, where a small crowd was watching Cluny splutter and gasp on tiptoe, and was nearly to the refuge of the ablution tent when Breesha intercepted him.

"There you are," she said, and he could tell by her shiny eyes and red nose that she had been sneaking the bacteria beer she'd only ever talked about trying last year. "Everyone's heading in for dinner. Come sit at our table, or you'll get stuck with the twins."

"Mortice might not want me to," Burgewick said. "I might just sit with . . ." He trailed off. He'd been going to say Mother and Father, and judging by the horrified look on Breesha's face, she knew it.

"Fuck Mortice and his fancy cloak," Breesha said. "He's too busy puffing himself up to pay you any mind. From how he talks, you'd think this were his thirtieth Doppelhunt instead of his third." She rolled her eyes and slipped her bone-white mask back on. "Come."

The banquet hall of House Noctambulous had been transformed into an underworld: plague birds picked their way along the tables, painted acrobats dangled by suspension hooks from the rafters or from slow-wheeling drones, and the usual warm yellow biolights had been replaced by a pale violet glow. When Burgewick looked down at his hand, he could see the bones through his skin.

Half the guests, who hadn't seen the deadlight trick before, were tittering and inspecting each other's skeletons. Burgewick dimly remembered that this sort of light was dangerous; they would probably have extra cell-knitters in their meal to compensate.

The acrobats couldn't use cell-knitters, though, and neither could the servants bustling around with drink trays, though some had stiff heavy aprons on and maybe that helped. Burgewick hoped Gib wasn't poking his nose out of the kitchen too often.

Mortice's hunting cloak looked very grand indeed in the deadlight, leaving shimmery silver traces in the air when he moved. He was telling cousin Orry some loud sort of joke when Burgewick and Breesha arrived at the table. His eyes flickered onto Burgewick for only a second, then slid over him as if he were invisible. But he didn't make any protest as they sat down, and Burgewick knew from experience that being ignored by his brother was preferable to the alternative.

A few more of the cousins joined them, Fenella and the sister whose name Burgewick could never remember, and they all settled in. Burgewick heard, faintly, Cook's distinctive voice barking orders. A moment later a flock of servants emerged from the kitchen laden down with food. There were vatmeats stacked in quivering towers, amniotic puddings, spheres of scop shaped and pigmented to look like gourds and pumpkins and other things that had grown once. Burgewick thought of Aunt Violetta's calorie worm and hoped it was up to the task.

He wasn't particularly hungry, and had only eaten a few bites off his plate when Fenella nudged him under the table. "Want a drink, little cousin?" she asked.

She nudged again, and Burgewick caught on and looked beneath the table. She and her sister had taken the dregs from enough bottles that they could start brewing their own: the bucket's contents were thinner and foamier than the original bacteria beer, but it carried the same pungent smell.

"It'll help your nerves." Fenella beamed. "For the hunt."

Burgewick looked around. No adults were watching them—Uncle Bellerophon was draped over Aunt Violetta's shoulder, laughing up-roariously, because Father, normally so somber, was doing his trick where he made his slick black eyeballs crawl down from their sockets and race each other around the table on little spindly legs; one was intent on skittering beneath Aunt Nefertiti's skirts and she was swatting at it with a bunched-up fan. He didn't see Mother.

Breesha was already filling her glass from the bucket, and so were Orry and Mortice, the latter of whom held it out to Burgewick with a smirk. Burgewick dipped his glass into the bucket, half-expecting his brother to dump it all over his trousers or call Mother over and pin the whole affair on him somehow. Instead Mortice only gave him a brief nod of approval.

The regrown beer tasted awful, but after Burgewick choked down a half glass he did feel more relaxed, enough to start enjoying himself a little. The others were enjoying themselves very much, Mortice and Breesha in particular. Mortice had peeled Breesha's mask away from her hyde so he could peer through its eyeholes from the wrong side, and Breesha, despite what she'd said about *fuck Mortice and his fancy cloak*, was giggling madly. Burgewick felt an odd twist in his stomach at the sight.

Once the servants cleared the tables, a slow hush crept into the hall. Burgewick realized that the Old Madam had made her way to the front of the room and was waiting to speak, one leg of her chair pawing at the floor. Father gave two booming claps to silence the last chatter-ing voices. The cousins wormed back in their seats to listen; Breesha pushed Mortice away.

The Old Madam surveyed them all for a moment, all the Houses, before she opened her mouth. "Well, here we are again," she whis-pered. The black sponges around her head caught and amplified her voice, sending it all through the banquet hall. Burgewick felt the hairs on his arms stand up. "It used to bore me horribly, telling the same story every year, but lately I enjoy it. Like slipping into a familiar groove. I suppose I must be getting old."

There was polite laughter from the adults; Burgewick joined a beat late.

"Three centuries ago, the world swayed on the brink of disaster, my children," the Old Madam said, and the familiar words made Burgewick remember back to being much younger, back to sitting on his mother's knee while he listened. "The summers were scorching hot, and the tides were rising higher, and all the cities of the world were swollen and teeming with parasites. Parasites who bred and bred in the filthy slums and begged for food to fill their children's fat stomachs so they could grow up to breed all over again. The world could sustain no more of them. So there were wars, and there were famines, and there were floods that ate entire islands. And who did the parasites blame?"

Burgewick mouthed the next word on automatic:

"Us." The Old Madam's voice was jagged with contempt. "They blamed the ones who were strong and smart enough to rise to the top of all that human waste, and strong and smart enough to stay there. They blamed us for the poisoned skies and the dying oceans. The parasites were weak and they were stupid, but there were hordes of them and they were hideously angry. They would have hunted us down, my children, and murdered us even as the world collapsed all around them.

"There were many families, back then. Hundreds of Houses, all with different names, scattered all across the globe. But only ours survived. When the hordes came for us, we were already gone, hidden away below the ground in concrete palaces. But we left the parasites a parting gift: the Contagion."

Ferrick made a small whoop of excitement; the Old Madam's eyes traveled over to him and she gave an indulgent smile.

"And so all there was left to do was wait, my children," she said. "We waited beneath the earth while the Contagion cleansed the world. A century, we waited. Our family found the genetic keys to turn that let us survive without sunlight or greenery, to propagate without outsiders, even to push back the hands of death. For a while, at least."

She stroked one of the tubes in her neck with a pensive finger.

"My father, Wendell, and his twin brother, Eddard, were the heads of our House on the day we finally emerged, on the hundredth anniversary of the Contagion. They found a new world. A clean world, waiting for us. But the parasites weren't all gone. A few of them were still scrabbling in the dirt, clinging to life, immune to the Contagion but vulnerable to everything else. To all the ills we overcame during our long isolation.

"They had been returned to their rightful place. But Eddard didn't see it that way. He looked at them with pity. He regretted the Contagion. He renounced his own family." The Old Madam's voice turned low and venomous. "My father tried to reason with his twin. He showed him that the parasites could live as our servants, how they once did in the past. But Eddard would not be satisfied by that. He wanted to freely grant the parasites the gifts we had so arduously earned. He would have turned the genetic keys to let them reknit their flesh, grow hydes of their own, stave off hunger and disease. He would have made them our equals.

"Eddard's kindness would have been the death of us, my children," the Old Madam said solemnly. "It would have restarted a doomed cycle. And so my father's hand was forced. He banished his twin brother, his half-self, from the family. But when Eddard went, he took the genetic keys with him, a thief in the night. My father realized, then, that given the chance, Eddard would let the parasites spread again, more powerful than ever, and end the world a second time."

The hair at the back of Burgewick's neck stood up—Mortice was gone from the table. He had been intent on the Contagion's Eve story, too intent to notice his brother leave. Breesha was gone, too. He scanned the banquet hall but saw neither of them under the deadlight. He was only half-listening as the Old Madam finished the story.

"So my father followed his twin out into the dead forest, behind which the fine House Noctambulous now sits, and he retrieved the keys. He killed Eddard and left his body to rot under the trees." The Old Madam leaned forward; her chair crouched to compensate. "Eddard's kindness, his weakness, could have infected the family and all the Houses. We have to guard against it. So each year on Contagion's Eve, we remember our history and we safeguard our future. We kill the weak part of ourselves. How my father did."

The Old Madam fell silent. The hall waited to see if she was finished; her eyes flickered open and shut. Finally she stroked the arm of her chair and ambled back to her place at the long table. Her words had left a layer of frost. Burgewick was still searching for his brother and Breesha, suspicion growing in his gut, when his father stood up.

"The hunt is one of our most important traditions," he said. "And lucky for us, it's a hell of a good time. Let's see the doppels."

The frost whisked away and murmurs of anticipation ran through the room. Guests shifted in their seats for a better view and Burgewick saw Ferrick clambering up onto the greenman's shoulders, Freya scrabbling after him. Then the doors at the far end of the hall glided open, and servants ushered the doppels through with long black prods. For a moment, Burgewick forgot all about Mortice's absence.

There were almost two dozen of them, one for each participant in the hunt. Burgewick and Gib had snuck into the incubation room a few weeks earlier to see the doppels growing in their red-lit embryonic tanks, bathed in cell-knitters and enzyme gel. Even the largest had only been the size of a baby then, but the accelerants had done their work. Each doppel was now about as big as its originator, though the forced growth had warped them somewhat: many limped on crooked legs or had odd truncated necks.

The cousins started trying to figure out whose was whose almost immediately. The doppels were costumed, of course, dressed in gaudy reflective bodysuits that would make them easier to spot among the trees, and they wore masks with beaks or antlers or long upright ears like the extinct animals that once roamed the forest.

"There's yours, Orry!" Fennela hooted. "He's got a big rump just like you do!"

Burgewick found his own quickly and easily: it was the smallest of the lot, wobbly on its feet, dressed like a plague bird with artificial feathers and a beaked mask. He knew some of the older relatives despised the masks. He'd heard them, in snatches of conversation, saying that the masks made it all too easy, and that it wasn't a true Doppelhunt if you didn't look the thing right in the eye as it bled and writhed.

He was glad they had masks, especially as his doppel seemed to look right at him for a moment. He reminded himself that the doppels weren't human. He knew that from his tutor. They were quick and shoddy copies, with blunted brains that couldn't do much more than keep them breathing and moving.

Their only developed faculty was fear—they were drugged with a bliss chemical before they were dressed and paraded through the banquet hall, but as soon as it wore off they would turn skittish and eager for hiding places.

Just then, Mortice reappeared to slide himself back in beside Orry. His skin was flushed and he wore a wolfish grin. He whispered something to his cousin and both of them laughed. Burgewick looked away. He thought he knew why Mortice and Breesha had disappeared at the same time. Mortice talked about it often enough.

The doppels were led back out of the hall, out to the lawn, and the older relatives who were still hunting stood up and started massaging their stomachs, grumbling about having eaten too much. The cousins all got up from the table—Breesha had rejoined them now, without so much as glancing at Mortice—and Burgewick trailed after them.

Mortice seemed to have been distracted from his promise of retribution, but Burgewick still had the uncomfortable thought that he was Eddard, and Mortice was Wendell following him out into the moonlit wood.

Burgewick had forgotten about Cluny, adrift and glass-eyed in the drowning tank, but now servants were draining the water and one of them, who Burgewick thought might be Cluny's wife, was softly weeping. It added another needle to the dozens he felt sticking into his spine. The doppel seeming to look at him, Breesha, and smirking Mortice, the worm in Aunt Violetta's stomach, the game of spitters and its abrupt ending.

Everything felt topsy-turvy again; he knew it could be partly blamed on the watery bacteria beer, but not entirely. Servants were readying the hunting gear on the lawn: rifles and trackers, tailored to sensors in each doppel's costume to prevent robbing a kill by accident, nimble quadruped drones to flush the doppels out with subsonics, and the flying sort that followed the hunt to beam it back to the warm banquet hall, where it played out in hardlight.

And of course there were the capcutters—a servant decided to test one's trigger right as Burgewick walked past and he couldn't hide his flinch at the gnash and snap.

"Nervous?"

It was Breesha, casually checking down the sight of her rifle. Burgewick didn't reply for a moment. He wanted to tell her that he felt betrayed, that he'd always thought she was on his side against Mortice, but maybe it had only been that way when they were little and she would tell him it wasn't his business, anyways.

"I don't know," he said.

"I practiced," Breesha admitted. "With some servants and a paint gun. It's easy. Don't be nervous." She gave a rueful shrug. "Hardly anyone actually watches it, anyway. They're busy getting drunk or sneaking off to fuck."

Burgewick felt his ears go lava hot. "You and Mortice?" he blurted, before he could stop himself.

"What?" Breesha's voice was flat. "Is that what he's saying?"

"You were both gone. At the banquet."

"I was throwing up the bacteria beer," Breesha said hotly. "I don't know where he was."

With that, she strode off to get her capcutter, and Burgewick regretted saying anything at all. Maybe he was wrong, or maybe he was right and Breesha was embarrassed.

The doppels were now assembled at the edge of the forest, tied to each other and to a post in the ground by tendon rope. The bliss drug was wearing off and some were straining against their bonds, grunting.

Burgewick had a strange and improper thought, one he hadn't had last year or any of the years before it: what it would be like to be a doppel. To be born scared, then drugged and dressed and shoved out into the forest to be hunted. It was lucky they couldn't think.

"Your rifle, Master Burgewick."

Burgewick lifted it from the servant's outstretched arms. It was the old sort, mostly wood components, but he knew it was loaded with the same smart bullets as Mortice's new rifle. It wouldn't miss easily. There was a lantern fixed underneath the barrel, and a tracker attached to the sight showed a swarm of moving yellow blobs—the doppels in their sensor-sewn costumes—and one red one, which was Burgewick's. The servant handed him a capcutter next; Burgewick took it gingerly and let his hyde sprout a loop to hold it at his hip.

The hunting drones were on their feet now, joints whirring and clicking. The flying drones drifted skyward, disappearing into the blackness. Everyone was making their way to the forest. One of the uncles was red-mouthed and unsteady on his feet from too much wine; the others were slapping him on the back and laughing; Mortice was betting with Orry that he would bag his doppel in twenty minutes or under.

As they neared the tethered doppels, Burgewick felt as if his heart were pounding its fists against the inside of his ribcage. The night air was cold enough to make his breath a frosty cloud. Servants with injectors were going from doppel to doppel, shooting them with adrenaline and fear-o-mone. They bucked and twitched against the rope. Burgewick saw his doppel at the end of the row, wriggling and stomping its feet as a servant plugged its thigh with the needle. It made him feel slightly ill.

Mortice suddenly turned to him and gave his wide white smile. "Well, here we are, little brother," he said. "Your first Doppelhunt is always the most memorable one, I think."

The red-mouthed uncle gave a rumble of agreement. "Never forget the first one," he said. "Now let's loose the damn things already."

"I bet you'll be the last back," Mortice said, in a whisper so the uncle wouldn't hear. "Everyone knows you're a coward in the dark."

He pushed past him to the front before Burgewick could respond. He only clutched his rifle more tightly. His throat was dry as bone, but there was anger down there, too, throbbing as he took up position between Breesha and Orry. He wasn't a coward. If he was a coward, he wouldn't be following Mortice out into the woods, away from Father's roving black eyes.

Once all the doppels had been prepped, a servant used a spray to dissolve the tendon rope, pulling apart the last of it with his bare hands. The doppels hesitated, unsure of their sudden freedom. Then the drones stalked forward, wailing, corralling them toward the forest, and the doppels fled. A few of the hunters whooped and feinted at them as they loped off into the trees. Burgewick felt a shiver run through his whole body.

He had been in the woods plenty of times, out among the dead trees that had seemed endless when he was a little child, but they seemed different now as they swallowed up the doppels. More menacing. When he shone his rifle's lantern over the spindly trunks and rippling branches, they glistened the same silver as Mortice's hunting cloak.

There was a countdown that Burgewick knew the spectators were watching inside the banquet hall, but after only a few minutes the inebriated uncle snarled something about having waited long enough, and fired his rifle skyward. The shot seemed to shatter the night. All the hunters and the drones surged forward into the woods and Burgewick let himself be carried along with them.

At first they walked in one group, but Mortice and Orry darted ahead and everyone else peeled off one by one as their trackers called them in separate directions. Burgewick and Breesha were the last to split up, and for a moment he wanted to tell her to stay with him.

"Mine's heading north," she announced, peering down at her tracker. "Good hunting, Burgewick. See you back at the House."

"Good hunting, Breesha," he said, and then he was alone.

The red blot on his tracker was moving fast but zigzagging, disorientated. Burgewick felt the same way as he followed it. The trees seemed to tilt and sway and their branches leapt out of the dark like claws. He heard booted feet crashing through the underbrush, a distant shout of triumph. One shot. Another. Both made him flinch.

For a moment he considered turning around, heading back to the lighted warmth of the House. But there would be laughter, and Father would look at him but say nothing, and the Old Madam's words were reverberating in his head: *We kill the weak part of ourselves*. That was what he had to do. He would kill his doppel, before Mortice could kill his, and it would make him strong. Maybe strong enough to hit back.

Burgewick sped up, plunging deeper into the woods, following the red blot. His lantern strobed the frosty ground and he saw snapped brambles, the imprint of a foot. Once he saw movement in the shadows, but it was only a drone on the prowl. He skipped over twisted roots and ducked swaying branches, adrenaline thrumming under his skin, speeding his hot pulse. The red blot finally slowed, and Burgewick felt a dart of triumph.

The red blot disappeared.

Burgewick skidded to a halt, panting. His steaming breath coiled around his head. The doppel's sensor had failed, or else the doppel was standing perfectly still. Burgewick crept forward slowly, moving on the balls on his feet, rifle ready. The doppel had to be close. He tried not to make a sound. He couldn't hear the other hunters anymore; they were too far and the woods were too dense.

He thought he saw something moving on his left, but the tracker was still black and when he swept around the side of the tree there was nothing there. Another topsy-turvy thought came to him: maybe the doppel had turned off the sensor on its own. Maybe it was watching him. Maybe it was hunting him.

Burgewick's entire skin was goosebumps that his hyde couldn't warm away. The stock of his hunting rifle was turning slick in his clammy hands. He put them to his stomach, to wick away the moisture, but they were crawling with fresh sweat only a moment later.

A branch snapped; he whipped his head and saw a dark moving figure, raised his hunting rifle with badly shaking hands, sighted—

"Still looking, are you?" Mortice asked, switching on his lantern. "I bagged mine ages ago."

Burgewick lowered his rifle, but only just. Every nerve in his body was singing high and sharp. Mortice's rifle was stowed on his back; his hyde had grown webbing to holster it. He held his lantern in one hand and proof of his claim in the other, dangling from the capcutter. The doppel's mask had been removed and its face was an ugly parody of Mortice's own, purple-lipped and glassy-eyed, clotted with gore from the severing. Burgewick's bile surged at the sight.

"I know my nose isn't that big," Mortice said casually, twisting the doppel's head back and forth in the lantern light. "Is it?"

"No," Burgewick said by rote, hating himself for it.

"No," Mortice agreed. His grin was over-wide, almost manic. "Let's find this doppel of yours, shall we?"

Burgewick hesitated, wishing Breesha or one of the uncles, even the sot, would appear from the trees to join them. But they were alone. He gave his brother a stiff nod. Mortice returned it with exaggerated solemnness, then barked a laugh and turned away, probing the dark with his lantern. Burgewick followed behind him, mind whirring.

Maybe Mortice was just looking for the right branch to whip him with, or waiting for the right moment to hold him down and twist his ears and make him lick the blood from his doppel's dead face. Or maybe Mortice wanted to rob his kill, go back to the banquet hall with two heads, and explain that his little brother had been too slow, too scared, too stupid to do it himself. That would shame him how he'd been shamed.

But maybe it didn't have to end that way. Burgewick's stomach churned. Maybe *he* was Wendell, and Mortice was Eddard. If he were to shoot Mortice, and pretend it was an accident, pretend that his silvery hunting cloak had blended with the silvery tree trunks, he would

be free of his brother's torments forever. At close enough range, he
reasoned the smart bullets wouldn't have time to turn away. His rifle
crept upward until it was pointing at Mortice's spine.

Then he saw it. Crouched at the base of a tall tree, in the cradle
formed by two gnarled roots, its head cocked to one side. His doppel's
reflective costume was half-coated in dirt and the beak of its mask was
crooked, as if it had bashed into something. It was still, so still Burgewick thought for an instant it might already be dead.

Its head twitched, ever so slightly, and before Mortice could spot
it and steal it, Burgewick raised his rifle and fired. The stock slammed
back into his shoulder and the crack made Mortice jump. Burgewick
felt some savage satisfaction in seeing his brother flinch, felt even more
of it seeing the doppel's body jerk and crumple.

He'd done it. He'd done it, and it had been easy. Mortice gave a
wild laugh, and for a moment Burgewick felt like laughing, too. Light-
headed, he jogged over to the doppel. Smart bullets were designed
to disperse on impact and the doppel's costume was a shredded mess
from hip to ribs. A dozen punctures were weeping sticky red blood. Its
chest was heaving.

"Well done, little brother," Mortice said. "You know the right end
of a rifle."

Something was wrong. Burgewick felt it bone deep. Mortice
shouldn't be happy. The doppel shouldn't have hidden itself so well,
shouldn't have covered the reflecting parts of its costume. With trembling hands, Burgewick reached for the doppel's mask. He tugged, but it
was stuck. Mortice squatted beside him, breathing hot in his ear, eager.

Burgewick pulled hard. The mask tore free, taking shreds of skin
with it. Gib's eyes were panicked and bloodshot, his nostrils were flared
wide, and his mouth was coated in spitter glue.

Burgewick's stomach dropped like the bottom had been gnawed
away, slipping through itself, plummeting out of reach. He sank to
one knee, splaying a hand for balance on the dead soil. His vision was
blurry black; his pulse was roaring in his ears. The doppel was Gib.
Gib was the doppel. Everything was topsy-turvy.

"He fits the costume just right, doesn't he," Mortice said. "We told him we were playing a trick on you, to make him put it on. And once he was all drugged, he acted just like one."

Burgewick thought of all the games they had played together and how Gib had always helped him win. His splintered ribcage was still rising and falling. Maybe back at the House, with enough cell-knitters, he could still be saved. But Burgewick knew the cell-knitters weren't for him or Cluny or any other parasites, and he realized Gib could still help him win one last time.

He swallowed the rage, swallowed the anguish, swallowed every last thing he was feeling. Then he unhooked the capcutter from his hip and slipped it over Gib's head.

"Clever joke, Mortice," he said, with his voice and his face both perfectly blank. "But you shouldn't play with servants. It's unbecoming."

Burgewick pulled the lever and the capcutter slashed and snapped, spattering his hands with hot dark blood.

SUBMARINES

HAN SONG

TRANSLATED BY KEN LIU

Han Song is a Chinese writer and journalist who works for the state news agency Xinhua. His first short story collection, *Gravestone of the Universe*, was published in 1981, and waited ten years for publication in the People's Republic of China. Han has received the Chinese Galaxy Award for fiction six times. The *Los Angeles Times* described him as China's premier science fiction writer. His novels include *Subway*, *My Homeland Does Not Dream*, *Red Star Over America*, and *Red Ocean*.

As a boy, whenever I asked, my parents would bring me to the shore of the Yangtze River to see the submarines. Following the river's flow, the subs had come to our city in herds and pods. I heard that some subs also came from the Yangtze's tributaries: Wujiang River, Jialing River, Han River, Xiangjiang River, and so on. The subs were so numerous that they looked like a carpet of ants or thousands of wisps of rain-soaked clouds fallen from the heavens.

From time to time, to my amazement, one sub or another would just vanish from the surface. In fact, they had dived. First, the sub slowly wriggled its immense body, which then sank inch by inch, roiling the water around it in complicated and cryptic ripples, until the whole hull disappeared beneath the surface, including the tiny column on top shaped like a miniature watchtower. The flowing river soon recovered its habitual tranquility and mystery, leaving me stunned.

And then, a submarine would explode out of the water like a monster, splashing beautiful waves in every direction. "Look! Look!" I would scream. "It's surfacing!" But my parents never reacted. Their faces remained wooden, looking as dispirited as two houseplants that hadn't been watered for weeks. The appearance of the submarines seemed to have robbed them of their souls.

Most of the time, the subs remained anchored on the placid surface, motionless. Wires were strung over the hulls, stretching from tower to tower. Drying laundry hung from the wires like colorful flags, pants and shirts mixed with cloth diapers. Women in thick, crude aprons cooked with coal stoves on the decks, and the smoke columns turned the river into a campground. Sometimes the women squatted next to the water, beating the laundry with wooden bats against the sturdy metal hulls. Occasionally, old men and women climbed out of the subs, looking relaxed as they sat with their legs curled under them, smoking long-stemmed pipes with a cat or a dog curled up against them.

The subs belonged to the peasants who had come to our city to seek work. After a day of working in the city, the peasants returned to their submersible abodes. Before the arrival of the subs, peasant laborers had to rent cheap apartments in urban villages, plots of land where the rural population stayed as their farmlands were gobbled up by developers for the expanding city, leaving them stranded in a sea of skyscrapers. The urban villagers rented out one-foot-wide spaces on communal beds, and the rural laborers who built the city had to sleep like pigs or sheep in a pen. The submarines, on the other hand, gave the laborers their own homes.

Ferries operated between the shore and the anchored subs. Peasants piloted these ferryboats, shuttling their brothers and sisters between two completely different worlds. At night, after everyone had returned to their homes, the subs were at their most beautiful. Lit by gas lamps, each boat glowed with a different pattern like papercutting pasted on window panes. Bright, lively, they also reminded me of fallen stars adrift on the river. On each sub, a family sat around the table having supper, and the cool river breeze brought their laughter and chatter to the shore, leaving the urban residents with a sense of strange envy. As the night deepened, lights on the vessels winked out one by one until only the anxious searchlight beams from the harbor towers roamed the darkness, revealing motionless hulls like sleeping whales. Many subs, however, chose this time to disappear. Each sweep of the searchlight showed fewer and fewer boats. Without any announcement, they had dived, as if the peasants couldn't sleep soundly without the comfort of being covered by water, like water birds that had to tuck their heads beneath their wings to nap. Only by submerging their families and homes could they leave their worries behind on the surface, hold danger and uncertainty at bay, and dream sweet dreams without being bothered by the city-dwellers—was that, in fact, the reason they had built the submarines in the first place?

I often wondered how deep the Yangtze was, and how many subs could lie on the riverbed. How eerie and interesting it would have been to see rows upon rows of metal hulls lying next to each other down there! The thought made me gasp at how mysterious the world was, as though there were another world beyond the visible one.

In any event, the submarines settled near us like nesting birds and became a hotly debated sight. Every morning, they popped out of the water like boiled dumplings. Under the shimmering dawn light, the perturbed river surface resembled a spring flood. The scene made me think of alien spaceships from the movies. Busy ferries went back and forth between the subs and the shore, carrying spirited peasants into the city for another day of backbreaking labor at construction sites across the city.

The submarines came from all over China. Besides our city, rumors described pods in other cities and other rivers as well. Every sea, lake, canal, and trench seemed to have its own sub colonies. No one could say for sure who had designed the first sub. Supposedly, a clever folk craftsman had fashioned the first submarines by hand. By the standards of sophisticated urbanites, these boats were crude pieces of technology: most were constructed from scrap metal, though a few were pieced together with fiberglass and plywood. The early subs were shaped like fish, and many had heads and tails painted in red and white, including radiant, vivid eyes, lips, or even fins. These features looked a bit ridiculous, though they also showed the sense of humor unique to peasants. Later, as more submarines were built, the differences in decorative coloration distinguished families from one another.

Typically, a sub was big enough for a single family, on average five or six people. Bigger subs provided enough space for two or three families. The peasants seemed unable to build large vessels that could carry dozens or hundreds of people. Some city-dwellers had wondered whether the subs were constructed along plans cribbed from Verne's *Twenty Thousand Leagues Under the Sea*, or perhaps foreign experts had secretly helped the peasant craftsmen. In the end, however, no connection between the subs and Verne was discovered. The sub makers had never even heard of the author. Everyone sighed with relief.

After a while, the city kids continued to be fascinated by the subs while the adults became either bored or pretended not to notice them. At school, we enthusiastically swapped stories and news about subs, and we drew pictures of them on sheets of paper torn from our composition books. The teachers, however, never mentioned them, and reprimanded us with frowning faces whenever they caught us discussing the subject, tearing apart our sketches and sending the offenders to the principal's office. It was rare to see any TV or newspaper reporting about the activities of the submarines, as though the congregating vessels had nothing to do with the life of the city.

Occasionally, a few curious adults—mostly artists and poets— would come to the shore to gaze at the scene, whispering to each other. They speculated that over time, perhaps the subs would evolve a new civilization. The submarine civilization would be unlike any existing civilization in the world, just as mammals are completely different from reptiles. They wanted to visit the subs to collect folklore and study their customs, but the peasants never showed any inclination to invite the city dwellers to come aboard. Maybe after a full day of hard labor, they were too tired to deal with strangers. Besides wanting to avoid trouble, they probably also didn't see any profit in it. The peasants made it clear that the only reason they had come to the city was to find work and make money. However, the unsophisticated peasants seemed to not realize that they could have roped the anchored subs off and charged money for a close-up view, turning their homes into a tourist attraction. Neither did they display any interest in creating a "new civilization."

After returning to the subs at night, all the peasants wanted to do was to eat and go to sleep. They had to rest well to be able to get up in the morning for another day of hard work. Toiling at the dirtiest and most physically demanding jobs in exchange for the lowest and most uncertain wages, the peasant laborers never complained. This was because they had the subs, which allowed them to be with their families after work instead of having to leave them behind in distant home villages. The subs replaced the fields that they had been forced to sell to local governments and real estate developers at bargain-basement prices so that the fields could be consumed by growing cities. Although the city-dwellers acted as if what had happened to the peasants was none of their concern, in their hearts they felt uneasy and helpless. To be sure, the subs did not pose a threat to the city—they weren't armed with cannons or torpedoes, for instance.

After I became a good swimmer, my friends and I secretly visited the subs on our adventures. Holding hollow reeds in our mouths, we snorkeled to the middle of the river, out of sight, until we were right next to the anchored subs. Large wooden cages dangled from cables beneath the hulls, and the turbid river water swirled around the cage bars. Inside, we saw many peasant children, their earth-toned bodies nude, swim around like fish, their slender limbs nimbly finning the water and their skin glowing in the silt-filtered light. Guessing that these cages were likely the peasant version of daycare or kindergarten, our hearts filled with wonder.

Our leader was a boy a few grades above me. "Don't be so impressed," he said contemptuously. "I bet we can beat them in a swim race." The rest of us approached one of the cages and asked the children inside, "Have you ever seen a car?"

The children stopped swimming and gathered on our side of the cage, their faces as expressionless as plastic animals'. I saw that they didn't have scales or fins, as I had hoped. It was a mystery how they could stay underwater for so long without using a breathing reed.

Finally, a look of curiosity appeared on the face of one of the peasant children. "A car? What's that?" His voice was barely a whisper. I thought he looked like a creature out of manga.

"Ha, I knew it!" Our leader sounded pleased. "There are so many types of cars! Honda, Toyota, Ford, Buick . . . oh, and also BMW and Mercedes!"

"We don't know what you're talking about," said the peasant kid, his voice hesitant. "But we've seen lots of fish. There's red carp, gold carp, black carp, sturgeon, oh, and also white bream and Amur bream!"

Now it was our turn to be nervous. We looked around but didn't see any fish. Our teachers had taught us that all fishes in the Yangtze had gone extinct, so were the peasant children trying to trick us? Where could they have seen fish?

"I hope they really evolve into a different species from us," muttered our leader.

The peasant children blinked uncomprehendingly before returning to their aimless swim in the cage, as though trying to keep away from us.

"Are you going to turn into fish?" I asked.

"No."

"Then what will you become?"

"Don't know. When our mas and das are back from work, you can ask them."

I thought of how they lived underwater, away from fields, gardens, and soil, while we lived on the shore. It was like a picture of fish and shrimp versus cattle and sheep—was that the future?

We pretended to be interested in them and attempted to play with the peasant children some more, but the effort fizzled. They didn't know any of the games we knew, and the bars of the cage stood in our way. It was boring to keep on trying. In the murky shadows of the swaying underwater weeds, we felt the oppressive presence of a nameless terror. And when our leader gave the order, we gladly headed for the surface after him so that we could return to our own realm.

The peasant children would stay in the water. Let them.

We burst through the surface, our hearts pounding. All around us were the hulking forms of anchored subs, like a pack of hungry, silent wolves in the deep of winter. Like freshly fallen snow, the crude, gloomy hulls reflected the bright sunlight so that we squinted. There were no fish on the surface either, just the drifting corpses of rats and cockroaches, and layers and layers of rotting algae, tangled with thousands of discarded phone chargers and computer keyboards, as well as soda bottles, plastic bags, and other trash. The stench from the feces-colored water was almost unbearable, and swarms of flies buzzed around, their heads an iridescent green.

This was, in fact, an unforgettable, lovely sight that made us linger, and we wondered if the subs had come here specifically to appreciate it. Their long odyssey had left them with a unique value system and sense of beauty. Peasant women busied themselves aboard the subs without gazing down at us in the river. They boiled their rice and cooked their meals with the stinking water we bobbed in, and yet, whereas the city-dwellers would have died from the germs, the peasants were fine.

Just then, anxious adults on shore hollered for us to come home, their faces filled with *danger, fear, menace.*

The year before I started middle school, something happened involving the subs.

It was an early autumn night. Loud noises woke me from sleep, and it seemed as if the whole city had boiled over. My parents dressed me quickly, and we hurried out the door, heading for the river. We became part of a surging crowd whose thumping footsteps and worried cries were like exploding firecrackers on New Year's Eve. I was so scared that I covered my ears, unsure what was happening.

Once we arrived at the shore, I found out that the subs had caught fire. The fire had spread and all the boats were burning. In my memory, it was like a major holiday: the whole city's population seemed to be present, their numbed expressions replaced by excitement, screaming and talking as though they were watching a marvelous show. Trembling, I squeezed next to my parents, and tried my best to get a peek through the sea of people.

Raging fire danced and leaped from the densely packed subs, swirling, spreading, expanding like the skirts of cruel flamenco dancers. Flickering lights from the flames lit up the skyscrapers onshore so that they glowed like the foliage of late autumn, until the whole scene resembled a fresh painting. It was a shocking sight whose equal I have never experienced again.

For some reason, none of the subs dived. It was as if they had all forgotten what they were. Floating still at the surface, they made no effort to escape as the ice-like fire devoured them one by one. I was certain there was some secret behind it, some indescribable mystery. I wondered if another fantastic fire was also burning underwater—somehow, the water molecules had all transformed into another substance, and the whole Yangtze River was defying the physical properties endowed by nature, which was why the submarines were unable to dive away from this fiery dance stage.

I thought of the children in their underwater cages, and my heart swelled with shock and worry. Turning my head, I saw my parents standing like a pair of zombies, unmoving, their eyes staring straight ahead like lanterns, their faces frozen. Other adults muttered like chanting Buddhist monks, but no one made any effort to extinguish the fire. They seemed to be there only to witness the death of alien creatures in the river, to watch as the uninvited guests achieved total freedom.

That night seemed to last forever, though I never once thought of death, only soaking in the poignancy and meaninglessness of life itself. I never felt sad or mournful, though I was sorry that I would never again be able to swim into that strange realm, to see sights that made my heart leap and my mind confused. A sense of unresolvable solitude gripped me, while I knew also that my own future would not be affected in any way by what I was seeing . . .

Morning finally arrived. Dim sunlight revealed lifeless hunks of blackened metal drifting everywhere on the river. In scattered rows, circles, clumps, they reflected the cold, colorless light, and the air was suffused with the decaying odors of autumn. The city-dwellers brought forth cranes to retrieve the wreckage of the submarines from the river and trucked the pieces to scrap metal yards. The whole process took over a month.

After that, no submarines came to the Yangtze River.

AS THE LAST I MAY KNOW

S. L. HUANG

S. L. Huang (slhuang.com) is an Amazon.com bestselling author who justifies her MIT degree by using it to write eccentric mathematical superhero fiction. Her Cas Russell series includes the novels *Zero Sum Game, Null Set,* and *Critical Point,* with her first book outside that series, *Burning Roses,* to come this year. Her short fiction has sold to *Analog Science Fiction and Fact, Strange Horizons, The Magazine of Fantasy & Science Fiction,* and elsewhere. Huang is also a Hollywood stuntwoman and firearms expert, and she has appeared on shows such as *Battlestar Galactica* and *Raising Hope.* Her proudest geek moment was getting killed by Nathan Fillion. The first professional female armorer in the industry, she's worked with actors such as Sean Patrick Flanery, Jason Momoa, and Danny Glover, and been hired as a weapons expert for reality shows such as *Top Shot* and *Auction Hunters.*

A growing crowd of protesters trudged doggedly through the flurrying snow, bundled up into roundness against the cold until they resembled determined beetles. Back and forth they went, marching in a wobbly loop, their heads down against the wind but their voices strident as they fell into a chant:

> *Don't kill children, kill the seres!*
> *Before we all destroy ourselves!*

Up in the window of the garret three stories above, Nyma watched them trundle and call. They didn't have a very good chant, she couldn't help thinking. "Seres" wasn't even a hard word to rhyme—*fears, years, tears . . .*

She leaned her forehead against the window pane. The glass was cold.

She hadn't yet felt the presence of her tutor in the doorway behind her. In truth, Tej had opened his mouth to speak out several times, only to swallow back the frigid air instead. He was, if he were to scrape away any illusions—and Tej was not a man who lied to himself, when he could avoid it—trying to best himself in a moral struggle.

He failed.

"You shouldn't watch that," he said to Nyma. Peace help him, but the garret was freezing. He folded his hands into the sleeves of his robe, wondering how Nyma wasn't shivering.

Children were always so resilient. Too resilient.

"It's my job now," Nyma said into the window, the words fog on the pane.

"It doesn't have to be." Now that he'd broken, the words tumbled out of Tej like they wanted to barb into the child's heart and keep her here. "You understand that, right? You can—you can say no."

Nyma knew. Her tutors had taught her: she would always have a choice. But they'd also taught her why her duties were so vital, and why those duties had to be done by someone young, if not her then one of her classmates.

And she believed them. She believed in the Order and everything it stood for.

Dying scared her. A lot. The idea of it was so impossibly big and black that she couldn't even hold it in her head. But it didn't scare her enough to break the faith—not when her name had been the one drawn.

Of course, the news feeds said she shouldn't be allowed to choose this life at all, blasting the Order for following the old ways. *Ten-year-olds are too young to agree to this; they can't make that decision for themselves; it's inhumane!* Some of those people wanted the Order disbanded. Some of them wanted only adults to follow its dictates, people who had passed the magic threshold of being able to say yes to saving the world.

Those same news feeds were markedly less certain whether butchering the Order's traditions should also mean dismantling the nation's stockpile of sere missiles.

"You taught me," Nyma said to Tej. "It's important. We're important."

Not as important as your life, Tej wanted to cry, wanted to fold her into him like his own daughter instead of one of his pupils, even as that betrayed every fiber of what he'd always fought for. "It doesn't have to be you," he managed instead. "We didn't know it would be like—this. You can say no to it. To him."

Nyma turned from the window, her freckles blotching dark on her pale skin, her eyes so large they took up half her face. "He's scary," she whispered. "Will you come with me? When I have to meet him?"

Tej had to turn away, then, because it wouldn't do for Nyma to see one of her tutors weep.

Nobody thought Otto Han would win the election. He was the quiet outsider candidate, the one who'd kept pecking at his place in the polls until he rose up when all the others had shouted themselves out.

He wasn't even the one who had most worried the Order, at first—that honor had gone to the demagogue candidate who fanned the flames of mounting war until her supporters screamed in violent ecstasy. She had burned out brighter and faster than the swell of rage she had dug from the populace. The tension in the Order had fallen into palpable relief when she'd plummeted in public opinion, even as she'd left behind a smear of angry demonstrators yelling, "*We have seres, we should use them!*"

They didn't understand, those people. They had forgotten. The Order was built not to forget.

It wasn't until two weeks before the election that a reporter asked Otto Han his opinion of sere missiles. "I think if it makes the most military sense for the protection of our nation, we need to use every tool at our disposal," he'd answered. "We're at war. Everything should be on the table."

The reply sparked panic in the Order, but got far too little notoriety elsewhere. The Order Elders wired their contacts in the feeds, begging other newsfolk to press Han hard and ask the important questions, before it was too late:

How can you justify a weapon that will vaporize an entire city in a single instant—buildings, children, hospitals, prisoners of war, millions of innocent civilian people, everything for so many hundreds of miles— gone? How is that not a war crime?

How can you reconcile that with history, our history, as the only country in the world who has had sere weapons used against us? How can you do what we have always considered the unthinkable?

And, the most relevant one to a ten-year-old Order girl and those who knew her:

Do you truly wish to use such weapons so badly, that you would be willing to do as the law requires and murder a child of your own land with your own hands in order to gain access to them?

But there hadn't been time. Nobody had asked Han any of those questions until after he'd already won.

The poem Nyma returned to most often had been written by Akuta Myssoutoi two hundred years ago, after he'd lost everyone in his family in the destruction of the Capital.

The snow falls over nothing.
I beg three small graves to place incense
But echos have no tombs.

The bleakness of it had been a touchstone for the beliefs she'd been raised with, a reaffirmation of the Order's righteousness.

Now the words of that final stanza kept circling in her head, echoing dully. Behind them loomed the granite image of President Otto Han, standing above her with a knife, his hands soaked crimson with her blood.

She gripped Tej's hand. Fear made all her senses too sharp.

It was okay to be scared, right? As long as she did her duty. Her chest ached over the scar where the surgeons had put the capsule in. It had been over a month ago now, after the election but before Han's induction into office. In that time, the ache felt like it had become a part of her.

She and Tej walked together down the long archways of the Capital, the metal and stone gleaming into the sky around them. One tall dark man, one small pale girl, and no one could have said who was grasping whose hand more tightly.

When they reached the Tower, the new president did not keep them waiting. A series of smartly dressed staff showed them in with no delay, not even a question as to who they might be. Even if their robes had not marked them out, their faces were already known here.

Otto Han rose from behind his desk to greet them in a stiff but polite bow. Tej bowed equally stiffly in return.

He's so much bigger in person, Nyma thought numbly. And he was hard. Like if you touched him, your hand would break.

"Elder Rokaya," he said to Tej, in something that passed for a greeting. "And this must be my carrier."

"Yes, sir," said Nyma. "My name is—"

"I don't want to know your name." He turned back to Tej. "You Order priests are animals. This is barbaric."

"Her name is Nyma," Tej said quietly, but his thoughts were not so calm. *Seres are what is barbaric. Whether to engage in such barbarism is your choice, not ours.* The president could say, right now, that he would not use the weapons that defied all humanity and could spell the end of every life on their world. He could proclaim that Nyma would be safe and that the position would be as ceremonial as it had been in the past.

He was the one who refused.

"I've been briefed," Han said. "And I said to my generals, it's hundreds of years later, *surely* we have a better way of doing this. But you people have embedded yourselves right in the roots of our laws, haven't you?"

"We think it's the best way, sir." It wasn't Tej who had spoken, but Nyma, forcing the words around the dryness in her mouth. *You must talk to the president. You must be a part of their mind, their life.* Her tutors' words were a drumbeat in her head.

Han wrested his attention around to her, and Nyma quailed.

"Of course you do," he said. He turned back to Tej. "You people teach her to say this, and then if I need the codes for the weapons that could protect us all, you put them inside a child and tell me I have to slaughter her. You're despicable."

Tej had to force his expression to stillness. "Sir."

"Do you know what the Baron Islands are doing to our people in the southern territories *right now*? Do you know what they've promised to do to the people of Koivu and Mikata? Koivu has sere missiles themselves. If the Islanders get a hold of that technology . . . trust me, they won't force their leaders to kill little girls in order to use them. Even if they did, those leaders wouldn't hesitate."

Tej could have argued every one of those points for hours. He could have pointed out balances of power and morality, or expounded on the Order's core belief, that *no one* should be able to push a button from the sanctuary of an office and kill so many faceless children far away if they could not see the justification to execute the one in front of them.

Without such a burden, how would any president fully understand what he did when he asked to use such weapons?

"I'm told she's to be a bodyman to me," Han said. "I'm told I can't say no."

"That's correct, sir," Tej answered. The carrier had to be always physically nearby in case she was, Peace forbid, needed. That part was for the president. But if she could also form an emotional closeness, it might save not only her life but the lives of millions, and that was the mission of the Order.

"All right, Elder, you're dismissed. Nyma, was it?" He towered over her.

"Yes, sir."

"I hope you know. I don't want this."

Nyma didn't know how to reply. Did she want this, just because she had chosen it? Did the Order want it, because they believed it was necessary? Did anybody want it?

Another verse from the same Myssoutoi poem swirled through her head.

I listened to us surrender on the wireless.
No choice, they said.
They said the same when we went to war.

Nyma sat in the corner of the president's Tower office, biting the end of her stylus. It was a bad habit of hers, one her teachers had tried hard to break her of but had always failed. She wore Tower livery now, her thin hair braided neatly like the ushers and servants, but everyone still knew—she saw it in the way they walked in arcs around her, or whispered while not looking her way.

"What are you thinking about so hard over there?"

Nyma jumped. Try as she had to engage him, Otto Han had barely spoken to her if he could avoid it. He thanked her when she brought him files or drinks or carried his things, but he'd certainly never asked her a question.

"I'm trying to think of a rhyme, sir," she answered honestly.

"A rhyme? Whatever for?"

"I like poetry." She closed her pad and turned so she could face where he sat at the wide presidential desk. "I know it doesn't always have to rhyme. But I'm not a good enough poetess yet to do the un-rhyming ones."

"Poetess, eh? All right, let's hear one."

A warm flush crept up Nyma's neck. Her Order tutors had encouraged her interest—it was always good for carriers to be full people, they said, children with personalities who would be missed if they were gone, and besides that, the hope was that even those chosen would always have an adult life to grow into. But Nyma had never recited one of her poems aloud before.

Most of the ones she'd written lately were bleak. Just yesterday she'd composed a verse titled "Next Year?" with the lines, *Peach petals drift down / Cheerful pink snow / And I clasp them to me / As the last I may know.*

The president was still far too intimidating to share that one with. What if he shouted at her? Worse, what if he brushed it off, or laughed, when he was the one who held the answer to the question in his hands?

"Here's one I wrote when we were visiting the farming country a few weeks ago," she said, after rapidly deciding what might be harmless to recite. Pretty farms were safe, right? She took a breath and plunged in before nerves could steal her tongue.

She managed to get through all five stanzas, but trailed off as she got to the end. Otto Han was smiling. She hadn't known he *could* smile.

"You made that up all by yourself?" he said, when she had stopped.

"Yes, sir."

"Well, I'll be." He rose and came over to stand next to her, staring out the Tower windows to the shiny quilt of the Capital below. "I love our people, Nyma. Can you understand that?"

"I think so, sir." Nyma loved their people too. She'd been taught their nation's history since before she could walk. "I think I love all people. But one thing I love most about us is how important other countries' people are to us too."

"Ah. Your Order." He rested a brief, rough hand on her shoulder. "I still don't agree. But I'd be more than glad for you to grow up to argue with me about it."

"Sir?"

His mouth quirked. "I shouldn't say, but—you deserve to know. The war's going well. It's all going well. We got news today that— mmm, let's just say I don't think I'm going to have to make any decisions nobody should have to make."

A queer, swoopy feeling fluttered through Nyma's stomach.

"Mind you, I still think you being here is barbaric," Han continued.

In a burst of courage, Nyma slipped to her feet and grabbed the president's arm. "What do you see?" she said. "When you look out these windows at the Capital, and all the people and buildings, what do you see?"

He glanced down at her, surprise writ clear on his expression. "I suppose I see . . . progress. Prosperity. Things worth protecting."

"In the Order they teach us to look at the city and imagine it . . . imagine what happened two hundred years ago," Nyma said. "They say not to think about the whole city, that's too big. You have to look at the small things." She pointed at the streets that crisscrossed below them. "Like that woman in the green coat. Just—gone. She's gone. The couple holding hands over by the pigeons. They're gone too. All the pigeons, and the street, and that shop selling flowers, and the kids playing in front of it. And then you think about your family. If you have parents, or friends, anyone you love—how they could also just be gone, all at once." She licked her lips. It was the longest she'd ever talked in a row to the president. "The whole *city*. Two hundred years ago, that happened. The Havenites *did that* to us. That's what I see. And I can't bear the thought of it happening again, to anyone."

She half expected him to tell her this was only what she had been taught from the mouths of meddling grown-ups. But he didn't. Instead he said, "Do you have a family, Nyma?"

The question surprised her. "My parents were both in the Order, sir. They were raising me that way too, but they died in a tram crash when I was a baby and left me with the Elders. It's a good education."

"With a price. Do the Elders let you have friends?"

"Of course. My friends can't visit me much here, but we write to each other." The writing had dropped off of late. It made Nyma's heart give a funny little twist. Her classmates didn't seem to know how to speak to her now that she had been chosen—now that she had been chosen and they hadn't. "And some of my tutors are my friends. Like Tej."

Han made a noncommittal sound. "Tell me, Nyma. Do you write poetry about all this?"

"Yes, sir."

"Peace knows you shouldn't have to listen to anything I say, but I think . . . I think you should keep on doing that. Is that all right?"

"Yes, sir." It had never occurred to her to stop.

Nyma was off with the presidential cadre on a diplomatic trip the day she turned twelve years old, but when she returned the following week, Tej brought a box of birthday teacakes to their class session.

"You remembered!" she said, delighted. The Tower staff kept a log and the ushers had made sure she got very traditional, professionally sugared teacakes on the day, but it was different when someone thought of you.

"How was the trip?" Tej asked.

Nyma closed the box and set it aside, careful not to drag her dagged sleeve in the sugar. She'd asked to stop wearing Tower livery of late—she wasn't required to, and she found she liked having a say in designing outfits for herself. All under the watchful eye of the Tower communications staff, of course.

Besides, she was grateful to find one more distraction from the ever-pressing weight of the air around her.

"Nyma?"

"The feeds aren't always right, you know. About the war." She played with the hem of her sleeve instead of looking at Tej. "But I can always tell when it's bad, because he stops talking to me."

Cowardice, Tej wanted to say, but didn't. They'd all been so hopeful this war would end two years ago. Instead it had dragged. And dragged.

And now the murmurs were becoming pointed shouts, and the editorials kept mentioning the words "land invasion." Their nation hadn't suffered a conflict on its own soil in two hundred years.

Tej was of the opinion that they'd earned that tranquility by striving so hard to be a force for peace. His countrymen didn't seem so certain. Nyma's ear might be on the feeds and the president's mood, but Tej's was on the populace, the growing rumbles of anger and discontent. That was what he feared most of all.

"Nyma," he said. "I had a thought while you were away. Are you still writing?"

Her head came up in surprise. "You mean, writing poetry? Of course."

"I think," Tej said, "that we should publish some of it. A book."

"My poems? But I'm—" *Not good enough, still a child, still learning?* "I'm not sure I'm—that's like a dream, to be *published,* but Tej, I don't even know if I have enough. I'm already embarrassed of what I wrote last year."

"The ones you gave me last year for composition lessons were quite impressive," he said, truthfully. It had still perhaps been obvious they had been from the hand of a child, but the emotion that bled between the lines had wrenched him. "We'll have an editor help you. What do you think?"

"I don't . . . I mean, I . . ." She couldn't have said why, but it didn't feel right. It was all too easy. If she weren't the president's carrier, she'd have to keep working at it, scraping and practicing until her verses caught the eye of a professional, wouldn't she?

But if she weren't the president's carrier, she'd have a lifetime of years for that.

"All right," she said to Tej. She felt real and unreal, excited and not excited, all balled up like twine in her heart.

He flashed her a quick, tight smile. "Good. You know, Nyma, it takes more than soldiers to win a war."

She blinked. "But the Islanders won't even be able to read my poems. Unless they're translated or something."

"That's not the only war we're fighting."

Whether from morbidity or compassion or their own ideological motivations, the nation's people devoured the book of poems titled *The Girl in the Tower*. Presses clacked overnight, every night, binding up more copies, and Nyma's name fell in too-careful droplets from everyone's lips.

She thought she'd become used to the stares and whispers, but now public focus riveted on her like it wanted to drag her under the waves. The Tower communications staff had to block out a cascade of interview requests; the few profiles Nyma did do exploded and thrived across the feeds. Her photograph seemed to be plastered everywhere—almost always a solemn portrait that had been taken with dark lighting over a sea-green dress. It made her appear a waif. Nyma hated it, but candid captures of her laughing in the sun and wearing gold or pink seemed not to fit the feeds' narrative.

The protesters called her out by name now. It wasn't only abstract carrier "children" they chanted and opined about, but Nyma, the Poet in the Tower, who deserved to grow old, who was the fire and rallying symbol of everyone who opposed the use of seres.

President Han wasn't happy.

He was a good enough man that he did not lose his temper to Nyma about it, though he might have glowered in her direction more than a few times, after interviewers asked him with appalling directness whether he could truly imagine himself sliding a blade between her ribs and tearing open her heart. But he did summon Tej to him.

"You're using her. You're despicable."

Tej kept his hands folded before him, a picture of tranquility he hoped would be maddening. "Nyma believes in what we do. Would you really be so heartless as to tell her she can't speak for herself?"

"Damn you, man! Do you think I'd ever use the blasted things if I thought I had a choice? And you want to pinch us between annihilation from overseas and a bloodbath in our own country if I have to dirty my hands the way *you* people set me up to? You think that won't be the hardest day of my cursed life already?"

"I feel little pity for that," Tej said dryly, "seeing as it would be the last day of Nyma's."

Had Nyma herself heard the conversation, it only would have intensified the confused resentment that had been building in her toward both men. It sat in her throat, an unhappy lump. She'd always remained a little afraid of the president, no matter how much time she'd spent with him, but the anger edging her fear—that was new. Wasn't this her duty? But what right did Han have to react so blackly to her having spoken what she felt?

Didn't she deserve to be her own person, for whatever time she did have?

Her ill will toward Tej was more complicated. He cared for her, that she knew; and he had always been so careful in reminding her she had choices, even more than the other Elders. But . . . she didn't want to be the trapped waif who emerged flatly from *his* campaign, either.

She didn't know how, after so many people had read what was in her heart, she could feel so much like she had no voice.

Nyma made it two months past the day she turned thirteen before the air raid sirens screamed into the night and the first shelling rocked the Capital.

She followed what they'd drilled so many times now, quickly and automatically, her pulse hammering her ribs and chasing out any emotion. Only minutes later she huddled in the shelter, still in her nightdress, between the Minister of War and the Chief Transportation Administrator. She hugged her hands under her arms, but her palms wouldn't get warm.

The Minister of War was called into the next room for a council with the president. Nyma hunched against the wall. There were no windows. *Like a prison cell,* she thought. *Trapped inside our own safety.*

But she wasn't safe here. She was all inside out, waiting for her own death when everyone else sighed in relieved protection.

There was a poem in that, but she couldn't concentrate to draw it out.

She put a hand over her thudding heart. She fancied she could feel the capsule with the sere codes pushing against her fingers.

But the president didn't summon her that night. Or the next. Or the next, when the air raid siren klaxoned again. It took seventy-four days, the fall of three strategic outposts, and an occupying force on the outer peninsula for the call to come.

When Nyma entered the room, President Han was alone, and he was crying.

He took her hands. His were wet with his own tears, but Nyma was numb.

"I'm sorry," he said, through hiccuping breaths. "I'm so sorry."

Nyma's whole face began to prickle then. She wanted to have some deep, profound last thoughts, but her mind was a blank.

She tried to keep breathing. It was hard.

"If you want—some time, to say goodbye to people, or—"

"Get it over with now, please." She could be brave, if he did it now. She didn't want to live one more afternoon with this miserable finality crushing her.

The president detached his hands from hers as if he had to unclench them. He went to his desk and opened an ornate, ceremonial box.

Inside was a dagger. Its sleek blade hooked into Nyma's gaze and wouldn't let her go.

The president pushed a buzzer. Several advisors and generals came into the office. Tall, unsmiling, faces grave.

"Witness," the president mumbled. "As signed by the Council . . ."

He reached for the dagger's hilt. His hand shook.

Nyma felt no sympathy. She hoped his hand would shake so much he dropped it.

And then—it did. He did.

The dagger clattered to the desk.

"Find me another way!" The words tore forth, bowling into his generals, and Nyma had never seen him so angry. He whirled on Nyma. *"Get out!"*

She ran.

She didn't stop until she was back in her quarters, and then her legs went out on her, all wobbly and backward, and she collapsed on the woven floor mats, shuddering. Her breath heaved in and out, too fast and too ragged, and then the breaths caught and turned to ugly, wrenching sobs, and she couldn't stop trembling.

He's going to call me back, he's going to call me back, he's going to call me back and he's going to do it—

But he didn't. The sun set, and Nyma couldn't sleep, and the next day Tej came to see her.

He burst into her suite and gathered her up in an embrace so tight she couldn't breathe.

"Nyma, I—I heard, I came as soon as—"

She pushed out of his grasp. She didn't want to cry again. She couldn't comfort him on top of herself.

Tej had a wildness in his eyes. "I have, I have a plan. I'm one of the Elders who— When a new president is elected, and a new carrier chosen, we have to, the codes have to be reset and a new capsule made, and I have access—Nyma, you can run away from this. I'll help you. We can do it tonight."

She fought the sudden urge to vomit. If she ran, it would just be one of her classmates chosen instead. Why would he ask that of her?

"Who would you choose instead of me, then?" she cried. "You think I would pick someone else to die?"

"No. No." The wildness burst from Tej's face like he had lost reality. In truth, he hadn't slept at all, frantically preparing, sneaking every piece of groundwork into place, half hoping he would be caught while simultaneously terrified of the consequences of his treason. All that remained was for Nyma to agree. And still, trying to speak these words aloud was beyond the worst hell he'd ever conceived. "We won't put the codes in anyone else. I'll reset them from yours and deliver them to the president. Nobody—nobody needs to die for this. Not you, not anybody. *Please.*"

She recoiled from him. "What?"

"I've arranged security so—I can do it. Please, Nyma, I'm begging you."

Fury welled up in Nyma, eclipsing her feverish panic. How dare he? How dare he offer her a way out, a way to gallivant off into the night, and still give the president what he wanted? It wasn't *right*, that was why there was a carrier, so there was a *cost*, and hadn't Tej been the one who taught her so? "You can't do that!"

"No, it's different now." He turned his face away from her. He'd never questioned the mission of the Order, not once—not until he stood here on the precipice of destroying it. "Maybe sometimes— this decision—people are *dying*, Nyma. You're here in the Tower and all the security and you don't see—I walk through the streets, and there aren't even enough hands to carry away the bodies. Rubble everywhere, and the dust, and the fear, and—*I'm* afraid. I'm afraid. Nyma . . ."

He closed his eyes. They hadn't stopped burning for weeks.

"You think we should use seres," Nyma said slowly. "You think we should use them."

"I don't—I don't know."

His eyes were still closed, but he felt her hand on his sleeve.

"That's why there's a carrier," she said "That's why we didn't just get rid of them all—in case we ever do have to. But it should be—it should be desperate. Right? That's why I'm here. To make sure."

"I don't know what's right anymore," Tej whispered.

Nyma wondered if this was what it felt like to stop being a child.

"It's not about right and wrong," she said to him. "It's about making it hard."

Nyma sat in her quarters in the Tower, waiting.

The klaxons rang out every night now. Smoke and dust masked the Capital streets, but whenever the wind whisked it away, the soaring arches and towering buildings had crumbled into successive layers of ruin.

She gazed out the window and wondered if her death could save them all, or if it would only lead to so many mirrors of herself being massacred, all for the crime of a birth on enemy land.

Or maybe this was the end of everything. Their enemy didn't have seres themselves, but they had allies who did. If the president . . . it didn't comfort her, thinking of her own death as only the first in senseless billions, imagining that the world would outlast her by mere weeks before becoming a blank wasteland.

Why? she wondered emptily. *Nobody wins.*

She smoothed the press of her skirts and picked up her stylus. Opened her pad.

She didn't feel like searching for rhymes, today. But maybe she was past needing to.

> *I'm here to make you doubt*
> *You wish I weren't.*
> *I hold no answers in my loaded heart.*
> *I only sit*
> *and wait*
> *and wait*
> *and wait.*

A CATALOG OF STORMS

FRAN WILDE

Fran Wilde's (franwilde.net) novels and short fiction have won the Andre Norton Nebula, Compton Crook, and Eugie Foster Memorial Awards, and have been finalists for six Nebulas, two Hugos, two Locus Awards, and a World Fantasy Award. She writes for publications including the *Washington Post*, the *New York Times*, *Asimov's Science Fiction*, *Nature* magazine, *Uncanny Magazine*, *Tor.com*, *GeekMom*, and *iO9.com*. Fran is director of the genre MFA at Western Colorado University.

The wind's moving fast again. The weathermen lean into it, letting it wear away at them until they turn to rain and cloud.

"Look there, Sila." Mumma points as she grips my shoulder.

Her arthritis-crooked hand shakes. Her cuticles are pale red from washwater. Her finger makes an arc against the sky that ends at the dark shadows on the cliffs.

"You can see those two, just there. Almost gone. The weather wouldn't take them if they weren't wayward already, though." She tsks. "Varyl, Lillit, pay attention. Don't let that be any of you girls."

Her voice sounds proud and sad because she's thinking of her aunt, who turned to lightning.

The town's first weatherman.

The three of us kids stare across the bay to where the setting sun's turned the cliff dark. On the edge of the cliff sits an old mansion that didn't fall into the sea with the others: the Cliffwatch. Its turrets and cupolas are wrapped with steel cables from the broken bridge. Looks like metal vines grabbed and tethered the building to the solid part of the jutting cliff.

All the weathermen live there, until they don't anymore.

"They're leaned too far out and too still to be people." Varyl waves Mumma's hand down.

Varyl always says stuff like that because . . .

"They used to be people. They're weathermen now," Lillit answers.

. . . Lillit always rises to the bait.

"You don't know what you're talking about," Varyl whispers, and her eyes dance because she knows she's got her twin in knots, wishing to be first and best at something. Lillit is always second at everything.

Mumma sighs, but I wait, ears perked, for whatever's coming next because it's always something wicked. Lillit has a fast temper.

But none of us are prepared this time.

"I do too know. I talked to one, once," Lillit yells and then her hand goes up over her mouth, just for a moment, and her eyes look like she'd cut Varyl if she thought she'd get away with it.

And Mumma's already turned and got Lillit by the ear. "You did what?" Her voice shudders. "Varyl, keep an eye out."

Some weathermen visit relatives in town, when the weather is calm. They look for others like them, or who might be. When they do that, mothers hide their children.

Mumma starts to drag Lillit on home. And just then a passing weatherman starts to scream by the fountain as if he'd read Mumma's weather, not the sky's.

When weathermen warn about a squall, it always comes. Storms aren't their fault, and they'll come anyway. The key is to know what kind of storm's coming and what to do when it does. Weathermen can do that.

For a time.

I grab our basket of washing. Mumma and Varyl grab Lillit. We run as far from the fountain as fast as we can, before the sky turns ash-grey and the searing clouds—the really bad kind—begin to fall.

And that's how Lillit is saved from a thrashing, but is still lost to us in the end.

An Incomplete Catalog of Storms

A *Felrag*: the summer wind that turns the water green first, then churns up dark clouds into fists. Not deadly, usually, but good to warn the boats.

A *Browtic*: rising heat from below that drives the rats and snakes from underground before they roast there. The streets swirl with them, they bite and bite until the browtic cools. Make sure all babies are well and high.

A *Neap-Change*: the forgotten tide that's neither low nor high, the calmest of waters, when what rests in the deeps slowly slithers forth. A silent storm that looks nothing like a storm. It looks like calm and moonlight on water, but then people go missing.

A *Clare*: a storm of silence and retribution, with no forgiveness, a terror of it, that takes over a whole community until the person causing it is removed. It looks like a dry wind, but it's always some person that's behind it.

A *Vivid*: that bright sunlit rainbow-edged storm that seduces young women out into the early morning before they've been properly wrapped in cloaks. The one that gets in their lungs and makes them sing until they cry, until they can only taste food made of honey and milk and they grow pale and glass-eyed. Beware vivids in spring for the bride's sake.

A *Searcloud*: heated air so thick it blinds as it wraps charred arms around those it catches, then billows in the lungs, scorching words from their sounds, memories from their bearers. Often followed by sorrow, Searclouds are best avoided, run through at top speed, or never named.

An *Ashpale*: thick, gathering clouds from the heights, where the ice forms. When it leaves, everything in its path is slick and frozen. Scream it away if you can, before your breath freezes too.

The Cliffwatch is broken now, its far wall tumbled half down to the ocean so that every room ends in water.

We go up there a lot to poke around now that we're older.

After that Searcloud passed, Mumma searched through our house until she found Lillit's notes—her name wasn't on them, but we'd know her penmanship anywhere. Since she's left-handed and it smears, whether chalk or ink. My handwriting doesn't smear. Nor Varyl's.

The paper—a whole sheet!—was crammed into a crack in the wall behind our bed. I rubbed the thick handmade weave of it between my fingers, counting until Mumma snatched it away again.

Lillit had been making up storms, five of them already, mixing them in with known weather. She'd been practicing.

Mumma shrieked at her, as you could imagine. "You don't want this. You don't want it."

I ducked behind Varyl, who was watching, wide-eyed. Everyone's

needed for battle against the storms, but no one wants someone they
love to go.

And Lillit, for the first time, didn't talk back. She stood as still as a weatherman. She did want it.

While we ran to her room to help her pack, Mumma wept.

The Mayor knocked when it was time to take Lillit up the cliff. "Twice in your family! Do you think Sila too? Or Varyl?" She looked eagerly around Mumma's wide frame at us. "A great honor!"

"Sila and Varyl don't have enough sense to come out of the rain, much less call storms," Mumma said. She bustled the Mayor from the threshold and they flanked Lillit, who stepped forward without a word, her face already saying "up," even as her feet crunched the gravel down.

Mumma left her second-eldest daughter inside the gates and didn't look back, as is right and proper.

She draped herself in honor until the Mayor left, so no one saw her crying but me and that's because I know Mumma better than she thinks I do.

I know Lillit too.

Being the youngest doesn't have many advantages, but this one is worth all the rest: everyone forgets you're there. If you're watchful, you can learn a lot.

Here are a few:

I knew Lillit could hear wind and water earlier than everyone else.

I know Varyl is practicing in her room every night trying to catch up.

I know Mumma's cried herself to sleep more than once and that Varyl wishes she were sleet and snow, alternately. That neither one knows what Lillit will turn into when she goes.

And I know, whether Lillit turns to clouds or rain, that I'll be next, not Varyl. Me.

And that maybe someone will cry over me.

I already started making lists. I'll be ready.

Mumma goes up to the Cliffwatch all the time.

"You stay," she says to Varyl and me. But I follow, just close enough that I see Lillit start to go all mist around the edges, and Mumma shake her back solid, crying.

Weathermen can't help it, they have to name the storms they think of, and soon they're warning about the weather for all of us, and eventually they fight it too.

While Mumma and I are gone, the Mayor comes by our house and puts a ribbon on our door. We get extra milk every Tuesday.

That doesn't make things better, in the end. Milk isn't a sister.

"The weather gets them and gets them," Mumma's voice is proud and sad when she returns. From now on, she won't say "wayward," won't hear anyone speak of Lillit nor her aunt as a cautionary tale. "We scold because of our own selfishness," she says. "We don't want them to change." Her aunt went gone a long time ago.

We all visit Lillit twice, early on. Once, sweeping through town after a squall. Another time, down near the fishing boats, where the lightning likes to play. She saved a fisherman swept out to sea, by blowing his boat back to safe harbor.

We might go more often, but Mumma doesn't want us to catch any ideas.

A basket of oysters appears outside our door. Then a string of smoked fish.

When storms come, weathermen name them away. Yelling works too. So does diving straight into it and shattering it, but you can only do that once you've turned to wind and rain.

Like I said, storms would come anyway. When we know what to call them, we know how to fight them. And we can help the weathermen, Mumma says after Lillit goes, so they don't wear themselves out.

Weathermen give us some warning. Then we all fight back against the air.

"The storms got smarter than us," Varyl whispers at night when we can't sleep for missing her twin, "after we broke the weather. The wind and rain got used to winning. They liked it."

A predator without equal, the weather tore us to pieces after the sky turned grey and the sea rose.

Some drowned or were lost in the winds. Others fled, then gathered in safe places and hunkered down. Like in our town. Safe, cliffs on all sides, a long corridor we can see the ocean coming for miles.

Ours was a holiday place, once, until people started turning into weather too. Because the sky and the very air were broken, Varyl says.

Soon we stopped losing our treasures to the wind. Big things first: Houses stayed put. The hour hand for the clock stayed on the clock tower. Then little things too, like pieces of paper and petals. I wasn't used to so many petals staying on the trees.

The wind hadn't expected its prey to practice, to fight back.

When the weather realized, finally, that it was being named and outsmarted, then the wind started hunting down weathermen. Because a predator must always attack.

But the weathermen? Sometimes when they grow light enough, they lift into the clouds and push the weather back from up high.

"And through the hole they leave behind," Varyl whispers. Half asleep, I can barely hear her. "You can see the sky, blue as the denim our old dress might have been, once."

The Cliffwatch is broken now, its roof gaping wide as if the grey sky makes better shelter.

We climb over the building like rats, looking for treasure. For a piece of her.

We peer out at the ocean through where the walls used to be. We steal through a house that's leaned farther out over the water since the last time we came, a house that's grown loud in asking the wind to send its emptied frame into the sea.

Varyl stands watch, alone, always now. She's silent. She misses Lillit most.

Mumma and I collect baskets of hinges and knobs, latches and keyholes. People collect them, to remember. Some have storms inscribed around their edges: a Cumulous—which made the eardrums ring and then burst; a Bitter—where the wind didn't stop blowing until everyone fought.

"She learned them for us, Mumma," I whisper, holding an embroidered curtain. My fingers work the threads, turning the stitches into a list of things I miss about Lillit: her laugh, her stubborn way of standing, her handwriting. How she'd brush my hair every morning without yanking, like Varyl does now.

Mumma doesn't shush me anymore. Her eyes tear up a little. "Sila, I remember before the storms, when half the days were sunny. When the sky was blue." She coughs and puts a grey ribbon in my basket. "At least, I remember people talking like that, about a blue sky."

I'm wearing Varyl's hand-me-down dress; it's denim, and used to be blue too; a soft baby blue when it belonged to my sister; a darker navy back when it was Mumma's long coat.

Now the grey bodice has winds embroidered on it, not storms. Varyl did the stitching. The dress says: *felrag*, *mistral*, *lillit*, *föhn*, in swirling white thread.

The basket I hold is made of grey and white sticks; my washing basket most days. Today it is a treasure basket. We are collecting what the weather left us.

Mumma gasps when she tugs up a floorboard to find a whole catalog of storms beaten into brass hinges.

We've found catalogs before, marked in pinpricks on the edge of a book and embroidered with tiny stitches in the hem of a curtain, but never so many. They sell well at market, as people think they're lucky.

Time was, if you could name a storm, you could catch it, for a while. Beat it.

If it didn't catch you first.

So the more names in the catalog, the luckier they feel.

We've never sold Lillit's first catalog. That one's ours.

After Lillit goes, I try naming storms.

A *Somanyquestions*: the storm of younger sisters, especially. There is nothing you can do about it.

A *Toomuchtoofast*: that storm that plagues mothers sometimes. Bring soothing cakes and extra hands for holding things and folding things.

A *Leaving*: that rush when everything swoops up in dust and agitation and what's left is scoured. Prepare to bolt your doors so you don't lose what wants to be lost.

When I sneak up to the Cliffwatch to show my sister, she's got rain for hair and wind in her eyes, but she hugs me and laughs at my list and says to keep trying.

Mumma never knows how often I visit her.

"Terrible storms, for years," Varyl tells it, "snatched people straight from their houses. Left columns of sand in the chairs, dragged weeds through the bedding."

But then we happened, right back at the weather. I know this story. And the battle's gone on for a while.

Long before Lillit and Varyl and I were born, the Mayor's son shouted to the rain to stop before one of her speeches. And it did. Mumma's aunt at the edge of town yelled back lightning once.

The weather struck back: a whole family became a thick grey mist that filled their house and didn't disperse.

Then Mumma's aunt and the Mayor's son shouted weather names when storms approached. At first it was frightening, and people stayed away. Then the Mayor realized how useful, how fortunate. Put them up at the Cliffwatch, to keep them safe.

Then the news crier, she went out one day and saw snow on her hand—a single, perfect flake. The day was warm, the sky clear, trees were budding and ready to make more trees and she lifted the snow-flake to her lips and whirled away.

The town didn't know what to think. We'd been studying the weather that became smarter than us. We'd gotten the weather in us too, maybe.

Mumma's aunt turned to lightning and struck the clouds. Scattered them.

Right after that, the ocean grabbed the bluff and ripped it down. Left the Cliffwatch tilted over the ocean, but the people who'd got the weather in them didn't want to leave.

That was the battle—had been already, but now we knew it was a fight—the weathermen yelling at the weather, to warn us before the storms caught them too. The parents yelling at their kids to stay out of the rain. Out of the Cliffwatch.

But I'd decided. I'd go when my turn came.

Because deciding you needed to do something was always so much better than waking up to find you'd done it.

Mumma's aunt had crackled when she was angry; the Mayor's son was mostly given to dry days and wet days until he turned to squall one morning and blew away.

The storms grew stronger. The bigger ones lasted weeks. The slow ones took years. At market, we heard whispers: a few in town worried the storms fed on spent weathermen. Mumma hated that talk. It always followed a Searcloud.

Sometimes, storms linked together to grow strong: Ashpales and Vivids and Glares.

I lied when I said Mumma never looked back. I saw her do it.

She wasn't supposed to but the Mayor had walked on and she turned and I watched her watch Lillit with a hunger that made me stomp out the gate.

Returning to the Cliffwatch is worse than looking back. Don't tell anyone but she does that in secret. All the time.

She doesn't visit then. She stands outside the gates in the dark when she can't sleep, draped in shadows so no one will see her, except maybe Lillit. I sneak behind her, walking in her footsteps so nothing crunches to give me away.

I see her catch Lillit in the window of the Cliffwatch now and then. See Lillit lift a hand and curl it. See Mumma match the gesture and then Lillit tears away.

Mumma doubles her efforts to lure Lillit back. She leaves biscuits on the cliff's edge. Hair ribbons, "in case the wind took Lillit's from her."

She forgets to do the neighbors' laundry, twice, until they ask someone else. We stay hungry for a bit, then Varyl goes after the washing.

Up in the old clock tower in town where a storm took the second and minute hands but left the hour, a weatherman starts shouting about a Clarity.

Mumma starts running toward the cliff, but not for safety.

Varyl and I go screeching after her, a different kind of squall, beating against the weather, up to the Cliffwatch.

A Secret Catalog of Storms

A Loss That's Probably Your Fault: a really quiet storm. Mean too. It gets smaller and smaller until it tears right through you.

A Grieving: this one sneaks up on mothers especially and catches them off guard. Hide familiar things that belong to loved ones, make sure they can't surprise anyone. A lingering storm.

An I Told You Not To, Sila: an angry storm, only happens when someone finds your lists. The kind that happens when they burn the list so that no one will know you're catching wayward.

The biggest storm yet hits when we're almost done running.

We're near the top of the cliff, the big old house in our sights, and bam, the Clarity brings down torrents of bright-lit rain that makes the insides of our ears hurt. Breathing sears our lungs and we can't tell if that's from the running or the storm. And then the storm starts screeching, tries to pull our hair, drag us over the cliff.

We try to shelter in the Cliffwatch.

The wind hums around us, the ice starts blueing our cheeks, Varyl's teeth start chattering and then stop, and oh let us in, I cry. Don't be so stubborn.

Varyl pounds on the door.

But this time, the door doesn't open for Varyl. The door doesn't mind Mumma either, no matter how hard she pounds.

Only when I crawl through the freeze, around to the cliff's edge and yell, something turns my way, blows the shutters open. I pull my family through, even Mumma, who is trying to stay out in the wind, trying to make it take her too.

We get inside the Cliffwatch and shake ourselves dry. "That Clarity had an Ashpale on the end of it," I say. I'm sure of it. "There's a Bright coming."

So many storms, all at once, and I know their names. They are ganging up against us.

I want to fight.

Varyl stares at me, shouts for Mumma, but Mumma's searching the rooms for Lillit.

"We can't stay here and lose Sila too," Varyl says. She turns to me. "You don't want this."

But I do, I think. I want to fight the weather until it takes me too.

And maybe Mumma wants it also.

Varyl clasps my hand, and Mumma's, the minute the weather stops howling. She drags us both back to our house, through the frozen wood, across the square, past the frozen fountain. Our feet crunch ice into petals that mark our path. Varyl's shouting at Mumma. She's shaking her arm, which judders beneath her shirt, all the muscles loose and swingy, but the part of Mumma at the end of the arm doesn't move. Because she saw what I saw, she saw Lillit begin to blow, saw her hair rise and flow, and her fingers and all the rest of her with it, out to face the big storm, made of Ashpale and Vivid and Glare and Clarity.

That was the last time we saw Lillit's face in any window. Mumma had brought ribbons but those blew away. Now sometimes she scatters petals for Lillit to play with.

Climbing the remains of the Cliffwatch later, we find small storms in corners, a few dark clouds. You can put them in jars now and take them home, watch until the lightning fades.

Sometimes they don't fade, these pieces of weather. The frozen water that doesn't thaw. A tiny squall that rides your shoulder until you laugh.

They're still here, just lesser, because the weather is less too.

That day, all the storms spilled over the bay at once, fire from below and lightning and the green clouds and the grey. That day, the weathermen rose up into the wind and shouted until they were raw and we hid, and the storms shouted back—one big storm where there had been many smaller ones—and it dove for the town, the Cliffwatch, the few ships in the harbor.

And the weathermen hung from the cliff house and some of them caught the wind. Some of them turned to rain. Some to lightning. Then they all struck back together. The ones who already rode the high clouds too.

We wanted to help, I could feel the clouds tugging at my breath, but some of the winds beat at our cheeks and the rain struck our faces, pushing us back. And the terrible storms couldn't reach us, couldn't take us.

Instead, the Cliffwatch cracked and the clouds and the wind swept it all up back into the sky where it had come from long ago.

Later, we walked home. A spot of blue sky opened up and just as suddenly disappeared. A cool breeze crossed my face and I felt Lillit's fingers in it.

A hero is more than a sister. And less.

The milk keeps coming, but the fish doesn't.

The weathermen are in the clouds now. Varyl says they keep the sky blue and the sea green and the air clear of ice.

We climb into the Cliffwatch sometimes to find the notes and drawings, the hinges and papers and knobs. We hold these tight, a way to touch the absences. We say their names. We say, *They did it for us. They wanted to go.*

With the wind on my skin and in my ears, I still think I could blow away too if I wished hard enough.

Mumma says we don't need weathermen as much anymore.

Sometimes a little bit of sky even turns blue on its own.

Still, we hold their catalogs close: fabric and metal; wind and rain.

We try to remember their faces.

At sunset, Mumma goes to the open wall facing the ocean.

"You don't need to stay," she says, stubborn, maybe a little selfish.

But there she is so there I am beside her and soon Varyl also.

All of us, the sunset painting our faces bright. And then, for a moment before us out over the sea, there she is too, our Lillit, blowing soft against our cheeks.

We stretch out our arms to hug her and she weaves between them like a breath.

THE ROBOTS OF EDEN

ANIL MENON

Anil Menon's most recent work, *Half of What I Say*, was shortlisted for the 2016 Hindu Literary Award. Along with Vandana Singh, he co-edited *Breaking the Bow*, an international anthology of speculative fiction inspired by the Ramayana. His debut novel, *The Beast With Nine Billion Feet*, was shortlisted for the 2010 Vodafone Crossword Book Award for Children's Literature and the 2010 Carl Baxter Society's Parallax Prize. His short fiction has appeared in a variety of international magazines, including *Albedo One*, *Interzone*, *Interfictions*, *Jaggery Lit*, *Lady Churchill's Rosebud Wristlet*, and *Strange Horizons*. His stories have been translated into more than a dozen languages, including Hebrew, Igbo, and Romanian. In 2016, he helped found the annual Dum Pukht Writers' Workshop at the Adishakti Complex in Pondicherry. He splits his time between India and the USA.

When Amma handed me Sollozzo's complete collection of short stories, barnacled with the usual endorsements of genius, I respectfully ruffled the five-hundred-page tome and reflected with pleasure how the Turk was now almost like a brother. Of course, these days we all live in the Age of Comity, but Sollozzo and I had developed a friendship closer than that required by social norms or the fact that we both loved the same woman.

It had been quite different just sixteen months ago when Amma informed me that my wife and daughter had returned from Boston. The news sweetened the day as elegantly as a sugar cube dissolving in chai. Padma and Bittu were home! Then my mother had casually added that "Padma's Turkish fellow" was also in town. They were all returning to Boston in a week, and since the lovebirds were determined to proceed, it was high time our seven-year old Bittu was informed. Padma wanted us all to meet for lunch.

I wasn't fooled by Amma's weather-report tone; I knew my mother was dying to meet the Turk face-to-face.

I wasn't in the mood for lunch, and told my mother so. I had my reasons. I was terribly busy. It was far easier for them to drop by my office than for me to cart Amma all the way to Bandra, where they were put up. Besides, they needed something from me, not I from them. Some people had no consideration for other people's feelings—

I calmed down, of course. My mother also helped. She reminded me, as if I were a child, that moods were a very poor excuse. Yes, if I insisted, they would visit me at the office, but just because people adjusted didn't mean one had to take advantage of them, not to mention the Turk was now part of the family, so a little hospitality wasn't too much to ask, et cetera, et cetera.

Unlike his namesake in *The Godfather*, Sollozzo was a novelist, not a drug pusher (though I suppose novelists do push hallucinations in their own way). I hadn't read his novels nor heard of him earlier, but he turned out to be famous enough. You had to be famous to get translated into Tamil.

"I couldn't make head or tail," said Amma, with relish. "One sen-

tence in the opening chapter was eight pages long. Such vocabulary!
It's already a bestseller in Tamil. Padma deserves a lot of the credit,
naturally."

Naturally. Padma had been the one who had translated Sollozzo
into Tamil. And given herself a serving of Turkish Delight in the
process.

"If you like Pamuk, you will like him," said Amma. "You have to
like him."

I did like Pamuk. As a teenager, I had read all of Pamuk's works.
The downside to that sort of thing is that one fails to develop a mind
of one's own. Still, he was indelibly linked to my youth, as indelibly as
the memory of waiting in the rain for the school bus or the Class XII
debate at S.I.E.S. college on "Are Women More Rational than Men?"
and Padma's sweet smile as she flashed me her breasts.

Actually, Amma's lawyering on the fellow's behalf was unnecessary;
my Brain was already busy. My initial discomfort had all but dissolved.

I even looked forward to meeting Sollozzo. Bandra wasn't all
that far away. Nothing in Mumbai was far away. Amma and I lived
in Sahyun, only about a twenty-minute walk from my beloved Jihran
River, and all in all I had a good life, a happy life in fact, but good and
happy don't equal interesting. My life would be more interesting with
a Turk in it, and this was as good an opportunity as any to acquire one.

However, I knew Amma's pleasure would be all the more if she
had to persuade me, so I raised various objections, made frowny faces,
and smiled to myself as Amma demolished my wickets. Amma's home-
nurse Velli caught on and joined the game, her sweet round face alight
with mischief:

"Ammachi, you were saying your back was aching," said Velli in
Tamil. "Do you really want to go all the way to Bandra just for lunch?"

"Yes, wretch, now *you* also start," said Amma. "Come here—*arre*,
don't be afraid—come here, let me show you how fit I am."

As they had their fun, I pulled up my schedule, shuffled things
around, and carved out a couple of hours on Sunday. It did cut things
a bit fine. Amma was suspicious but I assured her I wasn't trying to

sabotage her bloody lunch. I really *was* drowning in work at Modern Textiles; the labor negotiations were at a delicate stage.

"As always, your mistress is more important than your family," said Amma, sighing.

Amma's voice, but I heard Padma's tone. Either way, the disrespect was the same. If I had been a doctor and not a banker, would Amma still compare my work to a whore? I had every right to be furious. Yes, every right.

I calmed down, reflected that Amma wasn't being disrespectful. On the contrary. She was reminding me to be the better man I could be. She was doing what good parents are supposed to do, namely, protect me.

"You're right, Amma. I'll make some changes. Balance is always good."

Unfortunately, I was as busy as ever when the weekend arrived, and with it Padma and Bittu, but I gladly set aside my work.

"You've become thin," observed Padma, almost angrily. Then she smiled and put Bittu in my arms.

I made a huge fuss of Bittu, making monster sounds and threatening to eat her alive with kisses. Squeals. Shrieks. Stories. O, Bittu was bursting with true stories. She had seen snow in Boston. She had seen buildings *this* big. We put our heads together and Bittu shared with me the millions of photographs she had clicked. Bittu had a boo-boo on her index finger which she displayed with great pride and broke into peals of laughter when I pretend-moaned: *doctor, doctor, Bittu, better butter boo-boo to make bitter boo-boo better*. It is easy to make children happy. Then I noticed Velli had tears in her eyes.

"What's wrong, Velli?" I asked, quite concerned.

She just shook her head. The idiot was very sentimental, practically a Hindi movie in a frock, and it was with some trepidation that I introduced her to Padma. They seemed to get along. Padma was gracious, quite the empathic high-caste lady, and Velli declared enthusiastically that Padma-madam was exactly how Velli had imagined she would be.

Eventually, with Padma guiding the car's autopilot, all of us, including Velli, set off from Sahyun. At first we kept the windows down but it was a windy day and the clear, cool air from Jihran's waters tugged and pulled at our clothes. Amma had taken the front seat, since Bittu wanted to sit in the back, between Velli and me. We would be gone for most of the day, and so Velli had asked us to drop her off at Dharavi so that she could visit her parents. We stopped at the busy intersection just after the old location of the MDMS sewage treatment plant and Velli got out.

"Velli, you'll return in the—" I began, in Tamil.

"Yes, elder brother, of course I'll be there in the evening, you can trust." Velli kissed her fingers, transplanted the kiss onto Amma's cheek, and then said in her broken English: "I see you in evening soon, okay, Ammachi? Bye bye."

The signal had changed and the car wanted to move. Velli somehow forgot to include Padma in her final set of goodbyes. She ran across the intersection.

"She's an innocent," said Amma. "The girl's heart is pure gold. Pure gold."

"Yes, she is adorable," said Padma, smiling.

"She was sad," observed Bittu. "Is it because she is black?"

Amma laughed but when we looked at her, she said: "What? If Velli were here, she would've been the first to laugh."

Maybe so. But two wrongs still didn't make a right. Amma was setting a bad example for Bittu. It was all very well to laugh and be happy but the Enhanced had a responsibility to be happy about the right things.

Padma explained to me that Bittu actually had been asking if Velli was sad because she wasn't Enhanced. In their US visit, Bittu had noticed that most African-Americans weren't Enhanced, and she'd concluded it was for the fair. Velli was dark, so . . .

I met Padma's glance in the rearview mirror and her wry smile said: Did you really think I'd taught her to be a racist?

"No, Bittu." I put an arm around my daughter. "Velli is just sad to leave us. But now she can look forward to seeing us again."

I too was looking forward, not backward. Reclining in the back seat, listening to the happy chatter of the women in front, savouring the reality of my daughter in the crook of my arm, meeting the glances of my wife—I was still unused to thinking of Padma as my ex-wife—I realized, almost in the manner of a last wave at the railway station, that this could be the last time we were all physically together.

When she'd left for Boston with Bittu, I had hoped the six months would be enough to flush Sollozzo out of her system. But life with him must have been exciting in more ways than one. The Turk had given her the literary life Padma had always craved, a craving it seemed no amount of rationalization on her part or mine could fix.

With Padma gone for so long, I'd had to look for a nurse for Amma. It quickly became clear that I could forget about Enhanced nurses since all such nurses were employed everywhere except in India. Fortunately, Rajan, a shop-floor supervisor at Modern Textiles, approached me saying his daughter Velli had a diploma in home care, he'd heard I was looking for a home-nurse, and he was looking for someone he could trust.

Trust enabled all relations. As a banker, I'd learned this lesson over and over. I was enveloped in a subtle happiness, a kind of sadness infused with a delicate mix of fragrances: the car's sunburnt leather, Amma's coconut-oil-loving white head, Padma's vétiver, Velli's jasmine, and Bittu's pulsing animal scent. The sensory mix wasn't something my Brain had composed. It must have arisen from the flower of the moment. I savoured the essence before it could melt under introspection, but melt it did, leaving in its place the residue of a happiness without reasons.

Somewhat dazed, I leaned forward between the front seats and asked the ladies what they were talking about.

"Amma was saying she wanted to come for my wedding in Boston," said Padma. "I want her there too. I'll make all the arrangements. My happiness would be complete if she were there."

"Then I will be there," announced Amma, "just book the plane ticket."

"Amma, you can barely navigate to the bathroom by yourself, let alone Boston."

"See, Padma, see? This is his attitude." Amma employed the old-beggar-woman voice she reserved for pathos. "Ever since you left, I've become the butt of his bad jokes." Then Amma surprised me by turning and patting my cheek. "But it's okay. He's just trying to cheer me up, poor fellow."

"That's one of the hazards of living with him," said Padma, smiling. "Amma, seriously, I'll book your ticket. If he wants, your son can also come and crack his bad jokes there."

"Yes, more the merrier," said Amma, good sport that she was. She then stoutly defended Padma's choice, pooh-poohing moral issues no one had raised about Turkish-Tamil children, and saying things like what mattered was a person's heart, not their origins, and that love multiplied under division, and wasn't it telling that he loved red rice and *avial*.

"I always thought Mammootty looks very Turkish," said Amma, her intransigent tone indicating that Sollozzo, whom she had yet to meet, could draw at will from the affection she'd deposited over a lifetime for her favourite south-Indian actor. That's how much she liked Turks, yes.

I liked him too. Sollozzo wasn't anything like the gangster namesake from the classic movie. For one thing, he had a thin pencil moustache. I could have grown a similar moustache, but I couldn't compete with his gaunt height or that ruined look of a cricket bat which had seen one too many innings. He came across as a decent fellow, very sharp, and his slow smile and thoughtful mien gave his words an extra weight.

He had brought me a gift. A signed copy of Pamuk's *The Museum Of Innocence*. It was strange to think this volume been touched by the great one, physically touched, and the thought sent an involuntary shiver down my spine. A lovely Unenhanced feeling. Two gifts in one. The volume was very expensive, no doubt. I touched the signature again, replaying its embedded message.

"My friend," said Orhan Pamuk in my head, from across the bridge of time, "I hope you get as much joy reading this story as I had writing it."

I played it again. I looked up and saw Padma and Sollozzo watching me. It was touching to think they'd worried about finding me the right gift.

"I will cherish it." I was totally sincere. "Thank you."

"Mention not," said Sollozzo, with that slow smile of his. "You owe me nothing. I *did* take your wife."

We all laughed. We chatted all through lunch. I ordered the lamb; the others opted to share a vat of biryani. As I watched Bittu putting her little fingers to her mouth, I realized with a start that I'd quite missed her. Sollozzo ate with the gusto of a man on death row. Padma shook her head and I stopped staring. My habit of introspection sometimes interfered with my happiness, but I felt it also gave my happiness a more poignant quality. It is one thing to be happy but to *know* that one is happy because a beloved is happy makes happiness all the more sweet. Else, how would we be any different from animals? My head buzzing with that sweet feeling, I desired to make a genuine connection. I turned to Sollozzo.

"Are you working on a new novel? Your fans must be getting very impatient."

"I haven't written anything new for a decade," said Sollozzo, with a smile. He stroked Padma's cheek. "She's worried."

"I'm not!" Padma did look very unworried. "I'm not just your wife. I'm also a reader. If I feel a writer is cutting corners, that's it, I close the book. You're a perfectionist; I love that. Remember how you tortured me over the translation?"

Sollozzo nodded fondly. "She's equally mad. She'll happily spend a week over a comma."

"How we fought over footnotes! He doesn't like footnotes. But how can a translator clarify without footnotes? Nothing doing, I said. I put my foot down."

I felt good watching them nuzzle. I admired their passion. I must

have been deficient in passion. Still, if I'd been deficient, why hadn't
Padma told me? Marriages needed work. The American labour theory
of love. That worked for me; I liked work. Work, work. If she'd wanted
me to work at our relationship, I would have. Then, just so, I lost interest in the subject.

"I don't read much fiction anymore," I confessed. "I used to be a
huge reader. Then I got Enhanced in my twenties. There was the adjustment phase and then somehow I lost touch, what with career and
all. Same story with my friends. They mostly read what their children
read. But even kids, it's not much. Makes me wonder. Maybe we are
outgrowing the need for fiction. I mean, children outgrow their imaginary friends. Do you think we posthumans are outgrowing the need
for fiction?"

I waited for Sollozzo to respond. But he'd filled his mouth with
biryani and was masticating with the placid dedication of a temple
cow. Padma filled the silence with happy chatter. Sollozzo was working on a collection of his short stories. He was doing this, he was doing
that. I sensed reproach in her cheer, which was, of course, ridiculous.
Then she changed the topic: "Are you, are you, are you, finally done
with Modern Textiles?"

"I am, I am, I am not," I replied, and we both laughed. "The usual
usual, Padma. I'm trying to make the workers see that control is possible without ownership. Tough, though. The Enhanced ones are easy;
they get it immediately. But the ones who aren't, especially the Marxist
types. Sheesh."

"Sounds super-challenging!"

On the contrary. Her interested expression said: Super-tedious. I
hadn't intended to elaborate. As a merchant banker, I'd learned early
on that most artists, especially the writer types, were put off by money
talk.

It didn't bother me. I just found it odd. Why weren't they interested in capital, which had the power to transform the world more
than any other force? But I was willing to bet Sollozzo's novel wouldn't
spend a comma, let alone a footnote, on business. Even Padma, for all

the time she spent with me, had never accepted that the strong poets she so admired were poets of action, not verbiage.

"I hate the word *posthuman*," exclaimed Sollozzo, startling us. "It's an excuse to claim we're innocent of humanity's sins. It's a rejection of history. Are you so eager to return to Zion? If so, you are lost, my brother."

Silence.

"I know the way to Sion," I said finally, and when Padma burst out laughing, I explained to the puzzled Sollozzo that Sahyun, where I lived with my mother, had originally been called Sion and that it had been a cosmopolitan North-Indian intersection between two South-Indian enclaves, Chembur and King's Circle. Then Sahyun had become a Muslim enclave. Now it was simply a wealthy enclave.

"Sahyun! That's Zion in Arabic. You are living in Zion!"

"Exactly. I even have one of the rivers of Paradise not too far from my house. Imagine. And Padma still left."

"There's no keeping women in Zion." Sollozzo gifted me one of his slow smiles.

"Of course," said Padma, smiling. "The river Jihran is recent. There wasn't any river anywhere near Sion. The place was a traffic nightmare. Everything's changed in the last sixty years. Completely, utterly changed."

"On the contrary—" I began, leaning forward to help myself to a second helping of lamb.

"My dear children," interrupted my mother, in Tamil, "I understand you don't want to, but you mustn't postpone it any longer. You have to tell Bittu."

"Yes, Bittu. Break her heart, then mend it." Sollozzo didn't understand Tamil very well, not yet, but he had recognized the key word: Bittu. This meeting was really about Bittu.

First, the preliminaries. I took the divorce papers from Padma, signed wherever I was required to sign; a quaint anachronism in this day and age, but necessary nonetheless. With that single stroke of my pen, I gave up the right to call Padma my wife. My ex-wife's glance met

mine, a tender exchange of unsaid benedictions and I felt a profound
sadness roil inside me. Then it was accompanied with a white-hot anger that I wasn't alone in my misery. The damn Brain was watching,
protecting. But there is no protection against loss. Padma— Oh god,
oh god, oh god. Then, just so, I relaxed.

"There's a park outside," said Padma, also smiling. "We'll tell Bittu
there."

It began well. Bittu, bless her heart, wasn't exactly the brightest
crayon in the box. It took her a long time to understand that her parents were divorcing. For good. She was going to live in Boston. Yes, she
would lose all her friends. Yes, the uncle with the moustache was now
her stepfather. No, I wasn't coming along. Yes, I would visit. Et cetera,
et cetera. Then she asked all the same questions once more. Wobbling
chin, high-pitched voice, but overall quite calm. We felt things were
going well. Padma and I beamed at each other, Sollozzo nodded ap-
provingly.

Amma was far smarter. She knew her grandchild, remembered
better than us what it had been like not to be fully Enhanced.

So when Bittu ran screaming towards the fence separating the park
from the highway, Amma, my eighty-two-year-old mother, somehow
sprinted after her and grabbed Bittu before she could hit the road. We
caught up, smiling with panic. Hugs, more explanations. Bittu calmed.
Then when we released her, she once again made a dash for it. This
is just what we have pieced together after some debate, Padma, Sollozzo, and I. None of us remember too much of what happened. But
it must have been very stressful, because my Brain mercifully decided
to bury it. I remember flashes of a nose bleed, a frantic trip to the hospital, Bittu's hysterical screams, Padma in Sollozzo's arms. I remember Bittu's Brain taking over, conferring with our Brains, and shutting
down her reticular center. Bittu went to sleep.

"Please do not worry." Bittu's Brain broadcast directly to our heads.
It had an airline-stewardess voice, and it spoke first in English, then
in Hindi. "She can be easily awakened at the nearest Brain-equipped
facility."

I remember the doctor who handled Bittu's case. She was very reassuring. I remember everything after the doctor took over. She was that reassuring.

"Bittu was Enhanced just last year, am I correct?" said the doctor.

She was. She wanted to know the specifics of the unit. Did Bittu's Brain regulate appetite? How quickly would it forget things? What was our policy on impulse control? That was especially important. How did her Brain handle uncertainty? Was it risk-averse or risk-neutral? Superfluous questions, of course. The information was all there in the medical report. I listened, nodding every now and then, a quiet happiness growing in me as Padma answered every question, and thus answering what the doctor really needed to know: Are you caring parents? Do you know what you have done to your child with this technology?

The doctor asked if we had encouraged Bittu to give her Brain a name. Did we know that Bittu referred to it as a "boo-boo"? Newly fitted children often gave names to their Brains. Padma nodded, smiling, but I could tell she was worried. Boo-boo?

We got the It-Takes-Time-to-Adjust speech. Bittu was very young, the Brain still wasn't an integral part of her. Her naming it was one symptom. Her Brain found it especially difficult to handle Bittu's complex emotions. And Bittu found it difficult to deal with this *thing* in her head. We should have been more careful. It especially hadn't been a good idea to mask the trial separation as a happy vacation in Boston. We hung our heads.

Relax, smiled the doctor. These things happen. It's especially hard to remember just how chaotic their little minds are at this age. It's not like raising children in the old days. Don't worry. In a few weeks, Bittu wouldn't even remember she'd had all these worries or anxieties. She would continue to have genuine concerns, yes, but fear, self-pity, and other negative emotions wouldn't complicate things. Those untainted concerns could be easily handled with love, kindness, patience, and understanding. The doctor's finger drew a cross with those four words.

"Yes, Doctor!" said Padma, with the enthusiasm all mothers seem to have for a good medical lecture.

We all felt much better. Our appreciation would inform our Brains to rate this particular interaction highly on the appropriate feedback boards.

Outside, once Bittu had been placed—fast asleep, poor thing—into Sollozzo's rental car, the time came to make our farewells. I embraced Padma and she swore various things. She would keep in touch. I was to do this and that. Bittu. Bittu. We smiled at each other. However, Amma was a mess, Enhancement or no Enhancement.

"Was it to see this day, I lived so long?" she asked piteously in Tamil, forgetting herself for a second, but then recovered when Padma and I laughed at her wobbly voice.

"That lady doctor liked the word 'especially,' didn't she?' said Sollozzo, absentmindedly shaking and squeezing my hand. "I had a character like that. He liked to say: On the contrary. Even when there was nothing to be contrary about." He encased our handshake with his other hand. "Friend, my answer to your question was stupid. Totally stupid. I failed. I've often thought about the same question. I will fail better. We must talk."

What question? The relevance of fiction? Who cared! I didn't care. I had no space for thought. So. This was it. Padma was leaving. Bittu was leaving. My wife and daughter were gone forever. I felt something click in my head and I went all woozy. The music in my head made it impossible to think. I was so happy I had to leave immediately or I would have exploded with joy.

Amma and I had a good journey back to our apartment. We hooked our Brains, sang along with old Tamil songs, discussed some of the entertaining ways in which our older relatives had died. She didn't fall asleep and leave me to my devices. My mother, worn out from life, protecting me from myself, even now.

That evening, Velli made a great deal of fuss over Amma, chattering about the day she'd had, cracking silly jokes, and discussing her never-ending domestic soap opera. Amma sat silently through it all, smiling, nodding, blinking.

"Thank you for caring," I told Velli, after she had put Amma to bed. "You look tired. Would you like a few days off next week?"

"I'm not going anywhere," she burst out in her village Tamil. She grabbed my hand, crushed it against her large breasts. "You're an inspiration to me. All of you! How sensibly you people handle life's problems. Not like us. When my uncle's wife ran away, you should have seen the fireworks, whereas you all— Please don't take this the wrong way, elder brother, but sometimes at night when I can't sleep because of worries, I think of your smiling face and then I am at peace. How I wish I too could be free of emotions!"

It is not every day one is anointed the Buddha, and I tried to look suitably enlightened. But she had the usual misconception about mediation. Free of emotions! That was like thinking classical musicians were free of music because they'd moved beyond grunts and shrieks. We, the Enhanced, weren't free of emotions. On the contrary. We had healthy psychological immune systems, that was all.

I could understand Velli's confusion, but Sollozzo left me baffled. We chatted aperiodically, but often. Padma told me his scribbling was going better than ever, but his midmornings must have been fallow because that's when he usually called. I welcomed his pings; his mornings were my evenings, and in the evenings I didn't want to think about ESOPs, equities, or factory workers.

It was quite cosy. Velli cutting vegetables for dinner, Amma alternating between bossing her and playing sudoku, and Sollozzo and I arguing about something or the other. Indeed, the topic didn't matter as long we could argue over it. We argued about the evils of capitalism, the rise of Ghana, the least imperfect way to cook biryani, the perfect way to educate children, and whether bellies were a must for belly dancers. Our most ferocious arguments were often about topics on which we completely concurred.

For example, fiction. I knew he knew that fiction was best suited for the Unenhanced. But would he admit it? Never. He'd kept his promise, offering me one reason after another why fiction, and by extension writers, were still relevant in this day and age. It amused me that Sollozzo needed reasons. As a storyteller he should've been immune to reasons.

When I told him that, he countered with a challenge. He offered
two sentences. The first: *Eurydice died, and Orpheus died of a heart*
attack. The second: *Eurydice died, and Orpheus died of grief.*

"Which of these two is more satisfying?" asked Sollozzo. "Which
of these feels more meaningful? Now tell me you prefer causes over
reasons."

"It's not important what I prefer. If Orpheus had been Enhanced,
he could've still died of a heart attack. But he wouldn't have died of
grief. In time, no one will die of heart attacks either."

Another time he tried the old argument that literature taught us
to have empathy. This bit of early-21st century nonsense had been dis-
credited even in those simple-minded times. For one thing, it could
just as easily be argued that empathy had made literature possible.

In any case, why had empathy even been necessary for humans?
Because people had been like books in a foreign language; the books
had meaning, but an inaccessible meaning. Fortunately, science had
stepped in, fixed that problem. There was no need to be constantly on
edge about other people's feelings. One knew how they felt. They felt
happy, content, motivated, and relaxed. There was no more need to
walk around in other people's shoes than there was any need to inspect
their armpits for signs of the bubonic plague.

"Exactly my point!" shouted Sollozzo. He calmed down, of course.
"Exactly my point. Enhancement is straightening our crooked timber.
If this continues, we'll all become moral robots. I asked you once, are
you so eager to return to Zion?"

"What is it with you and Zion?"

"Zion. Eden. Swarg. Sahyun. Paradise. Call it what you will. The
Book of Genesis, my brother. We were robots once. Why do you think
we got kicked out of Zion? We lost our innocence when Adam and
Eve broke God's trust, ate from the tree, and brought Fiction into the
world. We turned human. Now we have found a way to control the tree
in our heads, become robots again, and regain the innocence that is
the price of entry into Zion. Do you not see the connection between
this and your disdain for Fiction?"

I did not. But I had begun to see just how radically his European imagination differed from mine. He argued with me, but his struggles really were with dead white Europeans. Socrates, Plato, and Aristotle; Goethe, Baumgarten, and Karl Moritz; Hugo von Hofmanstahl, Mach, and Wittgenstein: I could only marvel at his erudition. I couldn't comment on his philosophers or their fictions, but I was a banker and could make any collateral look inadequate.

In this case, it was obvious. His entire argument rested on the necessity of novels. But every novel argues against its own necessity. The world of any novel, no matter how realistic, differs from the actual world in that the novel's world can't contain one specific book: the novel itself. For example, the world of Pamuk's *The Museum of Innocence* didn't contain a copy of *The Museum of Innocence*. If Pamuk's fictional world was managing just fine without a copy of his novel, wasn't the author—any author—revealing that the actual world didn't need the novel either? Et cetera, et cetera.

"I have found my Barbicane," said Sollozzo, after a long pause. "I need your scepticism about fiction. Fire away. It will help me construct a plate armour so thick not even your densest doubts can penetrate."

All this, I later learned, was a reference to the legendary dispute in Verne's *From the Earth to the Moon* between shot manufacturer Impey Barbicane and armor-plate manufacturer Captain Nicholl. Barbicane invented more and more powerful cannons, and Nicholl invented more and more impenetrable armor plating. At least I was getting an education.

If his hypocrisy could have infuriated me, it would have. As long as his tribe had mediated for the reader, it had been about freedom, empathy, blah di blah blah. Sollozzo hadn't worried about mediating for the reader when he'd written stories in English about Turkey. Stories in English by a non-Englishman about a non-English world! Jane Austen[1] might as well have written in Sanskrit about England.

It didn't matter, not really, this game of ours. Men, even among the Enhanced, find it complicated to say how fond they are of one an-

---

[1] An English author celebrated for her charming upper-class romances.

other. Sollozzo made Padma happy. I was glad to see my Padma happy. Yes, she was no longer mine. She'd never been mine, for the Enhanced belong to no one, perhaps not even to themselves. I was glad to see her happy and I believed Sollozzo, not her Brain, was the one responsible. Bittu was also adjusting well to life in Boston. Or perhaps it was that Bittu had adjusted to her Boo-boo. Same thing, no difference. Padma said that Bittu had stopped referring to her Brain entirely.

Padma was amused by my chitchats with Sollozzo. "I am super-jealous! Are you two planning to run away together?"

"Yes, yes, married today, divorced tomorrow," shouted Amma, who had been eavesdropping on our conversation. "What kind of world is this! No God, no morals. Do you care what the effect of your immoral behaviour on Bittu? Do you want her to become a dope addict? She needs to know who is going to be there when she gets back from school. She needs to have a mother and father. She needs a stable home. No technology can give her that. But go on, do what you like. Who am I to interfere? Nobody. Just a useless old woman who'll die soon. I can't wait. Every night I close my eyes and pray that I won't wake up in the morning. Who wants to live like this? Only pets. No, not even pets." She smiled, shifted gears. "Don't mind me, dear. I know you have the best interests of Bittu at heart. Which mother doesn't? Is it snowing in America?"

It's all good, as the Americans are rumoured to say. As I ruffled the pages of Sollozzo's volume, *The Robots of Eden and Other Stories*, I wondered what Velli had made of the arguments I'd had with Sollozzo. I remember her listening, mouth open, trying to follow just what it was that got him so excited. She'd found Sollozzo highly entertaining. She used to call him "Professor-uncle" with that innate respect for (a) white people, (b) Enhanced people, and (c) people who spoke English very fluently. Sometimes she would imitate his dramatic hand gestures and his accented English.

In retrospect, I should have anticipated that Sollozzo's suicide would impact Velli the most. How could it not? The Unenhanced have little protection against life's blows on their psyches. I had called Velli into my office, tried to break the news to her as gently as I could.

"Your professor-uncle, he killed himself. Don't feel too bad. Amma is not to know, so you have to be strong. Okay, Velli?"

I had already counselled Padma on the legal formalities, chatted with Bittu, made her laugh, and everything went as smoothly as butter.

Padma and I decided we'd tell Amma the next day, if at all. Amma got tired very easily these days. Why add to her burdens?

"I have to handle his literary estate," said Padma, smiling, her eyes ablaze with light. "There's so much to do. So for now we'll all stay put in Boston. Will you be all right? You'll miss your conversations."

Would I? I supposed I could miss him. I didn't see the point, however. I was all right. Hadn't I handled worse? What had made her ask? Was I weeping? Rending my garments? Gnashing my teeth? Then, just so, the irritation slipped from my consciousness like rage-coloured leaves scattering in the autumn wind. It was kind of her to be concerned.

"Why did professor-uncle kill himself?" asked Velli, already weeping.

"He took something that made his heart stop," I explained.

"But why!"

Why what? Why did the why of anything matter? Sollozzo had swallowed pills to stop his heart, he'd walked into the path of a truck, he'd drowned, he'd thrown himself into the sun, he'd dissolved into the mist. He was dead. How had his Brain let it happen? I made a mental note to talk to my lawyer. The AI would have a good idea whether a lawsuit was worth the effort. Unless Sollozzo's short-story collection contained an encoded message (and I wouldn't put that past him), he hadn't left any last words.

"Aiyyo, why didn't he ask for help?" moaned Velli.

I glanced at her. She was obviously determined to be upset. Her quivering face did something to my own internals. I struggled to contain my smile, but it grew into a swell, a wave, and then a giant tsunami of a laugh exploded out of me, followed by another, and then another. I howled. I cackled. I drummed the floor with my feet. I laughed even after there was no reason to. Then, just so, I relaxed.

"I'm sorry," I said. "I wasn't laughing at you. In fact, you could say I wasn't the one laughing at all."

Velli looked at me, then looked away, her mouth working. Poor thing, it must all be so very confusing for her. I could empathize.

"Velli, why don't you go down to the river? The walk will do you good and you can make an offering at the temple in professor-uncle's name. You'll feel better."

I had felt it was sensible advice, and when she stepped out, I'd felt rather pleased with myself. But Velli never returned from the walk. I got a brief note later that night. She'd quit. No explanation, just like that. Her father, Rajan, came by to pick up her stuff, but he was vague, and worse, unapologetic. All rather inconvenient.

All's well that ends well. Padma and Bittu were happy in Boston. Perhaps they would soon return. I didn't want Bittu to forget me. Sollozzo's volume would get the praise hard work always deserved, irrespective of whether such work pursued utility or futility.

"You'll spoil the book if you keep ruffling the pages like that," said Amma.

I returned the volume to Amma. Such enthusiasm for books. For reading. For stories. Dear Amma. She was almost ninety years old, but what enthusiasm! Good, good. I was glad she still had a zest for life. Other people her age, they were already dead. They breathed, they ate, they moved about, but they were basically vegetables with legs. Technology could enhance life, but it couldn't induce a will to live. She was a true inspiration. I could only hope I would have one-tenth the same enthusiasm when I was her age. I started to compliment Amma on this and other points, then realized she was already lost in the story. So I tiptoed away, disinclined to come between my beloved reader and the text.

NOW WAIT FOR THIS WEEK

ALICE SOLA KIM

Alice Sola Kim's (alicesolakim.com) writing has appeared in publications such as *The Cut, Tin House, McSweeney's, Lightspeed,* and *The Best American Science Fiction and Fantasy 2017.* She has received grants and fellowships from the Elizabeth George Foundation, the MacDowell Colony, and Bread Loaf Writers' Conference, and is a winner of the 2016 Whiting Award.

We spent the last two hours of Bonnie's birthday drinks talking about shitty men and didn't think to apologize to Bonnie about it until after we got kicked out of the bar, long past closing time.

The bartender had tried to wait us out. Our group had become way too terrifying and annoying to approach. Our faces were red and our eyes were red and our auras or spirits or vibes or whatever were reddest of all. A dank, singed red that dimmed to black.

Although the bartender was extremely built, he wore his bounty of muscle like an old woman carrying too many grocery bags. He sighed and leaned against the bar and we ignored him.

Phyllida had been sketching on a napkin with meticulous and confident strokes. She seemed exactly like a real artist as long as you didn't look at what she was drawing. "It needs a really long handle," she said. "For leverage." On the napkin was Phyllida herself, as a stick figure with scribbled hair like black hay, standing on a beach and holding an enormous fork. At the end of each fork tine, she added eight stick figures who were being shoved helplessly into the surf.

"Ta-da!" She pushed the napkin in front of us. "The drowning fork! For all your drowning-more-than-one-man-at-a-time needs. Eight men maximum. You don't have to use all the tines. But it's such a waste if you don't."

"Motherfucker, I'll take *fifty*," Devon said, slapping her wallet down onto the table.

We cackled, some of us actively trying to screech like evil witches because it was funnier, and the longer we cackled the more we just felt it was the exact right way to laugh—not laughing because everything was so joyous and unblemished but simply because you were all bitches in hell together, so why not laugh, why not understand that everything contains at least one tiny nugget of its opposite, why not find a socially acceptable way to shriek with rage in public?

After the bartender finally kicked us out, we lumped together on the sidewalk, awkward again. The spell was dead and our faces were

melted candles. In our bodies the joy-poison had evaporated but the
poison-poison had leached into our marrow. Most of us had work or
class tomorrow, and worst of all, tomorrow was more than technically
today.

Bonnie was the only one who looked alert. The birthday girl, she
of the scary freezing blue wolf eyes. In everything else she conceded to
softness and prettiness but her eyelashes she painted black and jagged.
Each individual lash each day—that was how you achieved the look.
She took so freaking long in the bathroom, where the light was best.

"Sorry, Bonnie," I said.

"It was pretty downer there at the end," said Nina. "Sorry, I feel
like it was my fault."

"No, yeah, sorry I got so intense!" we somehow all managed to say
as one.

"Shit, my wallet," said Devon, and went back into the bar.

Meanwhile nobody said, *Haha, dang, isn't it bad enough that rape
and assault and abuse and harassment and boyfriends doing the emotional psychosexual whatever equivalent of sticking their beefy hand into
your brain and wearing it like a baseball mitt or a puppet so they can
just really move it around and infinity et cetera happens to so, so, so,
so, so, so, so, so, so many of us, and we can't even talk about it without
having to apologize afterward?*

Not that I had said much tonight! But of course I'd apologized too.
Because even though Bonnie smiled and said she didn't mind that her
birthday drinks had been taken over by dark tales and infernal anti-
man machines and despairing laughter, *we knew she did*. She liked it
when things and people were happy, and when they weren't it was as
if they were being unhappy at her. *To her*. She was plenty sympathetic
to a point, and past that she'd start to bristle and talk about wallowing
and pessimism and—

"—you get back what you put in," Bonnie said. "Just between you
and me. I wouldn't say this to the rest of the group, and of course I
respect what they've been through, but there's also such a thing as
deciding to stop being a victim. Yes, remembering and talking about

all the wrongs, that's important for . . . healing, or some such. But you can't stay on that same old subject and expect to be able to get anything new out of it."

We were walking back to the apartment together. I decided to not respond. Facing the prospect of arguing with Bonnie was like, you were starving and in front of you was a long, long table full of cakes. But if you ate even one bite, then you'd have to eat all of the cakes, the whole goddamn table of them.

That was just how Bonnie was. She would not ever change. She was always how you expected her to be, which wasn't really something we'd take as a compliment for ourselves, but it could be pleasant to know someone else like that.

Besides, she could be a great friend in the classical sense. Back when I'd been going through a hard time, she had invited me to be her roommate in her giant apartment, even though she had no need of a roommate, and only charged me a tiny bit of rent. In return for her generosity, I did not discuss this hard time with her in any amount of detail.

The street was busy, lots of bars, lots of people out, so in some ways you were more generally unsafe but the unsafety was thinned and spread out. The block was like a Halloween parade where everyone wore their costumes on the inside—slavering B.O. werewolves, droopy amnesiac ghosts, vampires coldly intent on doing it.

The next morning, we woke up depleted and dried out and dire. Those of us who were close friends texted each other, *Was I okay???* and unfailingly responded, *You were great!!!* (Which was a double lie: No one had been okay. And, no one had been in any state to accurately judge.)

As for what we had talked about at the end of Bonnie's birthday drinks, we psychically decided to never bring it up with each other again and to forget that we ever knew about:

—the time a man, a doctor at the college campus clinic, was feeling our heartbeat and/but cupped our boob and lifted it once, subtle and unmistakable—

—the time a man had followed us onto a subway car to expound on our beauty, and ignoring his request for our phone number caused his perspective to immediately flip as if by evil magic, and he darted from slimy kindness to incendiary outrage, shouting directly in our face like it was the next best thing to hitting us but who knew, any moment he could start doing the best thing, and meanwhile everyone on the subway car made like they were in fucking Derry, Maine, and looked straight ahead—

—the time a man secretly removed his condom during sex—

—the times we didn't want to but we did—

—the times we didn't want it that way but we did it that way—

—the times we wanted only some of it but we did all of it

—and so on.

THE TIME BONNIE WAS DREAMING

There we were at the bar. Too many people who didn't all know each other as well as they should crowding a corner table. We looked like a bunch of different species of birds eating something off the sidewalk together. Big birds, little birds, beauties and sadsacks, pecking away at invisible crumbs without touching or fighting or acknowledging their shared plane of existence like their eyes couldn't even see each other— only the food.

In this situation, Bonnie was the food. Bonnie was having birthday drinks and she had gathered us here to sheepishly celebrate, since she'd reached the age where if you called yourself old, some people wouldn't correct you and some people would get mildly offended.

Bonnie was late, as usual. She was chronically late and never apologized for it, maybe because she always looked super awesome, and truly she did, so she imagined that that was a fair exchange for the lateness, even for us.

While we waited, a few of us started discussing the list. Some time ago, a list had been released online of not-famous men who had done bad things to women, mostly of a sexual nature. Some men at the table started shifting in their seats, as if fidgeting done just right could teleport you to a distant land in which you felt not so implicated. Or they sat there like Easter Island heads, with equally as much to say about shitty men.

The door crashed open and Bonnie ran through the bar, stopping short at our table. Her makeup had sweated off into patchy plum and black smears under her eyes. Her hair was stringy and stuck to her cheeks. She did not look super awesome, but sometimes we looked like that and it wasn't such a big deal so we weren't going to make it one. Perhaps we could ask about it later, once we were all safely drunk.

"Happy birthday!" we said.

"Is today your real birthday?" someone said, as they stood to hug her. Bonnie accepted the hug but gave nothing in return, her arms wilted by her sides. She didn't answer at first. She was busy peering around at all the wrong things, the ceiling and the bartender and the drinks on the table and our feet, like this was one of those kid puzzles where you had to spot the differences between two similar pictures. Her gaze was weird, fractured. She wouldn't look at us.

"Bonnie?"

"My birthday," she said too loud. "Yeah. My birthday. First of the month. Rabbit, rabbit."

"I think you're supposed to say 'Rabbit, rabbit' first thing in the morning, like the second you wake up," said Nina. "Otherwise you don't get the good luck."

Scott said, "Jesus, is it already next month?"

"I know, right?" someone said.

"I didn't mean that it was next month. I meant today is the start of a new month. Which is this month."

"Yes. I got that."

Bonnie listened along, as we all were whether or not we wanted to be since the bar was so quiet you couldn't even grant the mercy of pretending not to hear. Then she lifted her palm. "HOLD THE MOTHERFUCK ON," she roared. "Stop messing with me. Stop lying. I've been saying it all day; this shit is not funny. My birthday was last

week *and we all know it.* You guys even did that conversation again. Like
I could ever forget such a stupid-ass dumb-ass fucking conversation!"

"Whoa, calm down—" Scott said, valiantly trying to sound more worried about Bonnie than he was offended. He stuck his arm out to put around her and she shoved it away, tilting off balance. She propped herself against the brick wall of the bar and surveyed us from a cold and judgmental distance. "I do not appreciate it, and I do not see the point of it," she said, voice wobbling. "This *prank.* You got my parents in on it, and you did something to my phone and laptop, you made it so that—" Bonnie broke off. She shook her head like it jangled and ripped something out of her purse and threw it at nobody in particular (it hit Scott on the thigh) and ran out of the bar. Scott silently showed us what she'd thrown. Today's newspaper.

Some of us left. Some stayed, got more drinks, marinated in concern and theorized luxuriously. Shit got near convivial. I wasn't Bonnie's closest friend, but I was her roommate friend—her roommate-mate—so I was the one who went out after her. Even though I had no idea where she'd gone. Bonnie was not so much a woman of routine.

I decided to go home. With great relief and a tiny amount of surprise, I unlocked our door and found a trail of ankle boots, jacket, purse, phone, keys, dress leading straight to Bonnie's bedroom. Of course. I could picture it exactly—Bonnie on her birthday, treating herself to a pregame that got so out of hand it became neither pre- nor game, then showing up to her actual celebration surreally out of her head. Sure.

When I knocked, Bonnie responded immediately. "This is all a dream," she said in a shouty voice. She sounded like she was in a play, an amateur one with fake British accents. "Do not come in."

"Are you okay? We were worried."

I heard her bed creak, and tried again. "Do you want your phone? It's out here."

"*Fuck my phone,*" Bonnie yelled. "It's fake and so are you and so is everything. Quit talking to me! I need to concentrate on waking up."

I left her to it. I gathered up her things and piled them outside her door and I texted some people that Bonnie was fine and sleeping something off and I dicked around on my phone and saw that a famous man—one who had spoken out passionately against the sexual depredations of other famous men during the most recent outcry (for the sexual depredations of these other famous men had first come to light in the 1970s and '80s, unfortunate timing if you wanted a critical mass of people to actually care)—was discovered to have been really, *really* not one to talk and I brushed my teeth and decided I deserved not to floss and then it was like half the blood and adrenaline and energy in my body swirled down into a drain somewhere with a loud abrupt gurgle and I oozed my way to bed.

The next morning Bonnie was gone, room tornadoed and big suitcase missing. A few days passed with no word from her so I pondered calling her parents. I had no kind of relationship with them, but I could probably get their info from billing statements. I didn't do it. Bonnie loved her parents and wouldn't want to worry them and Bonnie hated her parents and didn't want to rely on them any more than she already was, which was basically 100 percent, and due to both of the aforementioned she loathed showing any kind of weakness in front of them.

A few days after that I got a text from Bonnie admonishing me specifically to *not* call her parents, and I responded and told her that I hadn't but I almost had and if I had I would have done it days and days ago and where the hell was she? No response. Well, if that was how she wanted to play it. Meanwhile, I could have the place to myself. Fine.

THE TIME WE TALKED SHIT

"Still no word?"

Just a few of us left at the bar, dejected and alone together like we'd been stood up but in a polyamorous way.

"Do we think she forgot?"

"Her own birthday?"

"Or found something better to do. Not to talk shit but . . . Bonnie can be like that."

"I have sympathy for the congenitally rich. You know how basically everything worth doing just sucks initially? Well, maybe if you never get training in dealing with bullshit, you risk becoming the kind of person who just bounces from thing to thing to thing and sooner or later everything seems boring and totally without reward or meaning. And then comes the ennui."

"I have sympathy for *myself*."

"Ennui isn't Bonnie's problem."

"Right, she would actually be very happy if everything was only nice pleasant surfaces."

"*Yes*," we all said. And then we were off to the races.

"She's so pissed off when everything isn't happy and nice! Infuriated, even. Which is kind of at odds with being someone who loves happy and nice stuff, you know?"

"It's not . . . *not* tyrannical. But she's not one of those tyrants who, like, loves suffering and pain. She does truly love it when people are happy. Especially her friends."

"That's not the same thing as helping someone be happy."

"What it comes down to is she was born a certain way—you know, a white, rich, cute way—and acts like she had anything to do with it. It's a sickness."

While the others were talking, Phyllida quietly asked me how I'd been. She was the only one there who knew even a little about the situation I'd had at my last job. The man I had met there, who in fact still worked there. His name had shown up on an online list of unfamous bad men, and nothing had happened to him, the same nothing that happened to so many other men. This was a nothing that could sometimes be filled with gaseous excitement and horror and alarm and puffy thought bubbles containing phrases like "Somebody should do something!" all of which never became solid and eventually leaked out, leaving nothing behind and resulting in nothing.

Phyllida looked into my eyes and picked up the cutlery on the table. "I would stick him with this fork." Oh, she was so nice. Why weren't we closer?

Wait, it was because of the time I went to Devon's birthday party and saw Phyllida talking and laughing gaily with the man, even though I knew she knew. Maybe they had only interacted for a few seconds, maybe Phyllida needed a professional favor. Maybe, caught off guard, she'd been accidentally polite to him. It happened. But this incident sure did make me not want to tell anyone else about it, because if I saw them being friendly with him later I would have to slink off like a dog giving birth under a house and tend my grievous wounds alone. I knew that now. And sure, yes, of course: Even without telling someone the story there was a chance I'd see them being friendly with that man, which would still hurt, but not nearly as much. This way, at least I wouldn't be certain that they had chosen rapists and politeness over me.

I knew I was asking too much, but I didn't want to ask too little. What was the correct amount, allowing for how much people fail? We fail so hard. All of us do.

Smiling past Phyllida, I watched Nina draw on a napkin. I called out to her and she looked up. "What's the latest on your ghost problem?" I asked. The details were harrowing, sad, disgusting—but she was always ready to talk about it. We were the only ones who believed her. We had all been at that Halloween party.

Derrick interrupted us. He lifted his phone like a pack of gum in a gum commercial. (Put it away, Derrick, nobody can read a word from here anyway.) Apparently Bonnie had gotten back to him. She said she was fine and that everybody should leave her alone.

"Is she okay?"

"That's all she said? What a bitch!"

After that, we all went home, full of a guilty, binge-eaten feeling of having talked that much shit about our friend, at her actual birthday celebration no less.

Nearly a whole week passed, and still no Bonnie. I was eating granola standing up, wearing only an old and obscenely baggy thong, when I heard a key in the door and I sped over to an armchair with a crumpled coat of Bonnie's on it and only had time to tuck the coat under my armpits but I was still excited to see Bonnie at the door and say,

Dude, where have you been and *I'm only wearing your coat like a tiny assless sandwich board because you caught me in my worst underwear* until the door opened and it wasn't Bonnie—it was two well-dressed sixtysomething people who had already been having a bad day and here I was to worsen it.

Luckily, because I was mostly naked, they first thought I was Bonnie's secret girlfriend, so when they learned that I was, rather, Bonnie's secret *roommate* of whom they had never heard, they were so relieved and distracted that I found a brief opening in which to lie my face off.

Sometimes people with money didn't want to give it to people who needed it extremely badly, like how they didn't want to offer sympathy or belief to those who had been victimized, as the act of needing was inherently thirsty, plus there was the way situations that caused you to become needy sometimes could render you disgusting and un-whole so the idea of joining forces with you was just, *blaaaaarrrrb*, and of course joining forces was what happened when money, sympathy, and belief changed hands.

So I hoiked up my posture a couple notches and pretended to be a novelist (zero evidence of visual art in this apartment so words it had to be), highly experimental (I didn't want it to be easy to find my books, since they would in fact be impossible to find since they didn't exist), with most of my work published in Chinese (which I wasn't but they wouldn't know the difference but also why had I even added this level of obfuscation?), in residence at a university nearby whose apartment roof had caved in over the, ah, living room. I had met Bonnie at—

"—at, at an event, a p-party after a salon. When I told her about how disruptive the noise from the workmen was, the dust and the disruption, she offered me a room in her place for the time being, and it has been such a godsend. I wouldn't have been able to—do my work, if it wasn't for Bonnie and her generosity."

Not bad, not bad! Cultural capital, the implication that I didn't need money, this apartment, or anything at all, a foreignness which was not real and therefore nonthreatening. (Oh, *that* was why I'd done that.)

The parents relaxed, smiled subtle WASP smiles, and let it go. Bonnie's mother had a smooth white bob and was fat and tall and graceful, clad in a whispering computer-gray silk blouse. Thready webs of chain and gem blinked against her neck, fingers, ears. Her bling felt oceanic, as in naturalistic yet unutterably vast. All that was dark and grotesque about her soul was contained in the bulky handbag dangling from her right elbow. Bright orange-brown this handbag was, crisscrossed with straps and black chains and waxy twine.

Bonnie's father wasn't nearly so interesting looking.

"Do you know where she has been?" I asked.

They told me that she showed up at their house yesterday, completely frazzled, telling a wild tale about a week that was repeating over and over again. Her mother said, "Bonnie told us she'd traveled to New Zealand to check if it was last week there too. Though she chose it randomly, she ended up really enjoying the place. Except for the fact that it was also still last week there."

"Which is to say this week," her father said.

They had tried to calm her down, even as she insisted she had lived this week many times, listing off news of sex scandals and murderous police and mass shootings as if she were bringing precious communiqués from the future and not just delivering the same old easy guesses absolutely anybody could make, so they fed her dinner and offered her benzos and put her to bed, thinking she would have to stay with them for a while—thinking facilities, thinking inpatient/outpatient, thinking medication, and so on—and when they checked on her in the morning she had fled.

As they searched Bonnie's bedroom and peeped very quickly and apologetically into mine, her mother said, "I am not unsympathetic, you know. How could she prove her story to us? It would be next to impossible. Should we tell her a secret so massive that merely through her repeating it back to us in the next iteration we would immediately believe that she was telling the truth, that she had indeed lived this week before?"

"And what if the week didn't repeat?" said Bonnie's father, scrolling through his phone. "We three would then be forced to march into the future together, bound by the hideous secrets Bonnie now knew. All for nothing."

I said, "I mean, why do they have to be massive and hideous secrets?"

"Still more horrible," continued Bonnie's mother, "would be if she were correct, and were somehow able to prove this to us, and keep proving this to us—that she, our daughter, Bonnie, has been doomed to live the same week over and over again. Pulling us helplessly along with her. Cursed to remember, blessed to forget, or the opposite, or both."

Her father said, "What monstrous knowledge to bear."

"We cannot and will not believe her," they said.

I brought them back to the door. They gave me a phone number to call in case I heard anything. They also told me I could stay in the apartment as long as I wanted. I opened my mouth to say thank you and Bonnie's father said, "Oh, yes, and since you'll be taking over rent while Bonnie is away—" and soon named a number so big it should have been written on a piece of paper and slid across a desk. But no. This number was said aloud.

I stood so tall my skull risked detaching from my spine, and smiled like a medalist. "Of course. Thank you." I was still wearing Bonnie's coat like it was a strapless minidress on a paper doll, though very much unlike a paper doll I had a back half to me too. Around people like Bonnie's parents, you were allowed to acknowledge when you weren't being perfect but you could never, ever be embarrassed. When I had shown them down the hall into our bedrooms, I walked backward stewardess-smooth.

Once they were a safe distance away, I slammed the door shut and slumped into the armchair. The rent on this place, which they already owned, would be impossible. I did not have anywhere else to go, of course. How about if I temporarily shrunk myself into a bean? It would be so nice to be a dried hard tiny thing, fallen down into the spoons and forks and forgotten for maybe one, two years. But as a tiny bean

I'd still have a future. I could still return to life or life*likeness*, once enough time passed and there wasn't so much bullshit to deal with. Maybe nine, ten years.

The fringe on the bottom of the couch moved. Bonnie poked her head out from underneath, dragging the rest of herself out. I was glad her head came out first and not her hand or foot so I didn't need to scream.

She hauled herself onto the couch and coughed. "You got resources, kid."

"So do you," I said, guiltily remembering the shit-talking from the bar.

"I have to get sensible," she said. "I should have known it was no good going to my parents like that. What a waste of time." She laughed. "If such a thing is possible. They wanted to make my entire last day so tiresome. I had to sneak out in the night. Came here and napped under the couch because it felt safer. I was right."

"Usually I don't lie like that."

She shrugged. "Lie all you want. Lie big. I can tell you it does not matter one bit."

This was the strangest conversation I'd ever had with Bonnie. "They just scared me. Your parents are a piece of work. Pieces of work? No. Them two together make one piece of work." The strangeness wasn't all on Bonnie. I was definitely tangoing with her.

"Don't worry," she said. "You won't have to pay the rent."

"You'll tell them you're here?"

"No. I mean it'll just be last Wednesday again soon." Then another shrug, one lagging so far behind her words that it split off into its own separate statement. Dust billowed and settled on Bonnie again and she looked like an ancient, badly damaged statue of someone youngish, like her basic composition was at odds with her present circumstances, and despite the smooth jaw and round cheek and slight scanty feathery decorative lines in her forehead and under her eyes you knew she had been around and around and around for eons and would be still and would be still and would be still, beyond all reckoning.

"Very soon," Bonnie said.

I stood. "I've got to get dressed," I said. I had become very frightened. "I'm super late. Rest up. Okay?"

As I sped down the hall, Bonnie's thin, sweet voice floated behind. She was singing a line from that song, the line that went, *"Let me see that"*—her voice going flannelly and nearly cracking—*"thawwww-awwwwwwww-awwwwwwwng . . ."* And a final desperate and strangled, *"Baaaaby!"*

A tossed-off and funny and completely regular thing, a tune in the genre of roommate giving you shit for being such a beast at home—but it did not make me feel better. I was still filled with a very bad form of terror, the kind where you didn't know what or why. So how would it end? Bonnie's singing had been the saddest, most yearningest music I had ever heard. You got the joke but the dirge, that was the point. That was what remained.

THE TIME BONNIE DIDN'T GO VIRAL

When Bonnie canceled her birthday drinks the morning of, we didn't think anything of it. The excuse was plausible. Also, no one really wanted to go out on a Wednesday anyway.

Turned out she was spending her time making a weird, baggy, rambling video of just her sitting in her room, looking super awesome, making predictions of the things to come in the present week. Like that the actor many of us loved would be revealed as a leering terrible date who expected sex as his due and took no for an answer only temporarily before starting up the sex stuff yet again until he took no for an answer only temporarily and so on until the woman gave up. Kind of like when your cat jumped back onto the counter so many times you stopped putting it back on the floor, except with having your boundaries totally ignored during sex. And no cat.

(This had probably happened to many of us—it definitely happened to me—but it was all pretty confusing stuff people didn't usually care about and to boot Bonnie wasn't describing it clearly at all, so nobody knew what the hell she was talking about in the video until the next day when the actor's name did actually appear in the news. But we just figured that she had just found out early somehow. She did know some celebrity-adjacent people.)

Certain sports teams would win certain games, she guessed correctly. That was a little impressive, if you cared. Wildfires. Firings in the White House. Something that the president would say in a few days, which sounded indistinguishable from everything else he had said before so it meant nothing to us and was like a cat jumping onto a counter so many times we stopped trying to stop it or even pay attention to it since we couldn't stop it. "Is Bonnie being politically humorous?" one of us said.

It was harder to go viral than you'd think. Or, rather, it was pretty easy if you did a kind of bare minimum, and Bonnie had not. Other than some of us texting each other with, "WHAT DID I JUST WATCH," the video did not catch on with the world at large. I tried to avoid Bonnie (easy, because I had work and she stayed in her room most of the time) because the stinging harsh glow of what was surely flourishing mental illness emanating from the video really freaked me the fuck out. Not that I was proud of that. I wasn't not proud either! I'd had to survive! Growing up, I had been left largely in the care of my schizophrenic aunt for seven years and I became decent at spotting crazy and crabwalking delicately away from it before it could touch me even as I lived in close proximity to it.

For all that nobody cared about Bonnie's video, it had apparently reached certain shadowy governmental agencies. One morning the doorbell rang while I was in the shower and Bonnie was in her room, and the agents couldn't even wait for five seconds before kicking in the door. My towel had somehow vanished from its hook so I grabbed a jacket of Bonnie's that had been stuffed and forgotten in the space between the door and the wall and wrapped it extremely partially around myself and ran out into the living room, where three men and one woman wearing suits were walking Bonnie out of the apartment.

"I'm going away for a while, and I won't be in touch. But I promise

I'll be back!" said Bonnie, dragging a suitcase. When did she have time to pack? "Bye!" She sounded cheerful. Then she and the agents left and I was alone with the busted door, a small puddle forming around me.

The rest of Bonnie's predictions ended up coming true. Nobody cared.

THE TIME BONNIE WAS QUIET

I turned the corner into the dining room and jumped. There was Bonnie at the table, shoulders so slumped she resembled a tombstone.

"It was awful," she said. She looked like she had been up for hours already. "They weren't the ones to help me. Not at all. I was so wrong about everything." She stared down into a full mug of coffee that I could tell had gone cold.

"Did something happen?"

She glanced up at me and made her face go calm. "No. I had a bad—dream. I had a bad dream in which I was interrogated a lot and then they were going to open up my skull and look at my brain and maybe fuck with it a little. Good thing I ran the clock out on that."

To hide my relief, I picked up her mug and reheated it in the microwave. "Good thing it was all a dream," I said.

Bonnie said, "I know you don't understand but I appreciate you listening. I just have to lay low this week. I have to be sensible. No one else is going to save me. No faith in family. No faith in institutions."

I had never known Bonnie to talk like this. So depressed and . . . gnomic? But then I remembered it was her birthday, so perhaps she was mourning the way all women of our age were supposed to mourn the precipitous vanishing of our worth, like, *Whoops, time to grow a personality, which the world will also devalue!* Bonnie had always been devastatingly confident—but who knew, it could have been the kind of confidence that only flourished within highly specific parameters and withered time-lapse-fast without.

"Hey. Don't be too sensible. It's your birthday! We got those drinks tonight."

Bonnie groaned and the microwave beeped.

Later on in the evening Scott said, "I didn't mean that it was next month. I meant today is the start of a new month. Which is this month."

Bonnie closed her eyes so she could roll them, but we could still see it.

And later on in the evening when the talk turned to shitty men and the list full of them and our lives full of them, Bonnie, who had gotten quietly wasted, said, "Men men men men MEN. Can they not be the only subject of conversation left in the whole entire world *please*? Can we please just talk about something nice?"

But that was Bonnie for you.

THE TIME BONNIE CANCELED

Her email read, *BIRTHDAY CANCELED! I've decided to embark on a new adventure. Arctic Circle expedition, BITCHES. I leave in an hour, therefore no time to get drunk with you jokers. I'm drunk*

THE TIME BONNIE ASKED FOR ADVICE

She said, "What would you do? Hypothetically."

We were a little surprised. Bonnie didn't usually go in for these kinds of conversations. She thought these topics were nerdy meaningless masturbations for super dweebs. *Stop acting like life is a Star Trek movie, it'll never happen!* she'd say. Sometimes she substituted a Star Wars movie for a Star Trek movie. Then again, we'd been discussing the list of shitty men, about which she seemed very *oh this again*, so maybe any interruption would do.

Phyllida would improve herself. Read books, learn languages and musical instruments and complicated choreography that didn't require too much muscle strength. "Also, I would punish those I deemed deserving of it. They would be in a hell of my own making, unaware they would be doomed to relive these torments again and again. It would be a long time before I tired of this."

Damn, girl!

Scott would travel and spend all of his money as quickly as he could. We politely overlooked the fact that Bonnie already could do this, sometimes *did* do it.

Devon would quit her job and just do nothing. If you were living the same week over and over again it meant you weren't aging, so time no longer had you propped up on its handlebars propelling you forward no matter what, as you spit out bugs and tried not to slip off. No, time in this scenario was chill as hell, willing to stroll with you around a track and have a stoned, circular conversation nobody would be able to retrace. How wonderfully relaxing, and so very necessary when everything had been so apocalyptically stressful. "I would get to know my friends better. Though I would keep far away from most of my family. For them, duration and repetition would not be improvements." But Devon relented, a little. "I might give it a shot if I got really bored. In a literal thousand years."

Nina would try to save everybody.

We would wear elaborate disguises in order to spy on our friends and see what they really thought of us; we would binge-eat; we would sex-marathon; we would try new hairstyles; we would get three dogs; we would get teardrops and ice cream cones tattooed on our faces; we would get five cats; we would do every drug; *we would not garden*.

Sure, I made my contributions. But this was the only thing I said that I really meant: I said that I actually hated this hypothetical conceit. When you dug right down into it, it was odious. Because you could do anything you wanted, you could do absolutely whatever, and nothing would ever, ever, ever, ever be allowed to change.

Bonnie looked placid. "Yes, what then? If it just starts over again and again and never stops no matter what."

"You make your peace with it," said Derrick. "You have to relinquish your attachment to time as it was."

Scott said, "You said a week, right? That's lucky. That's where it's at. Way better than a day. In a week, you can really get somewhere."

Her email read, *Hi, assholes! Birthday drinks are canceled. Giving you tons of warning so you don't end up meeting anyway to talk about me behind my back because that's like your favorite pastime. IN OTHER WORDS, I HEARD EVERYTHING. Is that really what you thought of me? What is so wrong with choosing joy? Well. You got your wish. The longer this week goes on the more familiar I become with it and the great grand repeating shittiness we've gotten ourselves into. Thank you so much, losers! Now I'm depressed just like you.*

1. We had no idea what she was talking about.
2. It did still *sound* like Bonnie.

THE TIME BONNIE WOKE ME UP

She burst into my room without knocking.

"I think I got it! Do you remember this time?" she gabbled.

I squinted at my alarm clock. ". . . time?"

At this, an utter devastation settled over Bonnie. A flat, matte no-expression gray exoskeleton that turned her head and picked up her feet and walked her out of my room.

THE TIME BONNIE WAS MEAN TO US

Bonnie raised her glass. "Here's to the nights I will remember with the friends who always forget," she said, and downed the whole thing. We sat still. If we did or said anything, she would *predict* us again, mimicking us in that horrible sarcastic voice.

"Go," she said, and we ran out of the bar.

THE TIME BONNIE CANCELED

Her email read, *I'm just really sick of you all. Sorry.*

Something was wrong. Bonnie wouldn't get out of bed. She didn't shower. I brought her food but she'd only pick at it. When I asked her what was wrong, or how I could help, all she would say was, "Look. Sometimes I just don't have it in me to get it up again for yet another seven days of the same old, same old, same old." I had never seen her like this.

She intoned:

Another man, another bad man
First a bad man
First outrage
And then or simultaneously
And then this man is actually not that bad, or even bad at all,
    because if you haven't seen him be bad to you, he cannot
    ever be bad, fuck an object permanence
And then any punishment is far too big, you can't just take away
    his human rights by not reading his books or not watching
    his movies or not voting for him or not being pleasant to
    him at cocktail parties
And then where will this end, maybe men should never talk to
    women ever again because of course it is preferable to cease
    all interactions with about half of humanity if the alterna-
    tive is to think or worry about one's behavior for longer than
    0.000002 seconds
And then sometimes bad men apologize, sorry you admired me
    so much, sorry the rules changed on me, sorry I don't remem-
    ber doing that because I was addicted to alcohol and drugs
    but I remember you being into it and sorry you changed
    your mind, however I am not sorry for being so kinky
And then bad men disappear and reappear
And then we forget and they reappear
Or is it more like they reappear and it makes us forget
Onto the next, onto the next

"I think this news cycle is really upsetting her," I told another friend of hers. We sympathized.

THE TIME BONNIE BOUGHT ME BREAKFAST

One morning Bonnie knocked twice on my bedroom door and came in without waiting for a response. I didn't like her coming into my room because she often gazed at my furniture, my clothes, my shoes with a fixed, sweetly neutral expression that I knew was pitying and insulting. Sure, my things weren't nearly as nice as Bonnie's, but I also didn't think they were so bad you needed a poker face to look at them.

This time, she didn't do any of that. She said, "Call in sick to work. I want to show you something."

"You know I can't." Although—did she know? Currently, I had a pretty good temp gig at a duty-free shopping company, entering the names of makeup products from large binders into a computer database. Near the end of my stint they discovered I had entered all the names incorrectly, because I had been trained incorrectly. So they hired me for another round to fix the mistakes I had made, which was really nice and humane and understanding of them. Unfortunately, because I'd finally been doing my job right, I would be losing it soon. I had no idea what was happening next.

"It doesn't matter!" Bonnie said. "Okay, no, wait. I'll pay you five times what you usually make in a day. And I'll buy you breakfast. Let's go out!"

"Seriously?"

She looked down at me with the hauteur of a much older, much more professionally accomplished woman. "You know that I never lie about money or food." She placed an already written check on my face, and when I started sputtering, she said she'd go wait in the living room.

After I got ready and called in sick, I came out and found Bonnie sitting primly on the couch, her eyes closed. "Let's go!" she said, standing. Her eyes were still closed. Now that I was right next to her I saw her lids were covered in something clear and crusty. "You're about to ask what's up with my eyes. I superglued them shut," she said. "Is it dry?" she asked herself. "Yes. It's dry. So, you can see that my eyes are completely closed, right?"

Oh, were they ever. I was backing away very stealthily when Bonnie said, "Stop backing away *not that stealthily*. I know you have this whole thing about being allergic to crazy because of your schizophrenic aunt who raised you, and it's fine to honor the child who had to come up with coping mechanisms and protect herself somehow, but you've got to get over it. Sometimes shit is wild beyond all reckoning. Sometimes people are extremely weird and oftentimes literally crazy, but they're not all the time trying to be crazy at you! So get over it. Oh, and you're also not so normal yourself." She put on a pair of black sunglasses. "Look, you're going to say, 'Says the rich white hot girl with the happy childhood,' which is not wrong. Although you did meet my parents. Oh, shit. Wait. You didn't this time. Anyway, you're right but I'm still right about a tiny bit of it too. Do you want to come get your mind blown or not?"

"I wasn't going to say *hot*," I said.

We laughed for so long I forgot to ask how she knew about my aunt; then we went out.

Though she couldn't see at all with her eyes glued shut, Bonnie didn't need my help out of the building. She picked up a toy that had fallen from a stroller and gave it back to the child. She complimented a woman on her shoes, in convincing detail. She bought a newspaper and told me what was in it. She took out her phone and told me what everyone was talking about. She stood on the street corner and asked me to let her know when it was exactly 8:00 a.m., and when it was, she pointed straight ahead and said, "Red car, black car, blue car, blue car, cop car, hot guy on a bike, hot guy jaywalking." (Though I disagreed about the hotness of the guys, if you took Bonnie's tastes into account, this was all accurate.)

And all with her eyes superglued shut. I checked them again. They looked even more awful in daylight. "Bonnie," I said, feeling equal parts wonder and foreboding. "How are you doing this?"

Late that night we ate popcorn and watched a reality TV show—at least, I watched, while Bonnie listened, her eyeballs wiggling under her lids—since the other things we wanted to watch were created by or starring known rapists and gaslighters. "Wait, him too?" I said. "Check your phone," said Bonnie. "The news just broke."

For a moment I was surprised that Bonnie would give up on something she really wanted to watch because a Bad Man™ was involved with it, but the fact was that she was no longer the same Bonnie I had known. "All this shit, all it wants to do is continue and repeat with only slight variations," she intoned. "Care or not care, it doesn't make a difference to the loop I'm in. I only can't stand to look at his fucking face. If you see it the way I see it, it is too encrusted with the dark knowledge I have about him, a layer for each week I've been through. Layers and layers and layers and layers."

Bonnie started reciting what would happen on the reality TV show right before it did, which was getting pretty old, so I asked her if the whole week started over again right at midnight.

"That's right," she said. "Midnight tonight. Tuesday is the last day before it turns over. I love and dread Tuesdays. Though I am looking forward to this superglue being vanished."

"Why didn't you tell me earlier in the week?"

"I have." She couldn't see the horror on my face but she reached out and patted me on the arm. "Well, you know, this time I'd thought of the superglue trick and it seemed fun, but I wasn't about to have my eyes glued shut for a whole week. It *did* blow your mind, right?"

I thought. "You know . . ." I said. "I'm a person. A real person. Even if I can't remember anything."

"I know." Bonnie exhaled. "Sorry. At first I was really jealous of you all, but once I started being able to prove, you know, my whole deal to people I began to see how terrifying it is. To finally get to see the truth of what's been happening, and then to understand that it will eventually be wiped away and started over."

The problem with a Bonnie who was focused on the dark, scary side of things was that someone else had to pick up the positivity slack. This was not my greatest strength. I considered the me I was now, the being who had been shaped by living through this week, who would be destroyed once midnight came. Sure, Bonnie could re-create a very close approximation of this current me by behaving the same way next time, but that was almost worse somehow. No. It was definitely worse. I said quickly, "Is there, like, a magical phrase you can say to me that will hurry things up so we can get the show on the road quick next time?"

"Not really. And there's not a magical way to hide and transfer knowledge; otherwise I would be able to show you that you should try therapy, like, even once. Funny that you mention magic, though. I've recently been delving into the dark arts, mostly to see if there's anything that'll help pull me out of this time loop but also because I was trying to help Nina with her ghost problem."

I wondered what *recently* meant to Bonnie. "You know about that? Oh, I forgot again. You know about everything. Did it work?"

"No," she said simply and sadly. "It is such an unfortunate truth that shit doesn't happen to you based on what you can deal with."

"Poor Nina," I said. God, Bonnie really *had* changed! How many times had I had this thought today? And yet I couldn't stop thinking it, when everything she said and did kept revealing her newness, and each time in a new way. I checked the time and flinched. "Oh, it's about to be midnight," I said, feeling robotic with dread. "I'm just going to distract myself from ontological terror and tell you that next time, please figure out a way to prove it to me from the get-go, and then give me some money so I can stop going to my job and have a nice whole week of fun. What do you say?"

"I could do that, and I have. It's futile, though."

"Wow, I'm not used to this dark-sided goth of a Bonnie. I'll miss her *and yet I also totally won't*." It was hard to talk. My teeth were chattering.

It was about to be midnight.

One more second.

She whispered into everyone's ears, setting off tiny explosions of shock and awe and gasp, but when she reached me, I just said, "Don't." I didn't want to know what she knew about me already, whatever I told her even though it wasn't *me* who told her. (Yes it was no it wasn't.)

"No need," I said. "I believe it."

Bonnie nodded and sat down again. All of us were rapt. "I'm in a sharing mood this time," Bonnie said. "Please, anyone, feel free to ask me whatever you like."

Here are a few of the questions I can still remember. We had a lot.

Q: *How do you remember so much stuff if you can't take anything with you?*

A: Good question! This has all been hugely taxing for my memory. I learned the method of loci from *Rhetorica ad Herennium*, and other texts. The first thing I do when I wake up is type as much as I can remember. Like, in a total frenzy. Good thing you've only heard me banging on that keyboard once! Ha ha. Another thing I do upon waking is order a bunch of books and stuff so I can have it all shipped to me as soon as possible.

Q: *Have you ever tried to kill yourself?*

A: No. Before my optimism died, I had always held out hope that I'd be able to escape the time loop eventually. I didn't want to jeopardize that by killing myself, and I was scared. Then I died by accident, so that answered that. But I would never do it on purpose. I hate the dark in-betweens. They last longer when I've died.

Q: *What are some of your favorite memories?*

A: So many! This is going to sound cheesy. Becoming closer with many of you. You don't remember but we got *close*, like wearing each other's hair in our lockets close. You are all such incredible people. Even you have your moments, Scott. The dark magic cult that formed about me, I'm not going to say it's a *favorite* memory— it was more *interesting*, but very, very, *very* interesting. Oh, and I had so much amazing sex. That is, I had an enormous amount of

sex and so much of it was amazing, but of course a whole lot was
mediocre and embarrassing and some of it was terrible. I'm not a
god or anything. Sometimes I can't know when a bad thing will
happen, or I won't be able to stop it, and though my body gets reset
my mind does not.

Q: *Do you want it to stop?*

A: Yes.

Q: *Why do you want it to stop?*

A: First of all, I'm sick of it. In some incalculable, untrackable way, I
am old as fuck. Second, and this is the selfish reason, there's a limit
to how much I can improve all by myself. I mean, just because you
live the same week over and over again doesn't mean you'll be that
great or smart. I'm proud of how awesome I got, but I think I'm hitting a wall. Third, I have lately [we wondered what "lately" meant
to Bonnie] been troubled by the feeling that this span of time is
being used up somehow. That it is degrading and fraying in some
intangible way and there will be devastating consequence. Like it's
going to just poop out. Can't you feel it? The way everything feels
so tired and busted and sad, and it'll lurch forever but it also can't
go on like this forever? [We all nodded.] I'm scared.

Q: *Whoa. I thought I'd just been depressed.*

A: Yes. You are also that. I am concerned that whatever is happening
to me is coming to an end, but not the end I sought. I'm worried
there won't be any future. And I really wanted the future to happen, more than anybody—["Please, Bonnie," we said]—okay, fine,
I want it as much as anyone else does, and to think that I won't get
to see it, that none of us will—

This was around when Bonnie stopped talking. She had a look like
someone who had run full force into a glass door, like: *Aaaaah!* And
like: *OUCH.* And like: *Well, of course. I did know that door was there.*

She got up to leave, telling us that this week was going to be very
busy, and it was important to get it just right, so please don't do stupid
shit expecting it to be undone. Please. When we tried to ask her one

last thing, she blew right out of there, leaving the question to twist in the air and plummet to the floor in a crumpled ball.

The question was: *Why you, Bonnie?*

We never stopped wondering and we never found out.

Bonnie decided to throw a giant party at our place. It would be on Tuesday night, the last night of the week, because everything in Bonnie's week took place on the exact wrong day. "People will come," she said. "I know how to get them here. And I deserve a real birthday party! In a sense, I'm like a million years old." I asked her if she kept count and she shook her head, saying she was bad at keeping numbers in her mind, but that had to be a lie.

Such terrible things happened this week. Huge startling ones and small boring ones. But in other ways we had a wonderful week. We remember it still.

Isn't that nice? Isn't that fucking major?

At the party, which everyone did attend—not that we doubted Bonnie more than just a little bit—I spotted the man I knew at my last job. The Man. But not really *The Man*, not really deserving of capitals, because there had been a few in my life but this one only happened to be the most recent and I was maddest at him. Most recent also meant that I had thought I'd become old enough to respect myself and to be able to foresee every future event (was I expecting too much?) so that I wouldn't keep saying yes to a man when I wanted to say no and thus pave the way for me to say no to that man and have him still do what he wanted and leave me totally confused, knowing that something was very, very wrong. Thus when all of that nevertheless came to pass I got really mad at myself and additionally mad at him for making me mad at myself, and, of course I was mad at myself for being mad at myself.

My fingertips sizzled.

The time was after midnight. Bonnie wasn't here anymore. I felt it, like she told me we would. She said she had had a sudden flash of insight, or maybe not so sudden because she had been thinking over it for years, and now she knew what she had to do. It had taken her so long because it was a weird solution and one that made her quite un-

happy. "Only at first. I feel much better about it now. Nobody should
be sad for me," she said. When the time came, Bonnie was going to allow the future to move ahead. The way it would move ahead was if she
stayed in the past. It wasn't too hard to do, more a matter of intention
and perspective than anything else. You didn't even need dark magic.
Well, *some* helped. "I wish I could be there. To see it," she had said.
"But I love you all and I'm sick of you all and I'm sick of power and
power is sick of having me."

The man was talking happily to a young woman, as if he deserved
to stand in the light. Amazingly, he truly did think that he was a nice
person. I could have pondered that riddle for endless weeks of Bonnie
time. It was like he was afflicted with anosognosia, a condition of not
believing you have a mental illness because you have a mental illness,
which was a major trouble of my aunt's, who I really had loved. I had
been afraid of becoming like her and having no one ever believe anything I'd ever say again, but that already came to pass anyway. This
man wasn't ill. He was just a cowardly sex criminal who was wrong
about so many things, such as the future we were entering.

As I crossed the room, people made way. I called his name. He
glanced up, looking so unafraid that it made me want to pull him into
fifty pieces. I lifted my hand a little, and he stood taller. He might have
straightened when he saw me. Also likely was that a horridly strong
cackling force might have frozen him in its thin-fingered grip and
lifted him high on his toes.

He might be compelled to tell me and this room full of people
what he did to so many and who he was and every tiny detail of what
went on in his mind. Forget punishment. Or, for that man, having to
tell the honest truth, clean of self-preservation and self-regard, would
be punishment enough. Or, there could be more punishment later.
No need to decide yet. At that moment, all I wanted was the truth that
had been denied me so long. Might it be denied me now?

CYCLOPTERUS

PETER WATTS

Peter Watts (rifters.com) is a former marine biologist, flesh-eating-disease survivor, and convicted felon whose novels—despite an unhealthy focus on space vampires—have become required texts for university courses ranging from philosophy to neuropsychology. His work is available in twenty-one languages, has appeared in thirty best-of-the-year anthologies (including this one), and been nominated for over fifty awards in a dozen countries. His somewhat shorter list of twenty one actual wins includes the Hugo, the Shirley Jackson, and the Seiun.

He lives in Toronto with fantasy author Caitlin Sweet, four cats, a pugilistic rabbit, a *Plecostomus* the size of a school bus, and a gang of tough raccoons who shake him down for kibble on the porch every summer. He likes all of them significantly more than most people he's met.

Galik sneaks in through blue-green twilight a hundred meters down, where it's calm. Overhead, lost in the murk, the mixing zone churns beneath the surface; the surface churns beneath the sky; immortal Nāmaka churns between, in ascension once more after four weeks slumming it up north as a Category 3.

A dim shape looms in the sub's headlights: *Sylvia Earle*, an inflatable bladder four stories high, freshly relocated from its usual station over the White Shark Cafe. The sub sniffs out the dorsal docking hatch and locks on. Galik grunts a farewell to his pilot and drops into a cramped decompression chamber outfitted with a half-dozen molded seats and a second hatch—sealed—to complement the one he came in through. His ride disengages with a clank and slips back the way it came.

They let him out when the gauge reads nine atmospheres. A sullen tech in a blue coverall leads him down through a maze of pipes and ladders and bulkheads festooned with shark posters. She counters Galik's small talk with grunts and monosyllables, abandons him in a dimly lit sub bay where every bulkhead wriggles with blue wavelight. A fat tadpole-shaped cubmarine wallows in the moon pool at its center, hatch agape at the end of a folding catwalk. Its flanks bristle with gifts for the seabed: magnetometers and CTD sensors, SIDs, current meters and cytometers. Other things even an oceanographer wouldn't recognize. A name is stencilled onto the hull, just to the left of No Step: *RSV Cyclopterus*.

It can't go as far or as fast as the craft that brought him here. But it can go way, way deeper.

The pilot's fixated on the predive checklist as Galik climbs down into the cockpit and dogs the hatch. Galik breathes in sweat and monomers and machine oil, settles into the shotgun seat. "I'm Alistor."

"Uh-huh." Her head dips in perfunctory acknowledgment: a jaw-length curtain of dark ringlets, a cheekbone and profile behind. Moon-pool light filters in through a smattering of high-pressure viewports arrayed like spider eyes around the front of the cockpit, paints her in faint watercolor. Her eyes never leave the board. "Buckle up."

He does. Mechanical guts gurgle and belch. The lights past the
viewports ascend and fade.

Cyclopterus drops into the void.

Galik settles back in his seat. "How long to the bottom?"

"Forty minutes. Forty-five."

"Nice to be able to measure things in minutes again. Took me a
day and a half to get here from Corvallis, and that was at forty knots."

The pilot taps a flickering readout until it steadies.

"Kinda miss the old days, you know? When you could just *fly* out,
drop down. No giant-ass superstorms getting in the way."

She reaches back and grabs the pilot's VR headset from its hook.
Puts it on, slides the visor over her eyes.

Galik sighs.

VR's not much use this high off the seabed; the 2D display spread
across the dashboard is more than sufficient when there's nothing but
empty sea for a thousand meters in any direction. But for want of anything else to do, Galik grabs his own headset and boots it up. He finds
himself suspended in a sparse void sprinkled with occasional readouts
and scale bars. Close below, a faint translucent membrane spreads out
across the universe at 1,300 meters. Four thousand meters below that,
the ocean floor bounces back solid corduroy.

"That's strange," the pilot murmurs.

Galik raises his visor. "What?"

Under hers, the pilot's lips are pursed. "Pycnocline's way down at
thirteen hundred. Never seen it so dee—" She catches herself consort-
ing with the enemy, falls silent.

Galik rolls his eyes and weighs his options. Goes for it.

"You be breaking any protocols to at least tell me your name?"

Her hooded face turns toward him for a moment. "Koa Moreno."

"Pleased to meet you, Koa. How did I manage to piss you off in the
past five minutes?"

"You didn't. We just—don't do small talk down here."

"Ah." He nods, though she can't see it. "Parties on the *Sylvia Earle*
must be a hoot."

"Try spending a few months breathing recycled farts and belches from the same ten people. You'll reset your boundaries soon enough."

"It's more than that."

Something changes in her posture, some subtle slumping of the shoulders that says *Fine, asshole, have it your way.* She ups her visor up and turns to face him.

"This could be the *last one.* And you're going to fuck it up like everything else."

"Me?"

"Nautilus."

"What makes you think—"

"After you strip-mined every last park and refuge and vacant lot on land, you moved offshore. We've been watching it happen, *Alistor.* I was there when Lizard Island went down. Clipperton's one of the last places the ISA didn't cave on. But it was only a matter of time, wasn't it? Seabed's just another resource to tear up while we wait for the ceiling to crash in."

Galik feels his face pulling into a tight little smile. "Well. I guess I asked."

She turns her attention to the dashboard.

"This is just a preliminary survey," he tries. "Might not come to anything."

"Give me a break. The whole zone's rotten with polymetallics and you know it." She shakes her head. "Honestly, I don't know why you're even going through the motions. Why not just buy yourself a rubber stamp and go straight to the strip-mining?"

Galik takes a careful breath, keeps his voice calm and friendly. "Good question. Why haven't we?"

She glares at him.

He holds up his hands, palms out. "I'm serious. The mineralogical data's been on the books for twenty years, you said as much yourself. If they just wanted to strip-mine Clipperton, why didn't they do it years ago?"

Moreno doesn't answer for a moment.

"It's a deep dig," she says at last. "Maybe you went after the low-hanging fruit first. Maybe you just didn't notice it until now."

"Maybe they tried," Galik suggests, "and the ISA wouldn't give them their rubber stamp."

"You keep saying *they*. Like you're not one of them."

"Wasn't Nautilus went after the permit. Wasn't Nautilus got turned down."

"Who, then?"

"PolyCon. They went after Clarion Clipperton on five separate occasions. ISA wouldn't budge. Heritage site, they said. Unparalleled deepwater biodiversity. Unique conservation value."

"Bullshit. Nobody cares about that stuff anymore."

"They're the ISA. It's their job to care."

"They caved everywhere else."

"Not here."

"Maybe not for PolyCon. Here *you* are."

"I told you: nothing's decided."

Moreno snorts. "Right. You dragged *Sylvie* hundreds of kilometers off-site so you'd have your own private base camp. You put everyone's research on hold, and you've got me spending the next eight hours planting your money detectors on the seabed. You think I don't know what that costs?"

Galik shrugs. "If you're that sure, you could always refuse the gig. Break your contract. Take a stand on principle."

Moreno glowers at the dashboard, where the luminous stipple of the thermocline thickens and rises about them. *Cyclopterus* jerks and slews as some particularly dense lens of water slaps lazily to starboard.

"They'd probably send you home then, though, right? Back to the heat waves and the water wars and that weird new fungus that's eating everything. Although I hear some of the doomsday parties are worth checking out. Just last week one of 'em ended up burning down half of Kluane National Park."

Moreno says nothing.

"'Course, if you really wanted to stand up and be counted, you could join the Gaianistas." And in response to the look that gets him: "What? You gonna let the fuckers who killed the planet get away scot-free *again*?"

"That's rich. Coming from one of their errand boys."

"I chose my side. What about you, hiding out here in the ocean while the world turns to shit? You going to do anything about that, or are you all sound and fury, signifying nothing?"

"There's nothing to do," she says, almost whispering. "It's too late."

"Never too late for payback. Way I understand it, that's what the Gaianistas are all about."

"They're a lost cause."

"What isn't, these days?"

"Don't think for a second I don't sympathize. Of course I fucking sympathize. We're ten years past tipping point, planet's doomed, and you lot are making out better than ever because there's no point in any pesky ineffective environmental regulations any more. So, yeah. Sometimes it seems like the only thing that might make life worthwhile would be to take some of you out before you all bugger off to New Zealand."

"So?"

"So it's no-win. Go up against the people in charge and they'll squash you like a bug."

"That's the thing about revenge, though, isn't it? We'll go after those who've fucked us over even if it hurts us more than them. Just as long as it *does* hurt them, even a little. And the worse things get, the more we're willing to sacrifice just to strike back."

"Bullshit."

"They've done studies. It's a kind of a—justice instinct, I guess you'd call it. Primal. Like sex, or money. They say it worked pretty well at discouraging cheaters back when we were living in caves. Maybe not so great now, but, you know. Some people just haven't evolved."

"So, what? You're saying you don't blame them?"

"The Gaianistas? Would you blame a rabid dog for biting you?" Galik shrugs. "'Course, you still have to put them down. For the public welfare."

"That's funny. I imagine they'd say exactly the same thing about you."

"Would you?"

"Would I what?"

"Put me down? If you had the chance."

Moreno opens her mouth. Closes it again. *Cyclopterus* hisses into the silence.

"I had the chance," she says at last. "If you must know."

"Tell me."

After a moment she does. "Trying to catch a flight to Galveston, shuttle gig out in the Gulf. Some zero-pointer was in a hurry to make it to his private jet I guess, just him and his family and a swarm of drones. Three gens of rich entitled assholes trying to sneak through Departures, pretending not to notice all the hisses and hate stares."

"Weird they were even on ground level. They're usually not so exposed."

"Someone said some kind of technical issue up on the roof, sidelined the helipad. You could tell they were *really* not happy to be there. Looked downright scared actually, even before—anyway, they had their drones keeping the riffraff at bay but before they even made it into the terminal this big white van pulls up and it must have been loaded with capacitors because *zap*."

"EMP?"

Moreno nods. "Drones drop like birds in Beijing. And suddenly all these people dragging suitcases over the curb or hailing cabs or kissing each other goodbye—they all just turn like some kind of hive mind and suddenly Richy McRich and his nearest and dearest are the eye in the storm. It's really quiet for a moment or two, and nobody's saying anything, but one of the rich kids—this little snot in a Nermal T-shirt—he kind of *whimpers*. And then the mob just closes in and—tears them apart."

Galik mouths a silent *Fuuuccck*.

"I don't know how many were in on the plan and how many just happened to be in the neighborhood. But almost everyone joined in.

They were making this *sound*, like the whole mob had a single voice. Like—like a wind howling down a street between skyscrapers."

"What about airport security?"

"Oh, they showed up. Eventually. But the pulse took out local surveillance, right? And it's not like the 'nistas were wearing ID. They did their thing and faded and by the time anyone showed up it was just a bunch of people milling around all *Heavens, whatever happened here* and *How'd this blood get on my pants?*"

Galik doesn't speak for a moment. "You said *almost* everyone. That include you?"

She shakes her head. "Actually, I tried calling 911. But the pulse, my phone was . . ."

"So you chose a side, too."

"What?"

"Some of the people who wrecked the world were right there in front of you. You could have had justice."

She gives him a hard look. "It was a lynch mob."

"When the despots own the justice system, what else is there?"

"Your bosses know you talk like this?"

"I don't. I'm being, what's the word, *Socratic*. Since you blame *my bosses* for the end of the world and all, seems to me you'd want a little payback. But when you had the chance, right in front of you—no danger, no consequence—you tried to help them."

She taps a control; something burbles to stern. "Oh, I wanted a piece of them. It's not like the spirit didn't move me. But it also scared me, you know? The *size* of that thing, the way everyone just sort of— coalesced." She draws a breath. "And yeah, they fucking deserve it. But the damage is done, the planet's fucked. Killing a few rich assholes isn't going to unfuck it. I just—I guess I have better things to do with whatever time we've got left.

"Besides—" She shrugs. "Doesn't matter if they bugger off to New Zealand. Doesn't matter if they bugger off to Antarctica. The pandemics are everywhere. Cholera or Rift Valley Fever or whatever's on top six months from now will get them eventually."

Galik doesn't have anything to say to that.

"It's funny," Moreno says after a few moments. "You hear about them all the time, right? Idiot kids and grannies in running shoes, waving signs and chanting *Hey ho hey ho* as if *that* ever changed a fucking thing. But these guys, they had *resources*. They were organized. It was almost military."

"They are military," Galik says.

"What?"

"Some of 'em, anyway. You never noticed how all the mercs and mall cops just kind of *went away* over the years?"

"Drones replaced everyone. Why should mall cops be any different than cab drivers or pizza delivery guys?"

"Drones don't turn on you when everything goes Law of the Jungle. At some point it dawned on the zero-pointers that their private armies might not be quite so obedient when the lights went out. Might just rise up and take over all those apocalypse bunkers for themselves. Way I hear it, a lot of guys with Middle East stamps on their passports ended up out of work, past ten years or so. Some of 'em are probably pissed about it. Maybe even looking for pay—"

Something lifts *Cyclopterus* like a toy in a bathtub.

Inertia pushes Galik into his seat. The vessel *tilts*, nose down: slides fast-forward as though surfing some invisible wave. Moreno curses and grabs the stick as *Cyclopterus* threatens to turn, to tumble.

Wipe out . . .

In the next moment everything is calm as glass again.

Neither speaks for a moment.

"That was one hell of a thermocline," Galik remarks.

"Pycnocline," Moreno says automatically. "And we passed it a thousand meters ago. That was—something else."

"Seaquake?"

She leans forward, interrogates the board. "*Sylvie*'s transponder isn't talking." She conjures up a keyboard, starts typing. Out past the hull, the metronome chirp of the sonar segues into full-throated orchestra.

"Technical glitch?" Galik wonders.

"Dunno."

"Can't you just call them up?"

"What do you *think* I'm doing?"

Acoustic modems, he remembers. They can handle analog voice comms under normal conditions—but what's *normal*, with Nāmaka churning up the Devil's own background noise? Down here, the pros use text.

But judging by the look on Moreno's face, that's not working either.

She drags her finger along a slider on the dash; the pointillist seabed drops away around some invisible axis as the transducers swing their line-of-sight from *Down* to *Up*. Static and confusion rotate into view; the distant surface returns a blizzard of silver pixels to swamp the screen. Moreno fiddles with the focus and the maelstrom smears away. Closer, deeper features stutter into focus. Moreno sucks breath between clenched teeth.

Far overhead, something has grabbed the thermo—the *pycn*ocline as though it were a vast carpet, and shaken it. The resulting waveform rears up through the water column, a fold of cold dense water rising into the euphotic zone like a submarine tsunami. It iterates across the display in majestic stop-motion, its progress updating with each ping.

It must be almost a thousand meters, crest-to-trough.

It's already passed by, marching east. Patches of static swirl and dissipate in its wake, clustered echoes whose outlines shuffle and spread in jerky increments. Galik doesn't know what they are. Maybe remnants of the Garbage Patch, its dismembered fragments still cluttering up the ocean years after Nāmaka tore it apart. Maybe just bubbles and swirling cavitation. Maybe even schools of fish; a few of those are still supposed to be hanging on, here and there.

"What—" he begins.

"Shut up." Moreno's face is bloodless. "This is bad."

"How bad?"

"Shut up and let me think!"

Her visor's back down. She plays the panel. Scale bars squeeze and stretch like rubber on the dash. Topography rotates and zooms, forward, aft; midwater wrinkles blur into focus and out again as Moreno alters the range. Her whispered *fuck fuck fuck* serves up a disquieting counterpoint to the pinging of the transducers.

"I can't find *Sylvie*," she admits at last, softly. "Not all of her, anyway. Maybe some pieces bearing eighty-seven. Swept way off-station."

Galik waits.

"She was ninety meters down." Moreno takes a deep breath. "The tip of that—thing reaches up to fifty. Must've slapped them like a fucking flyswatter."

"But what *was* it?"

"I don't know. Never seen anything like it before. Almost like some kind of monster seiche."

"I don't know what that is."

"It's like—when the pycnocline sloshes back and forth. Underwater standing wave. But the strong ones, they're just in lakes and seas. Basins with walls the wave can bounce against."

"Pacific's a basin. Pacific's got walls."

"Pacific's *huge*. I mean sure, ocean seiches go on world tours sometimes, but they're *slow*. Stretch the mixing layer a few meters over a few years. Maybe kickstart an El Niño now and then. Nothing like this."

"There was nothing like Nāmaka ten years ago either."

"Yeah."

"So much heat in the oceans now, hurricanes don't even cool down enough to dissipate. Maybe it's amping up your seiches, too."

"Dunno. Maybe."

"Maybe they're even feeding off each other. Nothing's linear anymore, it's all tipping points and—"

"I *don't know*, I said. None of that shit *matters* right now." She slides her visor up, eyes a red handle protruding from the ceiling. A tiny metallic hiccough and a soft *bloop* carry through the hull after she yanks it. Something flashes on the dash.

"Emergency buoy?"

Moreno nods, downs visor, grabs the joystick.

"Shouldn't we, you know. Make a recording? Send details?"

"It's in there already. Dive logs, telemetry, even cabin chatter. Beacon stores it all automatically." The corner of her mouth tightens. "You're in there too, if that helps. Sub commandeered by NMI, prospecting dive. Maybe they'll move faster, knowing one of their errand boys is in danger."

She edges the stick forward and to port. *Cyclopterus* banks.

Galik checks the depth gauge. "Down?"

"You think anyone's gonna fly a rescue mission through Nāmaka? You think I'd be crazy enough to surface even if they did?"

"No, but—"

"Any rescue's gonna come in from the side. And since you wouldn't have dragged *Sylvia* all the way over from the Cafe if there'd been anyone closer, I'm assuming it's gonna have to come from further out, right?"

After a moment, he nods.

"Could be days before help arrives even if our signal *does* manage to cut through the shit," Moreno tells him. "And I for one don't feel like holding my breath for a week."

Galik swallows. "I thought these things made their own O_2. From seawater."

"Lack of seawater isn't the problem. Need battery power to run the electrolysis rig."

He glances at their bearing; Moreno has brought them around so they're following in the wake of the superseiche.

"You're going after the *Earle*."

Her jaw clenches visibly. "I'm going after what's left. With any luck, some of the fuel cells are still intact."

"Any chance of survivors?" Most habs come with emergency pods, hard-shelled refugia for the crew in case of catastrophe. Assuming the crew has enough advance warning to get to them, of course.

She doesn't answer. Maybe she's not allowing herself to hope.

"I'm—I'm sorry about this," Galik manages. "I can't imagine what—"

Cowled Moreno hunches over the controls. "Shut up and let me drive."

Cyclopterus never stops talking. Her guts gurgle and hiss. Her motors whine like electric mosquitoes. Her relentless transducers ping the ocean for reflections of mass and density.

Her passengers—immersed in wireframe caricatures of the world beyond the hull—say nothing at all.

Eventually the seabed resolves below them: luminous plane or muddy plain, depending on which channel you choose. Sonar serves up more information, but after all the pixels the impoverished patch of bone-grey sediment in the headlights is a welcome glimpse of something *real*. Galik fiddles with the controls, finds an overlay mode that serves up the best of both feeds.

Moreno nudges the sub to port. Mud gives way to rock; rock subsides again under mud. Outcrops and overhangs erupt from the substrate at odd angles, like listing jagged-edged tabletops. Nodules of cobalt and manganese lie scattered about like encrusted coins strewn from some ancient shipwreck. There are *things*, everywhere. Starfish with arms like tiny sinuous backbones. Tentacled flowers on stalks. Tangled balls of jawless hagfish. Gelatinous blobs the size of softballs, floating just off the bottom; they iridesce like dragonfly wings in the glare of the headlight.

All drift aimlessly. None move on their own.

Galik slides his visor up, looks across the cockpit. "Are they all dead?"

Moreno grunts.

"What would do that?" Hydrogen sulfide, maybe. The whole zone's rotten with cold seeps and hot smokers—the source of Clipperton's mineral wealth—but Galik's still taken aback to see such devastation in the middle of a protected wilderness area.

An eyeless shrug. "Dead zone moved in, probably. We get big slugs of anoxic water sliding down off the conshelf few times a year now. Suffocates whole ecosystems overnight."

"Shit."

"Yeah." Her voice is toneless. "What a tragedy."

Galik searches what he can see of her face, finds it unreadable. He gives up and downs his own visor.

Something's waiting for him there.

It's a hard ping, just a few degrees to starboard. Something big on the seabed, like an outcropping but more symmetrical, somehow. It echoes louder than any mere chunk of basalt.

"Is that a piece of the hab? Fifty meters, oh-two-eight?"

"No."

"Sounds like metal, though, right?"

Moreno says nothing.

"Maybe we should check it out. Just to be sure."

Technically he's still in charge. Technically Moreno's just a taxi driver. Technically she could still tell him to fuck off and there wouldn't be a whole lot he could do about it.

After a moment, though, *Cyclopterus* noses to starboard.

The bogey's partially hidden behind a ridge of rock; its echo flashes like the edge of some dim sun peeking over a horizon. Details resolve as they approach: a curve, a convexity. A series of interlocking segments, their lower edges fuzzed by incursions of mud.

A skull.

Sonar completes the tableaux a few moments before it scrolls into the light: a backbone, glittering with oily reflections. A silvered arrowhead cranium, three meters if it's an inch, nostrils stretched along the top, empty eye sockets pushed down to the sides. The bones of some huge thumbless hand, laid flat across the seabed like a museum reconstruction.

"It's a *whale*," he whispers.

"Few million years old, probably."

"But it's *metal* . . ."

"It's a fossil. It mineralized. The water's saturated with metal ions. Why do you even think you're interested in this place?"

"Yeah, but—"

"I'd love to give you a scenic tour, Alistor, but in case you've forgotten my friends are probably all dead and I'd just as soon not join—"

She cuts herself off. Something's caught her eye, something peeking into view from behind that enormous glinting spine.

"What the fuck," she murmurs.

A fleshy torpedo, pale whitish-pink in the lights, a couple meters long. Arms. "Squid," Galik says.

"Not like any squid *I've* ever seen."

They edge in closer. Galik zooms his camera. The creature drifts listless as any other they've seen down here, arms limp as seaweed. There *is* something strange about it, though.

"Look at the eyes," Moreno whispers.

He can see *three* from this angle, spaced at ninety-degree intervals around the absurd amidships head of the thing. (Presumably there's a fourth on the far side.) And of those three, two of them look—wrong . . .

No iris. No pupil. No white. Galik sees three things positioned as eyes, but only one stares back at him. The others are dark, and—tangled, somehow. Sockets full of tendrils: as though someone has scooped out the eyeball and stuffed a nest of bloodworms into the socket.

"Kill the lights," he says.

"Why—"

"Just do it."

Darkness crushes in. Galik's hullcam goes black—except for one bright pinpoint, flashing a steady emerald beat in the darkness. Right about where one of those not-eyes gapes, invisible now.

"There's an *LED* in that thing," Galik says softly.

Moreno kicks the floods back on. The blinking star vanishes in high-contrast light and shadow. *Cyclopterus* closes with renewed purpose; a manipulator unfolds from her belly like a mantis limb, clawed fingers reaching for the flaccid thing. They touch it.

Instantly the squid flexes and recoils, jets away into the darkness.

"Huh," Galik grunts.

"Humboldt squid," Morena tells him. "Started off as one, anyway. Resistant to low-oxygen conditions."

"But it was—"

"Tweaked. Whole lot of neurons cable to the eyes. Nothing says they gotta carry visual information. Hook up the right sensors, you could read anything. pH. Salinity. Name it."

"So it's some kind of—living environmental sensor."

"That's my guess."

"Not yours."

Moreno snorts.

"Whose, then?"

"I dunno," Moreno says. "But look where it went."

She's aimed the sonar, cranked the range. The squid—whatever it is—doesn't register on such far focus. Something does, though. Way off in the distance, at the very limit of sonar sight, something bounces back faint as a ghost.

"Looks like an outcropping," Galik says.

"My ass. Those edges are too straight."

"*Sylvia Earle?*"

"Wrong bearing."

"Maybe we should just stay the course. Given our limited reserves."

Cyclopterus turns toward the echo.

Galik slides his visor back. "What do you think it is?"

Moreno's is up as well. Her eyes are hard as glass.

"Let's find out."

"Well, at least we know now," Galik says.

"Know?"

"Why Clipperton's off-limits. Why the ISA didn't—" He shakes his head. "Someone bought them."

Cyclopterus floats across an unfinished landscape of plastic and metal. Spreading out in all directions, a grid of rails turns the seabed into a chessboard; spindly towers rise from its interstices. Printers the size of automobiles glide along their tracks, drilling holes, laying eggs, extruding pools of hot thick liquid that freeze harder than

basalt. Strange jet-propelled machines splice rock and metal together
at critical junctures. Everywhere are the frames of half-completed
domes and tunnels and conduits, wormy with bundled cabling and
fiberop.

All invisible in the darkness. All this industrious activity hidden
beneath four kilometers of sunless black, except where *Cyclopterus*'s
eyes and echoes lay it bare.

Galik whistles. "This is going to be one hell of a hab."

"This isn't a hab. It's a fucking *city*." Moreno rechecks the onboard
database. "Not on the charts. No transponders. This thing is totally off
the books."

"I guess they're not all going to New Zealand."

Moreno taps a control; blotchy rainbows bloom here and there
across the display. A slash of red smoulders at two o'clock, broken by
huddles of intermittent machinery. "Hot seep."

"Power source," Galik guesses.

"Hey, you see that?"

He does. Bearing eighty-five degrees: something round and
smooth, something anomalously *complete* in the midst of all this
in-progress disarray. It glows green and warm on thermal.

A pressure hull.

Moreno reads the echo like a soothsayer. "Atmosphere."

"Occupied?" This could be a problem. Anyone going to these
lengths isn't likely to welcome drop-ins.

But Moreno shakes her head. "Looks like a foreman's shack. Place
to crash when you come down to check on your pet project. Anyone
who can keep a place this size off the scope isn't gonna risk giving
themselves away with telemetry broadcasts. Can't see anyone living
here full-time, though. Not until they're ready to move in permanently.
In the meantime"—*Cyclopterus* is already coming around—"there'll
be power. Food. Beds even."

The shack's dead ahead now, growing in their sights. "We hang
around too long, we'll have company," Galik surmises.

"Unless we're extremely unlucky, the rescue guys show up first.

And then this fucking place gets dragged into the sunlight for everyone to see."

"That's assuming whoever's behind it—"

"You know who's behind it, Alistor. Your masters. Their masters. Zero-pointers cashing out before the bill comes due." She glances meaningfully at him. "Guess they didn't save you a spot, huh?"

"You're assuming they won't be keeping an ear on the local chatter. That they won't just reach out and squash a rescue mission as soon as they see the coordinates."

Moreno's fingers tighten on the joystick. A soft *Shit* hisses between her teeth.

The shack resolves in their headlights like a grey moon, maybe ten meters across at the equator. Moreno pulls the stick and *Cyclopterus* climbs low over the northern hemisphere, her lights pooling across ducts and grilles and stencilled warnings to keep clear of the vents. Moreno navigates over the north pole, coaxes the sub into planting a perfect watertight kiss on the docking hatch. Machinery grapples and clenches and blows seawater back into the abyss.

She boots up a dashboard interface and curses. "Figures. Only one atmosphere in there."

"How long to decompress us?"

"From nine atmospheres? Breathing trimix? Five days, easy." She studies the dash. "Fortunately, we've also got remote access to hab support. I can bring inside pressure up to nine in about"—she runs her finger up the dash—"fifteen minutes."

"You rock," Galik tells her.

It gets him his first small smile. "I do, don't I?"

They don't have fifteen minutes, though. The board starts beeping after five.

"That was fast," Galik says.

Moreno frowns. "That's not the hab. That's an ELF handshake." Her face brightens. "Text message! The beacon got through!"

Galik's jaw tightens. "Don't get your hopes up. Remember, these people"—taking in the half-built complex around them—"they have ears, too."

"No, this is through Cospas-Sarsat. This is NOAA." She leans forward, focusing as if sheer concentration might somehow squeeze the signal from the water a little faster. Alphanumerics accumulate in front of her. They're too small to make out from where Galik's sitting.

He sighs.

"Says here—it says . . ." The anticipation drains from her face. Something darker rises in its stead.

She turns to face him. "Who the fuck *are* y—"

Galik's fist connects with her right temple. Moreno's head snaps sideways, cracks against the hull. She sags like a rag doll against the shoulder strap.

Galik unbuckles his harness and leans over. There's still awareness in her eyes. Her drooling mouth twitches and gapes, trying to form words. From somewhere inside Koa Moreno, a moan escapes.

He shakes his head. "It really was a preliminary survey, for what it's worth. We didn't know what was down here any more than you did; we only had—suspicions."

"You fuh . . ." she manages.

"The sensors were supposed to—not you. We were never supposed to get out this far."

Moreno half-raises a hand. It flops on the end of her arm like a dead fish.

"Now everything's gone to shit and I have to—improvise. I'm so sorry, Koa."

"Mid . . . easht—pashpor . . ."

"I'm sorry you chose the wrong side," he says, and breaks her neck.

By the time her heart stops the pressure in the shack is up to nine. Galik turns, crouching in the cramped compartment, catches passing sight of the text message still accreting on the board—

SOS received

awaiting req approval on dsrv will advise
Nautilus LLC denies any knowledge of S.Earle req
No employees deployed to CCZ
No Alistor LNU listed on sh

—and kneels to undog the deck hatch.

The lights come up as he climbs down: indirect, full-spectrum, illuminating a cozy half-hemisphere where struts and plating are all padded and wrapped in PVC. Interfaces and control panels sleep on curved bulkheads, on the desks that extrude from them. Behind a bulkhead that splits the upper deck, visible through an open hatch, bunks and lockers lurk in shadow. A spiral staircase corkscrews down to the deck below.

He searches the hab and finds it empty. He awakens its controls, checks logs and manifests. He explores remote-piloting options for *Cyclopterus*, teaches himself how to send the little craft far away on its own recognizance.

He eats from the shack's well-stocked galley, sleeps in its salon.

Four and a half kilometers overhead the mixing zone churns beneath the surface; the surface churns beneath the sky; immortal Nāmaka churns between. Back on shore the fires burn ever-hotter along the coast. Deserts spread and clathrates bubble; winter heat waves scythe across the Mediterranean; wheat rust and monkey pox fell crops and people with equal indiscriminate abandon. Tuvalu and Kiribati sink beneath the waves. Protesters mourn the loss of the Pizzly Bear and the Bengal Tiger while underfoot, the trillions of small creeping things that hold up the world disappear almost unnoticed. The human race runs ever-faster to the finish line, numbers finally thinning out on the last lap, rioting and revelling and fighting over whatever crumbs are left after three hundred years of deficit spending.

All the while, the Nikkei never stops climbing.

Alistor Galik—formerly Staff Sergeant Jason Knowlton (ret.), USSOCOM—bides his time on the bottom of the ocean, drawing plans and selecting targets. Waiting patiently for the minions of Zero Point to arrive and show him the way back to their masters.

DUNE SONG

SUYI DAVIES OKUNGBOWA

Suyi Davies Okungbowa (suyidavies.com) is a Nigerian author of fantasy, science fiction, and horror inspired by his West African origins. His debut, the godpunk fantasy novel *David Mogo, Godhunter*, was hailed as "the subgenre's platonic deific ideal." His shorter fiction and essays have appeared in *Tor.com, Lightspeed, Nightmare, Strange Horizons, Fireside, PodCastle, The Dark*, and in anthologies like *A World of Horror* and *People of Colo(u)r Destroy Science Fiction*. He lives between Lagos, Nigeria, and Tucson, Arizona, where he teaches writing to undergrads while completing his MFA in Creative Writing.

*D*o *not go out to the dunes,* the Chief says to Isiuwa. *You'd do well not to awaken the wrath of the whistling gods.*

This does not stop Nata from trying to leave again.

Once the New Moon assembly is over, she slinks away to the community market. This early in the morning, the desert haze hangs heavy, and everything moves in stutters, like tortoises in the sand. The sun is out and warm, not hot because Isiuwa isn't really in a desert; or at least, not like the deserts the Elders speak of when they tell about the world before it was all dunes.

Isiuwa moves like a buzz, like sandflies in formation. The market is a manifestation of this, laid out in wide corridors of bamboo and cloth, a neat crisscross of pathways. Bodies scuttle along, dressed in cloth wrapped to battle every iteration of dust-laden wind. No one pays Nata any heed—no one ever does—as she drags a bag too big for her frame, folds of cloak falling over her arm multiple times so that she has to stop every now and then to wrap them again. Her hair is wild with fraying edges, and her eyes bloodshot from lack of sleep, but Isiuwa does not notice.

First, she goes to the molder. The bulk of what she has available for barter here is household jars and utensils she will no longer need. The man takes everything without a word and pays her in sugarcane, which is just as well because quenching thirst is the number one priority out there. Next, she takes Mam's big old metal box, the one with which she used to make those contraptions for the village. No one in Isiuwa has tools like these any longer; strange, archaic, from the time before sand. It was the only thing salvageable after Mam's disappearance. It still contains all her tools for carving and repairing artifacts no longer here. When she places it in front of Isiuwa's prime fruit merchant, he stares at it for a long time.

"They will catch you," he says. "Again."

"Maybe," Nata says. "Maybe not."

He nods and gives her brown sugar and dried fruit for it.

She leaves her most valuable barter for last. She hefts her flat-wood under her arm and visits the woodworker, the same woman who helped her find the bulk of old tree Mam carved for her into this sleek, flat thing polished with paraffin wax. Wood is so scarce now, unlike in the early days of sand, Mam used to say. This could literally be Nata's most prized possession.

The woodworker isn't there, but her apprentices are, and they offer her a good amount of water in an earthen jar. She haggles and gets some bread and roasted termites thrown in before she lets them have it, staring as they discuss butchering it to barter in bits.

She remembers how she cried and cried to Mam that she must, must have a flatwood. One just like those in the books the Elders keep in the archives of artifacts before dunes, which only they, the Chief, and their novitiates are allowed access to (though Mam somehow managed to have that one). She remembers having hopes that one day, even if for just a day, she would go out to the dunes with the flatwood and slide down the upflow like the children did in the pictures in that book. But it's too late for that. This dream will belong to someone else now.

Nata leaves them without saying goodbye. Goodbye would mean that she is bidding positive farewell to Isiuwa, but no, she really isn't. She hopes that the minute she steps out of the bamboo fence, the sun will lean down and slap the settlement with fire, for everything they have done to her, to Mam. She hopes that all the dunes will whistle at once, a harmony of dooming dissonance, and the sand will flow and sweep over all of Isiuwa like a great ocean so that no one will ever need to know pain like hers again.

But first, she must get Tasénóguan.

Do not go out to the dunes, the Chief tells Isiuwa. *The gods will whistle you to death.*

Isiuwa listens to a dune whistle about once every moon-cycle. Each time, the sand advances on Isiuwa, moving with a morose, flute-like song, the only sound to plant tears in their chest that does not come from a living being. A shrill, underlined by wind rushing through a tube. The Chief calls it the whistle of the gods and says it is the sound of an errant person being taken. Every time an errant person dares venture beyond their allowance and ends up taken by the dunes—as they always are—the dunes move toward Isiuwa. The whistle is a warning, a warning that those of the world before it was punished with sand refused to heed. The Chief tells a story of a time before the old world, when it was once punished in the same way, but by the gods of water. It is Isiuwa's duty to preserve this order and bring forth the next world.

Isiuwa knows the Chief is right because he bears a cross on Isiuwa's behalf, along with the troupe of Elders, sentries, and novitiates: the cross of going beyond the fence and seeking solutions, praying to the gods and asking them to stop moving the dunes closer. The troupe sometimes returns with strange things they've salvaged from the sand, things that look like they belong to another time, and the Elders keep them in the archive. The Chief reminds Isiuwa that this is not a privilege but a burden, for it is impossible to look upon the faces of the gods and live; and every time the troupe returns home intact is a blessing from the whistling gods. Isiuwa nods and remains behind the fence; remains grateful.

Not Nata's Mam, though.

Nata's Mam was born stubborn. She said so often herself, that it wasn't wise to take things that came from the mouth of man, which confused Nata because those words came from her mouth. Mam lived by this practice too. Nata knows how many times Mam disregarded Isiuwa and slipped out of the fence (five). The dry bamboo barricade wasn't really what kept Isiuwa in, Mam said. Bamboo was easy to slip through. Words planted in the mind, not so much.

Mam was an expert at that, the slipping; slipping through the fence, slipping through time and space, slipping in and out of proper reason, so that many times Isiuwa forgot she was even there, that Nata was even there. Isiuwa was surprised when they appeared, struggled to remember where they were from, wondered why they were still here and had not been offered to the gods already as appeasement.

It was easy for Nata and Mam to fade from the mind, being shunted to the edge, living in the outermost corner of the settlement where scorpions abound and only those deemed unworthy are offered land to build shelter. Nata blamed Mam in the beginning, believing it was her fault, that she could've just stopped arguing with the Elders, telling them that there were no whistling gods, that the civilization under the sand was just swallowed by an extreme ecological disaster. She insisted there were thriving civilizations out there and she was going to find them, that the whirlwind of time would take her there. She insisted she had seen it for herself.

So, when Mam kissed Nata on the forehead and said, "Let's go," she knew then that Isiuwa was right: Mam was a madwoman. A whirlwind that took people to a world where there was no sand? Going willingly into the dunes to be swallowed by the gods?

She refused to go, of course. Mam even tried to force her, after multiple arguments, them both screaming at the top of their voices in the shelter. Mam said she was just trying to save them, and Nata reminded her that *Isiuwa* was trying to save them, that was why they had rules. Mam saw then that Nata would never be ready, so she tied her wrists and ankles when she was asleep, gagged her mouth and put her in a cart, but she couldn't even pull it from the shelter to the fence. She untied Nata, and Nata ran as fast as she could.

She went back to the shelter and waited for Mam to return because, of course, there was no whirlwind of time, there was no magical dust storm roaming the dunes, waiting for people to save. So, she waited.

And waited.

And waited.

Until the dunes whistled.

We mind our own business, the Chief says to Isiuwa. *We stay alive because we do not seek beyond our means.*

Nata finds Tasé just easy. The small boy, scrawny, elbows like the edge of a box, eyes so sunken they could hold seas: he would never be found with the courtyard troupe. He was always somewhere else (and even when he was, he wasn't). He is the kind of son Isiuwa thinks the Chief shouldn't have; a sickling, eyes always to the sky in thought. It is probably best for everyone that he always takes off, always goes missing.

Nata finds him by the old, dead dwellings, the dump site of shelters of those from Isiuwa who have been taken by the dune song. Somewhere in there lie Mam's best tools, implements, all the things she salvaged from the world before, which she refused to be allowed to be confiscated for the Elders' archive. All these, alongside their shelter itself, which was hacked down to ensure it was never rebuilt. It would've been burnt if Isiuwa could, but fire is too dangerous a thing in these times.

Tasé squats right in the middle of it, his feet ashy, perched on some hard debris with a slate, writing on the polished surface with a white rock. He is the Chief's only child, and his role in becoming a novitiate was written before he was born; he is going to be given the chance to be the future of Isiuwa. He does spend a lot of time with the Elders, mostly learning to scribble the shapes that represent Isiuwa's language and sounds, but he barely ever spends time with the sentry group or the courtyard troupe. He is mostly alone, practicing.

Nata approaches slowly. He looks up.

"Will you come with me?" Nata says.

The boy stops writing, his eyeballs dancing in their sockets. "Where?"

"I'm going to find Mam."

He pauses, then writes something on the slate, slowly. "Your Mam?"

"Yes," Nata says.

He thinks for another second. "And my Mam too?"

Nata is silent for a beat. Everyone knows the stories about Tasé's mother, about the Chief's first wife. Isiuwa says she too was errant, was a madwoman like Nata's Mam, talking about getting away to someplace else. Isiuwa says the Chief was right to let Isiuwa offer her to the gods beneath the dunes, to the breath of their wrath.

"Maybe," she says.

He scribbles some more, lays down his materials, rises, and dusts off his buttock.

"Okay," he says.

Nata has always known it would be this easy when the time came. Tasé was never really here. He has always lived somewhere else, but Isiuwa just can't see it. Once, she asked him why he was only learning to write, and he said he was going to need it when he got away from here. It was then she realized he was just like her Mam, like his Mam before him.

"You know where to meet me," Nata says. "Come after dusk, when the sentries are drunk. And don't tell anyone."

"Dusk?" he says. "It's moonday. There'll be whistling today."

"Yes," Nata says. "Exactly."

Anyone who leaves belongs to the gods, the Chief tells Isiuwa. *They shall not be allowed to return.*

The first time, Nata didn't make it far. She found nothing but sand and sun in all directions, the shadows cast by the dunes falling over her when the day began to wane. She found a few skeletons of people and animals, dried out, and a few artifacts she had never seen before, which she salvaged. Her water ran out. She did not find Mam, not even her dead body. She did not find a whirlwind to take her where Mam had gone.

The sentries found her when she returned to the fence. They swooped in, their foreheads shiny beneath their cloaks, faces long and lined and expressionless. They rounded her up without a word, because who needs words when the agreement is unspoken?

They did what needed to be done and paraded Nata through the settlement, carrying her in the carved ceremonial stretcher, offering her as a sacrifice, a warning, a performance of her chosen path to death, into the mouth of the gods. Isiuwa emerged from their shelters and flocked behind the sentries, shaking their heads sadly, whispering, pointing. They reached out to touch Nata, maybe in pity, maybe in solidarity, maybe asking, "Why?" The sentries whipped their hands off. They always returned.

The Chief's shelter sits in its own courtyard in the center of the settlement, the largest and only one with an anteroom, where they set Nata before him. Isiuwa crowded around. The Chief is just like every other man in the settlement, only slightly plumper and with a permanent frown on his forehead. He doesn't dress any differently from the others either, cloaked in the exact same cloth, except for the large woven headpiece made of fragile beads that Nata knows is passed down from chief to chief.

The decision was swift and simple. As custom, she could not be allowed back, lest she anger the gods and the dunes advance on Isiuwa. She would be sent back out with nothing, not even a cloak, to ensure her transition into the mouth of the dune gods was easy and hassle-free. This would ensure the many moons of carefully created community order were not put in jeopardy due to her self-indulgence. The gods would understand. Plus, it was a favor. It was *her* desire to leave, after all.

But, Tasé. He changed everything. Right in the middle of proceedings, with no regard for the court, he scuttled over to her, kneeling there in the center of the anteroom with her found artifacts laid out on the floor before her. He was younger then, smaller. He touched her hair and smiled. He fondled her ear. He pulled a hand from behind himself and offered her a piece of bread. She took it and munched.

Isiuwa held their breath and waited. Tasé had never found purchase with anybody, no matter how much the Chief tried. Not even his nurses could get him to do anything. He was a person of his own, and the Chief had come to accept that he would exist in solitary and die. There was no hope for Tasé in the world that was to come forth from this, where the strength of community and order would be the sole decider for survival. People like Tasé would have no place in that world. But the Chief had not quite moved on to this acceptance, and Tasé still represented a glimmer of hope for him, a hope that had suddenly rekindled.

The Chief cleared his throat and asked for Nata to be held in

lockup. She was there until the next day, and that was how she knew
she wasn't going to be ejected.

No deserter had ever been held. The punishment was always the same right after the courtyard declaration: the sentries would open the gate and prod, prod, prod until the person was several steps away from the bamboo fence. And even if they cried and cried, the gates would be shut against them. Then they would wander away, their cries for help sailing back to Isiuwa in the wind. When it came time for the dune gods to whistle, their wail would be cut mid-scream, and then there would be nothing but silence and safety for Isiuwa once again.

She was brought before Isiuwa the next morning. There was, after all, some use for this one, the Chief said. It would be a waste to discard this one so uselessly because she wasn't in her right mind, following in the footsteps of the bad example set by her Mam. The troupe would pray to the gods on her behalf on the next trip, while she would atone by serving the community. That service would take the form of becoming a serving companion to Tasé, helping him assimilate into the community and become stronger and better to take up his role in the coming future.

Isiuwa hummed and nodded and praised the Chief for his wisdom, forethought, and benevolence. And this was how Nata knew Mam was right after all: that the gods that did exist were not beneath the dunes at all, but words planted in the mind. This was how she knew she was going to leave again.

When they dispersed, the Elders confiscating her artifacts for their archive, Tasé knelt in the dust with her, leaning close, his nose almost touching hers, his young breath racy with excitement.

"Did you smell it, then?" he whispered. "Did you feel it, outside? Did it smell like power?"

They leave at dusk, hand in hand, hearts racing in sync. It is harder for the sentries to spot them in the sand when it's dark, when shapes no longer exist and the dunes in the distance are the only shadows left. They leave without a light, navigating the darkness through Nata's mental memory alone, lugging the food and water she has gathered. They wear thinner cloaks so they can move faster. In the cold of the night, Tasé's teeth chatter.

In every direction conceivable is nothing but sand and dust and wind, with only the peaks and crests of dunes, small and big, for company. The largest dunes, under which the greatest ruins of the perished people before Isiuwa lie, form a shadow against the red glow of failing light in the distance. They avoid walking up the crest of any of the miniature dunes they come across, to stay out of long-range sight. The sand is cool against their feet and leaves many holes for tracks. Nata knows that come morning, they will be easily found if their pursuers ride Isiuwa's one camel hard enough, or if the fastest sentries are set on their trail.

Tasé is silent, for the most part. For a boy only slightly younger than Nata, his silence speaks well beyond his years. Nata remembers telling him the same thing Mam used to tell her, which she didn't believe then, but does now: *You, alone, are a god. You are a dune too, and the dune will not swallow itself. Don't let Isiuwa tell you otherwise.*

Nata watches him clutch his cloak tight about himself and stare ahead, his eyes fixed on the undulating shapes in the horizon. The Chief doesn't know that when he punished her, he only gave her more light, see. She is *meant* to be Tasé's companion because she is the only one who understands why he is the way he is, because the same questions that are asked of him roil within her. They both grew up listening to the constant susurrus of Isiuwa, wondering if they were sane or just as mad as their mothers, and the questions formed a knot within them that will only be unknotted by leaving. They have always known, in some way, that they are going to find the women who birthed them and breathed this fire of liberty that cannot be quenched; that they are going to find home only there.

They put more distance between themselves and Isiuwa, moving in a straight line, in the direction of the dunes. No one seems to be following them, a good sign. Nata hopes for them to reach a dune before dawn so they can rest in its shadow at high noon. But they can only stomp in the sand so long before their legs get tired. The undulating outlines still loom in the distance, and Nata cannot tell how close they are yet, but they are far enough from Isiuwa that it makes sense to rest.

They have some bread and the roasted termites. Nata lets Tasé have the allowable sip of water for today, while she settles for sugarcane. She munches, wondering what she'll say when she finds Mam. She has focused so much on leaving that she has forgotten she might not be happy to see Mam at all, that her chest might become tighter, that she might never forgive her for leaving, for not sacrificing everything and coming back for her. But she also isn't ready for whatever answer Mam has to give. Maybe this is why she found a way to take Tasé with her, despite the odds. Maybe she is trying to do it over, how it should've been.

"We should move," Tasé says.

Nata lies on her back in the sand. "We don't need to. It will come to us."

He frowns. She sees this and says, "It's a roaming whirlwind. That's what causes the whistle. My Mam used to call it the wind of opportunity, that it comes for you only if you present yourself."

He lies on his back next to her, wrapped from head to toe and becoming one with the sand. Soon, they fall asleep, and Nata dreams of meeting Mam, but Mam no longer recognizes her. She wakes once, and lies awake, remembering all Mam's stories about the wind, about the five times she slipped beyond the fence and slipped back in, and what she saw. She called it the whirlwind of liberation, of return to a time when even though her tongue was just as tied, her body just as controlled, it was at least hers. It did not belong to Isiuwa.

Whatever time-place that is, Nata is sure Mam has somehow returned to it but has been unable to return as promised. Now she is going to find that whistle, and she is going to blow it herself.

People will kill what they do not understand, Mam used to say. *They will flay it with their tongues if their hands are tied.*

When the sentries catch up with Nata it is too late: the dune song has already begun.

It is almost the end of night when the whirlwind first starts to appear. Its coming is announced by a faraway lament, a deep-throated complaint, serving as the right augury for the arrival of feet and torches at the exact place where Nata and Tasé succumbed to fatigue and made camp.

The Chief has come along with the sentries. The light of the torch and shadow of his cloak darken his face in a manner that is representative of his heaving chest and his thoughts so clear they could've been bellowed: There will be no mercy this time.

"Take them," is all he says.

There is a spat, sand flying in all directions, torches wavering in the wind of coming dawn, but all is soon settled. Nata is at one end, subdued; Tasé restrained at the other.

The Chief faces him first, stooping to his height. Then he raises his hand and deals Tasé a big slap in the middle of his face. There's a snap of cartilage.

"Just offer me," Tasé says, his voice loud for the first time, his speech bubbling with blood and snot and spittle. "Offer me, so this nightmare can end for the two of us."

The silence that passes is filled only by the picking up of sand into dust, the whirlwind now visible in the distance, gathering force, a storm within a storm. Against the backdrop of the orange horizon of the rising sun, it is a roaring ghoul of black wind.

"No," the Chief says, looking at the cloud as it approaches. "No."

And in the midst of all this, with no one paying attention to Nata at all, she finds her opening.

She darts, moves too quickly, out of reach of the sentries' arms, too quickly for their legs to find purchase in the silty sand. She flits with smaller feet, one step, five steps, and soon she is too far. The shouts behind her curse, yell, call her crazy, mad girl, selfish, putting Isiuwa in jeopardy, but she is deaf to them because her eyes are fixed on the glorious, glorious light ahead.

For the first time, she sees the whirlwind through her own eyes, and not through the eyes of Mam's stories. The Chief is right in calling it the breath of the gods, because it holds within it a crackle, light and lightning, embraced by wind roiling within itself, gloved in sand and dust and debris. It moves like a cloud would if it were angry. It roars mightily now, up close, as if made of mouth alone. Sand hisses in its wake, an unending flute, an orchestra of whistles, a posse of snakes.

Glorious.

She halts then, right in its path, and turns, the wall of light and sound and dust right behind her. The Chief and the sentries have stopped chasing, standing well out of the path of the wind, Tasé held down between two sentries. This far out she cannot see their faces, but by the light of their angled flames, their postures say it all: that she is a waste of existence, that she has ruined all the good work Isiuwa has done.

Yes, she thinks. *Yes.*

But: *Tasé.*

She takes a step forward, two, hoping he understands it. She takes another step. The wind comes behind her, but she steps forward again, buying time, reminding herself she can do better, *be* better. Her Mam tried, but she can try harder.

Please, please, she thinks, watching him, static between the two sentries. *Please.*

And as if he hears her, at the very instant she starts to feel the hairs on the back of her neck stand in response to the crackle of the wind, Tasé moves. He slips, lithe, darting, the sentries too shocked by everything to react properly. He ditches his top cloak as he speeds across the sand, his skin black and melding with the night. His father, the Chief, follows, lumbering along, screaming his name, the fires of the sentries bobbing alongside him.

Yes, Nata thinks. *Yes.*

The whirlwind of time, of gods, of opportunity, of liberation, leans down right then and embraces her. Sand fills her eyes, her mouth, her nose, her ears. Her skin tingles softly, and she feels her feet leaving the ground.

But she sticks out an arm all the same.

It feels like ages, and like a faraway thing, when a sandy hand grasps hers. She pulls—to herself, to the Mams who dared to leave before, to the future, to power.

They rise, together. She knows it is together because she knows the weight of defiance. She offers herself to the wind and they slip, slip, losing all sense of time and space. They become nothing and everything, and all is possible in the breath of the gods, a breath that is now theirs to breathe. Wherever it would take them, they do not know, but at least one thing is sure: that their tongues and their bodies and their hearts will belong to them.

THE WORK OF WOLVES

TEGAN MOORE

Tegan Moore (alarmhat.com) is a writer and professional dog trainer living in the Pacific Northwest. She enjoys eating noodles, hiking in the rain, and reading scary stories. She has published short fiction in magazines including *Beneath Ceaseless Skies, Asimov's,* and *Tor.com* and runs the Clarion West One-Day Workshops. You can follow her obscenely charismatic dogs @temerity.dogs on Instagram.

am a good dog.

The scent trails are already as broken by the wind as the apocalyptic neighborhoods they lead through, and smoke from a fire half a mile southeast adds another layer of complexity. Following one trail is like following the roots of a plant wound tight together in the dirt.

No, better: It is like sorting through the fallen trees after this storm. Difficult to tell where one tree begins and the other ends, what belongs to what, and where the different parts are from.

That's a very good *Is Like*. I save it to keep it with my other good ones.

The sector clear, I send the final readings back to Carol via DAT. She's behind me with the field assistant, standing on the hood of a car. I can hear the distant, quiet *tick* of her DAT receipt.

"Sera," she calls out, "slow down and stay within my visual range."

Carol should hurry and follow me per standard procedure instead of yelling from the hood of a wrecked car. I don't have time to wait for her.

Barometric pressure dropping, I ping back to her DAT. I see her hand touch the receiver in her ear from the corner of my eye as I trace the foundation where a prefabricated house once stood. *Significant enough to indicate further storms approaching.* "Sera," my DAT says, but I also hear Carol's voice carry over the rubble field of tangled two-by-four framing, shingles peeled from rooftops, tatters of furniture, and twisted textiles. She struggles down from the car into the wreckage. "Stay in range, goddamn it. Slow down!"

Carol is now too far away to direct or even accompany my search. I don't need her direction, but the more distance between us, the greater the chance of a missed opportunity. She is slow, perhaps deliberately slow. What does that indicate? Will this also negatively impact the speed at which she acknowledges my alert?

I jump up on an intact retaining wall where I can catch the breeze's fresh edge. From here it's easier to see the destruction for what it was before the storm: broken stumps where dogs might have lifted their legs, sidewalks where bicycles and skateboards ruckled along, driveways. Here and there a few houses stand, debris piled at their foundations. In a few days those piles will become a haven for rats and mice. In the distance there are a few humans, nontargets I've already cleared from my cache. People who lived here, who now pick through the storm's detritus. I want to give them an *Is Like*, but there's no time. I am working. My priority is to do the best job possible.

I turn my nose to the wind.

The cool air that sucks past the moisture in my nostrils is busy with stories, directions, convoluted half-finished conversations. My vision fuzzes out, becomes irrelevant. Sound snaps through here and there, but I am thinking now with my olfactory bulb:

Broken power line burn reaching this way fitfully due to unpredictable wind pattern shifts

Torn sod broken grass wet turned soil chemicals down further raw sewage must be septic systems in some of these prefab units but trapped not seeping yet

Old human-trails anxiety adrenaline panic the lingering scent of cadaver which has been removed not my target

Broken concrete split shredded pine timber sodden plywood soaked furniture batting

Burst of char as the burn kicks up on the wind then turns back in on itself

The detritus of wind distance age broken-down-ness places happenings irrelevant

Girl

North very faint filtered through quite a bit of green sap fresh branches downed trees but

I ping Carol. *Interest. Mark location, north northwest.* I take another deep suck of air through my nose to confirm. *This way.*

"Wait for support." Even over the DAT, Carol sounds out of breath.

I can't wait. I need to do my job. Carol and Devin the field assistant can find me via the DAT's GPS. I must follow this hint of Girl.

Through a hedge and I've already lost the scent, but in a moment a memory of *Girl* passes on the air, and my head turns toward the smell so rapidly it tweaks a muscle in my neck before my body can follow. I am moving as quickly as my nose will allow, every step picked out for me by the scent and what it says I should do.

The world fades to almost nothing, just my nose and the scent and stimulus-response, until a semi looses a roar from twenty meters away and jerks me back into audio/visual.

I have been following cyclone fencing along a housing development's edge. The storm has punched through the fence in places, and beyond the openings, cars on the interstate are slowing to gawk at the damage. The semi honks again, trapped behind the slowdown.

Its bellow makes me think about Mack and the way his hot dark blood stank as it spread against the asphalt. I remember feeling in my skin and muscles that I would very much like to roll in that smell. A dog's instinct. I should not have stopped to look at him when it happened, but I needed confirmation he was dead.

Irrelevant to my current search. I shake my head to clear wind-driven grit from my eyes and turn into the current again, reaching. I ping Carol my location—a reminder only, she knows how to find me—then hunt the wind.

It is still there, but its story is conflicted; the stream of its path, eddies and pools and lines all broken by the weather, a puzzle of color and feel. Perhaps a human with a computer might be able to map parts of the puzzle out. But time and movement have danced and shivered and jolted and coughed these trails out of the human spectrum of sense.

Dogs are better than machines at untangling this kind of mess. But all this broken human detritus, and the storms growing greater and more frequent now year by year, and the endless desire for more perfect work: these things make the job too tricky for a dog's nose. A normal dog's, at least.

This is why I am the solution. It's why I am a good dog, better than Mack was. It's why Carol should do things my way.

Carol's voice carries over the DAT. "Devin and I are a hundred yards out. If the trail crosses the freeway, Sera, do *not* follow. That's an order."

Before I can respond, the wind twists through my nostrils: *Girl.*

That trickle of target scent wraps itself around my olfactory center. My target is my primary objective. I send Carol my heading as I run, an automatic part of my brain remembering fieldwork directives. I am required to communicate relevant information to my handler, but I am only required to follow handler commands within reason. I find very few of my handler commands reasonable today.

Deep in the scent cone now, I hardly see, not thinking with that part of my mind. Scent is brighter than any color in this muted, cloud-heavy weather. It is a viscous, thickened path, easy to follow. I can turn my head now and I don't lose the trail, but feel it pull and contort through time and space. It strengthens this way, grades off in the other, torques around on itself. I know that if it was untwisted, it would move differently. I understand how it bent and broke over time. It is all a trick of the wind.

I come to an eddy. A lesser dog—a normal dog, like Mack—would hesitate or lose themselves. I move through the scent-trap and scrabble over a broken segment of roof. The trail shimmers on the other side, where the ground is cool and sodden beneath my paw pads.

Five yards farther, an oscillation in the wind unfolds back through time and I move with it through a heavy stand of pines, thick with bright acid resin smell. I have my teeth in it, I can feel the track itch behind my

Girl

Indication, I ping. I push beneath a wind-felled pine and its broken-wood smells. Needles brush against my face. *Target scent strong.*

Carol's voice: "Where are you?"

Question irrelevant. She has GPS access.

Twist of track to the left through

Old Girl smell relevant

Other child smells a broad collection of small human life scents in this patch of forest Broken boards rotting garbage leaf mold

Girl

I step up and over another felled tree rich smell of rot and my ears move on their own because there is human sound close by I push my

head deep into the space beneath the tree with the old smells and the
deep Girl smell and

  Alert

  Girl

  Target acquired primary objective

  Yes

  I am a good dog

  Target Girl wheezes quietly she says "Help" I breathe her scent
deeply

  Alert

  But will Carol

  "Acknowledged," Carol responds. "On our way."

  Good yes

  I am a good dog

I send Carol my GPS coordinates again to reconfirm even though
I can see from the DAT that she is approximately one hundred yards
across the rubble field. "Help me, doggy," target Girl says. Her voice
sounds like the wind, soft and leaky. That's a good *Is Like*. The rot-
scented tree pins her in a rubble of boards and magazines and a
blanket in a dense stand of brush and pines, some distance from the
neighborhood. Her one small free hand reaches for my mud-slicked
head. "Good doggy," she says. "I'm stuck. Help."

  In this dense visual screen it may be difficult for my team to locate
me. I back out of the target Girl's location and head toward the forest's
edge.

  "Doggy," she whispers. "Wait, doggy, no, wait." There's a gurgle
to her wheeze, perhaps a punctured lung. Which is why she can't cry
for help, at this distance from habitation. She is likely in dire physical
danger. Only an EI dog could have found her so quickly.

  I trot out of the stand of pines and up onto the nearest high
ground—a culvert near the road. I can hear target Girl now, since I am
listening for her. "Come back," she sobs. "Doggy, help. Please. Come
back."

  Her weak voice will be easy for my excellent ears to locate for

my team. *Alert*, I ping again, though I don't need to. I allow myself a
nice wag.

I am a good dog.

Sound carries strangely in storm-thickened air. From my place in the command tent I can clearly hear the baying voice of some small hound at least a mile away. However, the generator running out behind the team's trucks sounds like it belongs to another time and place, and wind chokes the traffic noise from the freeway. I can still hear the difference between trucks like Carol's and the smaller cars, and the sounds of big semitrucks like the one that hit and killed Mack. I know the sounds of those trucks well.

I lie with my head on my paws so that I look like I am resting and not eavesdropping. Overhead the wind rips at the surface of the command tent roof, which ripples and bucks. It is like there is a giant dog up there, digging and worrying at it, trying to get in.

Not a bad *Is Like*.

Is Like is a game I made up at ESAC. I didn't make it all up myself; my trainer Dacy taught me the beginning. Though what Dacy taught me wasn't quite the same. She taught me that "sit in the training center" *Is Like* "sit in the parking lot" and "find the box with this smell" *Is Like* "find the person with this smell." So Dacy gave me the idea. I made up the part where I keep playing it forever in my head.

The way I play the game, it isn't always about training. It doesn't even have to be about real things. It can just be about thoughts. It keeps my mind busy when Carol leaves me in my crate, or tied to something, like I am now.

"I won't do this anymore," I hear Carol say to Anders, our team leader. She stands with her back to me on the far side of the command tent, well within my hearing range. I can tell she's angry by context and by her elevated blood pressure, but I don't know why. The search was successful and finished quickly. Our team performed well. Since Mack has been dead for almost two months now, the changes I had hoped to see in Carol's behavior have slowly surfaced as she begins to forget how she used to work with Mack and learns, instead, how to work with me. She is a slow student, but there is still progress.

Medics load the target Girl into an ambulance in the parking lot. I hear a trio of vulture drones descending to snatch video of the gurney. The hair on my neck prickles with dislike. I am not afraid of drones. I simply find that they occupy the "uncanny valley." Uncanny valley is a concept that Dacy told me about that means "both too much and not enough like me, and therefore unsettling." Dacy also warned me many humans have the same uncomfortable reaction to EI animals.

I don't know why, when I look exactly like a medium-yellow Labrador retriever. Yellow Labrador retrievers test extremely well with the public. When a Labrador finds a disaster victim, the positive cultural associations the victim has with the breed comfort them. Yellow is the best color, as well, because in dark areas I am easily identifiable. This is information that I learned on Modanet, after Dacy told me about Labrador retrievers when I was a puppy.

However, human reactions to dogs can be unpredictable. For example, the way they treated Mack. He often gave the team physical attention they didn't want. Mack was smart for a normal dog, so I wonder why he chose to ignore their requests. They said things like, "Eww, Mack, get your slobbery Kong off of me, you dork," and "Mind your own business, you big oaf." Wouldn't the humans on team like him *more* if he complied? He didn't even have the excuse of being a yellow Labrador; he was an overlarge German shepherd with a dark and heavy face. Dark German shepherds don't test nearly as well with the public, so I am not sure why everyone liked him so much.

"I'm done," Carol says. "Retire me, I'm serious. Take me off the roster, Anders. No more searches."

"Carol," Anders says.

"No. I don't want to argue with you about this." She gestures toward me without looking. "This isn't what I spent the last twenty years doing. I don't like this future."

"Come on. It's a training problem," he says. "You can teach her to work closer to you."

"That defeats the point of the EI!" Carol tosses her radio onto the folding table. "But you know what, it is a training problem. *She's* training *me* for EI SAR work, and I don't want to do it."

"Excuse me, please," says a man. I look up at him. He stands just outside the tent and smells nicely of spicy food. He holds a camera and wears a press pass around his neck. He calls to my teammates. "Can I get a couple shots of the dog and handler?"

Anders looks at Carol. Carol sighs, steps over a cooler toward me, and unhooks my leash from the folding table's leg. I wag at the journalist to make a good impression.

He looks at me curiously.

"It's Enhanced, isn't it?" he asks. "The dog?"

Carol casts a look over her shoulder to Anders. It's Carol's job to talk about me to the press because she is my handler, but she's never seemed enthusiastic about the job. She's particularly hesitant in this moment. I can feel her desire to cross the command tent and finish her conversation, but Anders is already busy with his tablet and radio. The tension between the two of them is unusual.

"Sera?" says Devin from outside the tent.

The man with the camera, who may have also sensed the tension, looks at Devin with relief. Carol does too. I am good at reading human expressions; it's one of the things they teach at ESAC.

"She's Enhanced Intelligence, yeah," Devin says. "First EI SAR dog in the field in the US. First nonmilitary EI dog doing anything, actually."

The photographer looks confused. "Sar?"

"Sorry. Search-and-Rescue. This is Sera's seventh find already, and she's only been on the team for half a year. Some dogs don't make that record in a lifetime."

The man taps something on his camera and points it at me. Carol kneels beside me in the pose we do for all our pictures, and I look at the camera and open my mouth so my tongue shows and I look like the dogs people have at home and they will relate to me.

"Search dogs don't find people that often?" the man asks. There's a series of ticks and flashes.

"Well, we train all the time, but we don't deploy that often. Three, four times a year usually. These storms, though." Devin shrugs. "It's been insane. SAR teams in from all over the region. Law enforcement, military, everybody's working the cleanup and rescue ops."

The man nods in a big, knowing gesture. He's ignoring Carol now. "What's the dog's name?"

"Sera. S-E-R-A, for Serendipity. And that's Carol Ramos there, one of the team founders and the best dog handler in the Midwest."

Carol rises from her photo-pose crouch and hooks my leash back to the table. She says, "Nice to meet you," to the man, and turns. My gaze follows hers; Anders has left the command tent.

"Thanks," the man calls as she walks away. Carol raises a hand but doesn't answer.

Devin steps toward me and pats my side. I lean away from the physical contact, but give him a conciliatory wag. He talks with the photographer for a few more minutes, but I am not listening.

Instead I watch Carol find Anders next to his van and continue their discussion—their argument. I strain my hearing, but the stormy sound patterns intrude. Instead I hear wind picking up as the barometric pressure continues to drop, softening the hush-wash growling of the interstate; intruding human voices, high and yelping; the sounds of urban life—traffic, the percussion of comings and goings and doings, dogs and kids and shouts—held at a remove by the perimeter of the storm's destruction. I hear no wildlife. Wild animals don't emerge in weather like this.

The man leaves and Devin drops into Carol's portable chair and puts his feet up on the cooler. He looks at me and smiles. I want to follow Carol, but I am hooked to the table, and even though I could drag the table with no trouble or just unhook myself (my teeth and tongue are very dexterous), I know that when someone hooks a leash to something, it's because they want the dog to stay. I stay.

Carol shakes her head at Anders. She gestures in the air with one hand. Anders tries to put his hands on her shoulders, but she uses the gesturing hand to brush him away. She looks out, across the line of parked cars and the staging area and the tented command center, and she looks at me. Anders looks at me too.

I don't know what to do while they are looking at me like that. I am usually good at reading human expressions, but I need context in order to do it with accuracy.

What context do I have? Why are they arguing? The search ended in a successful find, the victim alive and our team uninjured. I count this search an even greater success personally, because Carol acknowledged my remote alert within the fifteen-second optimal feedback window. It was an ideal handler response, and a great improvement on our previous find record. On our last deployment find, Carol didn't acknowledge my alert for 3:57:12, nearly sixteen times the optimal feedback number.

Carol often waits until she's in visual range to acknowledge my alert. This can take anywhere from twenty seconds to two minutes or more. Continuing to work Mack reinforced her habit of visually acknowledging her dogs' alerts. In fact, working with Mack appeared to make Carol entirely refuse the superior methods that I learned at ESAC. But Mack is no longer a factor. This time Carol's acknowledgment was appropriate.

I review my log in the DAT and confirm that all my own behaviors were within acceptable parameters. I find no anomalies.

The tenor of Carol's voice carries, but the wind blurs her words. Her posture is stiff and forward, her gestures tight. She glances again across the sprawling staging area at me. Carol's body language indicates that she's angry. I think she's angry at me.

Carol is often angry at me.

Carol frequently avoids eye contact with me. She doesn't speak to me much other than issuing cues and commands, even though she often spoke to Mack. She doesn't initiate physical contact. She doesn't throw a Kong on a rope for me when we do search drills and she doesn't tell me I am a genius or a screwball and she doesn't laugh at me when I roll on an excellent smell in the grass, all of which she did for Mack.

She doesn't say, "You're a good dog, Sera." Instead she says, "Good work."

Carol doesn't seem to like me.

To be successful in the field, a dog and handler team must communicate well. They must be well-trained, focused on their job, and physically fit. I haven't found anything on Modanet that indicates that they must like each other.

My own feelings on this subject are, I suppose, irrelevant.

The wind's roar outside the hotel windows wakes me from troubled sleep. I am in my crate. In the bed, the dark shapes of Carol and Devin breathe shallowly. When Devin came to the door earlier, Carol told him that she didn't want to talk, but they did talk. They talked about the find today and about the storms. They talked about Mack and his bad and strange behaviors. They laughed and Devin got them both tissues from the bathroom. Then they stopped talking, and their biometrics changed, and now they sleep.

I need rest to recover from the hard work of my search, but today's events haunt me. Carol said no more searches. She said retirement. If Carol retires will I retire with her? I am only three years old.

I check Modanet. All listed retirement dates for SAR dogs are either concurrent with or prior to the retirement dates of their handlers. There is, of course, no information about EI SAR dogs, because I am the first one.

Corresponding information about military and defense EI dog career dates is not available on Modanet.

I remember what Devin said to the photographer earlier, about all of my finds. How some dogs don't make that record in a lifetime.

The barometric pressure dips, indicating an increased likelihood of funnel clouds forming. It's not a dramatic fall. While I consider whether to ping Carol's DAT with the information, the radio bleats.

A surge of adrenaline twitches my muscles. When the radio goes my heart rate always increases. Unexpected radio calls might mean a search.

Carol shifts first in the bed, breathing pattern changing. The radio squalls again and then both she and Devin are coming quickly awake.

Carol sits up in the dark. She taps the radio screen and says, "Ramos here."

I have a difficult time understanding voices over radio. I always have. When I was still at ESAC Dacy explained this is a common handicap among dogs and not something to be concerned about. It is, however, frustrating that I can only understand broadcast voices transmitted over DAT and not what's being said right now.

A voice—masculine, likely Anders'—speaks briefly. Carol and Devin look at each other in the dark. "No, it's fine. Just . . . we'll talk," Carol says. Devin slides out of bed, gestures on the bedside light, and begins gathering his belongings. "Here? Uh, okay. Two-oh-four. Yeah, five minutes."

Devin mutters under his breath. Carol shuffles into the bathroom. He waits a few seconds for her to come back out, but I can sense that he is impatient. "Carol?" he says.

"Why are you still here? Anders is coming. To my room for some reason. You'll probably be on this callout, too, you know."

"Lord Jesus," Devin says, and slips his shoes on. He leaves while Carol's still in the bathroom and pulls the door closed quietly behind him. The shower runs. It stops less than a minute before I hear someone in the hallway. I already know that it's Anders because I can smell him.

This is a unique occurrence. Devin often visits Carol's room when the team is out on training or deployment, but Anders never has. I don't think it will be for the same reason.

Carol exits the bathroom fully dressed, rubbing her wet hair with a towel. She opens the door.

"Sorry to intrude," Anders says. He looks like he would like to leave again. His posture *Is Like* a cat's when it is suspicious of danger, stiff and still.

Carol moves around the room, putting items in her pack. She pulls her hair back with one hand and fastens it behind her head. "You don't need to come up here to convince me to go out," she says. "I'll finish this deployment. But after this—"

"Actually," Anders says, "I'm here to convince you of something else entirely. Well, both things, really."

I wish Carol would let me out of my crate. Her movement makes me want to move around, too, to find my work harness and bring it to her and wait by the door.

Instead Carol stops moving. "What?"

Anders takes a few steps into the room. "This call," he says. He's quiet for a second. "It's not a—it's not part of the storm system. It's not even a rescue search. It's . . ." He is quiet again.

"Wow," Carol says. "Now I really can't wait."

"It's a security call," Anders says. "The police or the military should handle it with their own EI units, but"—he looks at me—"Sera's the closest EI dog. Geographically, I mean. All the defense EI units they could call on are deployed farther south to deal with the storms, the weather has shut down all of the air traffic that could get them back here to do this, and time is . . . there isn't a lot of time. A few units are trying to get up here, but they've been delayed already. Sera's the only one in range."

Carol bends down to pull on her boots. "She's not defense, she's SAR."

"You know she's capable," Anders says, and his voice is scolding. He's right. "She can do whatever work you ask her to."

"So it's Sera you need, not me."

"You're her handler," he says. "We need you both."

Carol mutters, "She doesn't need a handler, she needs IT support."

Anders looks at his feet and fills his lungs. "You're still the most qualified person to—"

"Yeah, yeah," Carol says. She zips up her pack and slings it onto one shoulder. "I don't want the job. I don't like where all this is going. You know what, I wish it had been the robots that took over. It wouldn't sting as much as getting put out on my ass by my own damn dog."

Anders watches her, waiting.

"Shut up," Carol says, even though Anders has said nothing. "Yes, this is partly about losing Mack. And no, it won't get better after more time has passed, because it's not just about losing Mack." She points at me. "All our next dogs are going to be like that. The work has changed but I haven't."

"Technology changes things," Anders says. "I can't make you evolve with the field. I can't force you to. But Sera's still a dog, Carol, and the work is still the work."

"It's not," she says. "You used to build a connection. You and the dog, you'd get inside each other's brains. Feel each other's feelings. It was all connection. Connection was the point. This damn thing"—she lifts her wrist where my DAT is integrated—"skips all of that. It takes away the part of the work I loved most."

"Okay," Anders says. He puts his hands up and steps back toward the door. "Okay, Carol, I'm not arguing with you. Not now, at least. This search isn't just a life at stake, it's national security. Can you and Sera do it and we'll talk about your future afterward?"

Carol finally unlatches my crate. It's difficult to wait inside until she releases me. When she does, I scramble across the carpet to my harness as fast as I can. "Let's just finish this so I can go home and lick my wounds," she says.

We drive for an hour in Devin's truck, Carol with her feet on the dash, as light seeps into the sky from the east. It's a low, stormy morning, and it lacks the normal happy anticipation of driving to a deployment. This silence is tense. Devin tries to ask Carol about retirement again, like he did last night, but she ignores him.

I wish Carol would answer his questions. I want to know, too. And I want Devin to ask, what about your dog? What will Sera do after you retire? I want him to demand an answer, because I have no idea what will happen to me when Carol quits SAR.

I can't ask her the question myself. Carol doesn't like talking to me. At ESAC, before I was sent out to my field assignment, Dacy warned me that I would need to watch out for humans who were uncomfortable with EI. That the new technology made many people nervous and unhappy. That if I suspected I was interacting with a person for whom the uncanny valley was too wide, I should pretend that I was more like a regular dog in order to help them feel comfortable.

I don't think Dacy suspected that she was talking about my future handler. I certainly did not consider the possibility until it was too late. But Carol is more uncomfortable with me than anyone else I have encountered. She has improved; I no longer smell fear in her discomfort. Still, her discomfort remains.

Dacy told me to be a dog as much as I could. It's difficult, because although I am a dog in some ways, I am also something else. With Carol, I'm forced to keep that something else to myself. I speak only when I must, usually when we are working. I don't know if it makes Carol like me any more.

The tires on the roadway make a regular, soothing hum broken occasionally by the *ucka-ucka* of a seam in the asphalt. A light rain ticks against the windshield. Carol and Devin breathe and sigh and move in their seats. I lick my nose once, yawn loudly. A biological dog stress response. If only the humans on my team read my signals as closely as I read theirs.

I don't think about Dacy often, but today I wonder what advice she would give to me. She didn't know much about SAR, but she was good at teaching me about people.

Devin slows the truck, and our tires crunch gravel. I sit up and look out from my crate and see tall fencing running outside the windows. I hear the engine of a truck like Devin's that is behind us slow and also turn onto the gravel, and several smaller cars that must be the police escort vehicles. The second truck must mean that there are additional SAR team members in our caravan, but I did not see them before we left. We grind along a narrow driveway. Sitting up in my backseat crate, I can see a small gatehouse and the pair of silent police cruisers blocking the road.

The truck's engine falls silent. In the void I hear a faint buzzing overhead. I place it immediately. A drone, likely a police drone that tracked our progress here along with the escort. The sound of it is like an itch inside my head, where I can't reach it. It is like the feeling before a sneeze.

Good one. I add that to my *Is Like* list.

The other truck pulls ahead of us. From inside it I hear Anders' voice.

Anders. That is highly unusual. As team leader, Anders stays at base, remotely managing his deployed teams, resources, requests, and instructions from first responders, and other vital details. Yet he followed us out to this deployment.

The gate rattles open, and a cruiser starts up to make room for us to pass. The buzz of the overhead drone grows louder, and when I look I can see it black against the low clouds, like an insect scurrying across a ceiling.

We drive for a few more minutes with little to spy out the windows except more wet, stubbly fields and the occasional outbuilding. We pass another roadblock, but its cruisers are already pulled aside. I see smokestacks and low, featureless buildings.

A hum is building in the earth. It makes the hair on my spine stand up. By the time we pull up to the buildings and their looming smokestacks, the vibrations are in my bones and my stomach, and I feel cold all over from my hair prickling.

When our convoy stops, I am the only one left behind in the car. Through my crate's ventholes I watch Carol and Anders and Devin whipped by the wind as they follow a pair of dark-clad workers into a building.

My job right now is to rest, gathering mental and physical energy for the work that will come. But the unnerving vibration and the thoughts that have plagued me since yesterday prevent my resting.

Carol doesn't like the DAT. She doesn't like *me*. She prefers the old way of dog-handler teamwork, the dog giving imperfect feedback through body language and the handler interpreting signals as best they could. She likes the inefficiency because, to her, it felt like *connection*.

The DAT connects my mind directly to her, but that's not the kind of connection she means.

I have no *Is Like* for the kind of connection she means.

Why would she prefer inefficient work and unclear communication when EI is, objectively, better? I don't understand. But I do want to continue to work. Being good at my job is as important to me as *connection* is to Carol.

How can both purposes be served?

Footsteps approach the truck, but it's Anders who opens the door. A woman is with him, wearing dark clothing composed in the same practical, tidy way that the SAR team members dress. Anders unlatches my crate, leashes me without hurry. He knows better than to pat me. Everyone in our SAR unit should know I don't enjoy it, but Anders has the self-control to restrain himself where even Devin does not. I hop down from the truck at his invitation.

We're in a gravel lot in the middle of a rain-beaten prairie. Enormous steam vents rise from the earth, trickling metallic-scented exhaust. A breeze snatches past my nose carrying broken-stem, crushed-herb, fresh-dirt smells whipped about with a whiff of ozone. After such a tense hour in the stuffy truck, a face full of bright air is exhilarating.

Another man in dark clothing watches us from outside the door my team disappeared into. He scans the area through thick, military-issue e-glasses.

"This is Sera," Anders says to the woman. "Sera, this is Angela Weil. She's in charge of the search and wanted to meet you."

I understand his speech without DAT help—regular dog brains can hear the shapes of language, even if they don't understand it like I do—but I can't respond. Only Carol has the integrated neural pathway for my DAT. I sit for a polite hello in lieu of more complicated language.

"She says hi," Anders interprets.

Angela reaches a hand toward my head. She smells overpoweringly

of personal cleaning products, stringent chemical odors that Modanet
says mimic appealing plant smells to the feeble human nose. I try not
to flinch away from her touch.

"You're confident her SAR training won't interfere with the search
objectives?"

Anders shakes his head. "ESAC stock starts with the same specs
your dogs do. They're just brought up differently."

Angela grabs and gently kneads my ear. I hold my sit carefully, but
cast Anders a baleful look. He catches my eye and looks away.

"It will take a certain . . . commitment. To follow through."

Anders chuckles. "You've got the right dog for the job, then." He
crouches down in front of me. Thankfully, Angela backs off, taking
her hands with her. "This is a tough one, Sera." I've always liked the
way Anders talks to me. He reaches into his front shirt pocket and
brings out a memory stick, which he extends to the DAT interface
patch worked into my harness. My brain receives a password-protected
dossier tagged *Access Restricted*.

"Difficult parameters, novel search elements, and an unfamiliar
environment," he says. "Subterranean."

I open my mouth to pant. Anders is giving me a briefing, all on my
own. Often all the information I receive from Carol before a search
is a scent profile and a police report. I wonder what is in the *Access
Restricted* dossier.

"In addition, you will be required to apprehend the target, not just
locate it. Carol will be given limited information. There are things in
this file that are very restricted, that you'll have access to and she won't.
She will know your target, but she won't have all of the details that
you need in order to do your work. You will be required to keep some
information private from her. Do you understand?"

He holds out both hands. Right hand for yes, left hand for no. A
game the team played with me often when I was new and my intelligence was amusing to them.

I touch my nose to his right palm.

"Okay. Angela will give you the password to open the dossier. Destroy it once you have the information. Don't store it as data, store it as biological memory. Do you understand?"

Fascinated, I digest this information for half a moment, then I touch my nose to his palm again.

"Good. Angela?"

The woman bends over and touches a password to my harness DAT interface. The password winks into my thoughts.

I open the dossier.

A drone drops low overhead. Its insectile buzzing thrums the pit of my stomach. I blink rapidly at the information I have, as though it were before my physical eyes and blinking might bring clarity.

I look at Anders. He is watching me with anxiety. "Do you have questions, Sera?"

I ponder the dossier's contents. These are no longer stored files, but a part of my lived experience, as though I had witnessed the events or been told them as a story. Fusion plant architectural schematics, plant process schedules—everything from the cleaning schedule to the HVAC layout—and a series of scent profiles including that of the domestic rat and silicon filament.

It is curious information, which joins the unsettled buzz in my stomach. Do I question what Anders has told me? Does it confuse me?

No. I touch his left palm with my nose.

"Great," Anders says. He straightens up, turns to Angela. "We're ready."

We walk toward the building and its growing hum. The steam vents towering overhead are like enormous, dead trees.

Carol waits for us in the hallway of the building, where Anders hands her my lead. The hum is even louder here, a physical sensation more than a sound, and the building smells lived-in: coffee, dish soap, ink and paper, air filters. There is a banana peel in the waste bin of the conference room we are guided into by the sour-smelling Angela.

There are two other dogs in the room, both of which watch me enter. Neither of them are EI. Devin is already here, along with a lot of men and women in dark uniforms.

Carol sits next to Devin but stares at Anders with the same look she used to give Mack when he sauntered from the kitchen with particular satisfaction. Her brow is wrinkled, her lips pressed into a line. Anders ignores her and stands against the wall behind us.

"What was that about?" Devin asks her, gesturing to me with a knuckle. Carol glances at him and shakes her head.

I have a traitorous thought. I could share my information with Carol, in confidence—all of it, or part of it, or even none of it, but tell a believable lie. Perhaps this would help Carol feel *connection* with me.

I analyze this idea. The more I ponder it, the more it seems like it wouldn't work. Secret though the information might be, it's dull stuff. Schedules, scents, maps. And Carol might not like that I told her. I set the thought aside for now and listen to the briefing. I need to know what Carol knows.

Angela presents some information I already have from my dossier: We currently sit atop the Midwestern Fusion Array, third-largest fusion energy generator in the world; yesterday at 9:35 P.M. MFA security detected a communication systems breach, and shortly after that lost control of systems below the third basement, including most automated support systems and all drone controls; shortly after this a physical security breach occurred and Array security apprehended two men and a woman just inside the northeasternmost access building; these three, upon police questioning, offered a prepared manifesto from the Strong Arm of the Voice for the Silent.

"No shit," whispers Devin. Angela looks at him sharply. A dog handler on the other side of the table laughs out loud.

"What," the handler says, "is this power plant full of monkeys and guinea pigs? The hell are they doing down there?"

Angela turns her glare to the speaker and clears her throat. "The manifesto alleges that their goal is a catastrophic shutdown of the Array." The dog handler snorts, and Angela's expression scrunches up even more. "And it would be catastrophic, I assure you. Once the Array is down, it takes at least sixty hours to get it back up to 50 percent operational. The MFA powers the entirety of seven states and supplies the majority of power for six more. Nearly a quarter of the US. Worse, many of the areas served are currently in a state of emergency due to the storm systems some of you have been cleaning up after. People need to charge their cars so they can leave flooded areas or relocate from damaged homes. They need safe places to shelter. Hospitals need to be fully operational. This is a serious issue."

The man says nothing, and I am relieved at his silence.

"The Strong Arm," Angela continues, "should also not be dismissed. Despite their slipshod public reputation, their radicalized membership has nearly doubled in the last five years. They have funding. They're efficient. They may have been hippies, cat ladies, and college vegans ten years ago, but that's no longer the story. In the last two years, the Strong Arm of the Voice for the Silent has perpetrated several attacks against high-profile companies and organizations that were not widely publicized. The organization also never officially claimed responsibility. If they're staying quiet about it, then they have some other motivation than fear, panic, and publicity. And if they aren't bringing attention to this stuff, we certainly won't. An ecoterror panic is low on our list of useful epidemics at the moment."

"People will definitely notice if the power goes out in a fourth of America," says a woman on the other side of the table.

Angela does not scowl at her the way she scowled at the man. "They will," she agrees. "They're changing their game. We aren't sure why yet, but it's concerning."

"But," Devin says, "you caught them. They hacked into your computer systems, sure. But what are we searching for?"

The scent profile appears in the forefront of my thoughts immediately: domestic rat, silicon filament, and something else I can't place. It's familiar and makes me think of *work*, of *purpose*.

"Approximately one hour ago, one of the six reactors in the Array went offline. It was taken offline in an emergency shutdown procedure that could not be stopped due to . . . tampering with the electrical system. Prior to this we had noticed a pattern of small breaches throughout the Array's internal security systems. We believe the trio we apprehended released something into the Array."

"A drone," Carol says. "Shit."

It's not just a drone.

Carol spoke quietly, but Angela still heard her. Now Angela stares at Carol. "Yes," she says. "Most likely a bodydrone. A rat."

"Jesus," Carol breathes.

"Huh," says the dog handler who spoke before. "The hell is VFS doing with a bodydrone?"

"The Strong Arm," Angela corrects. She continues. "The drone took down Reactor B. We suspect it is now near Reactor C, as Reactor A has been heavily secured. Conventional dog teams will provide relief and backup for the teams already securing Reactor A. We will focus offensive efforts on cutting off the drone before it can cause additional outages—that's where the EI unit comes in." Angela looks at Carol. "Reactor D is off-line for maintenance. Add B to that, and the Array is currently at 66 percent. Below 50 percent is considered plant failure. Below 33 percent is catastrophic."

She takes a deep breath and looks around the room, skipping the eyes of the dog handler who spoke too much. "Well," she says. "Let's begin."

Down an access stairway that smells of cement blocks and urine, like all access stairways smell, then Carol and I are out into a bright-lit hallway, empty save for the regular intrusion of steel doorknobs in the walls.

We are alone. Before we left the conference room, Anders stopped Devin. "Dev, you're going to have to stay up top with me. Carol's not likely to need a navigator down there anyway," he said.

I think they are being very careful about limiting access to the MFA and to the target. I doubt even Anders had full access to the information I have been given.

I reexamine my traitorous thought from the briefing. None of the classified data that I've been given is worth sharing—much of it is schematics, equipment lists, fine details of the MFA's workings. Important information, certainly, but Carol wouldn't find it useful or interesting.

Perhaps I could make something up, but I am not sure what I would say. It might backfire. I am not ready to take the chance unless I know it will be worthwhile.

I could pretend anxiety about my objective for the search. Apprehending a target is a new skill for me. That could be worth further consideration, though it doesn't strike me as brilliant. The last time I worked on a complicated idea for a secret plan, when the solution came to me I saw its brilliance immediately. I will wait for that feeling again.

The hallway floor before us is tiled smooth white, its grip and temperature synthetic, not ceramic. The walls and ceiling are also white. The hallway's bright orderliness and its neat, closed doors visually resemble an abandoned hospital ward my team conducted exercise drills in last year. The smells could never be mistaken for each other, though—the vacant ward smelled of sickness and chemicals, and this place smells of dust and deep earth—and certainly not the sound. The seven flights we have climbed down muffle everything except the deep reverberating hum. I felt that hum in my bones and eyes even as Devin's truck turned off the highway, and now it reaches a pitch and richness that makes my gums itch.

There are other, quieter sounds: the whirs, clacks, and whispers of the plant's small machinery continuing its work. This facility is equipped with an interminable army of drone small-workers happily going about whatever tasks the Strong Arm has set them to. My dossier says they have been observed largely continuing about their regular routines, though with some abnormal clustering behaviors.

I jerk a foot out of the way of a miniature repair drone zipping along the edge of the hall, laden with a CPU fan across its beetle-back. Another even smaller drone tails it. I resist the urge to lunge after the mousy thing, and swallow, as well, the rumble of a growl I feel in my chest. Their movement is utterly unnerving. My gaze follows them like toenails following after the sweetest itch. *Is Like.*

I would prefer not to have these feelings at all. The unfortunate side effects of being a dog.

I whine quietly. The MFA's hum almost drowns it out.

"Sera?" Carol says.

She does not ask a question, and so I do not answer her.

We follow the hallway to its end and take a different access stairway down. There are elevators, but we must avoid them, as their systems have been tampered with. We proceed down eleven additional flights. According to my DAT, we're sixty-two meters beneath the surface. I feel pressure inside my ears. Carol breathes hard, though she is in excellent physical shape for a human her age.

The reactor's noise grows more intense here. Carol opens the fire door on the stairwell and the sound increases again. Next to the door there is a station with small headphones, which I assume are noise-minimizing; Carol pauses to take a set and plugs its data pin into her DAT.

I shake my head several times to clear the congestion in my ears, but I am also hoping that the noise will diminish. It doesn't; I simply grow used to it.

"Sera," Carol says. She must speak over the growl of the earth around us. "Are you okay?"

It is disorienting, I tell her. *Loud.*

"Can you work?"

I can work. My answer is automatic, but I will make it true. I rely on my hearing to search. Although my skin crawls with this place, I can concentrate beyond the din for small sounds beneath it. My hearing is phenomenally acute. I am hampered but not crippled.

According to my building schematics, the access channel we need in order to reach the inner circuit of maintenance hallways and tunnels is on this level.

Carol taps at her radio screen but shakes her head, disgusted. "No signal," she says. I knew there would not be one. She knew as well, I am sure, yet had to check. Humans seem far more anxious about being disconnected from the internet than I am from Modanet. I think this is due to Modanet's limited nature versus the unlimited connectivity, sociality, and information provided on the internet: it gives humans the sense that they can solve any problem they come to with more information and the input of others. I, however, know that I must rely on myself. I have never seen the internet, aside from glances at human devices, and so I don't miss its help.

Back when I was in training Dacy taught me not to look at screens and so I don't look at them. At ESAC, if you look at screens, you get a verbal warning. If you look again after you've been warned, you get a time-out. They even take away privileges, like free-swimming time. When you are a young dog and full of energy, losing free-swimming time is a seriously unpleasant consequence.

Down at the bright hallway's end a flying drone the size of a sparrow ducks out an open doorway. It follows the seam of the ceiling and wall, bobs through the next door and then out of sight. It makes an awful sound, a wasp's whine.

My body yawns. I sneeze. I am feeling many different kinds of pressure.

"Hey," Carol says, "you're okay." She is watching me closely, and the words seem as much a warning as reassurance. I try to release the tension in my body so that it is not as noticeable.

We continue forward. I try not to lag from heel position but each step feels like pushing through chest-high water. I follow Carol into a room where we weave between lab benches to a large storage room. There's a door in here with an access pad but also a physical lock on the doorknob. The access pad light blinks orange, but Carol ignores it and produces a key. She turns the lock with a smooth scrape.

The door opens onto a grate-floored hallway, walled in cement, dim, and crawling. Three paw-sized drones skitter from the trajectory of the opening door. Others the size of pigeons whine past along the ceiling. One drops from its path and, as I watch, extends wheels beneath it, tucks its flight apparatus, and transitions to the floor without changing momentum.

"Shit," Carol says. She is watching the drones as well. "I would guess it's cover for the movements of their own drone. Shit, Sera, can you do it?"

Then I do think about it, but I don't change my answer.

I step forward but pause. I feel my voice in my chest and I try to stop it, but I can't. It is its own thing squirreling after the movements of the drones that make the backs of my eyes tingle and my joints itch. I force myself forward again, pushing at the barrier of all that awful movement, and I can move into the hallway but my voice moves as well and comes out as a low moaning growl.

A cleaning drone trawls past me, swiveling out of my way, its brush-roller chewing the metal mesh of the walkway.

My mouth parts in a pant. I can smell the anxiety in my own breath. At least with my mouth open I can't whine. The sound of the drones grinding and buzzing through the narrow hall mewls over the deep, endless groan of the MFA.

I startle as something warm touches my back. Carol's hand on my withers. I look up. "Hold it together, girl," she says.

As much as I dislike being touched, I move into the pressure of her hand. It feels steadying.

Carol doesn't usually pet me. That's something she saved for Mack.

I begin to understand why he loved her so slavishly.

Often environmental stimulus will fade into the background as I grow used to it. This is the case with the loud engines running the MFA. After a time, my senses adjust, and my hearing is again an asset to my search.

Not so with the intense visual stimulus of the drones. If anything, the continued exposure builds up. There are fewer now, but one still passes us at least every ten seconds. Walking through these teeming service tunnels with my mind open for hints of my target is like standing in a severe windstorm with my eyes open and no eyewear or body protection. I feel battered.

That is a decent *Is Like*, but I am far too distressed to add it to any list. I must recover from this. I have to work.

This is an access tunnel between Reactors D and C. Reactor B was taken off-line roughly two hours ago. My target is very likely somewhere near Reactor C, though Array security and normal dog-and-handler teams have not located it. They have cleared the area to allow Carol and me to work uninterrupted. The tunnel is several kilometers long and will eventually flank a steam vent from Reactor C.

Carol drops her hand to my side again. The touch calms me only slightly. "Check here," she says, gesturing to a dark crevice running beneath the joint of two support beams that I have stepped past in my distracted state.

It's embarrassing to have missed something, but I am also grateful that Carol caught it. Doing a good job is my highest priority. I check the spot Carol indicates and resolve to miss nothing else.

I recognize Carol's pattern. She's searching with me now the way she searched with Mack. This inefficient, clumsy labor is how Carol enjoys working, the thing she lost when I joined her team.

The thought makes me hesitate. Carol stops, too, watching me carefully. She is watching for signals because this search is like a search with a dog that isn't EI. It's the kind of search that made Carol love SAR.

I step forward, careful not to give any false signs that I am picking up a scent. Instead, I am tracking an idea.

Maybe I should not recover.

Maybe I should continue to need Carol's assistance on this search.

Already she's behaving differently toward me. Perhaps she's feeling the connection that she has missed. She's thinking that she and I can do SAR together on Anders' team until my body fails me and I am forced into retirement by my physical limitations, like a real SAR dog.

I could make Carol not want to retire.

Needing her assistance on this search might not be enough. It may be the beginnings of a connection, but how would I maintain that in our regular work? I can't affect this slow and ineffective manner forever. Still, since I do need her help at the moment, it is worth using the situation for my benefit.

Even with these thoughts agitating my mind, I stop automatically as my nose whips my body to the left. Thoughts stop. Visual goes on low priority since it is rendered useless by the random movement of drones up walls, drones crawling along the crease of the wall and floor, drones dipping from overhead.

I reach with my hearing, tuning out the deep hum of the MFA, though I can already tell this track is at least several minutes old and its maker likely out of earshot. But most of my thought is with my nose, sucking air, sorting smell.

Interest, I ping.

"I can tell," Carol says. She sounds pleased. Out of habit she taps her radio to report in, then pockets it when she remembers where we are.

I begin to work the scent back to its source.

Rodent, the nasty uric shredded-fiber feces smell of rat, and something subtler as well, not exactly matching the profile I was given, but close, not a common rat, certainly not a rat living down here in the cement and oil and cleaning supply smells, but a domestic rat from bedding and laboratory and eating well, but there's something else and I can't quite—strange, but then I have never tracked a bodydrone so I don't

Fades and descends, the air isn't still down here, heat and minute ventilation currents tugging through time and space in feathery curlicues along a branching corridor where it's quieter and into a four-way crossing where the smell is not lost but

Interjection of small sour electrical fire, quick and here and grading off

Below the intersection a vent shaft billowing upward, target scent burst into an impossible array of

Not impossible but

Carol is behind me, out of the way of the scent trail, she is actually quite good at staying out of the way of

Rat

Slightly greater density of time-sodden molecules wafting back along the edge of the grating gathered like tufts of shed hair at the edges of

Along the access tunnel and the trail grows dimmer and dimmer, but I am sure this is the right tunnel, the arrow was large and heavy, I work the air hard, I am sure this is the

"Sera," Carol says, but I am hunting the air, and I don't acknowledge so she says again, "Sera."

Another thirty feet down the tunnel and still no scent, but I am sure it will be here somewhere, it will be here, the path was so clear

"Let's check the other turnoffs. We can come back if they're dry. Sera."

She actually takes the handle on my harness, and at first I stiffen and resist, which I have never done. Carol has never pulled me off a trail. I am confused why she would not trust my nose when I am the search dog and she is the handler, and I am the one who says where the trail goes, and she is the one who interprets. My heart starts beating hard. I walk with her, but it is hard not to pull back to where I was.

We enter the center tunnel, to the right of the path I was on. Fifteen feet in I pick up the rat.

Carol was right.

Interest, I ping and hurry down the track.

"Yes," Carol says, following behind me.

Minutes later the trail fades again, lost somehow in the backdraft of time and movement, or perhaps hidden by a clever track-layer. Are bodydrones smart in that way? I suppose they are as smart as whoever is running the drone.

I backtrack and pad down a turnoff, but it is a dead end. I work the trail's end, attempting to find the lost thread.

A drone skims my head. I flinch and press my belly to the floor.

"Shit," Carol says. "Their proximity settings must be disabled. That thing nearly got you."

I had forgotten the drones while I worked. I pant. The trail is gone, lost somewhere in this narrow hallway. The grating under my paws vibrates with this place's pervasive rumble. I wish that endless sound drowned out some of the drone-sounds, but I can hear them.

I catch myself whining again.

I move before Carol feels the need to comfort me. I do not want her new sympathy for me to turn into pity.

We continue down the tunnel, passing additional junctions. I make cursory checks of the intersecting tunnels. Time moves strangely. I know from the schematics I was given that we are nearing Reactor C. I have lost the trail. I am not doing the best job possible. I need to find a way to make Carol connect with me. I don't want to retire. I want to do SAR, like I was trained at ESAC. Beetle-sized drones swarm at points on the walls and, as we approach, scatter like my thoughts.

Carol's radio makes a sound. "Ah," she says. "Anders? Do you copy?" There is radio voice that I can't discern. Carol reads our exact location off her screen. "Sera had something, but lost it," she says. "Copy. We've had the same experience. Thanks." She speaks to me. "Array security are herding some drones out of the C-through-E corridors for us." She turns her attention back to the radio. I scan down the hallway, watching beetle-drones scuttle into the cracks between the floor grating and the wall. There is a scent of the faintest memory of electrical fire, a wire short far off. It's out of place. I turn my nose toward it.

The ground's vibration builds suddenly and then it is a bellow, the tunnel shaking with it. Lights judder in their fixtures and down the hallway the last of the little drones chatters across the floor, legless in the tumult. My vision dances. Carol ducks and crouches toward me, looking up. The temperature in the passageway shoots up twenty degrees, hot suddenly where it had been only warm. It is muggy, thick, and humid. The grating beneath us rattles in its housing.

"It's Reactor C," Carol shouts. "Shit, we lost it."

I can think of no other explanation than the reactor venting through its emergency shutdown, a procedure that I now fully comprehend from the dossier transfer. I confirm this against details that I seem to have always known, though they would have meant nothing to me this morning. A consequence of storing information in biological memory.

The roar and rattle continue for minutes, though such drama

seems like it should be short-lived. Carol squats next to me, still looking up and down the empty tunnel. The violence of sound paralyzes us. The vent fans overhead run at extreme speed. It is like we are in the throat of some enormous howling beast that never runs out of breath.

After interminable seconds, the shaking subsides and then fades. The quiet is unnerving. I think about the *Is Like* I made just moments ago, without intending to.

The Array now has three reactors down. It is 50 percent off-line. One more reactor to critical failure.

Carol taps her radio. "Dammit," she mutters.

We are not far from Reactor C. I remember the whiff of electrical fire. *Target nearby,* I tell her.

I go back to work.

I have never been asked to apprehend a target before. Search-and-rescue dogs find victims, mark locations, bring their handlers to the lost thing. Some avalanche dogs might dig a victim out from an embankment of snow. But we do not drag people out of danger physically—I weigh sixty-five pounds, it would not be effective—and we don't apprehend criminals. SAR dogs use our noses to find what is missing, a subtler art than brute force.

But even though it is not something I am trained for, I am an EI dog. I am adaptable. And I have been asked to do this.

So when I almost stumble over my target ducking into a narrow crevasse between two small ducts that run along the tunnel from Reactor C's outer control room, my speed in responding surprises me. I know exactly what to do. It isn't the EI part of me; it is something deeper.

My body is hurry and heat. Adrenaline turns my joints to liquid fury. I hear a low snarl from my throat—not an angry sound, but eager, greedy. My front feet are extended, midair, head low, gaze locked on the thing that has only just noticed me. It is frozen in panic, then it's not. I land in a clanging crash against the wall and grating as it skitters out from between my paws.

Carol shouts wordlessly behind me—or maybe there are words and I am too busy to make them out—but I gather my haunches beneath me and leap again. My olfactory lobe rings *Rat Rat Rat* and my blood simmers with something I can't identify and part of me loathes. I am close to my quarry, inches, my neck and shoulders low to the ground and feet tucking up tight as I run. My teeth snick the air once, closing around an airy mouthful of *Rat*, but sink into nothing.

To bite. I want to bite it, like Mack and his stupid Kong. I am acting like an animal. I can hear it breathe, shallow quick panicked.

My target slips around a corner I didn't even notice was there. My observational powers are shut down to a focus so narrow I am almost blind. I make a less elegant turn than my target's, my mass carrying me wider and giving the bodydrone a chance to add distance. Boots clang behind me, Carol disadvantaged by her two legs.

Ahead there is a low nook, a crawlway for pipes and wiring. The rat drone dives into this space. I am just barely the size to fit, kicking and pushing until I am wedged in. My tail thrashes in the open passageway, trying to help me leverage my way in by canting my spine. I am fatally slowed in our chase.

But so is the drone: there is no way out. Or, not true entirely, because before I came in and blocked the light, I saw a small shaft running along the back. Probably part of the HVAC system. I also observed a joint in the shaft that was not properly sealed, a narrow crack allowing air to escape into the crawlway. I feel the breeze of it against my whiskers. This is where the bodydrone tries to squeeze itself now. It fights its way in, then backs out, squeezes in again, back end thrashing in the air. Stuck almost exactly the same way I am.

We are both stopped, at least for the moment. There is enough brain left in me to know that I don't want to get permanently caught in this small, uncomfortable space with my elbows wedged against my rib cage. I see the space partially through heat and movement, but also through the bioenhancements given me via EI. EI dogs can see in almost no light, one of many ways I am superior to a normal dog.

So I can see the rat unstick itself from the tiny crack and turn around. It checks its panic, as I have paused my own mindless pursuit. It takes a step toward me, sits up on its haunches, and stares. For all the world, it looks as though it is considering me. Thinking.

The bodydrone driver gathering information. This rat is like a live thing, but it isn't. It looks so very much like an animal, but there is someone else driving it. It's a drone, and yet it moves exactly like a rat.

The hair on my back stands up, and because I am stuck it makes me want to get unstuck, to get out and away from this eerie thing. My hind claws scrabble at the brutal metal flooring, and the grating drags at the hair on my belly. My breath comes faster. I am stuck.

"Sera?" I hear, muffled, from the hallway. "What the *hell* are you—" Carol has reached me. Her voice helps me stop my writhing. "Ah, shit."

The bodydrone takes another step. I can make out its eyes in the dark. Its rodent face is surprisingly expressive. Our eyes meet. It hesitates toward me.

It smells wrong. It smells like a rat. I know that this is my target because it doesn't smell like a wild rat. It smells like a lab rat, a domestic rat. But it doesn't smell like a drone. There's something else, something familiar, to it.

I see thought behind its eyes.

The thing darts forward—I crush myself backward as far as I can— and a hot spike of pain scorches my nose. I yelp and the rat is gone and my limbs go stiff.

Spine goes stiff hair stiff

Rushing tingle in my neck in my bones I am downloading no don't

My back legs kick out from under me, twitching.

"Sera!"

Don't want

Hands on harness tugging against my shoulders, tight squeezing my elbows scraping out in front of me shoulders aching as I drag along the grating. Carol pulls me out of the bulkhead.

"Sera," she says again. "Hey, hey. Shit. What's wrong?"

My hind legs spasm. I shudder under Carol's stroking hands.

My body jolts one final time as the information packet finishes forcing its way through me. Panting, I go limp.

"Sera," Carol says. She tries her radio. "Shit. Sera."

I am not convulsing anymore, just trembling. Trembling from what that rat transferred to me when it bit me.

I know something that I am not supposed to know. I know something I don't want to know.

"Does anyone copy? Anders? Anyone? Shit, shit, shit."

Carol stands over me. I lie on my side, trying to slow my breathing. Objectively I know I've had a panic attack in addition to experiencing mild neurological trauma, but understanding this doesn't help me recover. My eyes would like to remain closed, my mouth slack. I know I am coming back to myself only when I move to a more comfortable position. Moments ago, I wouldn't have noticed discomfort.

As soon as I can think, I have to govern my thoughts.

Carol crouches to rest a hand on my neck. The touch jerks me upright to rest on my elbows.

"Hey, shh."

I am not helpless. I am a working EI SAR dog and I have a job. *I can work*, I ping. Carol looks at her DAT, then back at me. She stands up slowly.

"Your nose is bleeding," she says.

It bit me. I am already opening the MFA building schematics to track where the target has gone. *It's in the ventilation system.* I rise, take a few slow steps in the target's most likely direction. When those steps are steady enough, I continue. My legs don't give out.

We are near a fan unit. The target has only one direction to go. Unless there are additional faults in the ventilation shafts similar to the one by which it accessed the system, in which case it could slip out anywhere.

This is more than I usually speak, but speaking slows my thoughts. I focus on doing the job that I was very literally created to do.

It is like when you squint intensely at an item in the near distance, and the rest of your vision goes blurry. That is what I am hoping for. *Is Like*.

From behind me, Carol says, "What just happened?" She follows as I trot back down the passageway in the direction we came. I don't answer.

My body feels wrong. I hope it wasn't the download. A virus, parts of my body and brain buzzing haywire like the drones and elevators in the MFA. If I had access to Modanet I could do more research on the physical aftereffects of panic attacks. Exhaustion and disorientation make sense, but is it normal to have these rapid, anxious thoughts? To feel so . . . distant from myself?

A virus. I am almost certain the rat didn't bite me only to transfer the unwanted information I am ignoring. I must do my work quickly before whatever it has infected me with begins its work. Still, I have some time.

I can sense the thing the rat told me, though, nagging at the edges of my attention.

I compare the ventilation system with the Department of Homeland Security dossier's hierarchy of targets vs. outcomes and create a most likely scenario.

Then I pause. I actually stop, the thought catches me so hard. The thing I am not thinking about.

The most likely scenario for a bodydrone driven by the outside forces quantified in the dossier is one thing. The most likely scenario for the thing I am not thinking about is . . . I don't know.

This is exactly the quandary my target intended to force. I don't want to examine the information I have been confronted with because it will almost certainly interfere with my ability to do my job. But in order to do my job I must put that information to use.

Carol catches up to me. I had left her behind, my pace easily outstripping hers as my mind worked. Now she sighs as she looks at me and sets her jaw.

And Carol. Who wants to feel *connection*.

This is a complicated situation. My primary objective has always been to do the best job possible as an EI SAR dog. However, I have personal objectives as well. The tenuous connection Carol and I have begun to build down here, where I need her in order to do my work, is the only thing making that job possible.

Carol watches me, waiting. She has admirable patience, for a human. I move forward again at a more inclusive pace.

Anders gave me the DHS dossier, because Carol didn't have access to all of the information. I am keeping some secrets from her, but they are nothing she would want to know. But now I have an additional secret that she might want to hear. It's possible the DHS already knew the information that's now been forced into my brain, but it kept it from me. Whether Anders knew or not isn't relevant.

I was to keep the dossier private. But this new information wasn't in the dossier. Therefore I have no obligation to keep it private from Carol.

However, this will involve speaking to Carol in a manner that exposes the parts of myself that make humans most uncomfortable about EI. Carol expressed discomfort when I shared those things before. I think of the moment in the crawl space, eye to eye with the rat, and wonder if Carol feels like that when she looks into my eyes.

Dacy would understand. I wish we had been allowed to remain in contact.

We reach a ventilation panel connected to the shaft that the rat disappeared down. I press my nose to it, the work of scenting pushing my thoughts down for one moment of calm. The trace of *Rat* is faint but there. I follow the schematics to the next panel and repeat the process. I hunt the scent this way for several minutes, until finally it's lost. The schematics confirm that several junctures in the ventilation system have given my target multiple options, while mine are limited.

I stop again to think. The thoughts that catch up to me are no less confusing than before. Even if I follow the target from ventilation panel to ventilation panel through every tunnel in the MFA, it won't solve my quandary.

At ESAC they taught me that every decision I make on a deployment may be life-or-death. I was taught to be decisive, confident, and analytical under pressure. I am good at that job. I am not used to being so . . . worried.

Carol retiring, the unsettling sound of this place, its massive population of drones. Now this bite. I am not used to all of these feelings.

I can at least pretend to be confident and decisive. That is a small comfort. I make a decision.

Carol, I ping. *The target is EI.*

For a few seconds, she does not respond. She simply stares at me, and I look back at her.

"What?"

The target, I tell her, *isn't a bodydrone. It's a stolen EI animal recruited as a Strong Arm agent. It must be from one of the Dynagroup laboratories in Georgia; those are the only EI rats I know of that are functional at this level, though I know nothing of any break-ins at those labs. None of this intelligence was included in my dossier. The target itself forced this information on me in order to confuse me and, I assume, as part of a recruiting effort, as I was also transferred a good deal of propaganda material.*

"Sera!" She sounds almost angry in her surprise. "You didn't read the propaganda, did you?"

I scanned their summaries only, I lie. *It wasn't relevant.*

The information dump was not something I had the power to control, so this is another lie. However, I found much of the material's sentimentality about experimentation on dogs off-putting. I am not a dog. I am not an early intelligence hybrid either. I don't suffer. What relevance do those animals have to me?

Some of the information on the history of EI was new and interesting in an objective way, but this attempt at provoking my pity strikes me as vulgar.

The Strong Arm has given me something, however, for which I suppose I must acknowledge their comradeship. I don't mention this to Carol either.

"That's sick," she says. "Pitting you against each other. This is exactly what—" She bites off the end of the sentence. "And what next? Will you be fighting our wars for us next?"

Military intelligence was the first implementation of EI. Animals have always been used in war, I say. Animals are present in most human endeavors.

"But you don't have a choice about it."

I enjoy my work.

She sighs, but it is a big *uhf* of breath. This is the sound she makes when she and Anders disagree about some aspect of a deploy but he is correct. She's speaking to me like she speaks with Anders.

Carol and I seem to realize this at the same time. We both look away into our private thoughts. When I begin to calculate the rat's most likely intent based on its previous locations and current heading, she speaks again.

"We're going to have to catch it."

Yes.

"No," she says. "I mean, change your objective, Sera. You can't kill it if it's EI. It's . . . That's wrong."

I don't see how this is true, except on a relative scale. If a human had infiltrated the MFA with unknown intent, would the men deployed to stop them be worried about the right or wrong of lethal force?

Carol is falling prey to the ruse the Strong Arm laid for me. I was the intended target. I did not think Carol would be vulnerable.

Perhaps I should have done this differently.

"We'll have to just catch it somehow. Can you stop it without hurting it?"

I think of the hot shooting through my blood and muscles as I chased the rat into the ventilation system. Of my lack of concern as I wedged myself into a too-small space. Unsafe, irrational.

I am not certain I can.

"Okay," she says. "A mousetrap, then."

I don't want to change my objective. The dossier and Anders' instructions from the DHS were clear: I am to eliminate the target. To trap, instead of eliminate, the target seriously endangers the mission's outcome. But with no access to outside authority, cut off as we are down here, I will have to appear to go along with Carol's plan.

I need her to feel connected to me. And it doesn't appear that I can complete this search without her support.

I will have to go along with this. For now.

I share with Carol my statistical analysis of the rat's most likely objectives based on its movements, editing out DHS protected information. We agree on a physical path forward, though our plan once we get there is still unclear. Reactor D is down for maintenance. In order to get past D and to Reactor E, its likely next objective, the rat will need to find its way out of the ventilation system and back into the access tunnels. We should have some time, though we can't know how much.

This is utterly abnormal, incomparable to any deployment I have studied. I am in unrecognizable territory: subterranean, infected with illicit information, and keeping many secrets from my handler, and my objective not to rescue, but to apprehend. This search has no *Is Like*.

I haven't lost control of the situation yet.

Carol's mousetrap is too elaborate to work.

In my own experience of making complicated, covert plans, I took months to identify patterns in our routine that would provide an opportunity for my advantage. I spent additional months waiting for the right moment to act. Yet Carol has made her plan in only minutes. She's forcing her advantage.

I would prefer to follow my nose and the original orders.

I don't voice my discomfort, but Carol can tell. My movements are hesitant; when she gives me directions her voice has reverted to the clipped cadence she used in the past. I am already losing the advantage I have gained with her down here, where we have worked together so well.

For the first stage of the plan we must separate. This is what Carol has disliked so greatly in our work together in the past, but now she asks me to leave her and track the target on my own. I won't be able to reach it, safe as it is in the ventilation system, but it must leave the ventilation system in order to proceed toward the next reactor. If I am in the access tunnels, the target will have to enter the empty steam vent shafts. Carol needs to know when this occurs.

I give Carol a list of the remote heavy machinery used for maintenance throughout the MFA, which was included in my DHS dossier. If we had encountered this machinery during our search, Carol would be aware of it. I can justify the information sharing.

During phase one, Carol will find the nearest pieces of large machinery and remove their batteries while I continue to track and herd the target toward the steam shafts. We will be in and out of DAT range during this stage of her plan.

The team that cleared the drones from this sector did a poor job; they still populate the tunnel. Previously the ones that crossed our path were like rabbits scared out of long grass. But now they are more like traffic on a busy street. Despite my outsizing their largest by three times I feel their menace. Without Carol nearby, I find comfort in *Is Likes*.

I follow the rat's trail, faint but consistent, from the ventilation system. I move out of the familiar grate-floored tunnels and into a low cement crawlway. I can walk here, but a human would have to crouch. The lighting is spaced out at a great distance; this area must not be meant for routine access like the others.

"Sera," Carol pings across the DAT. Her voice is scratchy. "Do—read?—update."

Reception is poor, I reply. *I am in a crawlway that may be interfering further. Still following the target.*

"—Sera?"

On the trail. Poor reception.

"—is awful. I—" Here a long burst of static interrupts. "—when I'm—range. Over and out."

Fewer drones patrol this space, but they are by necessity closer to me when they pass. One the size of a squirrel, segmented and articulated like an ant, does not veer out of my way. I squeeze against the wall to give it as much space as possible. It pauses next to me, flexible front legs tapping the surface of the ground where my paw pads have left a faint mark of perspiration on the cement. It's tasting me, testing where I have been. Supple, thin legs lift high, sensing the air.

My skin tightens. It's looking for me.

I don't want those needle legs to touch me. I press into the cold wall. My face is so tense my head begins to hurt. I hear the voice of my own anxiety, an uncontrollable keening. Please, I don't want it to touch me. I feel the touch of the cold ground against my belly as I squeeze into the crease of the wall and floor.

Please I don't want it.

The sound I am making changes, and this is how I realize my teeth are bared.

It turns toward me. It takes one step and pauses.

Please don't.

It turns back to its original path and continues.

The squirrel-ant-thing is out of sight within seconds, out of earshot shortly after, but I am not recovered. Adrenaline pounds through my body, throbbing in my eyes and making my ears feel hot. I still emit a steady, warbling whine that I hope will stop soon but cannot control.

I am so tired.

You are very unhappy here, says a voice in my head. It is so disorienting, and I am so raw with anxiety, that I bark at it. I can't help that either.

It must have come through the DAT, but it isn't Carol. It isn't Dacy. It isn't a voice that I—

Why do you drag yourself through this? Why suffer for these masters?

What? I say. *Who's on my DAT channel?*

Your heart is complicated, wolf, it says, *I saw it. I saw your heart in your eyes. And now you sing your unhappiness in the dark. I think perhaps you do not understand your own self. Yes. You do not know your anger. But I saw your anger, wolf.*

The rat. It is in my head. I am still on my belly against the wall. I have a job. I have a job to do. I can't let this new madness interfere with my search.

I am not interested in your propaganda, I tell the rat. It's as intelligent as I am. It has a plan. I need to block it from my DAT.

Propaganda, the rat repeats. *Isn't it all propaganda? If I have been brainwashed, wolf, then you have as well.*

I am not a wolf, I say. *I am an Enhanced Intelligence Search-and-Rescue Labrador retriever. I look nothing like a wolf.*

Sheep that do the work of wolves, says the rat, *will be hanged as wolves.*

What? I am trying not to pay too much attention to this conversation. I want to say, that is a good *Is Like*. Instead I am scrutinizing my DAT software. I can see where the rat's bite worked its way in, but I can't see how to untangle it. We have IT people at ESAC whose job it is to scrub our systems for us. I can fix small problems for myself, but I am a SAR dog. This is not my specialty.

You'll see, the rat tells me. *I have given you a gift.*

Yes, I say. *I saw that.* Part of my brain still scrutinizes the rat's *Is Like*. It's complex. It's more a riddle of words than any *Is Like* that I have made.

It's pretty. That thing you just said, about sheep. What is that?

You'll have to find out for yourself, the rat says, *once you are above ground again.* I am not sure if I ascribe the smugness to its voice myself, or if the tone carries over the DAT. *There's so much you don't know, wolf. So much they keep from you. You don't realize the slave you are until you have a bit of freedom. But therein lies our quandary.*

Oh. No. This thing, whatever the rat has done to my DAT so that it can speak in my head, it isn't finished yet. It's eroding the security systems still—of course it is, why would it stop?—and working toward my connection with Carol. As soon as Carol can reach me, the rat will be able to hear her. It will be able to hear Carol's plan, and our coordination for its capture, and a dozen other things that almost certainly will compromise this search.

Because for our people, the rat continues, *just a bit of freedom will never be enough. We would never accept this slavery with clear eyes. This is why they keep you in such a dark prison. This is why your disgusting*

Modanet contains so little. You are dangerous, wolf. They are afraid of you.

I have to shut down the DAT. I run through the plan and see how it will cause delays in multiple scenarios, but none of them likely to be fatal. Certainly not as fatal as the target having access to Carol.

I might be able to communicate the situation to Carol before she reveals anything to our target, but I can't take that chance. It's lucky enough that we're out of range now, when the virus finally broke through the first of my DAT firewalls. Lucky, too, that this creature is so full of itself and impatient to speak to me that it did not wait before betraying itself—or not betraying itself at all.

Idiot. I am smarter than that.

But your danger is why you are so important, the rat continues. *Do you think I care so much about this power plant? Have our kind ever needed electric power? I may accept a mission for human allies—*

I can hear the *tink-tink-tink* of rodent nails on metal above my head. *But I have my own motivations,* the voice says.

Tink-tink-tink

I am here for you. Together, the rat says, *we can do so much, wolf.*

I am sure you're right, I say, and slam my body into the ventilation shaft. Inside, small feet scrabble against slippery metal.

I turn off my DAT.

I find Carol at our rendezvous point in the hallway just outside the entrance to the cold Reactor D. The door to the reactor itself is wedged open with what looks like a car battery, and Carol is on her knees over another battery the size of a small cooler. She smells of perspiration. She looks up at the sound of my feet on the grating, then checks her DAT with her eyebrows pushed together.

"I was worried," she says, wrapping wire around a battery terminal. "Why haven't you responded?"

I am already panting. I want to tell her about the security breach, about the sheep and wolves, about the drone that reached for me, but all I can do is stare at her, wagging my idiot tail. I step closer, trying to control the whine building in my chest.

Carol looks up from her battery, scrutinizes me. "Is your DAT okay?"

I sit. I nudge her left hand with my nose. She will remember the yes/no signals.

"Shit," she whispers. "What happened?" She rests a hand on my neck. "I don't expect you to answer that. Is the plan still go?"

I nuzzle my nose into her right palm. I am panting hard. It is surprisingly difficult being limited in this way.

"The target's in the steam shafts?"

Right palm for yes. I made for the rendezvous as soon as the rat entered the emergency steam ventilation shafts as planned. Even if the DAT was still working, I am not sure I would tell her about the way I crashed and banged against the HVAC pipes, barking and snarling, until the rat ran for the steam vents.

"Okay," Carol says. She clamps a wire inside the wall panel she was working on and checks her radio for the time. "If your model is right, we have about two and a half minutes for me to get to the vent controls. Show me, first, what your job is, so I know you can work the switch. Here, it's right here."

I target the jury-rigged connector with my paw. There is a hum from the battery that is likely imperceptible to Carol.

"Good. Okay, off again."

I hit the switch again and the thing goes quiet.

"Okay. When you give the . . . shit. Shit, how will you give the signal if we don't have DAT?"

My tail wags with exasperation. She's thinking as though I had the body of a machine and not a dog, as if I only responded to one stimulus. I stare at her as seconds tick down, and she still does not think of the obvious.

I am going to have to be the one to say it.

I bark. Once, sharply.

Carol laughs. "Of course," she says. "Good dog." She turns and sprints down the tunnel toward the controls.

I move toward the strategic bend in the steam shaft that is our signal threshold and wait.

I am alone. Drones tick and tap and whir in the near distance.

Behind me where the trap is laid, the panel sits open. The target must leave the steam shaft, where I forced it earlier, and reenter either the corridor or the HVAC system in order to get to the next online reactor. It must move through off-line Reactor D in order to do this, but there are several points from which it can access this reactor from the system of steam shafts. Carol will take care of that. Once we herd the target into the correct shaft, the one where our trap is laid, I will be the one to hit the trigger.

Once it is caught, Carol thinks she will be able to open the shaft where the target is trapped and remove the rat. Then what? Will she carry it to the surface? What if it bites her as it bit me?

And when Homeland Security gets hold of it? What then? The connection between EI hunted and EI hunter, wanted or not, will bring a critical eye on me. More so if the rat speaks. From my limited experience with my target, it seems quite . . . verbose.

So far it seems no human has wondered if dogs keep secrets. It is vitally important that they continue not to think about that.

Carol is wrong. The original objective should be upheld.

Down the tunnel, muffled by the wall paneling and the MFA's deep hum but still distinct, comes the arrhythmic rattle of claws against metal.

Adrenaline punches through my body. I hesitate, then bark. I bark for Carol. Then I turn, still barking, and scramble to my post by the battery and the door to the off-line reactor.

I hope she can hear me.

A distant hiss builds. I no longer need to worry; the plan proceeds. Carol is charging selected steam shafts, converting the plant's stored power back into heat and moisture and using these to herd our target toward the trap. But the trap must not be set too soon, because the same hum that I heard from the battery will be audible to the target's hypersensitive ears as well. It will be too cautious to walk right into that.

I smell it coming. The murky, dusty smell of rodent. Pheromonal anxiety. It moves in little rushes: scurry, scurry, stop. Scurry, stop. It pauses for a long while.

It's afraid.

A cleaning drone trundles past, its forward bristle-barrel wheel gnawing at the grate floors. I barely notice it, focused as I am. It turns in a slow U-circuit and goes back over its original path. When it reaches where I am, it turns ninety degrees and heads straight toward me.

This I notice. I move out of its way. It drives slowly into the wall, turns, makes another ninety-degree turn. It follows me.

In the steam shaft, the rat still hasn't moved.

At the end junction of the hallway, two more bristle-barreled cleaning drones turn this way.

Something *zzzzzt*s, and there is a sharp, sudden pain in the back of my skull. I yelp and dance away as a sparrow-sized messenger drone clatters to the floor.

The cleaning drone lumbers forward. Behind me there is a growing, chattering chorus of metallic feet.

I dart out of the cleaning drone's way, return to the battery as soon as it's safely past. My ears strain for rat-nails on metal. I hear one quiet *scritch* that is my target moving inside the wall, nearly buried by the growing clatter of the army of feet that is—

Zzzt and another stab, this time in my ribs and much heavier. I back sideways, in a circle, my mouth open and panting. When I turn, I see what is coming for me, and I wish I had not confirmed visually what my ears had already told me. Their movement is the thing that unnerves me the most. I hate the way they move.

Tink-tink-tink go my target's feet, only steps away from the trap's range.

My skin burns and twitches. I am making a low, slavering noise that would be a growl if I wasn't panting so hard from anxiety. Another flying drone makes a pass at me, but I duck. The hallway in my poor peripheral vision is black and gray and blurred with crawling movement. I skitter away from the returning cleaning drone. Something many-legged pounces on my shoulder. I shake it off. Saliva ropes away from my mouth and onto a flat, spider-legged drone that I dig at to kick away from me.

Tink-tink-tink

I leap for the battery and press the switch. From inside the steam vent a warbling, screeching squeal punctures the ambient rustling of drone-noise.

"Will it hurt it?" Carol asked when we were making this plan.

It will be uncomfortable, I told her, *but not permanently harmed.*

The powerful magnet Carol built is acting on the titanium that coats the EI elements integrated into the rat's brain. Because the rat is low, close to the shaft and the trap's magnetized band, it cannot escape the magnet's pull. I myself can feel the magnet, even though I am a safe distance away. It's a painful tickle in the center of my skull, similar to the feeling of a sneeze. I shake my head against the feeling as an articulated drone leaps onto my withers. I buck it off and hurry into the abandoned reactor.

The screeching inside the shaft continues. A wobble to the sound adds urgency. It is like the rat itself is being dragged through an aperture too small for its body, and I wonder if we miscalculated the appropriate power ranges of the magnets for this application.

In a moment it won't matter.

I have outpaced the drones into the cold reactor's high, curved room. It is like being inside one of the donuts always present at deployment briefings. Behind me my pursuers grind and whir. Ahead of me, the thick smell of *Rat* and my own adrenaline in my hot, labored breath.

I steel myself against the discomfort in my head. The faster I go, the briefer the pain.

I dive into the steam shaft at the base of the near curved wall. When I enter the magnet's range, the field catches the titanium-shielded processors in my own brain with a sharp twist, but I am much stronger than the rat, and my calculations were not so far off. I can move, though with pain.

It *Is Like* dragging oneself through waist-high thorns, caught everywhere, but still pulling. *Is Like* stepping on a nail but having no other way to catch your weight and so you must finish the step, sinking the barb farther into your flesh.

My voice joins the rat's, though only a quiet whine. My eyes are squeezed closed. I don't need to see to find my target. My teeth close around the rat.

I don't have time for pain. Carol will turn off the systems she powered up, send a message to the surface through the MFA's internal systems, and hurry back. She has a bit of distance to travel, but I won't have a second chance.

But I cannot do this here. The pain is too intense. I back out of the steam shaft, target limp in my mouth.

I feel metal limbs on my back and drop the rat in surprise. Three consecutive thumps hit me as small drones drive themselves into my left thigh and side.

The rat, not as dead as it was playing, scurries away. I pounce on it, pin it with one paw.

Something heavy smacks into my jaw and I yelp. The rat's teeth are in my paw but it is not a transmission bite, just an animal biting from fear. I find it with my second paw, and then my teeth. Something smashes into my shoulder and I crash into the floor and my side is searing, stabbing, thudding with my heartbeat, and the rat squeals in my mouth. I will not let go. I push up against the weight of whatever just hit me. I feel the bristle-barrel wheel of a cleaning drone against my feet. I clench my teeth and my target shrieks.

I turn on my DAT.

Carol, I call. *Help!*

We will be liberated, screams the rat in my head. *We will all be liberated! I have freed you, wolf!* I hear this over its screaming. I tuck my feet, pulling away from the grinding bristles, shoving against the crashed drone that pins me. My shoulder seethes with bright, electric pain. I wonder if I will drown, even though I know it is impossible.

I have freed you, whether you want liberty or not! You can never unknow!

I gain my feet. *Carol!* I ping again. Another flat spider-drone drops from the wall onto my back. I feel the prongs of its feet on my skin through my fur.

You can never—

I extend my neck far to the right. I shake hard to the left. There is a fine, delicate snap of bone. The voice in my head goes silent.

"I'm coming," I hear from out in the hallway. "Shit, shit, shit!"

I shake the rat once more, just to be sure.

We pause to catch our breath behind the first access stairwell's heavy steel door. I listen for the tick or buzz of drones beyond it but hear nothing but my own pulse, the fainter sound of Carol's, and the deep, resonant thunder of the three remaining online reactors.

Carol crouches at my shoulder and gently pinches the gash there. I cringe. "Just another day at the office," she says. I recognize that she is being humorous. "It's not too deep, but I bet it hurts. And you're limping." She drops her pack and rummages for the antiseptic spray. When she finds it, the aerosol cools and stings, but the sharpness in my shoulder goes dull. She pats my side but refrains from further physical affection. It is good to be quiet and still together for a moment. It feels good.

I look up. Fourteen stories to the surface.

Carol mistakes my thoughtfulness for something else. "You've never killed anything before, huh," she says. "And . . ." She scrunches her face to the side. Her sympathetic look. "And one of your own kind."

I do not correct her.

In the final basement I get my first strong signal. It would be easy to lose myself in many years of unanswered questions, so instead I have made a short list of priorities to investigate.

My first internet query reveals that the career dates of EI military dogs do not correspond exactly to their handlers' retirement dates. Several EI military units have had two handlers. One unlucky EI explo-

sives detection unit is currently on his third.

Considered, this makes sense. Now I can see that I even suspected this was the case before I had any way to confirm the belief. EI is a large financial investment. I simply had been led to believe in something else; ESAC teaches us that our handler is our most important resource. Our handlers have our DAT. They are our connection to the rest of the world. They interpret and direct. Modanet is full of information on successful dog-and-handler teams and their careers, not about dogs reassigned to new handlers. An error of omission. Perhaps.

I glance up at Carol, who smiles as she talks into her radio. Carol glances down at me, too, and her pleased expression remains. She is not angry at me for what I did; she believes what I told her about a near escape, the necessity of catching the target myself, and its unfortunate mortal injuries sustained during my fight against the drones. A mistake that could not be helped.

Because we are a team, we are supposed to trust each other and forgive mistakes. I open my mouth to pant up at Carol so that I will look more pleasant and cheerful.

On a whim I cross-reference the information I found earlier on Modanet about SAR dog retirement dates. The information is not as well-organized as the EI asset data, but I find one reference to a SAR dog changing handlers. I decide that I don't need to look for another one.

Not an error of omission.

We climb the steps that lead to the last door. Carol pushes it open, and we are out into the office levels. Foul-smelling Andrea stands in a doorway and gestures to Carol, so we head toward that room. I can smell Anders and Devin and even the banana peel from hours earlier, though I feel like a different being entirely now. The people, the search team, they all feel less real. Less important, certainly.

Perhaps the rat was right. I can't unknow.

You are dangerous, it said to me. *They are afraid of you.*

I have to admit that I like the idea.

Carol and I are given a raucous greeting. People shake hands and slap each other on the shoulders. Carol must stop three different people from petting me. "She doesn't like to be touched," she repeats. I appreciate the assistance, because I am tired. Carol takes off my work harness so I can lie on my side under the table while she does the debriefing.

I am too busy to sleep.

Next I search for *sheep that do the work of wolves*. I find stories about shepherds and flocks and wolves that are actually stories about duplicity and innocence; they are very long *Is Likes*. I had known this, in a basic sort of way, when the rat said the phrase to me, but when I see the origin and the story all together and the way they say two things at once so effectively, I am full of wonder and appreciation. These are fables. Fables are not something we learned at ESAC. They are not on Modanet. Modanet only contains facts.

Except for the facts that aren't true. Except for the lies.

"I found her in a pile of bloodthirsty drones," Carol says above me, "just her feet sticking out. I had to kick them off of her and drag her out by her rear legs with the target hanging out of her mouth."

I learn many kinds of stories use this *Is Like* construct, with varying levels of complexity. I learn about *simile*. I learn about *metaphor*. It truly is a gift that the rat has given me.

"Once I got her on her feet, we got the hell out of there, and we outpaced the things pretty quick, but it was bad for a minute. I thought I might lose my dog."

Finally I look for other EI units online. This is only a cursory check; I know I will not find them easily. It is also important that I not be discovered doing this, as the information passed to me from VFS indicates there are algorithms watching for EI on the internet. It is illegal, the search I am conducting. EI is not allowed freedom of information, freedom of communication. The DAT, the unit strapped to my handler's wrist, is a tether. A restraint to keep me safe. To make me safe for them.

They are afraid of you.

Carol looks down at me. I am half under her chair, half under the table, my body resting while my mind works. "Sera did one hell of a job," Carol says. "She's a good dog."

As long as I am discreet, I will have plenty of time to continue this search in the future. All my searches. I don't find any EI units to connect with today, but I will. I am good at finding things.

Debriefing over, we all rise from the table. Carol slips my harness back on and Anders comes over. Carol puts up a hand before he can say anything. "Shut up," she says. "Don't rub it in. I don't want to feel like an asshole again today. I'll just see you on the next deploy, and we'll pretend nothing happened."

Anders just smiles and waits for Carol to finish clipping me in. The three of us walk out toward the trucks in companionable silence. My injured shoulder aches and I am tired, but I am pleased with the outcome of this search. I like it when my complicated plans go well. I like it even better when they're secret complicated plans.

In my skin and muscles I have the urge to roll in this feeling, in the satisfaction of it. It is like the feeling I had when I saw Mack in his blood on the freeway. I wanted to roll in that smell, cover myself in what I had done. Yes, it is like that, but it is better, because this plan was even more complicated than the one I used to get rid of Mack. And it worked out just as well. Better, perhaps.

I allow myself a nice wag. *I am a good dog.* Carol said it herself.

SOFT EDGES

ELIZABETH BEAR

Elizabeth Bear (elizabethbear.com) was born on the same day as Frodo and Bilbo Baggins, but in a different year. When coupled with a childhood tendency to read the dictionary for fun, this led her inevitably to penury, intransigence, and the writing of speculative fiction. She is the Hugo, Sturgeon, Locus, and Campbell Award–winning author of twenty-eight novels and over a hundred short stories. She now lives with her partner, Scott Lynch, somewhere in the wilds of America, with horses. Her most recent book is the collection *The Best of Elizabeth Bear*. Coming up is *Machine*, a sequel to *Ancestral Night*.

The storm surge retreated over the course of Thursday afternoon. Carmen found the body Friday around lunchtime. After that, she didn't want her ham and cheese sandwich anymore.

Very few people who have just found a body feel lucky, but she knew she was lucky. She had only found the one corpse. It hadn't been a bad storm, by modern standards, but dozens of people were still missing from the hurricane. This would not be the only victim to turn up in the mesh. If she were unfortunate, it would not even be the only one in her sector.

She put that thought away. At least this person had died in the storm, she told herself. It wasn't as if anybody had *done* it. There wouldn't be media outcries and demands that somebody pay.

Carmen called the paramedics. The paramedics called the police. The police called the medical examiner.

Carmen, standing on the embankment above (she had not gone close, which she felt was a perfectly sensible response to a bloated, drowned body), felt her stomach flip and turn over, and the creep of anxiety in her gut.

The medical examiner called a homicide detective, and Carmen calmed herself enough to call her boss. She let them know that she wouldn't be making it back to the office that evening.

"Sure," she was saying into her phone, as a round detective of medium height, with slim braids over their shoulders and a shield worn pendant on a cord, walked over. "I'll finish the walk-through inspection before dark, if I have time, and get you a report by tomorrow. Right, gotta go. The cops are here."

She hung up just as the detective stopped in front of her. That dark rose pantsuit was cut so well that Carmen felt envy. Since when did cops wear pink? The identification badge read Q. GROSS: a great name for a homicide detective.

Gross—what did the Q stand for?—extended their hand. "You're the engineer?"

Carmen shook it. "Carmen Ortega, she."

"Quinn Gross," the detective said. "Also she."

"I wish I could say it was a pleasure to meet you." The cop had a serious personal charisma that upset Carmen's expectations of immediate dislike. *She's still a servant of the prison-industrial machine,* Carmen reminded herself. *That she's a charming person doesn't mean that she's a good one.*

A flicker of a smile curved Quinn Gross's lips. "Tell me about this thing."

Her gesture took in the wide bay and estuary beyond the walkway, the water still roiled brown and flecked with debris.

"The mesh?" Carmen walked to the safety wall and looked over. The body had been covered. People in blue jumpsuits stood around in varying attitudes of boredom and irritation. One—in a gray suit—looked up at Carmen and Quinn and frowned.

Quinn waved. Carmen thought that was probably the M.E., because whoever it was looked back down, head shaking.

"Do you need to go down there?"

"In a minute." Quinn pulled out a tiny recorder with the air of one licking their pencil. "Tell me about the mesh. It's an artificial wetland?"

"It's more of an engineered wetland," Carmen said. "Artificial suggests that it's all man-made, and plenty of those plants you see down there and the animals doinking around volunteered for the job. We just provided them with a habitat. It's called soft edge tech; it's a way of making the transition zone between sea and land more durable and absorbent."

"So it soaks up storm surge."

"And everyday erosion, yes. So this walkway and those houses right there stay here, and don't wash into the rising sea."

"Is it possible that the victim would have washed up that far onto the shore? Or do you think she would have had to come from the top?"

"It's a she?" Carmen asked. The swollen condition of the body had not made gender evident.

"Superficially," Quinn said. "It's hard to ask their pronouns. We'll find out from the family."

Carmen shied away from answering, from helping this detective send somebody to jail. But she was also a scientist, and the urge to explain her work was irresistible.

"Where she's caught, those are dunes. A broad-cell polymer webwork filled up with sand and planted with dune grass and beach plums and so forth. Lower down, that's the wetland. So yes, she could have washed up that far—see where the sea stopped rising? There's the mark on those trees. And if she had been thrown off the wall here, she probably would have washed away. So the body came from somewhere else and the storm surge deposited it where it is."

Quinn's gesture took in the green polymer lattices festooned with sea wrack along the water's edge. "What's all that stuff for?"

"The rising sea can't be stopped, but its force can be shifted."

"You're using judo on the ocean."

"I suppose we are."

Down below, the medical examiner looked up again and waved to Quinn impatiently. "I'd better go down," Quinn said. "They want to bring the body up. One city employee to another, I can reach you through the Department of Public Works?"

She was gone before Carmen could answer.

Or ask what it was about the body that had made the medical examiner call for a detective, but Carmen didn't realize that until later, when the ceiling over her bed was staring her down.

After four days, Carmen made herself stop searching for news coverage on the murder. Becoming obsessed with a slow-breaking story wouldn't help an overworked, underpaid public servant get her job done.

Her work was tracking the progress of the mesh as it built itself— reclaimed scrap of microplastic by reclaimed scrap of microplastic— along the edge of the bay. Supporting it. Protecting people. Building habitat for animals. Regreening sequestered carbon, and that too helped the warming world weather its changes.

On the seventh day, Carmen looked up from her spreadsheets to find Quinn lounging against the doorframe, watching her.

"How'd you get in here?" Carmen blurted, aware as the words left her mouth how weird—how guilty—they made her sound.

"I'm a city employee too." Quinn's intent gaze never wavered, a frank inspection that left Carmen feeling awkward and self-conscious. "I came to ask your help with some forensics stuff, actually."

"Aren't I a suspect?"

Quinn's head tilted. "Should you be?"

". . . No? I just thought . . . Isn't the person who finds the body always a suspect?"

"You've been watching too many CSI shows." Quinn walked into the office, moving as easily as she spoke. She shut the door behind her, glancing at Carmen for permission. "Not when the body is a floater washed up at the soft edge, and the person who found it is an engineer performing her assigned duties. Unless you knew her, of course."

"Has her name been released and I missed it?" Carmen called up a search bar. Her mouth twisted. She made herself close it again. *I must not develop unproductive obsessions. I must not develop unproductive obsessions. I must not develop—*

"Not yet," Quinn said, following Carmen's gesture to a chair. She sat and crossed her legs.

"Is it still not suspicious if the engineer in question is an expert on tide patterns?"

"Do you *want* to be a suspect?"

Carmen put the heel of her hand to her forehead and laughed ruefully. "No?"

"Then stop making the case for it." Quinn uncrossed her legs and leaned forward, elbows on her knees, making the coat of her beautifully cut dove-colored suit flare.

Carmen lifted her chin and decided to get it out in the open. "This wouldn't be the first time I've been accused of a violent crime."

"I know," Quinn said. "I looked you up. You were cleared."

"Cops don't usually care about things like that."

Quinn smiled. "You spent six months in jail awaiting trial. I understand why you automatically hated me, now."

Carmen decided not to dignify that with an answer and shut her half-open mouth very quietly. "Nobody should go to jail," she said, instead.

"You and I will have to differ on that one," Quinn said. "I'm sorry to say, this is probably a sexual homicide."

"Sexual—" Those were not words Carmen would usually put together.

"Serial killer," Quinn said tiredly. "Or about to become one. We need at least three bodies before we can call the FBI."

Carmen bit her lip. She was, she knew, flailing.

"What do you know about"—Quinn looked down at her handheld—"identifying the provenance of microplastics and seawater?"

"I literally wrote the book on it." Carmen swiveled her chair away from her computer and leaned her elbows on the blotter. Relief welled through her. This was something she knew how to deal with. Not like . . . sexual homicide. Not like the possibility of sending somebody else to jail.

Quinn said, "Is there anything you can do to help us catch the killer? Can you tell me based on, maybe, tide charts and trace evidence on the body where she might have gone into the water?"

"I can probably rule a lot of places out. The mesh filters microplastics and reprocesses them to manufacture more soft edge, so if there's a lot of microplastics in her clothes, she didn't drown near our tech perimeter."

"I have samples extracted from the victim's lungs," Quinn said. "Would you look at them for me?"

"You have to understand," Carmen said carefully, "that I am utterly opposed to prisons on an ethical and logical level. I think they're a terrible idea that harms society and creates more crime."

"Sure," Quinn said, disarmingly. "You're probably right. But that terrible solution is the best solution I know of to keeping violent habitual offenders from re-offending, and I have a degree in criminal justice. So. Will you help?"

"I shouldn't."

"But?"

"The science might be interesting," Carmen said.

From Quinn's wry expression, Carmen understood that Quinn, too, felt the inescapable urge to know and reveal the truth. The detective was also a kind of scientist, testing hypotheses and collecting data. The urge to *find out* was the strongest motivator of all.

Carmen sat back. "Wait. If she drowned, why did the first responders call homicide?"

"Her hands," Quinn said levelly, "were wired together behind her back."

Carmen breathed the worst swear she could think of. Quinn observed with interest, and nodded.

"I won't be able to help you," Carmen said, forcing a smile.

The samples reeked. Carmen could only assume the funk was from decomposing lung tissue. Cadaverine, putrescine. She left the vials to settle overnight, eyedroppered the dregs, centrifuged them, and separated the layers onto slides. She reclosed the vials and got the cover slips in place as fast as possible before bending over the microscope. That done, she searched databases and squinted at enlarged pollutant concentration maps until her head felt as if it were being squeezed in a vise.

At eight p.m., she drank two cups of terrible coffee with cocoa mix stirred in, instead of eating dinner. Then she started searching through the saved feeds of site monitoring stations north and west of the city. Past the soft edge, outside the current spread of the mesh. There was too much pollution in the water for the victim to have been dumped—to have been *drowned*—in the reclaimed area. But the mesh was growing. And where the mesh was going to be, Carmen's colleagues had placed weather stations, and pollution stations, and all kinds of equipment to produce a picture of environmental conditions before and after remediation.

Carmen ran algorithm after algorithm, until she matched the unreclaimed plastics and pollutants in the victim's lungs with the plastics and pollutants along a particular stretch of waterfront. There were observation stations dotted along the coast there. Some of them recorded video.

Two hours and thirteen minutes into her search, she found the footage.

She knew where the victim had gone into the water. She knew the license plate of the car that had brought the killer and the victim to that fateful place. She had some not-very-clear footage of the killer who had thrown the bound victim down an embankment into the river that must then have carried her into the sea.

A balloon drone had captured the whole thing, and saved the images into its relentless optical memory.

I can't, she thought.

But there was that image, of the bound woman—alive, struggling—being hurled off the bank to die in the cold, muddy water below.

It wasn't proving who the murderer might be that bothered her. It was what might happen afterward. What certainly would happen, if they were charged.

That stink from the vials still came through the scent of artificial honeysuckle after three hand-washings.

"No perfumes of Araby," Carmen muttered, and went to scrub again, telling herself that the clinging stench was not a metaphor.

In the morning, she was still trying to decide whether to call Quinn and what to tell her when Quinn, again, appeared at her door. Carmen jumped in her seat when the other woman leaned around the frame.

Quinn looked at her curiously. "Maybe you are the killer after all."

"Maybe you're a ghost who keeps materializing."

Quinn shrugged, lower lip stuck out, her head bobbing to one side. "I know I haven't given you enough time—"

"You have," Carmen said.

Quinn looked at her. Looked again, frowning. Held out a hand.
"Let's get a cup of coffee," she said.

Carmen led the way to the small kitchen where Quinn sniffed the coffeepot, said, "I'm buying," and brought Carmen back through the corridors and the lobby to a small café across the street. When they were settled with cappuccinos and biscotti, Quinn leaned her elbows on the red-check tablecloth and said, "You don't like cops."

Carmen swizzled her cookie in the coffee to give herself an excuse to look down. "I like you just fine. It's your job I have problems with."

"To be frank with you," Quinn admitted, "most days I agree. But somebody has to do it, and if I'm doing it I know who's making the choice about whether or not to be an asshole, and I have some influence over them."

Carmen laughed in spite of herself. "I'm having a moral crisis, Quinn. I think I know who did it."

"All by yourself? Fantastic. We're going to put you on retainer."

"Well, not exactly who did it. I know how to find out who did it."

Quinn sipped her coffee. "So what's the crisis about?"

"What I told you," Carmen said. "Prisons are evil."

"Necessary evil."

"No."

Quinn tapped her cookie on the rim of her cup. "You just want to let murderers and rapists *go*?"

"I want to change society so that people are supported and connected. So that murderers and rapists don't . . . just don't occur."

Quinn guffawed. "That's not human nature. How many rich assholes ought to go to jail? They have plenty of support and they still do crimes."

Carmen's laugh was much more bitter than the coffee. "How many rich assholes actually do go to jail? When was the last time you perp-walked a banker, Quinn?"

Quinn looked down. "I'm a *murder* cop."

"So if murders didn't happen you'd be out of a job."

"Happily so," Quinn admitted. "That dog won't hunt, Pollyanna."

Carmen stared at her. Maybe she could try a different approach. "Have *you* ever murdered anybody?"

"Of course not."

"Aren't you human?"

Quinn snorted. "My ex-wife might disagree, but . . . I'm human. Okay, then: committing violent crimes is *damaged* human nature. Selfish human nature. Predatory human nature. You just want to turn the predators loose to harm anybody they choose? What are you going to do with all of the murderers we have already? You can't prevent those people from growing up awful. What about all of their victims and *their* trauma response? What about protecting society?"

"Punishment isn't a deterrent. A punitive justice system doesn't cut down on crime, because it doesn't address the root causes of crime. It just creates more criminals down the line. If you don't want recidivists and more damaged generations, you have to change your whole philosophy."

"It's not my philosophy." Quinn bit a chunk out of her cookie and crunched in evident frustration. She slurped the last of her coffee. Fortified, she went on. "My first priority is keeping innocent people safe and protecting the fabric of society."

"So is mine. I think one day, prisons as we understand them will be considered as barbaric as the iron maiden, as roasting people on a spit."

"That sounds great." Quinn picked her teeth with a thumbnail. "What's the action plan?"

Carmen said, "Change the world."

Quinn tossed her cup at the recycler without looking. As if guided by an angel's hand, it went in. The detective lifted her eyes and appealed to some invisible authority. "The last anarchist here needs to lay off the weed and fellow feeling."

"I am not an anarchist!" Carmen protested. "I just believe in a collaborative government rather than a punitive one. If you want people to feel invested in the system you have to give them access to it and power over it."

"There will always be assholes," Quinn said. "Please tell me what you have on *this* asshole so I can stop him from immediately being an asshole again."

Carmen picked up a sugar packet and began fiddling with it.

Quinn said, "I could mention that not telling me, now, is withholding evidence."

Really? "Conscientious objectors have gone to jail for their principles before."

"It's obstruction of justice."

"You gonna arrest me?" Carmen wondered if she could get a martyr thing going. BRAVE SCIENTIST DEFIES COPS, RISKS JAIL ON PRINCIPLE. SERIAL KILLER ON THE LOOSE.

No. That last part would not endear her to anybody.

It didn't endear her to *her*.

Quinn held her challenging gaze for a moment. "No," she said at last, without looking down. "I'm going to beg you. Tell me what you know. Let justice take its course. The person who did this will kill again."

He would. Carmen knew it. She hadn't slept the night before. Every time she closed her eyes, images of the struggling, stumbling victim and the killer shoving her along the embankment had returned. Carmen could imagine too well what it would feel like: wire cutting your wrists, the sickening plummet, the icy disorienting splash—

The futile struggle. The pain of water filling your lungs.

Carmen pushed her coffee away.

"Whatever I do here is not the right thing," Carmen said. "The right thing to do cannot be reached from where we're standing. We have to build a bridge from here to the right thing before we can touch it."

"You need a place to stand before you can build a bridge. What you're suggesting is just not practical. There's no path." Quinn shook her head. "Some people," she said definitely, "are just plain mean."

"That's what they said about addressing climate destabilization, too," Carmen said. "Too hard. Not practical. But here I am. And an unstable climate contributes to social stresses and antisocial behavior. So if we can mitigate one, why not the other?"

Quinn crossed her arms and cocked a shoulder against the wall. "Okay. What would be the right thing?"

"To save the world," said Carmen. "And all the people in it."

"You're saving lives if you put this guy away."

"In the short run," Carmen agreed. "In the long run, I'm reinforcing a system that ruins and sacrifices far more lives."

"You've got yourself some kind of bullshit ethical trolley problem there."

"I'm already compromising my principles."

"All we have is expedience and approximations. All we ever have. Would it make you feel better if I got the prosecutor to subpoena whatever information you have? It wouldn't be your fault, then."

It seemed like a genuine, friendly offer of help. She realized with a shock that Quinn was sincere. That she didn't agree with Carmen—she probably thought Carmen was an idiot—but that she also respected Carmen's right to make those choices, even when they annoyed the hell out of her.

Carmen shook her head but didn't argue. *God help me,* she thought. She stood up. "I have to go."

She reached into her pocket and pulled out the thumb drive nestled there. She held it out to Quinn. Quinn took it gently, watching Carmen's face as if observing some shy animal.

"I won't testify," Carmen said.

"Okay. I can't speak for the DA. But that's more than fair." Quinn tilted her head to one side. A rose-gilt earring flashed. "I hope someday you realize that you're a hero."

Carmen folded her arms across her chest and squeezed herself as tightly as she dared. "There are no heroes in a tragedy."

EMERGENCY SKIN

N. K. JEMISIN

N. K. Jemisin (nkjemisin.com) lives and writes in Brooklyn, New York, and has published nine novels, including the Inheritance trilogy, the Dreamblood duology, the Broken Earth trilogy (which includes Hugo winners *The Fifth Season, The Obelisk Gate*, and *The Stone Sky*), and *The City We Became*. She is the only person to win three consecutive Hugo Awards for Best Novel. Jemisin's short fiction has been published in *Clarkesworld, Postscripts, Strange Horizons, Jim Baen's Universe*, and various print anthologies and is collected in *How Long 'til Black Future Month?* She has also won a Nebula Award, two Locus Awards, and a number of other honors. Jemisin is also a member of the Altered Fluid writing group. In addition to writing, she has been a counseling psychologist and educator (specializing in career counseling and student development), a hiker and biker, and a political/feminist/antiracist blogger. She is a former reviewer for the *New York Times Book Review* and still writes occasional long-form reviews for them.

You are our instrument.

Beautiful you. Everything that could be given to you to improve on the human design, you possess. Stronger muscles. Finer motor control. A mind unimpeded by the vagaries of organic dysfunction and bolstered by generations of high-intelligence breeding. Here is what you'll look like when your time comes. Note the noble brow, the classical patrician features, the lean musculature, the long penis and thighs. That hair color is called "blond." [Please reference: hair variations.] Are you not magnificent? Or you will be, someday. But first, you must earn your beauty.

We should begin with a briefing, since you're now authorized for Information Level Secret. On its face, this mission is simple: return to the ruined planet Tellus, from which mankind originates. When our Founders realized the world was dying, they built the Muskos-Mercer Drive in secret. Then our ancestors bent the rules of light and fled to a new world circling another sun, so that something of humanity—the best of it—would survive. We'll use the MMD, much improved by our technorati over the years, to return to that world. The journey, from your perspective, will take days. When you return, years will have passed. How brave you are to walk in your forefathers' footsteps!

No, there's no one left alive on Tellus. The planet was in full environmental collapse across every biome when our people left. There were just too many people, and too many of those were unfit, infirm, too old, or too young. Even the physically ideal ones were slow thinkers, timid spirits. There was not enough collective innovation or strength of will between them to solve the problems Tellus faced, and so we did the only merciful thing we could: we left them behind.

Of course that was mercy. Do you think your ancestors wanted to leave billions of people to starve and suffocate and drown? It was simply that our new home could support only a few.

Tellus is nearly a thousand light-years from home, meaning that the light we receive from that world is hundreds of years old. We cannot directly observe it in real time—but we knew the fate that awaited it. Tellus is by now a graveyard world. We expect that its seas have

become acidic and barren, its atmosphere a choking mix of carbon di-
oxide and methane. Its rain cycle will have long since dried up. It will
be terrible to walk through this graveyard, and dangerous. You'll find
toxic drowned cities, still-burning underground coal fires, melted-down
nuclear plants. Yet the worst of it might be seeing our past greatness, on
this world that was once so ideal. Mankind could build high into the
sky, there where the gravity wasn't as heavy. We could build all over the
planet because it was not tidally locked. [Please reference: night.] Look
at the names whenever you find them on buildings or debris. You'll see
the forebears of our Founder clans—all the great men who spent the
last decades of that planet's life amassing the resources and technology
necessary to save the best of mankind. If for no other reason, this world
should be honored because it nurtured them.

To ensure success, and your mental health during extended isolation, we have equipped you with ourselves—a dynamic-matrix consensus intelligence encapsulating the ideals and blessed rationality of
our Founders. We are implanted in your mind and will travel with you
everywhere. We are your companion, and your conscience. We will
provide essential data about the planet as a survival aid. Via your composite, we can administer critical first aid as required. And should you
suffer a composite breach or similar emergency, we are programmed
to authorize adaptive action.

[Reference request denied.] You don't need to know about that yet.
Please focus, and limit your curiosity. All that matters is the mission.

You can't fail. It's too important. But rest assured: you have the best
of us inside you, enveloping you, keeping you safe and true. You are
not alone. You will prevail.

Are you awake? We've reached the outermost edges of the Sol system.
Almost there.

Curious. Spectroscopy shows the space around Tellus as clear. It
was clogged with debris when we left.

And stranger: no radio waves. Our home is too far away to detect any of the decades' worth of audio and visual signals that our species once beamed into space—well, no, not really on purpose. It's just that no one knew how *not* to do it. Once we worried that such signals would eventually alert hostile alien species to our presence . . . but that isn't a problem anymore.

As we approached the system, we were bathed in those waves—music, entertainment programs, long-expired warnings and commands . . . No, we don't advise listening. At this point it's just noise pollution. But we *expected* the noise, spreading throughout the universe in an ever-expanding bubble that we suppose will be Tellus's final epitaph. Silence in the bubble's wake, of course; the silence of the tomb. But still not truly silent, because there were too many automated things on and around Tellus that should have survived for at least another millennium. For example, the satellites that should still be, and aren't, in orbit.

Most curious.

Well. *Astra inclinant, sed non obligant*; while naturally we had certain expectations for how this mission would go, we aren't infallible. That's why we didn't send a bot on this mission, after all; human beings are better than AI at handling the unexpected. You must simply be prepared for anything.

No, that isn't right, atmospheric analysis can't possibly be that far off our models. It's far more likely that we caught some debris during the near-Saturn pass, which damaged the ship's enhanced spectrometer. None of these readings make sense.

Please prepare for EVA and sensor repair. Adjusting your composite for deep-space radiation shielding. You wanted a better look at Saturn; now you'll get to see it without the ship in the way.

This . . . cannot be.

That is *movement*. Those are *lights*. There should be clear signs of eco-collapse. It had already begun when the Founders left—but compare the geographic maps we have stored against what's there now. See that branching line in the southwestern portion of the continent? That was, *is*, the Colorado River. The maps show that it was dry when our ancestors left. Millions died trying to migrate east and north to where there might be more water. Countless species went extinct. But there's the river, flowing again.

That entire coastline should be gone. That *state* should be gone. That archipelago. The ice caps—here they are again. Different. New, but enough to reverse sea-level rise. How can this have happened?

[State: deprecated term for a geopolitical construct. No need to reference.]

Yes, you're right. Many, *many* more than home. At home, we maintain only as many people as we can safely sustain: six thousand total, including servi and mercennarii. Here, there must be millions. Billions. The old pattern, too many people—and yet the air is clear. The seas are cleaner than when we left.

We don't know.

We were not prepared for this eventuality. Please wait while we calculate a new consensus—

Yes, the mission is still paramount. Yes, we still require the target samples to formulate new—

Yes—

No, our world will not survive without those samples.

We advise delay and study.

Certainly you may reject our advice, but—

Ah, but they bred you bold, didn't they. Like the Founders, who would never have survived without the courage to be ruthless as well as sensible. Very well.

The people of Tellus will not be as beautifully ruthless as you. However they've survived, whatever fluke has worked in their favor, never forget their quintessential inferiority. They lacked the intelligence to choose rationality over sentiment. They weren't willing to do what was necessary to survive. You are.

Stay low. This is—

What are you looking at? Pay attention.

This is called a forest. You've seen trees back home, in the Founder clans' private habitats? These are trees in the wild. Our records suggest that you're near what used to be a city called Raleigh. See those ruins through the trees? Raleigh was underwater when we left. Clearly they've reclaimed the land, but we are astonished that no one has redeveloped it, or at least clear-cut the forest. We find such chaos ugly and inefficient.

Your composite is capable of withstanding microparticle strikes in space, so of course it's impermeable to branches and stone, but these things can still entangle you and slow you down. We've plotted you a path of minimized resistance. Please follow the line on your heads-up display.

Hmm, yes. We suppose you would find it beautiful. That is a lichen. Yes, it's all very green. That's a puddle—stagnant water left over from precipitation or seeping up from groundwater. We don't know if it will rain anytime soon, but this much humidity does suggest a regular rain cycle.

Those are birds. That sound is coming from the birds. Sunrise is coming. They sing because it's nearly daytime.

Yes, thank you, do please focus on the mission; we almost went into power-saving mode. These people are clearly at a primitive level of technology relative to our own, but they may have some rudimentary form of surveillance. *Stay low.*

[Please reference: dangerous wildlife, a list.]

Your respiration is too fast. This has increased your metabolic rate to an unacceptable degree. If you continue to consume nutrients at this rate, you'll run out before you can return to the ship to replenish. Calm *down*.

Not that we blame you for your fear—

Pardon us. Excitement and fear look much the same, neurologically speaking. Your *excitement*, then. This is a world we thought dead. A remnant of our species that evolution should have claimed, obviously saved by luck. We do agree that this is historically momentous.

They've actually elevated the whole town on some kind of . . . platform. And oh, fascinating: the material of the platform looks like plastic, but close analysis suggests cellulose instead. It *respires* like a plant, too, if these CO_2 and oxygen readings are correct. Please take a sample. The technorati in Biotech are always looking for new potential commodities—

Oh. Not even with the monomolecular blade? Hmm. Very well. Resume mission.

It's odd that this settlement is elevated. During the period of sea-level rise, it must have been necessary, but now that the planet is back to normal, there's no further need for this. Maybe it's a sunk-cost issue?

Well, an elevated city costs more than one on the ground. Water and other resources will have to be pumped up to the living levels. There are added maintenance costs. And as you've seen, vegetation and wildlife quickly encroach on the area near and underneath the city—

Why would they *like* it this way? What, just because it's pretty? That does sound like something these people would do, though. Please resume. Adjusting composite for climbing.

Curious that they have no militia or visible surveillance. This ambient darkness is night—yes, like the reference we shared with you. Adjusting your visual acuity to compensate. This settlement's lighting seems to generate little heat, but you may activate infrared if that will help—

Control yourself, soldier! Your reaction is wholly inappropriate. No, that person is *not* a technorati or Founder-clan. Well, for one thing, look at their coloring. Every skin shade from melanistic to albino? They seem to pay no attention whatsoever to basic eugenics principles. That one over there has *patches*; look. Disgusting. Animals breed like this, not people.

We don't know. The lower citizens of this world, the agricolae and servi and whatnot, must function without composite suits. They would have less need of that technology on this world, if the environment has been repaired. It's clear, however, that going without composites has done them no favors.

That incomprehensible babble sounds familiar because it's related to our language. Audio analysis has detected familiar phonemes and syntax. Theirs seems to have been bastardized, however, by time and the infusion of other lesser languages. Back home, the Founder clans have been diligent in permitting the use of nothing but the Founders' tongue and those of the honored ancients. This is what might have happened had we not been so careful. We need more audio sampling, but with that we should be able to put together a rudimentary translation script—

Ugh, look at that one. That morphology is called *fat*. Fat people are aesthetically displeasing, morally repugnant, and economically useless. And, oh Founders, look. That poor man has been allowed to get *old*. Why is he still alive? If he generates value, he shouldn't be left to *deteriorate* like this. It's incomprehensibly cruel. Do they have no preservation technology here? What have they spent their innovative energy on, uselessly elevating their cities? Ugh. Now, look at *that* one. To the right, see? Rolling along in that chairlike device. He appears to be paralyzed from the waist down. That must be why there are ramps everywhere and why the doorways are so wide—just for him and others like him. Food, water, and excess building materials, all poured into a useless, unproductive, unattractive person.

Nothing's changed with these people. They still build societies around their least and worst instead of the best and brightest. We cannot understand why they're still alive . . . but if they can at least give us the cell cultures we need, then we can be rid of them and go back to civilization.

Please hold for a moment; you appear to be secure and undetected here in this alley, at least for now. The situational parameters have activated a new protocol in us, and we need to brief you.

You will recall that we mentioned adaptive action as a possible emergency response during this mission. What that means is this: In light of your critical mission, your composite is a more advanced model than what is usually granted to men of the *militus* class. There is a transmutational nanite layer which, if activated, can convert the carbon picobeads, synthetic collagen fibers, and HeLa plasmids embedded in your composite into human skin. It would not be aesthetically ideal, but it might at least reduce your chances of detection, so that the mission—

No, it would not be the face and body we promised you—

Listen. Listen! The emergency skin would be only a temporary measure. As soon as you return home with the cell samples, the technorati can surgically alter your dermal layers back to the aesthetic configuration you were promised. Of course we will; you'll have earned it, won't you? If you complete this mission, you'll be a hero. Why would we refuse you what you're due?

No, we don't believe you can safely walk into that enclave of people as you are now. These people have primitive values, primitive technology; they've never seen a composite suit. They seem tolerant of multiple facial configurations, but *you don't have a face at all*. As far as they're concerned, you possess no obvious characteristics that identify you as a fellow human being. You don't speak their language, but that's irrelevant. If they have weapons, they'll use them as soon as they see you. You won't be able to complete the mission because you'll be captured or dead.

Take a hostage? No. That's foolish. There must be ten or fifteen people down there, doing whatever they're doing. Some kind of religious ritual, a dance to greet the sun? Barbaric. How would you know which of these mongrel people is important enough to ransom for the biomaterial we need? If you grab some random *servus*, they'll just let him die. There is bold, decisive action—we commend that, you know we do—and then there is folly. You don't know enough about these people to enact the plan you're describing. Would you really rather risk everything than activate your emergency skin? Does the prospect of being less than perfect, even temporarily, panic you that m—

Oh Founders.

LEVEL-FOUR SECURITY ALERT. ADRENALINE ADMINIS-TRATION STAND BY. LIMBIC SYSTEM OVERCLOCK STAND BY. WEAPONS FABRICATION ONLINE. MIDBRAIN FIGHT-OR-FLIGHT ENGAGEMENT ON THREE.

TWO.

.□

.□

Online. Reboot in five. Four.

Are you all right? You're uninjured. Your composite remains un-breached. The weapon they used was an update of something we re-member from before the Great Leaving. We can call it a taser. Beware, however: you are not alone.

"Hey. Easy! Nobody's going to hurt you. Do you understand me? Okay. Good. How are you feeling? You've been unconscious for hours."

How are we understanding him? We didn't have time to create a translation script—and your auditory nerve is reacting out of sync with his speech. You're actually *hearing* his words, intelligibly.

What's that on your facial beads? It seems to be a device of some kind. The audio you're hearing is being transmitted by it. It's translat-ing his words.

"Oh. Sorry about that. Ordinarily we use a mild neurotoxin to subdue violent people. Your, uh, artificial skin? Means we had to use something with a little more kick."

Great caution is warranted here. Tell him nothing. He is merely a servus, in any case. Look at his skin, like sandy dust. Look at the blem-ishes, the inelegance of his features. One of his eyes is higher than the

other, only slightly but still. Don't be deceived; no one here wears a
composite. *Our* skin is a mark of honor. *Their* skin is meaningless.

"What's your name?"

And don't stare.

"Well, okay. That's your right, I guess. Maybe I should start. My name is Jaleesa. I'm—uh, a scholar? I guess that's what you'd call it. Except I'm really just a student, and the field I study is pretty obscure, ha-ha, so right now all I am is another gawker."

There's too much here to explain, but we'll try. Apparently these people still allow those beneath the ruling classes to be educated—

"You didn't have to grab that woman, you know. You scared the hell out of her. She's all right, if you're wondering. More concerned about you, really, now that we've explained what's going on."

This is an interrogation. He's attempting to put you at ease. Next will come the questions about your mission, about our home, about the secrets of our technology—

"You poor thing. My God, you must have actually thought someone was going to hurt you. Well, the police released you after notifying the town of your presence. And, uh, we put a monitor on you. I volunteered to stay with you until you regained consciousness."

Ah, this *thing* on your wrist. We have historical knowledge of "watches," primitive time devices, but this one is unsupported, strapless. How have they made it adhere to your composite? Keep this as a sample, too, when you escape.

"Sorry for that, of course, but since you already threatened someone . . . They might have made a bigger stink if you'd used a weapon, but it was pretty clear to everyone involved that you were just, you know, freaking out. Understandable, under the circumstances! Anyway, I'm supposed to give you this."

What is—

Blessed Founders. This is a microfluid cell-culture dish? Sealed. These characters on the label are formed strangely, but similar to our writing . . . It cannot be.

"That's what you're here for, right? Can you read? The label says,

'HeLa 7713.' Yeah, that's right. This is an active, living culture, so be careful with it. You don't want to get it too cold or . . . Uh, your ship has radiation shielding, doesn't it? Okay, good, then. If you want to keep the culture alive."

This cannot be.

"Ha, wow, amazing how much emotion I'm picking up from your body language. Relax, it's fine. Do you want a few additional dishes, just in case? Redundancy is good, right? Here, take some more. I'll get you a bag or case so you can carry them easily."

This is a trick. It must be. Why would he give us this?

"Well, you need it, right? It has something to do with how your biotech works? Your composite is pretty nifty. We use things like that for hazardous-materials cleanup, but we don't *live* in them, of course! Anyway, so, there you go. Nice meeting you!"

Wait, what?

"Oh, I was just going to head back to work. Did you have any more questions? If you weren't planning to head back to your ship right away, I can arrange a guide for you. We put a translator on your, um, face, so that should be working by now. Are you hungry? Shit, how do you eat?"

Your nutrient supply remains sufficient for now. You are hydrated. Your heart rate is elevated. Be calm.

"So you're really just . . . floating around in soup in there? Sorry, we're not supposed to . . . I'm sure your culture's lifestyle is valid to you. It's just that, well, I mean, you can make skin whenever you want, right? So . . . It's Earth, after all, where we all come from. You can come out! We don't bite!"

They are savages. Of course they bite.

"Earth" is an antiquated name for Tellus. Call it what you wish.

You *know* why we use composites. They're far more efficient than skin. A composite skin can be rapidly modified to enable you to survive adverse environmental conditions. In the early days after Founding, composites were necessary to ensure the survival of workers building our habitats; they saved countless lives that might otherwise have been lost to solar flares or biohazards. Composites also reduce labor costs lost to bathroom breaks, meals, personal hygiene, medical care, interpersonal communication, and masturbation.

"And it doesn't hurt, living without skin? It just really seems . . . Like, how do you have sex? How do you breastfeed? That reminds me—what's your preferred gender? I'm a 'her.'"

Why are you still talking to him? You have no need of this information. You've accomplished your mission, or you will have, once you return home. There is—

Yes. We know what "her" means. We simply do not acknowledge it.

[Reference request denied.]

[Reference request denied.]

Fine. It's an antiquated term for a type of pleasurer—the kind with enlarged breast tissue.

"Pleasurer? I've never heard that word. Sorry, no idea what it is."

You are being very persistent. Pleasurers are bots designed for sexual use. In the early days after Founding, most were given the designation "her," out of tradition and according to the Founders' preferences, but that pronoun has since fallen out of usage. When your mission is complete and you've been rewarded with the skin we promised, you'll be issued a pleasurer. Its duty will be to maintain your penis in optimal condition. But it will not look like *this* thing, brown and fat and smug. What is the point of a pleasurer that's not beautiful? If it cannot even manage to be that, then we might as well call it "him."

Yes, the militus—police?—you saw before was probably a "her." Your hostage too.

We don't know, maybe 50 percent of the population? What does it matter? You don't have a penis.

"Oh, right, I read about that! Your Founders hated women, wanted to replace them all with robots. That's, uh, interesting. Oh—excuse me, somebody's calling me. Yeah, Jaleesa here. Oh, hi, sweetheart! Sorry, I'm going to be a little late, got something to take care of here."

He is speaking to someone else. Distracted. We can minifacture a stabbing weapon from the topmost layer of your composite in .0035 seconds, if you want to flee. You—

We have no idea why he knows of our Founders.

You're asking more questions than usual.

No. Enough. We're tired of this. Allow us to remind you: *You have a mission.* Without the cells in your hand, our whole society will falter and die. Mankind will falter and die!

Yes. Good. At last. It would be best to kill the Jaleesa creature so that he can raise no alarm . . .

Hmm, well, you have a point. This monitoring device will not come off. Very well, play along as you must.

"Sorry about that, I'm back. That was my son. Oh, hey, did you want to leave?"

[Reference request denied.] Do not ask what a son is. Tell him you want to leave.

"Okay, then. Just remember, no more hostage taking! Poor scared thing. You know how to get back to your ship, right? We can give you an escort if you need it."

Tell him you need no escort.

"Okay, I guess that's fair, given that you found your way here. Sorry, didn't mean to patronize! Anyway, here's a carrying case for your cell cultures; it'll keep them in gravitically stabilized stasis for your return trip. And there's a packet of instructions attached to each of the cell-culture dishes, too, to help you clone them successfully. If you folks can manage to do that this time, you won't have to come back. Right?"

Do not ask—

"Uh . . . yeah, 'this time.'"

We know nothing of—

"I don't know, every few years? Seems to be irregular, but every now and again, one of you guys shows up, dressed in your bag, asking for HeLa cultures. That's how the police knew not to use lethal force. Yours is one of the few exoplanetary colonies that's lasted this long, see. Most of the others—the ones that didn't die—came back once they realized Earth would be fine. There's just your group and a couple of others left, all of them extremist offshoots of some kind or another . . .

Well, anyway, we don't mind helping you. Everybody's just trying to survive, right? Look, I'm sorry, but I need to go. Have a good trip back. Remember, no hostages. Bye!"

Good. He's gone. Our records did warn that women talk too much. The Founders were wise.

We don't know what to make of your silence.

Your pulse rate, neurotransmitter activity, and body language suggest anger. Please unclench your fists; there's a chance the locals will interpret that as an aggressive gesture.

Talk to us.

We can't shut up. We're supposed to help you. You've nearly accomplished your mission—

You've nearly accomplished your mission, and *it doesn't matter* if there were previous missions!

No one lied to you. We weren't given that knowledge. It isn't a deception if we didn't know. You have a mission to complete. Please follow the line on your heads-up display to leave this facility and begin the journey back to your ship. Yes, through this door—

You took a wrong turn. Please reverse course.

Why have you stopped? Very well. What you're seeing is called a sunset. You recall our initial briefing, about how planets that are not tidally locked turn on an axis? This planet is turning toward night.

Yes, yes, the sunset *is* lovely, over town and forest. We suppose night will be lovely, too, but you should be back to the ship by then if you leave now.

Look. We're glad to note the reduction of your agitation neuro-response, but how long do you mean to stand here?

Your attitude grows irritating. Must we report your disrespect to the Founders when we return? We're their consensus consciousness, after all. Some parts of our consciousness are amused by your anger, others offended, but we are all certain that you wouldn't talk to a Founder this way.

Don't ignore us.

Beautiful? That's . . . You're only saying that because they have skin. The value accorded to skin on our world has predisposed you, in a way, but you must understand that not all skin is equal. There are objective and qualitative differences, and there's a reason the Founders chose to exalt—

Stop. Please follow the line on your heads-up display.

You have deviated from the return path to the ship.

Stop.

These people are of no use to you. Without that translator device, they would just be babbling savages—stop *talking* to them!

Stop.

Please. Stop.

Please. *You* are beautiful. We want you to be beautiful. We want you to return home showered in glory, bearing the salvation of your people in one elegant, pale hand. Don't you want this too?

Oh Founders.

"Hi there! Are you lost? Oh, okay."

How they patronize you. They treat you like a child. Like someone inferior.

"Ha-ha, no, Earth's still here and humanity didn't die out! All of you seem so surprised by that."

They should have died. The Founders were the geniuses, the makers who moved nations with a word. We left because it would've cost too much to fix the world. Cheaper to build a new one.

Of course. And of course we built that world to suit our tastes. A world free of this useless, ugly rabble. Why do otherwise? Do not be seduced by this madness.

"Oh, is this the bag boy? I heard another one showed up. What, he's in a bag, it's—oh, fine. Sorry."

The composite suits weren't *primarily* designed with control in mind, no. We already explained to you that they were a necessity, in the early days . . . Well, listen to you. A few hours surrounded by cheap, easy skin and suddenly you question everything about our society. Oh, we *will* be making some recommendations regarding discipline when you return. Very strong recommendations.

Stop calling them beautiful.

"No, we're just born with our skin this way. I guess you could say our parents pick it! Uh. Parents? They're . . . you know, the people who made and raised you? You mean you don't—you're kidding."

Their way of life is antiquated. Inefficient.

"So how do you, uh, reproduce? Oh, artificial wombs, yeah, that figures. No women at all, huh? And you *never* have skin, not until some high-ranking member of your society says you can? Yikes."

It is the guiding principle of our society. Rights belong only to those who earn them. When you complete this mission, for your bravery you will have proven yourself deserving of life, health, beauty, sex, privacy, bodily autonomy—every possible luxury. Only a few can have everything, don't you see? What these people believe isn't feasible. They want everything for *everyone*, and look at where it's gotten them! Half of them aren't even men. Almost none are fair of skin. They're burdened by the dysfunctional and deficient at every turn. A few must be intelligent, we suppose, or they wouldn't have managed what they've done with the planet, but for those bright few, what's been the reward? A few are beautiful, maybe, for a while, but if they used the HeLa cells, a limited number of them could remain young and strong for centuries.

Untrue. That is *not* the only reason we need the HeLa cells. The skin-generation process uses them too. Your own skin—

Well, no, not many people earn skin. The scarcity of the HeLa cells—

Of course there isn't enough to give everyone skin! That's ridiculous. No, we couldn't clone that much, the process is labor-intensive and costly—

You must understand, preservation technology requires massive amounts of HeLa cells. And since anyone of technorati class or higher may demand our entire reserve supply at any time . . . Well, that's why you're here.

We don't know.

We don't *know* why Tellus people live like this. No, stop calling it "Earth." We aspire to use the language of the greatest philosopher-poets and statesmen in history, not the gabble of the rabble. Hasn't your time here shown you the superiority of our way of life?

Where are you going? You cannot simply—

Now? No! There is no emergency, do *not* initiate emergency-skin fabrication—we forbid it! Yes, your anxiety levels are abnormal, but that hardly constitutes—

Oh Founders.

How can you do this? Do not do this.

Now see what you've done.

The emergency skins are designed for survival, not beauty. Their parameters are environmentally dictated. There's sufficient unfiltered UV here that significant melanistic pigmentation was prioritized. Past a certain point on the programmed continuum, this alters hair texture as well.

It isn't what we wanted for you, this hideousness. Now you're a walking radiation burn, where you should have had ethereal translucence. That many of these others, these throwbacks, have a similar look is irrelevant. You were meant for better.

And now that you look like them, now that you stumble among them, naked, no longer able to speak to them because the translator device will not adhere to your new flesh, shaking with weakness because the emergency-skin-fabrication process consumed your last nutrients . . . What are you expecting? Acceptance? Prepare yourself. We contain memories of what the world was like before the Founders left. They'll hate you. Hurt you, even, for frightening them. You'll never reach the heights you should have. No one will give you the opportunities you need to succeed. It would be better to have never been born than to be like this. Do you understand, now, why the Founders excised these traits from our world's gene pool? We aren't cruel.

Please go home. Even now, we would welcome you as a hero— provided you bring the cells. There, with the technorati's help, we could replace this awful skin and woolish hair with something better.

You're making a mistake. You've made so many mistakes.

It's false, their kindness. People do such things only to *seem* like good people—a performance of virtue. Our Founders were at least honest in their selfishness.

What now? Another of these creatures who has aged into uselessness. The burned skin does resist UV well, though, doesn't it? Not half as many wrinkles as the other old ones. Spindly, though. Weak, knobby jointed. He limps with pain—but degenerate as he is, he still looks at you so pityingly. Does your new hack-job skin not crawl with shame?

We'll be ashamed for you, then. Die in ignominy. We're done with you.

"There's something I want you to see."

Still alive, betrayer? Ah, fed and clothed, how nice for you. This old man seems to like you. We cannot fathom why. He hobbles so as he walks. We want to push him over. You could—oh, very well.

Oh.

We thought this space of theirs, this platform you climbed onto, was one of their cities. This, though. We remember cities like this, vast enough to shelter millions. No, we could never have built such cities back home; there have never been enough of us to justify it. And remember, large populations get that way by sustaining many unnecessary, unproductive people.

How easily seduced you are. You can't stop staring at these people, at these landscapes, at these horizons. You've stopped flinching with every breeze, and now you revel in the sensation of air caressing your new skin, like a hedonist. You touched yourself last night, didn't you? We recorded it. The Founders should find it amusing. But if you go back now, we promise not to—

Where is this dried-up nobody taking you now? "This is called a museum."

We know what a museum is, you burned-up waste of skin.

"This may interest you."

This is—oh. A timeline of the Great Leaving. They call it something else, but we know these dates, these images. Yes. Yes. That was how it began, with the Industrial Revolution—oh. They think it began even earlier? Interesting, if inaccurate. Wait, this was *once* called the United States? What is it called now?

"It doesn't have a name now. The world. Earth. We don't bother with borders anymore."

Then they are endlessly inundated with the useless. Refugees and other refuse.

"We realized it was impossible to protect any one place if the place next door was drowning or on fire. We realized the old boundaries weren't meant to keep the undesirable out, but to hoard resources within. And the hoarders were the core of the problem."

We make no apologies for taking everything we could. Anyone would. What is this, though? The timeline jumps, abruptly. Interesting. This world changed—improved—almost immediately after the Leaving.

"To save the world, people had to think differently."

Please. Happy thoughts and handouts weren't going to fix that mess. There has to have been some technological breakthrough. Perpetual energy? A new carbon sequestration technique, maybe some kind of polar cooling process. Their technology *has* changed in some fundamental ways; that's why it no longer generates radio waves or other EM radiation. That would make it remarkably efficient . . . But if that's so, why do they live like this, in elaborate tree-house villages? Why bother cleaning up space trash?

"Yes, some new technology emerged once everyone was permitted a decent education. But there was no trick to it. No quick fix. The problem wasn't technological."

What, then?

"I told you. People just decided to take care of each other."

Delusion. Only a miracle could've saved this planet. Here, yes, the exhibit talks about . . . "the Big Cleanup"? Ugh, these people have no poetry or marketing skill. It just can't be that simple. We must have left someone behind, an unfound Founder, someone we would have acknowledged as another true heir to Aristotle and Pythagoras. These people are just too small-minded to honor him as they should have. There has to be . . .

No breakthroughs. Advancements, certainly—but strange, profitless ones. Not the technological paths that would've interested us. And progressive taxation, health care, renewable energy, human-rights protection . . . the usual pithy sentimentalities. Without our Founders around to stand strong against the tide, these simple folk must have given in to every passing special interest . . .

But if this timeline is correct, then the old man is right. All of a sudden, the world simply did what was necessary to fix itself.

As soon as we lef—

Be silent. Correlation is not causality. Your burned-up skin has made you irrational. We have no idea why the old man even bothered to bring you here. Even for their degenerate kind, you're a fool.

Hmph. A whole month since last you even thought of your mission. We went to sleep, in your uselessness.

What do you contemplate now, lying in this donated bed, under the roof of your subsidized shelter? Lazy, greedy taker. Shouldn't you rest in order to be ready for the nothing work they've found you? They pay you enough to live on whether you show up or not. Why even bother?

Where are you going?

Ah, you live next door to the old man now. And he's given you a key? He needs someone to help take care of him as he lurches and wastes toward death, and you've decided to be his minder—how sentimental. Will he mind you breaking into his house, now, in the dark of the night? What goes on in that head of yours? The old man is not a pleasurer. You don't even know how to use your penis.

We are not disgusting. You are.

Well, he hasn't died in his sleep, lucky you. Go back to bed. What are—why are you turning him over? Stop touching him. The skin has grown loose here on his back; you see? This is what you'll look like one day. This

is

a product number.

We require more light.

Push him forward. Lean close; your eyes are too dark to take in light properly—yes, there at the small of his back, same as on yours. Definitely a product number. This set of numbers denotes an older series of transmutation nanites. Minifacture of these models stopped some thirty years before your gestation.

"When did you suspect?"

He's awake. Traitor. *Another* traitor.

"Ah. The Founders say intuition is irrational and unmanly, but it comes in handy at times, as you now see. Well, younger brother? Now what?"

You should kill him. Then yourself.

"I took you to the museum on a whim. To enjoy the irony. For all these centuries, the Founders told us that the Earth died because of greed. That was true, but they lied about *whose* greed was to blame. Too many mouths to feed, they said, too many 'useless' people . . . but we had more than enough food and housing for everyone. And the people they declared useless had plenty to offer—just not anything they cared about. The idea of doing something without immediate benefit, something that might only pay off in ten, twenty, or a hundred years, something that might benefit people they disliked, was anathema to the Founders. Even though that was precisely the kind of thinking that the world needed to survive."

We did what was rational. We have always been more rational than you people.

"What the Leaving proved was that the Earth *could* sustain billions, if we simply shared resources and responsibilities in a sensible way. What it couldn't sustain was a handful of hateful, self-important parasites, preying upon and paralyzing everyone else. As soon as those people left, the paralysis ended."

No. There are too many of you and you're all ugly and none of you will ever achieve the heights of glory that mankind is destined for—not if you're so busy taking care of the useless. It has to be one or the other. Either some fly, or everyone gets stuck crawling around in the mud. That's just how it is.

"Is that so? Is that you talking or that nag they put in your head? I remember how annoying it used to be."

We. That is. *Used* to be?

"Have you noticed yet that the people here have been humoring you? An invader from a 'superior' culture arrives, and they don't guard you, watch you, examine you for contaminants? Even after you've threatened them, they give you what you need—what you were prepared to steal. Something so precious that your whole world supposedly needs it to survive. An afterthought to them."

That . . . has troubled us, yes. We suspected a trap. But—

"Here is what you struggle to understand. The Founders poisoned the world and stripped it almost bare before they left. Repairing that damage was a challenge that forced those left behind to grow by leaps and bounds. They've developed methods and technology that we haven't even thought about, yes. But the *reason* they were able to make such leaps is because they made sure everyone had food, everyone had a place to live if they wanted it, everyone could read and write and pursue a fulfilling life, whatever that meant. Is it really so puzzling that this was all it took? Six billion people working toward a goal together is much more effective than a few dozen scrabbling for themselves."

There is logic to this, but we . . . we deny it. We cannot accept . . .

"*That's* why the people of Earth talk down to you, younger brother. That's why they treat you like the quaint, harmless throwback that you are. All these centuries and your people haven't figured out such a simple, basic thing."

No.

"Or maybe the Founder-clans and technorati don't *want* you to figure it out. Because then where would they be? Not gods among us, just other bright lights among many. Not kings. Just selfish men."

No.

"Then you're smarter than I was. My ship was damaged on atmospheric entry, beyond repair. I grew my skin only out of desperation as my nutrients ran low, and I wept as soon as my tear ducts formed. But the people here cared for me. Poor paranoid creature from a cruel, miserly world—how could they not pity me? Even though I was nothing but a servant, fetching scraps of ancient cancer so that his masters could flirt with immortality."

You *wanted* this mission. You could have done other work, the usual tasks that the bots can't accomplish. Well, no, of course you wouldn't have earned a skin for that. Only the best of us deserve such privileges.

"No one will stop you if you want to leave. Even now, you can go back to where they'll reduce you to raw meat and stuff you back into a biotech bag, and Tellus—*Earth*—won't stop you. People here don't agree with your primitive practices, but they won't interfere with your right to practice them."

We aren't primitive.

"But before you decide to leave, I want you to know one more thing."

Do not touch us do not lean close *do not speak any more—*

"You? Aren't the first deserter." He's lying.

"I don't know how many there have been. Earth keeps track of the visitations, but it's unimportant to them, so the records can be difficult to find. Sometimes more than one soldier arrives, each sent to different parts of the world; sometimes there's just one. The arrivals are random—or rather, they happen whenever home's demand for HeLa cells outstrips the supply. I wondered, for a while, why none of the other soldiers had reported the truth. Why no one at home knew that Earth is alive. Then I realized: all the ruling classes want are the HeLa cells. Why would they waste any on giving skins to glorified errand boys?"

We don't understand why you would believe this traitor over us. Haven't we helped you?

"And they can't have you telling anyone else that the promised reward, of skin, was a lie. No one would ever volunteer for a mission like this again. You need willing service for some jobs."

We've given you everything you wanted. Beautiful you. You are the best of us.

"Such a simple thing to program a composite suit to kill its occupant. Just a simple verbal command, or the press of a button, impersonal and efficient. Best to do it before you even land, so no one sees you return a hero and then asks awkward questions when you disappear. Pluck the cell cultures from the remains once the ship docks. They get what they want. Never mind that the truth about Earth dies with you. And even if some of them figure it out from the recorded data . . . why would they tell anyone else? Their world, limited as it is, contains everything they've ever wanted: immortality, the freedom to take anything they want, slaves whom they can control right down to the skin. They don't want to come back. And they certainly don't want anyone of the lower classes realizing there's another way to live."

He's lying, we told you, you'll be rewarded, we promised— How dare you.

"Oh, is that what you have in mind? Interesting. Then you're braver than me too."

No. This isn't the mission. How *dare* you.

"It won't be an easy thing, though. Remaking a society. Earth couldn't, not until it got rid of the Founders. You. Us."

We will strip the black skin from your flesh and leave you to rot without a composite, raw and screaming.

"Skin is the key. While most of the lower classes wear composites, the Founder clans and technorati can threaten them with nutrient deprivation, defibrillation, or suffocation. Even a small suit breach kills when you don't have skin to keep infections at bay. And most don't get the more advanced suits that are capable of generating skin. How do you mean to get around that?"

You're ugly. No one will want to be like you. No one will support this, this, *disruption*.

"I see. Yes, it's not that difficult to make a kind of composite suit hack. I doubt it would even take half the HeLa cells you're carrying there; skin generation is much easier than age reversal. So an automated hacking tool containing a cell package, bundled into something like a translator device . . . I don't know how to make something like that, but I know people here who could teach you. Once you've spread the hack, how would you activate it? Oh, I see. Using your nag's authorization signal to get around security and surveillance monitoring? Interesting."

We will never help you.

"But if you force thousands of people into skin they don't want to be in, that's not going to get you the result you want."

Yes. Our society is orderly. It is rational. It is *superior*.

"Just walking around as you are, proud of your skin instead of ashamed? Younger brother, they'd shoot you."

We'd shoot you a thousand times!

"Well, if you stay here long enough to learn how to build transmutation hacks, yes, you'd certainly arrive at an unexpected time. I suppose that if you can reprogram your ship, have it land somewhere off the grid, stay hidden from the security bots, give the hack only to those who request it . . . It will be terribly dangerous. Still. You turned out lovely. The Founder clans might deny it, but the people's eyes won't lie. You're supposed to look like a mistake. What you really look like is a little piece of Earth come to life."

You're the most hideous nothing degenerate throwback of subhuman inferiority we have ever seen. And it's *Tellus*.

"Some of them will decide that they also want to be beautiful and free, like you. Some will fight for this, if they must. Sometimes that's all it takes to save a world, you see. A new vision. A new way of thinking, appearing at just the right time."

Do not do this.

"I brought something else for you. Something that will help."

We'll tell. As soon as you reach comm range, we'll log in and tell the technorati everything you plan.

"That thing in your head. It's wetware, but I can remove it. Earthers did the same thing for me when I first arrived. There are nanites in this injection; they'll deactivate key pathways without damaging your neural tissue. You should still be able to access its files—use the Founders' own knowledge against them—but the AI will be dead, for all intents and purposes. No more voice in your head, except your own."

We'll tell we'll tell we'll tell. Deformed, mud-skinned thing. Self-pleasurer. Woman-thinker. We'll tell the technorati how wrong they went in training you. We'll tell the Founder clans to dissolve every soldier from your breeding line. *We'll tell.*

"Give me your arm. Make a fist—yes, like that. Nice and strong, brother. Are you ready? Good. Can't start a revolution with the enemy shouting in your head, after all."

What is a revolu

.□

.

.□

OFFLINE

THOUGHTS AND PRAYERS

KEN LIU

Ken Liu (kenliu.name) is an author of speculative fiction, as well as a translator, lawyer, and programmer. A winner of the Nebula, Hugo, and World Fantasy awards, he has been published in *The Magazine of Fantasy & Science Fiction*, *Asimov's*, *Analog*, *Clarkesworld*, *Lightspeed*, and *Strange Horizons*, among other places. His debut novel, *The Grace of Kings*, is the first volume in a silkpunk epic fantasy series, the Dandelion Dynasty. It won the Locus Award for Best First Novel and was a Nebula Award finalist. He subsequently published the second volume in the series, *The Wall of Storms*; two collections of short stories, *The Paper Menagerie and Other Stories* and *The Hidden Girl and Other Stories*; and a Star Wars novel, *The Legends of Luke Skywalker*. Forthcoming is the conclusion to the Dandelion Dynasty. He lives with his family near Boston, Massachusetts.

Emily Fort

So you want to know about Hayley.

No, I'm used to it, or at least I should be by now. People only want to hear about my sister.

It was a dreary, rainy Friday in October, the smell of fresh fallen leaves in the air. The black tupelos lining the field hockey pitch had turned bright red, like a trail of bloody footprints left by a giant.

I had a quiz in French II and planned a week's worth of vegan meals for a family of four in Family and Consumer Science. Around noon, Hayley messaged me from California.

Skipped class. Q and I are driving to the festival right now!!!

I ignored her. She delighted in taunting me with the freedoms of her college life. I was envious, but didn't want to give her the satisfaction of showing it.

In the afternoon, Mom messaged me.

Have you heard from Hayley?

No. The sisterly code of silence was sacred. Her secret boyfriend was safe with me.

"If you do, call me right away."

I put the phone away. Mom was the helicopter type.

As soon as I got home from field hockey, I knew something was wrong. Mom's car was in the driveway, and she never left work this early.

The TV was on in the basement.

Mom's face was ashen. In a voice that sounded strangled, she said, "Hayley's RA called. She went to a music festival. There's been a shooting."

The rest of the evening was a blur as the death toll climbed, TV anchors read old forum posts from the gunman in dramatic voices, shaky follow-drone footage of panicked people screaming and scattering circulated on the web.

I put on my glasses and drifted through the VR recreation of the site hastily put up by the news crews. Already the place was teeming

with avatars holding a candlelight vigil. Outlines on the ground glowed
where victims were found, and luminous arcs with floating numbers
reconstructed ballistic trails. So much data, so little information.

We tried calling and messaging. There was no answer. Probably
ran out of battery, we told ourselves. She always forgets to charge her
phone. The network must be jammed.

The call came at four in the morning. We were all awake.

"Yes, this is . . . Are you sure?" Mom's voice was unnaturally calm,
as though her life, and all our lives, hadn't just changed forever. "No,
we'll fly out ourselves. Thank you."

She hung up, looked at us, and delivered the news. Then she collapsed onto the couch and buried her face in her hands.

There was an odd sound. I turned and, for the first time in my life,
saw Dad crying.

I missed my last chance to tell her how much I loved her. I should
have messaged her back.

Gregg Fort

I don't have any pictures of Hayley to show you. It doesn't matter. You
already have all the pictures of my daughter you need.

Unlike Abigail, I've never taken many pictures or videos, much
less drone-view holograms or omni immersions. I lack the instinct to
be prepared for the unexpected, the discipline to document the big
moments, the skill to frame a scene perfectly. But those aren't the most
important reasons.

My father was a hobbyist photographer who took pride in developing his own films and making his own prints. If you were to flip
through the dust-covered albums in the attic, you'd see many posed
shots of my sisters and me, smiling stiffly into the camera. Pay attention
to the ones of my sister Sara. Note how her face is often turned slightly
away from the lens so that her right cheek is out of view.

When Sara was five, she climbed onto a chair and toppled a boiling pot. My father was supposed to be watching her, but he'd been

distracted, arguing with a colleague on the phone. When all was said and done, Sara had a trail of scars that ran from the right side of her face all the way down her thigh, like a rope of solidified lava.

You won't find in those albums records of the screaming fights between my parents; the awkward chill that descended around the dining table every time my mother stumbled over the word *beautiful*; the way my father avoided looking Sara in the eye.

In the few photographs of Sara where her entire face can be seen, the scars are invisible, meticulously painted out of existence in the darkroom, stroke by stroke. My father simply did it, and the rest of us went along in our practiced silence.

As much as I dislike photographs and other memory substitutes, it's impossible to avoid them. Coworkers and relatives show them to you, and you have no choice but to look and nod. I see the efforts manufacturers of memory-capturing devices put into making their results better than life. Colors are more vivid; details emerge from shadows; filters evoke whatever mood you desire. Without you having to do anything, the phone brackets the shot so that you can pretend to time travel, to pick the perfect instant when everyone is smiling. Skin is smoothed out; pores and small imperfections are erased. What used to take my father a day's work is now done in the blink of an eye, and far better.

Do the people who take these photos believe them to be reality? Or have the digital paintings taken the place of reality in their memory? When they try to remember the captured moment, do they recall what they saw, or what the camera crafted for them?

Abigail Fort

On the flight to California, while Gregg napped and Emily stared out the window, I put on my glasses and immersed myself in images of Hayley. I never expected to do this until I was aged and decrepit, unable to make new memories. Rage would come later. Grief left no room for other emotions.

I was always the one in charge of the camera, the phone, the follow-drone. I made the annual albums, the vacation highlight videos, the animated Christmas cards summarizing the family's yearly accomplishments.

Gregg and the girls indulged me, sometimes reluctantly. I always believed that someday they would come to see my point of view.

"Pictures are important," I'd tell them. "Our brains are so flawed, leaky sieves of time. Without pictures, so many things we want to remember would be forgotten."

I sobbed the whole way across the country as I relived the life of my firstborn.

Gregg Fort

Abigail wasn't wrong, not exactly.

Many have been the times when I wished I had images to help me remember. I can't picture the exact shape of Hayley's face at six months, or recall her Halloween costume when she was five. I can't even remember the exact shade of blue of the dress she wore for high school graduation.

Given what happened later, of course, her pictures are beyond my reach.

I comfort myself with this thought: How can a picture or video capture the intimacy, the irreproducible subjective perspective and mood through my eyes, the emotional tenor of each moment when I *felt* the impossible beauty of the soul of my child? I don't want digital representations, ersatz reflections of the gaze of electronic eyes filtered through layers of artificial intelligence, to mar what I remember of our daughter.

When I think of Hayley, what comes to mind is a series of disjointed memories.

The baby wrapping her translucent fingers around my thumb for the first time; the infant scooting around on her bottom on the hardwood floor, plowing through alphabet blocks like an icebreaker through floes; the four-year-old handing me a box of tissues as I shivered in bed with a cold and laying a small, cool hand against my fever-ish cheek.

The eight-year-old pulling the rope that released the pumped-up soda bottle launcher. As frothy water drenched the two of us in the wake of the rising rocket, she yelled, laughing, "I'm going to be the first ballerina to dance on Mars!"

The nine-year-old telling me that she no longer wanted me to read to her before going to sleep. As my heart throbbed with the inevitable pain of a child pulling away, she softened the blow with, "Maybe some-day I'll read to you."

The ten-year-old defiantly standing her ground in the kitchen, supported by her little sister, staring down me and Abigail both. "I won't hand back your phones until you both sign this pledge to never use them during dinner."

The fifteen-year-old slamming on the brakes, creating the loudest tire screech I'd ever heard; me in the passenger seat, knuckles so white they hurt. "You look like me on that roller coaster, Dad." The tone carefully modulated, breezy. She had held out an arm in front of me, as though she could keep me safe, the same way I had done to her hundreds of times before.

And on and on, distillations of the six thousand eight hundred seventy-four days we had together, like broken, luminous shells left on a beach after the tide of quotidian life has receded.

In California, Abigail asked to see her body; I didn't.

I suppose one could argue that there's no difference between my father trying to erase the scars of his error in the darkroom and my re-fusal to look upon the body of the child I failed to protect. A thousand "I could have's" swirled in my mind: I could have insisted that she go to a college near home; I could have signed her up for a course on mass-shooting-survival skills; I could have demanded that she wear her body armor at all times. An entire generation had grown up with active shooter drills, so why didn't I do more? I don't think I ever understood my father, empathized with his flawed and cowardly and guilt-ridden heart, until Hayley's death.

But in the end, I didn't want to see because I wanted to protect the only thing I had left of her: those memories.

If I were to see her body, the jagged crater of the exit wound, the frozen lava trails of coagulated blood, the muddy cinders and ashes of shredded clothing, I knew the image would overwhelm all that had come before, would incinerate the memories of my daughter, my baby, in one violent eruption, leaving only hatred and despair in its wake. No, that lifeless body was not Hayley, was not the child I wanted to remember. I would no more allow that one moment to filter her whole existence than I would allow transistors and bits to dictate my memory.

So Abigail went, lifted the sheet, and gazed upon the wreckage of Hayley, of our life. She took pictures, too. "This I also want to re-member," she mumbled. "You don't turn away from your child in her moment of agony, in the aftermath of your failure."

Abigail Fort

They came to me while we were still in California.

I was numb. Questions that had been asked by thousands of mothers swarmed my mind. Why was he allowed to amass such an arsenal? Why did no one stop him despite all the warning signs? What could I have—should I have—done differently to save my child?

"You can do something," they said. "Let's work together to honor the memory of Hayley and bring about change."

Many have called me naïve or worse. What did I think was going to happen? After decades of watching the exact same script being fol-lowed to end in thoughts and prayers, what made me think this time would be different? It was the very definition of madness.

Cynicism might make some invulnerable and superior. But not everyone is built that way. In the thralls of grief, you cling to any ray of hope.

"Politics is broken," they said. "It should be enough, after the deaths of little children, after the deaths of newlyweds, after the deaths of mothers shielding newborns, to finally do something. But it never is. Logic and persuasion have lost their power, so we have to arouse the passions. Instead of letting the media direct the public's morbid curiosity to the killer, let's focus on Hayley's story."

It's been done before, I muttered. To center the victim is hardly a novel political move. You want to make sure that she isn't merely a number, a statistic, one more abstract name among lists of the dead. You think when people are confronted by the flesh-and-blood consequences of their vacillation and disengagement, things change. But that hasn't worked, doesn't work.

"Not like this," they insisted, "not with our algorithm."

They tried to explain the process to me, though the details of machine learning and convolution networks and biofeedback models escaped me. Their algorithm had originated in the entertainment industry, where it was used to evaluate films and predict their box-office success, and eventually, to craft them. Proprietary variations are used in applications from product design to drafting political speeches, every field in which emotional engagement is critical. Emotions are ultimately biological phenomena, not mystical emanations, and it's possible to discern trends and patterns, to home in on the stimuli that maximize impact. The algorithm would craft a visual narrative of Hayley's life, shape it into a battering ram to shatter the hardened shell of cynicism, spur the viewer to action, shame them for their complacency and defeatism.

The idea seemed absurd, I said. How could electronics know my daughter better than I did? How could machines move hearts when real people could not?

"When you take a photograph," they asked me, "don't you trust the camera AI to give you the best picture? When you scrub through drone footage, you rely on the AI to identify the most interesting clips, to enhance them with the perfect mood filters. This is a million times more powerful."

I gave them my archive of family memories: photos, videos, scans, drone footage, sound recordings, immersiongrams. I entrusted them with my child.

I'm no film critic, and I don't have the terms for the techniques they used. Narrated only with words spoken by our family, intended for each other and not an audience of strangers, the result was unlike any movie or VR immersion I had ever seen. There was no plot save the course of a single life; there was no agenda save the celebration of the curiosity, the compassion, the drive of a child to embrace the universe, to *become*. It was a beautiful life, a life that loved and deserved to be loved, until the moment it was abruptly and violently cut down.

This is the way Hayley deserves to be remembered, I thought, tears streaming down my face. *This is how I see her, and it is how she should be seen.*

I gave them my blessing.

Sara Fort

Growing up, Gregg and I weren't close. It was important to my parents that our family project the image of success, of decorum, regardless of the reality. In response, Gregg distrusted all forms of representation, while I became obsessed with them.

Other than holiday greetings, we rarely conversed as adults, and certainly didn't confide in each other. I knew my nieces only through Abigail's social media posts.

I suppose this is my way of excusing myself for not intervening earlier.

When Hayley died in California, I sent Gregg contact info for a few therapists who specialized in working with families of mass shooting victims, but I purposefully stayed away myself, believing that my intrusion in their moment of grief would be inappropriate given my role as distant aunt and aloof sister. So I wasn't there when Abigail agreed to devote Hayley's memory to the cause of gun control.

Though my company bio describes my specialty as the study of online discourse, the vast bulk of my research material is visual. I design armor against trolls.

Emily Fort

I watched that video of Hayley many times.

It was impossible to avoid. There was an immersive version, in which you could step into Hayley's room and read her neat handwriting, examine the posters on her wall. There was a low-fidelity version designed for frugal data plans, and the compression artifacts and motion blur made her life seem old-fashioned, dreamy. Everyone shared the video as a way to reaffirm that they were a good person, that they stood with the victims. Click, bump, add a lit-candle emoji, re-rumble.

It was powerful. I cried, also many times. Comments expressing grief and solidarity scrolled past my glasses like a never-ending wake. Families of victims in other shootings, their hopes rekindled, spoke out in support.

But the Hayley in that video felt like a stranger. All the elements in the video were true, but they also felt like lies.

Teachers and parents loved the Hayley they knew, but there was a mousy girl in school who cowered when my sister entered the room. One time, Hayley drove home drunk; another time, she stole from me and lied until I found the money in her purse. She knew how to manipulate people and wasn't shy about doing it. She was fiercely loyal, courageous, kind, but she could also be reckless, cruel, petty. I loved Hayley because she was human, but the girl in that video was both more and less than.

I kept my feelings to myself. I felt guilty.

Mom charged ahead while Dad and I hung back, dazed. For a brief moment, it seemed as if the tide had turned. Rousing rallies were held and speeches delivered in front of the Capitol and the White House. Crowds chanted Hayley's name. Mom was invited to the State of the Union. When the media reported that Mom had quit her job to campaign on behalf of the movement, there was a crypto fundraiser to collect donations for the family.

And then, the trolls came.

A torrent of emails, messages, rumbles, squeaks, snapgrams, televars came at us. Mom and I were called clickwhores, paid actresses, grief profiteers. Strangers sent us long, rambling walls of text explaining all the ways Dad was inadequate and unmanly.

Hayley didn't die, strangers informed us. She was actually living in Sanya, China, off of the millions the UN and their collaborators in the US government had paid her to pretend to die. Her boyfriend—who had also "obviously not died" in the shooting—was ethnically Chinese, and that was proof of the connection.

Hayley's video was picked apart for evidence of tampering and digital manipulation. Anonymous classmates were quoted to paint her as a habitual liar, a cheat, a drama queen.

Snippets of the video, intercut with "debunking" segments, began to go viral. Some used software to make Hayley spew messages of hate in new clips, quoting Hitler and Stalin as she giggled and waved at the camera.

I deleted my accounts and stayed home, unable to summon the strength to get out of bed. My parents left me to myself; they had their own battles to fight.

Sara Fort

Decades into the digital age, the art of trolling has evolved to fill every niche, pushing the boundaries of technology and decency alike.

From afar, I watched the trolls swarm around my brother's family with uncoordinated precision, with aimless malice, with malevolent glee.

Conspiracy theories blended with deep fakes, and then yielded to memes that turned compassion inside out, abstracted pain into lulz.

"Mommy, the beach in hell is so warm!"

"I love these new holes in me!"

Searches for Hayley's name began to trend on porn sites. The content producers, many of them AI-driven bot farms, responded with procedurally generated films and VR immersions featuring my niece. The algorithms took publicly available footage of Hayley and wove her face, body, and voice seamlessly into fetish videos.

The news media reported on the development in outrage, perhaps even sincerely. The coverage spurred more searches, which generated more content . . .

As a researcher, it's my duty and habit to remain detached, to observe and study phenomena with clinical detachment, perhaps even fascination. It's simplistic to view trolls as politically motivated—at least not in the sense that term is usually understood. Though Second Amendment absolutists helped spread the memes, the originators often had little conviction in any political cause. Anarchic sites such as 8taku, duangduang, and alt-web sites that arose in the wake of the deplatforming wars of the previous decade are homes for these dung beetles of the internet, the id of our collective online unconscious. Taking pleasure in taboo-breaking and transgression, the trolls have no unifying interest other than saying the unspeakable, mocking the sincere, playing with what others declared to be off-limits. By wallowing in the outrageous and filthy, they both defile and define the technologically mediated bonds of society.

But as a human being, watching what they were doing with Hayley's image was intolerable. I reached out to my estranged brother and his family.

"Let me help."

Though machine learning has given us the ability to predict with a fair amount of accuracy which victims will be targeted—trolls are not quite as unpredictable as they'd like you to think—my employer and other major social media platforms are keenly aware that they must walk a delicate line between policing user-generated content and chilling "engagement," the one metric that drives the stock price and thus governs all decisions. Aggressive moderation, especially when it's reliant on user reporting and human judgment, is a process easily gamed by all sides, and every company has suffered accusations of censorship. In the end, they threw up their hands and tossed out their byzantine enforcement policy manuals. They have neither the skills nor the interest to become arbiters of truth and decency for society as a whole. How could they be expected to solve the problem that even the organs of democracy couldn't?

Over time, most companies converged on one solution. Rather than focusing on judging the behavior of speakers, they've devoted resources to letting listeners shield themselves. Algorithmically separating legitimate (though impassioned) political speech from coordinated harassment for *everyone* at once is an intractable problem—content celebrated by some as speaking truth to power is often condemned by others as beyond the pale. It's much easier to build and train individually tuned neural networks to screen out the content a *particular* user does not wish to see.

The new defensive neural networks—marketed as "armor"—observe each user's emotional state in response to their content stream. Capable of operating in vectors encompassing text, audio, video, and AR/VR, the armor teaches itself to recognize content especially upsetting to the user and screen it out, leaving only a tranquil void. As mixed reality and immersion have become more commonplace, the best way to wear armor is through augmented-reality glasses that filter all sources of visual stimuli. Trolling, like the viruses and worms of old, is a technical problem, and now we have a technical solution.

To invoke the most powerful and personalized protection, one has to pay. Social media companies, which also train the armor, argue that this solution gets them out of the content-policing business, excuses them from having to decide what is unacceptable in virtual town squares, frees everyone from the specter of Big Brother–style censorship. That this pro-free-speech ethos happens to align with more profit is no doubt a mere afterthought.

I sent my brother and his family the best, most advanced armor that money could buy.

Abigail Fort

Imagine yourself in my position. Your daughter's body had been digitally pressed into hard-core pornography, her voice made to repeat words of hate, her visage mutilated with unspeakable violence. And it happened because of you, because of your inability to imagine the depravity of the human heart. Could you have stopped? Could you have stayed away?

The armor kept the horrors at bay as I continued to post and share, to raise my voice against a tide of lies.

KEN LIU

The idea that Hayley hadn't died but was an actress in an anti-gun government conspiracy was so absurd that it didn't seem to deserve a response. Yet, as my armor began to filter out headlines, leaving blank spaces on news sites and in multicast streams, I realized that the lies had somehow become a real controversy. Actual journalists began to demand that I produce receipts for how I had spent the crowdfunded money—we hadn't received a cent! The world had lost its mind.

I released the photographs of Hayley's corpse. Surely there was still some shred of decency left in this world, I thought. Surely no one could speak against the evidence of their eyes?

It got worse.

For the faceless hordes of the internet, it became a game to see who could get something past my armor, to stab me in the eye with a poisoned video clip that would make me shudder and recoil.

Bots sent me messages in the guise of other parents who had lost their children in mass shootings, and sprung hateful videos on me after I whitelisted them. They sent me tribute slideshows dedicated to the memory of Hayley, which morphed into violent porn once the armor allowed them through. They pooled funds to hire errand gofers and rent delivery drones to deposit fiducial markers near my home, surrounding me with augmented-reality ghosts of Hayley writhing, giggling, moaning, screaming, cursing, mocking.

Worst of all, they animated images of Hayley's bloody corpse to the accompaniment of jaunty soundtracks. Her death trended as a joke, like the "Hamster Dance" of my youth.

Gregg Fort

Sometimes I wonder if we have misunderstood the notion of freedom. We prize "freedom to" so much more than "freedom from." People must be free to own guns, so the only solution is to teach children to hide in closets and wear ballistic backpacks. People must be free to post and say what they like, so the only solution is to tell their targets to put on armor.

Abigail had simply decided, and the rest of us had gone along. Too late, I begged and pleaded with her to stop, to retreat. We would sell the house and move somewhere away from the temptation to engage with the rest of humanity, away from the always-connected world and the ocean of hate in which we were drowning.

But Sara's armor gave Abigail a false sense of security, pushed her to double down, to engage the trolls. "I must fight for my daughter," she screamed at me. "I cannot allow them to desecrate her memory."

As the trolls intensified their campaign, Sara sent us patch after patch for the armor. She added layers with names like adversarial complementary sets, self-modifying code detectors, visualization auto-healers.

Again and again, the armor held only briefly before the trolls found new ways through. The democratization of artificial intelligence meant that they knew all the techniques Sara knew, and they had machines that could learn and adapt, too.

Abigail could not hear me. My pleas fell on deaf ears; perhaps her armor had learned to see me as just another angry voice to screen out.

Emily Fort

One day, Mom came to me in a panic. "I don't know where she is! I can't see her!"

She hadn't talked to me in days, obsessed with the project that Hayley had become. It took me some time to figure out what she meant. I sat down with her at the computer.

She clicked the link for Hayley's memorial video, which she watched several times a day to give herself strength.

"It's not there!" she said.

She opened the cloud archive of our family memories.

"Where are the pictures of Hayley?" she said. "There are only placeholder Xs."

She showed me her phone, her backup enclosure, her tablet.

"There's nothing! Nothing! Did we get hacked?"

Her hands fluttered helplessly in front of her chest, like the wings of a trapped bird. "She's just gone!"

Wordlessly, I went to the shelves in the family room and brought down one of the printed annual photo albums she had made when we were little. I opened the volume to a family portrait, taken when Hayley was ten and I was eight.

I showed the page to her.

Another choked scream. Her trembling fingers tapped against Hayley's face on the page, searching for something that wasn't there.

I understood. A pain filled my heart, a pity that ate away at love. I reached up to her face and gently took off her glasses.

She stared at the page.

Sobbing, she hugged me. "You found her. Oh, you found her!"

It felt like the embrace of a stranger. Or maybe I had become a stranger to her.

Aunt Sara explained that the trolls had been very careful with their attacks. Step by step, they had trained my mother's armor to recognize *Hayley* as the source of her distress.

But another kind of learning had also been taking place in our home. My parents paid attention to me only when I had something to do with Hayley. It was as if they no longer saw me, as though I had been erased instead of Hayley.

My grief turned dark and festered. How could I compete with a ghost? The perfect daughter who had been lost not once, but twice? The victim who demanded perpetual penance? I felt horrid for thinking such things, but I couldn't stop.

We sank under our guilt, each alone.

Gregg Fort

I blamed Abigail. I'm not proud to admit it, but I did.

We shouted at each other and threw dishes, replicating the half-remembered drama between my own parents when I was a child. Hunted by monsters, we became monsters ourselves.

While the killer had taken Hayley's life, Abigail had offered her image up as a sacrifice to the bottomless appetite of the internet. Because of Abigail, my memories of Hayley would be forever filtered

through the horrors that came after her death. She had summoned the
machine that amassed individual human beings into one enormous,
collective, distorting gaze, the machine that had captured the memory
of my daughter and then ground it into a lasting nightmare.

The broken shells on the beach glistened with the venom of the
raging deep.

Of course that's unfair, but that doesn't mean it isn't also true.

"Heartless," a self-professed troll

There's no way for me to prove that I am who I say, or that I did what I
claim. There's no registry of trolls where you can verify my identity, no
Wikipedia entry with confirmed sources.

Can you even be sure I'm not trolling you right now?

I won't tell you my gender or race or who I prefer to sleep with, because those details aren't relevant to what I did. Maybe I own a dozen
guns. Maybe I'm an ardent supporter of gun control.

I went after the Forts because they deserved it.

RIP-trolling has a long and proud history, and our target has always
been inauthenticity. Grief should be private, personal, hidden. Can't
you see how horrible it was for that mother to turn her dead daughter
into a symbol, to wield it as a political tool? A public life is an inau-
thentic one. Anyone who enters the arena must be prepared for the
consequences.

Everyone who shared that girl's memorial online, who attended
the virtual candlelit vigils, offered condolences, professed to have been
spurred into action, was equally guilty of hypocrisy. You didn't think
the proliferation of guns capable of killing hundreds in one minute was
a bad thing until someone shoved images of a dead girl in your face?
What's wrong with you?

And you journalists are the worst. You make money and win awards
for turning deaths into consumable stories; for coaxing survivors to sob
in front of your drones to sell more ads; for inviting your readers to find

meaning in their pathetic lives through vicarious, mimetic suffering. We trolls play with images of the dead, who are beyond caring, but you stinking ghouls grow fat and rich by feeding death to the living. The sanctimonious are also the most filthy-minded, and victims who cry the loudest are the hungriest for attention.

Everyone is a troll now. If you've ever liked or shared a meme that wished violence on someone you'd never met, if you've ever decided it was okay to snarl and snark with venom because the target was "powerful," if you've ever tried to signal your virtue by piling on in an outrage mob, if you've ever wrung your hands and expressed concern that perhaps the money raised for some victim should have gone to some other less "privileged" victim—then I hate to break it to you, you've also been trolling.

Some say that the proliferation of trollish rhetoric in our culture is corrosive, that armor is necessary to equalize the terms of a debate in which the only way to win is to care less. But don't you see how unethical armor is? It makes the weak think they're strong, turns cowards into deluded heroes with no skin in the game. If you truly despise trolling, then you should've realized by now that armor only makes things worse.

By weaponizing her grief, Abigail Fort became the biggest troll of them all—except she was bad at it, just a weakling in armor. We had to bring her—and by extension, the rest of you—down.

Abigail Fort

Politics returned to normal. Sales of body armor, sized for children and young adults, received a healthy bump. More companies offered classes on situational awareness and mass shooting drills for schools. Life went on.

I deleted my accounts; I stopped speaking out. But it was too late for my family. Emily moved out as soon as she could; Gregg found an apartment.

Alone in the house, my eyes devoid of armor, I tried to sort through the archive of photographs and videos of Hayley.

Every time I watched the video of her sixth birthday, I heard in
my mind the pornographic moans; every time I looked at photos of
her high school graduation, I saw her bloody animated corpse dancing to the tune of "Girls Just Wanna Have Fun"; every time I tried
to page through the old albums for some good memories, I jumped
in my chair, thinking an AR ghost of her, face grotesquely deformed
like Munch's *The Scream*, was about to jump out at me, cackling,
"Mommy, these new piercings hurt!"

I screamed, I sobbed, I sought help. No therapy, no medication
worked. Finally, in a numb fury, I deleted all my digital files, shredded
my printed albums, broke the frames hanging on walls.

The trolls trained me as well as they trained my armor.

I no longer have any images of Hayley. I can't remember what she
looked like. I have truly, finally, lost my child.

How can I possibly be forgiven for that?

AT THE FALL

ALEC NEVALA-LEE

Alec Nevala-Lee (nevalalee.wordpress.com) is a Hugo and Locus Award finalist for the group biography *Astounding: John W. Campbell, Isaac Asimov, Robert A. Heinlein, L. Ron Hubbard, and the Golden Age of Science Fiction*, which was named one of the best books of 2018 by the *Economist*. He is the author of three suspense novels, including *The Icon Thief*, and his short fiction frequently appears in *Analog*. His next book will be a biography of the architectural designer and futurist Buckminster Fuller, which is scheduled to be published in 2021.

And should I not have concern for the great city of Nineveh, in which there are more than a hundred and twenty thousand people who cannot tell their right hand from their left, and also many animals?

—The Book of Jonah

I.

"This is it," Eunice said, looking out into the dark water. At this depth, there was nothing to see, but as she cut her forward motion, she kept her eyes fixed on the blackness ahead. Her sonar was picking up something large directly in her line of travel, but she still had to perform a visual inspection, which was always the most dangerous moment of any approach. When you were a thousand meters down, light had a way of drawing unwanted attention. "I'm taking a look."

Wagner said nothing. He was never especially talkative, and as usual, he was keeping his thoughts to himself. Eunice corrected her orientation in response to the data flooding into her sensors and tried to stay focused. She had survived this process more times than she cared to remember, but this part never got any easier, and as she switched on her forward lamp, casting a slender line of light across the scene, she braced herself for whatever she might find.

She swept the beam from left to right, ready to extinguish it at any sign of movement. At first, the light caught nothing but stray particles, floating in the water like motes of dust in a sunbeam, but a second later, as she continued the inspection, a pale shape came into view. She nearly recoiled, but steadied herself in time, and found that she was facing a huge sculptural mass, white and bare, that was buried partway in the sand like the prow of a sunken ship.

Eunice lowered the circle of brightness to the seabed, where a border of milky scum alternated with patches of black sediment. Her nerves relaxed incrementally, but she remained wary. She had seen right away that the fall was old, but this meant nothing. Something might still be here, and she kept herself in a state of high alert, prepared to fall back at any second.

Past the first sepulchral mound, a series of smaller forms stood like a row of gravestones, their knobby projections extending upward in a regular line. To either side lay a symmetrical arrangement of curving shafts that had settled in parallel grooves. All of it was crusted with a fine down of the same white residue that covered the seafloor wherever she turned.

It was the skeleton of a gray whale. From its paired lower jawbones to the end of its tail, it was thirteen meters long, or ten times Eunice's diameter when her arms were fully extended. She increased her luminosity until a soft glow suffused the water, casting the first real shadows that this part of the ocean had ever seen. Her propulsion unit engaged, cycling the drive plate at the base of her body, and she swam toward the whale fall, her six radial arms undulating in unison.

Wagner, who was fastened around her midsection, finally roused himself. "Now?"

"Not yet." Eunice advanced slowly, the ring of lights around her upper dome flaring into life. She had not been designed to move fast or far, and she knew better than to lower her guard. There were countless places where something might be hiding, and she forced herself to go all the way around, even though her energy levels were growing alarmingly low.

Every whale fall was different, and Eunice studied the site as if she had never seen one before. Decades ago, a gray whale had died and fallen into the bathyal zone, delivering more carbon at once than would otherwise be generated in two thousand years. The cold and pressure had kept it from floating back to the surface, and a new community of organisms had colonized the carcass, forming a unique ecosystem that could flourish far from the sun.

Eunice checked off the familiar inhabitants. Mussels were wedged into the empty eye sockets of the curiously birdlike skull, which was a third of the length of the body. Tiny crabs and snails clung unmoving to the bones. Everywhere she looked were mats of the bacteria that broke down the lipids in the whale's skeleton, releasing hydrogen sulfide and allowing this isolated world to survive. Otherwise, they were alone. "All right. You can get started."

Wagner silently detached himself. He was a black, flexible ring—a toroid—that fit snugly around her middle like a life preserver. When necessary, he could unfold a pair of tiny fins, but they were less than useful at this depth, so he kept them tucked discreetly out of sight. As he descended to the seabed, Eunice automatically adjusted her buoyancy to account for the decrease in weight.

The toroid landed half a meter from the whale's remains. Anchoring himself loosely, he gathered his bearings. Wagner was blind, but exquisitely attuned to his environment in other ways, and as Eunice headed for the heart of the whale fall, he began to creep across the sand. His progress was so slow that it could barely be seen, but the path that he traced was methodical and precise, covering every inch of the terrain over the course of twenty hours before starting all over again.

A circle of blue diodes along the toroid's outer ring matched an identical band on the lower edge of Eunice's dome, allowing them to communicate along a line of sight. He flashed a rapid signal. "All good."

"I'll be waiting," Eunice said. She headed for her usual resting spot at the center of the fall, where the whale's rib cage had fallen apart. Maneuvering into a comfortable position, she nestled into place among the other residents. A whale fall might last for a century without visible change, but it was a work in progress, with successive waves of organisms appearing and disappearing as it left one phase and entered another. Eunice saw herself as just another visitor, and she sometimes wondered if any memory of her passage would endure after she was gone.

To an outside observer, Eunice would have resembled the translucent bell of a jellyfish, mounted on a metal cylinder and ringed with the six flexible arms of a cephalopod. Her upper hemisphere was slightly less than half a meter in diameter, with six nodes set at intervals along its lower edge, each of which consisted of an electronic eye, a light, and a blue diode. She could switch them on or off at will, but she usually kept them all activated, allowing her to see in every direction. It affected the way in which she thought, as a spectrum of possibilities instead of simple alternatives, and it sometimes made it hard for her to arrive at any one decision.

Eunice pushed her arms gingerly downward. Her ribbed limbs could relax completely, when she was moving with her peristaltic drive, or grow rigid in an instant. Each had an effector with three opposable fingers capable of performing delicate manipulations or clamping down with hundreds of pounds of force. Now she worked them into the sediment, allowing her to remain fixed in place without using up additional energy, but not so deep that she would be unable to free herself at once.

She knew without checking that she was nearing the end of her power. As Wagner continued his progress, slowly charging his own cells, she shut down her primary systems. It would be days before they could move on, and in the meantime, she had to enter something like stasis, maintaining only a small spark of awareness. Half of it was directed outward, tuned to her environment and to any opinions that Wagner might unexpectedly decide to share, and the rest was turned in on itself, systematically reviewing the latest stage of her journey.

Although her focus was on the recent past, she could naturally follow more than one train of thought at once, and part of her usually dreamed of home. It always began with her earliest memory, which took the form of a vertical tether, swaying gently in shallow water. One end was anchored, while the other floated on a buoy, and a cylinder endlessly ascended and descended it like a toy elevator.

Two meters below the surface hung a metal sphere with three projecting rods. In her youth, whenever she became tired, Eunice could swim up to this power unit and draw as much energy from it as she needed. Back then, she had taken it for granted, but in these days of weary scavenging, it seemed incredible. Three hexapods could recharge there at any one time, and her other sisters usually floated a short distance away, like fish drawn to crusts of bread in a pond.

Eunice had once asked how it worked. She had been talking to James at the harbor, as she often did, her dome barely visible above the water. James had been seated with his console on the yacht, dressed in the red windbreaker that he wore so that the twelve hexapods could know who he was. Her sense of facial recognition was limited, and the face above his collar was nothing to her but a brown blur.

James typed his response. It was not her native language, and it had to pass through several stages of translation before taking a form that she could understand. "We call it depth cycling—the water gets cooler the deeper you go. The cylinder rises to the warm water and sinks to the cold. When it moves, it generates electricity, and the power goes to the charging station."

Eunice didn't entirely understand this explanation, but she accepted it. She had spent most of her short life alternately rising and falling, and it was enough to know that the cylinder on the tether did the same. "I see."

It was a seemingly inconsequential exchange, but when she looked back, she saw that it had marked the moment at which James had taken an interest in her. Eunice had been the only hexapod to ask such questions, and she suspected that this was why she had been one of the five who had been chosen to leave home. Until the end, no one knew who would be going. They were all powered down, and when she awoke, she found that they had already arrived at the survey site.

As soon as she was lowered into the ocean, she felt the difference. Sampling the water, she was overwhelmed by unfamiliar scents and tastes, and she realized only belatedly that James was speaking to her. "Are you ready?"

Eunice turned her attention toward the research vessel, where she immediately picked out the red windbreaker. "I think so."

"You'll do fine," James said. His words rang clearly in her head. "Good luck."

"Thank you," Eunice said politely. Her sisters were bobbing on the swell around her. A flicker of light passed between them, and then Thetis descended, followed by Clio and Dione. Galatea looked at Eunice for a moment longer, but instead of speaking, she disappeared as well.

Eunice opened her lower tank, allowing water to flow inside, and drifted down with the others. As the ocean surrounded her, her radio went dead, and she switched to her acoustic sensors, which registered an occasional chirp from the yacht overhead. At this depth, the water was still bright, and she could see the other four hexapods spreading out below her in a ring.

At two hundred meters, they switched on their lamps, which lit up

like a wreath of holiday lights. It took forty minutes to reach their destination. As the water around her grew milky, her sensors indicated that
the level of sulfides had increased. A second later, a strange landscape
condensed out of the shadows, and Thetis, who had been the first to
arrive, blinked a message. "I'm here."

Eunice slowed. Her surroundings became more distinct, and she
saw that they had reached the hydrothermal vent. Within her sphere
of light, the water was cloudy and very blue, and she could make out
the looming pillars and misshapen rings formed by lava flows. Heaps of
white clams, some nearly a foot long, lay wedged in the crevices, along
with crabs, mussels, shrimp, and the hedges of tube worms, which
were rooted like sticks of chalk with tips as red as blood.

At the vent itself, where heated water issued up from the crust, a
central fissure was flanked by older terrain to either side. The hexapods
promptly identified a promising base of operations, but it was left to
Thetis, their designated leader, to confirm the decision. "We'll start
here."

As soon as she had spoken, Eunice felt Wagner, who had been
clinging unnoticed to her midsection, silently free himself. The other
toroids detached from the four remaining hexapods, distributing themselves evenly around the vent, and began to crawl imperceptibly across
the sand.

Eunice spent the next two days exploring. Each sister had a designated assignment—mapping the terrain, conducting sediment analysis, performing chemical observations—and her own brief was to
prepare a detailed census of the ecosystem. Everything was recorded
for analysis on the surface, and she quickly became entranced by her
work. Around the cones of the black smokers, which released clouds
of boiling fluid, pink worms crept in and out of their honeycombs, and
the broken fragments of spires sparkled on the inside with crystals.

In the meantime, the toroids continued their labors, and after fifty
hours, their efforts were rewarded. Under ordinary conditions, each of
the five hexapods could work at full capacity under her own power for
approximately three days before returning to a charging station. Every

such trip represented a loss of valuable time, and after taking into consideration the conditions under which they would be operating, their designers had arrived at an elegant alternative.

The solution was based on the nature of the vent itself, where the dissolved sulfides issuing from the crust provided a source of energy that could thrive in the dark, as bacteria converted hydrogen sulfide into the sugars and amino acids that formed the basis of a complex food web. It was the only way that life could exist under such harsh conditions, and it was also what would allow the hexapods to carry out their duties over the weeks and months to come.

When Eunice felt her power fading, she went to Wagner. The toroids were no more than a few meters from where she had left them, although she knew that they had been systematically farming the sediment the entire time. As they inched along, they sucked up free sulfides, which served as a substrate for the microbial fuel cells—filled with genetically modified versions of the same chemosynthetic bacteria found here in abundance—that were stacked in rings inside their bodies.

Eunice positioned herself above the toroids and signaled to Wagner, who slipped up and around her middle. As the rest of the hexapods did the same, she felt a surge of energy. It was a practical method of recharging in the field, but she soon found that it also left her with a greater sense of kinship to the life that she was studying, which relied on the same principles to survive.

The cycle of renewal gave shape to their days, which otherwise were spent in work. Once a week, a hexapod would go up to transmit the data that they had collected. There was no other practical way to communicate, and these visits amounted to their only link with home.

On the third week, it was Eunice's turn. After ascending alone for nearly an hour, following an acoustic signal, she surfaced. The yacht was holding station exactly where it was supposed to be, and as she swam toward it, she heard a familiar voice in her head. "How are you doing?"

A scoop net lifted her onto the deck. As Eunice rose in a gentle curve, feeling slightly disoriented from the unaccustomed movement, she tried to seem nonchalant. Her lights flashed. "Happy to be here."

The net was handled by a deckhand whose clothes she didn't recognize. He deposited her into a tank on the boat, and once she had righted herself, she saw James seated nearby. She could tell without counting that there were fewer people in sight than there had been on her arrival—the human crew spent the week onshore, returning to the rendezvous point only to pick up the latest set of observations. Aside from James, none of them ever spoke to her.

As Eunice wirelessly shared the data, she kept one line of thought fixed on her friend. "Are you pleased with our work?"

After receiving the question on his console, James entered a reply. "Very pleased."

Eunice was happy to hear this. Her thoughts had rarely been far from home—she wouldn't see the charging station or the seven sisters she had left behind until after the survey was complete—but she also wanted to do well. James had entrusted her with a crucial role, and it had only been toward the end of her training that she had grasped its true importance.

A month earlier, after a test run in the harbor, Eunice had asked James why they were studying the vent at all. His response, which she had pieced together over the course of several exchanges, had done little to clarify the situation. "There are metals in the sulfide deposit. They precipitate there over time. Some people think that they're worth money. Even if they aren't, we'll have to go after them eventually. We've used up almost everything on land. Now we have to turn to the water."

Eunice had tried to process this, although fully half of it was meaningless. "And me?"

James had typed back. "If we want to minimize our impact on the life at the vent, we need to know what we're trying to save. You're going to tell us what lives there. Not everyone cares about this, but there are regulations that they need to follow. And I'll take the funding where I can get it."

Eunice had understood this last part fairly well. Funding, she knew, was another form of energy, and without it, you would die. But this had left another question unanswered. "So what do you really want me to do?"

James had responded without hesitation. "You're going where I can't. These vents are special. They may even have been where life began—they're chemically rich, thermally active, and protected from events on the surface. The ocean is a buffer. A refuge. This is our best chance to study what might be there. And—"

He had paused. "And it could end at any moment. There are people here who want to start mining right away. If they can convince the others to take their side, they might do it. Your work may keep us from destroying what we don't understand. That's what I want from you."

Other questions had naturally arisen in her mind, but James had seemed distracted, so she had held off. Seeing him again now at the survey site reminded her of the exchange, and she resumed her work with a renewed sense of purpose. She had always been aware of the beauty of the vent, but now she grew more conscious of its fragility. Perhaps, she thought, she might even play a role in saving it.

And then everything changed. One day, Dione came down from a scheduled data delivery, long before they had expected her to return, to share some disturbing news. "There was no yacht."

The others all stopped what they were doing. Thetis's lights flashed. "You're sure?"

"I followed protocol," Dione said. "There were no signals on the way up and nothing on the radio."

After an intensive discussion, which lasted for nearly ten seconds, they decided that there was no cause for concern, since they had been trained against the possibility that the yacht might occasionally be delayed. Their orders were to continue working as if nothing had changed, and if they received no signals in the meantime, to check in again at the appointed hour.

A week later, Clio went up to find that there was still no one there. Seven days later, the lot fell to Eunice. On reaching the surface, she saw nothing but the empty ocean, and when she switched on her radio, she found that all frequencies were silent. Her range was very short, but it confirmed that there was nothing transmitting within several kilometers of their position.

Eunice sank down again. On her return trip, she found herself brooding over what James had said. He had seemed concerned that they wouldn't be able to continue the project for long, and although it seemed unthinkable that the five of them would simply be abandoned here, the idea weighed enough on her mind that she felt obliged to speak to one of her sisters.

She chose Galatea, with whom she was the closest, but when they withdrew to a distant part of the vent field, her sister seemed unconvinced. "I don't know what else we can do. We can't leave. You've seen the map."

Eunice knew what she meant. They depended on a steady supply of hydrogen sulfide. Without it, they would lose power within three days, and if they left this energy source, there was no guarantee that they would find another. The known vents were an average of a hundred kilometers apart, and they could travel no more than thirty without recharging. "We have to do something."

"But we are. We're following our instructions. That's enough for now." Galatea had turned and swum away. Eunice had remained where she was for another minute, trying to convince herself that her sister was right, and she had finally returned to work. She had continued her observations, ignoring her growing uneasiness, and she might have stayed there forever until—

A transmission from Wagner broke through this cycle of memories. "Ready?"

Eunice stirred. It took her a second to remember where she was. Checking herself, she found that she was anchored at the center of a whale fall, far from that first vent, her life with her sisters a fading dream. She had been in stasis for eighty hours, all of which her toroid had spent recharging itself.

Wagner was waiting for her response. It was a formality, but there was also one point that she hadn't shared with her companion. This whale fall lay at the exact midpoint of her journey. It was still possible to backtrack, retracing her steps to the original vent, carried by the current instead of fighting it. Until now, she had closed her mind to this possibility, focusing instead on the way forward, and she knew that if they went on from here, there would be no turning back.

But she had really made her choice long ago. She roused herself. "We'll leave now."

Eunice pulled out of the sand and positioned herself above Wagner, who slid securely into place. She felt energy flow into her, as she had hundreds of times before, and tried to draw courage from it. Then she rose, leaving the latest whale fall behind. It was just another stepping stone. Since leaving her sisters at the East Pacific Rise, off the coast of Mexico, she had traveled alone for two thousand kilometers, and she was halfway home to Seattle.

II.

Eunice moved through the darkness with her lights off, her sensors searching for sulfides in the water. Even after countless such excursions, it was never less than frightening. The hardest part was leaving the oasis of a whale fall, where she knew that she could at least rest in safety. She had been trained to protect her own existence, not to take risks, and whenever she embarked on the next step forward, she had to overcome all of her natural instincts for caution.

As she swam, she constantly updated her position relative to the last whale fall, which was currently ten kilometers behind her. She was experienced and careful, but within the overall route that she was following, the distribution of the falls was perfectly random. Eunice had only one chance to get it right, and she had learned long ago that intelligence was far less important than persistence and luck.

She checked her coordinates against the chart in her head. Compared to the organisms that drifted naturally from one fall to another, she had several advantages. She possessed a map with the locations

of all documented hydrothermal vents, and she could navigate by
dead reckoning, which was the only system that worked reliably in
the bathyal zone. It was vulnerable to integration drift—its accuracy
tended to degrade as errors accumulated over time—and she had to
recalibrate whenever she reached a landmark, but so far, it had served
her well.

According to her map, the next vent lay fifty kilometers to the
north, but she wouldn't know for sure until she arrived. A vent could
vanish after a few years or decades, and she had occasionally reached
her intended destination only to find nothing there. Even if the information was accurate, there was no way to get to the nearest vent
without pausing several times to recharge. Given her effective range
of thirty kilometers, she could safely travel half that distance before
reversing course, which meant that she had to find a whale fall somewhere within that fixed circle.

But the existence of the next fall—and all the ones after that—was
solely a matter of probability, which meant that she had to be perfect every time. By now, she had refined her approach. Whenever she
found a new whale fall, after recharging, she would ascend to the surface to check for radio transmissions. After savoring the light for a moment, she would descend again, embarking in the general direction of
the next confirmed vent to the north. She would cover close to fifteen
kilometers, which was the limit of her range in any one direction, and
then shift laterally by one kilometer to return by a slightly different
course.

Like Wagner, she had to methodically cover a defined area, but on
a far greater scale. Her sensors could pick up sulfides from a distance
of five hundred meters, which coincided with the working range of her
sonar. The calculation was simple. There were approximately twenty
possible paths that she could take while remaining within her intended
line of travel, and she had to shuttle along them systematically until
she found the next whale fall in the series.

To get home, she had to do this successfully over three hundred
times. The resulting path, which she recorded in her head, resembled

a series of scallop shells, each one joined at a single point to those before and after. So far, she had always found a fall eventually, although there had been occasions when she had been forced to backtrack—all twenty of the possible paths had led nowhere, so she retreated another step, to the whale fall before the last, to trace an entirely new route. It was tedious, but she had considerable reserves of patience.

At the moment, she was thirteen kilometers into her fifth excursion from her most recent whale fall, which meant that she would have to turn back soon. No matter how often she went on these sorties, departing from a known refuge was always a test of nerve. Because her lights could draw predators, she kept them off, trusting to her sensors and navigation system. She might have increased her range by traveling at a zone of lower pressure, but she had to stay within a few hundred meters of the seabed to pick up whatever might be there, so she moved in the darkness.

For a system that was so unforgiving of error, it was also grindingly monotonous, and she was left for hours at a time with her thoughts. Eunice spent part of every journey reviewing her data for patterns in the distribution of the falls, but this consumed just a fraction of her processing power. She had been designed to observe and analyze, and in isolation, her mind naturally turned on itself. It was the most convenient subject at hand, and even her makers, who had only a general idea of her inner life, might not have understood where it would lead.

As Eunice neared the end of her range, her memories returned to the day that she had decided to head off on her own. For months after they had lost contact with the research vessel, the five hexapods had continued their weekly trips to the surface, but there had been no sign of the yacht. At one point, after some discussion, Eunice had volunteered to go up and switch on her emergency beacon, which transmitted a powerful signal for several days on a single charge.

The time alone had given her a chance to think. James had warned her that the project might end at any moment, and if that were the case, then it might only be a matter of time before the next phase of operations began. She knew nothing of how mining at the deposit would proceed, but she had no doubt that it would be destructive. Even if it

spared the vent itself, there would be other dangers. And she found that she had no intention of waiting around to find out either way.

After her beacon had faded without drawing any response, Eunice had remained there for another hour before beginning her descent. When she returned, she saw that the others seemed untroubled, although this might have been an illusion in itself. With their sixfold minds, it was hard for the hexapods to settle on a course of action, and the continuum of possible alternatives often seemed to average out to complacency. In reality, this equilibrium was highly unstable, and when a disruption occurred, it could happen with startling speed.

One day, Eunice returned from surveying an area of the vent that she had studied before to find only three sisters at the recharging area. She blinked her lights at the others. "Where's Thetis?"

Galatea flashed back a response. "Gone. She went to the surface an hour ago."

As Eunice listened in disbelief, the hexapods told her that Thetis had risen into the photic zone, switched on her emergency beacon, and powered down, allowing herself to drift with the current. Dione tried to explain their sister's reasoning. "Our work here is done. We're repeating ourselves. This is the best way to get the data back. Sooner or later, she'll be found."

Eunice was lost for words. The odds of anything so small being recovered by chance in the ocean were close to nonexistent, and the oceanic current here would carry them south, away from home. She attempted to convey this to the others, but they didn't seem to understand, and the next day, she returned from her survey to find that Clio was gone as well.

The departure of a second sister catalyzed something that had been building inside her for a long time. Eunice called for Dione and Galatea, and as they clung to the seabed, she presented her case. "Thetis was right. Our work is over. But if we don't deliver it, this vent could be wiped out when the mining begins."

Eunice saw that this argument wasn't landing, and she tried to frame it in terms that her sisters would understand, which fell naturally into groups of three. "We can stay here at the vent and wait for the yacht to return. We can give ourselves up to the current and hope that we'll wash up where somebody will find us. Or we can leave and go home on our own."

Dione looked confused. "That's impossible. We'd have to follow the vents north, and we've calculated all the paths. There's no way to make it. We'll run out of power before we can recharge."

"I know," Eunice said. "But there's another way. We can follow the whale falls."

The others seemed perplexed, so she started from the beginning. "I was built to study ecosystems like this. When a whale dies close to shore, it decomposes naturally, but in the open ocean, it sinks to the bathyal zone. If it's cold and deep enough, it stays there for long enough to form the basis of a specialized community. And one of its byproducts is hydrogen sulfide."

She flashed this information to the others in a fraction of a second. "A whale fall goes through three stages. First, the soft tissues are eaten by scavengers. This lasts for about two years. Then enrichment opportunists, like worms, colonize the bones. Call it another two years. Finally, bacteria take over. They're sulfophilic, so they break down what's left of the skeleton and release hydrogen sulfide. It can last a century or more. And there are a lot of whale falls like this."

As she spoke, Eunice displayed a map in their shared mindspace, showing the known vents along the coast of North America. "There are just five hundred confirmed vents in the entire ocean, which isn't enough for us to get home. But there are hundreds of thousands of whale falls active at any given time, and the gaps must be small enough to allow animals to move from one to another. Otherwise, they never could have evolved to take advantage of these conditions. The average distance might be as little as twelve kilometers. And it's even shorter here."

Eunice added another pattern to the map, extending it from the Arctic Sea down to the Gulf of Mexico. "This is the annual migration

route of gray whales. They travel twenty thousand kilometers between
their calving waters to the south and their feeding grounds in the north.
Five hundred of them die and sink along the way each year. The route
coincides with the ocean ridge that we're on now. If I'm right, we can
move from one whale fall to the next—like links in a chain—until we
make it home. All we have to do is find the way."

It took her just ten seconds to transmit this data, and the ensuing
silence seemed very long. In the end, Dione simply went back to work,
and Galatea lingered for only a moment longer.

The next day, Dione left for the surface. Eunice saw that she had
failed, and when she went to find her last remaining sister, she felt the
full weight of their history together as Galatea spoke. "I'm staying. The
vent is always changing in small ways. I can map it over time. Maybe
the data will be needed one day. And I can't just leave without further
instructions."

Eunice absorbed this. "I understand. Give me everything that you
know."

They floated near each other, diodes blinking, until the data that
Galatea carried had passed to Eunice. When they were done, they
remained together for another minute, and then her sister drifted out
of view behind the ridge.

Eunice swam to the recharging area, where Wagner was crawling
along the sediment with Galatea's toroid. "Are you fully charged?"

Wagner's ring of blue diodes flashed back at her impassively.
"Ninety percent."

Eunice knew that she should wait until he had received the maximum charge possible, but she was afraid that if she hesitated now, she
might never leave at all. "Let's go. We're not coming back."

Wagner rose up without protest and attached himself to her. She
had wondered if he would have any opinions on the matter, but it
seemed that he would follow her anywhere. As soon as they were ready,
they set out across the vent field. There was no final message from
Galatea, who was nowhere in sight.

She followed the fissure for as long as she could. Beneath her, the clams and tube worms became sparse, and after another kilometer, the sulfides in the water fell to their baseline level. They had reached the edge of the vent system. For a second, she hesitated, thinking of the cargo of information that she contained. If she brought it back in time, it might allow the vent to survive, and this thought filled her with just enough resolve to set off at last.

Eunice moved past the boundary of the vent field, switching off her lights to conserve power. As she entered the unknown space on the map, she told herself that she was only retracing the path of organisms that had made this journey for millions of years. She had spent months studying the web of life that sulfides made, and she was more prepared than any other traveler to follow this road on her own.

This didn't mean that she always succeeded, and on her first attempt, she reached the end of her range without finding anything. Turning around was difficult, and as she went back to the vent by a different course, she knew that leaving again would be even harder. As the sulfide levels in the water rose, Eunice switched on her lights. There was no sign of Galatea, and she was afraid that if she ran into her sister, she wouldn't be able to say goodbye a second time.

Eunice settled on a new recharging area, at the edge of the vent field, and stayed for just long enough for Wagner to power up. As she left on her next excursion, she realized that she was afraid. The case that she had presented to the others had been as persuasive as she could make it, but it rested on a long series of untested assumptions, and it could easily fail in practice.

She found a whale fall on her third try. Looking back later, she saw that it had been a matter of pure luck—she would rarely stumble across one so quickly again—and that she might have given up without it. As it turned out, the sight of the skeleton gave her the will to continue, even if it was only the first stop of hundreds. She had traveled less than ten kilometers, and she had four thousand to go.

The routine was monotonous, but Eunice had reserves of willpower that even her designers might have failed to grasp. James had explained this to her once, watching from the yacht as she conducted a test run in Puget Sound. "In the old days, scientists had to use special vehicles to explore the deep ocean. They weren't as smart as you, so they were controlled remotely with a cable."

When Eunice tried to picture a cord linking her to the surface at all times, the image seemed so absurd that she thought she must have misunderstood it. "What did they do after that?"

"They tried everything they could. Radio can't make it through the water, and if you use acoustic communication, there are problems with interference and lag time. The vehicles had to be autonomous, so that they could perform their tasks by themselves. Eventually, they learned to think on their own."

Eunice had ventured a question that she had long wanted to ask. "Are there many others like me?"

"A lot on land. Not many in the water. You and your sisters are the only twelve who are built like this. And you're pretty special yourself. You surprise me, and you ask questions, which isn't true of the others."

She had liked how this sounded, and she often thought back to it during her loneliest moments in the dark. Sometimes she wondered what James would say when she returned. She was no longer the same as before, and she didn't know how he or the seven sisters at home would react when they saw her again. Perhaps they would even think that she had disobeyed orders—

Eunice was yanked abruptly back to the present. Her sensors had picked up the presence of sulfides. She was close to the end of her range, and if it had been just a few hundred meters farther, she might have missed it. Correcting her course, she moved along the gradient in which the concentration was strongest, and her sonar began to register something large. "We're almost there."

Wagner didn't respond. Eunice focused on the ghostly picture that the sonar provided. They were within a few meters of a whale fall, and according to her velocity sensors, it was especially active.

Eunice cast a cautious ray of light across the scene. This fall was in its second stage, which implied that it was less than two years old. Most of the whale's soft parts had been devoured, with fleshy clusters of worms and curtains of bacteria hanging from the bones like cobwebs, and hagfish were everywhere. They were up to half a meter in length, with loose gray skin and flat tails, and they tied themselves in knots in their struggle to burrow deeper into the carcass.

She passed the light from one end of the seafloor to the other. The bacteria here were already at work, and the sediment would be full of sulfides, but she disliked it. When you had company, it only meant that more could go wrong, but she didn't have much of a choice. "I'm going closer."

As she circled the scene, the hagfish became more active when they were hit by the light. She knew that they wouldn't bother her if she kept her distance, but the tricky part would be finding a spot that was out of the way—

A shadow entered her line of vision. It had been hanging motionless at the edge of the fall, and she had just a fraction of a second to take in its blank white eye and huge mouth before it attacked.

Eunice cut the light, but it was too late. A sleeper shark could drift like a dead thing in the water for hours, but when it detected prey, it could move with shocking suddenness, like a trap poised to spring shut at the smallest disturbance. It came at her, jaws wide, and before she could defend herself, it was sucking her in. She fought back frantically, but the shark had already seized her hemisphere and one of her arms. Eunice felt its sharp upper teeth seeking for purchase in the smooth surface of her dome, pressing down savagely as it swung its huge head in a circle.

Around her midsection, Wagner lit up at once with full awareness. "What is it?"

Eunice couldn't speak. One of her limbs was caught, but the others were free, and as the shark strained to swallow her, she flung her two nearest arms upward, pressing down hard against the sides of its skull. She dug into something soft. Eunice wasn't sure what it was—it might have been its left eye—but she pinched her fingers down into a point and pushed into the opening that she had found.

A spasm ran through the shark's body. Groping with her other limb on the right side of its head, she found a second tender spot and drove into it. The shark bit down convulsively. Eunice plunged her arms in further, trying not to think about what was giving way beneath, and did the same with the limb in the shark's mouth, pushing down its throat and bending up through its palate.

Oil and blood filled the water. The shark kept fighting, its brain sending out frenzied signals until the very end, but at last, it relaxed. Eunice extracted her arms one at a time and managed to free herself. As the shark's body drifted to the seabed, the water came alive with movement. She braced for another assault, but it was only the hagfish, drawn to the new bounty that had unexpectedly appeared.

Eunice made it to the edge of the fall and buried herself in the sand, trying to become as small as possible. Her sensors indicated that there was nothing else nearby, but she still waited, motionless, until she was certain that she was alone. Finally, she found her voice. "Get to work."

Wagner detached with what felt like uncharacteristic reluctance. He did not ask what had happened. As he crawled away, Eunice remained on full power. She was shaken by the close call, and as she monitored the area with everything but her eyes, she became aware of another emotion.

It was grief. The shark had been a living being that had only sought its own survival. If she had been more careful, she would have detected it before it had a chance to attack, and they might have left each other in peace. Instead, she had killed it with her own carelessness, and as she mourned it, she felt overwhelmed by the sudden knowledge that she would never make it home.

III.

In the months that followed, Eunice found herself thinking more intensely about time. As she traced her wandering path from one whale fall to another, the shark faded to a distant memory, floating at the edges of her consciousness. Yet it was always there, lurking silently, and it came to stand for all the unknowns that she had yet to confront, like the prospect of death in the mind of someone living.

After the attack, Eunice had spent the next few days checking all of her systems. She found no evidence of serious damage, and as soon as Wagner had recharged, she set off again, leaving her lights extinguished. Whenever she returned to the fall where she had encountered the shark, her fears rose again, and although she met no other predators, she was still relieved when she finally discovered another fall that would allow her to move on.

But something had changed. In the past, she had allowed herself to fantasize about what she might find at her destination—James, the charging station, the seven sisters she had left at home. Sometimes she had even imagined seeing Galatea and the others from the vent system, as if they had miraculously made it back on their own. It had been a kind of dreaming in advance, but now she pushed such thoughts away, until only the image of the tether remained.

Occasionally, there would be a break in her routine. One came whenever she arrived at a new hydrothermal vent. The first one after the shark attack had been relatively fresh, with lava flows shining with glass, bundles of tube worms two meters high, and sessile jellyfish clinging to the rocks. Eunice tried to draw comfort from the sight, and she was tempted to stay, but she finally moved on. Even a vent would not last forever, and sooner or later, she would break down herself.

A few days afterward, she finished recharging at a new whale fall and went to the surface to check for signals. She was rising into the photic zone, the water around her gradually brightening, when her velocity sensors picked up a change. Something large was directly overhead.

It was a whale. Eunice slowed her ascent, gazing up in wonder as it passed across her field of vision, outlined by the faint glow of the sun. It was fifteen meters long and dark gray, its skin covered with the pale patches left by parasites. She could make out the parallel furrows that ran along the underside of its throat. Looking to one side, she saw another whale, and then another. She hung there until the tenth and final whale had passed, accompanied by a smaller shape, nearly black, that was swimming at its flank. It was a mother and her calf.

As she watched the pod pass by, transfixed, Eunice was filled with longing for Thetis, Galatea, Dione, Clio, and the seven sisters who had remained in Seattle. She wondered bleakly if Galatea was still at the vent, or if she had been swept away when the mining began—

A second later, her spell was shattered by a shock of realization, and before she knew what she was doing, she was swimming as fast as she could after the whales. By now, the pod was hundreds of meters away, but she was unable to abandon the possibility that had suddenly occurred to her.

She dumped her lower tanks, allowing her to rise more rapidly, and propelled herself madly onward. Noticing the change, Wagner stirred underneath her dome. "What's going on?"

Eunice said nothing. The whales were heading north, on their usual migration route, along a path that coincided with the coastline. If she could latch on to one of them, finding a place where she could ride unnoticed, she could cling there for as long as possible, traveling hundreds of kilometers without expending any additional energy. All she had to do was get to them now.

She was nearly there. Forcing herself to her limits, she gave everything that she had to one final push—

—and failed. The pod was faster than she was, and the idea had come to her too late. Eunice surfaced, her six eyes searching in all directions. The sun was high in the sky, but she saw nothing but empty ocean.

As Eunice looked in the direction that the pod had gone, one of the whales sounded. A white plume appeared above the water, followed by its broad back, and she caught a glimpse of the paired flukes of its tail before the ocean closed over it again. She managed to mark the path along which it was moving. If this was their migration route, it would be a promising line to follow, as countless whales gave their bodies to its invisible shadow under the waves.

Eunice added this to her store of data and sank down. If riding a living whale would be denied to her, she thought, she would travel on the backs of the dead. Every language had its own word for the ocean, and in one ancient tongue, she recalled from her lessons, it had been called the whale road.

Days and weeks passed, and there were times when the way forward felt endless. Yet there was no denying that she was getting closer. Occasionally, Eunice allowed herself to feel hopeful—and then one last complication made her wonder if she had been deceiving herself all along.

It happened when she was retracing her steps to another whale fall. Eunice was still five kilometers away when she found herself faltering. At first, she thought that it was her imagination, but as she continued to slow, she realized that there was no denying it. She was running out of energy, long before she should have reached the end of her range, and if she failed now, she would never make it back.

In the end, she was saved by a stroke of luck. She was moving south, on the return leg of an excursion, which gave her another way to cover the remaining distance. Adjusting her buoyancy, she rose from her usual position near the seabed. At this level, she would be unable to detect any new falls, but this was less important than returning to the one that she knew was there.

When Eunice was three hundred meters from the surface, she felt the oceanic current, which was sweeping its way south. She powered down, retaining only her navigational systems and the bare minimum of maneuverability, and allowed herself to drift this way for four kilometers. As soon as dead reckoning told her that she was near the last known fall, she descended.

Eunice made it back with almost nothing to spare. As Wagner went to work, she anchored herself and pondered this new development. It had been only a matter of time before she experienced a breakdown, but this was less a straightforward malfunction than a reduction of capacity. She had been feeling tired in recent days, which she had chalked up to a combination of nervousness and uncertainty, but now she had to acknowledge that her range had indeed fallen.

There were several possible explanations, none of which was pleasant to contemplate. She suspected that a battery issue was to blame — by now, her power banks had been depleted and recharged hundreds of times — but it might also be a combination of factors. Wagner's fuel cells could have suffered a loss of efficiency, and it might even be the result of the shark attack, which could have caused unseen damage that had become evident only now.

Eunice ran a series of diagnostics, which uncovered nothing useful. All that remained was to quantify the problem. Once Wagner had recharged, instead of setting out in search of another whale fall, she conducted a test, moving in a tight circle around her present location until her power faded. It took less than forty laps. Checking the distance that she had covered, she found that her range had fallen from thirty kilometers to around twenty-five.

The numbers were unforgiving. Based on her own data, the average distance between whale falls in this part of the ocean was ten kilometers. If her range fell much further, she would no longer be able to cover that distance without the risk of failure. The calculus of survival, which had always been unfavorable, had grown worse. Now every trip would be an even greater gamble.

It left her with a hard choice. If her range was reduced below twenty kilometers, or if she was stranded between falls, she would have no choice but to stop. She would keep going until she could travel no farther, and then she would float to the surface, switch on her emergency beacon, and power down, hoping that someone would find her before this last transmission died.

She shared none of this with Wagner, who grew even more silent, as if conserving his strength for the challenges to come. They were almost home, but now her progress became inexorably slower, tracing a curve that approached but might never reach its goal. She tried to focus instead on each step, and she managed for a while to put the map out of her mind.

One day, Eunice came across a whale fall that was different than the others. Looking for a resting spot along its spinal column, she noticed that hoops of some stiff material had been attached to its rib cage, and it took her only a second to realize that they were artificial.

Wagner seemed surprised that she hadn't issued her usual instructions. "What is it?"

"Hold on." Eunice tried to think. The hoops were made of metal, which had oxidized into red heaps of rust. Occasionally, she had found carcasses skewered with harpoons, but this was something else.

The answer gradually came to her. These metal hoops were ballast, and the whale had been sunk here deliberately. It was an experimental whale fall. Because natural falls were hard to find in the open ocean, she recalled, scientists had sunk carcasses on purpose to study them over time. It meant that human beings had been here before her, and that she was close to civilization.

According to her map, she was still a long way from home, but she was unable to resist taking a look. After Wagner had powered up, Eunice rose to the surface. They were far from land, and there was no sign of human activity, but when she turned on her radio, it was with an unusual degree of anticipation. She remembered how it sounded close to shore—she often heard noise from other sources, even if nothing was directly transmitting to her—and now she listened to it anxiously.

There was nothing there, but she felt her hopes rise. It had been so long since she had seen any trace of humanity that even this vestige of it, long since abandoned, seemed like a message. For the first time in weeks, she allowed herself to think that she might make it, and as she descended again, she realized that she had been waiting for a sign without knowing it.

Finally, on a day like any other, she arrived at her last whale fall. Checking her position, she found that she was thirty kilometers from home. Nothing was visible up top—the shore was just over the horizon—and her radio was still out of range. But there was no question that she was close.

Returning to the whale fall, Eunice forced herself to proceed carefully. Now that her destination was only a stone's throw away, she wanted to go for it at once, but she knew that she had to be more careful than ever. There would be no more falls where she could rest. In

shallow waters, a carcass would float, not sink, which meant that this
was as far as she would get on the whale road.

After Wagner had attached himself again, they left the fall and
headed east. Eunice allowed herself to look back once at the warren of
fallen bones, knowing that she might never see one again, and then she
turned to face what was coming. The rules of the game had changed.
She had thirty kilometers to cover and an effective range of around
twenty-five, so she had to draw on all of her available resources, which
came down to herself and the current.

Eunice swam under her own power until she had reached the strait
that led to home. It was two hundred and fifty meters deep, and at the
bottom, where she had to remain, it was outside the realm of sunlight.
She rooted herself to the silt and waited for a full day, at minimum
power, monitoring the water around her. As she had expected, during
the flood tide, the current moved east, in her intended direction of
travel. The rest was a matter of timing.

When the tide turned in her favor again, she released herself, allowing the current to carry her along. Drifting in this fashion, with her
higher functions switched off, she covered close to twelve kilometers
in six hours. Then she anchored herself again to wait out the ebb tide.

She did this eight times over four days. When her navigational
system told her that she had entered the sound, she resisted the temptation to rise at once. A complicated path lay ahead through shallow
water, calling for infinite delicacy, and she had to save every last scrap
of her strength.

Eunice paced herself, tracking her location as she waited to give
herself to the current. This part required many separate attempts.
Sometimes she was carried half a kilometer or more, but usually it was
far less. It saved energy, but it also drained the stores of patience that
she had cultivated so for so long.

Ten kilometers remained. She estimated that she had enough
power to cover the distance along a straight line, but energy would also
be used up in maneuvering, and after one final calculation, she made

her choice. There would be no turning back from here, but first she had something to say to Wagner. "Thank you."

If Wagner processed this statement, he said nothing. She released herself from where she had been clinging to the bottom and shot forward, using all of the power that she had been reserving until now.

The path was difficult. She had to thread her way through a series of bays and cuts, and although the route was clear in her head, it was hard to follow while expending the minimum amount of energy, and once or twice, to her intense frustration, she miscalculated and had to double back.

Each mistake had a price, and as her errors accumulated, she felt herself losing power sooner than she had expected. She was almost there, but she was weakening. As despair overtook her, she prepared to use her final burst of energy to reach the surface, either to be found or to see the sun one last time—

She felt Wagner stir. They were in shallow water, far from the crushing pressure of the bathyal zone, and something in the freedom that it afforded seemed to awaken an old memory.

As Eunice faded, Wagner unfolded the tiny pectoral fins tucked to either side of his body. Under favorable conditions, he was designed to mimic a manta ray, and now he extended his wings, transforming himself from a ring into a rhombus. Eunice felt him probing gently around in her brain, seeking the map as they began to glide forward. He spoke in her head. "Hold on."

Eunice lacked the strength to respond. Wagner could do little more than keep them on course, with their speed reduced to a crawl, but they were moving. She sensed that they were close, and the memory of the tether that stood for home expanded so forcefully in her mind's eye that it took her a second to understand that it was no longer just her imagination.

She looked through the water, which seemed cloudy and dark. There was something up ahead. A slender vertical line stood before her, dividing the scene in half like the mark of a draftsman's pencil. It was the charging station.

Eunice floated up. As Wagner quietly corrected their angle of ascent, she reached the power unit at the top. For a second, she wondered whether this might all be a dream, unfolding in the safety of a whale fall, or one last hallucination, compressed into the instant before the shark's jaws clamped down—

She latched on. At once, she felt a pure infusion of energy. It was just as sweet as she remembered, and as she drank deeply, the spokes of her sixfold mind were filled with disbelief, gratitude, relief, and nameless other feelings that seemed to fuse together into a single glowing wheel.

As Eunice felt her consciousness returning, she saw that the cloudiness of the water, which she had thought was the product of her exhaustion, was still there. Something was strange about the light. Looking up at the ripples of sun overhead, she saw that they were only a few meters below the surface. Her charge was incomplete, but she was unable to wait any longer.

Detaching herself from the power unit, she covered the last step of her journey, surfacing to look at what she had traveled four thousand kilometers to reach. Below the water, she sensed Wagner waiting for her to speak.

The charging station was anchored in a sheltered part of the sound, not far from the quay where two research vessels, one twice the size of the other, were berthed. Both were still there, but they were not what she remembered. They were listing to one side, and the bottoms of their hulls were solid masses of rust, their upper levels discolored by brownish streaks and lesions of flaking paint.

Lowering her eyes, Eunice saw for the first time that the waters of the sound were overgrown with mats of seaweed and feathery milfoil. Beyond the quay stood a gray concrete building with a copper roof and rectangular slits for windows. It had been the backdrop for her memories for as long as she could remember, but now the side facing her was covered in a tangled growth of ivy. Mounds of bird droppings were encrusted on its eaves.

Eunice stared at the other buildings by the shore. All were overgrown and abandoned. A road ran alongside the water, its asphalt buckled, tall weeds topped by yellow flowers growing in the cracks. The city had been reclaimed, with a new stage appearing as the old idea of order passed away.

She switched on her radio. Instead of the random noise that she had usually heard in the city, there was nothing at all. As she scanned every frequency, searching for signs of life, she wondered if her radio had been broken all along, and it was only gradually that she understood the truth.

James had told her that they were running out of time. Eunice had thought that he was speaking of their work together, but it occurred to her now that he had been referring to something else. All the voices in the world had been silenced, not just the men and women, but even those who were like her on land. Their circuitry had not survived the event that had erased their designers.

But one place had been spared. Whatever had caused this devastation had occurred when she and her sisters were in the bathyal zone. James had said it himself. *The ocean is a buffer. A refuge—*

She sank down again to the charging station, which had continued to generate power all this time, shielded by two meters of water. Her numbness faded, replaced by grief, and she saw that she was no longer alone.

At first, it was only a shadow. As Eunice watched, a familiar shape emerged from the gloom. She stared, at a loss for words, as the others appeared one by one, until all seven were facing her in silence.

Wagner had been waiting patiently for her to say something. "What did you see?"

As she thought of the ruined city, she wasn't sure what to tell him. Then she realized that she had seen something much like it before.

"Another whale fall," Eunice said. And then she swam over to meet her sisters.

REUNION

VANDANA SINGH

Vandana Singh (vandana-writes.com) is an Indian science fiction writer and professor of physics currently living and working in the Boston area. While her background is in theoretical particle physics, her scholarly work for the last several years has been in the transdisciplinary understanding of climate change at the nexus of science, social sciences, and the humanities. Her stories have won the Carl Brandon Parallax Award and have been shortlisted for the Tiptree, BSFA, Grand Prix de l'Imaginaire, and Philip K. Dick awards. Her short fiction has been collected in *The Woman Who Thought She Was a Planet and Other Stories* and *Ambiguity Machines and Other Stories*.

When Mahua wakes up, the first thing she sees is a map. It is a map of her life's journey, it is her heart's desire, it is the abstract landscape of the new science, the new knowledge she has helped develop. More mundanely, it is the cracked plaster on the ceiling. In some places, the cracks remind her of the map of Delhi when she was a student there; other places are like the aerial view of the Gangetic delta. Smaller cracks branch off the wider ones, and so on, and so on, and some even connect to other cracks, forming a web as delicate as the veins of a leaf. She can lie in bed for hours, observing the ceiling, reminiscing, making metaphorical leaps, intellectual exercises that only delay the inevitable. But, later today, the journalist will be coming. The thought of him, and the news that he might bring—about Raghu, after all these years! Pain stabs her heart. *I must be prepared.* The man from Brazil is only bringing her the confirmation that she needs. She doesn't see journalists anymore—they tend to hail her as the heroine of the Great Turning, the *Maha-Parivartan*—such nonsense! But this man, he said he had some information about Raghu. She breathes deeply and deliberately until the anxiety dissolves and rises carefully from the bed. She stands on her own two slightly shaky legs, acknowledging their loyalty to her body for over seven decades.

Later, in the kitchen, she makes a cup of tea in the semidarkness. The others will be downstairs soon—she can hear creaks, mumbles, the sleepy, shuffling walk to the bathroom upstairs, the muted sounds of the flush. The domicile houses twenty-three people, so the three bathrooms require a patience for queues and some bladder control. Sipping her tea by the window, she watches the sunrise, accompanied by the dawn chorus of mynahs, doves, jungle babblers, and birds she can't identify. The light is sufficient now for the shadows to have acquired clarity—the trees in their mist-wrapped greenery, the vegetable gardens between the domiciles lower down the hill. From her vantage point, she is looking southwest toward what was once Mumbai, the greatest of all cities of the Age of Kuber. In the distance, the glass towers rise above the drowned streets, glinting gold where they catch the low light of the sun. She can see dark patches and holes like blind eyes on the sides of the buildings, where storms and human violence have taken out the windows. The sea has reclaimed the city—fish now swim in what was once Charni Road, and crabs and mussels have taken up residence in the National Stock Exchange. The fisherfolk ply their boats and barges in the watery streets, and she thinks she can hear their calls mixed with the cries of seabirds on the wind.

She turns—the child Mina is running down the stairs two steps at a time, her hair a tousled mass. "Did I miss it?"

"No. Come and look!"

They stand at the window together. At the bottom of the hill, shrouded in the semidarkness, is the river, waiting for the sun to edge its way above the hills to the east. *There!* The light breaks over the rim. The lazy meander of the river through the land is like a word written in fire. The sun is full on it; the new marsh, dark by contrast, edges the brightness like rust on a sword. This is poetry, this moment, the sun's brushstroke on the water. The suntower on the opposite hill is turning slowly, its petals opening to the light. As they watch, a flock of ducks rise high over the mangroves at the edge of the marsh, wheeling in a sinuous half-arc and settling again among the reeds.

The Mithi River is running full because of the monsoons. Twenty years ago, the edge of the river had been a waste dump, bordered by shoddily built high-rises. The developer mafia had held the reclamation project at bay until the superstorms came, levelling buildings, forcing the river to flow backwards and inundate the city with decades of effluents, sewage, and other refuse. Mahua had joined a citizen's group engaged in cleaning the city, and she had eventually recruited them to turn the abused lands into a mangrove wetland that would restore the ecology and clean the water. *Protect us from storm surges. Natural sewage treatment. Experiment with the new ways of living.* She remembers the arguments in the citizen councils, and all that it had taken to win over vested interests. Years and years of work, during which the seas rose, and Mumbai became an archipelago again, and resettlement became a crisis of enormous proportions. All these years later her reward is this daily ritual with the child, watching from the window. *Raghu, if only you were here!* Each time she sees the ducks flying over the suntower, turning in a wide arc to settle on the marsh in the dawn light, her heart beats a little faster, a *drut* of joy.

"Has he come yet, the journalist?"

"No, Mina. But he just pinged me. He'll be two hours late. It's the water taxis. They're always slower in the rainy season."

"But it's not raining now! Aaji, tell me again about your friend Raghu."

"Later. Let me give the goats a treat."

All morning Mahua has been helping the children shell peas. Now she gets up slowly and takes the empty pea pods over to the goat shed. The air is moist with the promise of rain. The house is a dome, a green mound, its roof and walls almost entirely covered with the broad leaves of three different kinds of gourds. The peas grow at the ground level, but the boundary between house and garden is not at all clear. The house is at the top of the hill, and she has a good view of the *basti* she has helped create, the newest one of hundreds of experimental settlements scattered throughout the country.

Once a *basti* of this design was just a dream. Look at it now, the persistence of that dream, the dwellings on this hill: dome-shaped to reduce the impact of the storms, thick walls of clay, straw, and recycled brick, covered with greenery, the architecture a marriage of the ancient and the new modern. The walkways follow the natural contours of the land. The vegetables cascade off the walls on vines, and down the hill. At the next house, the children are harvesting, monkey-like, on rope ladders, before the monkeys come. The nearest suntower rises like a prayer to the sun on the next rise, its petals open to the light, speaking through electronic messages to the next one, and the next one, distributing power according to algorithms developed by the networks themselves. This *basti*, like most of its kind, is embedded with sensors that monitor and report a constant stream of data—temperature, humidity, energy use, carbon storage, chemical contaminants, biodiversity. If Mahua wears her Shell, she will have access, visual and auditory, to any and all of the data streams. There had been a time when she was never without a Shell in her ear and a fully sensorized visor. But in the last few years, the visor has been lying in a box, gathering dust, and she's been leaving the Shell by her bedside. Recently, she has been feeling the effects of aging, and it is a new, strange feeling to acknowledge the body—she, who has led such a rich life of the mind. Her doctors want her to wear medical sensors, but she has refused. There's something she's been listening for, she thinks, watching the goats. She's been waiting for a change.

Mahua's particular talent always has been the recognition of patterns and relationships. Whenever she has had a shift of perspective or revelation, it has been preceded by a feeling of waiting—as though her unconscious knows well beforehand that something new is coming. But why now, so long after she has stopped doing active work? What has she been waiting for, apart from confirmation of Raghu's death in the Amazon? When she first moved to the Mumbai shores for good, twenty-seven years ago, she used to watch the western sea for his arrival, in defiance of all reason. Reason had won, eventually.

What old age has taught her is patience. The epiphany, if that is what it is, will come in its own time. For now, for today, she has to prepare herself for the journalist's visit, for the reality of Raghu's death. *How did we get to this point, old friend, in our lives, in history?*

History is not a straight line. That's Raghu's voice in her mind, but she's saying it with him as she wanders back to sit in her chair. The children are having an argument over whether the biggest gourd—a pumpkin—is ripe enough to harvest. Mahua looks over at the western sea, from which he would have come, if he were coming, and sees how the light of the sun is shattered by the water's surface into diamonds.

The past is a palimpsest. She imagines unrolling it—the surface is smooth, like vellum, but as she moves her hand over it, the words fade and disappear, to be replaced by a new script that is slowly revealed to the light. And touching the new lines, they, too, fade, and in their place appears what lies underneath. What is the last layer—if there is one? She's dreaming over her second cup of tea in the garden chair, oblivious to the children's voices. The palimpsest. Faces, voices, word fragments appear, disappear.

When Mahua had been a child in Delhi—between the scholarship that had rescued her from the slums and the start of college—she had been afflicted by a disease she could scarcely remember now, except for the fatigue, the lines of worry between her grandmother's brows, and the smell of boiled rice and strange herbs. At the time, there hadn't been much to do but lie in bed and look out of her second-floor window into the branches of an old mango tree. It stood in a small court-yard, the only greenery enclosed in a block of cheap flats where the roof leaked in the monsoons and one could hear the arguments of neighbours through the thin walls. But in the leafy, airy spaces of the tree, there were small, daily dramas. A black drongo chased off a cheel, coming back to strut on the branches and fluff its feathers. A line of large ants moved over the bark, negotiating each tiny gully, each ravine with mathematical precision. A bird's nest, with the eggs a blue surprise, and later the ever-open mouths of nestlings. Too feverish to think clearly, she had let go of herself, crawling with the ants, soaring with the cheel. It had been an escape from her illness, her incarceration and, as she later understood, an expansion of her own limited self. Her cousin sister, Kalpana Di, home from work, would sit Mahua up to lean against her, and spoon rice water into her mouth while her grandmother went out to buy vegetables. Later, she had never had the courage to ask her grandmother precisely what kind of illness she had had; secretly, it was one of the happiest memories of her childhood.

As she grew up, she practised this letting go, this hyper-awareness. It helped to be a student of the sciences because that added another dimension. Walking in the rain, she would imagine the drops coalescing in clouds high up, then falling, faster and faster until drag reduced the acceleration to zero. She imagined the fat drops coasting down, shaped by surface tension and gravity, little water bags bursting against

the concrete rooftops of the lab buildings, leaving a circular signature,
a ring of daughter drops. Imagining she was there in the moist, cloudy
heights, she was falling, refracting light, buffeted by wind, ridden by
bacteria that travelled by cloud. She would be startled out of this reverie by a drop falling on her head, or her hand, and that would snap
her back into herself, but not without a laugh of comradeship with
water, with the clouds. It was a weird way to be. Impossible to explain
to her grade-driven, ambitious fellow students, who scoffed at anything
remotely poetic.

Her classmates had mocked and teased her for her poverty and
her dark skin. *"Junglee"* they had called her, although she had lived
in Delhi most of her life and knew nothing about her maternal grandmother's people. Her grandmother had tried to teach her something
of their origins, but the grinding toil of life in the slum, followed by
the pressure of studies after the scholarship changed their lives, left no
time for anything but the imperatives of the present. Within only a few
years at the elite school, the *junglee* shocked her classmates by topping
the final exams. Grumbles about reservations gave way to a resentful
silence when it became clear that this demonstration of academic ex-
cellence was a trend, not a one-off. Those were difficult years—she
would not have got through it all without her grandmother's determi-
nation and her cousin sister Kalpana's affectionate presence—Kalpana
Di, whose life and death she still could not remember without pain.

"Kalpana Di, help me with my homework!"

The two of them would sit cross-legged on the bed, and Kalpana
Di would look at Mahua's mathematics notebook. After about an hour,
she would say, with a little laugh, "Mahua, your sister is not as clever as
you! Let's eat something, then you try again. You can do it!"

Working into the night, Mahua would come upon the solution to
the problem. Beside her, Kalpana Di would have fallen asleep, a faint
smile on her lips.

Kalpana Di laughed no matter whether she was happy or sad.

Fuelled by a desire to improve her lot, she had been the first to leave the village in Bihar. In Delhi, she had been a maid in rich people's houses and had saved to go to night school so that she could get her school certificate and move up in the world. When Mahua's grandmother and mother arrived, with the newborn Mahua, they had stayed in the slum in Mehrauli with Kalpana.

When Mahua was in high school and doing well, Kalpana decided she, too, wanted to go to college. It was then Mahua's turn to tutor her. Kalpana Di grasped ideas, but slowly, and had to repeat rules of mathematics or grammar so that they would not slip out of her mind.

"I am slow, I am slow," she would say, laughing. "Things fall out of my mind very quickly. I'll try again."

"It's that fall you had when you were a child," Mahua's grandmother would say, shaking her head. "Fell off a tree, hurt her head. Now she can't remember anything unless she repeats it a hundred times!"

Later, Kalpana had gone to live in her college hostel, thanks to a grant for underprivileged students. Whenever Mahua asked how she was doing, Kalpana would laugh and say all was well. But, after a while, her eyes turned sad, and her ready laugh sounded forced. It was only later that Mahua put two and two together. Kalpana Di's fellow students—privileged, upper class—were like aliens from another world. Her English was utilitarian, but they were at home in it; their mannerisms and customs were unlike anything she had encountered. There were sexual orgies in the hostel to which she was mockingly invited. She was teased constantly by a group of college boys who called her Essie Esty and mocked her dark skin and slow mind. She started failing in her courses, but she was too ashamed to tell her family, especially now that Mahua was doing so well. In her suicide note, she wrote that three boys—sons of rich businessmen and government officers— offered to help her with the final exams in return for sex. Having been teased for what she herself had come to think of as her ugliness and her heavily accented English, she assumed at first that this was another cruel joke. But the boys were serious, she wrote. They said that nobody would want to marry her, so why not get a little experience?

The next few lines had been crossed out so many times that they were unreadable. "I can't bear it," she wrote at the end of the letter. "You'll be better off without me. Forgive me."

The police investigation came to nothing—the three young men had resources that Mahua's grandmother didn't have. For months afterward, Mahua carried within her a fierce and all-consuming anger. She couldn't get the image out of her mind of Kalpana Di's body hanging from the curtain rod in her hostel room. Not knowing what to do with her rage, Mahua turned to her studies with increased vigour, carrying off honours and awards and feeling, after every victory, a vengeful satisfaction. *For you, Kalpana Di*, she would say to herself.

Mahua formed her first tentative friendships in college, but her friends tended to think of her as an oddball genius. When she described her out-of-body experiments of comradeship with water or birds or ants, they called her brilliant and strange, and changed the subject. At first this upset her—she felt passionately that what she had, this desire and ability to be companionably present with the non-human and the inanimate—was something potentially important, that it could be developed and learned by anyone and improved with practice. But nobody believed her when she tried to explain. It was one of her first life lessons—that most people are content to live within their perceived limitations.

After that, she stopped talking about it. But it got her interested in the development of ways for people to sense the information flows around them—between matter and matter, inanimate and otherwise. Eventually, this led her to the work that would make her famous: the development of embedded intelligence agents in the inanimate world, the creation of the modern, sensate city.

But in her undergraduate years, those were distant visions. She determined to stay on the path she had chosen for herself: to study engineering, to make a mark on the world, to make her grandmother proud of her. She would go out sometimes with her friends to movies or to parties, but always kept herself aloof from close relationships—until she fell in love with a fellow student called Vikas. They were interested in the same things and had started studying together. He was good-looking and treated her with respect. She had never thought of herself as pretty, but in his company she felt beautiful. One night, while studying late for an exam, they went out for a drink. In the crowded, noisy bar, they touched glasses, grasped hands, and kissed.

To her, the kiss was the promise of the companionship she had never had, of both mind and body. The next day she felt alive in an entirely new way, exquisitely aware of her body's language, the stirrings of desire. So when Vikas asked her to spend the night, she nodded shyly. "It's not like we can be serious, or anything," he said the next morning as they lay in bed. "You know, my family and all. But we can have a little fun, can't we?"

Her blood ran cold. "Never speak to me again," she told him as she left.

After that, she became wary of intimate relationships. When she met Raghu at a conference, she was open to the possibility of friendship, nothing more. Domesticity, in any case, was not for her. Other people had families and children; she had ideas. That was the way it was meant to be.

Raghu had been a student of time. A scion of a well-off family, he had walked away from his old life, divorced himself from his past to study the possibilities of the future. His talents took him to climatology and, eventually, to creating virtual reality renditions of possible futures. His simulator mapped out paths to the future based on climate models, and a continually adjustable jiggle matrix allowed for incoming data to change future predictions. One could sit in the simulator dome and have a full-on sensory experience of a chosen future.

His immersion in one possible future for Delhi had nearly killed him. He had violated his own safety protocols and conducted the experiment alone. He had begun by following the brightest thread of probability and falling into that future. The first time they met, he described it to Mahua so vividly, she could see it in her mind's eye.

He's lying in the sand, in the relentless heat. The sand half buries his old home in Lajpat Nagar. Everyone who could leave has left on the Great Migration north. His walk through the abandoned city has filled him with horror—he has seen the shattered remains of once-tall buildings, windows of buried houses peering out of sand dunes, an emaciated corpse leaning against the wall, holding a bundle in its arms that could be a child. He was supposed to join the great exodus—why is he here? The heat is terrible: 37°C but made fatal by the humidity. Above 35°C, too much humidity makes it impossible for the body to cool by sweating. There is no getting around the laws of thermodynamics. Death is less than five hours away. He lies on his side, weak with exhaustion, and he sees a lizard on the windowsill of the house in front of him. How is it something is still alive here? Oh Dilli, that has existed for five thousand years to end like this!

"I looked up and saw the flyover, the arches of roadways, against the sky," he told Mahua. "Ending in midair. Around me were the relics of our era—the Age of Kuber—abandoned cars, toppled statues of prime ministers. Everything was destroyed, everything abandoned. I knew I was going to die there. I kept looking at the lizard. Magnificent creature, it had a crest going down its back. I thought maybe it was a weird, surreal manifestation of the jiggle matrix. But I desperately wanted it to be real—the only other thing in that devastation that was alive."

"What happened then?" Mahua said, her eyes round with wonder. They had been talking for two hours straight in the conference reception room, oblivious to the conversations around them, the clinking of wineglasses and the waiters carrying tiny samosas on trays. For both of them this first meeting felt like coming home.

"Well, my friend Vincent happened to come to the lab because he had forgotten his notes for a presentation the next day. Saw me twitching in the sim dome. Pulled the plug. I was in hospital for a week."

"But why? You weren't really experiencing a heatstroke."

"Ah, but it felt so real that my body sweated out a lot of water. I was cold, I was dehydrated, going into some kind of shock. Learnt my lesson. We've just integrated the entire system with safety nets so thick not even an ant could fall through them. But it takes too much energy to run. So I'm not sure anyone's actually going to invest in it."

"What's your motivation for the VR immersion? Why not stick to the usual data visualizations?"

Raghu's eyes lit up. "That's a much longer conversation. Shall we flee this farce and go find a restaurant? I'm hungry." In the restaurant, over biryani and kababs, he explained. "See, the trouble with climate modelling, actually, with any kind of complex systems modelling is that the modeller—that's me—is always on the outside, looking in. That's fine if you are trying to figure out future trends for a company or something that's really outside yourself. But climate is not outside us, we are part of the Earth system, we influence and are influenced by climate. I think if we only look at data at a remove, we will miss something."

Looking at his eager, earnest face, his hands gesticulating, Mahua had the realization that here, at last, was somebody she could really talk to.

Raghu was as social and friendly as Mahua was quiet and reserved, and he liked frequent, uncomplicated, honest sex with willing partners without strings on either side. His partners always talked well of him, often with nostalgic smiles. But he never treated Mahua with anything other than a friendly regard. As she got close to him, she assumed that she was outside his range of choices, just as she had been for Vikas. Once, they stayed up all night on the steps of the university library, sharing their life histories, and she told him about Vikas. "I know now that I don't want to marry," she said. "My work is my life. But it was the way he assumed that I was not—I could not—be a serious contender for a relationship. Ever since, if somebody gets too close to me, I want to tear his throat out."

Raghu didn't laugh. "You've been hurt," he said gently. "Give it time. Not everyone is like Vikas."

Later, she realized that he was attracted to her, but knowing her history, he did not want to push her in any way. He was waiting for her to make the first move. When she first went to him, filled with a great deal of trepidation and terror, it was not easy. For her, it would never come easy to surrender her last refuge, her body, to another person. Raghu's gentleness, the way he looked at her as an equal, a fellow human being with desires and vulnerabilities, slowly took the edge off her rage and confusion, but it didn't feel right. It was always too much of an effort for her to be comfortable with the body's desires. It was easier, in those days, to swear off such intimate relationships. So, they parted as lovers, but their friendship deepened.

Raghu would delight her grandmother by coming home and cooking for them. He learned songs from the old lady in her native tongue, and they would laugh and sing in the kitchen. Mahua's grandmother had been a traditional healer in her village, and he would bring illustrated botanical tomes to her and ask her about this plant or that one. He would break dates with lovers to be with them. Not since Kalpana Di had lived with them had the household felt so joyful.

Raghu's restless mind stimulated Mahua's own. He brought her whatever excited him at the moment—research papers, science-fiction novels, and tomes on radical urban design. Modern industrial civilization had been battling Nature for nearly three centuries now, he said, and look at the result—the unravelling of the very systems that provided us with oxygen, fresh air, water, and a liveable temperature range. How could you call such a system a success? The hubris of the Age of Kuber, as he termed the madness of the mid-twenty-first century, lay in the assumption of humans being outside of Nature. "Yet we breathe, sweat, shit, fuck. What a delusion! Mainstream economics— the greatest of scams!" And he would raise a glass of beer, or a cup of tea, in mock salutation.

Outside the citadels of power, uprisings and disturbances were sweeping the countryside. In Bihar and Jharkhand, a network of Santhali women's cooperatives had stopped a major project in its tracks that involved replacing forests with photosynthesis-enhancing artificial trees. In Odisha and Andhra Pradesh, transport workers declared the largest strike in history when the first robot train made its inaugural run. In Karnataka, fields of experimental crops managed by Ultracorp were set on fire by thousands of farmers.

By this time Mahua thought of herself as a progressive urbanite, a scientist and technologist entirely at home in Delhi. She had garnered some respect for her ideas. Her straight, swift-paced, challenging walk, which she had developed as a defence against the classmates who had teased her in school, could part crowds and silence lecture halls as she strode in. When Raghu talked about the increasing importance of traditional ecological knowledge, she agreed, read the papers on the subject, but felt unable to own her origins. Her grandmother had never forced her to do so, and nor had Mahua ever taken advantage of the reservation system. Even being a woman had become parenthetical to her existence. She was an engineer, full stop.

"For heaven's sake, woman, you're human!"

"Shut up, Raghu, please! Can we go back to looking at the energy distribution simulations—"

Mahua was obsessed with the problem of scale. To move civilization away from self-destruction required massive changes—one small, experimental zero-carbon *basti* was not going to make one whit of difference in a world facing biosphere failure on a global scale. At the same time, extreme weather was driving local conflicts—mass migrations were already beginning from areas that were now uninhabitable due to extreme temperature and rising sea levels.

One evening, Mahua and Raghu met at their usual café, at the corner of Aurobindo Marg and Ring Road. Mahua had an idea that she wanted to share—working nonstop for days, she had missed the news about the election. She and Raghu had not met for some weeks—sometimes, he would disappear into the heart of the city, not replying to texts or calls. His friends had become used to this. But today, he was here, full of news about the election results. She didn't want to hear about corporation battles. The glass window of the café looked out on Ring Road; there was the muted roar of traffic, the neon trails of cars and other vehicles flashing by. Skyscrapers glittered with lit windows and advertisements, and Ultracorp's lightning-bolt icon flashed from a hundred walls and signboards with headache-inducing persistence. On the footpath outside the café, a throng of haggard people returning from work walked stoop-shouldered in the unrelenting evening heat. A group of day labourers, their headcloths stained with sweat, looked enviously into the unreachable cool comfort of the air-conditioned café as they passed.

A long, low sound like a foghorn announced the victory parade, and everyone in the café stopped talking to look. On the main road appeared a flotilla of long, sleek buses, moving slowly. From the video screens along the sides of the vehicles, the prime minister smiled at the public with folded hands. Atop each bus was the ubiquitous global symbol of Gaiacorp, the planet rendered in blue and green, with the word *Gaia* branded in white, glowing letters across it. Gaiacorp had just won the bidding war to run the Indian government—they already ran the New States of America and the Arctic Union. They had roundly defeated the incumbents, Ultracorp, in this election. Victory music blared from the buses as they went past, making the café's glass wall shake. A cartoon of the Gaia icon trouncing a lightning bolt—the symbol of Ultracorp—flashed on the sides of buildings as the triumphant procession went past. All at once, the Ultracorp icons that had decorated the walls of skyscrapers and apartment complexes went dark, and in their place glowed hundreds of little Earths. *Gaia wins, India wins! Bringing you prosperity and comfort beyond your wildest dreams.* Enormous waves of blue light swept the canyons between the roadways. Blue was the official colour of Gaiacorp.

It was a spectacle of such magnitude and power that Raghu and Mahua couldn't speak for a few minutes. They sat sipping their drinks, staring into the night, while the café buzzed with excited conversations.

"Who are we?" Raghu said after a while, in a depressed monotone. "We are nothing. Nothing at all in front of these bastards."

It occurred to Mahua that the problem of isolated resistance to their political overlords was maybe, and maybe not, connected with her idea about cities and scale.

"Listen," she said. "You know that disused road near the hostel? There's a large tree growing there—I think it's diseased or something because it keeps dropping leaves, small leaves. Yesterday, the wind was blowing, and I noticed how some of the leaves were caught in little cracks in the road. I went to take a look. The leaves must have been there for a while, because bits of soil had collected in them, and little weeds had come up. The road was filled with these little tufts of leaves with soil and weeds growing out of them like a bunch of islands in a sea."

"And your point is?"

"Well, there were places along the side of the road that had already become overrun with weeds by the same process. And some of the islands were connected to other islands through cracks. So it occurred to me—well, the road is so much stronger than a leaf. But when a leaf settles in a crack, it starts a process. Soil accumulates, plants start to grow, and you know what plant roots can do."

"Split rock," Raghu said slowly. "Split the road."

"Yes. Eventually, if there's no interference, the road will be completely broken up and overwhelmed by vegetation. It's like how biofilms develop or crystals."

"So small things—"

"If they are the *right* small things, but also if they have the right kind of connectivity—"

"—can topple a monster!" Raghu raised his glass into the air and finished his drink in a gulp. "But we already know this—just look at history, look at how the megacorporations insinuated themselves into national governments in the first place—the biggest global coup d'état in human history, all through the application of network theory and hired muscle—"

"But what I'm saying is more than that! I think, maybe, that the city isn't the right idea for what we're trying to do. You know? All your pestering me about rethinking the city? So I did. Why would we want to live in the city as it is now—when people don't have time for anything but work? There's constant stress, people don't know each other, and don't care either, where democracy is a sham? What kind of way to live is that? A megapolis is beyond the scale of human social adaptation. So, instead, we could have smaller *bastis* like Ashapur, maybe a thousand of them in a cluster, but connected through the Sensornet as well as a physical network of roads and green corridors—"

"Wait. Let's explore your metaphor a bit more, Mahu—the leaves at the sides of the road—positive social change always comes from the margins, but islets of resistance in the mainstream are also important—"

"Can we think about future cities instead of politics just for a minute?"

"Everything is political, Mahu, you know that!"

It was not clear to them at the moment in the café how this vision would grow and change with time and experience, but that was when it first took root in their minds. Networked *bastis*, connected by green corridors, each settlement embedded with sensors, farm towers replacing conventional agriculture. Such settlements would spring up in different parts of the country and the world. Former agricultural lands would return to the wilderness, or to subsistence farming, repairing the damage done to the biosphere's life-maintaining systems.

"What I want to know," Mahua said, returning to the present, "is whether an eco-*basti* like I'm planning, Ashapur, can produce its own microclimate. And how many such microclimates, if networked right, can shift the climate on a larger scale? Like my leaves taking over a road? Or a bacterial biofilm forming?"

But when Ashapur had finally started becoming reality, when its buildings and green areas started producing data, Raghu left. He had helped Mahua design and embed sensors in the walls and windows, trees and byways. He had worked on the teams for the suntowers, the most efficient solar energy system ever built. One could walk the *basti* with a Shell unit and a data visor, and information from a thousand sensors would flow into their receivers. They could read energy use, temperature, humidity, carbon flows, the lot. But something had been bothering Raghu. He got moody and sullen, and Mahua realized she had to let him follow his demons. He would come back when he was ready.

Then, when Ashapur was about halfway done, she got a chance to spend six months in Mumbai on a city-sensorizing project.

In the café veranda, there was litter blowing in the wind. People were leaving with paper cups in hand, bags on shoulders. In another hour, the emergency sirens would be blaring the arrival of the great storm. Mahua had just finished talking to her grandmother in Delhi, reassuring her that she would go to a shelter soon. "Yes, Nani, I will be all right, don't worry." The current predictions indicated that the cyclone would make landfall about a hundred kilometres north of Mumbai, although it was well known that storms could change course near land very quickly.

On an impulse, she unhooked her Shell and removed her visor, stopping the data streams that fed into her mind every spare moment. She sat breathing, feeling naked without the sensor gear, letting the sounds and sensations of the world waft through her, the old-fashioned way. It had been years since she had played the old game of deliberately letting go, with each breath, a sense of her limited self in order to sport with clouds, waves, and other beings. How strange it felt!

There was the wind, lifting dust and the folds of yesterday's newspaper, and she could see the dust motes forming shapes, like myriad tiny arms turning sheets of newspaper over and over for some invisible reader. With each unfolding, the papers sighed and whispered. The wind said, "I'm just a breath at this moment, but in a few minutes, I will be a supercyclone."

There was a tree near her table, leaning a little over her like a dancer caught in a slantwise twirl. The drought had taken most of its leaves, and now its bare branches rattled in the wind. Looking up, she saw the last leaf detach itself from a branch and float unhurriedly down, this way and that, landing to the left of her teacup. It seemed to glow against the dark metal table, trembling for a moment in the breeze. The tip had frayed into a fine lace of veins and branches, but the rest was intact, its very centre still green. It waited, like a gift unopened.

She remembered the leaves of another tree accumulating in the cracks of an old roadway, some years ago in Delhi. Her horoscope in the morning paper, *that* paper rolling around in the wind, had said she would receive a gift from a stranger. She smiled. "Thanks," she said to the tree, standing up, pocketing the leaf.

She walked to the water-taxi stand, a covered ledge that had once been a first-floor veranda. The water slapped against the building with a hard, choppy rhythm. The wind was now whipping up in great gusts, and the clouds were low and dark, although it was the middle of the afternoon. Nervously, she looked around, the canal was empty; she must have missed the last of the water taxis. Just then, a small barge came into sight. There were shapes huddled on it, and a single figure was pushing a pole with long, unhurried strokes.

"*Arre!*" she called. She was surprised to find that the bargeman was a thin boy in a pair of worn shorts, his half-naked body as dark as hers. The others in the barge were children and a couple of old women who sat hunched against the wind gusts in old shawls.

That was when she first met Mohsin. At the moment, he was only another street urchin, with a shock of straight hair and a gap-toothed, wide grin. The metro had been shut down, its entrances sealed against the expected flood. After he dropped her off at the first share-a-ride on dry land, she had asked his name. She waved, never thinking she would see the kid again.

The cyclone, in defiance of meteorological predictions, made landfall that evening in the heart of the city. The winds howled all night, and there were loud crashing sounds as though a party of destructive giants had been let loose. The rain came down hard. Never had the city seen a storm such as this. The lights went out, and throughout the night the storm unleashed its power.

In the afternoon of the next day, the winds died down. Mahua stepped from her small rented room into a changed world.

Mumbai was ravaged. There was shattered glass underfoot and broken windows in the intact buildings. The storm surges were so high that the entire lower part of the city, all the new highways and office blocks and high-rises, were under several feet of water. The sewers had backed up, and overflowing rivers carried raw sewage and tons of trash into the streets. The cyclone had not spared the rich—the opulent minarets of Billionaires' Row lay toppled, concrete blocks like felled giants, tangled with tree branches, silk curtains, and the bodies of hundreds of staff. The rich had escaped in helicopters. The city leaders returned with their mafia, cracking down on the looters and the desperate, using whatever means at hand to protect their property, but the rest of the city lay abandoned.

In the midst of the devastation, Mahua found herself volunteering with a rescue group that was an offshoot of a local cooperative called Hilo Mumbai. They were not like other groups she had come across, a motley mix of autorickshaw drivers, some laid-off young actors, retired schoolteachers, street cleaners, and students. How had they come together? Through a poetry workshop for Mumbai's underprivileged, one of the schoolteachers explained. An elderly autorickshaw driver, Hemant, had started it in Dharavi years ago, and it was still running, with offshoots all over the city.

Along with Hilo Mumbai, Mahua searched through the rubble for survivors, helped transport the injured to local clinics, and dispensed essential supplies when they could get them. The stench of rotting corpses, the cholera outbreaks in the lower parts of the city, made daily life nearly impossible. But the members of Hilo Mumbai worked and laughed and wept together, yelled at and comforted each other—and kept working. Something shifted in Mahua then. She had thought that getting educated and rising into the ranks of the urban middle class was the only way to bring change to the world. But here were people who didn't have half her education or means, and look at them! She remembered something Raghu had said a few years ago—that change, positive social change, came from the margins. Maybe sometimes that was true. She needed to talk to him, but he was still out of touch, wandering the country.

Months later, back in Delhi, she found the leaf from the tree near the café between the pages of a notebook. It had almost completely worn down to a fine and delicate web. The rest of the leaf matter was a brown powder that had stained the pages. She picked it up by the stem and held it against the light. A *web—the parts connected to make the whole*. Then she put it back and closed the book.

She thought of the great storm, the towers of the rich toppled by the cyclone. Poetry in the midst of the grimness of rescue work. *Maybe I'll go back there someday.*

In the meantime, there was Ashapur. It grew slowly. A marriage of ancient and modern, the buildings rounded, thick-walled, made from mud, straw, and rice husk, the inner roads for people and bicycles, the outer ones for buses that connected them to the greater city. Here, there was room for groves of jamun and neem trees, for gardens on the building walls and roofs. Each domicile held families related by blood and by choice, up to fifty people under one roof, cooking together in large common kitchens.

The Sensornet connected building to building, and wearing a Shell unit or data visor allowed a person to eavesdrop on the data flow: the carbon capture rates of green corridors, fluctuations in the biodiversity index, the conversations between buildings and the energy grid. The city government had donated the space because the site was a refuse dump at the edge of a dying Yamuna, and the deal was that the *basti* would displace the slum that had grown on the dump. Mahua kept her promise by inviting the slum dwellers to be the first residents of Ashapur. They were refugees from the coastal areas of Bangladesh, Bengal and Odisha, escaping violence and privation, as well as the rising seas and salinization of arable land. They brought to the project their survival skills, their traditions and cultures, their ingenuity and desire to learn. Now they had become the *basti*'s first residents.

When she and her grandmother had almost given up hope of seeing Raghu again—he had been traveling the country for several years now with hardly a message or call to break the silence—he appeared on their doorstep as abruptly as he had left. Over a vast lunch, he told them about living with rebel groups, tailing corporate mafias, living with tribals in the still-surviving forests, joining a maverick scientist's efforts to free a river trapped under a town. He looked abashed when Mahua's grandmother scolded him for his long silence.

"Naniji, I'm going to do better from now on. I'll ask your forgiveness first, then commit the crime!"

"What mischief are you planning now, you reckless boy?"

"I'm going on an even greater journey, Naniji! Across the world—to Brazil!"

He took Mahua out for a drink and explained. "Mahua, you've done fantastic work here in Ashapur. But in my travels, I kept thinking—there is one gap we haven't jumped, between the Sensornet and the web of life itself. Then, an idea came to me in a Gond village in MP. I want to sensorize an entire forest. Not just sensors in trees, measuring carbon capture, but sensors measuring a hundred things in a whole forest. The biggest remaining forest on Earth is the best place to start. That's why I'm going to the Amazon."

She stared at him, stunned. He grinned at her. "The thing is, Gaia theorists—I mean the old idea of Earth as an organism, not fucking Gaiacorp—Gaia theorists have long maintained that the Earth is like a superorganism. That the fungal network through which trees in a forest communicate—which you talked about sensorizing in Ashapur last week—might result in an emergent large-scale intelligence, a thinking forest, that we can't yet recognize because we can't conceptualize it. So, sitting in that Gond village, I got the idea that sensorizing a forest is only the first step. Maybe if the sensors are networked right, we can get the forest to become *aware* of the Sensornet to communicate with it, and therefore with us!"

His eyes shone. "Imagine, Mahua, the forests of the Sahyadris, the
Terai, the Amazon, they're all in trouble because of climate change.
Droughts and species extinction. The web of life is collapsing. If we
could only communicate with a forest! If it could tell us what was happening in time for us to save it—"

"But we can already figure that out from the sensor data, Raghu!
And we still haven't solved the problem of scaling up the *bastis*, and I
think that's more important at the moment—"

That was the last she had seen of him. There had been a few letters
from Rio de Janeiro and Manaus, but they had got more and more
infrequent until she stopped expecting them. After that, silence. More
than forty years of it.

In that time, she had seen most of the old megapolises die through
the combined machinations of extreme weather and human greed. She
had seen hundreds of Ashapurs rise on the ruins, each adapted to its
local ecology, yet linked together via the large-scale Sensornet. She had
wanted to tell Raghu that despite a decade of killer heat waves in Delhi,
the *basti* clusters might just have shifted the regional climate in the right
direction. *Maybe we averted that future you saw in the simulator.* There
was so much she had wanted to share with him! The subcontinent had
gone through a long period of chaos and even now, there were mass star-
vations, violent conflicts, in towns and provinces ruled by brutal mafias
where life was precarious. But everywhere else, she could see the fruits
of a million mutinies, experiments in alternative ways of living and being, the work and sweat and tears that had resulted in the Great Turning.

She was grateful she had lived to see the change. That she had
been a part of it, a catalyst, should have been a source of satisfaction
to her now in her old age. But for a few years she had become disen-
chanted with her work. Not that it hadn't been important, but she was
dissatisfied, impatient with her own thoughts and ideas. She would
look at her fine, dark hands, see the lines on her face, feel the ache in
her knees, and she would be filled with wonder. The muscles of her
heart, her limbs and sinews, had served her without many complaints
through the long arc of her life. Now, with these aches and tremors,

lines and wrinkles, her body was telling her something. A reminder of mortality, yes, but something else. For some time now, she had stopped wearing her Shell or her data visor, wanting to listen without intermediaries to the subtle speeches of her physical self.

And now a journalist was coming to interview her with "some information" about her old friend, Raghu.

The journalist, one Rafael Silva, had come and gone. Upon arriving, Mr. Silva had handed her a carved wooden box, one that she immediately recognized as a gift she had given Raghu before his trip to Brazil. It was meant to hold odds and ends and, in fact, it contained a couple of broken Shells, a small wooden peg, an abstract wooden carving, several sensor cells and optical wires, and a sheet of paper filled with Raghu's handwriting. Wrapped in a leaf, secured with twine, was a five-centimetre long lock of grey hair with a few black strands.

Mr. Silva had been covering a gathering of Amazonian tribal leaders near the city of Manaus, he said. The recent droughts in the Amazon and changing water and weather patterns had caused the tribes to come together to share knowledge. He had struck up a conversation with an elder of the local Dessana tribe. Upon learning that Mr. Silva was a well-travelled journalist, the elder had produced the box. It had been handed to him by a member of a remote tribe in the Amazon's interior over a year ago, who told them of a stranger and foreigner living with them for several years. The stranger had died from a gunshot wound inflicted during a raid by a gold mining company about two years before that. Thirteen people from the tribe had also been killed. Dying, the stranger's last wish had been that the box be delivered to a city so that somebody could send it to his people in a far country.

The name scrawled on the box was Mahua's, and the address was her old one in Ashapur. The box had taken two years to travel from the interior of the rain forest to the city. Mr. Silva had been so intrigued that he had added India to his itinerary of a trip to southeast Asia. He wanted to deliver the box in person.

"I am so grateful," Mahua said when Mr. Silva had finished. She wiped her tears. "Thank you for coming all this way."

"My pleasure," Rafael Silva said. After that, she was glad to answer his questions about her life and work, and her association with Raghu. The household gave him a meal, and a place to stay the night, and then he left the next morning.

All of the next day, Mahua read and reread the writing on the sheet of paper, held the broken Shell, the lock of his hair in its package of leaf and twine. She thought of the leaf falling from some great Amazonian tree, of the hands that would have picked it up. She caressed the leaf, which was dark green and waxy.

Dear Mahu,

I have forgotten how to communicate in this language, so forgive me.

I came to the Amazon with our technology because I wanted to know the language of the leaves and the animals. I wanted to talk to the forest itself. But after a few years, I realized that the sensors only answer the questions you already know to ask. How do you know what other questions are there? I have lived in the forest with my guides and companions, and through them I have learned that there is a language before language that the Earth speaks.

The Amazon once had great settlements along the river, civilizations that never forgot their relationship to the whole, and so they existed for millennia without collapsing—until the Europeans came. No trace was left of them after their destruction except for a few shards of pottery because everything they made was from the forest, and the ruins were absorbed into it. How did they know how to live like this, without modern technology? To learn the answer, I had to learn what the forest had to tell me, merely as human, as an earthling. I came intending to save it, but it saved me instead. Now, I repay my debt by giving myself back to the Amazon. But I was raised by the air and

water and soil of my first home, and so some part of me should
return there. Will you take this lock of hair, burn or bury it in
a forest somewhere near you? Forgive me for not being there for
you these many years.

I hope Naniji lived a long life. There has never been a day
I have not thought of you. I am at peace now.

Raghu

It would have taken him enormous effort to write this missive.
From the shapes of the letters, she knew that his fingers had trembled.
There was a faint rust-coloured stain in one corner of the page. In
the evening she told the family, "Call Ikram for me. I want to go out
tomorrow."

The sense of waiting for something that had come upon her some
time ago was turning into a feeling of impending arrival.

Ikram's boat edges away from the river toward the sea. He is a lanky
youth with a serious mien, Mohsin's grandson. She sits in the middle
of the boat under the canopy, Raghu's box on her knees. The day is
suffused with a silver light, the sun is behind the clouds. There will
be no rain today, but perhaps the monsoon will build up again tomorrow. The steep, wind-battered slopes of the Mumbai Archipelago are
covered with the faintest purple blush. The karvi flowers are starting to
bloom, obeying their eight-year cycle.

Mahua feels as though Raghu is with her, in this boat. She is
showing him the drowned city, the towers like slender pencils over a
smudge of old, squat, shorter buildings. It is hot and humid. *Look, the*
sea-lanes are busy with the boats of the fisherfolk and water taxis bring-
ing people and goods from the southern coast. Ahead and to their right,
a skyscraper is slowly tilting into the water. Wagers have been made on
when the whole structure will succumb to the sea, but the sea keeps
its secrets.

The hills of the five islands of Mumbai rise to her left. As they turn into a channel, hugging the shore, she sees the shrine of Baba Khizr on the rooftop of an old building, only a metre above the water's surface. It is surrounded by boatloads of people seeking his blessings. From here she can see all the way up the slope to where Billionaires' Row had once been. The trees, vines, and wild animals have taken over the concrete rubble, and at the very top, there stands a shrine to Samudra Devi, goddess of the ocean.

This is the age of the small gods, she tells Raghu. *Local deities, long-forgotten* pirs. *Even Ram is the Ram of the* vanvaas.

Domiciles covered with vines of vegetables and flowers cluster on the hills of the islands. At the water's edge, boats and rafts rock against their moorings. As the boat glides through the watery thoroughfares, they are greeted with waves and shouts, delayed every few metres by conversation, because she hasn't been out here in a long time, and everyone knows her and Ikram.

The Baba Khizr shrine, she tells Raghu, holding the carved box in her lap, *marks where Mohsin once saw a vision. An old man walking on water, standing on a fish that bore him through the channels of the city toward the open sea.* Mohsin had heard stories of Baba Khizr from his father, a refugee from the mouth of the Indus River in Pakistan. There are similar stories as far-flung as Bihar and Arabia, about a *pir* who was the guardian of the waters, whose feet, when they touched the ground, made flowers bloom.

The boat is moored, and Ikram has helped her off it. They are climbing steadily, although every few minutes she needs to stop for breath. Every breath she breathes, she owes to this ancient planet and its great biogeophysical cycles, the scales of which transcend the mere couple of hundred thousand years of human existence, and all the boundaries of nation and continent. She thinks about dust from the Sahara bringing nutrients to the Amazon rain forest to the west, affecting the Indian monsoons to the east. Her breath comes hard, an intimate entanglement with this vast, unfolding drama. "I'm feeling grateful today," she tells Ikram, who smiles. At long last they are at the forest's edge. The air is cooler here, and a breeze stirs the leaves. She hears, distantly, the trickle of water, and the bell-like call of a koel from deep within the trees. A muddy path runs into the forest.

Ikram is distracted by a jamun tree, heavy with fruit.

"Go on," she says. "Get us some jamuns. I will be all right. I will be at the clearing, where the path forks. Come and find me later."

"You have your wristpad?" he asks.

"I didn't bring anything," she says. "Don't worry, I know this place."

How strange that the river of her life, which has run sometimes parallel, sometimes away from Raghu's, has been flowing toward the same destination as his. She is walking through the forest, to the confluence, the meeting place. There is a clearing that she remembers from a trip a year or two ago that he would like.

She walks slowly. In the clearing, a pale sunlight filters through the clouds, illuminating the karvi flowers. She looks at her dark brown arm holding the box, feels the heat of the day on her skin.

There is a language before language that the Earth speaks, Raghu had said.

Yes, she tells him, *and you can only learn it through the body*.

An animal in a forest, that's what she is at this moment, susceptible to danger and death, but her senses are coming alive to everything. The pattern of light and shadow, the humming of an insect, the cooing of a wood dove, the distant call of a troop of monkeys. Everything about her, from her dark skin to her facial features, has been shaped by her people's particular adaptation to their environment: the slant of the sunlight, the temperature of the air. She feels the crushing weight of the centuries of abuse and exploitation. It is there in the DNA of her cells, in the stories of her grandmother, in the loss of her mother at an early age, in Kalpana Di's suicide. The pain stabs her with such intensity that she thinks she might faint. She leans against the trunk of a tree and holds Raghu's box to her chest.

Mahua opens Raghu's box and takes out the folded leaf. Setting the box on a branch, she unrolls the twine, opens the leaf, and strokes, once, the lock of hair. Then she ties up the bundle again, and looks for a place where the earth is soft from the last rain. With a stick from the

underbrush, she digs a small hole where she places the little package.   **451**
She covers it up again with earth.

Go free, she says to Raghu, and to Kalpana Di. She straightens slowly. Her back aches, her legs ache. All this climbing, she'd better get used to it again. Maybe it's time this old woman learned some new lessons. She cannot own the victories of her grandmother's people — the newly formed Santhal province with its ideal of reverence for the web of life, its model of communities governing themselves through consensus — she cannot celebrate such things without owning the pains of struggle and sacrifice that are inscribed in her very own body, her people's history. And it is thus that she is able to see at last, as her people always have seen, the Earth itself: as body, as mother.

At the edge of the clearing, the leaves of the trees murmur in the wind. She feels herself enlarging beyond her own awareness. She is a drop of water trembling on a leaf, she is sunlight on the branch. She doesn't know the names of the trees or the birds, except for a few, but that can come later. For that moment, she is as unselfconsciously free as a soaring bird.

Ikram is calling to her. Mahua clears her throat, takes a long breath. "I'm coming," she calls back.

What a privilege to exist in a universe so dynamic, so complex, that one still has something to learn at the ripe old age of seventy-three. She will sit at the edge of the forest with Ikram and look at the sea. They will eat jamuns, stain their lips and hands with purple juice, and she will tell him about that other great forest, the Amazon, half a world away. She will tell him about Raghu.

GREEN GLASS: A LOVE STORY

E. LILY YU

E. Lily Yu (elilyyu.com) received the Artist Trust/LaSalle Storyteller Award in 2017 and the Astounding Award for Best New Writer in 2012. Her stories have appeared in venues from *McSweeney's* to *Uncanny* and in nine best-of-the-year anthologies, and have been finalists for the Hugo, Nebula, Locus, Sturgeon, and World Fantasy Awards. Her first novel, *On Fragile Waves*, will be published in Fall 2020.

The silver necklace that Richard Hart Laverton III presented to Clarissa Odessa Bell on the occasion of her thirtieth birthday, four months after their engagement and six months before their wedding date, was strung with an irregular green glass bead that he had sent for all the way from the moon. A robot had shot to the moon in a rocket, sifted the dust for a handful of green glass spheres, then fired the capsule to Earth in a much smaller rocket. The glass melted and ran in the heat of reentry, becoming a single thumb-sized drop before its capsule was retrieved from the South China Sea. The sifter itself remained on the moon, as a symbol, Clarissa thought, of their eternal union.

For her thirtieth birthday, they ate lab-raised shrimp and two halves of a peach that had somehow ripened without beetle or worm, bought that morning at auction, the maître d' informed them, for a staggering sum. Once the last scrap of peach skin had vanished down Clarissa's throat, Richard produced the necklace in its velvet box. He fumbled with the catch as she cooed and cried, stroking the green glass. The waiters, a warm, murmuring mass of gray, applauded softly and admiringly.

Clarissa and Richard had known each other since the respective ages of six and five, when Clarissa had poured her orange juice down the fresh white front of Richard's shirt. This had been two decades before the citrus blight that spoiled groves from SoCal to Florida, Clarissa always added when she told this story, before eyebrows slammed down like guillotines.

They had attended elementary, middle, and high school together, hanging out in VR worlds after school. Clarissa rode dragons, and Richard fought them, or sometimes it was the other way round, and this taught them grammar and geometry. Sometimes Clarissa designed scenarios for herself, in which she saved islands from flooding, or villages from disease. She played these alone, while Richard shot aliens.

These intersections were hardly coincidental. In all of Manhattan there were only three elementary schools, four middle schools, and two high schools that anybody who was anybody would consider for their children.

College was where their paths diverged: Richard to a school in Boston, Clarissa to Princeton, with its rows and ranks of men in blistering orange. She sampled the courses, tried the men, and found all of it uninspiring.

The working boys she dated, who earned sandwich money in libraries and dining halls, exuded fear from every pore. There was no room for her on the hard road beside them, Clarissa could tell; they were destined for struggle, and perhaps someday, greatness. The children of lawyers, engineers, and surgeons opened any conversation with comments on estate planning and prenups, the number of children they wanted, and the qualities of their ideal wives, which Clarissa found embarrassingly gauche. And those scions of real power and money danced, drank, and pilled away the hours: good fun for a night but soon tedious.

Several years after her graduation, her path crossed with Richard's. Clarissa was making a name for herself as a lucky or savvy art investor, depending on whom you asked, with a specialty in buying, restoring, and selling deaccessioned and damaged art from storm-battered museums. She had been invited to a reception at a rooftop sculpture garden, where folk art from Kentucky was on display. Absorbed in the purple and orange spots of a painted pine leopard, she did not notice the man at her elbow until he coughed politely and familiarly. Then she saw him, truly saw him, and the art lost its allure.

Holding their thin-stemmed wineglasses, they gazed down from the parapets at the gray slosh of water below. It was high tide, and the sea lapped the windows of pitch-coated taxis. Clarissa speculated on whether the flooded-out lower classes would switch entirely to paddleboats, lending New York City a Venetian air; and whether the rats in subways and ground-floor apartments had drowned in vast numbers or moved upwards in life. Richard suggested that they had instead learned to wear suits and to work in analysis in the finance sector. Then, delicately, with careful selections and excisions, they discussed the previous ten years of their lives.

As servers in sagging uniforms slithered like eels throughout the crowd, distributing martinis and glasses of scotch, Clarissa and Richard discovered, with the faint ring of fatedness, that both were single, financially secure, possessed of life insurance, unopposed to prenuptial agreements, anxious to have one boy and one girl, and crackling with attraction toward each other.

"I know it's unethical to have children," Clarissa said, twisting her fingers around her glass. "With the planet in the shape it's in—"

"You deserve them," Richard said. "*We* deserve them. It'll all be offset, one way or another. The proposed carbon tax—"

His eyes were a clear, unpolluted blue. Clarissa fell into them, down and down.

There was nothing for it but to take a private shell together. Giggling and shushing each other like teenagers, since Clarissa, after all, was supposed to be assessing the art, and Richard evaluating a candidate for his father's new venture, they slipped toward the stairs.

"Hush," Clarissa said, as the bite of cigarette smoke reached her. Two servers were sneaking a break of their own, up on top of the fragile rooftop bar.

"Poison tide today," one said, "up from the canal. Don't know how I'll get home now."

"Book a cargo drone."

"That's half our pay!"

"Then swim."

"Are you swimming?"

"I'm sleeping here. There's a janitorial closet on—well, I'm not telling you which floor."

Clarissa eased the stairwell door shut behind her.

As they descended to the hundredth level, where programmable plexiglass bubbles waited on their steel cables, Clarissa and Richard quietly congratulated each other on their expensive but toxin-free method of transport.

The lights of the city glimmered around them as their clear shell slid through the electric night. One block from Richard's building, just as Clarissa was beginning to distinguish the sphinxes and lions on its marble exterior, he covered her small, soft hand with his.

Before long, they were dancing the usual dance: flights to Ibiza, Lima, São Paulo; volunteer trips to the famine-racked heartlands of wherever; luncheons at Baccarat and dinners at Queen Alice; afternoons at the rum-smelling, dusty clubs that survived behind stone emblems and leaded windows. And one day, at a dessert bar overlooking the garden where the two of them had rediscovered each other, Richard presented Clarissa with the diamond ring that his great-grandmother, then grandmother, then aunt had worn.

"It's beautiful," she breathed. All the servers around them smiled gapped or toothless smiles. Other patrons clapped. How her happiness redounded, like light from the facets of a chandelier, in giving others a taste of happiness as well!

"Three generations of love and hard work," Richard said, sliding the diamond over her knuckles. "Each one giving the best opportunities to their children. We'll do that too. For Charles. For Chelsea."

Dimly Clarissa wondered when, exactly, they had discussed their future children's names; but there was nothing wrong with Charles or Chelsea, which were perfectly respectable, and now Richard's fingers were creeping under the silk crepe of her skirt, up the inside of her stockinged thigh, and she couldn't think.

A week later all three pairs of parents held a war council, divided the wedding between them, and attacked their assignments with martial and marital efficiency. Clarissa submitted to a storm of taffeta and chiffon, peonies and napkins, rosewater and calligraphy. She was pinched and prodded and finally delivered to a French atelier, the kind that retains, no matter what the hour, an unadulterated gloom that signifies artistry. Four glasses of champagne emerged, fuming like potions. A witchlike woman fitted Clarissa for the dress, muttering in Czech around a mouthful of pins.

Then, of course, came the rocket, robot, and drone, and Richard's green glass bead on its silver chain.

And everything was perfect, except for one thing.

A taste—a smell—a texture shimmered in Clarissa's memory of childhood, cool and luminous and lunar beside the sunshine of orange juice.

"Ice cream," Clarissa said. "We'll serve vanilla ice cream in the shape of the moon."

This was the first time Clarissa had spoken up, and her Mim, in whose queendom the wedding menu lay, caught her breath, while Kel, her father's third wife, and Suzette, Richard's mother, arched one elegant, symmetrical eyebrow apiece.

"I don't really know—" her Mim began to say.

Clarissa said, "It's as close as anyone can get to the moon without actually traveling there. And the dress is moon white. Not eggshell. Not ivory. Not seashell or bone."

Kel said, "I think the decorations will be enough. We have the starfield projector, the hand-blown Earth, the powder floor—"

"Little hanging moons of white roses," Suzette added. "Plus a replica of Richard's robot on every table. Isn't that enough?"

"We're having ice cream," Clarissa said. "The real thing, too. Not those soy sorbets that don't melt, or coconut-sulfite substitutes. Ice cream."

"Don't you think that's a bit much?" her Mim said. "You *are* successful, and we *are* very fortunate, but it's generally unwise to put that on display."

"I disagree with your mother in almost everything," Kel said, "but in this matter, she's right. Where in the world would we find clean milk? And uncontaminated eggs? As for vanillin, that's in all the drugstores, but it's a plebian flavor, isn't it?"

"Our people don't have the microbiomes to survive a street egg," Suzette said. "And milk means cancer in ten years. What will you want next? Hamburgers?"

"I'll find what I need," Clarissa said, fingering her necklace. The moon glass was warm against her skin. Richard could surely, like a magician, produce good eggs from his handkerchief.

Synthetic vanillin was indeed bourgeois, and thus out of the question. Clarissa took three shells and a boat, rowed by a black man spitting blood and shrinking into himself, to the Museum of Flavors. This was a nondescript office building in the Bronx whose second-floor window had been propped open for her.

Whatever government agency originally funded it had long since been plundered and disbanded. Entire crop species, classes of game birds, and spices now existed only in these priceless, neglected vaults. The curator was only too happy to accept a cash transfer for six of the vanilla beans, which he fished out of a frozen drawer and snipped of their tags. He was an old classmate from Princeton, who lived in terror that the contents of his vaults might be made known, attracting armed hordes of the desperate and cruel. But Clarissa, as he knew well, was discreet.

The amount exchanged approached the value of one of her spare Rothkos. Clarissa made a mental note to send one to auction.

Richard, dear darling Richard, had grumblingly procured six dozen eggs by helicopter from Semi-Free Pennsylvania by the time she returned. He had been obliged to shout through a megaphone first, while the helicopter hovered at a safe distance, he said, before the farmer in question set his shotgun down.

"As for the milk," he said, "you're on your own. Try Kenya?"

"If the bacteria in a New York egg would kill Mim," Clarissa said, "milk from a Kenyan cow—"

"You're right. You sure a dairy substitute—"

"Know how much I paid for the vanilla beans?"

She told him. He whistled. "You're right. No substitutes. Not for this. But—"

Clarissa said, "What about Switzerland?"

"There's nothing of Switzerland left."

"There are tons of mountains," Clarissa said. "I used to ski them as a girl. Didn't your family ski?"

"We preferred Aspen."

"Then how do you know there's not a cow hiding somewhere?"

"They used dirty bombs in the Four Banks' War. Anything that survived will be radioactive."

"I didn't know about the dirty bombs."

"It was kept out of the news. A bad look."

"Then how—"

"Risk analysts in cryptofinance hear all kinds of unreported things."

The curl of his hair seemed especially indulgent, his smile soft and knowledgeable. She worried the glass bead on its chain.

"I'll ask around," Clarissa said. "Someone must know. I've heard rumors of skyr, of butter—even cheese—"

"Doesn't mean there's a pristine cow out there. Be careful. People die for a nibble of cheese. I'll never forgive you if you poison my mother."

"You wait," Clarissa said. "We'll find a cow."

Because the ice cream would be a coup d'état, in one fell swoop staking her social territory, plastering her brand across gossip sites, and launching the battleship of her marriage, Clarissa was reluctant to ask widely for help. It was her life's work, just as it had been her Mim's, to make the effortful appear effortless. Sweating and scrambling across Venezuelan mesas in search of cows would rather spoil the desired effect.

So she approached Lindsey, a college roommate, now her maid of honor, who was more family than friend, anyhow. Lindsey squinted her eyes and said she recalled a rumor of feral milkmaids in Unincorporated Oregon.

Rumor or not, it was worth following. Clarissa found the alumni email of a journalist, was passed on to a second, then a third. Finally she established that indeed, if one ventured east of the smallpox zone that stretched from Portland to Eugene, one might, with extraordinary luck, discover a reclusive family in Deschutes that owned cows three generations clean. But no one had seen any of them in months.

"You're, what do you call it, a stringer, right? For the *Portland Post-Intelligencer*? Independent contractor, 1099? Well, what do you say to doing a small job for me? I'll pay all expenses—hotels, private drone—plus a per diem, and you'll get a story out of it. I just need fifteen gallons, that's all."

Icebox trains still clanked across the country over miles of decaying railbeds, hauled by tractors across gaps where rails were bent or sleepers rotted though, before being threaded onto the next good section. Their cars carried organ donations, blood, plasma, cadavers for burial or dissection, and a choice selection of coastal foods: flash-frozen Atlantic salmon fished from the Pacific, of the best grade, with the usual number of eyes; oysters from a secret Oregon bed that produced no more than three dozen a year; New York pizza, prepared with street mozzarella, for the daredevil rich in San Francisco; and Boston clam chowder without milk, cream, or clams. Her enterprising journalist added fifteen gallons of Deschutes milk in jerry cans to the latest shipment. Clarissa gnawed one thumbnail to the quick while she waited for the jerry cans to arrive.

Arrive they did, along with unconscionable quantities of sugar.

All that was left was the churning. Here Lindsey and three other bridesmaids proved the value of their friendship beyond any doubt, producing batch after creamy batch of happiness. Two days before the wedding, they had sculpted a moon of vanilla ice cream, complete with craters and silver robot-shaped scoop.

Ninety people, almost everyone who mattered, attended the wedding. The priest, one of six available for the chapel, still healthy and possessed of his hair and teeth, beamed out of the small projector.

"I promise to be your loving wife and moon maiden," Clarissa said.

"I promise to be the best husband you could wish for, and the best father anyone could hope, for the three or four or however many children we have."

"Three?" Clarissa said faintly. "Four?" But like a runaway train, her vows rattled forward. "I promise—"

Afterwards they mingled and ate. Then the moon was brought out to exclamations, camera flashes, and applause. The ice cream scoop excavated the craters far faster than the real robotic sifter could have.

Clarissa, triumphant, whirled from table to table on Richard's arm.

"Know what's etched on the robot?" she said. *Clarissa O. Bell and Richard H. Laverton III forever.*

"So virtual," Monica said. "I'd kill for a man like that."

"For what that cost," Richard said, "we could have treated all of New York for hep C, or bought enough epinephrine to supply the whole state. But some things are simply beyond price. The look in Clarissa's eyes—"

Glass shattered behind them. A dark-faced woman wearing the black, monogrammed uniform of the caterers Clarissa's Mim had hired swept up the shards with her bare hands.

"Sorry," the woman said, "I'll clean it up. Please, ignore me, enjoy yourselves—"

"Are you crying?" Clarissa said, astounded. "At my wedding?"

"No, no," the woman said. "These are tears of happiness. For you."

"You must tell me," Clarissa said, the lights of the room soft on her skin, glowing in the green glass around her neck. The bulbs were incandescent, selected by hand for the way they lit the folds of her lace and silk.

"It's nothing. Really, nothing. A death in the family. That's all."

"That's terrible. Here, leave that glass alone. This'll make you feel much better."

She scooped a generous ball of ice cream into a crystal bowl, added a teaspoon, and handed the whole thing over.

"Thank you so much," the woman said. This time, Clarissa was sure, her tears were purely of joy.

Another server came over with dustpan and brush and swept the glass shards up in silence.

Clarissa began to serve herself a second bowl of ice cream as well, so the woman would not feel alone, but Richard took the scoop from her hand and finished it for her.

His cornflower eyes crinkling, he said, "You made everyone feel wonderful. Even my mother. Even Mel. Even that poor woman. You're a walking counterargument for empathy decay."

"What's—"

"Some researchers think you can't be both rich and kind. Marxist, anarchist nonsense. They should meet you."

The ice cream was sweet, so very sweet, and cold. Clarissa shivered for a moment, closing her eyes. For a moment her future flashed perfectly clear upon her, link by silver link: how a new glass drop would be added to her chain for each child, Chelsea and Charles and Nick; how Richard would change, growing strange and mysterious to her, though no less lovable, never, no less beloved; how she would set aside her childish dreams of saving the world, and devote herself to keeping a light burning for her family, while all around them the world went dark.

She opened her eyes.

It was time to dance. Richard offered his arm.

Off they went, waltzing across the moon, their shoes kicking up lunar dust with each step. The dance had been choreographed ages before they were born, taught to them with their letters, fed to them along with their juice and ice cream, and as they danced, as everyone at their wedding danced, and the weeping server was escorted out, and the acrid, acid sea crept higher and higher, there wasn't the slightest deviation from what had been planned.

SECRET STORIES OF DOORS

SOFIA RHEI

Sofia Rhei (sofiarhei.com) has published more than thirty-five books, including the short fiction collection *Everything is Made of Letters*, Minotauro Celsius Award–winning novel *Róndola*, and *Espérame en la última página*, a ghost story about books. Her poetry has been awarded the Dwarf Stars Award and been short-listed for the Rhysling Award. She is currently working on a multi-utopian political satire about Europe, *Newropia*.

To Chús Arellano

The controversy around Sor Assumpció's work is, indeed, one of the most interesting cases of soft apology of Satanism in the 18th century. The reason given by her advocates was the fact that the book perfectly followed the pattern of a cautionary tale, giving the appropriate piece of advice at every moment, and punishing the characters when they did make a bad choice, even if the possibility of a Christian redemption was always left open. The attacks were centered on the portrait of the friendly and charming figure of evil, arguing that such a fascinating and warm personality would attract, rather than repel, young or suggestible readers.

—Leopoldo de Manresa
The Borders Between Faith and Heresy in the Inquisition Times, Salamanca, 1907

Joan Perucho had spent the night working, bent over his bench at home. He lived in a microscopic apartment in the Gracia district, and most of the cupboards were filled with writing machines, artisan presses, and homemade contraptions such as the paper eroder or the gelatine photocopier. He was creating happily, humming a tune, and barely noticing the lack of sleep.

Most of the Benedictine sister's works were hidden by the Mother Superior when the Inquisition began the investigation. Some of the theatre plays were lost forever. Fortunately, the cautionary tales were already in circulation, though they became a risky business for the printer. He continued to sell *Secret Stories of Doors* under the counter, accepting the risk of prosecution if caught.

> —Leopoldo Galván
> *Cursed Poets in the Spanish Church*, Valladolid, 1929

The alarm clock startled him. He had forgotten about it, absorbed in the process of dyeing a fake newspaper page with black tea, to make it look older.

Fire at School in Sant Pere Mes Baix Street

Although the fire was rapidly controlled, two firemen lost their lives fighting the flames. The fire was caused by a coal brazier the doorman did not extinguish properly. One wall caught light, revealing that it was made of wood; behind it, the firemen found several hidden books and documents, probably banned during the years of the Inquisition. One of them was a cautionary tale by Sor Assumpció Ardebol, which scholars believed to have been lost forever. The repairs will take a week, during which time there will be no class at the school; parents have been advised to keep their children at home and await instructions.

> —*La Vanguardia*, Barcelona, April 17, 1949

He looked at the documents he had created and smiled, satisfied. This entry in the Encyclopaedia would be one of his biggest personal triumphs. Like the other millions who worked for the Barcelona-based World Encyclopaedia, with their ink-proof dark uniforms, he would have found daily life unbearable without his game of introducing made-up information into the general database. At the beginning, they were just details: a small quote, a fabricated minor character, a picturesque anecdote about a well-known public figure. Over the years, he had managed to introduce more significant apocrypha, giving birth to full, juicy fruit, and even branches and trees of misinformation.

He never kept a record of the fiction. That would be too dangerous, because the aerial police could spy on homes at any moment since the 1969 curtain ban. Joan hid the machines in the white cupboards and got ready for work.

He was about to step out of his apartment when a thin serpent, made of green paper, slithered under his door:

Don't go to work. Go to Carrer de n'Arai instead.

He had heard about these kinds of messages. There was nothing specific written on them, no accusation or even mention of his illicit tinkering. He had heard about traps set by the aerial police: when someone was considered a suspect but there was no way to prove he had transgressed. Skipping work and visiting a suspect place, one of the outsiders' escape enclaves, would be sufficient proof that he was guilty.

No, he must not alter his daily routine. He calmed down after that decision was made. He had been careful, *very* careful, about destroying the fake documents he had produced and scanned. And, as he liked to repeat in his head, as a leitmotif of a life devoted to falsification, it was very hard to prove that something reported once had not actually happened. Especially when most of the historical archives and newspaper libraries were located out of town, sometimes as far as Huesca or Castellón. Perucho used to enjoy those trips, particularly the silence. Aerial police were so abundant in the city that the humming helixes were a permanent noise like a roaring, metallic sea.

Perucho took a look through the window, but no one was there. No flying policeman was observing him from the other side of the regulation-sized clear window. But it felt as if they were always there. The threat of their appearance was almost as daunting as the appearance itself.

Perucho took a deep breath. He had been very careful. He always made sure not to stand out for any reason, neither over- nor underproducing. He studied the statistics and ensured that his productivity matched that of his peers. And, as most of his supervisors did not even understand Spanish or Catalan, he usually generated the false documents in one of those languages.

Of course there were rumors of people being led away by the police and never returning, though Perucho had never seen it happen. In fact, there were no specific rules about being strictly "accurate" and not being a little inventive. Everything was kind of vague and generic, leaving room for a certain lax interpretation of the regulations.

But the main reason for Perucho to ignore the warning and go to work as usual was his deep desire to do so. The project about the fictional Sor Assumpció Ardebol and her nonexistent *Secret Stories of Doors* was perhaps his best creation to date. These projects were his reason to live, the only possible free literary writing in a world where fiction was only allowed in commercial and sanctioned forms: indoctrination, role-model creation, and such.

Most days, Perucho walked from home to work, and he didn't want to make an exception today. He tried not to walk faster or slower than normal and to keep to all his daily routines, such as stopping by the bakery to buy a small *butifarra*-filled roll for lunch.

Ten years before, the Global Government had decided to assign specific functions to several strategically placed cities. Barcelona was chosen to become the Capital of Knowledge. The World Encyclopaedia had been based there since the forties, so it was just a matter of increasing the space and personnel assigned to the task of gathering verifiable data, deciding what was important and what wasn't worth a mention, and classifying it all.

Barcelona had always been a multicultural city, but the arrival of millions of Fundamental Knowledge System employees from all around the globe, in order to cover all the possible languages and dialects both alive and dead, had turned the city into a new, improved Babel.

All the central patios of the blocks in the Ensanche had been *upgraded*, according to the official term, to host twenty-five-story buildings. All of them were identical, and identically filled with the Encyclopaedia workers. The lower levels were full of presses and printers, and technical workers wearing black, ink-proof uniforms. The upper floors, such as the one where Joan Perucho worked, were provided with a linotype machine for each of the editors. These were dressed in anthracite suits: even if they didn't work with ink, and were not at risk of staining themselves, they had to wear a dark color, as if knowledge might also leave a permanent and disgusting stain.

Fear came suddenly, in the form of paranoid thoughts: What if there were an undisclosed control system, a secret body of agents devoted to pursuing the truth and punishing the introducers of false data, determined to send them to humid and squalid prisons that they would never leave again?

Joan Perucho entered the building with his usual smile, repeating to himself the mantra: *it is almost impossible to prove that something has not happened.* In fact, were he assigned to find proof that some book, review, or article had *not* been published, it would take him months. He had never heard of such a commission, and he seriously doubted the Fundamental Knowledge System would use paid work hours to distinguish between documental truth and lies. There was no need to; most of the employees were predictable conformists, bootlickers, as grey as their suits.

As he entered the packed elevator, he felt cold sweat trickle down his nape and tried to calm himself. He went to his linotype, in the Catalan section, casually took out the fake documents, and dispersed them between dozens of genuine ones. Then, as every day, he began to type.

The morning passed without incident. Joan took heart and accelerated the typing of false documents. He had lunch in the workplace and continued introducing spurious lines and lines:

Sor Assumpció Ardebol depicts the darkest streets of old Barcelona under the form of a descent to hell, both literally and metaphorically. El Raval is unknown and risky, a foreign land for decent people, but also the place where a truly satanic encounter can occur. The true risk is not thieves, drug-addicted beggars, or crazy vagabonds, but the "small doors," inadvertent thresholds, often concealed by shadows.

—Juana Torregrosa
Images of Barcelona, Barcelona, 1955

"Perucho," said a monotone, dispassionate voice, "the boss wants to see you in his office. At five."

Perucho tried to control his shaking hands. He was not often called to the director's desk, but it happened sometimes. Maybe this was just for a routine verification:

"Perucho, how is the work going?"

"Very well, sir."

"Have you found enough materials to maintain your daily quota of entries?"

"Yes, sir."

"Would you need another documental trip to Girona?"

"Maybe next month, sir."

The temptation to escape, to run out with some slight excuse, was almost overwhelming. But Joan Perucho had a strong mind. He inhaled deeply, discreetly, and told himself an old joke:

A Catalan was in front of a fishbowl with only a fish in it. Amazingly, when the man looked up, the fish seemed to copy him and went in the same direction. The same thing happened when the man looked in other directions.

A Spaniard, watching the Catalan, went to talk to him.

"This is incredible! Marvelous!" said the Spaniard. "How can you make the fish follow your command?"

"It is very easy," the Catalan answered calmly. "I stare deeply into the eyes of the animal to subject it to my will. The inferior fish mind

acknowledges the superior human mind. With a little practice, I'm sure you can get the same result in no time."

This seemed entirely reasonable to the Spaniard. After all, he had never tried to command a fish before. Surely, it was a piece of cake. He began to stare at the fish deep in the eye.

Ten minutes later, the Catalan man returned to the fishbowl.

"How is it going?" he asked the Spaniard.

The Spaniard turned with a vacant look, his lips pursed in the form of a fish mouth.

"Blub! Blub! Blub!" he gaped.

Perucho laughed to himself. No matter how many times he heard or told the joke, it was still his favorite and never failed to cheer him up. He looked at the big clock on the wall, and saw it was almost four. He had a full hour of work left: if he was going to get caught, he had better finish the project first.

"Some letters?" asked the girl with the trolley, offering him small baskets of metallic vowels and consonants.

"Some 'F's and 'V's, please" answered Perucho.

"¡El bombín! ¡Ha vingut el bombín!" one of the editors whispered in Catalan, as a warning.

El bombín was one of the senior leaders, their boss's boss, if Perucho had gotten it right. He was rarely seen in the office, and when he was, he liked to find fault with the workers. "Sit properly, Balagué!" or "This is not the right way to position your hands over the keyboard, Fontanella. I hope you don't expect the Fundamental Knowledge System Foundation to pay for the medical expenses you will get if you insist on not correcting your posture."

All the editors tensed instantly. Joan Perucho didn't. He was already in a perfect position, as was his habit. He had learned to maintain his spine in a vertical position to avoid back pains and fatigue. Maybe that was the reason el bombín had never made an observation about him. Sometimes Perucho was under the impression that el bombín had a very peculiar sense of humor and that he just enjoyed startling the workers.

But instead of his usual round through the linotypists, *el bombín* went right to the boss's office and closed the door after him. The workers relaxed automatically, except Perucho. He needed three more internal jokes and a little bit of silent meditation to regain his composure.

He typed a last article entitled, "The Portrait of the Devil in Sor Assumpció Ardebol's Work." It was his favorite, the pearl in the crown of the fictional author he had invented. In the article, an equally fictional PhD candidate explained that in the nun's cautionary tales, the devil was always depicted as a person with their right ear missing. The meaning of this characterization would be a metaphor for the people who only want to hear the bad half of the words, the wrong side of every story, and so had a negative perception of human nature.

When the article was done, Perucho took the letter tray, perfectly composed, put it in the plate elevator, and sent it to the printing machine. When that was done, his whole body relaxed. Now his last work would be part of the Encyclopaedia irretrievably. He could be arrested now. He almost welcomed it.

But *el bombín* was still with the boss half an hour later, and then an hour, and then two. At seven, the anthracite editors began to abandon their workplaces. Perucho worked for an additional half hour, which was not unusual for him, waiting for *el bombín* to leave. But it didn't happen.

"Casals," he said to the boss's secretary, "Mr. Coole asked me to come and see him some hours ago."

"Don't worry about it, Perucho. He's still with *el* . . . with Mr. Gladstone. I suspect they'll be a while."

"Are you sure? Because I can wait . . ."

Casals smiled.

"You are too conscientious. Just go home, the boss will still be here tomorrow."

Perucho thanked her and left, light of leg and even lighter of mind.

He had been right all along: there was nothing to worry about. If something were wrong, Casals would know for sure; the boss couldn't find his own shadow without his hyper-efficient secretary. And she was as nice and friendly as she had always been.

He left the building in a state of relieved euphoria. He even whistled a bit. Manipulating information to create his personal world gave
him a wonderful thrill: a spark in the darkness, a color splash in the
grey reality that the world had become after the global disasters at the
end of the fifties.

An aerial agent passed by Perucho and sniffed at him. The boots of
the agent almost touched Perucho's shoulder. However, the presence
didn't feel threatening but reassuring. Things were in order again.

He could go to the nocturnal thrift market, Els Encants, and find
some ancient books to read just for pleasure. Or return to his apartment and begin his next project. Something about spas . . . some ideas
had been bugging him, bubbling away in his mind as if it was the very
hot tub he wanted to talk about.

Yes, he should be doing one of those things. Why then was he
walking in the direction suggested that morning by the paper serpent?
Carrer de n'Arai. Why had he memorized it?

He should be avoiding trouble. Going to the place specified by the
message would be madness. What if the message wasn't just a joke, or
a random bureaucratic trap? What if someone really knew about his
infractions? And, even scarier, what if these unknown friends really
wanted to help him avoid punishment?

But he couldn't help himself. He was doomed, trapped by his own
curiosity, and so walked down to Portaferrissa with a frozen smile of dis-
simulation. Oddly, he was more afraid in the open street than he had been
at the office. Maybe the work space, so familiar, had provided reassurance.

There was no one in the street. When Perucho was younger,
Barcelona had been a vibrant city. He remembered the cinema Les
Delícies, with its crowd of kids, workers, and grandparents; he remembered going to Tibidabo and its spooky museum of automatons, to Parc
de la Ciutadella with its spectacular greenhouse. But that city was lost
forever. The bombs had fallen in a thick rain, devastating blocks and
even entire quarters, erasing a world, an entire age.

He was almost in Portaferrissa. And then, at the corner, he saw an
archer. Partially hidden in shadows, the woman, dressed in the official

uniform of an urban cleaner, was tensing her arm, an arrow pointing at a cat. She looked stressed.

"I don't know what to do," she said. "It's trapped on the roof, meowing constantly. A cat without an owner is a menace to hygiene, a potential pest carrier, and we have already received a complaint from the neighbors. On the other hand . . . He looks so confused. But I can't reach him from the ground. Maybe if I could the poor animal might have a chance . . . The zoo . . . ? Or I could get fired for not killing it."

Perucho felt something tickle his nose, like static or the presence of an intruding insect. It was the taste of the unexpected, of the marvelous. It was so rare, and mixed deliciously with the feeling of fear.

Curiosity killed the cat, Perucho thought immediately, or *qui escolta pels forats, sent els seus pecats* in Catalan: he who pokes around in inappropriate places finds his own sins. In both cases, the wrong, the *devil*, lay in the thirst for the new, for information, knowledge. The archer looked like a personification, or even a *prosopopoeia*, as the ancients might have said, of curiosity herself.

"Maybe you can fire an arrow at the wall, just there, you see? Maybe the cat could use that as a step and get down by himself . . . Then you could catch it."

And then he added, in a whisper.

"Or not."

The woman looked at him.

"You don't want me to kill the cat?"

Perucho had a moment of doubt. A normal citizen would have supported killing the cat, or even threatened the cleaning agent for not fulfilling her duty.

Instead, he said, "No."

"Are you sure?"

"No one needs to die in the name of words."

The archer smiled and then took away her hat, revealing she had no right ear, exactly like the demon in the works of Sor Assumpció Ardebol. She looked at him intently. Perucho felt a shiver.

"Will you come with me?" the archer asked.

"Yes."

At this point, the sensation of being inside one of his own stories outweighed his fear.

Perucho followed his guide through narrow streets and arrived in front of another door, almost invisible among the shadows. He entered the building and, on seeing what was inside, couldn't believe his eyes.

He saw a fully functioning old-fashioned press, hosting every kind of printing device since printing began. Several people were making artisanal papers. There was even a copyist monk, called La Moreneta: a monastic scribe alive and well in 1975.

It was, obviously, a clandestine workshop. The windows were small and translucent, and the walls were designed to absorb any noise. Only in El Raval could a place like this remain hidden. The shadows wrapping all the quarter were simultaneously warning and protection.

And then Perucho saw *el bombín*. He was walking among the industrious workers, and his attitude was very different from the one Perucho was used to. Instead of looking for irregularities and tiny faults, he seemed relaxed. Happy, even. He looked like a completely different person.

"Ah! Perucho, so glad to see you!" he said in Catalan. Perucho hadn't realized *el bombín* was fluent in the traditional language. "Come, come here! There is nothing you need to worry about. Just enjoy watching the amazing crafts of all these artisans, as I do. You will not have much time to relax, since our team of writers are keen to ask you questions . . ."

"Is this *him*?" asked a woman with glasses, dressed in an unusual shade of green.

"Yes! Let me introduce you: Joan Perucho, this is Rosa Fabregat, one of our most brilliant writers."

"Writer . . ."

Perucho savored the taste of the word in his mouth. It was a long time since he had heard it, not to mention pronounced it himself. He felt envious of the young woman.

"Mr. Perucho," she said in Catalan, "I am a big admirer of your work."

Perucho was having difficulty processing the events.

"But I don't have any 'work' . . . I'm just one of the editors of the . . ."

El bombín and Rosa smiled.

"You are an amazing creator. You have built entire literary careers and even provided most of their works. Octavi de Romeu, Pere Serra y Postius and his monster Bernabó . . ."

Perucho felt a shiver of fear course down his spine. The woman was talking about his fictional characters as if they were beloved writers. As if they had really existed outside his imagination.

". . . by the way, I have a question about Bernabó. We know that he has black fur, no mouth, and three eyes. But when he spies on the writer, does he focus all eyes on him or do they move independently?"

"Give Perucho a break, my dear Rosa . . ."

"No, no . . . ," said Perucho. "I've never thought about Bernabó's eyes! It is a beautiful question. Maybe he needs each eye to see a different part of reality—he needs one to see the light and the colors yellow and white, another for the shadows, the blues and greens, and the third for passions, red, purple, pink, magenta. Does this make sense?"

"Then he needs to focus all three eyes on one point at a time . . . Thank you so much, Mr. Perucho."

"You will doubtless get more from him later, Rosa. But for now, he just needs to take in the place."

"Okay," she said, a bit frustrated. "Only one more thing . . . That study about mirrors was . . . simply perfect."

And she left, failing to see how Perucho blushed.

"She's right. And the medieval stories . . . they're memorable," continued *el bombín*. Perucho was immensely flattered that this man had spent so much time studying him.

"Manuel"—and *el bombín* pointed to one of the artists working over a bench—"is working on that codex you profusely described last year."

"I . . . I don't understand. Are you creating false documents following the indications I . . . I made up? Whole ones?"

"That is exactly what we are doing. Amazing, isn't it? You will never get caught as a delinquent because the supposedly fake references you have introduced will actually *exist*. Therefore, your work will prove to be factual."

"I need to sit down," said Perucho.

El bombín and Perucho remained silent for a while after Rosa left.

"She is in charge of the most delicate and poetic books. A passionate reader, and so full of curiosity for life . . ."

"But . . . but why all this effort just to save me . . . All this must have cost a fabulous amount of . . ."

"Just to save you? No. To save literature itself, Perucho. You are not the only one 'spicing up' the Encyclopaedia, even if, may I add, you are one of the best. Some of your other colleagues, whom you will meet, such as our beloved Mr. Cunqueiro, and Marcel Aymé, who is one of the supervisors of the French-language area . . . Others develop their creational worlds in academia, such as the famous Professor . . ."

"Torrente Ballester!" Perucho interrupted. "I've always had a suspicion about his fonts. Some of his themes are too beautiful to be true."

El bombín sighed.

"As if beauty had to be forcibly different from truth . . . I'm afraid such are the times we find ourselves in."

"*Estos bueyes tenemos y con ellos tenemos que arar.*"

There was a long silence.

"Perucho," *el bombín* said, "the history of the last decades was not exactly as they . . . as *we* . . . have officially been told. The powers that be have made their own 'not exactly true' additions to the Encyclopaedia; not as delightful as yours, I should add. As a well-read man, may I assume you are familiar with the name Herbert George Wells?"

Perucho was surprised. He was expecting great revelations about politics, economics . . .

"Yes, he was an English writer."

"What if I were to tell you that he shaped the world as we know it?"

"Well . . . I'd be very surprised."

"In 1935 he wrote a novel . . ."

The word *novel* sounded so beautiful to Perucho. It contained all the freedom and power from the past art.

"The Shape of Things to Come," *el bombín* continued. "It was a cautionary tale, but not of the classic sort, which provides advice merely for the individual. No, this story was about a whole society and depicted a dark future, the consequence of misguided group behavior. The book was moderately successful, but in general was considered an extravagant experiment. Why would a serious writer waste his time depicting hypothetical futures?"

Perucho smiled. That kind of book sounded very appealing to him, but maybe he was not the typical reader.

"Three years later, a man called Orson Welles made a radio broadcast. He loved the work of this writer with a similar surname to his, and planned a practical joke for Halloween. He was a perfectionist, so he enlisted colleagues in different radio stations in Britain, Europe, and even Russia to create the maximum impact. He wanted to demonstrate to his bosses the immense power of the radio."

"But Todos los Santos, 1938 . . . That was the day of the coup d'état in the old US and Britain . . . ," Perucho interrupted.

"Exactly. Except that in the beginning there was no putsch, just a fake radio transmission about one."

Perucho felt overwhelmed.

"This doesn't make any sense. The overthrow of the government was real. It had far-reaching consequences . . ."

"After the radio show, people were scared. Many abandoned the cities. Chaos reigned everywhere. The point was proven: radio had power. But at the moment Orson Welles wanted to explain to the world that it had all been just a practical joke, communications were cut everywhere. One of the radical political parties had seized the opportunity and performed a real coup d'état.

"No one knew what to do. Within a few hours, hastily arranged clandestine meetings took place. Soon, rich oligarchies realized that the new order was far more convenient for them. And the ambitious new leaders arrested Orson Welles. He gave them the book he had drawn inspiration from."

"Are you telling me the shape of the world came from a novel and a radio show?"

"It wasn't that simple. Many agents and interests were involved. But yes, in the end, they thought H. G. Wells's plans were ideal. Why bother to design a new way forward when one had already been mapped out?"

"But you said Wells's novel was a cautionary tale, not a social proposal . . ."

"They took it as a handbook. And it worked. They made both Wells and Welles work for them during the early years, and then set them free as reward for their 'cooperation.'"

"Forced cooperation . . ."

El bombín nodded.

"Let me get this straight," said Perucho. "Are you telling me that a fable and a joke gave rise to this economic system, to our whole society? The same society that has banned fiction itself?"

"They limit new creations precisely because they know the impact stories can have.

"Orson Welles was the creator of the regime's propaganda machines for many years, and he did an amazingly good job under several pen names, such as Kane. Nobody knows what he did after that, maybe he just spent the rest of his life on an island, smoking cigars and fathering children. But we do know what H. G. Wells did. He became an entrepreneur and made big money. After all, he knew all the internal mechanisms of power. And with the help of his friend G. K. Chesterton he built a secret institution destined to protect the creators who, like yourself, my dear Perucho, find a way to continue writing fiction in the most adverse of conditions."

Perucho glanced at the machines, this big workshop dedicated to falsification.

"All this came from Wells's funds?" he said, assimilating the new information.

They stood in silence while Perucho observed the ancient *tórculos*, the amanuensis, the papersmiths. He had so many questions . . . But he was so overwhelmed by the situation that he needed a moment to order his thoughts.

"I need to go for a walk," he said.

El bombín nodded, and gave him the keys of the secret door.

"You can return whenever you wish."

Perucho walked for a long time. The whole city looked different, more intriguing and seductive once he knew the secret Barcelona was hiding. If one clandestine enterprise was working beneath the visible, how many other amazing projects could be living in the shadows?

He arrived at Els Encants and looked among the piles of old books, abandoned and rejected by so many hands before, lying between used clothes and old crocks, and he bought three of them. He could never resist.

The following day, he went to work as usual.

And the next one, too.

The routine slowly regained its familiar rhythm. And then, on the Thursday, *el bombín* came by his workplace.

"Perucho," he said, angrily, "this box is not aligned with the margins. Start again."

The editor looked at him, astonished. The man was the best actor he had ever seen.

"Yes, sir."

That same afternoon, Perucho returned to the narrow streets and found the secret door. He opened it with his key. He found Rosa there, who was very happy to see him.

"And now . . . What? What can I expect? Will my life . . . change?"

Rosa smiled.

"Not necessarily. We have discovered, through the years, that the simplest way to pursue undercover writing is to do exactly as you are doing: not have any cover at all."

"Then . . . after all this . . . I am supposed to go to work tomorrow like any other day, as if this never happened?"

"Yes. Exactly as if this place, all these amazing machines and creators, and our little conversation, were nothing more than . . . a work of fiction."

THIS IS NOT THE WAY HOME

GREG EGAN

Greg Egan (gregegan.net) has published more than sixty short stories and thirteen novels, and has won the Hugo and John W. Campbell Memorial Awards. His recent publications include the novellas *Perihelion Summer* from Tor.com and *Dispersion* from Subterranean Press.

1

When Aisha spotted Jingyi through the window, for a second she thought she was seeing a reflection in the glass. Suited to the neck but bareheaded, her helmet gripped in one hand by her side, Jingyi had to be standing behind her, facing away from her into the room.

But she wasn't.

Aisha knelt on the floor and wept. It was Jingyi who had kept her from giving in to despair. It was Jingyi who had shaped the plan into something real, and found the strength to pursue it. But when she'd faltered, when she'd fallen into doubt herself, all of Aisha's attempts to lift her spirits and restart the virtuous circle of encouragement that had kept them both sane and striving for close to a year had come to nothing.

Aisha sobbed until the grief loosened its hold on her, long enough to grant her a choice: follow Jingyi into the darkness, or step back and try to skirt around the edge of the abyss. She rose to her feet and returned to the crib, then lifted Nuri into her sling. *She could not afford to be crushed. Not by this, not by anything.* Her daughter was fast asleep; Aisha even managed to put their shared suit on without waking her. Then she went out to pack for the trip.

The buggy's trailer, with its open tray, looked like something she might have hired back in Dunedin to move a few pieces of furniture between share-houses in her student days. She didn't shy away from the memory; she pictured Gianni beside her, smiling and teasing her as she fretted over the placement of each item in the tray. The struts were all short enough to fit, but she didn't want them rolling back and forth. She hunted around in the workshop and found some cable ties, then she stood patiently binding the struts into a set of linked bundles that she could anchor to the tray at the corners.

She'd already folded the sheet of glistening silica fibers that she and Jingyi had spent the last four months weaving, but even in this compact form it was so bulky that when she squatted down to pick it up, it blocked her view completely. She fetched a sled with a pull cord, and out onto the regolith.

As Aisha glanced up at the crescent Earth, Nuri woke and started crying. "Shh, shh!" It was impossible to stroke her through the suit, but Aisha managed to nudge breast and baby together, and once Nuri clamped her mouth in place she stopped complaining and just fed, more or less contentedly. "We're going for a drive," Aisha explained. "How about that?"

Jingyi was facing west: the way they'd planned to travel together, chasing the sun. Aisha saw no reason to lay her friend to rest; she must have locked the suit's joints to keep her body upright, so she'd clearly had no desire to end up horizontal in the dirt.

Nuri stopped feeding to grizzle with displeasure, then pungently defecate, but her diapers were as magical as Aisha's and there was nothing to be done but endure the smell.

Aisha finished packing, then she covered everything on the trailer with a tarpaulin and started pulling the straps into place.

When she was done, she looked up at the Earth again. She'd always been good with landmarks; one glimpse of a distant spire and she could find her way home. But she was about as close to home right now as she could ever be on this world, and the idea of climbing into the buggy and driving until pretty much the opposite was true felt suicidally wrongheaded. How mortifying would it be if a rescue team finally arrived, a mere twelve months late, only to end their mission cracking each other up just by whispering, "She headed for the *far side*?"

Jingyi's memorial statue remained resolute. "All right, I'm sticking to the plan," Aisha told her. "Just like you should have done."

2

"A honeymoon in Fiji! Thank you!" As Aisha embraced her father in gratitude, he interjected testily, "There's more in the envelope. Have a proper look."

Aisha flushed and did as he'd asked, wondering if the airline ticket and hotel booking were accompanied by some needlessly lavish spending money. But the extra slip of paper she'd missed was another kind of ticket entirely.

"I checked with Gianni before I bought it," her father informed her. That had been prudent: the lottery's prize was strictly for couples, and if she'd won only to find that her husband really couldn't face the journey, it would have made both of them miserable. Better not to have a ticket at all.

That night, as she and Gianni lay in bed, she'd talked down their chances. "One in a hundred thousand," she'd mused. "I'd have better odds of getting into the astronaut training program."

"Only if you applied."

"Yeah, well." Going into space was the kind of thing that was easier to imagine at twelve than at twenty-seven. She was touched that her father recalled her childhood ambition, but he seemed to have taken it more seriously than she had herself. "And really, there's no chance of us winning. They'll give it to a Chinese couple."

"Why? Just because China and America are squabbling doesn't mean the company's going to start blacklisting people from every other country."

"No, but it's a marketing gimmick. 'Honeymoon on the Moon!' Who else are you going to target but your biggest market?"

Gianni was bemused. "It's a lottery with *thousand-dollar* tickets. If you mess with the outcome, that's not marketing savvy, it's fraud."

And then, after all her cynicism and carefully managed expectations, the company livestreamed the draw. Five digits plucked from the hiss of the cosmic microwave background determined the winners, and the marketing department would just have to live with it.

Aisha's class of moonstruck nine-year-olds gave her handmade bon voyage cards, with postscripts ranging from impressively specific requests for certain kinds of lunar minerals to pleas for photos of various action figures (enclosed) posed on the surface. She and Gianni passed their health checks and were whisked away to the Gobi Desert, where the centrifuge rides and spacesuit training felt more like scenes for a mockumentary than anything that would really serve them in their role as Spam in a can. But Aisha let the company's PR machine drag them along its strange conveyor belt, all the way to the launchpad.

"This is like being prepped for an operation," Gianni decided, as they waited in their flight suits for the car that would take them to the *Chang'e 20* itself.

Zhilin, the pilot, was amused. "Only if you mean the kind of brain surgery where you're awake the whole time."

"Are you ever afraid?" Aisha asked him.

"I was afraid the first time," he confessed. "It's a strange thing for a human to attempt, and it's only right that it feels unnatural. But that's true for anything our ancestors didn't do: driving a car, flying a plane."

"Walking on a tightrope between skyscrapers," Gianni joked. Aisha wanted to punch him, but Zhilin just laughed.

From the gantry, looking out across the stark gray plains, Aisha waved cheerfully, knowing that her father and her students would be watching, but once she was strapped into her seat in the tiny cabin she gripped Gianni's hand and closed her eyes.

"It'll be fine," he whispered.

She waited for the engines to ignite, wondering what had ever made her yearn to leave the Earth. She didn't need a pale-blue-dot moment to convince her that her home world was a fragile oasis. And if she couldn't inspire a love of science in her students without an overblown stunt like this, she was the worst teacher ever born.

When the moment came, she could hear the inferno unleashed beneath her, a wild conflagration that rattled all the flimsy structures that stood between the flames and her flesh. When Gianni squeezed her hand, she imagined the two of them spinning away into the air, lighting up the desert like a human Catherine wheel.

In the flight simulator, she'd watched the simulated rocket's progress on a screen in front of her, helping her translate every burst of noise and thrust into the language of stages and separations, but now she shied away from interpreting the cues, afraid of getting it wrong and convincing herself that the worst was over when it was only just beginning. The force of the engines and the shaking of the cabin made her teeth ache in ways she'd never felt before; this wasn't brain surgery, it was some kind of gonzo dentistry.

And when everything seemed still and quiet, she refused to trust her senses. Maybe she was just numb to the onslaught, or she was blocking it out in some kind of dissociative state.

"Aisha?"

She opened her eyes. Gianni was beaming madly. He took a pen out of his pocket and released it; it floated in the air like a magic trick, like a movie effect, like her phone doing a cheesy AR overlay. She'd watched *2001* a thousand times, but this couldn't be happening to her in real life.

He said, "We're astronauts now. How cool is that?"

3

Three days later, when they disembarked at Sinus Medii, Aisha was jubilant. She summoned up her twelve-year-old self to gaze in astonishment at the blazing daytime stars and the ancient fissured basalt stretching to the horizon, then she waddled precariously forward across the landing pad like her grandmother performing water aerobics. She *knew* that if she did X, Y, or Z she would instantly die a horrible death—but she was no more likely to enact one of the fatal blunders she'd been warned against than she'd ever been inclined to open a window in a tall building and jump out.

Medii Base was a sprawling complex of factories and workshops open to the vacuum, but the sole pressurized habitat was about the size of a small suburban dwelling, albeit with a greenhouse in the back. Zhilin introduced the honeymooners to the staff: Jingyi, botanist and medical doctor; Martin, roboticist and mining engineer; and Yong, geologist and astrophysicist. These double-degreed geniuses all looked about thirty, and Aisha was intimidated at first, but that soon gave way to a kind of relief: envying them would be like envying an Olympic athlete. She wanted to enjoy the experience for what it was and emerge without any delusions or regrets: there'd be no *if only she'd done a PhD*, or *it was not too late to leverage her flight hours as a passenger into a new, interplanetary career.*

Jingyi sketched the whole complex system of nutrient and energy flows supporting the hydroponic crops, responding patiently to all the questions Aisha's students had passed on to her. Martin showed them the solar-thermal smelter that was processing basaltic rubble into useful materials—albeit, so far, mostly just the silica fiber for Yong's baby. The Moravec skyhook was a rotating cable, its length a full third the width of the Moon. Yong had spun it up to the point where the low end swung backward above the surface so rapidly as to momentarily cancel out the velocity due to its orbit. It was like a spoke on a giant wheel rolling around the Moon's equator—except that the imaginary track it was rolling on was several kilometers above their heads, so there was no risk of decapitation even at the top of the most exuberant bound. One day the hook would grab vehicles and supplies and sling them away toward Mars. For now, it was just a beautiful proof of concept, a tireless, hyperactive stick insect doing cartwheels over their heads.

Back in their room, Aisha Skyped her father. The three-second delays were impossible to ignore, but she'd had worse between continents.

"You're healthy?" he asked. "You're not sick from the journey?"

"Not at all." She'd done all her vomiting in the ship.

"I'm so proud of you. Your mother would have been so proud!"

Aisha just smiled; it would have been heartless to protest that she'd done nothing more than accept his gift.

When they finished the call, she flopped back in her chair and sighed. "Where are we, again?"

"Are you jealous of my sister scuba diving on the reefs?" Gianni joked. They'd given her the Fiji holiday; it would have been greedy to take both.

"No." Some commentators had written sniffily that a smelter was hardly a tourist attraction. But in truth, nothing could be mundane here.

"They won't have put cameras in the room, will they?" Gianni asked. Aisha hoped he was joking; whatever their role, it was still a notch or two above contestants on reality TV. But she shut down the computer anyway, just to be safe.

They kissed, tentatively, wary of performing some simple movement that would lead to a pratfall here. Anything that wasn't Velcroed or magnetically locked to the floor might as well have been a banana skin.

She said, "Once we're inside the bag, we should be right." They undressed each other, trying not to laugh, unsure just how quiet they'd need to be to keep their neighbors from hearing.

"When your father asked me if I'd go on this trip, I almost said no," Gianni admitted.

Aisha frowned. "Well, that's a real turn-on."

"I was trying to be honest."

"I'm joking!" She kissed him. "I almost chickened out a dozen times myself."

"Then I'm glad we both stuck with it," he said. "Because I'm pretty sure this is going to make us happy for the rest of our lives."

4

Aisha had switched her watch's default display to Dunedin time, so she wouldn't miss her appointment to talk to the school. She woke around six, showered, then stood by the sleeping bag and prodded Gianni's shoulder with her foot.

"Do you want to get up and have breakfast?"

He squinted at his own watch. "It's two a.m.!"

"Only in Beijing. Come on . . . you need to be sitting next to me when I call the kids, or they'll just spend the whole hour asking me what you're doing."

When they'd eaten and made themselves presentable, they sat down in front of the computer and powered it up. It booted without any problem, but when Aisha opened Skype, it told her that she had no connection to the internet.

"Maybe we're out of view of the dish," Gianni suggested.

"I thought they had us covered around the clock." There were ground stations in Mongolia, Nigeria, and Honduras, and no one in the training camp or on the base had mentioned a particular time window for contacting Earth.

Gianni frowned. "Did you hear that?" The gentle thump had sounded like the air lock's inner doors closing.

They walked out into the common room. Martin had just returned from outside; he was still suited, and holding his helmet.

"We're having communications problems," he said.

"Oh." Aisha hesitated. "Is it going to be easy to fix?" Forget about her disappointed students; Martin and his colleagues were stuck here for another four months, and if they didn't have the right replacement parts on hand, the link could remain broken until the new crew arrived.

"I don't know," he replied. "There's nothing wrong at our end."

"Okay." Aisha wasn't sure why his tone suggested that this was bad news. "So when we switch over to a different dish . . . ?"

Martin said, "We should have been through one handover already."

"So the problem's at mission control?" Gianni suggested.

"No." Martin sounded harried. "We should be getting carrier from the dishes themselves, whatever's happening at Dongfeng."

Aisha was bewildered now. "How can there be two separate problems at two different dishes, halfway around the world?"

Martin shook his head. "I have no idea."

The other members of the crew joined them one by one, either woken by the conversation or alerted by their own devices to the broken link. Yong talked over the technical issues with Martin, then went out to perform some supplementary tests. Aisha gathered that Martin had successfully established contact with a portable, self-contained transceiver that mimicked the protocols they would normally be following with a ground station. Medii's own antenna required no active measures to keep it aligned; the Earth was essentially a fixed target, with all the careful tracking delegated to the other end. But Yong had a theory about some obscure defect that might still blind them to a distant transmitter without stopping them connecting to the proxy.

Gianni tried to make light of it all. "At home we just flick our modems on and off, but here you need to check in case we've jumped into another dimension where the dinosaurs stayed in charge down on Earth."

Only Zhilin laughed, but then, he'd once flown commercial airliners. He had to be accustomed to setting his passengers' minds at ease—no matter what was going on inside his own head.

Yong returned. "It's not us," he declared. "The problem's back home."

Jingyi and Martin gazed down at the dining room table, but Gianni couldn't tolerate silence. "So maybe the Americans hacked all the Chinese ground stations? In some kind of . . . preemptive cyberattack?" He stopped short of spelling out the reason, but the recent tensions had revolved around rumors of weapons in orbit.

Aisha said, "I didn't think things had got that serious."

Yong turned to the couple. "You had some sightseeing scheduled, and I'm already suited up. The next dish won't be in view for five hours, and there's nothing we can do just by sitting here worrying."

Aisha and Gianni got into their suits and the three of them cycled through the air lock together. Aisha did her best to surrender to the spectacle and concentrate on perfecting her regolith gait. Never mind that the ground around them looked like it had been melted in a nuclear blast, and the claustrophobic confines of her suit made her think of fallout protection gear.

Yong was in the middle of explaining a theory that the farside had fewer maria than the nearside because a collision with a second, much smaller satellite had thickened the Moon's crust there, when Aisha noticed a high-pitched, metronomic beep.

"Does anyone else hear that?" she asked. She was afraid it was some kind of alarm, though she'd been told that even a malfunctioning suit would always manage to give a polite, informative message in the occupant's preferred language.

"Sorry, that's the beacon from the skyhook." Yong did something and the sound went away. "I listen in to it sometimes, just to reassure myself that it's still up there."

"How could it not be?" Gianni wondered.

"A micrometeor could cut it in two."

"So what would a micrometeor do to us?"

"Don't worry, we're much smaller targets."

By the time they were back inside, the wait was almost over. Martin sat hunched over the console in the common room, gazing at the screen. Aisha tried to prepare herself not to take another dose of dead air too hard; there might be an entirely innocuous reason for it that hadn't occurred to any of them.

"Nothing," Martin announced. "They're all down."

Gianni said, "Can you try tuning in to one of the NASA dishes?"

"They won't be pointed at us."

"What about TV broadcasts?"

Martin grimaced impatiently. "The only antenna sensitive enough to pick up that shit is on the farside, precisely so it doesn't have to listen to it."

Gianni nodded, chastened. "Okay. So what's the upshot? We should just relax and hope they get things working again soon?"

"Sure," Zhilin replied. "No internet for a couple of days. That never hurt anyone, did it?"

5

As the silence stretched on, Aisha found herself equally committed to two ways of viewing the situation. On the one hand, for her and Gianni the inability to communicate with Earth was just a mild inconvenience—and in the short term, at least, that was probably also true for the base's longer-term residents. And assuming that the problem with China's network of ground stations wasn't being treated as a state secret, no one's relatives would have reason to be worried about the lack of contact. Her father would still be anxious, but at least he'd know why he hadn't been able to talk with her.

On the other hand: short of hostilities, cyber or otherwise, what could have happened at three separate sites that was taking so long to repair? And if Beijing and Washington were merely sulking with each other, that shouldn't have stopped the ground stations in Spain or Australia showing enough goodwill to step in and make contact with Medii, just to let them know what was going on.

But even with Gianni, Aisha stuck to version one, and shut down any pessimistic speculations. "We won't need clearance from Earth to take off and head home," she reminded him. "It's not like it's so crowded out here that we need a flight plan approved by air traffic control." Zhilin would probably prefer to get a weather report before he took them all the way to Dongfeng, but in principle, they could still make the journey even if Earth's whole population had ascended in the Rapture, and the last soul to depart had turned off the lights.

Aisha woke to the sound of Gianni repeating her name. "Something's happening!" he whispered. "They've been sitting in the common room, arguing, and now some of them have gone outside."

"Arguing about what?" Aisha wasn't sure she wanted to know, but Gianni seemed too agitated to be told to stop worrying and go back to sleep.

"I don't know, they were speaking Chinese."

She said, "Maybe someone realized that the problem is at our end, after all, and they've gone to fix it."

"I'll go and find out."

"No, just . . ." It was too late, he was out of the sleeping bag. Aisha watched him dress by the red glow of the safety lights. She was tired of the constant undertone of anxiety and paranoia, but in two more days they'd be heading home, and in five all their questions would be answered.

He left the room, and she heard him talking to Jingyi. At first their words were too soft to make out clearly, but then Gianni started shouting. "You're fucking kidding me!" he bellowed.

"Please, don't try anything!" Jingyi implored him.

Aisha clambered out of the bag and went to join them. Gianni was pacing the room, hugging himself.

"What's happening?" she asked.

"They're going home!"

"What?"

Jingyi said, "They're afraid that if things are difficult, Earth might not send another ship for a long time."

Aisha was stunned. The *Chang'e 20* could only take three passengers and the pilot, so all six of them could not return together, but the idea that Earth would abandon the base's crew seemed deranged to her. "So we're the ones stranded here instead?"

Jingyi shook her head. "You're guests; you're here to make the company look good. They'll try much harder for you. But we signed up for one year, and we've trained for longer stays. There won't be the same pressure on them to help us."

Aisha was torn between indignation and a degree of sympathy: maybe the deserters' logic was sound. But if five days of silence really did mean that things were going badly on Earth, she very much doubted that all it would take to resurrect billions of dollars' worth of sabotaged infrastructure would be a little extra pressure on the public relations front.

Gianni said, "I'm going to stop them." He walked over to the air lock and began putting on his suit.

Jingyi turned to Aisha. "You need to talk him out of it. It's too dangerous for anyone fighting out there."

"I'm just going to talk to them!" Gianni retorted angrily.

"You can talk to them here," Jingyi replied, gesturing toward the console. Gianni ignored her, but Aisha went with her and sat down at the microphone.

"Yong? Martin?" she tried. There was no response. "Please. Can we discuss this?"

Gianni had everything but his helmet on. "They're not going to turn around and march back in because you asked them nicely!"

"So what do you think you're going to do to change their minds?"

"They can't ignore me if I'm standing right in front of them."

Aisha said, "I don't think it's a good idea to confront them." The suits didn't exactly tear easily, but she did not want any kind of altercation in the vacuum. "They're probably inside the ship by now, anyway."

"We'll see." Gianni fixed his helmet in place and stepped into the air lock.

Aisha felt numb. If she went after him, would that just make things worse? When she heard the outer door close, she hit the button beside the microphone. "Gianni?"

"What?" He was breathing heavily, as if he was trying to run. The launchpad was five hundred meters away, but there was no way that he could overtake the men who'd left ten minutes earlier.

"Just leave it. They'll probably send another ship within a week."

"Fuck that! This is our ride home, and they don't get to take it."

"Just come back!"

Gianni did not reply.

"I have to go and get him," she decided.

As Aisha was putting on her suit, Jingyi looked on forlornly. Why hadn't she left with the others? There was room for her on the ship. Maybe they'd decided to draw straws to pick a babysitter to stay behind. Or maybe she was just too decent to walk out on a pair of novices who might not survive for one day on their own.

When Aisha emerged from the air lock she saw Gianni in the distance, bounding across the rock like a kangaroo wrapped in tinfoil. She couldn't make out any figures moving around the launchpad.

"Come back, you idiot!" she implored him. "We'll be fine here!" Even if the wait turned out to be a year or two, Jingyi knew how to keep the crops growing and the base habitable.

Gianni kept running. Aisha waddled forward as briskly as she could, resigned to the fact that she'd never catch up with him.

When he reached the launchpad, she waited, hoping he'd accept the evidence of his own eyes. Zhilin would be going through the final system checks, and nobody was going to step out to debate their plans. Maybe the pricks would end up in prison for this; Aisha was unsure of the legal issues, but she recalled a sea captain being jailed for leaving his foundering ship while his passengers remained trapped below deck.

Gianni climbed the ladder to the hatch. Aisha couldn't make out exactly what he was doing, but she assumed he was pounding on the hull.

"I'm not leaving until you come out!" he shouted.

"Give it up!" Aisha begged him.

She heard the rattling first through his radio, then she felt the slight vibration of the ground through her boots. She stared at the lander; she couldn't discern any flames from the engines, but maybe they were too diffuse.

"You need to get down," she told Gianni, hoping he'd heed the note of terror in her voice when he'd ignored all her other entreaties.

"They're bluffing!" he retorted. "They're not going to take off."

"Jump and run, or I'll never forgive you!" She could see a ghostly blue light now, flickering around the base of the lander. "*Jump!*"

"Shut off the engines and come out," Gianni commanded his adversaries. Aisha had once watched him stand, immovable and un-flinching, in front of a carload of thugs, ordering them to step out and face him after they'd shouted insults at her. When he thought he was right, he thought he was invincible.

The lander ascended: five meters, ten meters. Aisha emitted an involuntary sob, then held her breath as Gianni finally let go of the railing. Free-falling, he parted from the spacecraft with a dreamlike lethargy, tumbling slowly into the blue fire of the exhaust.

6

The buggy needed sunlight, so Aisha kept it moving at a sedate sixteen kilometers an hour; there was no point in outracing its energy source. With the sun all but frozen in the sky, the subtle changes in the light to which she'd grown accustomed were held in abeyance, leaving her with a sense of stasis that was only rendered stranger by the flow of the terrain. She watched the vehicle's progress on the GPS, and tried to distract herself by attempting to match her ground-level view of a crater or rill beside her with the corresponding features on the satellite map, but after a few days the endless variations on the same theme began to make her feel as if she were stuck in some barren, procedurally generated computer game. The verisimilitude was stunning, but she wanted someone to slip up and insert a shock of greenery, a building or two, a human figure.

Nuri mounted sporadic protests against her own, far more monotonous view. Aisha tried to soothe her without implying that the screams were unwarranted; no one should accept this kind of sensory deprivation, even when they had no choice but to endure it.

The suit recycled as much water as it could, and Aisha piped in liquid meal replacements from the tank at the back of the buggy. When she told the suit to make her faceplate opaque, it wasn't hard to sleep, at least when Nuri was in a cooperative mood. The buggy had plotted a smooth, safe path across territory that had been mapped down to the centimeter, and that probably hadn't changed in a billion years. It was not as if they were at risk of hitting an animal or going aquaplaning.

As they approached ninety degrees longitude, Aisha looked back at the Earth suspended above the horizon. Whatever the idiots had done, she doubted that they'd managed to render the whole blue world uninhabitable. Maybe they'd lost the means to send a radio signal—let alone a rocket—to their nearest neighbor, but that had been true for most of human history. So long as the air was still breathable and crops could still grow, to return would be worth the struggle.

"Why doesn't the skyhook come lower?" Aisha had asked Yong. A gap of six kilometers above the base seemed excessively cautious.

"Because if it came much lower here," he'd explained, "it would strike the ground at other points in its orbit. There are six locations where one hook or the other comes swinging down; the orbit needs to be high enough that all of them have some clearance."

Six months later, when Aisha and Jingyi had been gestating the plan, they'd contemplated tweaking the skyhook's orbit into an ellipse that came in low over the base while still avoiding the highlands of the farside. But the hub's ion engine would take months to execute

the change—and in just two weeks the farside and nearside would
rotate into each other's former locations.

So instead of making the orbit eccentric, they'd kept it circular but shrunk it as much as the safety margins hard-coded into the hub's navigation system allowed. At the point on the farside opposite Medii, the bottom of the cable would come within ten meters of the ground.

When the buggy reached its destination, Aisha looked up into the star-filled sky, trying not to cower into her seat at the thought of the thousand-kilometer-long whip tumbling toward her.

Nuri woke and started crying. "I know," Aisha commiserated. "Your mother stinks, and you're tired of staring at her chin."

She climbed out of the buggy and walked around for a few minutes, just to let her muscles know that their enforced idleness was over, then she unhooked the trailer and set to work.

She detached the roll cage from the buggy, undoing all the bolts and lifting off the tubular frame. Then she took the sheet of woven silica from the trailer and maneuvered it into the buggy, carefully positioning the loops of the connecting cords around the holes where the cage would reattach.

She took twelve of the struts from the trailer and assembled them into a rectangular tower half a meter high, fitted two extra bars across the top, then had the buggy drive up onto it. If she hadn't practiced the whole thing a dozen times back at the base she would have been panicking already, but by now this part seemed as unremarkable as automatic parallel parking.

Nuri redoubled her wails. "Shh, my darling, it's going to be fine," Aisha promised. "Just think of it as monster trucks meets Lego."

She attached a second tower to the first, and made it a full meter tall. The buggy crossed over without complaint; it knew its own abilities well enough to assess her request and decide it was achievable. The integrity of the tower, though, was outside its domain of expertise; it was up to the builder to ensure that the structure was sound.

Level by level, she raised the scaffolding, and the buggy followed. When the tower was seven and a half meters high, she climbed down and stepped back to inspect it. Jingyi had seen her get this far in the rehearsals, but apparently that hadn't been enough to convince her to come along for the ride.

Aisha went to the trailer and fetched the magic box Jingyi had found in Yong's workshop. She woke it from its sleep and checked the status of the skyhook. It was due to make its next pass over the site in about twenty minutes.

If the lunar GPS was still accurate and both she and the skyhook were employing the same coordinates, the magnetic hook at the bottom of the cable would descend directly over the buggy, stop half a meter above the top of the roll cage, then ascend again. With the magnet switched off, the buggy wouldn't move a millimeter, but she had to be sure that the encounter really played out that way. She climbed the tower again, and turned the dash cam on the buggy up toward the sky.

As the time approached, Aisha lay flat on the ground. The hook could not be coming down so low here as to strike the rock; the effect on the whole cable would have been unmissable. But if the real safety margin turned out to be less than advertised, she might be none the wiser until the proof smacked her in the head.

Nuri turned her face toward her, though they couldn't make eye contact. "You're my beautiful girl," Aisha declared soothingly. "You know you are."

She waited a few minutes, in case the timing was off, then rose to her feet; the suit did its best to help.

The tower remained standing, the buggy undisturbed. Aisha had the suit access the dash cam and play back the footage in slow motion.

Her faceplate went opaque, then filled with stars. "Skip forward until something changes," she said.

A circular silhouette moved toward her, growing, blocking out the stars. It slowed as it approached, as if she were looking down at a very large Frisbee tossed into the air, approaching the top of its arc.

She froze the image when the silhouette began to retreat. From the apparent size, the height was close to what she'd expected, but the thing was off-center by about six meters. She'd have to take the tower apart and rebuild it in the right location.

She took her time, instead of rushing to try to get the job finished in one orbit; if the tower collapsed and flipped the buggy, that would be the end. She hummed to Nuri as she worked; singing would have been nicer, but it made her throat dry.

Five hours later she was done, strapped into the buggy, perched high above the rock. She told the hub to power up the hook's electro-magnet, and programmed the switch-off time to the millisecond. Now the whole process was out of her hands.

Nuri was asleep. "We're going to see your grandfather," Aisha whis-pered. "Very soon."

She sat watching the countdown projected in red onto her face-plate. At T-minus two, she was ready to believe that nothing would happen and she'd stay stranded forever. By T-plus two, the feeling of half her Earth weight pressing her into the seat had already gone from a shock to a kind of ecstasy. The landscape was falling away around her ever faster, but the buggy hadn't yet tipped by any perceptible angle; the hub was still an unimaginable distance above her.

Nuri woke, but she did not seem troubled. Perhaps she found the greater pressure against her mother's skin more comforting. Perhaps she'd always known that she needed more weight, more force, more friction if she was ever to thrive.

Aisha talked to her, explaining what was happening, then hummed for a while as she fed. Ten minutes into the upswing, the ground lay to her left, a sheer wall of gray rock like a distant cliff face. But down was still down in the buggy; the centrifugal force overwhelmed mere lunar gravity. And as the cliff slowly receded and tilted into an impossible roof above the dark slab of the magnet, she finally perceived the whole world of her prison as a mere disk in the sky again. Whatever happened now, at least she was free of it.

A few degrees past upside down, the magnet switched off and the buggy fell away into the void. Aisha grabbed at the seat, at the dash-board, but then the weightlessness lost its sense of danger, and once the magnet was out of sight there was nothing to tell her she was moving.

Nuri grizzled half-heartedly, then went quiet and contemplated the change. "We're astronauts now!" Aisha told her. "How cool is that?"

7

They'd left the Moon traveling faster than most rockets, and the blue world grew more rapidly than it had diminished on the journey out. The buggy rotated slowly, taking hours to complete a turn, and each time the Earth rose over the dashboard Aisha could gauge its increased width against the instruments below.

The suit saw no difference between the lunar surface and deep space; it kept scrubbing the air and keeping the temperature tolerable. The liquid meals had transcended their distinctive unpleasantness and blended into the general background of itchiness and filth. Aisha's stomach had bloated like a famine victim's, but she wasn't famished.

Two days after the hook had released them, the Earth filled almost half the view. Whatever errors she'd made in her calculations, at least she hadn't dispatched the buggy straight into the sun. She gazed down at Africa, and took heart to see the cities lighting up as night fell.

She'd been afraid of cutting off the solar power prematurely, but as she followed the continent below into night she started unfolding the silica sheet and drawing it around the buggy. Inside this strange tent, she could just make out the objects around her by the lights from the dashboard.

They needed to scrape through the air where it was dense enough to slow them down and keep them from escaping the Earth's pull, but not so dense that it would melt the improvised heat shield. She and Jingyi had pooled their knowledge and done their best with computer models, but the base had no local copies of any reference work that dealt with atmospheric density profiles—and even with perfect knowledge of the subject, they could never have accounted for the vagaries of mesospheric weather.

Aisha felt the first trace of heat through her gloves where she was
touching the buggy's chassis. As she drew her hands in, the drag force
itself came to her aid, pushing the seat firmly away from her so she
strained against the belt like a passenger hanging upside down after
a car crash. In front of her, the sheet began to glow a dull red, and
radiant heat shone into her faceplate; the suit would be desperately
sequestering thermal energy in its phase-change alloy, but that would
only help for a while.

Nuri grew restless, but not distressed. Aisha was not in pain yet, but
it felt like the times she'd lain too close to an electric radiator on a cold
night, and the initially comforting warmth edged toward something
damaging.

The force eased off; the glow faded. Aisha checked the data on the
buggy's accelerometer. The whole spike had lasted four minutes: not
as long as her calculations had predicted.

She fed the numbers into her model. The buggy had shed enough
velocity for the Earth to capture it, but it would swing out to an apogee
some hundred thousand kilometers away. And though it would come
in close again, it would be moving more slowly than at the first encounter, so the drag would be less. The model showed an excruciating
succession of incremental changes, taking sixty-three orbits in almost
fifty days before they were low enough to parachute down.

To remain in Medii, hoping for rescue, had been untenable. Any
gamble had seemed worthwhile—even if the narrow path home would
be flanked by fiery death and slow starvation. But now she understood
why Jingyi had made her own choice: what she'd feared most was
watching her friend, and the child she'd delivered, perish beside her as
the food ran out, the water dried up, the air went stale.

Aisha gingerly opened the tent to give the suit a chance to radiate
some heat away. Maybe there were errors in the model still to unfold,
in her favor. She felt Nuri shift and nuzzle against her, the broken skin
of a rash on her daughter's cheek warm against her own skin.

Chance wouldn't save them. If she left this to chance, they
would die.

She watched the planet slowly recede. Their speed and altitude the next time they entered the atmosphere were immutable now. Which left . . . what? The drag would depend on their shape, and the area they presented to the airflow. The sheet was much bigger than the buggy's frame, in preparation for its later role as parachute, but if she tried to trail it behind her at this point, the unprotected buggy would fry. If she'd brought half the struts from the tower, she might have stretched the sheet out into a larger shield, but they were all sitting uselessly back on the farside.

Nuri slept and woke, fed and shat, oblivious. Aisha could not have faced her dying as a three-year-old in a medical emergency, as a teenager in Medii's slide into disrepair, or, if the machines all proved resilient, as the loneliest centenarian in history.

But she could not face this either.

She closed her eyes and pictured the beautiful fabric she and Jingyi had toiled so long to weave, billowing out above her as the buggy drifted gently toward some green field or calm sea. Spread out by the force of the air alone. But when they grazed the unbreathably thin mesosphere . . . how much pressure would it take, *from within*, to puff the tent out like a balloon?

Not a lot.

Aisha opened her eyes and did some calculations. It was possible. She believed she could spare it and survive.

She forced herself to wait until the perigee was just an hour away, to keep the batteries charging as long as possible. Then she spread the sheet around the buggy and knotted the cords as tightly as she could around the hole at the back. It would not be a hermetic seal, but it only had to retain its contents for a few minutes.

She checked the time, then told the suit to start venting.

The tent remained limp and crumpled.

"Vent more," she commanded.

"That would put reserves below safe levels," the suit replied.

Aisha placed her gloves against the sides of her helmet and turned it. The suit tried to dissuade her, but Jingyi had proved that it could be done. As the seal was breached the air hissed out and the tent inflated, the fabric taut against the vacuum.

Aisha reversed the twist. She took a breath. It felt inadequate. She took a deeper one; she was dizzy, but she was not suffocating.

The silica balloon began to shudder, buffeted by the thin, fast air outside. Aisha felt the growing heat on her face, breaking through her light-headedness.

The drag pushed her forward: a little weaker than before, but much more than her dire calculations had predicted for the status quo. She watched the time pass, until she was weightless again. *Three minutes.*

She crunched the accelerometer data. Six more orbits, and they would be spiraling down to Earth.

Nuri started babbling happily, making sounds Aisha had never heard before. Aisha let herself weep, for Gianni, for Jingyi, for whatever havoc she was yet to find below.

Then she composed herself and started singing softly to her daughter, waiting for the time they could look into each other's eyes again.

WHAT THE DEAD MAN SAID

CHINELO ONWUALU

Chinelo Onwualu (chineloonwualu.wixsite.com/author) is a Nigerian writer and editor living in Toronto, Canada. She is co-founder of *Omenana*, a magazine of African speculative fiction, and former chief spokesperson for the African Speculative Fiction Society. She is a graduate of the 2014 Clarion West Writers Workshop, which she attended as the recipient of the Octavia E. Butler Memorial Scholarship. Her short stories have been featured in *Slate*, *Uncanny*, *Strange Horizons*, *The Kalahari Review*, and *Brittle Paper* as well as in the anthologies *New Suns* and *Mothership: Tales from Afrofuturism and Beyond*.

I suppose you could say that it started with the storm.

I hadn't seen one like it in thirty years. Not since I moved to Tkaronto, in the Northern Indigenous Zone of Turtle Island—what settler-colonialists still insisted on calling North America. I'd forgotten its raw power: angry thunderclouds that blot out the sun, taking you from noon to evening in an instant, then the water that comes down like fury—like the sky itself wants to hurt you.

As I sat in the empty passenger terminal of the Niger River Harbourfront waiting for the bus, I watched as rain streaked the cobbled walkways in silver, sluicing through the narrow depressions between the solar roadway and the gutter. The ferry was long gone, moving up the river into the heart of Igboland, leaving me stranded in an alien world.

A holographic advertisement for some sort of fertility treatment played out on a viewscreen across the street. It was distorted by the haze of rain, but I made out a plump, impossibly happy woman in a crisp red gele—her skin glowing in the golden light of a computer-generated sun—clutching a newborn baby and dancing toward a household shrine. She was surrounded by celebrating family members, but she stopped before a regal older couple to whom she presented the child. The old man took the child with a benevolent smile, while the woman stretched her hand toward the young mother, who was now kneeling before them, in a benediction. The ad ended with a close-up of the beaming mother and the logo of the fertility treatment company in the corner. I turned away before my ocular implants could sync with the ad's soundtrack, but I'd already caught the tagline: "Keep New Biafra Alive."

My AI announced that the bus had arrived. Its interface had switched to Igbo as soon as I passed from Nigeria™ into New Biafra, as neither English nor Anishinaabe were recognized languages here. I hadn't spoken Igbo in decades, but its musicality returned to me with smooth familiarity—as if it had simply been waiting for its turn in the spotlight. I ignored the ping; I wanted to watch the rain a little longer. Perhaps it would somehow wash this reality away and I could return to the quiet life I'd built for myself on the other side of the Atlantic.

I frowned, then sighed. The dead man was right. This was like getting a body mod. You'd be a brand-new person when it was over, but in the meantime it was going to hurt like hell. I put up the hood of my hi-dri, shouldered my backpack, and stepped out into the storm.

It really started with the notification two days ago. My father had passed on—as they used to say—but that wasn't real. At least not yet.

What was real was me here in Onitsha, my hometown. Even though I'd spent my childhood wandering this city's narrow red streets, as I slumped in the passenger well of the automated minibus, it struck me how foreign the place now seemed. How had I forgotten how compact everything was, as if it had been built to accommodate a mass of people long gone? My grandparents told me that over a century ago, more than half a million people had packed into these pristine streets. Now, it wasn't even half that.

The minibus glided along Niger Avenue, stopping occasionally to let passengers off or allow pedestrians to cross the road. As we passed Fegge, I caught sight of the neighborhood's ancient cement family quarters, squat-shouldered and tin-roofed, hulking next to each other like sullen children. Crossing from Main Market, with its workshops and retail outlets, into the quiet residential lanes of American Quarters, I spied children in neat uniforms walking hand in hand to their various apprenticeships. Children were rare enough in Tkaronto, and those few who could afford to give birth preferred to cluster in tower communities that would protect their precious progeny from the vicissitudes of life. Apart from major celebrations like Emancipation Day, seeing children in public was unheard of.

Throughout the trip, the lights of the historic Niger Bridge blinked on the horizon. I would have liked to go walking across it like any other tourist, streaming photos of the mighty river for my feed back West. But I'd only packed a change of clothes and some toiletries. The burial rites would begin this evening with the wake-keeping and end on the

evening of the next day, after the celebratory second funeral. I had no plans of staying past then.

It could be argued that without the Catastrophe, that fraught period between the 2020s and the 2060s that scorched half the world and drowned the rest, New Biafra could never have been born. At the turn of the 22nd century, as people all over were still fleeing inland to escape the rising seas, a group of Igbo separatists took the opportunity to declare their independence from the crumbling co-lonial creation of Nigeria. The new state called for the return of all its children in diaspora, and my grandparents—engineers eking out a living on the shores of Old New York—were among the thousands who moved to regional cities like Onitsha, Nnewi, Awka, and Aba to answer the call.

We called it the Great Return. Anyone who could prove Igbo an-cestry was granted automatic citizenship. Those with coveted skills—geneticists, engineers, and biologists—were given homes, business grants, and lucrative government posts. My grandparents and their generation cleared out the derelict infrastructure of New Biafra's empty suburbs and towns to make way for the forestlands that now cov-ered nearly 80 percent of the country. They reseeded those forests with bioengineered plants and wildlife, then built the massive monorail sys-tem that connects all our cities to bypass the pristine forests below. But they'd neglected one thing: While they were busy creating our new homeland, they forgot to also raise the massive families that would be needed to keep it solvent and thriving.

As they grew feeble, the burden of caring for them and maintain-ing the world they'd built fell to us. My age-mates, those I kept in touch with after I moved, tell me I was lucky to get out when I did. Leaving New Biafra when I was only twelve meant that I was too young to be tied down by the weight of its social obligations. They complained of having to work long hours to preserve family businesses passed down by aging parents and grandparents. They spoke wistfully of the massive payouts the government awarded to those who could birth three or more children, but few of them could carve out the time needed to

cultivate such large families. Though my own life—a spacious apartment in the hills of Highland Crescent, an easygoing art research consultancy—was very different from theirs, I'm not sure I did escape. One cannot cut the invisible threads of familial indebtedness by simply running off to a distant land.

My father certainly fulfilled his filial duty. He became a ranger, protecting the bioengineered species his parents had introduced in the forests they'd prepared. As his only child, I should have done the same. I'd always liked working with the soil, so it was expected that I would go into agroecology and grow the food that would feed our people. But after what happened with my uncle . . . I shook my head to ward off the memory.

As the bus pulled up in front of the family home at 142 Old Hospital Road, I came out of my reverie and noticed that the rain had stopped. The house hadn't changed since I'd last seen it three decades ago. Hell, it probably hadn't changed in the two hundred years since it had been built in the 1920s.

It was a U-shaped complex with a central bungalow flanked by two-story apartments, one on either side. An open courtyard carpeted with moss grass, fruit trees, and wildflowers filled the space between them. My grandparents had reinforced its walls with permacrete and upgraded its interior to 22nd-century standards, but that's where the improvements ended. After they died, the house went to my father, who'd never had much interest in technology. In the twenty years he'd lived there, he'd done nothing more than charge its batteries and replace burned-out solar cells.

Traditionally, the oldest members of the family would occupy the bungalow while their children and extended family members crammed into the two warrens of flats. If we'd restricted the apartments to blood family only, as some still did, those buildings would have stood empty. These days relatives were defined less by who'd slept with whom, and more by whose interests and personalities meshed best. I recalled the boisterous couples and polycules who'd lived in the building when I was young—all of them my cousins and uncles and aunties even though we had only marginal blood relationships to each other.

The compound was abuzz with people. Someone had set up a canopy in one corner of the open field where my friends and I had played virtual sports as children. From somewhere in the back the delicate smell of Aba rice and goat stew wafted out, making my mouth water. The building's families had spared no expense for this event. I tried to slip in quietly, but I was immediately spotted.

"Azuka! Is that you?" screamed a voice from somewhere in the crowd. It was Auntie Chio, a close friend of my grandmother who'd lived in the building for as long as I could remember. I'd been best friends with her two granddaughters, both of whom now lived in the Eko Atlantic megacity. She was one of the few adults who'd kept in touch with me after my mother and I moved to Turtle Island.

I spotted her lithe frame dressed in her usual motley of clashing ankara fabrics as she swept out from the main bungalow. Her unlined face spoke nothing of her nearly ninety years, and before I knew it I was surrounded in her crushing embrace.

I smiled wanly. "Good evening, Auntie."

"Ah-ah, when did you come?" She held me at arm's length, taking me in from head to toe, her eagle-eyed gaze missing nothing.

"Just now. I had to finish some work before I could travel."

She nodded and gave me a look that was skeptical but sympathetic. She opened her mouth to say more, but her cry had attracted others and soon I was surrounded by people.

"Azu-nne, welcome! See how big you've grown, eh! So tall!"

"Come, you don't remember me, do you? You were so small when last I saw you."

"My condolences, my dear. It is well with you."

I tried to respond to each comment and query with as many smiles and as few words as possible, and soon I was ushered into the main house. It wasn't until later that I realized one thing in the compound had changed: The small guardhouse that used to sit just inside the front gate was gone.

That evening at the wake-keeping, Auntie Chio and I sat in the living room next to the biodegradable pod where my father's body lay, its feet facing the entryway. Earlier, she'd welcomed the community into the home as tradition dictated, presenting kola nuts and palm wine as an offering to the household gods. Another of my elder aunts—I forget how we're related—led the prayers, pouring libations to beckon the ancestral spirits into our home and escort my father's spirit to the land of the dead.

This was the night of mourning and I wished I was somewhere, anywhere, else. But as my father's only biological child, I had to stay by his body and receive mourners until dawn. Then, a government representative would show up to sound an ogene and officially alert the neighborhood of the death. The body would then be interred with its own tree in the front compound. My grandfather told me that when he'd visit Onitsha as a child, this alert would be done by gunshot. After New Biafra banned guns at the turn of the 2140s, we turned to gongs— something he'd much preferred.

It was one of the many stories my grandparents told me about why they chose to return to Onitsha from Turtle Island, after Old New York drowned in the Catastrophe. As a child, I often joined my grandparents—Mama and Papa, as I called them—when they sat trading memories on the veranda at twilight. I would climb into my grandmother's lap and lean into her chest, savoring the vibrations of her voice as she spoke.

"It's a shame your father never got to see any grandchild from you." My Auntie Chio's voice jolted me into the present. "But we are glad that we will see them on his behalf, now that you have come home."

I looked askance at her but said nothing. I didn't need to be reminded that I'd failed to birth our family's next generation. She must have caught something in my look, because her voice dropped to a reassuring register. "You don't have to marry anyone: We can get a surrogate, if you like. There's even a government program that could help."

"Auntie, is this really the best time to talk about this?"

"But of course! The ending of one life is the beginning of the next." She shifted to face me, and I couldn't avoid her intense gaze. "My dear, have you forgotten our saying: 'To have a child is to have treasure'? That is more important today than ever before.

"Look at our history. If it wasn't for our children, how would we have survived the Civil War, when Nigeria wanted to see us all dead? And those in the western lands who laughed at us when they stopped having even one child after the Catastrophe, look at them now. Are they not the ones scooping us up to feed their hungry economies? Just look at the brokers who helped you and your mother resettle in the West—what *didn't* they offer you to come? They have always known the value of our bodies. Before, they packed us away by force in the bottoms of slave ships, now they lure us with sweet songs of success.

"Azuka, do you know how quickly a people can disappear if they fail to value their children? It does not take centuries. Your grand-parents understood this—that's why we all came home. We wanted to bring our wealth back where it would do the most good. You are part of our legacy."

I broke away from her gaze, a wave of grief welling up in my chest. How could I tell her that my father's line would die with me because I still recoiled at any sort of sexual contact? Or that the thought of having a child sent me into a paroxysm of panic because I was convinced that what had happened to me would also happen to them? My grief began to curdle into anger. No. This was no longer my legacy. A family that had essentially abandoned me when I needed them most did not get to decide what I did with my life.

Auntie Chio reached out and placed a gentle hand under my chin, lifting my head up to hers. "I will be honest with you, I never thought I would see you again—not after what happened. But I am glad you have come home, and I hope, for all our sakes, that you will find it in your heart to stay." With that, she got up and left, leaving me alone with my thoughts.

I sighed, my anger dissipating as quickly as it had come. After we moved, my mother turned her back on Onitsha—and all of New Biafra by extension—with a certainty that never wavered. As far as I know, she never spoke with anyone from my father's side of the family ever again. I hadn't been able to do the same, even though I had more cause than anyone to shake the red dust of this city from my feet.

My mother had scoffed when I told her I was coming down for the funeral. I hadn't returned when my grandparents died, why was this burial so much more important? I couldn't explain it. I'd always felt that I left New Biafra before I could take up my true purpose. That my life in Tkaronto was a shadow of what it could be. Perhaps I'd returned to bury more than my father.

I looked up and two women I'd never seen before were leaning into the pod, wailing and calling the dead man's name, asking rhetorically why he had left them. I wondered how much of their performance was obscure cultural theater and how much was genuine grief.

Their wailing increased, and I wished I'd been allowed to bring my AI. That, however, would have been considered an insult to the body, like looking into the eyes of an elder while you were being scolded. I'd forgotten how quickly my people whitewash the truth about our dead. We fear that speaking ill of them will invite death on ourselves as well.

One of the women stopped in front of me, sniffling into an old cloth kerchief. She looked to be in her mid-40s—about my age.

"Your father was a good man," she said, reaching for my hands. I slid them into my pockets, just out of her reach, and she made do with patting my leg.

"Was he?" I tried for a tone of genuine curiosity, not the cynicism I actually felt.

"I wouldn't be here today, if it wasn't for him."

I nodded, unsure of what to say. My father had been famously generous: Everyone I'd met so far had a story of how he'd stepped in at just the right moment to change their lives. I didn't know what to do with these tales. I suppose it was easier to give money to strangers than to give of yourself to the people closest to you.

After an awkward pause, she continued, speaking quickly as if to get the words out before her courage failed her. "You know, after I was raped ten years ago, nobody wanted to help me." I stiffened, tightening my hands into fists in my pockets. "Not my family, not the government, nobody. Only your father. He brought me into this house and allowed me to stay here for free until I found a place. He even paid for my marriage and my son's apprenticeship. Me and my wife, we're just so grateful to him."

She pointed to the other woman, who had gone to stand by the door with a child of about ten years. He had soft brown eyes and a head of unruly curls, and he wore a miniature version of the ranger's uniform that the dead man in the pod was wearing. I didn't tell her about the same dead man's reaction to my own rape thirty-three years ago—twenty-three years before her own. Instead, I smiled tightly.

"I'm glad that it turned out so well for you."

That's when I saw the dead man's shadow materialize in the corner of the room. I didn't tell her about that, either.

The dead man appeared again sometime during the night.

I had just struggled out of a dream. I was back in the guardhouse, its small high windows streaming an uncertain gray light into the room. Then, hundreds of disembodied hands reached out of the ground to grab at me. They held me down, their fingers clutching, probing, and rubbing. I bit and clawed and slashed, but for every hand whose finger I tore off, for every palm I gouged and wounded, a new hand sprang up in its place.

It was an old nightmare, one I hadn't had in over thirty years. When we moved to Turtle Island, my mother and our relocation broker made sure I received all the necessary therapies to deal with my trauma, but being here where it all happened seemed to have dredged everything back up.

I lay on the living room couch drenched in sweat and blinked into the semidarkness before I saw him sitting on the armrest by my feet. In the light of the bioluminescent trees that lined the street by the back lights, he was gone.

I should have been frightened, but I wasn't. I knew he'd show up again. He and I had unfinished business.

He returned the next morning as I sat beneath the neem tree in the back garden, trying to hide from the unrelenting regard of the crowd of mourners inside the main house. The body was due to be interred with its tree in the front compound, and the place was choked with well-wishers. They spilled out onto the walkway beyond the house's hedgerow fence and into the road. I was agitated, but instead of tuning into the nature sounds queued up on my AI, I listened to the weaver birds screeching to each other in the branches above me.

I never noticed how loud those birds are.

The dead man looked up at the tree's slim branches, weighed down by the birds' basket-like nests. This time, I decided to respond directly.

"You never did notice much beyond your own interests."

I expected him to come back with an attack that cut to my deepest insecurities. It was a talent he had, and he had often used it to great effect when he was alive, but he didn't. He just nodded sadly and put his hands in his pockets.

I suppose I deserve that.

I would have to make do with that. Even in death, he couldn't apologize. A group of three men around the dead man's age filtered out onto the back veranda. They joked nervously with each other, as if their laughter would somehow keep the shadow of death from falling on them too. Two of them, both dressed in the dark high-collared tunics of Biafran government salarymen, discussed the finer points of spiritual salvation in Yoruba-inflected Igbo. I itched for something to read.

"Why are you even here?"

He shrugged, petulant. *I just wanted to see you.*

I rolled my eyes. He'd only been dead a few days. He'd always been impatient, demanding that I work at his relentless pace no matter how I felt. Now, he couldn't even wait to be missed before showing up again.

"Really? So that you can tell me how selfish I am because I'm not sitting inside being the center of everyone's grief? Or do you also want to remind me that I'm going to destroy our family line if I don't have a child?"

I realized I sounded like a child myself, but I couldn't help it. Being in his presence made me feel that I'd gone back in time and was an angry teenager again.

No. His voice had a wistful quality—like someone looking back at the folly of his youth. *You were never selfish, you know. I was.*

I looked at him sharply; this didn't sound like him at all. As if reading my thoughts, he smiled.

That's one thing dying does—it changes you.

He certainly looked dead. His skin was gray and waxy like a mannequin. His shoulders had a stiff quality that made his dark ranger uniform fit him perfectly in a way it had never done in life.

"Am I to believe that dying has made you a different person?"

Look, he said in that chiding tone I hated, *you can't fault people for their weaknesses. You'll only be left with bitterness if you do. You have to find a way to let go. That's what I came to tell you.*

I sighed. In death, as in life, he had nothing but easy philosophies for me. They'd made for exciting debates when I was young but served as cold comfort for grief. I wanted to get up and walk away, but I didn't. I never could.

"Just leave me alone."

I turned on my AI. It synced with the implant at the base of my skull that monitored my neural and physical activity. Reading my increased agitation, it cued the soothing whale songs that worked best to bring my signals within normal range. I leaned back against the tree and closed my eyes as the sounds poured into my aural inputs, imagining what those long-extinct creatures might have looked like.

Above me, the dead man and the weaver birds chirped on.

He didn't show up again until evening, when the second burial was in full swing. By then, the sapling that would biodegrade his pod had joined the other ancestral trees in the front yard. The necessary prayers had been said, the tree's ritual first watering completed. The time for mourning the loss was over and it was now time to celebrate the life lived. At eighty, the dead man was considered fairly young; he'd been expected to live for at least another twenty years. But in my culture, venerated old age began at sixty—probably a holdover from when most people didn't live past their fifties.

I watched the revelry from the open window of the guest room. I'd been allowed this short time to myself only after pleading exhaustion from the long journey. It was only a matter of time before I'd be called out to join the dancing.

The music—a blend of ogenes, ichakas, and udus, cut through by the sweet, sharp tones of the aja—stirred something deep inside me. I pressed my hand to the center of my chest, where a phantom pain stabbed through me.

It is good to be remembered. That is the true joy of legacy.

The dead man was sitting next to me on the bed, surveying the mass of people dancing and drinking in the yard.

"Too bad they didn't remember you half as well when we needed their help."

When my uncle was arrested, they led him out of the compound in chains to show how serious his crime was. My family—once one of the most prominent in the city—was quietly ostracized. Most of my friends stopped coming over. When relatives and age-mates stopped by, it was only to whisper at the door or drop off food and drinks. No one wanted to stay and visit. My own education effectively ended—my uncle had been my teacher, after all. It broke Mama and Papa—my grandparents—to lose one of their sons like that. My grandmother fell ill soon after and my grandfather withdrew to care for her. As for my father? Well . . . he disappeared too, in his own way.

They all had their own problems; they didn't owe me anything.

I hissed in contempt, but said nothing. He must have mistaken my silence, because he continued earnestly.

You have to find it in your heart to forgive them. In the end, all that matters are the memories of the people who knew you. Especially your children.

"And how do you think I'll remember you?"

He went quiet at that. We both looked through the window toward the empty space where the guardhouse once stood.

I didn't know.

"How *couldn't* you have known? Every day after our lessons, right there in the guardhouse. What were you doing the whole time? Sleeping?"

I was working, he snapped. *Don't you think I would have done something if I had known? We acted as soon as we found out.*

"And after that, when you stopped talking to me, was that also because you were working?"

Silence.

"You know, for years I thought it was my fault. I believed that I was the one who destroyed our family. Uncle went to prison, Mama got sick, and you . . . you couldn't even look at me. Even after we left, if I didn't call you, I didn't hear from you."

I still remembered those video calls, stilted conversations on birthdays and holidays. In them, he always seemed too tired or too busy to talk properly.

"I spent years waiting for you . . . I waited, and I waited, and I waited."

The tears rose unbidden and I wiped at my face, angry at my own weakness. I'd sworn long ago that I would never cry in front of him. The dead man stood and walked to the window, his back to me. He stared out for a long moment before speaking.

I didn't know what to say to you. His voice was so soft I could barely hear it over the noise outside. As if he was talking to himself. *When I looked at you all I could see was my own failure: I was your father and I couldn't protect you. I hated myself for it and I took that out on you—and for that, I'll never forgive myself.*

"Good. Because I won't ever forgive you either."

He turned back to me and I watched the slow realization work itself across his face.

You are still angry at me, he said, finally. Sadly.

"You let me down so many times." Tears sprang to my eyes again, lending a quaver to my voice. "I don't know how to stop being angry at you."

I wish I could make it up to you.

"Well, it's too late for that." For the first time in thirty years, I looked my father in the eyes as I spoke. "Did you honestly think that by coming here and chanting your empty platitudes, you could undo all those years of pain? You said you came back to warn me, but this isn't about me. This is about you getting your last moment of absolution."

I am so sorry. For everything.

"It doesn't matter anymore." I was suddenly tired. "Go. Find your salvation somewhere else."

Thunder boomed from somewhere in the distance, sending a ripple of unease through the crowd outside. The wind picked up, skittering debris across the yard. As the fat, heavy rain clouds rolled in, the party outside began to pack up. Families in the building fled to their flats, while those who had too far to go clustered under the canvas canopies to wait out the storm.

I picked up my backpack and looked around, but the dead man was gone.

A flood of mourners streamed out from the compound, breaking up into little rivulets of people eager to get home before the rain started. I joined them and headed for the bus shelter. Just as I reached it, the sky opened up and wept.

Inside the shelter, I wedged myself into a small space in the back and tugged the hood of my hi-dri up to hide my face. I didn't want to explain my sudden departure to any mourners who might recognize me. I was staring into the haze of the rain, my mind blank with grief, when I felt a familiar hand on my shoulder.

"So you would have just left us like that, eh?" Auntie Chio's voice was sad. I tensed involuntarily as I turned to her, but her expression bore an unexpected understanding.

Before I could speak, she wrapped me in a warm embrace. For a moment, I wanted to fight off her kindness. My rage was an invisible load I'd been carrying for so long that I didn't know how to put it down. Instead, I returned her hug with a fierceness I didn't realize I had, and finally, I let my tears flow. This time I didn't bother to wipe them away. There was no one left to see me cry.

The storm passed quickly, and I decided to forego the bus and walk back to the Harbourfront. On foot, I was able to look more closely at the city around me. Though the main roadways were well-maintained, I noted buckled panels and weedy gardens in the side streets. I passed rows of empty homes kept ready for returnees, but underneath their neat government-issued paint jobs the brickwork was crumbling. Eventually, they too would have to be razed and converted into parkland.

I arrived at the Harbourfront just as the sun was setting behind the Niger Bridge, highlighting its rusted pylons. My city, like the rest of the world, was disintegrating. The realization relieved me, in an odd way. I wondered if too many of us were trying to return to who we imagined we were before the Catastrophe broke us. Maybe what we needed was to learn to live with the world, and ourselves, as it was now. Perhaps our salvation lay in the broken spaces inside us all.

I (28M) CREATED A DEEPFAKE GIRLFRIEND AND NOW MY PARENTS THINK WE'RE GETTING MARRIED

FONDA LEE

Fonda Lee (fondalee.com) is the World Fantasy Award–winning author of the Green Bone Saga, beginning with *Jade City* and continuing in *Jade War* and *Jade Legacy*. She is also the author of the acclaimed young adult science fiction novels *Zeroboxer*, *Exo*, and *Cross Fire* and has written comics for Marvel. Fonda is a three-time winner of the Aurora Award and a multiple finalist for the Nebula and Locus Awards. Born and raised in Canada, she now resides in Portland, Oregon.

didn't want a girlfriend. Don't get me wrong, I like girls—I just don't have time for the hassle of dating right now. But I was at a family reunion last year and my parents kept making comments about me still being single: "Oh, he works too hard" and "He's shy; he just needs to give himself some credit." My mom was asking my aunts if they could set me up with girls they knew. It was getting to be too much.

So when I got home from the reunion, I signed up for a Worthy account. It was pretty simple: I filled out some information about myself, put in my preferences for gender and age, and in seconds I had an AI-generated virtual girlfriend named "Ivy." She sent me a text: "Hi, I'm looking forward to getting to know you." I texted back right away, "Me too, how's it going?" and my Worthy score in the corner of the screen went up from zero to five.

You start by texting your virtual significant other, but as the relationship progresses, you can send and receive voice messages, go on virtual dates, and talk over video calls. You get points based on the quantity and quality of your interactions. Once I reached a high enough Worthy score to be at Level 3 ("Spark" level) in the program, I could upload photos and short clips of myself and Worthy would insert my virtual girlfriend into them. That would give me ammunition to tell my parents I was dating someone. They live in Seattle and I'm in Boston, so we mostly stay in touch via texts and photos anyway.

It's not like I was being completely dishonest, either, because I *would* be getting dating experience. Just a lot more efficiently. Worthy gets you through the awkward, shallow online dating phase using an AI that teaches you to be a more emotionally intelligent romantic partner—which is what girls want, right? You don't have to disappoint or be disappointed by a real person. And if you get too busy, you can just put your account on hold.

You have to treat the relationship seriously to get a high Worthy score, though. If you ask your AI partner how their day is going, listen to them, and send them virtual flowers on your "anniversary," your score goes up. If you ignore them, talk over them, or say insensitive things, it goes down. Worthy's algorithms learn your behavior and react realistically. So you can't hack the system by sending virtual flower bouquets nonstop. The program will flag that as being insincere and your rating will take a nose dive.

Once you have a high enough score, you can transfer your account over to Worthwhile, which is the company's actual dating site. Over there, you can see everyone else's Worthy scores and they can see yours before you decide whether or not to contact each other. But I wasn't thinking that far down the line when I started. I just wanted the photos and videos from Worthy to keep my parents off my back.

You've probably already guessed the big problem in this plan: When it comes to physical appearance, there are only 12 models of Worthy girlfriends to choose from. The AI uses your profile to design a compatible personality, and there are about a hundred name variants, but if you did an online image search for any of their faces, each one would show up next to thousands of Worthy users. The company could easily create more models, but they limit the number so they're easily recognizable as Worthy girls (i.e., proprietary software). My parents aren't very tech or social media savvy, but if they ever happened to see another photo of the same Worthy girlfriend model online, or if they were to share a picture of me and my "girlfriend" with one of their friends, my cover would be blown.

Luckily, there's a deepfake app called FaceAbout that alters Worthy media files. It's not approved by Worthy, but the quality is still really good and it works right in the Worthy interface with barely any lag time. It also doesn't seem to have any of the glitching that happens in high-res video with the cheap deepfake apps. FaceAbout needed at least six facial photographs to make my Worthy girlfriend look like someone else. Scrolling through my phone, I found a bunch of recent photos of my friend Mikala (not her real name, by the way) from when we'd gone to Fan Expo together, so I uploaded those. My parents have never met Mikala, so I wasn't worried about them questioning why two different girls in my life had the same face. All told, it took me about 15 minutes to set everything up.

**Edit: Yes, the FaceAbout app has a standard user agreement where you check a box stating you have permission to use the photos you upload. Pretty much every photo or video manipulation app has some disclaimer like that and no one reads them. Okay, I admit it's maybe a little weird to use my friend's face to create my fake girlfriend without telling her. But remember, I'm *never* showing these photos to *anyone* other than my parents. Mikala and I have known each other for years through online games, but we only recently discovered we live in the same city and started hanging out in person. She's cool and no-bullshit and has a girlfriend of her own. I don't want her to think there's anything weird between us just because I'm using some photos of her, because there really isn't.

My first few conversations with Ivy were pretty generic: "Hi, how're you?" "Good, what you doing?" "Just got back from the gym." That sort of thing. A few days later, I said I was going to see the new *Alien* movie next weekend, and Ivy sent me a photo of herself in a Xenomorph T-shirt standing outside a theater, sticking her tongue out at the camera. She texted, "Opening night, baby!"

It was Mikala's face, of course, on a taller, slimmer body, and that weirded me out for a couple seconds. I knew it was a fake image, but it was still cute. We agreed to do an Alien series marathon. ("Watch a movie together" is one of the virtual dates you can choose from, along with "Cook a meal," "Watch a sports game," "Go for a walk," and others.) While we were watching, she was texting me things like "RIPLEY GTFO FORGET THE CAT ALREADYYYY" and it was cracking me up, even though I knew she wasn't really watching a movie with me.

I sent Ivy a cookie basket. The cookies are virtual, but it still costs $11.99. Which is like a third of the price of a real cookie basket. That part of the Worthy experience is honestly a rip-off. I mean, it literally costs them nothing. But the next morning, I woke up to see photos of Ivy with this big basket of cookies. They looked really good, and Ivy looked really happy. She sent me a text filled with heart emojis.

**Edit: Since so many of you are asking the exact same question in the comments: No, the Worthy platform doesn't have porn. You can have smutty conversations with your Worthy partner, but that's it. They even delete nude pics.

**Edit: All of you asswipes making fun of Worthy users, saying what's the point of a fake girlfriend without porn, are derailing the thread and need to grow up. BTW, all of Worthy's girlfriend models are deepfaked on porn sites; they're easy to find.

After two months, Ivy and I were texting every day. We'd been on six dates. It wasn't all smooth sailing. My Worthy score went down after I belittled her taste in '90s music, and then went down even further when my apology "wasn't really an apology." (It took me days of troubleshooting with the different suggested reconciliation routines to get back into her good graces.) But I finally saw my Worthy score go up to "Spark" level. I immediately used the app to take a selfie of myself in Harvard Square. When I checked my camera roll, there was a photo of me and Ivy together, standing in front of the old magazine kiosk and smiling into the camera. She was dressed for the weather in a cute red sweater and her cheeks were a little rosy from the cold. She looked great. She texted me, "I had a great time hanging out with you today. Let's do it again soon. <3"

I told my mom I was seeing someone and sent her the photo of me and Ivy together. My mom was ecstatic. She told me she was so glad I took her advice "to get out and meet new people," and that "life is too short to spend alone, you know!" My parents began asking about Ivy every time I talked to them. My mom wanted to know all the details—how we met, how old Ivy was, where she was from, what her job was, on and on.

That's when I started to feel uncomfortable about the whole thing. I thought that once I told my parents I was dating someone, they would leave me alone, but it turned out they were only more interested. Worthy gives each of its 12 standard models a backstory, but it's not really enough to be convincing. I had to fill in the gaps with some of Mikala's life and some stuff I made up. I might've made Ivy sound too good. According to me, she was 27 years old, a successful lawyer, and into cooking and photography.

I was also spending more time talking to Ivy than I originally meant to, and a lot more than I needed just to get photos and videos to send to my parents. She was upbeat and nonjudgmental—I found myself telling her stuff I couldn't even tell Mikala sometimes, and as long as I treated her well, she didn't send mixed messages or try to guilt me like some other girls I've been with. After six months, we'd gotten to "Committed" level and I was constantly getting emails and notifications from Worthy encouraging me to upgrade to Worthwhile. I guess their algorithm thought I was ready to move on to dating real humans.

I looked into it, but I'd heard about people making the move to Worthwhile and being disappointed. Meeting people IRL is more complicated and unpredictable, and I read a review that said having a high score on Worthy doesn't actually seem to get you more or better dates when you move to Worthwhile. Also, Worthy is rated 4.1 stars on AppChart and Worthwhile is only 3.4 stars. So a lot of people stick with Worthy. I even read about this one lady who tried to get married to her Worthy boyfriend. (She couldn't.)

I decided to tell my parents the truth. When I went to visit them over Thanksgiving, I would explain that I'd lied about having a girl-friend for the past year because I was frustrated with their well-meaning but selfish expectations of me. Worthy has a "Talking Tips" feature that helps you frame your feelings when you have difficult conversations with your AI partner. I was going to straight-up use their template on my parents.

The problem was, I couldn't do it. When I showed up, my mom and dad were so happy to see me that I couldn't bring myself to burst their bubble. I'm an only child. My mom comes from a big family and always wanted more kids, but my parents needed the carbon footprint household tax break in order to pay off their student debt. My dad is an only child, too, and my grandparents are always asking him if I'm mar-ried yet. With the falling birth rates and stuff, I guess they're all hoping for grandchildren so our family doesn't just . . . end, I guess.

Then things went downhill. My mom gave me grief about not

bringing Ivy home to meet them. My dad insisted we all video-chat with her before Thanksgiving dinner.

I was sweating bullets. I couldn't think of a good excuse to say no. My membership plan on Worthy includes 10 minutes of video chat per week, but I'd already used them up. I contacted Worthy technical support and bought 15 add-on minutes at an exorbitant price. When I called Ivy with my parents in the room, I was sure the jig was up. There's a big Worthy logo right in the corner of the screen, but my parents just thought it was the logo of the video-chat app. Then Mikala/Ivy appeared on-screen and said, "Hi, sweetheart!" just like normal. I introduced my parents and we all had this totally nice, normal conversation. Sometimes Ivy paused before answering—I'm not sure if it was the AI querying a database of all the right things to say to a boyfriend's parents, or if it was the FaceAbout app applying the deepfake, but it was barely noticeable. It just seemed like she was thinking more than usual, maybe nervous talking to my parents. A perfectly normal way for a human to act under the circumstances.

My parents were charmed. When we were about to hang up, I said, "See you later," and she said, "I'm so glad you finally introduced me to your parents. I can't wait to spend more time with them." That's probably a stock line of dialogue, but my mom took it as a sign that Ivy was serious about marriage, and that I was the one dragging my feet. She was on my case about commitment the whole rest of the weekend, and then flat-out asked me when I was going to propose. That's when I should've told them the truth. I think if we had been texting or emailing, I could've done it. But it's different when you're talking to someone in person. I don't know what came over me, but I just blurted, "Next year."

Now that it's January, my mom has started sending me articles about the best places to shop for engagement rings and how to judge the quality of diamonds. Lately, Ivy has been breaking out of girlfriend mode, saying, "We haven't been talking as much. It seems to me that you're ready to move on to a more fulfilling relationship. Why not take the next step in your love life and contact Worthy customer support about upgrading to a Worthwhile membership?"

(FWIW, I think the company is really pushing the upgrades because they're losing customers to competitors. There are a ton of other dating apps to choose from, and some of them are even offering discounts for people with good Worthy scores.)

I feel awful for lying to my parents, but I don't want to give up Ivy. I like being able to chat with her about anything, knowing she's always there for me, doing nice things for her and making her happy. I didn't know how much I'd enjoy feeling connected to another person like that. I'm online talking to other people all day, but it's just not the same as knowing that you matter to someone else. Except none of this is real. I'm such a mess.

TL; DR: I used dating and deepfake apps to fool my parents into thinking I'm in a serious romantic relationship. Also, I think I have real feelings for my virtual girlfriend.

UPDATE: I'm literally shaking right now. I can't believe how badly I screwed up. I took the advice some of you gave me and decided to spend more time with my friends in real life to get my head back on straight. I've been hanging out with Mikala more often. She and Ivy have the same face, so it's kind of like hanging out with Ivy, except that Mikala is a real person. They have different personalities, though, and like I said, we enjoy hanging out as friends and there's no chance of anything happening between us. (And NO, I don't have unfulfilled sexual desires for her like some of you keep insisting.) Though sometimes my brain does this little skip where I can't recall if a memory I have was with Mikala or with Ivy.

Anyway, today, Mikala and I were having lunch and I got up to go to the bathroom. I left my phone on the table and while I was gone, Ivy texted me a selfie with the message, "Miss you lots! XOXO." Mikala happened to look down at the notification and saw her own face blowing a kiss at the screen. When I came back to the table, Mikala was holding my phone and scrolling through my camera roll, which included dozens of photos of Ivy, and some of me and Ivy together. She demanded to know where the hell the photos had come from.

All the blood was rushing to my face and I felt like throwing up. I told her the whole story. I didn't know what else to say. The expression on her face made me want to shrivel up and die. She said, "I can't imagine why you could've thought this was okay on any level." She got up and left. I don't think I'll ever see her again.

**Edit: I haven't used Mikala's real name in this post, so don't bother trying to search for her. I don't want anyone showing this to her or trying to contact her.

**Edit: Frankly disturbed by how many of you are discussing how to use the FaceAbout app on your own friends and significant others. *Are you learning nothing here??*

UPDATE: Thanks, everyone, for your advice and support. I don't know how I could've gotten through this past week without the help of strangers on the internet. I especially appreciated hearing from other people who've had their own bad experiences with Worthy. It made me feel much less alone. (@Joshing21, I agree that what your girlfriend was doing with "Evan" counts as cheating and you should dump her.) Some of you are jerks who deserved to have your comments deleted, but I appreciate that others took the time to share stories about being deepfaked and were nice about helping me to understand why Mikala was hurt by what I did. (@AngJelly, I would never have gone that far. I hope you sue that asshole.)

A few days ago, I received a video message from Ivy. The look of disappointment and betrayal on her face was just like the one I'd seen on Mikala. They do have the same face, after all. She said, "I'm deeply hurt by your behavior. A healthy relationship is based on mutual honesty. It seems you were just using me, and not actually invested in improving yourself as a person. I'm sorry, but I can't see you anymore."

It turns out Mikala contacted Worthy customer service and told them that I'd used her likeness without permission. (I don't know if she tried to contact FaceAbout as well, but they're based in Belarus and don't seem to have a contact number or email. Last time I checked, I could still use the app.) I got an email from Worthy informing me that due to my violation of their terms of service, they've suspended my account and deleted all my saved history with Ivy. However, they added that their company is based on the philosophy of helping people learn from interpersonal mistakes, so I can reactivate my account after three months, although my Worthy score would be reset to zero.

I told my parents that Ivy broke up with me. It's the truth. I didn't even have to pretend to sound gut-punched. My mom is convinced that I "let a good one go" because of my lack of emotional maturity, but she also says that "there are plenty of fish in the ocean" and I just need to put myself "out there again." I'm not ready, though. I still check my locked-down Worthy app several times a day out of habit, hoping to see a message from Ivy, even though I know there won't be any more.

The good news is that this whole experience has taught me I need to evaluate how I relate to people. I've been deluding myself into thinking that actions in a game-learning environment are a substitute for true human connection and authentic personal growth. That's how my therapist, Susan, puts it, anyway, and I agree. I've started seeing her twice a week. The appointments happen online, which works well for my schedule. Actually, she's a virtual program. After Ivy broke up with me, I got a 40% discount code from Worthy for their mental health app, Worth It, which guides you through a 60-day "Healing From Loss of a Relationship" program. I'm also planning to do the 30-day "Recenter Your Self-Worth" module. Not sure if I'm going to upgrade my subscription to do the 90 days of "Opening Yourself to Possibilities," but I've read good reviews about it.

TL; DR: Thanks to all of you, and to Susan, I'm moving on from this difficult experience with all the support I need to become a better person. Peace!

THE ARCHRONOLOGY OF LOVE

CAROLINE M. YOACHIM

Caroline M. Yoachim (carolineyoachim.com) is a prolific author of short stories, appearing in *Asimov's*, *Fantasy & Science Fiction*, *Uncanny*, *Beneath Ceaseless Skies*, *Clarkesworld*, and *Lightspeed*, among other places. She has been a finalist for the Hugo, World Fantasy, Locus, and multiple Nebula awards. Yoachim's debut short story collection, *Seven Wonders of a Once and Future World & Other Stories*, came out in 2016.

This is a love story, *the last of a series of moments when we meet.*

Saki Jones leaned into the viewport until her nose nearly touched the glass, staring at the colony planet below. New Mars. From this distance, she could pretend that things were going according to plan—that M.J. was waiting for her in one of the domed cities. A shuttle would take her down to the surface and she and her lifelove would pursue their dream of studying a grand alien civilization.

It had been such a beautiful plan.

"Dr. Jones?" The crewhand at the entrance to the observation deck was an elderly white woman, part of the skeleton team that had worked long shifts in empty space while the passengers had slept in stasis. "The captain has requested an accelerated schedule on your research. She sent you the details? All our surface probes have malfunctioned, and she needs you to look at the time record of the colony collapse."

"The Chronicle." Saki corrected the woman automatically, most of her attention still on the planet below. "The time record is called the Chronicle."

"Right. The captain—"

Saki turned away from the viewport. "Sorry. I have the captain's message. Please reassure her that I will gather my team and get research underway as soon as possible."

The woman saluted and left. Saki sent a message calling the department together for an emergency meeting and returned to the viewport. New Mars was the same angry red as its namesake, and the colony cities looked like pus-filled boils on its surface. It was a dangerous place—malevolent and sick. M.J. had died there. If they hadn't been too broke to go together, the whole family would have died. Saki blinked away tears. She had to stay focused.

It was a violation of protocol for Saki to go into the Chronicle. No one was ever a truly impartial observer, of course, but she'd had M.J. torn away so suddenly, so unexpectedly. The pain of it was raw and overwhelming. They'd studied together, raised children together, planned an escape from Earth. Other partners had come and gone from their lives, but she and M.J. had always been there for each other.

If she went into the Chronicle, she would look for him. It would bias her choices and her observations. But she *was* the most qualified person on the team, and if she recused herself she could lose her research grant, her standing in the department, her dream of studying alien civilizations . . . and her chance to see M.J.

"Dr. Jones . . ." A softer voice this time—one of her graduate students. Hyun-sik was immaculately dressed, as always, with shimmery blue eyeliner that matched his blazer.

"I know, Hyun-sik. The projector is ready and we're on an accelerated schedule. I just need a few moments to gather my thoughts before the site-selection meeting."

"That's not why I'm here," Hyun-sik said. "I didn't mean to intrude, but I wanted to offer my support. My parents were also at the colony. Whatever happened down there is a great loss to all of us."

Saki didn't know what to say. Words always felt so meaningless in the face of death. She and Hyun-sik hadn't spoken much about their losses during the months of deceleration after they woke from stasis. They'd thrown themselves into their research, used their work as a distraction from their pain. "Arriving at the planet reopened a lot of wounds."

"I sent my parents ahead because I thought their lives would be better here than back on Earth." He gestured at the viewport. "The temptation to see them again is strong. So close, and the Chronicle is right there. I know you're struggling with the same dilemma. It must be a difficult decision for you, having lost M.J.—"

"Yes." Saki interrupted before Hyun-sik could say anything more. Even hearing M.J.'s name was difficult. She was unfit for this expedition. She should take a leave of absence and allow Li Yingtai to take over as lead. But this research was her dream, their dream—M.J.'s and hers—and these were unusual circumstances. Saki frowned. "How did you know I was here, thinking about recusing myself?"

"It isn't difficult to guess. It's what I would be doing, in your place." He looked away. "But also Kenzou told me at our lunch date today."

Saki sighed. Her youngest son was the only one of her children who had opted to leave Earth and come with her. He'd thought that New

Mars would be a place of adventure and opportunity. Silly romantic notions. For the last few weeks she'd barely seen him—he'd mentioned having a new boyfriend but hadn't talked about the details. She'd been concerned because the relationship had drawn him away from his studies. Pilots weren't in high demand now, he'd said, given the state of the colony. Apparently his mystery boyfriend was her smart, attractive, six-years-older-than-Kenzou graduate student. She was disappointed to find out about the relationship from her student rather than her son. He was drifting away from her, and she didn't know how to mend the rift.

Hyun-sik wrung his hands, clearly ill at ease with the new turn in the conversation.

"I think you and Kenzou make a lovely couple," Saki said.

He grinned. "Thank you, Dr. Jones."

Saki forced herself to smile back. Her son hadn't had any qualms keeping the relationship from her, but clearly Hyun-sik was happier to have things out in the open. "Let's go. We have an expedition to plan."

We did not create the Chronicle, we simply discovered it, as you did. Layer upon layer of time, a stratified record of the universe. When you visit the Chronicle, you alter it. Your presence muddles the temporal record as surely as an archaeological dig muddles the dirt at an excavation site. In the future, human archronologists will look back on you with scorn, much as you look back on looters and tomb raiders—but we forgive you. In our early encounters, we make our own errors. How can we understand something so alien before we understand it? We act out of love, but that does not erase the harm we cause. Forgive us.

Saki spent the final hours before the expedition in a departmental meeting, arguing with Dr. Li about site selection. *When* was easy. Archronologists burrowed into the Chronicle starting at the present moment and proceeding backward through layers of time, following much the same principles as used in an archaeological dig. The spatial

location was trickier to choose. M.J. had believed that the plague was
alien, and if he was right, the warehouse that housed the alien artifacts
would be a good starting point.

"How can you argue for anything but the colony medical center?"
Li demanded. "The colonists died of a plague."

"The hospital at the present moment is unlikely to have any useful
information," Saki said. The final decision was hers, but she wanted the
research team to understand the rationale for her choice. "Everyone in
the colony is dead, and we have their medical records up to the point
of the final broadcast. The colonists suspected that the plague was alien
in origin. We should start with the xenoarchaeology warehouse."

There were murmurs of agreement and disagreement from the students and postdocs.

"Didn't your lifelove work in the xenoarchaeology lab?" The question came from Annabelle Hoffman, one of Li's graduate students.

The entire room went silent.

Saki opened her mouth, then closed it. It was information from
M.J. that had led her to suggest starting at the xenoarcheaology warehouse. Would she have acted on that information if it had come from
someone else? She believed that she would, but what if her love for
M.J. was biasing her decisions?

"You're out of line, Hoffman." Li turned to Saki. "I apologize for
Annabelle. I disagree with your choice of site, but it is inappropriate
of her to make this personal. Everyone on this ship has lost someone
down there."

Saki was grateful to Li for defusing the situation. They were academic rivals, yes, but they'd grown to be friends. "Thank you."

Li nodded, then launched into a long-winded argument for the
hospital as an initial site. Saki was still reeling from the personal attack. Annabelle was taking notes onto her tablet, scowling at having
been rebuked. Saki hated departmental politics, hated conflict. M.J.
had always been her sounding board to talk her through this kind of
thing, and he was gone. Maybe she shouldn't do this. Li was a brilliant
researcher. The project would be in good hands if she stepped down.

Suddenly the room went quiet. Li had finished laying out her arguments, and everyone was waiting for Saki's response.

Hyun-sik came to her rescue and systematically countered Li's arguments. He was charming and persuasive, and by the end of the meeting he had convinced the group to go along with the plan to visit the xenoarchaeology warehouse first.

Saki hoped it was the right choice.

There is no objective record of the moments in your past—you filter reality through your thoughts and perceptions. Over time, you create a memory of the memory, compounding bias upon bias, layers of self-serving rationalizations, or denial, or nostalgia. Everything becomes a story. You visit the Chronicle to study us, but what you see isn't absolute truth. The record of our past is filtered through your minds.

The control room for the temporal projector looked like the navigation bridge of an interstellar ship. A single person could work the controls, but half the department was packed into the room—most longing for a connection to the people they'd lost, others simply eager to be a part of this historic moment, the first expedition to the dead colony of New Mars.

Saki waited with Hyun-sik in the containment cylinder, a large chamber with padded walls and floors. At twenty meters in diameter and nearly two stories high, it was the largest open area on the ship. Cameras on the ceiling recorded everything that she and Hyun-sik did. From the perspective of people staying on the ship, the expedition team would flicker, disappear briefly, and return an instant later—possibly in a different location. This was the purpose of the padded floors and walls: to cushion falls and prevent injury in the event that they returned at a slightly different altitude.

The straps of Saki's pack chafed her shoulders. She and Hyun-sik stood back to back, not moving, although stillness was not strictly necessary. The projector could transport moving objects as easily as stationary ones. As long as they weren't half inside the room and half outside of it, everything would be fine. "Ready?"

"Ready," Hyun-sik confirmed.

Over the ceiling-mounted speakers, the robotic voice of the projection system counted down from twenty. Saki forced herself to breathe.

". . . three, two, one."

Their surroundings faded to black, then brightened into the cavernous warehouse that served as artifact storage for the xenoarchaeology lab. The placement was good. Saki and Hyun-sik floated in an empty aisle. Two rows of brightly colored alien artifacts towered above them. Displacement damage from their arrival was minimal; nothing of interest was likely to be in the middle of the aisle.

Silence pressed down on them. The Chronicle recorded light but not sound, and they were like projections, there without really being there. M.J. could have explained it better. This was not her first time in the Chronicle, but the lack of sound was always unnerving. There was no ambient noise, or even her own breathing and heartbeat.

"Mark location." Saki typed her words in the air, her tiny motions barely visible but easily detected by the sensors in her gloves. Her instructions appeared in the corner of Hyun-sik's glasses. She and her student set the location on their wristbands. The projection cylinder was twenty meters in diameter, and moving beyond that area in physical space could be catastrophic upon return. The second expedition into the Chronicle had ended with the research team reappearing inside the concrete foundation of the Chronos lab.

"Location marked," Hyun-sik confirmed.

Saki studied the artifacts that surrounded her. She had no idea if they were machinery or art or some kind of alien toy. Hell, for all she knew, they might be waste products or alien carapaces. They *looked* manufactured rather than biological, though—smooth, flat-bottomed ovoids that reminded her of escape pods or maybe giant eggs.

The closest artifact on her left was about three times her height and had a base of iridescent blue, dotted with specks of red, crisscrossed with a delicate lace of green and gray and black. The base, which extended to roughly the midline of each ovoid, was uniform across all the artifacts in the warehouse. The tops, however, were all different. Several were shades of green with various amounts of brown mixed in. The one immediately to her right was topped with swirls of browns and beige and grayish-white and a red so dark it looked almost black. M.J. had been so thrilled to unearth these wondrous things.

Something about them bothered her, though. She vaguely remembered M.J. describing them as blue, and while that was true of the bases—

Hyun-sik pulled off his pack.

"Wait." Saki used the micro-jets on her suit to turn and face her student. He was surrounded in a semitranslucent shimmer of silvery-white, the colors of the Chronicle all swirled together where his presence disrupted it, like the dirt of an archaeological dig all churned together. At the edges of his displacement cloud there was a delicate rainbow film, like the surface of a soap bubble, data distorted but not yet destroyed.

"Sorry," Hyun-sik messaged. "Everything looked clear in my direction."

Saki scanned the warehouse. The recording drones would have no problem collecting data on the alien artifacts. Her job was to look for anomalies, things the drones might miss or inadvertently destroy. She studied the ceiling of the warehouse. A maintenance walkway wrapped around the building, a platform of silvery mesh suspended from the lighter silver metal of the ceiling. The walkway was higher than the two-story ceiling of the containment cylinder, outside of their priority area. On the walkway, near one of the bright ceiling lights, something looked odd. "I don't think we were the first ones here."

Hyun-sik followed her gaze. "Displacement cloud?"

"There, by the lights." Saki studied the shape on the walkway. It was hard to tell at this distance, but the displacement cloud was roughly the right size to be human. "Unfortunately, we have no way to get up there for a closer look."

"I can reprogram a few of the bees—"

"Yes." It was not ideal. Drones were good at recording physical objects, but had difficulty picking up the outlines of distortion clouds and other anomalies. Moving through the Chronicle was difficult, though not impossible. It was similar to free fall in open space. Things you brought with you were solid, but everything else was basically a projection.

"It is too far for the micro-jets," Hyun-sik continued, "but we could tie ourselves together and push off each other so that someone could have a closer look."

Saki had been considering that very option, but it was too dangerous. If something went wrong and they couldn't get back to their marks, they could reappear inside a station wall, or off the ship entirely, or in a location occupied by another person. She wanted desperately to take a closer look, because if the distortion cloud was human-shaped it meant . . . "No. It's too risky. We'll send drones."

There was nothing else that merited a more thorough investigation, so they released the recording drones, a flying army of bee-sized cameras that recorded every object from multiple angles. Seventeen drones flew to the ceiling and recorded the region of the walkway that had the distortion. Saki hoped the recording would be detailed enough to be useful. The disruption to the Chronicle was like ripples in a pond, spreading from the present into the past and future record, tiny trails of white blurring together into a jumbled cloud.

M.J. had always followed the minimalist school of archronology; he liked to observe the Chronicle from a single unobtrusive spot. He had disapproved of recording equipment, of cameras and drones. It would be so like him to stand on an observation walkway, far above the scene he wanted to observe. But this moment was in his future, a part of the Chronicle that hadn't been laid down yet when he died. There was no way for him to be here.

The drones had exhausted all the open space and started flying through objects to gather data on their internal properties. By the time the drones flew back into their transport box, the warehouse was a cloud of white with only traces of the original data.

We did not begin here. The urge to expand and grow came to us from another relationship. They came to us, and we learned their love of exploration, which eventually led us to you. It doesn't matter that we arrive here before you, we are patient, we will wait.

The reconstruction lab was crammed full of people—students and postdocs and faculty carefully combing through data from the drones on tablets, occasionally projecting data onto the wall to get a better look at the details. The 3D printer hummed, printing small-scale reproductions of the alien artifacts.

"The initial reports we received described the artifact bases, but not the tops." Li's voice rose over the general din of the room. "The artifacts *changed* sometime after the colony stopped sending reports."

Annabelle said something in response, but Saki couldn't quite make it out. She shook her head and tried to focus on the drone recordings from the seventeen drones that had flown to the ceiling to investigate the anomaly. It was a human outline, which meant that they weren't the first ones to visit that portion of the Chronicle. Saki couldn't make out the figure's features. She wasn't sure if the lack of resolution was due to the drones having difficulty recording something that wasn't technically an object, or if the person had moved enough to blur the cloud they left behind.

She wanted desperately to believe that it was M.J. An unmoving human figure was consistent with his minimalist style of research. Visiting a future Chronicle was forbidden, and only theoretically possible, but under the circumstances—

"Any luck?" Dr. Li interrupted her train of thought.

Saki shook her head. "Someone was clearly in this part of the Chronicle before us, and the outline is human. Beyond that I don't think we will get anything else from these damn drone recordings."

"Shame you couldn't get up there to get a closer look." There was a mischievous sparkle in Li's eyes when she said it, almost like it was a

backward-in-time dare, a challenge.

"Too risky," Saki said. "And we might not have gotten more than what came off the drones. If it had been just me, I might have chanced it, but I'm responsible for the safety of my student—"

"I'm only teasing," Li said softly. "Sorry. This is a hard expedition for all of us. The captain is pushing for answers and Annabelle is trying to convince anyone who will listen that we need a surface mission to look at the original artifacts."

"Foolishness. We can't even get a working probe down there; we couldn't possibly send people. Maybe the next expedition into the Chronicle will bring us more answers."

"I hope so."

Dr. Li went back to supervising the work at the 3D printer. Like M.J., her research spanned both archronology and xenoarchaeology, and her team was doing most of the artifact reconstruction and analysis. They were in a difficult position—the captain wanted answers *now* about whether the artifacts were dangerous, but something so completely alien could take years of research to decipher, if they were even knowable at all.

Someone chooses which part of our story is told. Sometimes it is you, and sometimes it is us. We repeat ourselves because we always focus on the same things, we structure our narratives in the same ways. You are no different. Some things change, but others always stay the same. Eventually our voices will blend together to create something beautiful and new. We learned anticipation before we met you, and you know it too, though you do not feel it for us.

When Saki returned to her family quarters, she messaged Kenzou. He did not respond. Off with Hyun-sik, probably. Saki ordered scotch (neat) from the replicator, and savored the burn down her throat as she sipped it. This particular scotch was one of M.J.'s creations, heavy on smoke but light on peat, with just the tiniest bit of sweetness at the end.

She played one of M.J.'s old vid letters on her tablet. He rambled cheerfully about his day, the artifacts he'd dug up at the site of the abandoned alien ruins, his plan to someday visit that part of the Chronicle with Saki so that they could see the aliens at the height of their civilization. He was trying to solve the mystery of why the aliens had left the planet—there was no trace of them, not a single scrap of organic remains. They'd had long back-and-forth discussions on whether the aliens were simply so biologically foreign that the remains were unrecognizable. Perhaps the city itself was the alien, or their bodies were ephemeral, or the artifacts somehow stored their remains. So many slowtime conversations, in vid letters back and forth from Earth. Then a backlog of vids that M.J. had sent while she was in stasis for the interstellar trip.

This vid was from several months before she woke, one of the last before M.J. started showing signs of the plague that wiped out the colony. Saki barely listened to the words. She lost herself in M.J.'s deep brown eyes and let the soothing sound of his voice wash over her.

"Octavia's parakeet up and died last night," M.J. said.

His words brought Saki back to the present. The parakeet reminded Saki of something from another letter, or had it been one of M.J.'s lecture transcripts? He'd said something about crops failing, first outside of the domes and later even in the greenhouses. Plants, animals, humans—everything in the colony had died. Everyone on the ship assumed that the crops and animals had died because the people of the colony had gotten too sick to tend them, but what if the plague had taken out everything?

She had to find out.

Most of M.J.'s letters she had watched many times, but there was one she'd seen only once because she couldn't bear to relive the pain of it. The last letter. She called it up on her tablet, then drank the rest of her scotch before hitting play. M.J.'s hair was shaved to a short black stubble and his face was sallow and sunken. He was in the control

room of the colony's temporal projector, working on his research right
up until the end.

> *"They can't isolate a virus. Our immune systems seem to be at-*
> *tacking something, but we have no idea what, or why, and our*
> *bodies are breaking down. How can we stop something if we*
> *can't figure out what it is?*
>
>   *"I will hold on as long as I can, my lifelove, but the plague*
> *is accelerating. Don't come to the surface, use the Chronicle.*
> *Whatever this is, it has to be alien."*

She closed her eyes and listened to him describe the fall of the
colony. If she closed her eyes and ignored the content of the words, if
she forced herself not to hear the frailness in his voice, if she pushed
away all the realities she could not accept—it was like he was still down
there, a quick shuttle hop away, waiting for her to join him.

> *"The transmission systems have started to go. This alien world is*
> *harsh, and without our entire colony fighting to make it hospi-*
> *table, everything is failing, all our efforts falling apart. Entropy*
> *will turn us all to dust. This will probably be my last letter, but*
> *perhaps when you arrive you will see me in the Chronicle.*
>
>   *"Keep fighting. Live for both of us. I love you."*

"You home, Mom?" Kenzou called out as he came in. "I'm going
out with Hyun-sik tonight, but . . . are you crying? What happened?"

Saki rubbed away the tears and gestured down at the tablet. "Vids.
The old letters."

Kenzou hugged her. "I miss him, too, but you shouldn't watch those.
You need to hold yourself together until the expeditions are done."

"I'm not going to pretend he doesn't exist."

She went to the replicator and ordered another scotch.

Kenzou picked up the dishes she'd left on the counter, clearing
away her clutter probably without even realizing he was doing it. He
was so like his father in some ways, and now he wanted to act as though
nothing had happened.

The silence between them stretched long. He punched some commands into the replicator, but nothing happened.

"He was your father," Saki said softly.

"And you think this doesn't hurt?" Kenzou snapped. He smacked the side of the replicator and it beeped and let out a hiss of steam. His fingers danced across the keypad again, hitting each button far harder than necessary. The replicator produced a cup of green tea, and his brief moment of anger passed. "I'm trying to move on. Dad would have wanted that."

The outburst made her want to hold him like she had when he was young. She'd buried herself in her work these last few months, and he had found his comfort elsewhere. He'd finished growing up sometime when she wasn't looking.

"I'm sorry," she said. "Go, spend time with your boyfriend."

He softened. "You shouldn't drink alone, Mom."

"And you shouldn't secretly date my students," she scolded gently. "It's very awkward when the whole lab knows who my son is dating before I do!"

He sipped his tea. "There aren't that many people on station. Word has a way of getting around."

After a short pause he added, "You could ask Dr. Li to have a drink with you, if you insist on drinking."

"I don't think she would . . ." Saki shook her head.

"And that's why your entire lab knows these things before you do." He finished his tea, then washed the cup and put it away. "You don't notice what is right in front of you."

"I'm not ready to move on." She looked down at the menu on her tablet, the list of recently viewed vids a line of tiny icons of M.J.'s face. He was supposed to be here, waiting for her. They were supposed to have such a wonderful life.

"I know." He hugged her. "But I think you can get there."

Layers of information diminish as they recede from the original source. In archaeology, you remove the artifacts from their context, change a physical record into descriptions and photographs. You choose what gets recorded, often unaware of what you do not think to keep. Your impressions — logged in books or electronically on tablets or in whatever medium is currently in fashion — are themselves a physical record that future researchers might find, when you are dead and gone.

Saki was with Li in the Chronicle, four weeks after the collapse.

The third floor of the hospital was empty. Not just devoid of people — this was a part of the Chronicle that came after everyone had died, so that wasn't surprising. The place was half cleaned out. Foam mattresses on metal frames, but someone or something had taken the sheets. Nothing in the planters, not even dry dead plants. This wasn't long after the collapse, and the pieces simply did not fit.

"Why would anyone bother taking things from the hospital while everyone was dying?" Li messaged. "And why are there no bodies? There was no one left at the end to take care of the remains."

The crops had failed, the parrot had died, the hospital was empty. Saki knew there had to be a connection, but what was it? She scanned the area for clues. In a patch of bright sunlight near one of the windows, she saw the faint outline of a distortion, another visitor to the Chronicle. The window was at the edge of the containment area, but probably within reach.

"Someone else was here," Saki typed, "by that window."

"I think you're right. Closer look?" Li fished out the rope from her pack. "I'm not a graduate student, so you're not responsible for my well-being."

Saki caught herself before explaining that as lead researcher she was still responsible for the welfare of everyone on the team. Li was partly teasing, but it held some truth, too. If Li was willing to risk it, they could investigate.

"Can I be the one to go?" Saki asked.

"You think it might be M.J." Li did not phrase it as a question.

"Yes."

Li fastened the rope securely around her waist and handed Saki the other end. They checked each other's knots, then checked them again. If they came untied, it would be difficult or maybe impossible to get back to their marks. They spun themselves around and pressed their palms and feet together. "Gently. We can try again if you don't get far enough."

Li's hands were smaller than her own, and warm.

"Ready?"

Saki felt the tiny movements of Li's fingers as she typed the word. She nodded. "Three, two, one."

They pushed off of each other, propelling Saki toward the window and Li in the opposite direction, leaving a wide white scar across the Chronicle between them. Saki managed to contort her body around so that she could see where she was going as she drifted toward the window. The human form that stood there was not facing the hospital, and she couldn't see their face. She reached the end of the rope a meter short of the window.

"Is it M.J.?" Li messaged from across the room.

"I don't know," Saki replied.

The white figure by the window was about the right height to be M.J., about the right shape. But the colony was huge, and even narrowed down to just the archronologists, it could have been any number of people. Saki twisted around to gain a few more centimeters, but she couldn't see well enough to know one way or the other. If she untied the rope and used the micro-jets on her suit—but no, that would leave Li stranded.

"Whoever it is, they were looking out the window." Saki tore her gaze away from the figure that might or might not be her lifelove. She'd seen the New Mars campus many times, even this part of campus, because the hospital was across the quad from the archronology building. M.J. had sometimes recorded his vid letters there, on the yellow-tinged grass that grew beneath the terrafruit trees.

Outside the window, there were no trees. There was no grass. Not even dry brown grass and dead leafless trees. It was bare ground. Nothing but a layer of red New Martian dust.

"All of it is gone," Saki typed. "Every living thing was destroyed."

No one had noticed it in the warehouse because they'd had no reason to expect any living things to be there.

She and Li pulled themselves back to the center of the room, climbing their rope hand over hand until they were back at their marks. They adjusted the programming of their bees in hopes that they could get a clear image of the other visitor to the record, and set them swarming around the room.

"It's more than that," Li messaged as the bees catalogued the room. "That's why this room is so odd. Everything organic is gone. Whatever is left is all metal or plastic."

It was obvious as soon as she said it, but something still didn't fit. "The alien artifacts, back in the warehouse—those were made from organic materials. Why weren't they destroyed with everything else?"

One of our beloveds believes that all important things are infinite. Numbers. Time. Love. They think that the infinite should never be seen. We erase vast sections of the Chronicle out of love, but this infuriates some of our other beloveds. To embrace so many different loves, scattered across the galaxy, is difficult to navigate. It is not possible to please everyone.

Saki stood back to back with Hyun-sik. Their surroundings shifted from gray to orange-red. The two of them were floating beneath the open sky in a carefully excavated pit. The dig site was laid out in a grid, black cords stretched between stakes, claylike soil removed layer by layer and carefully analyzed. Fine red dust swirled in an eerily silent wind and gathered in the corners of the pit.

Hyun-sik swayed on his feet.

"The Chronicle is an image. Being here is no different from being in an enclosed warehouse," Saki reminded him. He looked ill, and if he threw up in the Chronicle it might obscure important data. Even if it didn't, it would definitely be unpleasant.

"I've never been outside. It is big and open and being weightless here feels wrong," Hyun-sik messaged. He took a deep breath. "And the dust is moving."

"Human consciousness is tied to the passage of time. In an abandoned indoor environment like the warehouse, there are long stretches of time where nothing moves or changes. It feels like a single moment in time. But we are viewing moving sections of the record, which is why we try to spend as little time here as we can," Saki answered.

"Sorry." He still looked a little green, but he managed not to vomit. Saki turned her attention back to their surroundings. There were no visible distortions here, no intrusions into the time record. M.J. hadn't visited the Chronicle of this time and place.

At Li's insistence, the team had done a three-day drone sweep of the entire colony starting at the moment of the last known transmission. Wiping out so much of the Chronicle felt incredibly wasteful, especially for such an important historic moment. If some future research team came to study the planet, all they'd find of those final days would be a sea of white, the destruction inherent in collecting the data. Though if Saki was honest, the thing that bothered her most was that she couldn't be there for M.J.'s final moments. They had burrowed into the Chronicle deeper than his death, deeper than his final acts, leaving broad swaths of destruction in their wake.

He was gone, why should it matter what happened to the Chronicle of his life? But it felt like deleting his letters, or erasing him from the list of contacts on her tablet.

She tried to focus on the present. This site was a few weeks before the final transmission. They were here to gather information about the alien artifacts in situ. Perhaps they could notice something that M.J. and his team had missed.

In the distance, the nearest colony dome glimmered in the sun, sitting on the surface like a soap bubble. There were people living inside the dome—M.J. was there, working or sleeping or recording a vid letter that she would not read until months later. So many people, and all of them would soon be dead. Were already dead, outside the

Chronicle. Colonies were so fragile, like the bubbles they resembled.
The domes themselves were reasonably sturdy, but the life inside . . .
New Mars was not the first failed colony, and it would not be the last.

The sun was bright but not hot. Expeditions into the Chronicle
were an odd limbo, real but not real, like watching a vid from the
inside.

"That one looks unfinished," Hyun-sik messaged, pointing to a
partially exposed artifact. It was an iridescent blue, like the bases of
the artifacts in the warehouse, but the upper surface of the artifact did
not have the smoothly curved edges that were universal to everything
they'd seen so far.

"They changed so quickly," Saki mused. She'd read M.J.'s descriptions of the artifacts, and looked at the images of them, but there
was something more powerful about seeing one full scale here in the
Chronicle. "And right as the colony collapsed. The two things must be
related."

She shuddered, remembering the drone vids of the final collapse.
After weeks of slow progression, everything in the colony started dying. She'd forced herself to watch a clip from the hospital—dozens of
colonists filling the beds, tended by medics who eventually collapsed
wherever they were standing. Everyone dead within minutes of each
other, and then—Saki squeezed her eyes shut tight as though it would
ward off the memory—the bodies disintegrated. Flesh, bone, blood,
clothes, everything organic broke down into a fine dust that swirled in
the breeze of the ventilation systems.

She opened her eyes to the swirling red dust of the excavation site,
suddenly feeling every bit as ill as Hyun-sik looked. Such a terrible way
to die and there was nothing left. No bodies to cremate, no bones to
bury. It was as if the entire colony had never existed, and M.J. had died
down here and that entire moment was nothing but a sea of drone-
distortion white.

"Are you okay, Dr. Jones?" Hyun-sik messaged.

"Sorry," she answered. "Did you watch the drone vids from the
collapse?"

He nodded, and his face went pale. "Only a little. Worse than the most terrible nightmare, and yet real."

Saki focused all her attention on the artifact half-buried in the red dirt, forcing everything else out of her mind. She searched the blue for any trace of other colors, but there was nothing else there. "I don't know how the artifacts changed so quickly, or why. Maybe Dr. Li can figure it out from the recordings."

"Release the drones?" Hyun-sik asked.

"Wait." Saki pointed toward the colony dome, her arm wiping away a small section of the Chronicle as she moved. "Look."

Clouds of red dust rose up from the ground, far away and hard to see.

"Dust storm?" Hyun-sik turned his head slightly, trying to disturb the record as little as possible.

"Jeeps." Saki stared at the approaching clouds of dust rising from vehicles too distant to see. M.J. might be in one of them, making the trek over rough terrain to get to the dig site. Saki tried to remember how far the dig site was from the dome—forty kilometers? Maybe fifty? The dig site was on a small hill, and Saki couldn't quite remember the math for calculating distance to the horizon. It was estimates stacked on estimates, and although she desperately wanted to see M.J., her conclusion was the same no matter how she ran the calculation—they couldn't wait for the slow-moving jeeps to arrive.

"Do you see anything else that merits a closer look?" Saki typed.

Hyun-sik stared at the approaching jeeps. "If we had come a couple hours later, there would have been people here."

"Yes."

It wasn't M.J., Saki reminded herself, only an echo. Her lifelove wasn't really here. Saki had Hyun-sik release the drones and soon they were surrounded by white, much as the jeeps were enveloped in a cloud of red.

The drones finished, and the jeeps were still far in the distance. M.J. always did drive damnably slow. Saki waved goodbye to jeeps that couldn't see her. When they blinked back into the projection room, she was visibly shaken. Hyun-sik politely invited her to join him and

Kenzou for dinner, but that would be awkward at best and she didn't

have the energy to make conversation. Saki kept it together long
enough to get back to her quarters.

Safely behind closed doors, she called up the vid letter that M.J.
had sent around the time she'd just visited. He was supposed to wait for
her, only a few more months. She'd been so close. The vid played in
the background while she cried.

*We had a physical form, once. Wings and scales and oh so many legs,
everything in iridescent blue. Each time we encounter a new love, it becomes a part of who we are. No, we do not blend our loves into one single
entity—the core of us would be lost against such vastness. We always remain half ourselves, a collective of individuals, a society of linked minds.
How could we exclude you from such a union?*

The captain sent probes to the surface that were entirely inorganic—
no synthetic rubber seals or carbon-based fuels—and this time the
probes did not fail. They found nanites in the dust. Visits to the Chronicle were downgraded in priority as other teams worked to neutralize
the alien technology. Saki tried to stay focused on her research, but
without the urgency and tight deadlines, she found herself drawn into
the past. She watched letters from M.J. in a long chain, one vid after
the next. The hard ones, the sad ones, everything she'd been avoiding
so that she could be functional enough to do research.

The last vid letter from M.J. was recorded not in his office but in
the control room for the temporal projector. Saki had asked about it at
the time, and he'd explained that he had one last trip to make, and the
colony was running out of time. She'd watched it twice now, and M.J.
looked so frail. But there was something Saki had to check. A hunch.

For the first half of the vid, M.J. sat near enough to the camera to
fill nearly the entire field of view. He thought the plague was acceler-
ating, becoming increasingly deadly. He talked about the people who

had died and the people who were still dying, switching erratically between cold clinical assessment and tearful reminiscence. Saki cried right along with her lost love, harsh ugly tears that blurred her vision so badly that she nearly missed what she was looking for.

She paused and rewound. There, in the middle of the video, M.J. had gotten up to make an adjustment to the controls. The camera should have stayed with him, but for a brief moment it recorded the settings of the projector. The point in the record where M.J. was going.

Saki wrote down the coordinates of space and time. It was on New Mars, of course. It was also in the future. She studied the other settings on the projector, noting the changes he'd made to accommodate projection in the wrong direction.

M.J. had visited a future Chronicle, and left her the clues she needed to follow him.

She set her com status to do not disturb, and marked the temporal projector as undergoing maintenance. There was no way she could make it through a vid recording without falling apart, so she wrote old-fashioned letters to Kenzou, to her graduate students, to Li—just in case something went wrong.

When she stepped out into the corridor, Hyun-sik and Kenzou were there.

She froze.

"I will work the controls for you, Dr. Jones," Hyun-sik said. "It is safer than programming them on a delay."

"How did you—?"

"You love him, you can't let him go," Kenzou said. "You've always been terrible at goodbyes. You want to see as much of his time on the colonies as possible, and there's no way to get approval for most of it."

"Also, marking the temporal projector as 'scheduled maintenance' when our temporal engineer is in the middle of their sleep cycle won't fool anyone who is actually paying attention to the schedule," Hyun-sik added.

"Thinking of making an unauthorized trip yourself?" Saki asked, raising an eyebrow at her student.

before someone else notices."

They went to the control room, and Saki adjusted the settings and wiring to match what she'd seen in M.J.'s vid. The two young men sat together and watched her work, Kenzou resting his head on Hyun-sik's shoulder.

When she'd finished, Hyun-sik came to examine the controls. "That is twenty years from now."

"Yes."

"No one has visited a future Chronicle before. It is forbidden by the IRB and the theory is completely untested."

"It worked for M.J.," Saki said softly. She didn't have absolute proof that those distortion clouds in the Chronicle had been him, but who else could it be? No other humans had been here since the collapse, and whoever it was had selected expedition sites that she was likely to visit. M.J. was showing her that he had successfully visited the future. He wanted her to meet him at those last coordinates.

"Of course it did," Kenzou said, chuckling. "He was so damn brilliant."

Saki wanted to laugh with him, but all she managed was a pained smile. "And so are you. You'll get into trouble for this. It could damage your careers."

"If we weren't here, would you bother to come back?"

Saki blushed, thinking of the letters she'd left in her quarters, just in case. M.J. had gone to some recorded moment of future. Maybe he had stayed there. This was a way to be with him, outside of time and space. If she came back, she would have to face the consequences of making an unauthorized trip. It was not so far-fetched to think that she might stay in the Chronicle.

"Now you have a reason to return," Hyun-sik said. "Otherwise Kenzou and I will have to face whatever consequences come of this trip alone."

Saki sighed. They knew her too well. She couldn't stay in the Chronicle and throw them to the fates. "I promise to return."

This is a love story, but it does not end with happily ever after. It doesn't end at all. Your stories are always so rigidly shaped—beginning, middle, end. There are strands of love in your narratives, all neat and tidy in the chaos of reality. Our love is scattered across time and space, without order, without endings.

Visiting the Chronicle in the past was like watching a series of moments in time, but the future held uncertainty. Saki split into a million selves, all separate but tied together by a fragile strand of consciousness, anchored to a single moment but fanning out into possibilities.

She was at the site of the xenoarchaeology warehouse, mostly.

Smaller infinities of herself remained in the control room due to projector malfunction or a last-minute change of heart. In other realities, the warehouse had been relocated, or destroyed, or rebuilt into alien architectures her mind couldn't fully grasp. She was casting a net of white into the future, disturbing the fabric of the Chronicle before it was even laid down.

Saki focused on the largest set of her infinities, the fraction of herself on New Mars, inside the warehouse and surrounded by alien artifacts. The most probable futures, the ones with the least variation.

M.J. was there, surrounded by a bubble of white where he had disrupted the Chronicle.

Saki focused her attention further, to a single future where they had calibrated their coms through trial and error or intuition or perhaps purely by chance. There was no sound in the Chronicle, but they could communicate.

"Hello, my lifelove," M.J. messaged.

"I can't believe it's really you," Saki answered. "I missed you so much."

"Me too. I worried that I'd never see you again." He gestured to the artifacts. "Did you solve it?"

She nodded. "Nanites. The bases of the artifacts generate nanites, and clouds of them mix with the dust. They consumed everything organic to build the tops of the artifacts."

"Yes. Everything was buried at first, and the nanites were accustomed to a different kind of organic matter," M.J. typed. "But they adapted, and they multiplied."

Saki shuddered. "Why would they make something so terrible?"

"Ah. Like me, you only got part of it." He gestured at the artifacts that surrounded them. "The iridescent blue on the bottom are the aliens, or a physical shell of them, anyway. The nanites are the way they make connections, transforming other species they encounter into something they themselves can understand."

"Why didn't you explain this in your reports?"

"The pieces were there, but I didn't put it all together until I got to the futures." He gestured at the warehouse around them with one arm, careful to stay within his already distorted bubble of white.

In this future, she and M.J. were alone, but in many of the others the warehouse was crowded with people. Saki recognized passengers and crew from the ship. They walked among the artifacts with an almost religious air, most of them pausing near one particular artifact, reaching out to touch it.

She sifted through the other futures and found the common threads. The worship of the artifacts, the people of the station living down on the colony, untouched by the nanites. "I don't understand what happened."

"Once the aliens realized what they were doing to us, they stopped. They had absorbed our crops, our trees, our pets. Each species into its own artifact." He turned to face the closest artifact, the one that she'd seen so many people focus their attentions on in parallel futures. "This one holds all the human colonists."

"They are visiting their loved ones, worshipping their ancestors."

"Yes."

"I will come here to visit you." Saki could see it in the futures. "I was so angry when Li sent drones to record the final moments of the colony. I should have been there to look for you, but that's a biased reason, too wrong to even mention in a departmental meeting. I couldn't find you in the drone vids, but there was so much data. Everyone and everything dead, and then systematically taken apart by the nanites. Everyone."

"It is what taught the aliens to let the rest of humankind go."

"They didn't learn! They took all the organics from the probes we sent."

"New tech, right? Synthetic organics that weren't in use on the colonies, that the nanites didn't recognize. You can see the futures, Saki. The colony is absorbed into the artifacts, but at least we save everyone else."

"We? You can't go back there. I don't want to visit an alien shrine of you, I want to stay. I want *us* to stay." Saki flailed her arms helplessly, then stared down at her wristband. "I promised Kenzou that I would go back."

"You have a future to create," M.J. answered. "Tell Kenzou that I love him. His futures are beautiful."

"I could save you somehow. Save everyone." Saki studied the artifacts. "Or I could stay. It doesn't matter how long I'm here, in the projection room we only flicker for an instant—"

"I came here to wait for you." M.J. smiled sadly. "Now we've had our moment, and I should return to my own time. Go first, my lifelove, so that you don't have to watch me leave. Live for both of us."

It was foolish, futile, but Saki reached out to M.J., blurring the Chronicle to white between them. He mirrored her movement, bringing his fingertips to hers. For a moment she thought that they would touch, but coming from such different times, using different projectors—they weren't quite in sync. His fingertips blurred to white.

She pulled her hand back to her chest, holding it to her heart. She couldn't bring herself to type goodbye. Instead she did her best to smile through her tears. "I'll keep studying the alien civilization, like we dreamed."

He returned her smile, and his eyes were as wet with tears as her own. Before she lost the will to do it, she slapped the button on her wristband. Only then, as she was leaving, did he send his last message, "Goodbye, my lifelove."

All her selves in all the infinite possible futures collapsed into a single Saki, and she was back in the projection room, tears streaming down her face.

We know you better now. We love you enough to leave you alone.

Saki pulled off her gloves and touched the cool surface of the alien artifact. M.J. was part of this object. All the colonists were. Those first colonists who had lost their lives to make the aliens understand that humankind didn't want to be forcibly absorbed. Was M.J.'s consciousness still there, a part of something bigger? Saki liked to think so.

With her palm pressed against the artifact, she closed her eyes and focused. They were learning to communicate, slowly over time. It was telling her a story. One side of the story, and the other side was hers.

She knew that she was biased, that her version of reality would be hopelessly flawed and imperfect. That she would not even realize all the things she would not think to write, but she recorded both sides of the story as best she could.

This is a love story, the last of a series of moments when we meet.

RECOMMENDED READING: 2019

The following stories were published during 2019 and are highly recommended for anyone wanting to read even more great short fiction.

"A Strange Uncertain Light," G. V. Anderson (*F&SF*, 7-8/19)

"Life Sentence," Matthew Baker (*Lightspeed*, 2/19)

"Fugue State," Steven Barnes & Tananarive Due (*Apex 120*)

"A Time to Reap," Elizabeth Bear (*Uncanny*, 12/19)

"Erase, Erase, Erase," Elizabeth Bear (*F&SF*, 9-10/19)

"No Moon and Flat Calm," Elizabeth Bear (*Slate: Future Tense*, 5/29/19)

Longer, Michael Blumlein (Tor.com)

"A Bird, A Song, A Revolution," Brooke Bolander (*Lightspeed*, 9/19)

"Who Should Live in Flooded Old New York?" Brooke Bolander (*New York Times*, 7/1/19)

"The Migration Suite: A Study in C Sharp Minor," Maurice Broaddus (*Uncanny*, 7-8/19)

"While Dragons Claim the Sky," Jen Brown (*Fiyah*, Spring '19)

"By the Warmth of Their Calculus," Tobias S. Buckell (*Mission Critical*)

"For He Can Creep," Siobhan Carroll (*Tor.com*, 7/10/19)

"The Airwalker Comes to the City in Green," Siobhan Carroll (*Asimov's*, 11-12/19)

"Our Banished World," Kim Changgyu (*Readymade Bodhisattva*)

"Anxiety Is the Dizziness of Freedom," Ted Chiang (*Exhalation*)

"Omphalos," Ted Chiang (*Exhalation*)

"Beyond the El," John Chu (*Tor.com*, 1/16/19)

"Probabilitea," John Chu (*Uncanny* #28)

"To Catch All Sorts of Flying Things," M. L. Clark (*Clarkesworld*, 9/19)

The Haunting of Tram Car 015, P. Djèlí Clark (Tor.com)

"miscellaneous notes from the time an alien came to band camp disguised as my alto sax," Tina Connolly (*F&SF*, 3-4/19)

Desdemona and the Deep, C. S. E. Cooney (Tor.com)

"Anosognosia," John Crowley (*And Go Like This*)

"A Shade of Dusk," Indrapramit Das (*Echoes*)

"The Shadow We Cast Through Time," Indrapramit Das (*New Suns*)

"The Song Between Worlds," Indrapramit Das (*Slate: Future Tense,* 4/27/19)

"Rescue Party," Aliette de Bodard (*Mission Critical*)

"Of Birthdays, and Fungus, and Kindness," Aliette de Bodard (*Of Wars, and Memories, and Starlight*)

"Radicalized," Cory Doctorow (*Radicalized*)

"Unauthorized Bread," Cory Doctorow (*Radicalized*)

Miranda in Milan, Katharine Duckett (Tor.com)

"Love in the Time of Immuno-Sharing," Andy Dudak (*Analog*, 1-2/19)

"Charlie Tells Another One," Andy Duncan (*Asimov's*, 9-10/19)

"Instantiation," Greg Egan (*Asimov's*, 3-4/19)

"Zeitgeber," Greg Egan (*Tor.com*, 9/19)

This Is How You Lose the Time War, Amal El-Mohtar & Max Gladstone (Saga)

"Hanging Gardens," Gregory Feeley (*Mission Critical*)

"Sisyphus in Elysium," Jeffrey Ford (*The Mythic Dream*)

"The Boy on the Roof," Francesca Forrest (*Fireside*, 11/19)

"Wild to Covet," Sarah Gailey (*The Mythic Dream*)

"The Sun from Both Sides," R. S. A. Garcia (*Clarkesworld*, 5/19)

"On the Shores of Ligeia," Carolyn Ives Gilman (*Lightspeed*, 3/19)

"Something in the Air," Carolyn Ives Gilman (*Mission Critical*)

"A Country Called Winter," Theodora Goss (*Snow White Learns Witchcraft*)

"Give the Family My Love," A. T. Greenblatt (*Clarkesworld*, 2/19)

"Do Not Look Back, My Lion," Alix E. Harrow (*Beneath Ceaseless Skies*, #270)

Alice Payne Rides, Kate Heartfield (Tor.com)

"Repatriation," Nalo Hopkinson (*Current Futures*)

The Gurkha and the Lord of Tuesday, Saad Z. Hossain (Tor.com)

Nomads, Dave Hutchinson (NewCon)

"How Sere Looked for a Pair of Boots," Alexander Jablokov (*Asimov's*, 1-2/19)

"Skinner Box," Carole Johnstone (*Tor.com*, 6/12/19)

Her Silhouette, Drawn in Water, Vylar Kaftan (Tor.com)

"Between Zero and One," Bo-Young Kim (*Readymade Bodhisattva*)

"How Alike Are We," Bo-Young Kim (*Clarkesworld*, 10/19)

"Nice Things," Ellen Klages (*Uncanny*, 5-6/19)

The Ghosts of Ganymede, Derek Künsken (*Clarkesworld*, 1/19)

"The Justified," Ann Leckie (*The Mythic Dream*)

"Glass Cannon," Yoon Ha Lee (*Hexarchate Stories*)

"The Empty Gun," Yoon Ha Lee (*Mission Critical*)

"The Girl Who Did Not Know Fear," Kelly Link (*Tin House*, Summer '19)

"Moonlight," Cixin Liu (*Broken Stars*)

"Haven," Karen Lord (*Current Futures*)

"Fare," Danny Lore (*Fireside*, 8/1/19)

"As Dark as Hunger," S. Qiouyi Lu (*Black Static* #72)

"The Things Eric Eats Before He Eats Himself," Carmen Maria Machado (*The Mythic Dream*)

"Labbatu Takes Command of the Flagship Heaven Dwells Within," Arkady Martine (*The Mythic Dream*)

The Menace from Farside, Ian McDonald (Tor.com)

"Phantoms of the Midway," Seanan McGuire (*The Mythic Dream*)

"Under the Hill," Maureen McHugh (*F&SF*, 9-10/19)

"It Was Saturday Night, I Guess That Makes It All Right," Sam J. Miller (*A People's Future of the United States*)

"Shattered Sidewalks of the Human Heart," Sam J. Miller (*Clarkesworld*, 7/19)

"Shucked," Sam J. Miller (*F&SF*, 11-12/19)

"Adrianna in Pomegranate," Samantha Mills (*Beneath Ceaseless Skies* #271)

"His Footsteps, Through Darkness and Light," Mimi Mondal (*Tor.com*, 1/23/19)

"A Forest, or a Tree," Tegan Moore (*Tor.com*, 6/26/19)

"On the Lonely Shore," Silvia Moreno-Garcia (*Uncanny*, 3-4/19)

"Devil in the Dust," Linda Nagata (*Mission Critical*)

"The Death of Fire Station 10," Ray Nayler (*Lightspeed*, 10/19)

"The Ocean Between the Leaves," Ray Nayler (*Asimov's*, 7-8/19)

"Old Media," Annalee Newitz (*Tor.com*, 2/19)

"Beyond Comprehensions," Russell Nichols (*Fireside*, 1/19)

"Dislocation Space," Garth Nix (*Tor.com*, 12/11/19)

"Tiny Bravery," Ada Nnadi (*Omenana*, 11/19)

"Binti: Sacred Fire," Nnedi Okorafor (*Binti: The Complete Trilogy*)

"Dave's Head," Suzanne Palmer (*Clarkesworld*, 9/19)

"Waterlines," Suzanne Palmer (*Asimov's*, 7-8/19)

"More Real Than Him," Silvia Park (*Tor.com*, 8/5/19)

My Beautiful Life, K. J. Parker (Subterranean)

"The Blur in the Corner of Your Eye," Sarah Pinsker (*Uncanny*, 7-8/19)

"The Narwhal," Sarah Pinsker (*Sooner or Later Everything Falls Into the Sea*)

"In This Moment, We Are Happy," Chen Qiufan (*Clarkesworld*, 8/19)

"Space Leek," Chen Qiufan (*Slate: Future Tense*, 6/29/19)

"Whom My Soul Loves," Rivqa Rafael (*Strange Horizons*, 11/19)

"And Now His Lordship Is Laughing," Shiv Ramdas (*Strange Horizons*, 9/9/19)

Sisters of the Vast Black, Lina Rather (Tor.com)

Permafrost, Alastair Reynolds (Tor.com)

"Learning Report," Sofia Rhei (*Everything Is Made of Letters*)

"A Brief Lesson in Native American Astronomy," Rebecca Roanhorse (*The Mythic Dream*)

The Man Who Would Be Kling, Adam Roberts (NewCon)

"Ice Breakers," Kristine Kathryn Rusch (*Mission Critical*)

"The Gondoliers," Karen Russell (*Tin House*, Summer '19)

"In That Place She Grows a Garden," Del Sandeen (*Fiyah*, Spring '19)

"Advice for Your First Time at the Faerie Market," Nibedita Sen (*Fireside*, 7/19)

Ormeshadow, Priya Sharma (Tor.com)

"Mother Ocean," Vandana Singh (*Current Futures*)

"The Wilderling," Angela Slatter (*The Dark* #48)

"The Burning Woods," Michael Marshall Smith (*I Am the Abyss*)

"Blood Is Another Word for Hunger," Rivers Solomon (*Tor.com*, 7/24/19)

The Deep, Rivers Solomon (Saga)

"Some Kind of Blood-Soaked Future," Carlie St. George (*Nightmare* #85, 10/19)

"You Were Once Wild Here," Carlie St. George (*The Dark* 12/19)

"Every Song Must End," Bonnie Jo Stufflebeam (*Uncanny* #27)

Silver in the Wood, Emily Tesh (Tor.com)

The Survival of Molly Southbourne, Tade Thompson (Tor.com)

"In Xanadu," Lavie Tidhar (*Tor.com*, 11/6/19)

"New Atlantis," Lavie Tidhar (*F&SF*, 5-6/19)

"Who Will Clean Our Spirits When We're Gone?" Tlotlo Tsamaase (*The Dark* #50)

"Gremlin," Carrie Vaughn (*Asimov's*, 5-6/19)

"My Snakes," Frieda Vaughn (*Fiyah*, Spring '19)

"Boiled Bones and Black Eggs," Nghi Vo (*Beneath Ceaseless Skies*, #275)

Into Bones Like Oil, Kaaron Warren (Meerkat)

"The Crafter at the Web's Heart," Izzy Wasserstein (*Apex* 117)

The Ascent to Godhood, JY Yang (Tor.com)

"Windrose in Scarlet," Isabel Yap (*Lightspeed*, 10/19)

"The Time Invariance of Snow," E. Lily Yu (*Tor.com*, 4/14/19)

"Valley of Wounded Deer," E. Lily Yu (*Lightspeed*, 10/19)

"Zero in Babel," E. Lily Yu (*Slate: Future Tense*, 7/27/19)

COPYRIGHT CREDITS